Daybreak
The Dawning Ember

Books by Mary Summer Rain

Nonfiction:

Spirit Song
Phoenix Rising
Dreamwalker
Phantoms Afoot
Earthway
Daybreak
Soul Sounds
Whispered Wisdom
Ancient Echoes

Children's:

Mountains, Meadows and Moonbeams

Fiction:

The Seventh Mesa

Daybreak
The Dawning Ember

**Mary
Summer Rain**

HAMPTONROADS
PUBLISHING COMPANY, INC.

Hampton Roads Publishing Company, Inc.
891 Norfolk Square
Norfolk, VA 23502
Or call: (804) 459-2453
FAX: (804) 455-8907

If you are unable to order this book from your local book-
seller, you may order directly from the publisher.
Call 1-800-766-8009, toll-free.

Cover Art "Blessings of Dawn" Copyright © 1991 by
Carole Bourdo, Colorado Springs, Colorado

ISBN 1-878901-14-1

10 9 8 7

Printed in the United States of America

For one with a golden heart . . . for Art

Contents

Author's Foreword

No-Eyes foresaw a future that I continually held in wonder. She foresaw masses of spiritual seekers (both believers and skeptics alike) who were searching for that one glowing ember of light that would serve to pierce their darkened paths with the illumination of truth — the light that would ultimately unravel the tangle of life's spiritually perplexing mysteries and enigmas —the light of a new dawning Daybreak.

The visionary was like an excited pixie as she expressed my future work. Her animations were highly-charged displays of joy as she portrayed the light that would shine forth. Indeed I could see that very light radiating from her frail being at these times, for she was the visionary. .my own Daybreak Light.

And now, because I am the messenger, I will make her light manifest in the world. Therefore, through the thousands of questioning letters you've written, there is no better time to shed light on these than now.

I am not the visionary, but she remains at my side, ever watchful, ever being my guiding friend. In the silent early hours of morning, when I pour over the letters that were selected for this book, the light of my oil lamp flickers, the woodstove warms my being, and No-Eyes softly whispers as my pen comes alive with an animated life of its own and. . .the communion begins.

Therefore, these are your questions.

So then, these are our answers.

The Communion

The following questions have been taken directly from actual inquiries, comments, and statements contained in letters to Mary Summer Rain. They represent the most frequently asked questions from her readership worldwide and have been appropriately disguised to protect the identity of the correspondents.

The individual answers to questions are specifically worded according to the entity who chose to be the source for the particular response. These being the author or No-Eyes or The Advisors.

Whispered Wisdom

From her weathered face, the Light of Daybreak still shines forth. From her sweet breath the Wind Spirit still whispers her wisdom. Through her death does she still live. . .forever alive. . .forever the Light and the Breath.

What made you follow an old blind woman into her dilapidated cabin?

Looking back on that day with its strange encounter in the woods makes me think of little Gretel meeting the witch-of-the-candy-house. Then, in deeper retrospect, my ponderings turn more toward the encounter that Luke Skywalker had with the entity, Yoda. Indeed, I smile at this comparison, for Yoda has certainly taken on a new significance for me. He represented the high wisdom of truth and, he was small and so elfin-like. . .so much like No-Eyes.

In order to clearly understand why I'd follow an old woman into her dilapidated cabin, my frame of mind at the time has to be taken into serious consideration. Actually, I was well primed for the destined meeting. I had been plunged into a terribly deep and dark depression that morning. I had written a milestone book of spiritual truths and predictions. This book was "given" to me by Bill's guide and no publisher would touch it. . .it appeared that I was presenting something too new and before its time. . .before a time when "channelers" were a known word. And, because I'd received the last rejection for it in the morning's mail from the final publisher on my list — my book was dead. So much valuable information would never reach the public. So long had I worked to get the material down exact as dictated. . .all for nothing. And I despaired.

You have to understand the incredible amount of determination and faith a struggling writer is required to sustain. I could've been published long ago if I had written sexy romances or bloody horror fabrications, but my purpose took other directions and paths, paths that the "dark side" loved to play on, to block! Consequently, I again was defeated in a skirmish while trying to accomplish my spirit's mission here, and I felt like I could no longer cope with my powerful adversaries who were the warriors of darkness.

So you see, I already figured that things couldn't get any worse than they were. What did I possibly have to lose by going with the old one?

Then, as she spoke and gave me certain knowing looks, I began to have those familiar inner signals that kicked my awareness back into gear and sent my hopes soaring once again. As my spine tingled and hair stood on end, a warm wave of light washed through me. . .and I was shot like a cannon ball up out of my depression. . .I was catapulted back up into the Light.

As it turned out, No-Eyes did indeed sneak me through the battle lines that were drawn between the forces of Light and Dark. I did win. When she said that I'd get through like a snake in the grass she meant that I'd get the same truths published, only this time, by using **her** story instead of the one I'd previously written.

She was a wise visionary who possessed the spiritual powers that far surpassed those of my long-time evil opponents and, through her tutelage, I have learned how to attain the strength of power needed to continue my many ongoing battles. . .I have learned to wield the warrior's power shield.

You must be insane to willingly be led into hell by No-Eyes! You had everything to lose and nothing to gain. What was your reasoning?

It may appear that way; however, you are merely skimming the surface here. When we deal with spiritual realities, we have to go far deeper.

You say that I must've been insane. But what is insane? War is insane. Bigotry is insane. Prejudice, avarice, egotism, and jealousy is insanity. Insanity is one of those clever words that can be qualified, depending upon the individual personal viewpoint of the speaker. See?

Now, let's get down to the specific matter of the issue. Yes, on the surface, it would indeed appear to be insanity to follow through with the psychic exercise No-Eyes had planned out for me that day. She knew that it would be a most grave trip—the most grave trip I'd ever have to make. That diabolical journey was to be my ultimate test of endurance, concentration, development, and power. Surely you don't think for one minute that she would've had me go through with it if she wasn't absolutely certain that I could accomplish the feat without coming out of it unscathed. However, she hadn't anticipated that I'd use God's own image as my spirit's companion of protection — and *that* worried her then. You must never, ever, underestimate the tremendous power of the White Light protection though. Faith in that, in conjunction with one's strength of power and conviction, can work miracles!

You say that I had everything to lose and nothing to gain. Think! What is the spirit's ultimate goal? To gain perfection so that it will rejoin the pure essence of God. Right?

Listen carefully here. The "everything" you say I could've lost would've merely been the facets of my *physical life*. We all die someday. Perhaps tomorrow I'll be killed by a speeding car. We cherish our physical lives and those we love. Each day we give thanks for the blessings of those around us that we dearly love. We live each day as though it will be our last. This is how my family has done it for years. It's as everyone should live. This way, there's no regrets — nothing left undone or unsaid. Physical death can crook its finger at us at any time death is not a fearful entity. It's not anything to be afraid of. So, after the final analysis, I had *nothing* to lose.

Then you state that I had nothing to gain. Again I say, think deeper! If I had not been able to retain my powerful force of protection while my spirit had been on the plane of hell, I would've experienced physical death, thereby freeing my spirit to live in the light of God — I had *everything* to gain if I had failed my exercise.

However, I didn't want to fail, simply because I wasn't yet finished with my work on the physical plane of reality —I had much yet to accomplish, many people to help. Therefore, I *had* to be certain that I would succeed and complete my journey test. And, as it happened, I was richly rewarded.

Also, you haven't taken into account something else. . .one's own personal spirit guide. I may elaborate on my own guide's identity later on, yet suffice it to say that there would just be no way I could've been harmed by the exercise. He was right there to immediately take my hand. Although I hadn't visualized him right away, he was standing by. . .as always.

Who were No-Eyes' friends that took care of her?

No-Eyes was an extremely private individual. You have to remember that fact. She frequently reinforced this attitude by clamming up whenever I attempted to extract some information regarding her personal life. There were specific subjects that she flatly refused to discuss and there were others that she would give token information on. She'd give bits and pieces of information like someone carefully leaving a meager trail of bread crumbs through the woods.

In the two years that I spent with my teacher, she spoke of her private friends only a few times. They had come out from Minnesota. They had produced families whose younger members would travel up from Pueblo twice a month to check on her and to bring her supplies such as radio batteries, kerosene for her lamp, containers for her many botanical collections, etc. Once a month the elders would make the trip to visit with her.

She also had others of her kind who occasionally came to visit. These people took care of all her needs and gave her the deep emotional support and bonding that her heavy heart required.

How many others did No-Eyes teach before you came along?

I plied my fancy wiles on the old one to extract the answer to this very question. I would cleverly attempt to get the answer in subtle ways by skirting the main question and sneaking up behind and beside it. And, as always, she had eyes in the back of her head — she knew what I was getting at every single time.

I was foolish to think that my finite mind could trick or outsmart her. No matter what form I used to cloak the question, she'd merely grin and shake her head. Yet, one time after she chuckled at my feeble attempt, she finally admitted to the fact that I was her seventh student. To me, this seemed like a very low number, but after she informed me that most of my predecessors spent many, many years with her, the number was more in line with what I'd heard of traditional Native teaching.

Most of the students left their teacher's protective wing to travel throughout the world, settle down and become private teachers to those who were led to them. They are silently teaching the aware seekers in places both here and on foreign soils. They all remain anonymous and go about their work in a quiet manner. Many Heart was and is one of these, for in simple peace does he roam the country at will, spreading the visionary's high wisdom and light wherever needed.

No-Eyes was indeed a spiritual pebble that has caused her students to perpetuate the ripple of awareness to spread endlessly throughout the sea of humanity. It could not be otherwise, for she was indeed that kind of teacher.

Was No-Eyes ever sick?

There are many kinds of "sick," but it would be logical to conclude that you're referring to a "physical" illness of any type.

I cannot speak for the time prior to my meeting her, but during the time frame I spent with the visionary she never endured any form of physical sickness. You have to understand that her lifestyle was one of ancient tradition — the Indian way of living close to the earth.

She made sure she spent the majority of her day outside in the fresh mountain air. She walked her woods and mountainsides every day, no matter how inclement the weather was; heavy snowfall, blustery wind, or bitter cold had no adverse affect upon her extremely strong constitution. These less than pleasant aspects of nature merely provided her with vast diversity. Her mental faculties were forever being exercised and stretched to their limits (if indeed she had limits in this area). She ate of the healthful bounties that her Earth Mother lovingly provided, exercised her limbs in the deeper pools of the valley stream and rejoiced in the warmth of the sun. She was one with the entity of the earth and, in turn, earth nourished and sustained her.

But I saw another sort of sickness invade the being of No-Eyes. This was a sickness of the heart. She deeply longed for her homeland. She pined for the serenity of her lost heritage ways. She cried inside for her presently-oppressed people. She silently keened for the future of man.

Although I saw all this wrenching heartache within my gentle teacher, I also saw the healers — hope for mankind, knowledge of the final peace, joy for the "risen race," and the serenity of returning to her homeland where she would take her last walk into the woods of home. All this did I see and the seeing did soothe my own heart.

Could No-Eyes control the weather? I've read somewhere that some Indians know how this is done. Or is it a myth?

You certainly can't believe everything you read. And I hope that you don't. I hope you're more discriminating than that.

The theory that certain Indians knew (or know) how to control the forces of nature (weather included), however, is based upon fact. It would appear to be quite a preposterous feat for any one person to possess a power great enough to be able to affect the basic nature elements. Nevertheless, this power is not a physical one, but rather stems from the correct knowledge of same.

In the old tradition, the great shamans and medicinepeople obtained this highly secret knowledge from their powerful teachers. These secrets were considered strong medicine, consequently, they were carefully guarded and passed along only to those who had proven their goodness and worthiness. Indeed, such knowledge was (and is) sacred.

In answer to your question, yes, No-Eyes did know how to affect the weather at will. The mechanics of the feat are simple, just as all the laws of nature are once they're understood. And. . .no, I'm not planning on giving lessons on this, for as always, these things are sacred — they would be absolutely destructive in the wrong hands. Some knowledge must forever remain locked within the pure hearts of those who were chosen to guard them. Until mankind reaches the same heights of comprehension about the Earth Mother, certain laws governing nature will remain a baffling mystery.

Oh, you decry, Summer Rain is not "sharing" that which she knows! But Summer Rain is sharing. I share those things that are deemed to be shared and I retain those that *must* be retained. That fact has been shared, for I have not come to lay bare that which is too sacred to receive the light of day. There are laws to be strictly followed. I have not come to break these.

Why did the old woman want to be such a recluse? Why didn't she want you to tell anyone where she lived?

You've asked two questions here. In order to fully comprehend my answer, you would have to possess a deep understanding of the Indian mind and way of life. To begin with, the Indian people are quiet people. They have a unique awareness about them that is in a continual state of functioning. This means that they analyze and take in all the facets of their surroundings *at all times.* At least this is how it used to be. Consequently, they would appear to walk slow, make lengthy decisions, be seemingly lazy or reticent to speak. Awareness has a way of slowing down the physical responses — the exterior facade.

No-Eyes was a true Indian in every sense of the word, in that she was a traditional individual who treasured that singular characteristic of constant awareness. This caused her great inner turmoil whenever she ventured out into the busy modern-day world of haste and waste. She never liked what she saw and she always returned to her cabin with a very definitive irritation. She referred to this worldly irritation as , "bugs on her." So it was only natural for her to prefer to stay up within the serenity of the mountains and away from man's blatant unawareness.

In answer to part two of your question, I will let the words of the old one herself take care of that. "Summer gonna promise No-Eyes that she never never gonna tell peoples where lessons been. Peoples gonna come an' gawk. They gonna think this be some great sacred place. They gonna trample Earth Mother's breast tryin' to take bits of No-Eyes' house away. Peoples be stupid, Summer. They no see that lessons be most important here —they no see very good now. It not matter *where* truth come from. Summer gonna promise, huh."

And again her foresight has been borne out, for several people I've met with asked if they could see the cabin. Why, I asked, wondering if it was for personal verification of my story. It wasn't. They would lower their eyes and respond, I just wanted a little piece of her cabin.

There's another reason I'll never take anyone to the cabin, but that'll be covered in another response.

How could No-Eyes see without the physical use of her eyes? This would be a breakthrough in the medical field for all the permanently blind people of the world.

The sight No-Eyes possessed was a paranormal spiritual gift she was born with in order to compensate for her lack of physical sight and to hasten the comprehension of her spiritual instruction by her father.

Soul sight (don't like the word psychic) is a spiritual gift. It is given to those who would not misuse it in any way, essentially, that means those with a pure heart who have spiritually-related work to accomplish.

This soul sight is a fragmented aspect of paranormal functioning. It can be developed within the minds of those who were not born with it — those who did not inherit it. Yet this talent requires years of exhaustive efforts placed into its development. And, on the whole, those years could be put to better use by helping *mankind* rather than helping **oneself** to powers one may never fully attain.

No-Eyes' senses were the most acute I'd ever witnessed. She not only possessed soul sight, but also an uncanny hearing ability.

You must remember that until one has gained the prerequisites of total awareness, belief in the truths and an absolute acceptance of life, the gifts of the soul will remain out of reach.

The visionary could "split" her spirit awareness, thereby, "seeing" everything while half out of her body.

Are there more people like No-Eyes who teach willing seekers? I'd like to be one of their students.

Ones such as No-Eyes do not advertise their readiness to teach, for the Way of it is for the student to "appear" before them at the appropriate "destined" time. The Way is for all things to come about in a natural fashion without any conscious force placed on the issue or eventual encounter. This is the only method of operation for these ones.

As the visionary revealed, she taught six others besides myself. I was her seventh one. These former students are now in the world as teachers themselves.

Please understand that each of these former students of No-Eyes were spiritually developing for years and years. They were not novitiates on the spiritual path. They had the inner awareness to strike out on their own to follow their individual paths as their Higher Self urgings directed. They experienced many hardships along the way and underwent many years of longsuffering. They endured ridicule and participated in many battles with the Dark Forces in order to finally end up on the doorstep of No-Eyes' cabin. It was like playing Dungeons and Dragons, only it was *real.* And, after reaching the safety of the visionary's cabin, they spent many, many seasons studying under her strict intensive tutelage.

Now these people are out on their own, teaching those spiritual seekers who have been guided by their personal promptings.

I cannot direct you to one of these teachers, just as nobody showed me to my teacher. It must come from deep within self! It must come from the depths of the individual perceiving soul.

Out of all No-Eyes' students, I was the only one she wished to go public with her words — probably because I was a writer who had been previously defeated when I fought and fought to spread the truths. And, more probable, because she knew I was to be her last.

Also, do not entertain the idea that No-Eyes' students are the only teachers available. Be it known that there are many others who patiently await the right seeker to step upon their pathway. There are teachers of every race. Search your heart. Seek and you shall find. Knock and it shall be opened unto you.

Was the medicine woman a walk-in?

Before I respond to this question, two words need to be clarified. Familiarity with terms does not necessarily denote understanding of them.

The term "medicine woman" has been bastardized of late. It is used to define a broad scope of concepts. The term has become stirred in a big boiling pot that includes the ingredients of many other ideas. A medicine woman is not the same as a shaman or shamaness. Please separate your concepts and retain the proper nomenclature for such.

I prefer that No-Eyes not be referred to as a medicine woman, for she was so much more. Because of her all-encompassing wisdom and scope of knowledge, she was many things and she was all things.

The term "visionary" best suits her.

Now, the term "walk-ins" is not by any means a new one.

It has existed since spirits first gained the use of physical vehicles (bodies), yet "walk-in" is not the original terminology; but since it has already become popularized, we will stick with it here for the sake of clarity.

While spirits are existing in the transitional stage between incarnations, they must determine what accomplishments their next physical life will achieve. The spirit is determined and full of relentless energy and excitement to be about its new chosen work.

However, once the spirit is in the physical third dimension once again, life's adverse circumstances and conditions have a way of wearing down that determination and energy to such a low level that the physical mind now wishes to leave (suicide).

Now listen: this is very important. While the depressed and suicidal individual is asleep, his spirit offers the physical body to another spirit who is fired up to carry on in *place* of the original spirit. When both spirits agree, the switch is made — the spirit of the suicidal person withdraws to carry on in the spirit plane while the new spirit returns and enters into the dreamer's body. The "new" spirit has literally walked in to the body that the tired spirit *walked-out* of. See? Now when the dreamer awaked, it would appear to those around him that he has become a new person who no longer entertains the deeply depressive thoughts, but rather is now filled with a renewed vigor for life! This fact of the spirit has been going on for eons. It has been termed differently depending on the ethnic culture or timeframe. For centuries, the Native people have known it as "Trading Ghosts."

The unusual circumstances surrounding No-Eyes' birth, youth and educational upbringing do not support the theory that she was a walk-in or a ghost-trader. And, in fact, she was not.

What did No-Eyes wear and where did she get her clothing?

The visionary preferred to wear ankle-length skirts with long-sleeved peasant-type blouses. Of course, nothing she wore ever matched, but then that was part of her unique character — she didn't care and neither did I.

Her clothing was supplied by her Indian friends who either hand-made them or bought them for her. The old one had all her needs adequately taken care of. She was never in want for anything.

I met a woman who claims she'd been channeling No-Eyes before your books were published. This didn't strike me as being credible. Was it?

It was about as credible as the many other dozens of so-called channelers who are claiming the same regarding No-Eyes. I'm pleased that you had the intelligence to perceive the falsehood, for it would appear that many channelers believe the public is so gullible they'll believe anything.

No-Eyes has been with me in spirit since the day she made her transition. She is absolutely disgusted with those people who are claiming any sort of communication with her. She says it is clear evidence of the critical time we're in whereby many of the false prophets will be manifesting.

Although this very idea of people claiming communication with No-Eyes greatly distresses me, I too understand the deep void within people and their eagerness to make any claim that may serve self in filling that darkness within. But remember that falsehoods can never bring light. . .lies will never fill the void within the self.

Anyone claiming to channel No-Eyes is either lying or is being seriously duped by a lesser entity who is misrepresenting their identity. A channeler who cannot recognize a lesser entity shouldn't be channeling in the first place. . .either way, the channeler loses, as does his/her clients.

Be it served as Notice: *No-Eyes does not channel to anyone.* She is *still* my closest friend, companion, and advisor. So anyone claiming to be channeling No-Eyes had better pick another name out of the hat — and do it quickly.

Your teacher was very strict, yet she seemed to have a soft spot in her heart for you. Do you think she felt sorry that she had to leave you?

Yes, she could be so strict and demanding that some days I would actually be reduced to tears of frustration. And double yes, she did have a soft spot in her heart for me. She always attempted to put up a stern and unyielding facade, but her true emotions usually managed to break through it.

No-Eyes was a master at controlling and concealing her true emotions, especially those that were deep-seated within her tender heart. When we spoke about the day when she would no longer be with me, she made brave attempts to be the tower of strength, but when she saw my own crushed, devastated reaction, she faltered. She put my head down in her lap so that I couldn't witness her weakness, but I witnessed it all the same as her tear fell on my forehead.

I believe my friend felt sorry for several reasons. She very much wanted to teach more seekers. She wanted to touch a copy of my first published book. She wanted to watch me work in my future office. She wanted to join me in the falcon's eternal flight, to feel the warmth of many more suns, to inhale the woodsmoke in my home, and to continue our friendship forever.

Yes, No-Eyes was sorry that she had to leave, but maybe you'd like to know that she still inhales my woodsmoke, she still teaches me, she touched my first book and we still fly the falcon together.

No-Eyes hasn't left me at all — she's merely changed a little. . . her old bones no longer creak.

How did the medicine woman collect all her botanicals if she was blind?

The woman's physical blindness was not a handicap in any way! You must understand that she could see with her *spirit!* She could see hundreds of times better than if she possessed physical sight. The woman invented remote viewing!

Her spirit could see behind her, to either side, above, below, and *through.* Please know that this type of soul sight is common among the highly spiritually-developed individuals of enlightenment, even for those who also have normal eyesight.

Frequently, when we strolled through her woodlands together, she would switch off her soul sight in order to allow me to feel helpful to her by holding onto her arm and guiding her along. But when we sat to rest, she'd turn it back on and teach me about the forest and its ways.

As far as the gathering of botanicals went, she'd harvest whatever grew in her locale and the rest were provided by her friends from Pueblo who supplied those that were grown elsewhere around the country.

Did No-Eyes ever admit to any fears?

That's an interesting one.

Let's begin by stating that a highly intellectual individual would be a foolish individual if he did not give fear its due respect. Only a fool would continually throw caution to the wind. Therefore, No-Eyes was a cautious woman when it came to lessons or exercises where danger lurked in the shadowed sidelines.

The only fear she admitted to me (and that was *after* the fact I might add) was when I envisioned the wrong protection to shield me on my lonely journey into hell. Although she openly admitted how deeply that had frightened her, there were other occasions when I could tell by her tenseness that she was filled with an intense anxiety as to whether or not I'd be able to fully accomplish a dangerously difficult spiritual task successfully.

You have to remember that she worked me through complex lessons of the spirit and took me into various negative vortexes of dark forces.

I never saw fear on my teacher's face — not real fear —only serious concern and caution.

Did you ever meet with your teacher's friends or any other of her visitors?

No-Eyes could be secretive about her personal friends and she did prefer to keep her students and friends separated.

Students were supposed to be of one mind and that one mind was to be always centered on focused, serious learning rather than on the enjoyment of casual conversation — that constituted wasted learning time.

However, after I had been under her tutelage for some time, I was allowed to meet with her old friends and some of their younger family members. No-Eyes didn't receive any outside visitors except for these people and several other native elders.

Occasionally a hiker or wandering tourist would lose their mountain way and ask her for directions back to the road, other than that, No-Eyes was alone and that's precisely how she wanted it, because instructing the seekers was her only business and she didn't like her business interrupted by anyone.

When I was fortunate enough to have my days shared with the elder friends of No-Eyes, it was like being in the midst of a circle of shamans. Some of my answers brought on thundering peals of uproarious laughter, while other answers produced solemn nods. I loved those rare days spent in the company of No-Eyes and her wise friends. I learned from their deep wisdom and they were pleasingly amused to share a day with No-Eyes' famous "incorrigible" student.

What did No-Eyes eat and how did she do her cooking?

My friend did her cooking on her kitchen woodstove and, more often than not, she'd simply set her cast iron dutch oven in the fireplace.

Her food supply was most unlike that of our modern-day cupboard stock. Initially, when I first met her, she didn't have any form of processed market food available. She made wonderfully tasting breads from the ground seeds and nuts that were harvested from the land — hot cereals were also created from these wild edibles. Teas and coffees were converted from the local plants and seeds. Her vegetables and fruits were all from the Earth Mother's pantry.

After I got to know the lady better, I began bringing her items such as powdered milk, granola bars, raisins, fresh fruits and vegetables, and vanilla-flavored instant breakfast mixes.

No-Eyes became particularly fond of boxed oat and raisin cereal. She would eat them right out of the box while she rocked in her chair during my lessons. It was quite a comical sight and I had to frequently control my impolite urges to giggle, but then she understood, for she could see my smiling heart.

I read an article in the A.R.E. Journal that made reference to a popular writer who spent time with a blind Indian woman who talked like Tonto and named her botanicals in modern-day terms. I was shocked to see this cursory reference to No-Eyes.

As am I, especially since the writer of the article had only a cursory knowledge and superficial understanding of No-Eyes. If indeed this writer was referring to my visionary, she committed grave journalistic errors by not contacting me for deeper background information for her material. In essence, the writer assumed that which was in error. Consequently she passed on misinformation to all her readers. . .proof that many writers have lost the true art of journalism.

Now I must address and attempt to correct the aspersions against No-Eyes. In my frantic midnight hours of trying to capture my times with the visionary, it must be understood that I actually relived those experiences. In doing so, I mentally *heard* the old one's voice as memory sped to recall all the conversations we had. To alter her manner of speech would not make for an accurate record, I wrote down what I heard — what was spoken — and the *manner* of same. Therefore have I managed to bring the true essence of the visionary before the eyes and hearts of the readers.

In reference to the botanicals, No-Eyes termed these by her own unique language of classification such as "the blue ones," "the night ones," etc. It took a great deal of my time sorting out precise botanicals and attaching their modern-day names to each. If I recorded her exact terms for the botanicals, the reader wouldn't know what I was talking about. See? This has been explained in *Earthway* also.

What did you do immediately after you discovered that No-Eyes had finally left you?

After I had gently closed her cabin door for the last time, I stood alone on her empty porch and let my misted eyes scan the mountains that she had loved. I was numb from head to toe. A great cold lead weight had lodged deep within my chest, as if it had replaced my warmly beating heart. I was in shock. No thoughts came to me as I hypnotically panned the glorious sun-touched scenery around my old schoolhouse.

My next conscious memory was that of my secret valley. I don't even remember how I got there, but I was standing on the dew-flecked grass, staring down into the swift coursing stream that had caught the sun's blinding rays and reflected them up into my eyes — mesmerizing me. I stood and allowed myself to be absorbed by the gentle magic hand of nature. Then a shadow of a large bird passed over me, breaking the stream's charmed trance. I looked up into the deepness of the sky's blue eyes and their magnetic intensity drew out my painful grief as I sent up a long death wail — a wail that released my soul song into the waiting wings of the wind which carried it away so that my healing could then begin.

Was it hard learning how to fly with the falcon? I'd love to be able to do something like that.

The pleasurable benefits of awareness are rewards for those who have expended great efforts, diligence, and persistence toward attainment.

The feat of flying with the falcon can be accomplished in two ways. One is by "soul sight" which entails the concept of absolute observation when the individual's consciousness is voluntarily transferred to that of the object being observed; and the second method is by "soul flight," where the spirit is voluntarily sent to the desired object.

Both of these methods can be satisfactorily developed after intensive practice. It requires a strong control of the individual's mind. However, these talents will be extremely difficult to accomplish if the individual has not initially attained a certain high level of awareness. I'm sorry that I cannot simply say that everyone can do these things with ease, without a great expenditure of strenuous efforts of mental and spiritual control. But then, that is the way it is with all spiritual/paranormal functioning.

Soul sight is by far the easiest. It merely involves the complete transfer of one's centered and focused consciousness. It can be done by anyone. All that is required is for the individual to be able to observe an object and simultaneously forget all aspects of self. Soon you'll find that your own consciousness has been successfully transferred to that of the object, thereby sensing all stimuli affecting the object.

Soul flight is extremely difficult and involves complex efforts that cannot be strong enough if the awareness measure has not been developed to a certain degree of higher attainment.

I don't understand how No-Eyes could manage alone when she was blind, especially being so up in years.

This subject matter has been covered in one of my previous answers, however, because it was asked about so often, I'll take a moment to reinforce it.

Look around you. Senior citizens are not the sedentary folks of old. They're travelling, swimming, dancing, and jogging.

No-Eyes was a true Indian, in that she maintained a spartan lifestyle. Fresh air, daily exercise, proper diet, and good mental attitudes were her four basic rules of physical health and total well-being.

Her blindness never had any negative effects upon her lifestyle because of her sharp soul sight.

I supplied her with several market items and personal items such as shawls and afghans. Bill would spend occasional weekends up at her place splitting wood and restocking her fireside woodpile. No-Eyes' Indian friends visited her regularly to round out her stock of supplies.

When the old one was alone she managed without any problems. She kept busy, both physically and mentally.

No-Eyes might have appeared to be a blind old woman on the exterior — but inside, she was an eternal youngster.

What types of mystical lessons did No-Eyes receive from her father, Two Trees?

No-Eyes often had vivid flashbacks into her youth during my lessons that involved the mystical aspects of life's spiritual realities. When these recalled memories came to her, we'd digress from our current lesson and I'd excitedly listen to her memories with great interest.

Some of these flashbacks would be sad, some would be quite humorous and, of course, some would be most frightening, but no matter what their mood, No-Eyes would frantically animate the detailed re-telling with exaggerated expressions and actions. These moments of the past were especially enjoyable for me. Even now they are reserved as the sweetest of memories.

Two Trees taught his youthful daughter the mechanics of soul flight, and the young girl journeyed to distant realities to learn of their finer vibrations. The fledgling visionary was brought gently through the Corridor of Time where she witnessed her own future. She was taught methods of altering her consciousness so that she could effectively communicate with the entities of nature. She studied and practiced with beetles, rocks, and frogs — she practiced her weather-works until she was successful, every time. She journeyed to the Land of Ghosts where her learning advanced to still higher degrees.

Two Trees watched with held breath as his only daughter confronted a powerful shaman's destructive spirit. And No-Eyes learned how to help the wayward spirits find their way back home. Eventually the young woman was taught the complex process of teleportation.

All these esoteric lessons and more were recounted by my sometimes melancholy teacher. She loved remembering them and she knew that the re-telling also helped me obtain a deeper measure of comprehension.

Was No-Eyes' mother afraid to let her daughter travel so far away, especially when she knew she'd most likely never see her again?

An individual's spiritual awareness of another's mission in life does not necessarily eradicate their own personal fear for that person, particularly when that individual is a dearly loved daughter.

Remember that Pretty Weasel knew right from the moment of No-Eyes' birth that she was destined to accomplish great spiritual things. She knew her daughter would one day leave to be about her own business of the spirit.

And all through the youthful years of her daughter's life, Pretty Weasel practiced acceptance for what was to eventually come — the day No-Eyes would be on her own way.

Yes, she was fearful, but not because she had doubts about how well her daughter would care for herself in an unknown region.

She was fearful of the Dark Side that is ever watchful for the chosen entities of Light who have come to help the masses work their way toward the Great Spirit.

Two Trees comforted his worried wife by frequently utilizing his soul sight and soul flight to check up on their distant daughter. And, after awhile, Pretty Weasel had gained enough confidence to realize that her daughter could indeed handle herself in any situation — physical or spiritual.

Could the old medicine woman communicate with animals?

Yes, No-Eyes often communicated with the feathered and furred residents of her beautiful woodlands.

Of course you must realize that this communication takes place on a purely spiritual level.

Animals possess highly psychic instincts. They communicate with their own species in a language of physical signals and verbal sounds coupled with these psychic facets of their inner instincts. They communicate with each other and also with those humans who they perceive as being "one" (sympathetic) with all of nature.

This communication between man and animals is more like a "touching" of spirits. If a human has gained enough sensitivity he can actually perceive thoughts from an animal. In turn, the human's thoughts can be perceived by the animal.

Never entertain the false idea that animals cannot possess feelings and thoughts! Listen and you will hear for self!

Do you know if the visionary ever saw an extraterrestrial?

This is an extremely touchy subject for me. Especially since I've not fully written about the issue in any of the books yet.

When the time came for No-Eyes to introduce this subject, she initially extracted my own experiences with UFOs before speaking about her own personal ongoing encounters.

If you were a highly intelligent alien visiting and guarding the people of an alien planet, what type of people would you feel most comfortable with? A fearful person? A skeptic? A scientist? Military individuals? Of course not. You'd be fearful yourself that any one of these types would either pull out a shotgun on you or lock you up for a scientific autopsy! An intelligent alien would naturally be drawn to a highly enlightened individual who possessed an absolute understanding and acceptance of such foreign beings, one who would be totally comfortable and calm in the face of such an encounter.

And so it was with No-Eyes. She never sought out such beings, but rather they quickly found her. The remote cabin was ideal for their gatherings. They communicated in peace and total acceptance of one another, and she learned of their plans to protect the warlike earth people from their missile follies. She learned much from them and, they in turn, gained from knowing her.

Did No-Eyes ever see a nature being like you did?

It's not likely that I could have an experience that would not already have been experienced by my teacher.

There were many times when No-Eyes would be sitting alone within her deep woodlands and suddenly see the clear image of a nature person appear behind her. She'd mentally greet it and then send her spirit out to converse with it.

The environment is full of these little inhabitants. Deserts, plains, waterways, and especially the mountains.

Remember that all lifeforms that possess intelligence were created by God and, because of this aspect, they also possess souls. Just because you've personally never actually seen a different, intelligent lifeform does not prove that they do not or cannot exist.

Why are the small beings so nebulous — so secretive? Think what mankind would do if he ever got his hands on one! We are a collective civilization of skeptics and doubters and, when physical living proof is evidenced to validate a seemingly mythical entity, we are too inclined to take it apart to see how it ticks and then preserve its parts for all the world to view for validation. We are not ready for such encounters. We are still a primitive lot.

Did No-Eyes end up teaching you all she knew about healing with the wild botanicals?

After my amazement over my teacher's massive botanical supply finally subsided, I expressed a deep interest in learning about these wonderful healing and edible wild plants.

Yet, while we were on the subject, she'd watch me bottle up this plant and grind up that one. I worked long and hard with an excited fervor. And she'd silently look on.

Then, one day I realized that most of what I had collected would go bad, be ineffective, by the time I'd need them. I had masses of jars and odd-shaped containers filled with all manner of botanicals that I'd probably never use. That's when the visionary spoke up and smiled. I had finally come to the logical realization that I didn't really need all those plants.

After I did more intensive research, I discovered that most of my healing botanicals could be bought fresh in capsule form from most any local health food shop. I emptied my jars of dried up plants and replaced them with vials of capsules. Nearly every botanical had a capsule equivalent. This was easiest for me, though collecting them fresh was easiest for No-Eyes.

Although we now utilize the capsule form of No-Eyes herbals, we still harvest certain fresh botanicals, especially the plantain which a salve is made from for insect bites and all forms of skin rashes and irritations. And my youngest daughter, Sarah, is always on the lookout for newly-sprouted puffballs. She'll come in the door with a pocketfull, gently remove them, proudly display them to me in her dirt-covered palms and carefully place them, one-by-one, into the puffball jar. These little quarter-sized grey balls are found growing out of the damp ground. If you would accidentally step on one, a puff of dark grey matter would rise from its hole in the top like a puff of smoke. These puffballs are one of nature's naturalgrowing antibiotics and we use them as a poultice under bandaged abrasions, for burns and any infectious skin condition. They have proven to be miracle healers for us.

Do you think that No-Eyes was sent by God? She obviously was a great philosopher and was privy to sources that gave her deep wisdom.

Nobody can absolutely state that they know what is in God's mind. No-Eyes never said, nor even hinted, that she was sent by the Great Spirit. I don't say that she was either.

Please listen well here. Do not assume that merely because an enlightened individual presents himself and appears to be highly spiritual with deep philosophical comprehensions does not automatically signify that he/she is sent from God. I believe that anyone who would say this about oneself is egotistical, self-serving, and a false prophet. I admit to a few genuine messengers of God, one being Jesus.

You must be careful what you say or assume about others. Do *not* attribute sanctity upon anyone. Do *not* deify *anyone*. Only *God* deserves those highest attributes.

You must remember that many hundreds of spirits have well attained near perfection and have volunteered to return to the physical world to help bring truth and the light of awareness to the masses. It is these dedicated, one-minded individuals who have broken away from the norm and searched their path of destiny, their personal mission of enlightening the world. To claim that these individuals have been personally sent by God is highly presumptuous. They are simply near-completed spirits who have retained their memories of the truths and have returned to help light the minds of the world.

What did No-Eyes mean when she talked about the "mountains telling her things." What were her "voices on the wind?"

The visionary knew things that no person ever told her. She was aware of things that haven't been set down in any books. She was cognizant of personal happenings in my life that I never spoke to her about. How was this to be? How *could* this be?

Many times her reply would simply be, "mountains tell No-Eyes that!" or "voices on wind say so, they never speak untruths!" And, two or three times she even said, "little person in woods say so."

Know that the truths are constant. They are universal. They are basic and without complexity. Man confuses and complicates the truths by making many changes, translations, alterations, and updates. The truths cannot be altered. They undulate about the atmosphere in a continuum of pure energy within the fine current — a knowledge energy, and

No-Eyes could perceive these circulating truths as their fine vibrations emanated from the mountains and were gently carried on the wind. Indeed, the wind carries many voices upon its gentle breath. Listen and you'll hear their whispers of truth. Listen with the *soul* of self, for the wind and the mountains do indeed whisper.

What did your wise teacher think of our modern technological advances? Was she impressed?

Hardly. No-Eyes was far from impressed with mankind's technological advances. She viewed our current civilization as an extremely backward one. Our energy advancements were perceived as reversals rather than forward strides, our medical knowledge was backward, our governments were blind and untrusting to the point of being paranoid, our general attitudes were dark and our humanitarian views were completely nonexistent.

The old one laughed at the crude space program because she said that we would've been centuries more advanced if we only would've been more peaceful throughout development and hadn't been so inclined to divert efforts into preparataions for warfare. She was extremely appalled at our utilization of nuclear energy. She said that the scientists have been putting their heads in the air instead of on the ground where the real energy sources could be found in free abundance.

She insisted that the widespread utilization of computers were going to eventually prove to be a big part of humankind's downfall. Our televisions were archaic too. She said we should be at such a stage of development where we could *mentally* be viewing all information. And we had become synthetic people because of all the chemical drugs we were treated with, instead of the natural botanicals that had more effect upon our unique physiological systems. She said that chemotherapy often complicated a diseased condition and that *mental* efforts performed by the patient would be far more effective than being bombarded by intense radiation. More than once did she extoll the beautiful benefits of radio waves and sound waves for healing. Yet, it seemed to her, such simplistic methods were still too far beyond our comprehension or reach.

Our eating habits were disgraceful and our use of laborsaving devices was concrete evidence of our lazy attitudes.

Did No-Eyes ever tell you about any of her past lives? If so, what were they?

Yes. She detailed some to me so that I could grasp the concept of the carry-over soul with a more thorough comprehension. However,

I'm not at liberty to reveal them because they aren't really relevant to anyone.

What did No-Eyes do for money?

She never required money because all her needs were satisfactorily met by those who loved and cared for her.

What were some of your teacher's faults?

Her faults were insignificant compared to her beautiful qualities. I never speak of another person's faults. If you wished me to help you with yours, I'd be more than happy to, but do not concern self with the faults of others.

Did you ever take No-Eyes for a drive through your mountains?

What would either of us gain by this physical activity? She already could see and sense all of nature from her broken rocker. And, if I was driving, how could I then be free to participate in the sharing of the wonderful sensations of nature? We journeyed through many a mountain pathway together, but not by way of any physical vehicle.

No-Eyes always encouraged the utilization of absolute acceptance in one's life, Yet she herself couldn't accept man's ignorance. Wasn't that like telling people to do as she said but not as she did?

It is always judgement that creates problems.

The question signifies that one expected No-Eyes to be perfect. We forget that the woman was human.

You might recall that the most saintly person to have visited this earthly plane went against his own teachings. Jesus taught people to always control their anger, yet he became enraged with the sight of the moneychangers on the steps of his Father's holy temple. Jesus too became a human, therefore he became susceptible to the frailties that can assail the human condition. Would you expect No-Eyes to perform more perfectly than Jesus?

Some doctors claim that smoking may cause cancer, yet many of those same professionals smoke themselves. Dentists say to brush three times a day, yet many of them don't. Just because a person of authority tells you what is right — the truth about a subject, does not mean that they personally follow those same rules to the letter of the law — all the time! Still, that does not alter the truth of the matter, it does not make it any less concrete. See?

The question infers that you judge people. You must not concern yourself with the contrary actions of others, but rather with how you personally follow the law. My advice to you would be to monitor the actions of self according to the beliefs of self.

Why was your teacher so short with you on occasion? I would think that an enlightened spiritual teacher would be the epitome of patience and total serenity.

One must learn to see others as absolute individuals. . . unique in every way. You cannot place people into neat little cubbyholes and label them this or that.

Your mental picture of an enlightened teacher would make me think that you would have No-Eyes wear a loincloth, sit within a darkened cave high up in the cloud-covered mountains and fast until she was thin skin over bones. No-Eyes wasn't some bearded guru that feigned eternal holiness. Please stop classifying people by preconceived notions.

No-Eyes was strict. That was paramount for our often dangerous lessons. It was vital for a spiritual student to retain a severe seriousness and an exact control over all aspects of self.

Her frequent impatience stemmed from her high awareness and the continual caution of that deadly seriousness. Her methods of instruction were highly unconventional, yet they were most effective. She was a woman who possessed an intense love for her work and for her students, therefore, she freely displayed her joy and her excitement and even her impatience. She was a demonstrative individual who could show her moods and her intentions by simple silent animations. This was part of her beautiful personality — it was a part that I dearly loved. It made me laugh and it could make me cry. It was a big part of why I loved her. She was strict because she also loved me back.

Did No-Eyes ever speak about any other teachers that are here now? How about her former students?

The old one spoke about her students who are now teachers. She spoke of several Indian men who held the truths deep within the protective confines of their hearts. She mentioned black people who taught within their own communities. And she would speak of many races who had enlightened beings among them.

Returned teachers are everywhere. They just don't advertise, as that is not their way. They are silently going about their work of bringing the seekers up into a higher plane of awareness and vibration.

There are teachers who are well-known individuals, yet you don't recognize them as being teachers because they utilize their spiritual knowledge in ways that you don't perceive. These teachers are active in all sectors of our world. The slums, the executive suites of corporations, the cities, the suburbs, the beaches, the neighborhood you live in all have teachers.

Don't be searching for the "teacher" stereotype. If you do, you won't be in the company of a "real" teacher. Please remember that the truly enlightened teachers will not be toting a bible or wearing sackcloth robes, but will be one of those among you, they will be their own individual, one who is first true to self so they can then be true to others. Physical appearances can deceive.

Follow not the self-proclaimed, but rather the guidance within self, for the enlightened do not walk apart, but among.

Did No-Eyes ever say whether or not you'd personally meet any of her previous students who are now teachers?

After the old one finally gave in and spoke about her former students, she loosened up a little more and told me where some of them were. And I wouldn't be physically encountering any of them except for Brian Many Heart.

I accepted this completely. I thoroughly understood the seriousness of their purpose. They were to be of one mind as they instructed their own students. They now possessed an absolute centered and focused purpose for their lives. Many of them have left for foreign lands and have no intention of returning to this country in the future. No-Eyes mentioned the possibility of me moving to another country at some later date. Therefore, since all of her students are so widely scattered, it would be quite impossible to get together, and, it would deter them from their important tasks at hand.

No-Eyes said that you were so different from her other students. In what ways were you different?

From what little information she revealed regarding past students, they were serious, well disciplined, deeply respectful, and somewhat frightened by their teacher's powers. They performed their difficult exercises without question or challenge. This was what No-Eyes expected and demanded, except perhaps for the lack of her students' use of challenge, she contended that they were model seekers who became adept graduates.

Then I stumbled along and all that changed. I presented the wise one with an entirely new experience. I had inherited the quality of excited animation from my own ancestral grandmother. I was filled with an uncontrollable exuberance that hinged upon my deep sensual love for the mountains and all of nature. All my emotions were externalized, I never felt the need to contain them in the presence of my teacher.

So, I was far different from my model predecessors because I readily voiced my emotions, thoughts, and ideas. I frequently challenged my instructor's concepts or reasonings. I'd misbehave during lessons by allowing my spirit to join in an elated celebration of nature instead of keeping my mind chained to the lesson at hand.

I occasionally doubted some facets of the future that No-Eyes foresaw, consequently, we challenged one another like rams clashing their horns. I would rant and rave at her as I paced back and forth across her floor. I would pull my silent treatment on the old one whenever she proved me wrong. And, of course, I had the distinction of being the only one who swore.

Some evenings when I'd be driving home after having been a particularly troublesome and incorrigible student, I'd berate myself for giving the old one such a hard time. But then toward the time of our last months together, she confessed that it was my ecstatic love of nature — my intense love of life, my open sensitivities, my continual questioning mind and my open honesty that amused her so. She actually enjoyed my tirades and incessant questions and reasonings. I refreshed her. And I suppose that was why she initially called me Summer Rain.

Although she justified all of my undisciplined actions, she never could bring herself to overlook the swearing I did. She said that spiritual teachers didn't do things like that. Well, maybe not. I continue to insist that *she* was the wise spiritual teacher; I, merely the one she wished to write about her beautiful concepts. I'm not a mountaintop guru or master of deep wisdom. I'm simply a human — just like you.

Did No-Eyes psychically communicate with her parents after she relocated into the Colorado Rockies?

Yes, with her father. I could expand on this by describing their many sensitive conversations and precious moments of deeply moving "touchings," but that would be a direct invasion of their beautiful privacy, wouldn't it.

Did No-Eyes teach you any mystical things that weren't in your books?

Of course. But they'd have been in the books if they were meant for the public eye. Again, please understand that ones such as No-Eyes and

Joe Red Sky and Brian Many Heart are cognizant to the ways of nature and of the spirit. Being wise to such ways naturally opens up certain areas of higher wisdom and comprehensions, yet these must remain resting upon sacred ground where they silently await other enlightened individuals to discover them. They themselves cannot be taken out of their holy temple.

Did No-Eyes want you to write instruction books on the methods of attaining awareness and psychic development?

Absolutely not! Hers were not the simple childish techniques that are presently found within the current popular psychic how-to books. True paranormal functioning of the spirit is not a game for the parlor, nor is it any toy for the unaware to amuse self with. There is no learning of these techniques without the constant serious companionship and ever-watchful eye of an experienced enlightened teacher. Without this, you may find yourself in dark unfamiliar places of no return. There just are no clear-cut, step by step methods of obtaining psychic development and/or spiritual enlightenment. That is to say, no step-by-step formulas that can be applied and utilized by everyone.

Will you go to Minnesota to visit No-Eyes' gravesite someday?

This question doesn't show a firm grasp of the death concept.

One of the old one's most adamant complaints about our present-day traditions was that of the practice of attending long, drawn-out funerals and the burying of the bodies. She said that they were a backward custom that hinged on the barbaric. This custom was not in keeping with one's belief in the ongoing life of the spirit.

You must remember that an individual's personality, the unique emotions and personal attitudes are what you loved most about a deceased person. If you really comprehend this, then you will also understand that that deeply-loved personality still lives on in the individual's spirit. The physical body is now merely the spirit's shed cocoon casing. Would you give attention and respects to a dead cocoon casing and ignore the beautiful butterfly that was freed from it and flutters near your shoulder?

Our world will never attain its required level of awareness until people begin to realize the true concept of the spirit and its beautiful shimmering reality of eternal life. It merely undergoes a subtle change. Your deceased loved one is NOT dead, but has simply performed a beautiful metamorphosis.

Realizing the above truth, you can now understand why I would never consider traveling to view a corpse or its gravesite — anyones'!

When any one of my loved ones make their transition, I will rejoice in the beautifully free life they are experiencing — I will NOT grieve over their discarded shell.

Did No-Eyes chastise you for your smoking? And didn't that greatly hamper your psychic exercises?

The visionary chastized me for my over-exuberant ways, for my frequent wandering mind and spirit, for my swearing and for my occasional show of self-doubts. But never did she shake a finger over my smoking.

The negative effects of smoking are caused by adverse mental attitudes and emotions in conjunction with stress. She knew that I retained a healthy mental attitude, even though there were times when I could be deeply depressed. She knew that I handled the dark times by bringing my humor to the forefront, thereby accepting circumstances and carrying on with my life.

Some people have commented on my smoking in regard to it interfering with my paranormal functioning. That's pure and simple nonsense. Paranormal talents come from the spirit, and the spirit is entirely unaffected by any physiological manifestations. I've had no trouble with that type of functioning or spirit communications because of smoke. When you hear these off-handed ideas, use your fine reasoning and think deeper.

As an aside, you might be interested to know that my teacher often enjoyed quiet evenings puffing on her pipe. The pipe smoking is an important aspect of Native American ceremonies. Many words are raised on the evening prayer smoke. . .including mine.

Why was your teacher so touchy about your occasional swearing? I don't think "damn' and "hell" are so bad.

Neither do I, obviously. I don't say any other swear words either, although there is a long list I could use.

My teacher never had anyone in her company that used these expletives. I had utterly shocked her the first time I said one of them in her presence. Initially, she considered the verbalization of damn and/or hell to be a highly disrespectful manner of speaking, quite unlike the enlightened person I was supposed to be (or become). Then, after I continued their use, she'd stamp her foot or shake a knobby finger at me and clam up until I apologized and promised to refrain from using the offending words. I'd promise, then I'd find myself letting them slip out again.

This pet peeve of hers was simply a personal dislike for words that didn't become an aware person. Later on, she would completely ignore times when I said them, she even once became angered enough herself to copy me by using them. But basically, she remained true to her own attitude of negativity toward her wayward student's unbreakable habit. She didn't like it, but she accepted me as I was — bad words and all.

Did No-Eyes ever criticize you for any of your personal habits or mannerisms?

No-Eyes was ever watchful that my mental consciousness did not wander into nature, or that I didn't allow my spirit to take a sudden hankering to take flight and join with the falcon. She continually used her psychic awareness to monitor this undisciplined erring student. And my occasional swearing was a constant thorn in her tender side. She criticized my self-doubts about my own future because I had no say in what that eventual future would be — it would be whatever was meant in order to bring my purpose into full fruition. She was forever scolding me by reinforcing that the mission of my spirit took high precedence over the desires of my physical mind — my personal idea for the future.

Did No-Eyes ever say how well your books would sell?

It was, in the end, irrelevant how my books would sell. One of my spirit's goals was to record the truths in written form, to make the concepts available to more unaware people and to return the aware ones to the right path once again. Whether my books became bestsellers was not important, for I'm not in competition with anyone in that regard. What was important was that people could be exposed to how things really were and how they'd be in the future.

With the sale of the books, I was to set up a correspondence type of information-clearing center for the realities of life, both of the physical and of the spirit. This center was to be for correspondence only and meant to provide the public with its first "free" source to write to with their many questions. In the end, it mattered not whether I became a well-known writer, for only the publication of the material counted as being important.

However, she did show me the future that my books would one day experience.

Did you ever read to No-Eyes? If so, what sort of material did she enjoy hearing?

That's a question I never expected to get. Yes, I did read to my teacher. She enjoyed all I chose to read her, but was partial to hearing my own poems and writings from my woodswalking notebook.

I also read to her of Gandhi, Black Elk, and *Walden Pond.*

Did you make any attempts to ease your teacher's meager physical lifestyle?

Of course, what do you take me for?

Bill made a couple trips out to her place to split wood and stack it. He made any household repairs that he saw needing attention, both inside and out. Once he even attempted to surprise her by repairing her broken rocking chair, but she was way ahead of him. She quickly shuffled across her floor, plumped herself down into the chair and flatly stated, "Bill not gonna touch this! It already be way No-Eyes like it!" And so the rocker never lost its famous creak and thud voice. . .I'd sure like to have that old chair now.

I mistakenly introduced No-Eyes to aluminum foil. She wasn't at all impressed and severely cautioned me on the use of it with certain foods and, "never, never cook with it!" she'd warn. So then I brought her a small cast-iron Dutch oven which she then used to heat her food within the fireplace embers.

I once bought her a pair of knee-high moccasins and, although she marvelled over them, she never wore them. One day I questioned her why she continued to wear her old worn-out ones when she had brand new ones to wear, she simply said that the ones she had on were like old friends. But I knew that she didn't especially care for the hasty workmanship of the new ones.

No-Eyes liked her traditional lifestyle. She wasn't eager to make changes or new adjustments and we respected that. We helped where we could, otherwise, we left things as they were —just as they always were.

On the earthly plane, who is the real author of the No-Eyes books?

This one really surprised me. Yet when I thought deeper on the question, I wasn't sure how to respond to it. The wisdom was all No-Eyes, yet I wrote the words. We lived the experiences together as one entity. In essence, did *she* really write them?

Perhaps this would be best answered by relaying how they were written.

After No-Eyes left me, as devastated as I felt, her words kept hounding me until they began to haunt. "Summer gonna do them books? Summer promise to do them books? Huh, Summer?"

So like a woman possessed (or obsessed) I waited until the entire family was in bed one night and lit the oil lantern on the kitchen table. In the dark surround, illumined only by the flickering flame, I began at the beginning. Furiously the pen raced along the lines, page by building page, until I thought my hand wasn't my own. I desperately tried to recapture so much, God, there was just so *much!* Seasons, all the different concepts talked about, the shared emotions, the important times inbetween the visits when I learned so much through woodswalking or journeys with Old Blue. I found myself crying during the writing. . .all the old pains rose to tear again at my heart. Oh how the recalling and recording did open the deep wounds. And chapter after chapter appeared.

When I took the notebook the next morning to type it up on my old Penney's electric typewriter, I sat in a frozen mesmerized state. The writing in the notebook was so tiny I could hardly read it —the writing was not mine. Yet I distinctly remember spelling every word— the tears brought on by certain memories recalled—all gave evidence that I was consciously doing my own memoirs. . .yet. . . it was not in my hand-writing. So? Whose? Both our guides write completely differently than what I had produced. No-Eyes?

Eventually she admitted to helping me that night (and the subsequent nights) to recall the precise conversations and events. And after two weeks of furious writing, *Spirit Song* was complete. *Phoenix Rising* was put in the same notebook because the writing was so small both books fit. Each subsequent book became easier and easier to convert to my own hand. . .still the words flowed like clear stream waters rushing down a mountainside. Now all the books are written in my own handwriting, but while I'm writing in the wee hours of darkness, I feel her presence as she verifies and proofs the work.

So, does this resolve the question? I don't know. I guess I'll just leave that up to each reader to conclude whatever they want.

Does Summer Rain still communicate with No-Eyes?

The above response pretty well addresses that one. Although I haven't been in her physical presence since 1984, there are certain things I still hear and smell. I frequently hear a "tsk-tsk" and smell that special fragrance that only came from her fireplace. Sometimes when I'm in a discussion or business conversation with my publishing editor,

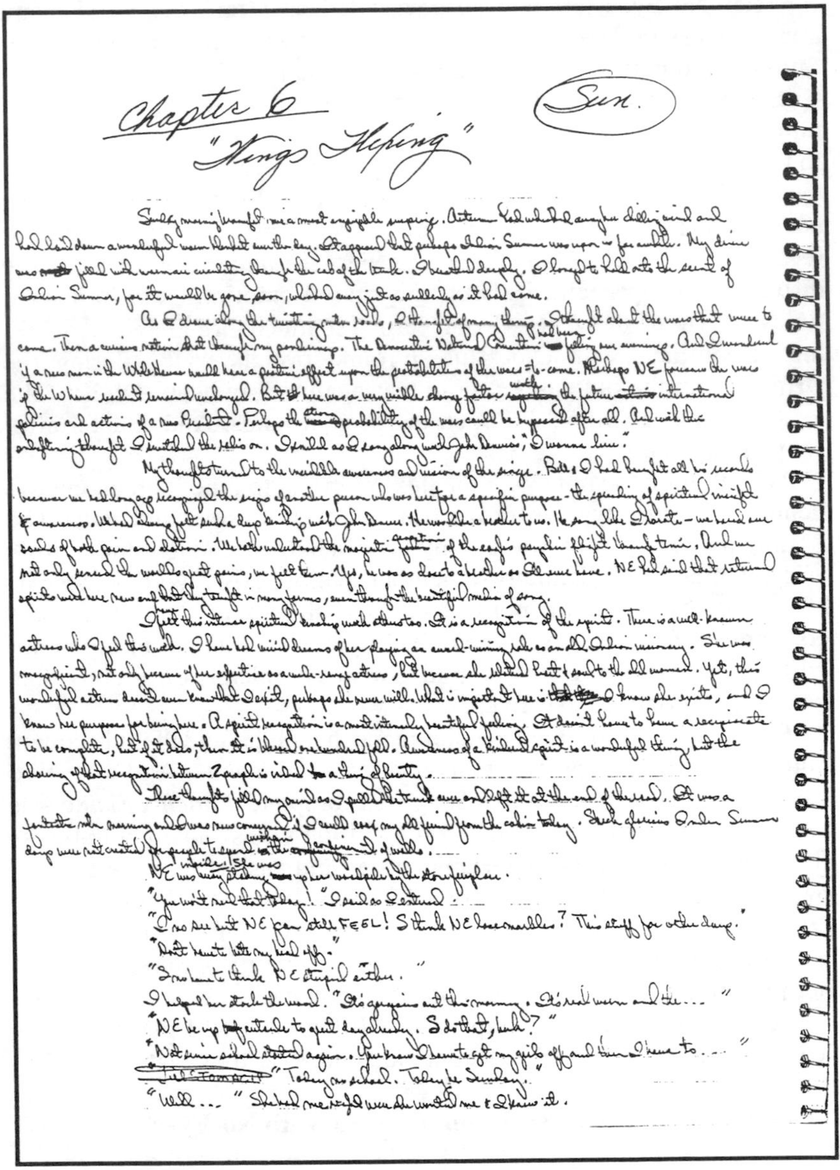
Chapter 6
"Wings Helping"
Sun.

Sample of notebook writing
(See preceding page)

I'll hear a distinct "Blah!" enter in. No-Eyes had not agreed with some editorial alterations to my books, however, she is living within Acceptance of the human condition and what I must work within.

When I'm down, I feel her enter my immediate surround to give comfort and support. When I'm happy I hear a faint "creak-thud." When things are going well, I feel her positive input that made it so.

Yes, No-Eyes is still with me. She communicates loud and clear.

Did No-Eyes ever speak of an inner earth or world? If so, did you go there?

The visionary spoke of many things. An inner earth was referred to when she talked about the nature spirits and other currently unknown entities. This was their domain where they could be protected from the skeptical and threatening civilization that thrived in the outer earth (us).

No-Eyes also spoke of different worlds in connection with Earth. This was in connection to altered dimensional vibrational frequencies. The final shift will soon be upon us. To say more would be breaking a confidence.

Where did No-Eyes learn her knowledge of the body's "power points" called the "Gates?"

This information came directly from her friends she called "her brothers." Clearly these brothers were other intelligences who had been communicating with her for a long time. It does seem interesting to me that all the "channelers" who are allegedly bringing in information from aliens haven't brought us really useful knowledge in areas of health. This makes me extremely cautious of these ones because their channeled information is always so vague and generalized.

Although the basic concept of the chakras enumerate seven centers of the body, in reality there are many more. . .but as revealed by The Brothers, the most important ones are the six outlined in the material given on this in *Earthway*. These six main chakras are the only ones that act as the body's gates for channeling direct healings. See? These six are the only ones that are in open alignment to specific vertebrae and can be easily treated.

Did No-Eyes do many traditional Indian ceremonies? Which ones?

No-Eyes, because she was cognizant to the universal truths and the collective wisdom, had discovered that some ceremonies were actual byways that skirted the direct path to enlightenment, therefore she didn't practice the medicine wheel. She did sweats and pipe ceremonies. Drumming and chanting was a vehicle for her to express her native soul.

The traditional ceremonies she did regularly practice were those lesser known ones of the tribal elders. These were more in line with shamanistic levels whereby the natural elements were utilized to bring about desired resolutions. You would call it magic.

Was your teacher a complete enlightened person when she lived?

Contrary to the question asking if she was sent by God, this one can be conclusively responded to. My teacher was indeed a completed and enlightened soul when she was in the physical plane. As such, she can now operate on the spirit plane by doing whatever spiritual work she so desires. I'm grateful that she's decided to be close to me, for her foresight and advice has been invaluable.

Will No-Eyes come back to experience another physical life?

I seriously doubt she would do that, however, I cannot say what she may decide in the distant future. Currently she is involved in spiritual work on many levels and has conveyed to me that it's been very rewarding. Don't forget that, before, she was a master living among a civilization she perceived as extremely backward. And now, now she is in her own realm of enlightened beings. She is surrounded by companions who speak her language. I doubt very much she would re-enter such a vibrationally heavy world again. Not when she's accomplishing so much where she is. She's so happy.

Do you believe everything No-Eyes taught was the absolute truth?

All truths are absolute. And yes, she was a completed soul. . . she knew the score on everything.

Could you show me No-Eyes' cabin if I came to visit you?

Could, but wouldn't. You have to realize that the place No-Eyes resided in was just a loan; it belongs to someone, therefore it's private property. You can't just go trampling around on someone else's property just because you once spent time there. She wasn't a squatter who just found a deserted cabin to inhabit. Her Pueblo people provided the living quarters for as long as she needed it. It was never specifically owned by the visionary.

The day I discovered her gone was the last time I've been there. That was in the spring of 1984. I have no reason to return. . .my friend is no longer there and I don't make shrines of objects. So you see, even I no longer have a right to go back on another person's private property.

Also there's a greater reason for not taking anyone to the cabin site. Please understand that I've shared so much of myself and No-Eyes through the books. I've opened my heart wide. I've exposed all the extremely tender experiences and most private times of my relationship. I've literally brought the public into the very, very private world of No-Eyes. And. . .the visual of the cabin is all I've retained for myself to remember. . .it's hidden within a sacred and private place in my heart. . .it's all I have left.

Did No-Eyes ever speak of "mystery" entities such as Bigfoot?

Sure she did. Although she didn't call these intelligent beings by that term. She thought the term was too crude for such sensitive beings. When she spoke of the Inner Earth, these were a segment of those inhabitants.

How did your teacher view the New Age movement? Or did she even know about it?

You're not going to like this answer.

Since I'd been getting my own spiritual information for nearly twenty years before meeting No-Eyes, I hadn't kept my eyes on what the movement was doing. One day No-Eyes asked about the public's awareness of the truths. I told her about Edgar Cayce and a few others, but that question got me thinking and I looked into it further. I was shocked to see that the tender communication between an individual and guide was now called "channeling" and that it appeared that just everyone was calling themselves a channeler. It seemed that the beauty of the concept had been so blown up that it had completely lost its specialness and high integrity.

I read everything I could get my hands on. People were authoring all manner of ridiculous material. They were making millions from their channeled information. I was in spiritual shock. . .and so was No-Eyes. She was extremely saddened to hear of the ugly turn it had taken. What pained her most was the fact that it'd become a commercial commodity to be bought and sold. She told me of the future she'd foreseen, after the Phoenix was free, when NO spiritual aspect would be sold for any price. She said that those who were now doing that would fall by the wayside like so many autumn leaves. The spiritual teachers of the Golden Age of Peace will give freely of all they know and can

46/*Daybreak*

share. . .that will be the law of the Golden Age of Spirituality. She viewed most of the current channelers as: "The White Medicine Man selling his snake oil to the gullible." Those weren't her exact words but she correlated the concept to snake oil being sold by the old time traveling medicine man. She was heartbroken, for she had thought the public was farther along in their spiritual perceptions.

No-Eyes'view of the channeled entities was laughable. She did laugh over it, but not without first dropping a tear or two.

I could say more, but I think you get the idea of what the visionary thought of the New Age movement.

No-Eyes revealed some of your future to you. Did she happen to foresee her story being made into a film? That'd be fantastic! There wouldn't be a dry eye in the audience.

Although she said that my books would flow like a warm current across the land, going from hand to hand and heart to heart, she never mentioned anything remotely sounding like a film of them.

I think every author has visions of a major film being made of his material, but this hasn't been on my mind; for just getting the written information out to the public has been my only goal in this. That in itself has been very rewarding.

There has been several actresses who've expressed high interest in doing the No-Eyes story, but Indian material appears to be of little interest to the powers-that-be called producers. Certainly, if it's meant to be, the right person will accomplish it.

Our group here in Florida thinks No-Eyes may have been an alien. Would you have any information on this?

Sure I would. She was as human as you. You have to be very careful about forming such kinds of opinions or assuming things that may be misleading on the surface. I say this because you've not been the only one to presume this. Granted, she did have an extraordinarily high degree of deep wisdom and her knowledge of many little-known aspects was broad in scope, but that doesn't necessarily make her not of this world. See? But a living Completed One who is indeed human may also carry with him the same knowledge and, indeed, some do.

I will concede that there are other intelligences living here among us, however, the entity known as No-Eyes was not one of them.

Did your teacher celebrate Christmas in any way?

The key to this question is "in any way." In her *own* way she celebrated Christmas *everyday,* for in her sensitive heart, she found the soul of the Great Spirit in all she saw around her. To one such as her, she viewed the birthing of the God-Essence in all her surroundings. In this manner did she celebrate the heart and soul of the God she saw as, not coming *into* the world, but rather His "being" in the world already manifested.

Did any of the medicine woman's former students ever come back occasionally to visit with her?

I know only of Brian Many Heart who did this. Although the visionary never mentioned any others visiting her, this cannot be interpreted as a negative response. They may have, I just wasn't told about any.

Please remember that her former students are very busy going about their work. As already mentioned in a former response, some are in other countries. But surely, out of sight/ out of mind, would not apply here. Her student-turned-teacher group would naturally think of her often.

Do you think that No-Eyes' former students knew of her death?

When someone such as No-Eyes comes into your life and you spend intense hours, days, weeks, months, and years with them, there is a living umbilical that is formed between you. When you've laughed and cried with another, when you've allowed someone to become a living part of your heart, the bond cannot be severed.

I imagine they experienced the same ripping pain that I did. They would naturally have felt the sudden emptiness and void that marked the growing distance of her final walk.

They had to know. . .it couldn't have been otherwise.

If No-Eyes didn't have any electricity, she couldn't have had a well pump. How'd she get water?

Sure she had water, it came from a hand pump at the kitchen sink. Her well had great production and the water was as good as it gets.

Is the cabin still there?

I haven't been back since 1984 but I see no reason why it wouldn't still be standing. It was a sturdy little place.

Did No-Eyes have any personal pets?

All the woodland animals were her "special" people. They were all her friends. Frequently a racoon or squirrel would wander in when she left the door open, but as far as "keeping" an animal, that just didn't set right with her.

In your opinion, what current New Age personality is on a par with the entity of No-Eyes?

Is this a trick question? Or if it's for real, say it isn't so. Is it so hard for the public to recognize an entity who comes once-in-a-lifetime? There have been a few who have come close to comparing to different aspects of the visionary, but nobody I'm aware of has evidenced the totality of her.

Edgar Cayce closely compares to the aspect of the spiritual knowledge and truths that No-Eyes spoke, however, most of his wisdom came through while he was sleeping.

Krishnamurti compares to No-Eyes in overall general philosophical concepts. Also he reminds me of her when he speaks his mind regardless of public opinion. This is as it should be with highly enlightened teachers or personalities because the truth is more important than stepping on a few toes.

This singular aspect is missing in the personalities of many current New Age personages. There are many reasons for this and they all hinge on the aspect of fear — fear of not being popular, therefore not having as many followers as the next teacher. To make your teaching concepts "go with the flow of public opinion" is a very dangerous philosophy. To tell folks what they want to hear is fatal in the end. To be afraid to tell it like it is, and not be courageous enough to contradict an erroneous spiritual concept if it is wrong, is spiritual suicide. Please realize that just because a spiritual concept is popular and generally believed to be the "real way," doesn't necessarily mean it's right — the Law of the One.

New Age personalities are fearful of presenting the new concepts because they feel safer staying with the tried and true. General public opinion is their livelihood. And so we've come to the bare crux of the matter.

No-Eyes wasn't afraid to state that her knowledgeable alien friends said that *six* chakras were the basic prime ones when all the world believed there were seven. She saw the truth for the beautiful light that it was and, therefore, took steps to enlighten the masses with it.

I can think of no other New Age notable to name here.

What did your guides think of No-Eyes?

Clearly they commended and supported her. I was "led" to the visionary's woods that first day. I let the spirit lead me into the mountains and found myself traveling narrow roads I'd never been down. My guides drove, I didn't, for my mind was far from concentrating on where I was going. I had reached the prescribed time in my life where destiny awaited. And so it was fulfilled.

The Guides were in collusion with her all along. And they remained so to this day. It was the guides who always gave me direction and clarification during the inbetween times of my cabin visitations. They verified No-Eyes spiritual completeness. They were the ones who referred to her as an old, old finished soul.

Did the medicine woman ever work with crystals?

Not in the manner known currently. She did have two special ones that were "knowledge programmed" in an ancient time. She found the present-day knowledge of crystals rudimentary and said the current work being done with them was sometimes erroneous and all the time elementary at best.

The practices were compared to Thomas Edison fooling around with his new phonograph. The refinements just are not here yet.

No-Eyes had certain stones that she worked with. These were not the gemstones so widely used today. They were normal-looking stones, but they were not of this world. These she carried with her in her medicine pouch. I don't know what they did, but do know that she was going to show me. . .and we never had the time.

Did you and your teacher ever drum and chant?

Rarely did we have the time to drum and chant, there were just too many more important concepts to cover. But when we did do this, it always served to be a vehicle that brought on spirit journeys. It was very moving.

Many Heart did magic. Did he learn it from No-Eyes? If so, did she teach you the same things?

What you call magic is actually no more than knowledge of natural forces and the elements of nature. The laws that govern these are simplistic, yet current knowledge of physics have not stretched far enough to reach these realities.

Many Heart did learn these laws from No-Eyes.

Did she teach me the same? Some, but when these are gone into and understood, they no longer hold any mystery. The so-called magic has only been necessary on rare occasions for me. I find it useful on occasion, but it's not a major part of my life or work.

How did No-Eyes know your name when she first saw you?

She knew the names of all her visitors, for none were ever unexpected.

Remember that the visionary was never completely alone. She had many friends, both of spiritual and physical vibrations, who she was in continual communication with. Two of these were members of The White Brotherhood — our personal spirit Advisors —who had been in collusion with her for several years before we were advised to move to Colorado. It had been foreseen that the visionary was to stand in the path of my destiny. She knew I would one day be led to her woods. Our Advisors knew of the plan. Everyone knew but me. It was as if some unknown play was being acted out. Only one player didn't know anything about it — yet still she followed all the right stage directions that brought her face to face with the one who awaited her entry cue. The timing was perfect.

As so much of one's life is the "playing out" of the course our spirit sets, one's path can be read as a script by others. In this manner, an individual's future trail is frequently as visible and clear as reading a screenplay or book. It's just that sometimes, the main character is the only player without a copy of the script. No-Eyes had such a copy — she knew the names of all the players.

At the end of SPIRIT SONG No-Eyes died. Did she physically come back to life? Or were the rest of your learning experiences with her done on the spirit plane?

Nobody comes back to life.

Since I thought *Spirit Song* was the only book I was going to do about my times with No-Eyes, I touched on most of the issues we spoke of and naturally concluded the book with her transition. Then, realizing how much I'd left out and how many important aspects I needed to publically convey, I wrote additional volumes that included vital conversations that covered these issues.

But no, the visionary did not come back to life for those. All the books cover the experiences we had in the physical together. Those experiences that continued after her death have not been made public.

A friend of mine is an Apache medicine woman who says she knew No-Eyes.

This could very well be so. Occasionally I receive letters from medicine people or elders of various tribes who've detailed the location of No Eyes' cabin. This was done to provide me with verification of their integrity. It's clear to see that the visionary had powerful contacts throughout the country. Her circle of friends spanned the length and breadth of the U.S. and Canada.

So if your Apache friend says that she knew No-Eyes, I could not confirm or deny it unless I personally received a letter from her that I could touch and extract impressions from. However, I've been advised that your friend had, indeed, known No-Eyes.

There have been some readers who've written to inform me that they knew No-Eyes. And the Advisors inform otherwise. Please be honest in your letters. One doesn't have to claim to have known No-Eyes to get my attention. Starting out with a falsehood is no way to begin our correspondence.

I was one of No-Eyes' former students. We must meet to talk more of your specific times with her.

Because of my many spiritual obligations and inability to hold to any type of scheduled meetings, I am no longer able to meet with those wishing this type of connection.

You, of course, would've known this if you were really who you're claiming to be. Please, don't humiliate yourself by saying you're someone you're not. Respect self. And. . . respect the insights of others.

Star Born

From Within and Without. . .even Among, the Earth Watchers have watched and waited. For centuries have they observed and intervened with their deep compassion to protect and guide, for our family is not only of this small earth. . .much of our Family is Starborn.

Have you seen differently-shaped space vehicles? How many have you seen altogether?

All of the space vehicles that I've seen have been identical in shape, only their size differed.

I can't give you an exact figure as to the total number of vehicles that I've seen because I haven't bothered to keep count. To me, they are simply another aspect to life's reality and to keep a record of my sightings would be implying that they are something totally unique and out of the ordinary.

Please remember that when a person is exposed to the many aspects of reality since childhood, it then becomes an accepted facet of one's life, of everyday living. "Unidentified" space vehicles *have* been iden-tified — they are the vehicles of an intelligent race of people and, being such, they are not to be feared but rather accepted as the normal part of reality we call life.

Have you ever seen any of the UFO occupants? Spoken to any of them?

This is a difficult question to respond to. I prefer to admit that communication has been established. At this time I wish to leave it at that and not elaborate further on it.

My young daughter said she saw a UFO one night. I passed it off as imagination, now I have regrets that perhaps I handled it wrong. Could you possibly tell me if she really did see one? I'd sure like to know so I can reassure her that her daddy believes her.

I'm pleased by your open mind and your acceptance of this fact of reality. Your daughter is fortunate to have such an understanding and aware dad.

Although my correspondence is not generally for the purpose of giving out such psychic information on individuals, I think an exception is in order here. I'll check this for you.

Your daughter did indeed see an alien vehicle. She has seen them several times but this was the first time she's ever spoken about it. Make sure that she understands that the people inside the ships won't harm her. Tell her that they are intelligent people who want to help keep our world a safe place to live. Tell her that they are compassionate and sensitive people.

I think you should compile verified statements from those people up in the mountains who have witnessed actual sightings, like telling their experiences. It would make for one heck of a good read.

Your suggestion leads me to believe that you are unfamiliar with the ways of mountain folk. These people are very private individuals who have chosen the remote mountain life in order to maintain their peace of mind. They are close to nature and all that nature represents. They don't like to be around a lot of people, nor do they appreciate strangers nosing into their business. They would tell me all they know because I am one of them, but for me to then turn around and publicize their experiences would be synonymous to treason. You just don't do things like that for the flimsy purpose of producing "a good read."

When I wrote *Phantoms Afoot,* I had to go with my conscience. I sacrificed verifiable testimonials in deference to the wishes of the good mountain folk. They requested that their names be altered and also the real names of the actual locations Bill and I "cleared." I did this because the specifics weren't all that important — the real happenings were. Whether that action hurt the credibility of the book is neither here nor there to me. If I had used the real names, the skeptics would *still* be doubting and my peaceful mountain friends would be inundated by noisey gawkers trampling their once remote and peaceful domain.

As far as writing a book on these encounters, I think the literary marketplace already has quite enough of them to give the public the general idea of the issue, however, I will state that I would write such a book if my "Brothers" ever suggested that I do so. This book would not be based on folk sightings, but rather on their direct information to me. So far they have not expressed any interest in such a book, but that is not to say that, at some future date, they will indeed express such a work for me to create.

I'm an officer in the Air Force. And...yes, we pilots have seen them! Don't think for one second that your government doesn't know too.

I appreciate your candidness and courage to speak the truth on this issue. I know about the world governments who are cognizant to the facts of the matter.

On this subject, I suggest the following books:

The Roswell Incident by Charles Berlitz and William L. Moore
Above Top Secret by Timothy Good
Dimensions by Jacques Vallee

What do you think the aliens look like? Or have you already seen them? Are they green?

They have basic similarities to the human physiological system, but they also possess evolutionary differences. Are they green? Actually, that's not a dumb question. Are not humans a rainbow of colors and shades?

The alien people also have varying shades of color depending upon the specific regional area they come from — but they are *not* lizards!

Although I wish to decline responding to an aspect of this question, I will state that it's possible for individuals to "spiritually" see these aliens in the Corridor of Time or through remote viewing at the time of a UFO sighting, these being in addition to actual physical contact and communications.

I live up in the mountains near you. One night when our group had taken a weekend backpacking trip, we crested a ridge and down in a secluded valley, there sat a ship with all its lights off except for a sort of ultraviolet beam shining down on the ground. It softly glowed. We were frozen with fright and quickly high-tailed it out of there, never caring to venture nearer. None of us have ever spoken about it to anyone other than amongst ourselves. We're relieved to be able to share our sighting with you because we know we won't be laughed at. If you ever relate this occurrence please don't reveal our names — we're medical professionals.

Don't worry, I'm known for not using "real" names. I respect your desire for anonymity and will uphold your confidentiality.

I know just the "secluded" valley you mean. I have some friends who have also been startled by a landed vehicle in that very same area. And I will admit that your first sighting does give one a fright, especially when you come up on it so unexpectedly like you did.

That particular area appears to be quite popular with the alien people. It is National Forest property and is well separated from the surrounding residential areas. There's not many people who hike in there or use it for trailrides. It would seem to be an ideal spot for their temporary layovers.

I wish your group hadn't been frightened away. You could've had some excitement by observing the vehicle from your ridge vantage point. Next time try to maintain an inner calm about it. You're fearing the unknown factor here — it has no aspects to fear.

If the aliens are so highly advanced, which they'd have to be, why would they want to bother with us ?

They don't think of humans as a "bother" at all . They are a living part of God just as we are, and as such, makes all of us " family" in the Universal Brotherhood .

The more advanced intelligences need to be viewed in the proper perspective as being an "extension" to the human family. And since they are more advanced, they naturally are interested in monitoring our development and helping wherever possible.

What do you think of the popular movies like "Close Encounters of The Third Kind" and "E.T."?

I saw both films several times. I think these two films were wonderful. They bestowed a small measure of awareness within the hearts and minds of the public. I thought that it was particularly important that

"E.T." went straight to the minds of children, and "Close Encounters" went to the adults.

The latter movie clearly depicted the government's view and its typical method of coverup. It showed how ignorant the human mind can be — the skeptics ridiculing the believers. It showed, to my amazement, the link between the alien people and those earth people who have disappeared within the boundaries of the Bermuda Triangle (although I doubt many people even made the factual connection). But, most importantly, the film gave a sense of "good feelings" toward the alien people. It showed their compassion and good will. And that is how it was depicted because that is precisely how it is.

You've actually seen several space ships. Would you also like to take a ride?

A ride? Take a ride? I can best answer this one by repeating what I've often said — there are many ways to fly. Although I don't take airplanes, there are other more reliable means that are less conventional.

Would I like to take a ride? Sure, everytime they're in my area.

How could an alien race be so much more technically advanced than ours?

How could it not be!

You're forgetting that, through our foolish handling of powerful energy sources, we have nearly annihilated ourselves several times. How far *could* a race advance when it has to begin over from scratch time and time again?

There are those civilizations that have never had to begin again. Wouldn't that fact alone give some indication as to why they would then be so much more advanced than we are?

Are UFOs noisy? I heard a strange sound in the sky one night, but it was too dark to see anything.

In response to this question, I have to say that, on the whole, the vehicles are perfectly soundless. The exception to this is when they create something like a sonic boom upon certain take-off conditions and when they sound like thunder under other conditions. The latter being a condition of choice.

At my current remote residence, their sonic booms shake our house on the average of several times a week.

How many other planets are there that support intelligent lifeforms?

Dozens. They are within other solar systems, at least most of them are.

Our scientists and astronomers doubt the alien's mere existence because of how they are forming their theories. Theories that, in themselves, are hinged on an erroneous database. They very authoritatively grin as they disclaim the possibility of an alien's existence anywhere within our solar system. But. . .we're not talking about our solar system here.

How come you know so much about the extraterrestrials when the learned astronomers continue to doubt their very existence?

I accept your rude inference. And I'll reply by saying that the tallest tree can see an eternity of life beyond it, while the forest perceives only the trees. One is enlightened to reality while the majority remains in darkness.

Of course this is not to imply that I am the *only* enlightened one, for there are many. This is to imply that there are also many unenlightened.

In the Corridor of Time you saw some intelligent beings that were from other worlds. What did they look like?

There were some mutated forms of intelligent life. These were the most highly advanced though. Most were not very different from ourselves in appearance.

Were the extraterrestrials created concurrently with humans?

You bet! But do not forget that *their* civilizations are *also* called "man." And so is the reality of the Universal Family of Man.

Are there evil aliens?

As with all intelligent life, there remains the capabilities of being influenced by the Sons of Belial or the powers of darkness. They too, like us, are working their way back into the Light of God.

Why haven't the aliens openly presented themselves to us?

And what would fearful earthlings do? Raise the trusty shotgun. Kill. Capture and detain. Dissect.

We are not yet mature enough for encounters of this kind. We yet need to grow up and reach new levels of enlightened awareness that would dispel our fearful ignorance.

Little by little, the public is becoming more and more aware of the existence of other intelligences who come from beyond our galaxy. All is going according to plan. The people of earth must be gently exposed to the reality of this issue.

If God created man in His own image, how do you intellectually explain aliens who look different from us? How many faces does God supposedly have?

God has no face, my friend. God is pure energy. God is the Nucleus of the Atom called Love.

In the beginning, God created man into his own likeness —His brilliant *spirit*. It was much *later* when God created the human *physical* form according to the *environment* that the individualized form was going to inhabit (planets). See?

On our own planet, Chinese look different from Americans, Hawaiians differ in appearance from Africans, and five different color races exist here on earth. So too do the other interplanetary beings differ from each other as well as from us. . .all according to their individualized environment.

Are there any aliens who are presently living among us? If so, how is this accomplished if their physical appearance differs from ours?

Yes, extraterrestrial beings are presently living among us. There are two types of beings who have this capability. One is a race that is capable of simulating the human physiological form. This is a technical feat of those aliens who are members of the highest advanced group. Their own appearances are undefined, rather like a spirit. This enables them to come among us.

The other type possesses a physical appearance much like we humans. The difference is so slight nobody would notice it unless you knew what to look for. . .which comes more as a spirit recognition than a physical affectation.

Do extraterrestrials also have spirits like we do?

Please remember that *all* life was created by God in his own image at the time of creation. Therefore, all intelligent life possesses the same God Spirit Force as humans.

This aspect is so often overlooked when we humans are involved in considering the issue of alien intelligences. This question clearly indicates that you are thinking along the lines of the spiritual truths of the collective wisdom as only being viable for earthlings and nobody else. But aren't these truths *universal?* What does "universal" mean if not intended to be all-inclusive?

Have you spoken to many people who have seen UFOs?

Yes, simply because they don't fear ridicule from me. However, be it known that everyone's tale did not originate from the real facts. The difference is easily perceived.

On the whole, most folks realize that I can tell a tall tale when I hear one, and usually they like to talk to me about their very private, unusual encounter experiences because they know that I can see that they speak the truth and that I'll understand.

It's important for people to share their encounter experiences with others because this then gives them a sense of camaraderie. Knowing that others have had similiar experiences, and being able to freely discuss them, is wonderfully therapeutic to all involved.

Don't you think that some UFOs aren't actually alien ships but are rather the military's secret inventions?

This would be a comfortable theory to settle on, however, the confidential files of various governments prove the opposite.

Do UFOs have colored lights?

Not the ones that I've seen around my mountains or when I was in Michigan. It would depend upon which alien civilization the specific vehicle hailed from. There are many such civilizations, all with varying types of vehicles. Hence it would stand to reason that some would have colored lights while others didn't.

What would be the purpose of aliens having different bodily forms than ours?

Environmental planetary adaptation and the subsequent survival of the species.

Are aliens telepathic?

Yes. All species are. Consider the telepathic abilities of some humans at the current time. Now multiply that novitiate ability by ten thousand years. Consequently, telepathy has become quite a normal functioning when considering all the additional psychic abilities that have been developed throughout their long lifespan.

I don't understand why people are so skeptical about the possibility of aliens existing. Is it because people think that they are the superior race?

Absolutely. Also, it throws a credibility wrench into some religious belief systems.

The general skepticism is enhanced by the government's denial of otherworld civilizations that has been generated because of the fear the public will panic to learn that all military weapons can be so easily rendered ineffective by alien intervention systems. No government wants to admit that they can be rendered completely helpless by an unknown alien power.

Could we ever be food for an alien race?

You've been watching too many monster movies!

That wouldn't indicate a superior race at all. *They're* not barbarians — we are. The unaware earth people are the only intelligent race that actually kills and eats their lower lifeforms. And that, my friend, says it all.

It's ideas like this that keep the alien people from attempting any sort of intelligent communications with us on an open scale.

You ought to write science fiction because you sure can come up with some fantastically entertaining stories!

Thank you. Reality *is* fantastic, isn't it.

Some folks consider *Phantoms Afoot* to be science fiction. Some folks consider all my books to be fiction. They haven't seen nothin' yet!

Actually, I have written two fiction novels, however, all my books are *based* on fact. The fiction will be tales of happenings that can occur. They will be dealing with spirits and other dimensional forces.

I appreciate your compliment. It's comforting to know that any fiction novels I do will be welcomed by the public.

Could aliens produce offspring with earth people?

It has already been done. Remember that some aliens can utilize the concept of spirit transfer, thereby being an alien intelligence within a human form. Another type of alien cannot physically accomplish this biological act. It merely depends on the specific species and how closely it matches with our own. But yes, it has been accomplished.

Why would you encounter aliens in the Corridor of Time? Because of their intellectual and technical advancements, wouldn't they have other means of traveling through time?

The truths are universal! They do not alter. They are constant throughout *all* universes.

Please understand that "time" is not of physical substance. The past cannot be driven to on a Sunday afternoon, neither can an alien vehicle gear up to warp speed into the past.

The future cannot be reached by a command module, neither can it be reached by an alien ship.

Listen. The timeframes of the future and the past are *dimensions*. Only the "present" can be physically experienced or physically reached because it is the moment that is being lived. The future and the past can only be reached through a means which "spans" dimensional frequencies. That means the Corridor of Time.

Would extraterrestrials ever invade us with the purpose of using our planet for their own civilization continuance?

That scenario is for the science fiction books — not for reality.

The key word in your entire question is "invade." A more apropos term would be "infiltrate" or "harmoniously blend." The aliens have no intentions of invading this earth. They are more interested in the establishment of a racially-unified civilization that will exist in harmony and peace.

War of the worlds is not a part of their consciousness.

Do extraterrestrials eat their own lower lifeforms like we do?

Although this has been addressed in a former response, I've included it again to stress the point.

Extraterrestrials have various originations. The lesser advanced species can be compared to the human species who do eat of certain lower animal lifeforms. However, the more advanced alien races are too intelligent for that sort of cultural barbarism. They are enlightened people who have learned to cherish and respect the worth of all life.

If the aliens are so advanced, why do they still exist? Haven't they been reincarnating their spirits a lot longer than we have?

Clearly, they exist to help the ignorant. Of course their spirits have also been advancing through incarnations. How else would they get to such an advanced level of development? Think how our own current civilization would appear to the cave man. He might have asked the same question of us.

Your question infers that perhaps you believe that extraterrestrials have been reincarnating their spirits a lot longer than we have. This suggests that you perhaps surmise that they "existed" *before* we did. Not so. *All* spirits were created in the beginning — all at once.

Think how far along we would be if we hadn't destroyed our civilizations throughout history.

Why does the idea of alien beings scare us so?

The idea doesn't have to be scary. But generally, the public is fearful because we are not enlightened enough to know better. Our realm of experience does not include the beauty of the paranormal dimensional realities, and our science of physics is rudimentary in that it has not stretched beyond its currently confining database.

So therefore, whenever some concept comes along that we have no foundation of proof for, we are treading an unknown path that has unknown boundaries and laws of physics. We believe we are in the Age of Technology. We would best serve ourselves if we moved out of the Age of Machines and Tangibles and up into the Age of Awareness.

We are scared to approach reality and perceive all that exists there. We are fearful to approach the unknown factors that govern reality.

I'd love to see a real UFO up close. Can you tell me where I could camp out in the Rockies to see one or two?

And then a hundred other campers would be there with their pup tents, motor homes, technical video equipment, radios, and movie cameras. Does that sound like the quiet remote place that an intelligent alien person would land his vehicle? Besides, the military might get there first and cordon off the entire area because of a serious "toxic substance leak."

How many UFOs have you seen at one sighting?

Three.

Once while I was driving down my mountain road around 6:30 on a summer evening, I spotted three coming directly toward me. They were in a vee formation. They were small vehicles the size of my pickup.

I pulled over to the side of the road and shut the engine off. I watched their approach.

The three maintained a slow steady pace. Smooth and straight. They sailed directly over me and continued up the deserted road. There wasn't a single sound emitting from the vehicles — not even a quiet whirring. I almost got out of my truck to wave at them, but I was too engrossed to move. I sent them friendly thoughts and wished them peace.

Since they were heading directly toward my cabin, I called home as soon as I reached a phone. The family ran outside to see if they could see them, but my call came too late.

Has anyone else in your family seen a UFO?

When we were living in Rainbow Valley, south of Divide, Colorado, Robin worked late as manager of a Woodland Park convenience store. She was driving up Highway 24 at 3 a.m. On her approach to Divide, her International truck sputtered out and she coasted over to the shoulder. She couldn't start it up again. There was nothing open in Divide to call from so she nuzzled down in the seat to await a passing motorist.

Soon she saw light beams spearing up off the rise in the road in front of her. She made ready to hail down the vehicle because she thought the lights were from headlights. . .they weren't. Instead of the vehicle coming "down" the hill ahead of her, they continued on right off the horizontal plane of the rise. A UFO was passing. It was a "good-sized" one from what she could see of it in the winter darkness. Soon after, the engine turned over when she started it again.

When we lived in Leadville, Colorado, a sighting occurred during the Fourth of July fireworks. My daughters, Jenny, Aimee and Sarah, with their friend Eric, were all sitting out on the hillside of our house watching the fireworks. Behind them on the property was a lighted utility pole which illuminated part of the hillside. Suddenly the light was different. They looked up directly above them and saw an enormous shadow hovering — it was solid black and obliterated the stars. They rushed indoors for Bill and I to go look, but by the time we got out, the stars were back.

A resident of Leadville relayed an incident that occurred about nine months before the above sighting. She happened to look up to our house one night and saw a UFO with a beam of light going directly down to the house. She called the police but they thought it was a prank call and did nothing. She said she never forgot that sighting.

Later I found out that the "beam" was for the purpose of clearing the radon and other metal radiation from the house and property for our arrival there. The house sat above Leadville and perched on mine tailings.

Has your husband ever seen a UFO?

Not up close as I have. He's seen them many times through binoculars. Their erratic movements in the night mountain sky are very distinctive. Bill has become an adept at picking them out quickly. One night he mentally communed with a passing vehicle and they immediately gave a responsive signal back when they flashed a beam of light toward him.

Would any of the recorded apparitions in the Bible be caused by the physical presence of aliens who had come to direct and to guide the people during that time?

Yes. I would like to go into deep detail on this issue but I've been cautioned against it at this time. Evidently this issue will be covered by the extraterrestrials themselves when the time is deemed right.

But consider this. In my former response, regarding the beam of light shining down on our house that the neighbor witnessed, how might that be interpreted by those in biblical times? A light from God? A heavenly light pointing out a place or person?

Scattered throughout our world are massive geographical intaglios. Were any of these made by the extraterrestrials?

Not merely *by*, but rather with the aid of.

Do UFOs go in and out of our oceans?

This question gets very close to an aspect of their reality that I cannot comment on at this time. Some extraterrestrial aspects are still "classified" until the time has ripened for their revelation. This "ocean" aspect is not an impossibility for them to manage.

Do the extraterrestrials have anything to do with the unexplained mystery of the Bermuda Triangle?

You inquisitive readers are going to get me into trouble yet. In response to your question — most definitely. It has to do with their communication transmissions and what effects this technology has upon our own physical environmental atmospheric conditions. The transmissions alter them. An altered dimension is temporarily created in this region. And that's all I can say at this time.

I don't swallow this extraterrestrial idea. There's absolutely no concrete evidence to support such an outlandish theory.

You don't have to swallow anything. Why not try just swishing it around in your mouth a little to get the taste of it. I'm not here to convince anyone of anything they don't wish to believe. I accept your belief in alien nonexistence. I'm not here to argue the issue. I wish you well in life. I wish you health. And I wish you one other thing — a sighting.

There are many of us here in (city withheld) who believe that Brian Many Heart was an alien. Will you confirm this?

I cannot confirm nor deny this. He never spoke of his clan or which tribe he was from. His history (or origins) never became an aspect of our discussions. He knew a great deal about the "other intelligences" and we talked about them in great detail, but that in no way proves that he was one of them.

I've finally found someone who'll believe me. Last year, while I was camping overnight in the Cascades, a tiny space ship landed nearby. I was transported into that ship. The people were lizards. My son is part alien but nobody believes me. I know you recognize the truth when you hear it. Please direct me to an enlightened person of authority who will help me cope with my experience.

It makes me feel good when people realize that I can recognize the truth.

And I can also direct you to a person of authority who is enlightened and has the professional experience to help you come to grips with your experience — a psychiatrist.

My friend, I see that you do not have an overactive imagination, but rather an altered view of reality. You dreamed that experience. Yes, you did. Please accept this for what it is. Your son is a normal healthy human boy, nothing more. If you cannot accept this, please seek professional counselling. The extraterrestrials that visit earth do NOT have the physical appearance of lizards.

Are YOU an extraterrestrial?

What if I actually said "yes?" So what? Nobody would believe me anyway. What a person *is* remains irrelevant. What a being does and says is what is important here. See?

When will the extraterrestrials make physical contact?

Since they already have made physical contact with many, many humans, I must interpret your question to infer to "public" contact.

This aspect is a fragment of the Phoenix Days issue and will manifest whenever they perceive the civilization of earth as being emotionally ready for such a physical appearance en masse. However, this option is only viable if certain aspects of the Phoenix Days do not manifest their probabilities. If certain events do indeed take place, the extraterrestrials will be much in evidence as their technological skills are brought into play to either interfere with an event or to rectify others by reversing negative effects. See?

What is the alien's purpose here?

Their purpose is to watch over their lesser-advanced family and to monitor human activities that could adversely affect the earth's viability of surface and atmospheric conditions. They are also here to expand human awareness of reality.

Where do alien's land?

Mountainous regions are most favorable because of the peaks and valleys covered with forests. Yet they land wherever they need to in order to fulfill specific missions. Not all landings are physically manifested and therefore are not perceived by the eye.

At what altitude do the aliens fly?

How can this be answered? Depending on the specific vehicle, they fly at all altitudes.

Are there good and bad aliens?

Are not there good and bad earthlings?

This question cannot be answered without clarifying terminology here. What is meant by "bad?" What is "good?"

Your concept of these may not coincide and verify with another being's perception of same. See? Their very appearance here may seem to be bad to you, yet good to them.

Within the general concept of good and bad, the extraterrestrials are not bad people. Generally they are good and have come with the best of intentions. These are the ones interested in earth and its inhabitants.

Now if you're thinking of a *Star Wars* film type of scenario, there are species of extraterrestrials who have taken the darker path with their technology and overall social belief systems. These ones are not interested in earth however.

Were the extraterrestrials created by our same God?

Same God? Are you saying that there's more than one God? I don't believe that was your intent here. There is but one God and He created all spirits at the same time. How those spirits manifested into the physical is as varied as the grains of sand on the beach.

Are the Earth Watchers you spoke of in PHOENIX RISING the aliens?

Yes. They have been instrumental in monitoring our actions for centuries. Likewise they have been instrumental in nullifying many negative effects our actions would have caused upon our planet and environment. But within the past two decades, they have been advised to hold back on their efforts in order for humankind on earth to visually perceive its erring ways and how they destruct the planet and human health.

This however, does not mean that they will continue to stand back and watch us destroy ourselves. They wouldn't do that. They will intervene whenever is necessary to insure the continuance of our civilization on a liveable planet.

Will the extraterrestrials help us during the final hours of the Phoenix Days?

This is one of the major reasons for them being here. There exists a future probability that they may be instrumental in an evacuation of some type. This will not be wide scale, but will rather be selective and contingent upon the individual human free will at the time. Nobody will be forced to leave against their wishes. This issue appears to be grossly misunderstood among the public, for many think they will be literally "captured" during the destructive days of the Phoenix. This is not so.

I've been told that I'm from another planet. Can you clarify this for me?

I think you already did clarify this concern. Your questioning reveals that you are a human born of earthly parents.

An extraterrestrial living here on earth *knows* what he/she is. They don't have to ask anyone. They know what they are and exactly why they're here.

Please be very careful and discerning with this issue. There are many humans who are psychologically convinced they're from another world. This cannot be so without the conscious awareness of same. See? One does not need to "convince" self of the matter if one is truly an alien here. Nor would a true extraterrestrial living on earth go about claiming such, for their work would be rendered useless if the public knew of their true identity.

A few of the experiences relayed in PHANTOMS AFOOT appear to be similar to certain aspects of alien contact. Do you think some of these actually were?

I'd be in a lot of hot water if I couldn't differentiate a wayward spirit from an alien encounter. This is not to be sarcastic with your question, for some alien manifestations are indeed much like a spirit one. However, when both realities are frequently experienced, there is really no comparison left. Their contrasts are immediately self-evident.

Had No-Eyes ever communicated with alien intelligences? That seems to me to be a likely event.

This specific aspect of the issue is extremely touchy and places me in a precarious position. Therefore, I've made it a policy to immediately tread "away" from this subject when it arises. Perhaps when, and if, the time comes to speak of this I will write of it. But for now, I can only state that there was indeed communication done on a frequent basis.

It's clear to many of us here in (state withheld) that you are an alien and that's why you feel so deeply that you don't belong here.

I'm glad you're so clear on this. Please, be careful of those aspects you accept as truth.

My feelings of not belonging stem from a spiritual level of development called The Knowing which brings on The Great Alone. In this state of being, one's heart and mind perceives the absence of like souls in the physically-manifested dimension. It is not unlike being alone for a long time in a foreign country. There are few who speak your language.

Will you be doing a book on aliens?

Although it's painful to see so much misinformation being penned about the extraterrestrials and so many alleged channelers bring in material from them, I cannot write on the issue until I'm given the signal that the right time has arrived. Let me just state that, if channelers were really giving alien information, they would be speaking of many, many more celestial bodies than the routine Orion and Pleiades.

I could write two or three books on No-Eyes' alien connection, however, this will not manifest until I have been given the okay on it, for I must stay within the guidelines I've been given in respect to revelations.

Have you heard of The Rapture? Will UFOs be involved in this?

Yes, I've heard of the belief in a Rapture that refers to the "taking up" or "ascension" of certain "saved" people. This concept is not at all the physical one that people believe it to be.

Will aliens share the earth with us at some time in the future?

This is a very strong probability at this time. Remember that they have much to share with us in the way of technology and medical knowledge. To coexist with beings who can easily bring about a more healthful and environmentally safe earth would be a beautiful beginning to the Age of Peace and Harmony.

The above response was associated with an "en masse" sharing, however, please remember that, currently, some aliens are walking among you.

I've experienced missing time. Does this always verify an alien contact experience?

Although many humans who have had an alien encounter may also experience missing time, the reverse does not always apply. Experiencing missing time does not necessarily indicate that an alien encounter was manifested.

There are other reasons for experiencing missing time. These are generated from psychological aberrations such as fugues, which are instances of pathological amnesiac conditions during which the individual is conscious of actions but on return to normal has no recollection of them. Great stress or emotional crises can cause fugue states which are interpreted as periods of missing time.

I've read several popular books on alien contact. Should I believe this material?

An individual's personal belief system is a very private thing. I cannot tell anyone what to believe. When you read something you must base your belief by how you feel about what you've read. The Higher Self must be your guide on such things.

Most of my UFO experiences have been connected with Indians. Why?

The intelligent extraterrestrials do not misrepresent themselves to those they manifest to. By the details of your letter, your experiences have not been with aliens, but rather with individual spirits manifesting as Native Americans.

What will be the true test that conclusively verifies aliens as real space beings?

Perhaps for you the true test will be an encounter of the third kind.

When our brothers on other planets manifest themselves during the Phoenix Days there will be no denying who they are or where they are from. They will have many ways to verify their true identity.

What will be the alien's message for us?

The same as they've been trying to give us for centuries —that of harmony and peace through unconditional love. And how living the Earthway is our natural heritage of health for both humans and the earth.

We here in our group believe you're a space-sister.

And so I am.

As are intelligent beings everywhere related through the Family of Spirits God manifested upon Creation. Indeed, you and I and they are all of one *root* family.

Where are the Earth Watchers from?

They're from places that have no current reference point. They are not of our small galaxy.

This is not to infer that no cosmic beings are from places within our galaxy, but you specifically asked about the Earth Watchers. You tightly qualified your question, so too has the response been likewise qualified.

I've always wanted an alien visitation because I know I wouldn't be scared of them.

Knowing and believing in an alien existence is not the same as coming face to face with it. Be it known that the first encounter will indeed strike real terror in you. . .*if* you are allowed to recall any of it. This is, of course, in reference to the smaller white ones who prefer to appear quite unexpectedly in your living room or next to your bed late at night. Subsequent visitations are not as stressful as the initial encounter.

There is no psychological or physical terror if the visitors are of the species that are much like us in their appearance. In that instance, it's much like conversing with an old friend.

Have alien beings ever been in Summer Rain's house? If Yes, were you aware of it and what transpired?

Three questions here.

Yes, they are frequently in our house.

Family members are usually aware of these times.

Depending on their purpose, various things transpire. Several of us have experienced a visitation to their vehicles on an individual basis. Other times their appearance is for the purpose of "clearing" or blocking negative vibrations from approaching or contaminating our dwelling or property. Once when Aimee got up during the night, she passed a hallway and subliminally took notice of a bright light shining down through the house. In her sleepy state, she didn't give it a passing thought other than knowing "they" were doing something in the house again. She returned to her bed and fell back to sleep. In the morning, she recounted seeing a brilliant beam of white light that speared right through the house.

One of the evidenced signs of them being in the house during the night is the scent of crisp, fresh air as if all the windows and doors are opened to the winter night. This sudden fragrance usually wakes one or more of us up. Usually we just take note of it and fall back to sleep (except for the individual who is intended to remain awake).

Everyone in the household has had some contact with them, whether it was just seeing them in the house or an actual communication.

Isn't it wonderful so many channelers are bringing in information from the alien beings?

There are many of our star brothers and sisters walking around among you in the physical. So then, why do we need channelers to tell us their messages? Why is this such a widespread practice when they themselves are speaking directly to walking, talking folks in the physical. They communicate in a face-to-face manner with us and, we, in turn, relay their information. Truly, our starborn brothers and sisters have little use for channelers.

So why the preponderance of them? I think the answer to that is very clear. Just be wary of any channeled information that's claimed to be coming from alien intelligences.

I read a book that was channeled by an alien intelligence who claimed to once be Jesus.

And I was once Kris Kringle.

My statement isn't meant to be a sarcastic one, but in this instance, if I know anything, this would be it. And it deeply depresses me to see so much misinformation being written without the slightest regard to the reality of the basic facts and truths.

FIRE KEEPERS

The Native American. The Original People.
Earthkeepers.
They still hear the buffalo thunder. They still feel the Earth Mother's breath. They still see the visions. And their hearts keep the Fire. . .still.

Spiritually speaking, I feel that the Native Americans symbolize something important in regard to their "return" yet I get off on so many different tracts that I can't exactly pinpoint the precise meaning. It seems to elude me. Would you please clarify this?

Long before the white man came to America, the Indian civilization enjoyed a universal lifestyle that was sympathetic with the Earth Mother. This civilization was ordered and serene. The people respected each other's boundaries. They possessed an intense regard for all of life. They knew the truths of the Great Spirit because their pure hearts were open and their spirits were free to join with the high-flying eagle as it soared through the deep canyons and wind-blown mountain tops. All of nature whispered of profound spiritual truths and the people listened with reverence. They were far from being ignorant savages.

Soon these people will rise again with the great Phoenix. Even today, as the Phoenix restlessly turns its embryonic form within the womb of the Earth Mother, the Indian nation is also moving restlessly above the earth. The people sense their bond with the Phoenix entity that will rise up free, taking the people with it. The Indian nation is full of anxiety for they are patiently awaiting their ultimate freedom to be.

For decades, the Indian people have been a literally forgotten segment of our nation. They have been misunderstood and pushed into darkened corners. Yet, if *any* race of people would've been chosen by God, it would've been the Indian people, for they possessed a true grasp of the spirit and its relationship to the Great Spirit and to all of life.

A great hue and cry is sent up when people remember the terrible atrocities of one Adolph Hitler, and how he exterminated those he didn't like. Who makes an outrage of what was done to the Indian? Nobody cares anymore. They were just savages. It was alright to herd them like animals from their own beloved lands. It was alright for the "civilized" soldiers to raid their encampments and slaughter the women and children who were running for cover. It was alright to give them gifts of warm blankets that were taken from soldiers who had died of smallpox and cholera. It was alright to give them "special" land areas that weren't good for anything but dust devils and lizards.

Today the Indian people are still treated as if they're a sub-class people. They still have the reservations. Are they not as human as everyone else? Are they not equal among men in the eye of God? Yet as soon as they begin to speak up for their equal rights —it's considered an "uprising." Our nation has opened its doors to all people of all races except to those who were here first. This is going to change. There is no choice. The gentle hearts and tender spirits of the Indian People are going to reign over their beloved land once again. When the Age of Peace and Harmony is upon us, it will be the way of the redman that survives —it will be the *only* way.

And that is the clarity you need to your question. The aspect of the Indian that will return is the "way". . .the belief in harmony and oneness between man and his earth. See?

Are most textbooks fairly accurate regarding Indian history and their treatment of the Indian personality?

Have you ever read an American History book written from the *Indian's* perspective?

It seems to me that Hitler was reborn a German AFTER he did his vile "thing" on the Indian people. Don't the two persecutions compare?

Your theory is accurate. It's a shame more people don't realize this. The horror of the evil entity also known as Hitler remains in evidence in our own nation's history, yet the public is blind to it.

It was our nation's duty to free those imprisoned in Germany, yet those imprisoned on reservations by that same entity are still suffering. We open our hearts to the starving poor in foreign countries, yet the Indian people of our own nation go unnoticed.

I think Indians are scary, creepy.

You are fearful of that which you do not understand. You fear the unknown factor. Do not continue in fear. Take the time and make the effort to *learn* about that which you fear. Do not continue in ignorance.

I'm a Native American who has tried to get my heartfelt thoughts published in magazines. My perseverance has been worn thin — nobody wants articles written by an Indian. I believe the publishing industry is prejudiced against us. I am sad about this. How did YOU break through their iron doors?

I was fortunate for my manuscript to land on Robert Friedman's desk (he is now president of Hampton Roads Publishing Co.). He recognized the importance of what I had to say and heard the voice of my spirit. He knew others would also hear that voice.

I sympathize with your situation. The publishing industry has been closed to native material for a great many years, however, in the last decade it has opened its doors wider and wider. I don't know what your articles are about, but I do know they must be upbeat in order to get accepted — no editor wants to print negative or emotionally-depressing material no matter what subject it's on. Perhaps you need to reformat your material so it's more acceptable. I wish you the best and encourage to keep submitting your work. . . don't give up.

It's an old belief (or myth) that Indians could walk through the woodlands without being heard. Is that true?

It's true.

And I could not begin to tell you how this is done because it is a physical ability that comes quite naturally once one has attained a spiritual union with nature. It is not a "learned" talent, but rather a naturally "acquired" one.

Indians are lazy and a bunch of derelict drunks!

Please tell me how *you* would feel if you were rousted out of your comfortable home, your possessions burned, your ancestors murdered, your family starved while being herded onto a barren land to live? How would you feel if your religious beliefs were outlawed and your children were forced to learn another language and never speak their own again? How would you feel if you accepted all of the above and then tried your hardest to make a better life for yourself by getting a job off the reservation and nobody would hire you? How would *you* feel if all the cards were always stacked against you?

Please, place yourself in another's shoes before you make such unkind and erroneous statements.

I would like to see more Native Americans represented in the literary field. Now that you've broken the ice, so to speak, do you feel that more of these people will come forward with their writings of the heart?

You will see a change as the nation's awareness awakens to its gentle brothers. It will not be long before the highly sensitive writings of Native Americans will be sought after by the publishing world. It is the wave of popularity that will sweep the literary field away into a more enlightened future.

After wallowing in the depraved issues of sex and horror, the literary field will have hit a solid bottom, it will have nowhere to go but "up" into a new sensitive awareness that touches the heart.

Why do Indian names usually relate to animals or nature?

This is so common because the Indian people on the whole relate so closely to nature and all of its innocently beautiful lifeforms.

In the days when Indians were free of the legal paperwork of the white man, they often changed their given names to a more fitting one that gave them personal identity which correlated to a specific aspect of nature in their lives. Usually these new names came to an individual after a vision quest whereby they joined their spirit with the spirit of truth. And, depending on their specific vision and subsequent spiritual experience, their name would be altered accordingly. You could tell a great deal about an individual's character just by what his/her name was.

If Native Americans are so respectful of nature and its wildlife, why is so much of their jewelry and clothing made from talons, teeth, and skins?

That is all that remains of their beautiful heritage. Would you also deny them that? Would you also take that away?

Indians relinquished their land rights when their leaders signed their binding treaties. Now they want to change those treaties to suit themselves. Don't they realize that a treaty is a legal contract and that it can't be altered upon a mere whim of fancy?

If you had put any effort at all into researching the historical treaty records, you would not be asking this of the Indian people, but rather of the United States government!

Indians belong on their reservations — they're nothing but a sub-class race anyway.

You're entitled to your personal opinions.
May your darkened path be shattered by the arrow of enlightenment, and may your eyes open up onto the brilliance of a golden daybreak.

I am a Caucasian, but love the Indian people. They are so deeply sensitive and possess such a deep understanding of nature and the secrets of the Earth Mother. I believe that they are the most misunderstood people of our time and I pray that our nation will open its eyes and hearts to the plight of these peaceful and oppressed people and come to realize their sensitivities and valuable worth.

I thank you for that. Your sentiments will remain within my heart.

My wife and I have vacationed in southern Colorado and in New Mexico. Our travels have brought us in contact with Indians who live on the nearby reservations. We've noticed how markedly quiet and reserved they are. Why don't they speak much? They merely sit and stare or grin. Why is this? What makes this race so withdrawn?

Oppression.
And prejudice. And misunderstanding and hatred by others.

All minorities have been able to effect changes for their race or sex except the Native American — the prejudices run too deep, prejudice that cloaks guilt.

The Indian merely sits and stares. He simply silently grins because he knows things — wondrous things that you do not. He knows the changes that are coming. He is merely listening to the drumbeat that you do not hear. He is merely biding his time —he's waiting. He's waiting for his sun to rise. . .for his Daybreak.

There doesn't seem to be very many articles about or by Indians. I've often wondered why they don't submit more of their sensitive thoughts to magazines so that the general public can benefit from them.

Flat facts will be stated here.

What makes you think that the native people don't submit their literary work to magazines?

Many editors of both magazines and publishing houses are biased. They don't think that their readers would be interested in what an Indian has to say — especially if it's about the past. Nobody wants to read about the depressing things that have happened to the gentle Indian — that could quite possibly be considered subversive material!

The truth hurts too much and editors don't want their readers hurt, offended, or feeling guilty.

But. . .the winds of change are blowing this way. And the changes cannot be stopped.

I think it's clear that Summer Rain is to be the new leader of the Indian nation.

I appreciate the thought, but it's not even logical. I walk the Shadowland where sunlight never fully shines on my heritage, for it is of the spirit. I have not come to be a leader of anyone, a people, or a nation. I am simply a voice in the wind. . . some hear and some don't.

Please, watch how you think of others. Take a care as to their specific purpose rather than trying to fit one to them.

What is the Sacred Tree?

The Sacred Tree is synonymous with the "Spirit" of a culture. It represents the living fruit of living the pureness of same.

What is the Hoop of Nations?

The Hoop of Nations is symbolic of the "unity" of the Indian people that bonds all tribes. . .ultimately, all people.

Who gave you your Indian name?

As you may know, one cannot just invent an Indian name to be known by. These are "given" in a sacred manner by a fullblood in ceremony.

Before I came to Colorado, the spirit of my grandmother appeared to me and called me by Summer Rain. I didn't know what she meant by that. It wasn't until I met No-Eyes that I heard the name spoken out loud. She knew of my destiny and gave me the name in a sacred ceremony that I'll probably never write about. Immediately afterward, I had the name made legal, for No-Eyes emphasized that it was my right of heritage to do so since it was my *real* name anyway.

What is a Dreamwalker? I thought it was someone who could "walk" through the dreams of others.

The term Dreamwalker was first brought to the general public in my book by the same name. Many readers misunderstood the term and began using it in reference to those who could enter the dreams of others. This is totally in error.

A Dreamwalker is one who is cognizant of the many dimensional aspects of spirituality and the metaphysical facets that accompany the universal truths of the collective wisdom. A Dreamwalker can quite naturally perform at optimum level within any dimensional realm. He can also enter dreams, however, that is but a small aspect of his abilities and in no way infers that his talents are confined to this manifestation.

A Dreamwalker walks through life with the will of the Great Spirit as his guide. He helps all those he comes across and is a great teacher. He never tells people what he is. . .never. You will recall that it was No-Eyes who told me about who Brian Many Heart was. . .he never made much of it himself.

Was No-Eyes a Shamaness, a Medicine Woman, or a Visionary?

I've noticed that literature has these terms very confused and, in turn, the public uses the terms as though they were interchangeable They are not.

A Medicine Woman works with healing aspects. A Shamaness manages the more metaphysical side of nature. And a Visionary is one who is wise to the future and possesses paranormal functionings.

No-Eyes was a synergic blend of all three, for her development was guided by many adepts, both of the physical and spirit realm. To say that she was only one of these would be to narrow and confine her personality to a thimble. She was all three and so much more.

What is a Skinwalker?

This would be synonymous to what you would understand as a witch. A skinwalker is also known by other names, most common is Shape Changer. This term is connected to the more negative use aspects of paranormal functioning such as spells that bring on illnesses and disease.

Do we all have Dreamwalkers in our dreams?

The term Dreamwalker does not infer this is what they do. Very few can actually enter another's dreamscape. We do not all have Dreamwalkers in our dreams.

The elders in our tribe have been watching you. So far they like what they're seeing but hold their breath about what else you might one day reveal.

My intent is to manifest a promise I made to my sweet teacher. My alternative intent is to bring the general public into a new awareness of the importance of the Native way and the people's belief in a bonded relationship with the Earth Mother. My intent is not to make magic nor expose any real sacredness. I pray that the public perceives Summer Rain as the shadow behind the living entity of No-Eyes who has lived only to share her wisdom. My intent is for the public to only see No-Eyes and to maintain the proper perspective of Summer Rain.

How come No-Eyes didn't do sacred Indian ceremonies and magic in the books?

Because these were not meant for the books, it does not infer that she didn't do these or that we didn't do them together. There was much of this and it will remain within my heart.

Does Summer Rain get letters from Native Americans? What is their tone?

I've received a great deal of mail from Native Americans who have all encouraged my work. I've received letters from almost every tribe, AIM members, and elders. They are written for a wide variety of reasons. Some offer me membership, some have requested permission to quote from the books, some are written simply to express their appreciation, many were written to say how grateful they were that I didn't expose the more sacred ways and ceremonies.

And, in turn, I have been equally grateful for their kind encouragement, for there appears to be an unspoken trust that has been forged between us. I know my place and I don't misrepresent myself as being something that I'm not. I hold the Native Way in great respect and I will always honor that attitude. I know where the line is drawn and also know never to even come close to crossing that important line.

Do you perform regular Indian ceremonies like the Medicine Wheel, Sweats, and the Pipe?

All ceremonies taught to me by No-Eyes and Brian Many Heart are done in absolute privacy. My pipe prayers and chanting/drumming are always a solitary performance. Such was the proper reverence taught to me in order to be alone with the Great Spirit Force.

I do not perform the Medicine Wheel, for my teachers repeatedly reinforced the fact that this particular ceremony was not necessary for me to expend energies on.

When can we expect a book on Native magic?

This material won't come from me. As No-Eyes so aptly put it: "This be Sacred Way stuff!" And that always denoted an aspect I would retain within my heart and not put to pen.

My Indian mother won't teach me her sacred ways because she says that every time Indians trust someone they end up getting hurt. Mother says there's nobody left to trust enough to teach, so why bother?

I'm sure your mother could trust *you*. It's so important for the Old Sacred Ways to remain vitally alive! What will you pass on to your own children? If these things are not handed down they will then indeed be lost forever. They must be preserved!

What Clan are you?

I am a descendant (both physically and spiritually) from the Spirit Clan of the Anasazi.

I was known as See-qu-aa-nu (Sequanu) of the Anasazi People in the year 650 A.D. It is from this life that much of my personal information has been recalled. The Spirit Clan was one comprised of the visionaries and wise ones who took their young ones into instruction from birth. Their purpose was to collaborate with the extraterrestrials in sequestering the articles of wisdom from the ensuing invaders they foresaw coming upon the land.

The following two lifetimes were spent as a member of the Shoshone tribe which was comprised of those Anasazi who left the original compound when the others left to return home.

No-Eyes confirmed this, as did Brian Many Heart. It would appear that the recording on my ancestors was tampered with. But I care not for this indiscretion for the sake of "propriety," for I'm comfortable to walk the Shadowland and not force the issue. My place is not here and not there. I, as do many during this time frame, walk the Borderland Trails.

Some aspects of your books, particularly parts of Dreamwalker, made me tingle and I actually have the hair stand on end. This is especially strong when Brian Many Heart is telling of the hidden articles. When you wrote Sphinx, Pyramid, Mesas, it was as if my mind was suddenly sparked by some inexplicable knowing. I had to put the book down until the trembling dissipated. Can you help me with this?

During this time frame of civilization, there are many who have once been members of the Spirit Clan. The memories of that time are spearing through the carryover soul and sparking the consciousness of many. There are those few who have had a psychic shock while reading some of my material because certain aspects have served to jar the former memory bank of the spirit. When this occurs, one trembles and the hair stands on end with recognition of long forgotten events that were experienced.

What does the word "Namaskara" mean?

It is a most beautiful word that connotates a Native phrase: "the divinity within me salutes the divinity within you."

Are Indian spirits more advanced than other races?

No, just a little more aware of the necessity of human bonding with the earth and all living things. The Indian spirit will possess a natural tendency toward the aspects of nature which many Anglos perceive as magic.

I was at a meeting in a metaphysical bookstore where a native American woman (name withheld) said that Mary Summer Rain was in physical danger because of the things she's written about and because she's not a fullblood. Can you comment on this?

You addressed two completely different aspects here. We need to take them separately.

I found it interesting that she said my life was in danger for what I've written, because I've not written of any of the Sacred Ways or revealed anything that hasn't already been printed at one time or another in different ways. It's also interesting that all my Native mail has been so encouraging and supportive of my works. One wonders what the underlying reason could be for this woman's negativity. Surely, to voice such a thing is serious business and infers a threat of some type.

I am not unfamiliar with the spiritual "magic" some native people possess, for I've encountered more than one skinwalker since my books have been published. But what few perceive is the surround of entities that protect me against such attack attempts. How does she know of these attacks? I've never spoken about them to anyone. Perhaps my life is precarious because of, not what I've "said," but rather of what I "represent." There are many types of threats and I've said nothing to be construed as revealing Sacred Ways. So? This would lead to the possibility that someone thinks I'm a threat to them personally. Someone definitely doesn't know what I'm all about.

The second part of your statement concerns the woman's view that I have no right to be writing of native issues because I am not a fullblood. I've heard this once before when a bookstore manager told me a customer was outraged that a "white" was writing of native ways.

Spiritually speaking, this attitude is so very petty. And generally speaking, it is so irrelevant.

If this were a valid statement, it would mean that nobody had a right to record their memoirs or write of any of their experiences. This is censorship of the very worst kind. It is evidence of extreme narrow-mindedness.

My meeting and subsequent times with No-Eyes was the bright highlight of my life. And I promised her I'd write of those times. Just because she happened to be a fullblood Indian, does this then mean I have no right to share the relationship and our experiences together? Does this mean that only Irish people can write of the Irish and only French people can author French literary works? This idea is generated from extremely false logic that serves to perpetuate racism.

If I hadn't kept my promise to No-Eyes and written of our times, who could benefit from her wisdom? The thousands of letters I've received have honored the visionary by how her wisdom and deep philosophical insight has literally changed their lives. Through her, many have been spiritually helped. How is it that this should be denied the public simply because I am not a fullblood? Ridiculous. Truth is truth. Wisdom is wisdom no matter who it comes from, no matter what culture or race it is generated from. See? The perspective of this issue clearly needs to be brought into an alignment with the Light.

Can you teach me the pipe ceremony?

This type of question is often asked and therefore needs some clarification.

First of all, I don't teach any Indian ceremonies because I follow a path that has very little ceremonial aspects. When one can mentally and psychically attain the dimensional level required without utilizing ceremonies, that one finds it expedient to forego the time-consuming rituals. Such was the way of No-Eyes and so it has been my method also.

Now, in regard to specific ceremonies, especially the pipe, it's important to remember that much learning and preparation goes into the learning of this ritual. There is seven year's preparation for one to be qualified enough to teach such a ceremony. And so it is equally important that the novice doesn't seek just anyone out who may know only a "little" of this ritual.

Learning cannot be rushed or forced just because we want to know something or participate in a ceremony. Indian ceremonies are sacred rituals that must be approached with the proper mental attitude of high respect. One must know the background aspects of such ceremonies in order to gain and appreciate the full facets of same. To participate just to say you did this ceremony or that one, is meaningless and, ultimately, is highly disrespectful.

I realize there is a growing interest in Native ceremonies and that many are flocking to "teachers" in order to pay their fee to participate in them, but my friends, the fee is not the value of the ceremony — learning the full background and reasons for the beautiful ritual is where the true value lies. And this learning can take several years in order to come into a full and respectful appreciation of it. This holds true with the Medicine Wheel and Vision Quests. One doesn't just journey to a teacher, pay a fee and spend two days participating in their "ceremony." One cannot attain the full appreciation and knowing by this method.

So if you truly want to learn the pipe ceremony. Seek first a bonafide Native teacher who has spent his seven years of learning the Way. In truth, few seekers will be accepted. Even fewer non-natives, for this is the way of it.

I've heard that certain Native Americans in the Southwest have harbored extraterrestrials in the past and that a few aliens may still be living among them. Is this true?

What is true is this: *If that were true, it would be public and common knowledge if it were meant to be known as such.* Be careful to guard your tongue where rumors are concerned. I'm not being sarcastic here. I understand you're asking for clarification of what you've heard, but I am not the one to resolve this for you. Although I'm familiar with the issue, it's outside my realm of authority to speak of it. I suggest you either put the subject out of your mind or else go and seek an elder in the Southwest. And, if you even find one who will speak of this. . .you will still walk away without your answer.

It's been theorized that the American Indian population originally journeyed across the Bering land bridge and then down into North America. This doesn't seem right to me.

Nor to me. There is a reason a native tribe calls themselves The Original People. . .and they don't resemble Eskimos at all either.

Most of the Native Americans were the race of North America, as such, they were placed here upon Creation. This is truly "their" land. . .their homeland. Those non-Indian races that find themselves now living in North America all came from somewhere else.

Why do you object to public Indian Pow Wows and parades?

This is a personal and very private feeling that has been generated from so many strong memories of how native life used to be. It involves many intertwining aspects that are extremely sensitive for me. . .aspects that make a painful heartsound that only I can hear.

Yet, generally speaking, I do think that, on the whole, the public Pow Wows and parades are a good thing because they bring a unique Indian exposure to the public. They serve to increase the public's interest in native culture and, in turn, many people then go home and do a little more research on the subject. I am therefore not opposed to the "theory" of these displays, but rather do they hold an individualized meaning that is specific to myself.

Your books have really opened my eyes in respect to the Indian issue. Now I find myself ashamed to have white skin.

No! This is all wrong! This was not my intent in writing of my experiences and memories. Please remember that, because all of us here now have been reborn, you yourself may have not at all been involved in history's Indian mistreatment. You may have been an Indian back then. You cannot blame yourself for what has been done in the past. What you *can* do is assist the public to move forward into a greater awareness of the plight of the current Indian population. Donate clothing or funds to Indian-run organizations. Share what you know with others. The reason for knowing anything like this is to *do* something about it, not just feel bad. We do not suffer the sins of our fathers if we make solid attempts at retribution or to "balance" out the racial karma. See?

Never be ashamed of who you are. Never be ashamed of the color of your skin or your belief systems. Each of us is such a unique individual that harbors the spirit of God within. As such beautiful individuals, we must all work to bring about a harmonious and peaceful society where it can be said that *all* races have equal rights including enough food, clothing, and societal opportunities to advance their lot in life. We must join forces to work on eradicating poverty and segregation among all in the Family of Humankind.

I have three Native American spirit guides. They all tell me that you were a great wise one in your last life.

There are two aspects that need addressing in your statement.

First . Spiritually speaking, it is the law that : *one* guide be assigned to each incarnated individual. One. Those who say they have more than one are revealing that they have wayward entities or mischievous spirits attached to them. These are "playing" with you and giving misinformation for the fun of watching you hang on their every word in belief. Please watch who you open self to. You have only ONE personal spirit guide.

Also on this same issue, I am amazed at the preponderance of "Indian" spirit guides. My own, and Bill's, are not Indian. No-Eyes has chosen to assist my work, but she is not my personal spirit guide. She is rather likened to a constant spiritual companion.

Spirit guides do not have specific names because they're comprised of pure spirit energy and in possession of "all" former life identities.

Therefore they are, in actuality, ALL the names they have experienced in their many physical lives. A spirit guide is a "composite mind" — never an individual. Therefore do they not have a specific name by which to be called, but rather an "essence" of the developed composition. See?

When communicating with their "charge," they may choose to pick a name that best corresponds with their essence." This is done for the convenience of the physical individual only, and the chosen name will only be represented as native if the guide had spent a great many incarnations as such. This is a rarity because a spirit must spend lifetimes in many different races in order to attain a rounded experience. Therefore, the preponderance of "Indian" spirit guides doesn't justify. . .doesn't wash.

So? What's my point? The point is that, because of the current popularity of "native" culture and issues, many "false" guides (wayward spirits and lower plane entities) are playing at being Indian. It's the "in" thing to do around etheric circles. But playing games is not what our spiritual advancement is all about. We must be absolutely certain of our "channeled" information and "who" is giving same. These times are too important to be opening self to whoever (or whatever) is around. Channeling is so popular and you're nobody if you can't do it. Wrong.

To be able to perceive a spirit guide is *not* where it's at — to be able to perceive your "true" guide is all that matters. It matters not what he/she calls self. And a warning signal should go up if *more* than one spirit claims to be your guide, and if they have Indian names. KNOW YOUR GUIDE.

Now, the second aspect of your statement needs addressing because your "guides" have given you false information.

I was not a wise one in my last life — great or otherwise. I was never a great anything in any of my former lives. I was a common individual in all lives. Just because She-Who-Sees could envision the future and the coming of Summer Rain as her next incarnation, does not infer that she was a "great wise one," for many native people were in tune with their Higher Selves. In all my former lives, as now, "great wise one" does not apply.

The native people were very primitive before the white man came, yet you would have us believe they were so wise, peaceful and competent.

In looking at your statement, I find we must define "primitive" first. What is primitive? Let's look at that.

Generally the term means simplicity and unsophistication. Mathematically speaking it means: a form in which another is derived. In geology it means: first foundation. In biology: beginnings. Linguistically: elementally first. In art: self-taught.

So if the native people were "primitive," according to the official interpretation of the word, they were a people who lived a simple life that was unfettered with extraneous aspects — all the better to be close to the earth and their spirit. Yes?

They also were a "foundation" by which other ensuing generations were born of. They were the very "beginnings," which set the "first elements" of that which followed. And, they were indeed "self-taught." My, how *wise* to be able to teach oneself how to survive without supermarkets, without gas heat, without clothing and shoe stores.

How "competent" would you be if you had none of the above and had to gather and hunt your own food without rifle or shotgun? How competent would you judge self if you had to provide for your family with an arrow? Make a shelter without brick and mortar? How far would you get without your "sophisticated" trappings of today?

If you didn't have to "depend" on another's knowledge could you be so self-reliant as to build your own two or three-story house? A car? A radio? A telephone? Could your mate gather botanicals or grow a garden for your food? Sew all your clothing? Make your shoes? You see how "primitive" your society is? You literally "depend" on other's knowledge for all your sophisticated goods and lifestyle. How wise would you be if you had to build everything for yourself and family from scratch?

As far as the "peaceful" aspect goes, how often do you ask forgiveness of the steak's essence that you're about to eat? How many times have you "felt" the earth breathe? Heard the wind whisper? How many times have you given away your most prized possession to another. How often do you consider the good of the "all" without ever considering the self? How often do you pray for the purpose of "thanking" instead of "asking.? All these things and more were the "primitive" Indian's way of life. They all contribute to a peaceful existence within the clan's society.

Please, attend more to deeper thought before making such statements. These times greatly demand the need to shed shallow thought. Surface thinking is dangerous and does not contribute to advancement of society or **of self.**

The joy Summer Rain and No-Eyes felt over the Indian nation rising again struck me as odd. It seems to me that the development and enlightenment of the spirit is what's most important, not the issue of one's skin encasement.

Ah, but you did miss the whole point of it. We weren't even talking about the "physical" race, but rather the "spiritual aspects" of it. See? Our great joy came from the "spirit" of the race rising. . .not the physical race itself, although that too will occur. Know that the spirit *always* takes precedence.

Some ancient Indian artifacts have been in my family for many generations. Finally I donated them to a historical museum.

What your family held were highly sacred objects. They should not have gone to a museum, but rather returned to their rightful owners.

I know of some buried Indian gold and I have a map to show you. I believe you can help me find this treasure. Please help. We can split the find. Enclosed is a Navajo blanket representing my friendship and goodwill.

It's important for you to understand that I don't use my spirituality to find treasure. Not for you and, certainly not for me. And, if this buried gold was found, spiritually speaking, who would it rightfully belong to? Or would it simply be finders keepers?

By the details of your letter, this has become a great quest for you. Beware of that which you choose as your quest in life. If you are meant to discover this treasure, the way will be shown to you. It will come quite naturally.

I wrote you about the gold treasure a few weeks ago. I'm coming to Woodland Park to talk to you about it.

In my last letter to you, I explained that I can no longer meet with people due to my many obligations. I'm frequently out of town on unexpected journeys. I cannot help you with this quest.

I'm the one with the buried gold quest. I made it to Woodland Park but everyone refuses to give me your address or phone number. I finally followed a blue pickup to where you used to live. I knocked on doors and someone gave me your phone number. Robin said you were out of town. I'll hang around a few days.

No comment, for Bill and I were out of town.

I can't hang around here any longer. You were no help. I want the Navajo rug back.

I accepted your give-away because it was sent as a sign of friendship and goodwill. I'm sorry to hear it was intended as a bribe. Next time think deeper about the reason behind your gift-giving, for a true Quest does not involve forcing the consummation through bribing others to help with it. A true Quest is resolved through inner introspection, contemplation, and by walking the Within Path.

I seriously caution you with this quest, for you're looking for that which may be protected by native spirit powers. . .still. Such things are not folklore. Such things are meant to be left alone.

I'm an Anglo woman and have been making some beautiful Navajo rugs. It gives me great pleasure to be able to imitate these.

Dear lady, I hope you're not also selling these. And if you are, I hope you're informing your buyers that they *are* imitations.

Most native women weavers do their work through spiritual means. There are ceremonies involved with the weaving. These frequently involve visions, spirits, and other members of the tribe. An Indian rug is NOT just a rug. It is a spiritual creation that carries great meaning with it.

This Weaver Way and the beautiful spirit process cannot be imitated nor duplicated by a non-native.

I've been looking for some Native American music. Most of what I've bought hasn't been very moving.

That's because you don't understand it. Native music and chanting is not like any other music. You must get "into" it before it can be appreciated. Some types of music must be listened to with the heart. . .with the spirit, not merely with one's physical ears.

Why do Native people still make clothing and ceremony objects from animal skins (leathers) and other body parts? That's not in keeping with the Earthway?

The term, Earthway, was specifically coined by No-Eyes and, never did she associate it with the issue of using animals skins or parts for clothing or objects. Didn't she herself wear leather moccasins? Didn't she herself have a doeskin medicine power pouch at her waist?

In your assumptions you've brought dark shadows upon the Earthway term. You cannot chastise an entire people because of your own misunderstandings and interpretations.

Know all the aspects of a concept before criticizing those factors that are assumed part of same.

Do Native people really believe in things as silly as Thunderbeings?

I would caution you to hold your tongue when referring to the spiritual beliefs of an entire race of people. We must show more respect for another's spiritual belief system. Know that "silly" is often associated with those concepts that are not understood. . .or to those concepts that one has no inclination to understand.

Also know that your world is populated by a multitude of entities. . .both seen and unseen.

There seems to be a flood of Native American literature directed to Female Power. As a man, I and many of my friends would like to see more directed to the male aspect as well.

As would I. This would be beneficial for the equalizing or "balance" of the duality of Inner Power. This was precisely why No-Eyes had me spend a span of time with Brian Many Heart. For one to center on a singular Power Gender is to create an unbalanced and greatly slanted spiritual aspect. Unity, an Inner Hoop of roundedness, cannot be attained through the study and practice of singular gender spirituality.

Men, like the females who've gained so much through the female Native literature, need equally inspiring and revealing texts to study and be inwardly touched by. The male ceremonies are very important. The male aspect must also be nurtured, but first it must be provided and made accessible for those thirsting for it.

Does the Native Sweetgrass have a Christian ceremonial counterpart?

The closest similarity would be the Christian "palms."

My first contact with a Native individual was when I journeyed to Woodland Park from my home in Detroit. I met the Native man who owned the jewelry shop there. He wasn't unusual at all — it was just like talking to any other shopkeeper.

Unusual? Did you expect an alien?
Clearly, you did hold some strange expectations before you walked through the jewelry shop door. Obviously you expected a Close Encounter of some kind. But, to your great amazement, there was no alien behind the counter. . .only another human. . .just like you. What a relief that must have been. Now you see how easy it was to just reach out and get to know another kind. Indeed, it's not so hard to see us all as siblings in the Great Spirit's Earth Family. . .brothers and sisters all.

Why isn't Summer Rain associated with any Native organization?

When one knows their place they don't try to force another. I'm what Many Heart referred to as The Ghost Dancer. . .I dance upon the Inbetween Trails. . .never solidly manifesting upon the Native or white paths. There is where I belong. There is where I walk. And there is where the greatest depth of The Great Alone is found.

I'm so excited. I'm going to a weekend Shamanism course next month. I'm really getting into this Native thing.

I certainly can understand your excitement, but I'm not really sure what "thing" you're getting into. A "weekend" course in anything can't begin to get anyone "into" anything. But a weekend course in *Shamanism?* This *can't* be *real.* Say it isn't so! Shamanism isn't some ethnic game to play. It's not even for non-natives to learn.
It takes a great deal of time — years and years, sometimes an entire lifetime — to learn and truly understand all the complex aspects of Shamanism. One does not learn it in a few years, months, or a weekend. It's truly a beautiful thing to gain knowledge of different ethnic ceremonies and spiritual belief systems, but what you're insinuating is that quick courses are being offered to anyone interested in learning to be a Shaman. This would be consistent with someone offering a

weekend course in becoming a Rabbi or a Catholic Priest. This entire issue has grown out of hand.

I've found that many so-called teachers of such courses are not well-versed in what a true Native Shaman is or what he does (*can* do). This involves so many traditional beliefs in spirits that anyone attempting to get "into" it without proper training has no idea what they're in for. One doesn't play with fire without first knowing what fire is. . .what it can do. . .how to handle and control it.

I've been quite disgusted with some of the popular Native American books I've picked up. Could you perhaps suggest some proper reading material on this subject?

Since you didn't mention the titles you've previously "picked up," I can't possibly comment on those. However, you may find the following titles worth your while.

Indian Country by Peter Matthiessen
Seven Arrows by Hyemeyohsts Storm
The World's Rim by Hartley Burr Alexander
God Is Red by Vine Deloria, Jr.
Daughters of the Earth by Carolyn Niethammer
Voices of Earth and Sky by Vinson Brown
Touch the Earth by T. C. McLuhan
Pumpkin Seed Point by Frank Waters
The Religions of the American Indians by Ake Hultkrantz
In The Spirit of Crazy Horse by Peter Matthiessen
Forked Tongues and Broken Treaties by Donald E. Worchester
Voices of the Winds by Margot Edmonds & Ella E. Clark
Encyclopedia of Native American Tribes by Carl Waldman
Atlas of the North American Indian by Carl Waldman

Do you recommend the native path as a way to enlightenment?

Not as a "way," but rather as a possible extension. The way to enlightenment must first come from walking the Within Path. That is to say, by going *within* via meditation and deep contemplation. This is where all the answers are. After you've walked this path for a great deal of time, you may like to round out your spiritual understandings by walking other "outside" paths.

You said that the Native American will no longer eat meat when the Phoenix Peace Days are here. All along this has been their Earthway lifestyle. Your statement appears to be a contradiction.

First it must be understood that, when I say "meat" I mean the red meats and pork. Fish and fowl are not included in this concept. This first aspect clarifies much of the seeming contradiction you thought you perceived. Secondly, it must be remembered that, when the Phoenix is flying free during the Golden Age of Peace and Harmony, God will be walking among us. Much will be different then, for all races will follow His Way. This includes our manner of eating as well as what we eat. . .both generated from God's own guidelines.

In PHANTOMS AFOOT, you quoted a part of Chief Seattle's speech. I had no idea the Indian people were so eloquent.

Yes, I understand, and this was one of the reasons I chose to include a portion of his speech. You may like to look the speech up some time and read it in its entirety. There are many such speeches by the historical Native leaders. They spoke with their heart and were not afraid to do so in public.

Historically, the Indian Chiefs sold out to the U.S. government. That's why they only have reservation land now.

I think you need to go back and hit the books again. You need to read about "how" the treaties were signed. You need to gain some important facts you missed, for many Chiefs were coerced into signing these by being lied to or being given the choice of signing or having their people massacred. Many of the "marks" on treaties that were supposed to represent so-called "Chiefs" were made by someone else altogether.

When you do your drumming and chanting out in the woods, what direction do you face and why?

My back is to the West. I face East. Why? I can't say why, I only know that that's what is inherent for me to do. That directional position is most vibrationally aligned to my spirit.

The story of White Buffalo Calf Woman is pretty preposterous to be credible, but somehow your message seems correlated with hers. Is there actually this correlation?

Truth does not alter. Men or the passing of time does not change it.

As far as the tale being preposterous; for some, I guess you had to be there. This then would be the saving grace of credibility that is retained within the spirit memory of one's essence.

Did the Shoshone People ever experience any massacres on the level of Sand Creek?

Oh yes, my friend, and worse too.

The Battle of Bear River (as it's erroneously termed) took place on January 29, 1863 outside of present-day Preston, Idaho. It was much more devastating than the Sand Creek massacre of 133 Cheyennes or the Wounded Knee slaughter of 153 Sioux.

In January of 1863, a large band of peaceful Shoshone led by Chief Sagwitch Timbimboo had gathered for their annual winter ceremony of the Warm Dance. This was a ritual to drive the cold away. In the night of the 27th, an elder by the name of Tin Dup awoke from a vision dream that showed soldiers killing his people. He warned the tribe to break camp and flee, but few believed their peaceful camp would come to such a horrifying end.

Two days later, on the morning of January 29, Chief Timbimboo rose early. He stood and watched a strange mist creep down the slopes of the surrounding hills. Then he saw Colonel Patrick Connor's 200 soldiers bearing down on the slumbering encampment. The Chief told his warriors not to raise weapons for, he believed, the soldiers come just to talk. His people had been peaceful, so what other reason would the advancing soldiers be coming for?

But little did the Chief know that the Colonel's mormon scout, Orin Porter Rockwell, had told his superior that more than 600 Shoshone warriors were "battle ready." And they stormed the unarmed camp.

Women fleeing with babies were shot and/or raped. Infants were swung by their heels, heads dashed against trees. Another chief, Bear Hunter, had a heated bayonet rammed through his head. In all, over 400 peaceful Shoshone were slaughtered that day. . ."Battle?". . . that word hardly applies. That word is currently the subject of recent efforts to be changed to massacre."

The Chief's twelve-year-old grandson, Yeager Timbimboo, lived to tell the tale. Today, his granddaughter, Mae Timbimboo Parry, has spent much of her 70 years trying to get a landmark for the massacre site. Mae is currently tribal secretary for the Northwest Shoshone. She says the tribe never recovered from that massacre because, today, they only number 350 in all.

I have been a long time active member of the American Indian Movement (A.I.M.) and I think your books have been a good thing for our people.

Your long letter has served as a beautiful "give-away" of encouragement to me. Such native sentiments serve to reinforce my purpose of enlightening the general public to the Native people's past and their current ongoing struggles.

I think it's a disgrace that so many non-Natives are trying to delve into Native religion and copy our ceremonies. [From a Medicine Woman.]

I whole-heartedly agree, but with tempered qualification.

Gaining knowledge of a different culture does not also infer that one must try to emulate it. The native ceremonies are held as highly sacred rituals. They remain sacred within the people's hearts throughout time because of the very deep traditions that accompany these rites. Therefore, these ceremonies should only be preserved and perpetuated by Native ones.

There is a tendency for such sacredness to be lessened when non-Natives attempt to perform the same ceremonies, for they do not and cannot appreciate the deeply philosophical and spiritual connections to them. When non-Natives begin performing such, the rituals then become a token performance, that is, a "surface" performance that lacks the true spiritual depth of the ritual.

I believe that non-Natives should study Indian history and Native culture to gain a more thorough understanding of the people.

This would be well when trying to learn about any ethnic race different from self, but to actually attempt to perform the Native ceremonies and sacred rituals is indeed crossing a very definitive line. . .one that trespasses upon a culture's holy ground. . .their sacred ground.

It is well to try to understand a culture, it is another to tread upon it. What I've seen going on in the so-called New Age movement has pained my spirit, for, it seems, everyone and anyone is or can be a medicine woman, Shaman, or Native teacher. It truly is a disgrace and must end now before it gets any worse. If the non-Natives truly understood the sacredness of these ceremonies they would never have attempted to copy them in the first place, for they cannot be copied.

If you care so much for the Native culture, do real in-depth historical studying, become cognizant to what is currently transpiring in the courts regarding the Native issues, do your part by contributing funds to the Native American Rights Fund, but don't try to be that which you are not — stop treading on their sacredness. In your attempts to be sympathetic, you've gone way too far along the wrong trail!

What Native ceremonies do you recommend doing?

Those that are "native" to the spiritual heritage of *self.* These then will have the most inner meaning and power.

The Indian practice of the "sweat" was suggested by No-Eyes as being an extremely healthful benefit to the system. However, the *native* way for these was not her intent, nor is it mine. Rather the *idea* of sweat baths was recommended as a natural health method of ridding the system of toxins and negative aspects. See? A regular sweat bath is *not* the same as a Native sweat, for the latter is much more of a sacred ceremony.

When will Indian rule begin?

You have misunderstood the concept. Rather we speak of the *Earthway* to begin. Living upon and *with* the earth will be the way. . .the rule of right living. This then will be the Native association inferred.

Have you heard from Brian Many Heart again?

Only second-hand from other Native people who know him. They tell me he still maintains we'll spend time together again after I'm finally settled. I'm looking forward to that day.

I think it was right for the government to abolish the Indian Sun Dance ceremony, don't you?

There is a little something called: separation of church and state. That would apply to *all* spiritual beliefs of *all* religions. Unless of course, this concept was uttered from a mouth that a forked tongue flicked from. . .or if it came with unwritten exclusions.

Of course I don't agree. It was the same government that tore native children from their families at a young age and placed them in white schools so they couldn't and wouldn't learn the newly-abolished Native tongue and spiritual ways in an attempt to slap a coat of whitewash over an entire generation!

I overheard some Indians telling jokes. They all laughed uproariously but I didn't get any of the punchlines? Am I dense or what?

A little of the first, and a lot of the last.

Indian humor can only be appreciated if you're Native. It has a hilarious quality to it. . .tongue-in-cheek. This is often blended with cynicism and Native history. Unless you know your Native history like the back of your hand. . .you won't get the punchlines. Like their sacred ceremonies, Native humor can best be understood by Natives. . .others need not apply.

Native people have negatively spoken out about certain New Age writers of Native ways. Yet nothing is heard about you. Why?

Someone once said: "Silence is Golden." And it is. Perhaps you've not heard anything because I don't tread all over another's Sacred Ground, whitewash it and then charge for the new view. I don't teach Native ceremonies nor do I condone the practice of doing so.

You have managed to walk softly so far. We're watching your footsteps. [From a Native elder.]

My spirit wants to call you Grandfather but my heart knows I've no right to the term. Therefore know, Old One, that I feel your eyes upon my trail and I shall not disappoint you nor betray you. You called me a Ghost Dancer as did Many Heart once. I know the term, but most of all, I understand the intent. It is a precarious position and place to live within, yet it is mine alone to inhabit. I accept the Inbetween World, for it is the one I was born to.

Can you recommend some workshops and classes on Native ceremonies and culture?

You would do well to avoid the non-academic type of these. In otherwords, steer clear of those teachers who are viewed as the New Age type, for many of these are merely taking profitable advantage of sacred Native ways.

If you wish to learn of the Native peoples, enroll in anthropology or ethnic college courses that are offered as Extension Courses or Adult Education Classes. Explore a culture from its foundation rather than picking and choosing a ceremony or rite to learn.

How does one receive their personal Indian name?

If you are biologically Native-born, the name comes from the parent or a medicine person. Later in life, it can be changed to correspond to the power entity of one's vision quest.

If you're a non-Native, a Native name can only come from a Native elder who performs the associated ceremony on your behalf.

Since the sixties, it has been fashionable for non-Native people to associate more closely with the Native American race by coming up with inventive Native-sounding names for themselves. These self-created names are not recognized by the Indian people and, in fact, are not looked upon in a favorable light. A Native name is a sacred aspect and must be obtained in the same manner. This high respect is not being accorded the issue in light of the current New Age penchant for individuals to gain a connection to Native culture — a "connection" that is not valid or in keeping with the long established Native traditions of same. You cannot just think up a Native-sounding name to go by. It also must be realized that many fullblood Native people do not have Native-type names.

I know you don't teach Native ways or make any money from No-Eyes' teachings, but if the Native people object to someone doing these things, how come some Natives are doing it? What's your opinion on this?

You've asked two questions here.

It's true that the real traditional Native people do deeply object to the selling of their sacred ways. Their tradition naturally demands a highly respectful attitude toward these sacred ways. And, indeed, they are absolutely right.

So. How come some Natives are selling these ceremonies and sacred ways? I can't answer that one. I can't even imagine how one justifies the practice. Perhaps they're not as traditional as they would have the public believe.

My opinion? I repeat: I can't imagine anyone selling Native ways or any form of their culture under the covering skin of "teaching," much less making a profit from it. I just cannot imagine it.

A Native Shaman said it would be easy for me to learn Shamanism. Does this mean he sees me as being psychically talented?

No. It means he sees you as an easy mark. You did admit to a $1,500 fee for this. Your so-called Shaman is a sham-man.

What's the deal with this Shaman/Shamaness thing? Is this some new bandwagon to get on?

The "deal" is a new cult interest for New Age folks to get into, except they seem to have forgotten all about the attendant respect associated with such high matters. They, in their unquenchable thirst to gulp down every new or exotic metaphysical type of drink, give no care to each precious ingredient nor how it was gathered. They merely guzzle it down just to be able to say they've partaken of the essence. And, once tasted, they then turn searching eyes for another new exotic drink to conquer.

Please understand that I'm not being cynical here, for I'm not of a mind to waste energies on such, rather I am of a mind for straight talk. Indeed, there has been no greater need for it than now.

There was once a wonderful native time, before the phrase of "New Age," when the concept of the Shaman was held as sacred to the highest degree. Shamans then, as today, were extremely knowledgeable and talented. Great respect was given to these special Native people. And, because of this high respect, one never walked up to one and asked to be taught the sacred Shamanistic way. . .certain ones were "born to" it and, at puberty, were recognized and "chosen" by the Shaman himself. When the instruction period began it was a great honor and the young student well expected to spend his entire youth and manhood upon the Path.

Then a movement stirred upon the land. People began calling it New Age, and after that, no sacredness was left for the Native people to call their own. Now, because of this travesty, non-Natives are claiming to be Shamans or Shamanesses. But tell me, how can that be true when none have spent a lifetime learning the way? Weekend courses? Absurd to the point of being laughable. People, please wake up!

Shamanism is not for non-Natives. Shamanism is *not* to be treated so lightly or carelessly! Shamanism must be respected, protected, and left alone in its sacredness!

The current "Native fad" has no rhyme or reason. I'm talking about the mass invasion into Native ceremonies and the rush for experiential one-upmanship. The New Age movement has indeed gone far astray, for the members are not seeking truths and the understandings of same. They are no longer content to learn and cherish their truths. . .they crave to be leaders. . .they've gone berserk.

It's time for some serious soul-searching. It's time to sit back and take a very serious and clear view of what's transpiring.

I know there was more between you and Many Heart, so you should write about more of the magic he did.

Why? So I can betray the sacredness I was entrusted with? And if I did write of those experiences, what would you do with that information? Attempt to duplicate? Claim expertise then sell the way to others?

Walk the Within Path, for there awaits all the magic you've ever dreamed possible.

What does the Native word "Chanunpa" mean?

This is Lakota for the Sacred Pipe. Anglos frequently confuse the Sacred Pipe with the "peace pipe." They are not one and the same.

A Native friend of mine gave me a string of colored tiny bags. I didn't want to appear ignorant, but what is it and what is it for?

Your friend gifted you with a "prayer tie" or "tobacco tie." These are made of 100% cotton one-inch squares of various colors. They're filled with tobacco while a prayer is said. These are then tied onto a string.

Usually these prayer ties are used as part of the required accessories for one's ceremonial altar. The number of colored pouches can vary from as little as five to as many as over 150.

What does "mitakuye oyasin" mean? My friend signs off all his letters with that.

This is a Lakota phrase that is uttered for many reasons; entering a sweat lodge, after smoking the Sacred Pipe, when a prayer is ended (as an Amen). This phrase means "all my relations" and means "the connectedness to all existence." Therefore, this phrase does not just infer one's personal blood relations, but rather all of life — everything above, below, and upon the planet.

Some native acquaintances of mine call me "wahshechew." Does that mean friend?

That's Lakota for "white man." The correct spelling for this term is washicu. You spelled it phonetically.

You referred to No-Eyes as being of the Chippewa Tribe. You should've used the correct term of Ojibwa.

No, no. The *correct* term is "Anishinabe." However, if I had used the correct term (or your term), few people within the circle of the general public would've known what tribe I was talking about. Sometimes, for clarity within the broad spectrum of knowledge, literary references must seek a corresponding common level. . .common terminology within the realm of general understanding. This serves the whole rather than the more knowledgeable few. See? Mine was not an anthropological treatise that demanded terminology exactness. Mine was a personal story told from the heart.

In your health book, EARTHWAY, you wrote about the astronomy beliefs of the Anasazi. How'd you do that?

With No-Eyes, many things were possible. This information was culled from the many carry-over memories of us both when we were members of the Anasazi Spirit Clan. Much lost historical data can be recaptured in such a manner. In truth, past civilizations should no longer present mysteries to us, for within the many facets of our spirits we each carry the imprinted memories of many lives lived. Once these are tapped, the mists of ponderable enigmas vaporize.

Will you ever do a book about the historical period of the Anasazi Spirit Clan as you recall it?

Many book ideas flutter about in my head. They are like Gypsy Moths drawn to the light. It seems that everytime I sit down to rest, a new idea is there trying to get my attention. So far I've got the books planned up to number twelve, but the way things are going, I can't say how many more I'll do after that.

The Anasazi memories are very strong. I wouldn't discount a future book being done on this time frame. I'm always guided by our Advisors on these books for they can see what's needed. And, in that context, I'm writing as fast as I can. Also, because this Anasazi issue is so closely tied in with alien intelligences, I still require *their* further input as to the appropriate time for this special book.

I think the Anasazi planet section in EARTHWAY was fantasy.

You are welcome to think anything you wish, for I always encourage free will choices as well as personal opinions. However, my editor will vouch for my reluctance to include such revealing information in

Earthway because of those such as yourself. Yet after it was all said and done, in my heart, I knew it was right, for the timing had manifested for same.

You are entitled to your opinion, but perhaps you'd rather prefer to hold it in silence until future archeologists prove me out with their "re-discoveries."

Remember those who once helped pile wood at the stake for the man who said the world was not flat. Ideas or concepts are not to be prejudged just because they are new. These must await judgement until history proves them out one way or another.

The idea of Native People (medicine people) communicating with various spirits and/or alien intelligences is a crock.

Perhaps so. Perhaps the reality of such can never fit into the manifested reality of your personal realm. And so it is a crock for you. And so it will always be so, for the mind has willingly blocked out all possibilities that cannot be intellectually or psychologically dealt with.

How come all Native People don't have the same traditional dress or design use? How come they have so many different languages?

That's very much like asking why all Europeans don't speak the same language or have the same traditional costumes. It's also the same to wonder why all Americans don't speak with the same type of accent. A New Yorker will dress and speak much differently than a Western cowboy or a Southern belle. Geographic locales and specific tribes make each Native people a little different. It's a beautiful difference, don't you think? Each one is so incredibly unique. All tribes have maintained their wonderful individuality through strength of character and pride of their long-protected culture. An Indian is not an Indian, no-no, that just wouldn't do. An Indian is proud of his or her special tribal tradition. An Indian is Hopi. Or Zuni. Or Acoma or Lakota. Or. . .

I heard that the Hopi believe their lands will be completely safe for the future. Is that just wishful thinking on their part?

Or maybe on *your* part? Hopi prophecies aren't fantasy. Hopi prophecies aren't "wishful" anything!

I wish I was a Native American.

Don't ever wish you were anything other than who you are. You're here for a specific purpose and, when in spirit form, you yourself chose which skin would best suit that individual purpose. Therefore, make the most of the skin you're in. Make it work.

Is Native chanting just another form of music?

Not at all. Most chanting has a specific purpose depending upon the chanter's need. Certain chants are what you would call magic, for they attract spirit helpers who are more than prepared to assist with the chanter's intention. Other chants are specific to the natural forces of nature.

Our Advisors and the Brothers have anticipated that my eleventh book will be the right manifested time frame for me to write of this issue.

What is meant by the Five Nations?

The Five Nations refers to a confederation of five Iroquoian Indian Tribes of the northeastern United States. These include the Mohawks, Oneidas, Onondagas, Cayugas, and Senecas.

Are you ever sorry you weren't born a Native fullblood?

My Higher Self knew what it was doing when it was planning out the destiny of my next incarnation. Nothing happens by chance, therefore did I enter the correct skin for my intended purpose during this time frame. All has manifested accordingly. When one realizes this, one doesn't wish to alter the initial decision which was made through extensive foresight of spirit perception. I do not wish to be anyone other than who I came to be.

There are many famous Native teachers who currently author books, give seminars, and have teaching centers. Are these in competition with Summer Rain?

No, no, not at all. I'm not even in the same category as they are. You're mixing apples and oranges here.

The Native ones you're talking about are strictly involved in the "native aspects" of spirituality. They are an entirely separate group of people who carry a specific type of message to the public. On the other hand, my own message is that of No-Eyes, which doesn't zero in on the singular *Native* aspect, but rather is broadscope enough to be all-inclusive of the totality of the spiritual truths as aligned with the precepts of the Law of One. Her unique spiritual purpose for being here was not to confine truths to a native slant, but to share the beautiful *totality* of them. In this light No-Eyes was more of an overall spiritual philosopher/teacher rather than being confined into a specific cubbyhole labeled: native, medicine woman, Shamaness or whatever.

The same holds true with Summer Rain because I'm here to share No-Eyes' spiritual philosophy and wisdom. I'm not here to walk a narrow path or suggest the same for others, for that in itself prevents one from expanding the spirit of self into the totality of the Whole. . .the All.

Why isn't Summer Rain ever among the speakers at special gatherings related to Native New Age events?

I don't participate in these because of what I'm about and what my purpose here is. Both go far beyond the narrow confines of ethnic aspects. As I've previously explained, just because No-Eyes was Indian and she gave me a Native name, this in no way becomes the center aspect of who I am or what I'm about. No-Eyes was the prophet I was supposed to encounter. My purpose is not and cannot be confined to a specific category of people or type of philosophy. Therefore, this is the sole reason I do not attend any kind of event that will serve to label me or my work as such.

I bought a couple Native American music tapes but they weren't quite what I was looking for. Can you suggest any?

Sure can. *Echoes* by J. C. High Eagle (Osage Cherokee). This tape is basically flute accompanied by such additional sounds as a Horned Owl, horse hoofbeats, drums, wind, chimes, and chant.

For a catalog of High Eagle's music and others, you can write for a free copy at: Panoramic Sound, P.O. Box 58182, Houston, TX 77258.

What does the native word Wakontah mean?

This is an Osage word meaning "great mysteries."

I've heard it said that non-Native people today were never Natives in previous lifetimes. In keeping with the universal truths, this doesn't seem like a logical theory. Can you clarify this for me?

I don't know where you heard this from or who initially said it, but you're absolutely right in your thoughts on it.

The conceptual aspect of the Precepts of the Law of One that relates to reincarnation does not ever segregate any specific race for the purpose of excluding it from the array of possible choices for the spirit to physically reenter. Therefore, in simple terms: *All races are subject to a spirit's choice for its next reincarnation.* The idea that the Native of yesteryear cannot be White today is an absolute fallacy. When an entity is in the Spirit Plane and planning out the best course for his/her next physical life, *all* races are an option. *All* ethnic groups are open choices for them.

Since childhood I've always heard the term "Indian-giver" but never quite knew the exact meaning. Does it have anything to do with the Native way of giving?

Quite the contrary. The term applies to two ways of giving: one is the giving of a gift then taking it back, the other is the giving of a gift with an ulterior motive in mind. Both are directly against Native traditional thought.

The term originated with the U.S. government giving gifts to the Indians, such as heavy and warm Army blankets that were riddled with smallpox. Or the promises of land gifts (which were barren). See? Also it relates to government promises to the Native Americans that were not kept — they were later denied (taken away).

So then, when you next hear reference to the term it means that someone has made a promise and then retracted it or else they've given some type of gift that had strings attached — usually selfserving strings.

I think the increased public interest in Native culture is good, but I also see a lot of low quality crafts being churned out by those trying to capitalize on the interest.

While that may be true in some cases, not everyone is involved in this. Kim FireBear Brennan and her husband create beautiful native items. Kim sculpts mask-type native faces and finishes them in warrior paint. Her husband completes the large plaques by adding traditional accessories such as beads, feathers, fur and suede. These masks make very impressive wall decorations.

Her husband, Leo, is equally talented and his work has been praised by Tribal Council Elders who remark on how well done his work is and that it's created in the traditional manner. Leo takes great care in creating medicine sticks, staffs, decorated skulls and Dream Catcher hoops.

For more information, please write to: Kim FireBear Brennan, P.O. Box 65, Pima, Arizona 85543.

I'm unable to get around but greatly desire to have some art work by real Native People. Do you know of any that have some type of catalog?

Yes! Nakoma Volkman of Rochester, Minnesota does beautiful work. He created a pen and ink poster entitled: *The Circle Is My Path.* This is done on parchment, and it has become a very popular item with both Natives and non-Natives. He also has composed and illustrated another parchment piece entitled: *An Indian Version of The Twenty-Third Psalm.* Both of these would be a beautiful addition to anyone's home. Nakoma's main subject matter is usually Indian portraits and subjects with spiritual and nature themes. He works in pastel chalks, pencil and pen and ink. Nakoma is presently preparing a brochure on his artwork.

For more information, please write to: Nakoma Art Traditions, P.O. Box 1421, Rochester, MN 55903.

Can my medicine bag protect me with the White Light? [From Sioux Elder]

Your medicine bag (and the power objects in it) can and does work the same as surrounding yourself in the White Light because your power objects are "of the spirit" and have much spiritual power.

This question is very different from the one asking about the power of ancient relics. Native medicine objects are indeed very powerful because of the spirit attachments they're associated with.

My heart goes out to the Native American People and I want to help them with monetary donations, but because of all the Native-sounding organizations that are actually run by whites or white churches, I'm confused. I want my money going directly to the Native people. Can you suggest an organization?

Yes I can and I'd be happy to suggest the Native American Center of Southeast Minnesota. Please send donations to: Native American Center, 102 So. Broadway, #8, Rochester, MN 55904.

Wing Beats

. . .and the Great Living Phoenix did rise up from the fire
burning in the people's hearts. The Fire did consume all, save the
Flames of Hope, Spirituality and Unconditional Love.

**I cried over SPIRIT SONG. My husband and I want to relocate,
but don't know where. Can you help?**

The matter of personal relocation is a highly individualized subject.
I cannot help you by way of suggesting geographic locations, but I can
assist you to find inner direction to this end.

When considering this specific issue, one cannot perceive it as being
a purely physical matter of where to live our lives. The spiritual aspect
is most important here and must, therefore, come into play as a determining factor to be evaluated.

We are all here for a reason. And spiritually speaking, a spiritual
purpose can be greatly enhanced by its corresponding geographical
location which is vibrationally correlated. This simply means that some
geographical regions can present a wider variety of spiritual opportunities than others in respect to one's specific purpose. See? This
therefore is a prime consideration when considering an alternate
residence for oneself.

Ah, you might say, but how does one know which region will best
enhance their spiritual purpose? The old adage still applies: seek within

and you shall find. I know how utterly simplistic this sounds, but in spiritual reality, all *is* simple.

To perceive where your spirit wishes to be in order to best fulfill its purpose is not a difficult or complex feat. The voice of the Higher Self or of one's personal spirit guide is always there to be heard. This is not an audible sensory aspect, but rather a subconscious perception of the individual's conscious mind. The Higher Self is always actively guiding us. The voice is always speaking to us. We just don't always hear or, if we do, we don't recognize the "given thought" for what it really is.

When considering a relocation, give yourself a short quiz. When you think of living somewhere else, what region seems to come into your mind the most? What area appears to have a particular draw or pull for you? If you could live anywhere in the country, where would that be? Do you find yourself ever thinking of one place more than others? Are you drawn to the Southwest? The New England area? Mountains? Lakes? Oceans?

The honest responses to the above questions will serve to point the way for your own individual geographic direction as related to your spiritual purpose.

This "guided" direction will in no way have anything to do with the future changes, in truth, these have no bearing on one's spiritually-guided geographical locale. It matters not if the spirit can best fulfill its purpose in the area of a major fault or the Atlantic coast. It matters not if your inner guidance leads you next to a nuclear plant. Being wherever your spirit needs to be is most important, for we are all here to advance our spirits, not worry about our physical shells. This is a very important concept to understand and accept within the heart. We're here to balance past incurred karma and, by listening to the Higher Self and our spiritual guide, we can actually reside in the geographical region that will best serve out this purpose.

Am I crazy for wanting to move to Montana?

I can't imagine why you'd think that, for the unwritten guideline is to be wherever you feel most drawn. When this important concept is thoroughly understood, each individual must walk toward the sound of their personal drumming and, as such, nobody can criticize where another is led to reside.

Montana is a most beautiful state. If there is where you are drawn, then you should make every effort to get there, for great opportunities of the spirit may be awaiting your arrival.

Was the fall of the Berlin wall foreseen by No-Eyes?

Phoenix Rising would've been a massive tome if I had listed and detailed everything the visionary spoke of during the weeks we spent on the future. Sure she mentioned this as a strong possibility. In fact, at the time, it was so improbable to me that we went into it quite extensively in order for me to understand the individual event. This was when she brought in the surrounding factors of the communist countries eventually going democratic in their reforms. It was one aspect she included in events that would happen in the "blinking of an eye." And, it would appear, one Communist country after another was swept by the "civil unrest" she foresaw bringing radical changes upon the face of Europe.

The Berlin wall event and the fall of communism comes under the heading of "civil unrest" in *Phoenix Rising*. At no time in our world history have we seen an outcry that was made en masse by the general populace of communist countries. . .and what a beautiful outcry it was! What joy!

And it does continue with Romania and Lithuania. It continues until all of communism falls away from our world. Even China's initial outcry will be heard again and again from the people.

Where is a safe place to live?

Safe? The term is an absolute. Although our language makes qualifying derivatives of it such as "safer" and "safest," this cannot apply in regard to this issue. Safe means "absolutely safe." And in that interpretation, there is no safe place to live, for all geographical regions quite naturally experience "unsafe" phenomena throughout time. Hurricanes. Tornadoes. Floods. Toxic chemical and radioactive pollution. Earthquakes. Avalanches and mudslides. Nature is not selective and does not "favor" one region over another. Manufacturing folly pollutes indiscriminately throughout the country. Acid rain contaminates regions far from its polluting sources.

I cannot tell anyone where to live. I cannot move people around the country like so many mindless pawns on a massive chessboard. I have no right to do such. Please remember that one's individual geographical choice MUST come from within the self as guided by the Higher Self or personal spiritual guide. Nobody, and I do mean "nobody," can tell another where they should live. This is a very private and privileged aspect of one's precious free will. Never place such decisions in the hands of another.

Although I cannot say where the "relatively secure" regions are (because everyone would move there without listening to their own inner voice), I can enumerate those aspects to stay away from. The *better* geographic regions will be located a *reasonable distance* from the following *negatives* foreseen by No-Eyes: **Coastal areas;** Oil Refineries; Missile Sites; Arsenals; Fault Lines; Germ Warfare Sites; Weapon Plants; Nuclear Dump Sites; Proving Grounds; Military Installations; Nuclear Power Plants; Historically-active Mountain Ranges; Civil Industry with defense contracts; Mississippi River regions; New Madrid region; Great Lakes states with high density missile silos; Fuel/Propane/Chemical facilities; Major rail lines; Mining regions; Naval ports; downstream and east of industries using toxic chemicals; East of central Kansas; lowlands; Downstream from dams.

When is war coming?

Look with open eyes. See that which is reality. War is a present reality. Or didn't you think the warring in other countries counted?

If we accept the changes as "inevitable," aren't we then "creating" them?

This question sounds an awfully lot like the "create your own reality" misconception.

Can a boulder falling down a mountain be stopped? Can one "wish away" an avalanche in progress? Please, solid logic is required here. Philosophic reason must be utilized.

Simply put, *knowing* does not mean the same as *creating*.

To *know* an event has a strong probability of occurring does not mean we *create* the reality just because we believe in the knowing. This is extremely important because of the preponderance of people believing in the false premise that "all" events that show a strong probability of making it into reality are "strengthened" by the collective belief in it doing so.

This belief, in essence, says that: if we don't believe in it and just put our heads in the ground it won't manifest. This is a grave and highly ignorant concept to subscribe to. It has spawned the "ego-generated" concept of "create your own reality." What of the reality of Reality? We must not create our own little worlds where everything is just as we wish to create them. We live in a very big world that encompasses the human family. We MUST not believe in the concept of "creating our OWN reality," but rather "creating the reality of the ALL." Wholeness and unity can only be so created by the unconditional attitude of "love". . .for all men — not just for self and the wants of same. See?

Let's go deeper into this term "inevitable." Let's look at this more closely.

Inevitable means "incapable of being prevented." This is the sole interpretation of the term. It does not say that it means incapable of being "altered" or "lessened." This is so important to grasp.

An event that is foreseen as one that cannot be prevented does not mean that additional probabilities may enter in at a later date to somehow "alter" the event. It may end up happening in such a manner that the event has little impact. . .although it "still" happens. See? Probabilities may alter the specific "location" of the foreseen event. Probabilities may even alter the "timing" of the event. But all events that are foreseen as "inevitable" WILL happen in some form, for they are too strong and are already set in motion as the avalanche is.

Will the changes affect the care of my young son who has cerebral palsy?

I don't envision any of the future changes negatively affecting you or your son. This is because of where you're currently residing. This is not to say that future probabilities may enter in, such as a geographical residence relocation or any number of affecting factors. But, as it is viewed from this moment, the future changes will not affect either of you in any major way.

Why bother with safe geographical areas when we'd just have to protect our supplies from unaware and scared neighbors?

If this is your perspective then your reasoning is valid. However, is this the spiritual attitude? Aren't we all working and expending energies for the reality of the All? Aren't we striving for a unified and peaceful humanity that lives in peace and shared love? Aren't we "here" to help our neighbor wherever and whenever we can? Or are we here for the self alone?

Your philosophy lends one to believe you'd seek out a remote cave in which to sequester yourself and hoard your goods. In striving to bring about the Age of Peace and Harmony that marks the best aspect the Phoenix Days, we must shift personal attitudes and perspectives from the reality of *self* to that of the *whole*. This is the foundation upon which harmony and humankind familial love will be supported by. Separatism will be ancient history.

Which mountain region is safe to relocate to?

Safe? We have that word again. As explained in a former response, "safe" is an absolute term and does not apply to the issue of foreseen future events.

All mountain regions will experience some effects of the future events, however, some will only quiver while other will roil from within and erupt.

Generally speaking, the Cascades are most vulnerable. The Sierra Nevadas will experience a lesser degree, yet still be active in the future. The Rockies will not activate as the above ranges, but will see greatly increased geothermal energy being released. This refers to those regions which emit surface evidence of such energy such as hot springs. Caldera locations and those areas consisting of high basalt content may see activity. The Appalachians will experience some quake activity due to the New Madrid region. This range is highly susceptible to airborne toxins that are carried in a westerly current from any accidents of chemical or nuclear origin that are generated west of there. The Shenandoahs and Alleghenys will be likewise affected. The Adirondacks were foreseen to experience quake activity, and these along with the Green Mountains and the White Mountains will see adverse affects from eastbound airborne toxins.

I'm a psychic. Please tell me which regions will be safe?

This will be known to you, for the answer lies within.

How much of the future can I tell my 15-year-old son?

By the age of fifteen an individual should be cognizant of the Collective Wisdom in all of its beautiful aspects, including the bright future after the cleansing of the Phoenix Days.

My own children have been raised with this knowledge and they are not fearful, but rather anxious for the Age of Harmony and Peace to begin. I cannot tell you precisely what to reveal to your son, but if done right, with love and the entirety of the truth of it, it can be a wonderful revelation that spawns anticipation instead of fear.

Are the North Carolina mountains and Massachusetts ones safe?

These will see activity (see former question). However they are in greater jeopardy from airborne toxins for the future.

How come the Earth Watchers' protection will be held back. I thought our Guides always protected each of us?

You have asked a valid question, however you are mixing conceptual terminology.

The Earth Watchers are NOT our spiritual guides. They are completely separate entities. Our spirit guides are always here to advise and protect. The Earth Watchers are the other intelligences who have been correcting or negating the negative effects of our erring ways throughout history.

Please understand that a child cannot learn from hazardous activities until the parent stops preventing the results from occurring. If every time a child reaches up for the handle of a hot pot on the stove and the parent immediately moves it back, the child will never learn that, if it is reached and pulled down, burns will occur.

Of course this is not to suggest that the parent should then allow the child to go ahead and pull the pot down, but it does suggest that the parent intervene in some effective manner in which the child understands the danger of his actions. So too have the Earth Watchers been advised to "pull back" on their interference of our collective ways in order for humankind to realize and assess the results of actions taken. When this is understood, it is not an unreasonable concept, for earth is truly our schoolroom whereby we learn the lessons of living a spiritual way of life, generating a harmonious and healthful continuum for both humankind and the school.

We're living in Florida and plan to move near you soon because we want to reside where it'll be safe for the future.

You have made an assumption that is in error. But at least I can say that you are not alone in your belief, for many have expressed much the same idea.

Please, this is very important. Where I live has absolutely no bearing on where YOU need to live in order to best fulfill your spirit's purpose.

Since we've not obtained the resources to be able to settle upon our sacred ground yet, we're guided to maintain a mobile status. Therefore we rent a house wherever we're directed to be. We were originally in Woodland Park for many years. Then Eagle for six months. Leadville for nine months and then back to Woodland Park. We follow the voice of Spirit and go wherever we're guided at any one time. This can only be accomplished through the devoted efforts of family members who take on any job they can in the different areas. We never worry about that aspect, for they work in convenience stores, grocery stores, or whatever. They pool the income to make the household expenses. All for the good of the all. And this allows us to move whenever and wherever spirit guides us.

So if you move to where I am, I may not be here when you arrive with your moving van. I could be anywhere in the state by then.

The second factor of this issue is the factor of "safe" places. When one follows the guidance of their spirit, the aspect of a geographic location's "safety" is not even considered. If I were guided to move tomorrow next to a nuclear plant. . .I would. . .without question. My spirit knows where I can best spiritually serve and fulfill my purpose, therefore that's where I want to be. I'm not here for the survival of my physical self, for I care not for that factor at all. I'm only here for a spiritual purpose, and that is all that matters to me.

So please, don't think that wherever Summer Rain is. . .is safe for the future. It may well not be.

How can you survive if the Rocky Flats plutonium facility will blow sky high?

This was foreseen by No-Eyes "at the TIME of viewing," which doesn't necessarily mean that probabilities cannot or have not already affected this event. I don't worry about such events becoming a reality. I've too much else to do.

What skills will be needed for the future?

Service skills. Medical and nursing. Blue collar skills such as electrical and repair. Teachers and counsellors. Sharing and loving skills. Skills of deep compassion and empathy. The arts skills. . .musicians and artists. And those who have deep unconditional love.

What Colorado areas will be safe for the future?

The Colorado regions that will be relatively secure will be those areas from Fairplay to the Utah border. This is nearly half the state, therefore, there will be pockets in this region that will be in jeopardy such as the mining districts, fault areas, and geothermically active regions. Also, the Glenwood Canyon region was foreseen as experiencing activity that may well tumble the new highway by falling boulders. Glenwood Springs may experience some increased geothermal activity.

Also within this large region, Aspen has a high probability that it's 200 faults beneath the town and ski lifts may activate. Several dams may break, the worst probability is that of the Ruedi Dam which would inundate the Frying Pan River and all of the town of Basalt.

These, along with the major mining areas, were foreseen as the regions with the highest jeopardy probabilities within the more secure section of the state.

I'm concerned about living in Utah because of the germ warfare research facility.

Your concern is not to be taken lightly; however, this aspect foreseen by No-Eyes was not a facility accident that involved that installation. It was on the east coast. This is not to say that probabilities couldn't affect a change in location, but she was not inclined to think that would occur.

Wasn't the Phoenix and the Harmonic Convergence connected in some way?

Definitely. No-Eyes was clear that she wanted the material of the Phoenix Days to be in the public's hands by the Harmonic Convergence. There are specified "timings" for events to become manifest in reality. This was one.

When I did my book signing in Glenwood Springs for *Phoenix Rising,* there were many, many who journeyed to the town for the Harmonic Convergence. They came to the signing and knew that the event and the book were connected.

Are the Rockies the only safe place for the future?

I never said that. It's just not true. Perhaps you assumed this because this is where I reside.

Is it right to bring a child into the world just to go through a holocaust?

There are a couple misconceptions in the question. The future of the Phoenix Days will not be a holocaust at all, but rather a gentle cleansing period that will span many years. Many will live through it. Whether they reside in a high-risk region or a relatively secure one, all will experience some type of negative effect, but many will survive unscathed.

Your overall perception of the Phoenix Days is in grave error. Much of the events foreseen will not affect you at all, for they will manifest in foreign countries. You have taken the predictions and overblown them into a holocaust of the world.

On the aspect of bringing a child into the world during the Phoenix Days — what better time? Please understand that, if a spirit didn't want to enter a newborn, the baby would be stillborn. But many, many spirits are eager to return during these times because they themselves have desired to do so for a multitude of reasons. Would you deny them their vehicle of entry? Were babies not born in the German camps?. . .they "wanted" to be there. But babies born during the Phoenix Days can in no way compare to the above situation, for one represents despair while the other, hope.

What events happened since PHOENIX RISING was published?

So many of the events No-Eyes foresaw and were recorded in *Phoenix Rising* have occurred that I could in no way list them all. Just because they haven't touched YOUR life doesn't mean they didn't occur. Please be more aware of your world and those events affecting your brothers and sisters in the human family.

It is interesting that many of the visionary's forecasts have received little or no mention on the national newscasts, for I could write a verifying tome on all the events that have taken place since *Phoenix Rising* was released.

I have sources from around the world that keep me posted to No-Eyes predictions that have manifested. A weekly *Earthweek* newspaper carries geologic events and "unusual" occurrences that happened around the world during that week. Most of these never make the news programs or major newspapers.

The information is there for everyone to perceive. Anyone having to "ask" another for such information to verify or "list" the events is not walking in "awareness". . .they are not perceptive of their world.

You never mentioned the Second Coming in PHOENIX RISING.

Your choice of wording is a fragmenting factor that suggests segregation of spiritual belief systems. This must be addressed before I can respond to your statement.

The phrase "Second" Coming infers that God already came to walk among mankind a "first" time. Many good spiritual people believe He has not come to us yet. These people believe in the existence of the entity of Jesus, but do not necessarily believe he was the "God" many generally refer to as "God." Nor do these good people believe he was the direct "Son" of God. Are we not *all* Children of the One? Are we not *all* sons and daughters of the one God?

So whether you choose to believe that God has come once before and are awaiting the "Second Coming" or whether you believe He never came before and are awaiting the "First Coming" is totally irrelevant to the question and should be stricken for the sake of clarity. This once done we can correctly and appropriately revise the statement as follows:

You never mentioned the Coming of God in *Phoenix Rising*. Now I can address the basic intent.

Tell me how humankind, being what it is today around the world, could actuate a Golden Age of Peace and Harmony *without* the presence of the One? Although this specific factor was not spelled out on the book's page in black and white text, wouldn't it stand to reason that a Great Unifying Force will manifest among humanity? For those who cannot read between the lines. . .Harmony comes. Peace comes. Unity comes. Love comes. GOD COMES.

After there is peace, will the world come to an end?

Why bother with the cleansing and the spiritual unifying into peace and harmony if we're all going to die in a big bang? Why would God bother coming to walk among us if this were made manifest?

No, God intends to walk in peace among us for a very long time afterward. . .the best part of the Phoenix Days will shine with the daybreak of God's loving light.

Since, in PHOENIX RISING, you said that people who will survive will be in the right place, does this then mean that since the information hasn't been shown to me that I'm not meant to survive?

You may have come to the wrong conclusion. How can you say that you're not *already* in the right place? Have you considered that scenario? Perhaps your Higher Self doesn't guide you elsewhere because you're where you need to be already.

What is survival anyway? There is no death for the living spirit. Please do not be so fearful of physical death, for it's hampering your perspective of what "life" is all about.

Please, trust your Higher Self more. Have more "faith" in your personal spirit guide's direction for you. Be not so fearful in life. Go forth with a heart opened to love and sharing, compassion and empathy for your brothers and sisters. LIVE each day without fear. . .LIVE!

You're cruel not to reveal all the safe places for the future. What good is knowledge if you don't share it?

I have listed all the jeopardy regions that are expected to present negative manifestations for the future. I have placed the food before you, now you must partake in the feast — eat and digest the food that has been given unto you.

Knowledge is nothing without a mind to analyze and discern it. Without these, knowledge is meaningless. My work is of the spirit, as such, the spiritual issue of this entire matter is for one to be wherever the Higher Self or spirit guide directs them. It is a matter of each individual's heart. . .it is a matter of free will of the self. . .it is a matter no other outsider can breach or interfere with.

I've already covered the issue of "safe" for the future. . .it is not in the realm of the spirit. Therefore I cannot emphasize the aspect of it.

I've waited 50 years for a detailed prophesy book like PHOENIX RISING. It paralleled the Bible and was so comprehensive it literally pinpointed the geographical regions to avoid.

Your astute observation has been received with heartfelt appreciation. There are many who have not expended the energy to "see" that which has been placed before them. Many "read" but do not read.

Will those who die during the Phoenix Days still have chances to balance out their karma?

Sure they will. God awaits the return of all the stray sheep. All will be gathered into the flock. All will be given time to return to the One.

What types of business will survive the economic aspects of the Phoenix Days?

Blue collar services. Medical services (restructured, of course). The arts will survive, for many will discover new talents by which to express their hearts and spirits through.

Life will go on much as it does today, only there will be no more industry or toxic/nuclear facilities to pollute. Society will be based on the philosophy for the All rather than for the one. Energy will be radically altered to utilize the natural earth forces. Medicine will re-discover the uses of sound frequencies and light in healing. All will be harmonious with the Earthway.

Is a meltdown expected at the Oswego nuclear plant?

At the time of viewing the future with No-Eyes, the Oswego plant was not the one to go; however, I cannot say that developing prob abilities will not alter the location envisioned at that time. Nuclear plants are on the jeopardy list.

Have more faith in wherever your Higher Self guides you to reside. Your spirit purpose is far more important than any other aspect of this future issue.

If many go into the wilderness for the future, who will be left to make changes in the new society?

Those who go into the wilderness for the future are not the ones you would wish to organize the new society. These ones represent the ego and therefore indicate a perception of "self" that will not be tolerated in the Golden Age. These ones will ultimately be the "students" . . . not the "teachers."

What sign would you consider to be the LAST warning to relocate?

A great "noise" from the Higher Self or one's guide.

False prophets will appear during the end times chaos. How does one tell the difference?

Your heart should tell you this.
True prophets share their power, while the false ones hoard it. True prophets walk within simplicity and speak of unconditional love. True prophets care not for material aspects of life, for only the spirit is the true reality. A true prophet will speak of the need for sharing self in all facets of one's life and to live in harmonious acceptance. A true prophet's life will reflect all that is taught.

Will there still be the pattern of reincarnation after the Phoenix Days are complete?

Of course, for God does love the babies and little children.

Will we still have our free wills after the Phoenix Days?

Oh sure we will. Just stop to think about this for a moment. If you were God, would you want to come and walk among a humanity of robots that have no will of their own? You see, that's the incredible beauty of it. We will all live in harmony while maintaining our own free wills. The will of God will quite naturally be our will. How wonderful the world would be now if we each awoke with these words on our lips: "I love you, God. I have no will but Your will for me." And so we each would live our life according to the voice of our spirits. The prayer does not mean that we have *no* will of our own, but merely that our own will is in complete accordance with the Divine Will. See?

When there is finally peace after the Phoenix Days, what will prevent mankind from making the same mistakes all over again to destroy each other and the earth?

Collective enlightenment. . .and God walking among us.

Will we still have metals for tools after the Phoenix Days? If so, won't we have to continue mining for them?

Yes to both. Please remember that our Earth Mother provides us with many assets. Her metals are one. It is the "manner" by which they are extracted that will be altered. This technique will not leave gaping holes and caverns nor separation processes that require cyanide or any other toxic chemicals. All will be quite natural and environmentally safe.

Will we be able to travel to other worlds after the Phoenix Days?

I need to clarify an aspect of this question before I can respond to the main concern.

Don't refer to "after" the Phoenix Days, for the "end times" of the Phoenix Days is when it is flying free *during* the Phoenix Days. Therefore, the Phoenix Days are "inclusive" of the Golden Age of Peace and Harmony. See? When speaking of the Phoenix Days you must be comprehensively accurate and include the Peace Time also. The Phoenix Days are NOT just the cleansing aspect at all.

So. . ."during" the "end time frame" of the Phoenix Days we WILL be able to travel to other worlds. This has been prophesied and so it will be done. Perhaps the "manner" of this travel will not be as you envision at this time, but the ability will be utilized just the same.

What will happen to the "doubters" after the Phoenix Days?

They will experience the reality of the beautiful end time frame of the Phoenix Days when they see the manifestation of the Golden Age in the world. The "doubters" will be no more, for they will exist within the reality of that which they had doubted.

Will those who die during the Phoenix Days have a chance to live upon the New Earth?

If this is their spirit's wish it may be manifested according to their free will.

What will become of some of the beautiful knowledge of the past earth, like music for example, will it have to be recreated?

This question clearly infers that the face of the earth will be wiped clean as a slate with nothing remaining. This just is not so. This one grave misconception enlightens me as to how people are so fearful of the changes. But is absolutely a false perception of the cleansing time.

When the worst is done, the libraries will still stand, symphony halls will remain, museums and archives will be untouched. This is not to infer that *all* of them will be unscathed, but it does emphatically say that most will remain untouched.

Will all people be totally aware of all things after the cleansing period or will some still have to be taught?

The collective conscious of humankind will be raised up out of its darkness, however the aspect of learning will be a much sought-after goal. There will be teachers and students. . .and many teachers will be students of THE Teacher.

Will the seasons still change after the Phoenix Days?

Absolutely, for that is the natural way of the earth's orbital revolution which will not alter, however, because of the new axis degree, the seasons will shift somewhat. This is due to the new equatorial position. See?

What will be the event that marks the final cleansing period?

Those geological events that result from the axis adjustment. These include the coastal inundations and inland flooding by events other than the Great Lakes drainage. Melting icecaps and bergs.

The Earth Mother will settle then.

If the Indian way will be society's way after the Phoenix Days, will everyone perform their ceremonies?

You have misinterpreted the entire issue of this. You have taken the "letter" of it rather than the "spirit."

Harmony. All for the good of the Whole rather than for the good of the One. Earth bonding. Sharing. These are the "spirit" of the issue. I speak not of ceremonies. I speak of the heart and spirit of the concept. See?

We live in San Bernardino, California. Should we move?

Please, don't ask this of anyone other than self. This is an extremely personal decision that MUST be based upon your own beautiful free will. Nobody can tell you where you need to be or where to go. Nobody but self.

If you feel comfortable there then perhaps that is exactly where you need to be. Don't doubt self. Don't look outside self for aspects that generate false fears. Trust self.

If everyone fled the cities and suburbs to prepare for the future changes, the remote areas would be as overcrowded as the cities are now!

This is true.

That's why I'm not specifically recommending such a mass exodus from the cities. Many cities will be perfectly good places to be for the future. However, even the relatively secure regions will experience brief interruption in delivered goods and/or periods of power outages. So it is well to have an emergency supply to accommodate this eventuality. An alternative heat source, battery-operated radios. Oil lanterns/oil. Camp stove with fuel (bottled propane). Canned goods. Medical supplies. Anything that you think you would need. A good way to envision these items is to mentally imagine such an emergency and then go through your day's activities to see what you use/need. Toilet paper. Water jugs. Source of news, heat, light, cooking. Country folks should have propane refrigerators.

You don't have to run right out and spend a fortune on these supplies all at once. Start gathering a little at a time and, every time you grocery shop, pick up a can or two to add to the stock. It can be a process that doesn't drain the finances, but when done, certainly brings a little more comfort to one's mind.

How could you write PHOENIX RISING if so many future occurrences actually hinge upon probabilities? Might not the probabilities change those foreseen events to such a massive degree that they never occur at all?

This is the type of false logic that is spawned from the concept of "creating your own reality." You want to believe the best, as most do, but you also refuse to accept the possibility of the more dangerous events. This is not evidence of "reality thought," but rather more of an immature fantasy world. You must pull your head out of the ground about this. Have you not also considered that probabilities may also alter the event to such a massive degree that the foreseen event might manifest ten times worse?

Therefore have I given out the information. Whether the information affects the manifestation in a better or worse degree is not germane. What is important is that people be made *aware* of the "possibility" of the event itself. This is shared so they can utilize their free wills to make individual choices.

Would you have someone such as No-Eyes or myself not say anything? Let the world go about its own little way? Not share the vision? Would you have me see a car coming at you and not pull you aside?

Regarding PHOENIX RISING — if the future can be foreseen, wouldn't that verify the existence of fate?

Not in the true sense of the word. Fate represents an "end" of something — the final outcome. And since all future events are affected by the altering aspects of infringing probabilities, we cannot make an *absolute* prediction of a future event in respect to the "exact conditions" of its ultimate outcome. Therefore, we can safely say that we foresee a "generalized" fate for certain happenings or individuals. We can safely say that we foresee a generalized "outcome," but because of the altering probabilities that can affect that foreseen outcome, we cannot be assured of its absolute finality. See? Therefore, we *could* use the word "fate" here, but only if we keep the perspective that it's a highly *generalized* one.

Now, in respect to one's spiritual "purpose" in life, the term fate can be used with some accuracy because one does "plan out" their life before entering into the physical. And, as one lives this life, their spirit tries to guide them along the right paths that were foreseen being taken. This then could be interpreted as one's "spiritual fate" or "destiny." See?

Is Pike's Peak going to blow sky high?

At the time of the viewing by No-Eyes, it was erupting much like Mt. St. Helens. However, since then, I've had strong feelings that the peak is simply going to do some "grumbling" and a little shaking. I don't think it's going to rock an' roll like was envisioned in 1984.

I don't see why people would want to live through the changes just to end up eating grass and doing things the old-fashioned way.

You're being cynical.

Through the advance preparations I've given I see no reason for this type of attitude. The warnings have been given in plenty of time for adequate preparations to be made.

Also, you're being sarcastic. I never said that people would be eating "grass." There will be a wide variety of nutritious foods available all during the changes. People will be consuming a healthier diet of fresh fruits, vegetables, grains, eggs and fish/poultry (if desired).

The Golden Age of Peace and Harmony will be a most beautiful time to experience. One that will be well worth striving toward. It will be a reward for those who have survived the changes by taking heed of the advance warnings.

Where does Armageddon fit into the future changes? You forgot to include it.

No I didn't. It was there all along. . .between the lines.

Isn't it rather obviously clear that an Age of Peace would naturally follow Armageddon? That all the "changes" would be a precursor to the Final Battle? That the Phoenix would be flying free *after* all evil had been banished?

Armageddon will be the "great conclusion" of the changes that was envisioned to coincide with the axis readjustment. It will be the "grand finale." I never actually spelled this out because my purpose was to make people *aware* of the changes, to *share* the "signs" of change in order for them to recognize the beginning of the end, and thereby, make corresponding personal preparations and free will choices. The "changes" can be prepared for, while there is absolutely nothing we can do about Armageddon —at least not physically. *Those* preparations must be done *within* self.

Do you see any racial problems in the future?

Unfortunately, yes. A growing faction will arise "before" the changes, and "during" the changes there will be times when these problems become very intense.

Won't the mountains entrap radiation between them? Can you clarify why some mountains will be safer than others in this respect?

Radiation entrapment will not generally occur because of the continual "dipping" of air currents in the mountains. The upslope and downslope winds constantly clear the air of the regions between ranges. Those valleys between ranges that are "extensive in width" *will*, however, experience a "hovering" type of atmospheric conditions.

As far as why some mountain ranges will be more secure than others is clearly evidenced by a good look at any map of the United States. Some ranges are too close to coastal areas that will experience tremendous plate movement, thereby activating not only the dormant volcanoes within those mountains, but also intensifying earthquakes as well. Other mountain ranges are simply situated too close to vast areas of land that are speckled with hundreds of underground missile silos. These areas are in prime jeopardy. Other mountain regions have too close a proximity to military installations that have been foreseen as being at a very high risk for the future. Other factors that will affect different mountain ranges are rainfall inundation (mudslides), airborne toxins from the west, and geothermal activity.

When the Phoenix is flying free, will there be a monetary system?

Eventually, yes, but nothing like is now utilized. First goods will be traded on a barter system. Then the general economic system will be revived and will prosper into a system that will be "just" for all people. There will be no more "have and have nots" to split society.

What will be the purpose of cattle if they will no longer be used for human consumption in the future?

Your question infers that you believe these beautiful animals have no reason to live other than to end up on your plate. At the time of Creation, before the spirits were created, all animals existed. What for? Certainly not to feed a non-existent people. God created life. And the life was good. Should our own perspective be any less?

Will there be things like television after the changes?

Yes, and more.

Eventually, when the new power source system had been perfected, which will utilize the concept of magnetic fields and electricity, power will be generated by "natural" means rather than coal and nuclear-powered generating plants. Each individual building will operate off its own separate unit and, it will be absolutely "free."

Technically speaking, advancements will accelerate as inventors and scientists are free to use their creativeness without restriction of having to work within the confines of present-day power sources. It will be amazing.

When I think about the future, I don't get any concrete impressions past the year 2004. Is this because the major upheavals will take place then?

Perhaps. That was a very clever way of trying to pin me down on the "date" factor. That was very good.

Some of your predictions for the future coincide with those of others like Edgar Cayce, yet some aspects are very different and completely new — why the discrepancy?

Some are different because probabilities have already affected them. And also, because God has extended the time frame — let out more rope for humankind, so to speak.

Some are new because more events are appearing now that weren't foreseen before.

You would do well to remember that *all* predictions are subjected to alterations, especially those that are affected by the will of God. We foresee certain events coming about for a specific time frame, but *God* can choose to hasten or hold these. See?

The basic *facts* of prior predictions remain; what has altered are the *dates*. And this is precisely why I won't give those out.

Also, events that were foreseen in the distant past frequently were based on the technology of the time. Now we have nuclear aspects to contend with. We have acid rain, industrial and radioactive pollution, and so much more now.

Will anything major happen to our sun?

Not that we have foreseen. Perhaps when the changes are ancient history and the Golden Age of Peace and Harmony is ready to draw to a close, God will reward us all by creating a Final Sunset for us to enjoy. Then there will be nothing left but God who will serve as our living earth. God will be our Sun.

Will acid rain destroy all our nature?

Rather the "causes" will be destroyed first.

After the cleansing, will nuclear power plants be in operation?

Absolutely not.
The ones that will be left standing will never operate again. They will serve as ghostly reminders as the monsters that caused much of history's destruction. They will serve as huge monoliths that represent humankind's former foolishness through ignorance.

I don't see how all people will live peacefully together after the cleansing period. There will ALWAYS be racism and the desire for money and power, best and biggest.

Ah, but you are speaking from a present-day perspective of society. These are negative attitudes that will have been long shed and forgotten. The Golden Age of Peace and Harmony will not recognize such unaware characteristics because Armageddon will have wiped them out.
Those who are left to carry on will be of one mind, and that will be for the improvement and betterment of humankind — not of self.

If the wild animals aren't hunted after the changes, aren't we then looking at a world that will be overrun with animals?

Nature will still keep its own house in order by maintaining the concept of natural selection and survival of the fittest.
Nature took care of itself long before the seasonal advent of sport hunting arrived. Nature will repeat and maintain the fine balance once again.

This may sound silly to you, but will there still be zoos after the cleansing?

The Golden Age of Peace and Harmony will bring about an intense awareness to the remaining population. This awareness includes the high respect for all life and the intelligence to perceive the folly of holding animals captive.

No. There will be no more zoos.

Will there still be movie stars after the Phoenix Days?

Eventually, such forms of entertainment will arise again, but the people involved will not reap the high monies that they do today, and the "type" of entertainment will be on a more cultural and aware level.

I live in Michigan. What would the closest safe state be to live in?

Out of all of Michigan's neighbor states, northwest Minnesota would be the best choice.

Will there still be professional people like doctors and scientists left after the Phoenix Days?

Physicians will be in great demand *during* the cleansing aspect of the Phoenix Days, and scientists will be useful afterward. These people will be instrumental in pulling the survivors together, but like the movie stars, they will *not* become famous, nor will they enjoy the higher salaries that they once had. They will not be considered any better than the common laborer. Everyone will be equal in *all* aspects of daily life.

I think you're trying to SHOCK the world into living better lives by saying all those bad and horrid things are going to happen to us. I don't believe them for one minute. You don't have ME fooled!

The choice is *always* yours. God gave each individual a free will and I expect each person to use it. You have the right to your opinions and judgements of any situation.

If you worked as a seismologist and your delicate instruments indicated sudden increased plate movement that was building up intense pressure, wouldn't you at least *attempt* to send out a warning of some kind? Wouldn't that be your moral responsibility? Once done, it is then up to the people themselves to decide if they should heed the warning or not.

I don't think people should cry wolf, indeed, I am not. I have simply attended to my moral responsibility. What others do with that information is completely up to their individual free will choices.

No. I haven't fooled you at all. I don't make fools of people — they take care of that all by themselves.

You mentioned that many coastal lands will be flooded, some far inland, but won't there also be new land masses?

Yes, many new land masses will appear quite suddenly. They will be accompanied by the major earthquakes and erupted volcanic activities. One of these possibilities is 300 miles off the Oregon coast where a string of volcanic cones will be found to encompass approximately twelve miles. These were foreseen to grow at a rapid rate, that is, rapid in respect to past geological calculations for such an event.

The Ring of Fire may eventually produce most of the land upthrust that has been foreseen.

If we'll still have electricity in the distant future, what will generate the power in the power plants?

You're assuming electricity will come from centralized generating facilities. This assumption is in error, for all appliances will have their own self-contained source of generated energy. Electrical power lines, like the old cable car lines, will be obsolete. This then also makes all gas appliances equally obsolete for the future, for no exterior connections will be required since each machine needing power will come equipped with its own self-contained generating device that utilizes the earth's natural magnetic field.

What will communication systems be like in the future?

To begin with, there will be no more telephone or electrical lines, nor will there be telephone companies. All communications will be powered by crystals that will directly connect with specific geographical coordinates of the caller.

In EARTHWAY, who did No-Eyes refer to when she said, "He will be returning?" Was she talking about Jesus Christ?

The spirit who spent a life as Jesus the Christ is now walking among you in the human physical form with another name and is not making himself known to you. The "He" No-Eyes referred to was not Jesus Christ, but God Himself — the distinction is very important.

When the different geological events are happening, I don't see how the insurance companies are going to cover peoples' property.

Or their medical insurance claims. Yes, you're using good logic.

Although in *Phoenix Rising,* I only mentioned the bank failures, there are always many, many more contingent aspects that naturally become involved and equally affected. It would indeed stand to reason that the insurance companies would also fail due to the bankrupt funds caused by massive nation-wide catastrophic claims being made. The numbers of claims will be staggering. A certain percentage of the public has already become aware of this manifestation.

When I had my gall bladder operation we had no medical insurance because our former insurance carrier went bankrupt and we were in the process of looking around for another company for our medical needs when the emergency occurred, therefore, I was caught with the large hospital bill with no insurance to cover it. In the future, many insurance companies will not be able to cover their client's claims for property damage and personal injury.

Won't the equator line be in a different placement after the earth changes?

Yes. Since the earth will shift between 23 and 24 degrees, the equator will most certainly be in a new position. This is why there will be massive temperate zone alterations after the axis shift. This will create the seasonal differentiations.

Will there still be books being printed in the future? In other words, will the publishing business survive?

When things settle down after the cleansing aspect of the Phoenix Days, life will begin to reorganize itself once again. Books will become an important means of recording events and cultural entertainment. It will survive, but in new geographical regions of the country, for the New York, east coast and California publishing companies will no longer be in operation.

Since you own one of the major publishing companies, I would suggest that you begin looking elsewhere to relocate your house, for the publishing companies that are established in the west and southwest areas of the country will be the only publishers of the future.

Before the future peace becomes a reality, what will be the last negative change — the final bad happening?

The Final Battle, of course.

What would happen if the Phoenix Days were prevented from becoming an actuality?

Humankind would continue taking advantage of one another, pollution would worsen, the ecosystem would be destroyed, ego and greed would rule the world and God would wage Armageddon tomorrow morning.

Is there time for another president to be in the White House before the Phoenix Days commence in full swing?

You're sneaking around and coming up behind me. You're hinting for dates.
Yes.

Will cars still be produced after the Phoenix Days are over?

The Phoenix Days will *never* be over, for the end times of the Phoenix Days will be the Golden Age of Peace and Harmony.
Eventually there will be new automobiles produced that are powered by a new source of energy — a "natural" source that utilizes the earth's powerful magnetic field. This is where our scientists come into play. They will then be developing their research along the proper channels — for the good of the all, rather than for those who can pay the most. There will come a time when vehicles are powered by a single small crystal placed within the chassis.

What type of businesses and/or industries will be obsolete after the cleansing time?

The gas industry. Coal mining. Power plants. Meat processors. The oil industry, including extraction operations, refineries, and distribution facilities. Cattle and sheep ranches. The stock market. Electric companies and associated operations. All the baser aspects of present-day life will vanish: hard drugs and associated businesses, illegal operations, prostitutes, pornography, child abuse, and organized crime factions.
In essence, all businesses or operations that aren't established for the "good" of humankind and the earth will vanish.

If we prepare well, why won't high density residential areas be safe? Isn't it how well prepared one is rather than WHERE one lives?

This could be perceived as good logic "if" one lived a "reasonable" distance *away* from the negatives that will severely affect an entire population. So the geographical location is still a major concern here. Those within a close proximity to nuclear plants, military installations, coastal regions, faults, etc., would NOT be secure no matter how extensively the preparations were. See?

It's taken me years of hard blood-and-sweat work to obtain the material comforts that I now enjoy. There's just no way I'm going to sell these things for a basement full of canned food and toilet paper!

I'm not suggesting that you sell anything. I commend your hard work.

Ultimately, your decisions are what you and your family will have to live with. I don't tell people what to do, I only advise of the signs and the aspects that may cause future harm. Each individual must then decide for themselves what they must do.

I don't tell anyone to sell their material possessions. I merely stated that they will be of little use to them in the future.

After reading PHOENIX RISING, I bought a large parcel of land for our future survival days. My friends have contributed considerably to finance our own little community where we can all go and live comfortably during the bad times ahead. Thanks for the forewarning.

I'm pleased that you and your friends will be comfortable when the time comes. I'm pleased that you had the awareness to heed the warnings. And I sincerely hope that your responsibility will not wane or falter when the homeless and hungry stumble across your compound.

Should we include several types of guns in the house as part of our survival supplies?

If you require such a weapon to shoot down a ferocious bear that attempts to break into your house — but certainly NOT for people!

During the worst of the Phoenix Days cleansing time, should we hide and defend our house or should we admit people who stray onto our remote property?

You don't need *me* to answer this.

If you were the one to "stray" onto someone's well-supplied remote property, what would you want "them" to do? Shoot you or admit you?

Will there be electricity available during the bad times?

This depends on your specific geographical location and the extent of devastation. Some regions will not experience any interruption in power. Some, only brief periods. Others will be out for many weeks.

Will the Rocky Mountain Arsenal be a major negative aspect for Colorado in the future?

This facility has been permanently closed down for several years.

Your predictions of increased earth movement doesn't seem to be happening. When will this begin?

It already has begun and is manifesting on an ongoing basis that is increasing in both intensity and frequency. You need to make yourself more aware of that which is happening upon and within your world.

Please refer to the Phoenix File VIII in the second section of this book for a look at some of the earth movements that have occurred in 1990 and a portion of 1991. This section also lists some of the more devastating floods that happened during this time frame.

I see a new consciousness growing in the general public's eating habits. It seems more and more people are cutting down on the ingestion of beef and other red meats. Will cattle ranches be a thing of the past in the near future?

My answer is a regrettable one. Before cattle ranches become a thing of the past, *buffalo* ranchers will try to get their share of the market. These beautiful four-leggeds will be fattened for the slaughterhouse. There will be many steps taken in a backward direction before the final advancing ones are manifested, yet in the final analysis, the responsibility for making changes rests solely upon the shoulders of the consumer. If the demand isn't there, neither will the supply be necessary.

Will gas mains explode during the worst of the Phoenix Days?

Certainly. But also there will be a "seepage" coming to the surface from displaced lines resulting from earth movement.

Many of your letters show a great concern for these natural gas mains that run beneath your streets and up to your homes, but few inquire about "propane" gas. These also will present a grave danger. When the earth trembles, the massive propane storage tanks will be shaken off their supports, resulting in tremendous explosions that will level entire towns. Please, be advised of this actuality for the future. Be aware of where you live. People become too complacent. All propane facilities should never be located "within" any residential area — rather they be set up in open land outside of the town.

Why wouldn't you and your husband want to establish a survival community to help your fellow men?

The "spirit" of man is what survives physical life. The spirit is our most valuable possession. We have come for the express purpose of enlightening the spirits of our fellowmen —NOT for the purpose of saving the physical bodies. The spirit is far more important than physical needs. So my purpose is far more important than any survival community could ever be.

You may like to mull something over — my Advisor has stated that there are not enough people with pure and unconditional hearts to gather together for a "community." Please remember that, when times are prosperous and no sacrifices are demanded, people are eager to join survival communities. The collective attitude is one of gaiety and helpfulness. However, when the worst of the future is upon us, people will be tested to their limits. Few will pass.

When I speak of survival communities, I do not include such groups as the Quakers or the Amish, for they are of pure heart and have been tested all their lives. They know the face of sacrifice.

I think that Ute Pass in Colorado is a safe area because of the valley between the two mountain ranges. Am I right?

You've not thought this through. To begin with, Ute Pass is one long fault area that extends North of the Forestry Experimental Station all the way south to Cheyenne Mountain where NORAD is sequestered. If earth movement caused Pikes Peak to tremble and rumble, if it actually did become active, you would be inundated with ash showers and possible lava flow. The Pass would be impassable. Most of the structures would experience damage.

What will the shape of the United States look like after the axis shifts?

Please refer to Phoenix File XIII in the second section of this book. This configuration represents the coastal outline and interior alterations due to flooding immediately after the shift.

When No-Eyes spoke of clergy dictating to the government, was she referring to the Pope in Rome, the Moral Majority, born-again fundamentalists, the 700 Club, or Moslems, etc?

Actually, she foresaw interference coming from many different religious factions. Some of these have already manifested. We must keep a close watch on this aspect, for it will have grave ramifications if they intensify.

Will the undeclared wars be directed to a specific target such as communism, socialism, state-financed terrorism, or will they be as vague as the reasoning behind being in Viet Nam, which was for the enrichment of a few hundred men?

There will be diverse reasons for the U.S. to be involved in future undeclared wars. The people must be aware of what is transpiring so they may have a voice in how deeply we involve ourselves with this aspect.

Will the land devaluation only affect this country?

No-Eyes foresaw the world economy affected. Most all countries will be involved in this aspect.

Is the Utah push for religion in schools inevitable? If so, will it pave way for paranormal inclusion?

The Utah push for religion in schools is evidence of how religious leaders and factions will attempt to impose their wills on the government. This though, will not be totally successful.

The inclusion of paranormal functioning in schools will be begun as "optional" courses and not be required by all students. When this manifests, it will not be presented as a "spiritual" or "religion"-type class, but rather will be associated with "psychology" and science.

Will there ever be a world religion?

Rather there will be a world "spirituality."

I've heard that there is a plan to destroy world currency through the implementation of something called System 2000, a credit/debit government ID card. Did No-Eyes ever mention this matter?

This issue was indeed covered, although she did not tag it by the specific term System 2000. When this subject was broached, No-Eyes considered it to be a slight possibility because of the more dominating probabilities that could negate it. These being aspects that would thoroughly disrupt and cease all banking computer systems, such as atmospheric nuclear detonations targeted at broadscope electrical functionings, computer virus epidemics, international computer terrorism, etc. These she foresaw coming *before* the System 2000 had any chance of manifesting into a full-blown reality.

Frequently, when correspondents write to me saying that cash will not be good in the future, this is what they're referring to. Yet they've not given adequate consideration to the negating aspects of interfering probabilities from other sectors.

Where can I find listings of U.S. nuclear plants?

Larger libraries have reference departments that contain information on this subject in their listings of materials regarding "utilities — nuclear."

Please refer to The Phoenix Files (File I) in this book where I've listed them by state for the reader's reference convenience.

The New Madrid Fault is no little thing. How many states will be affected if this does manifest as a major upheaval?

Eight states will be affected. Please refer to The Phoenix Files (File V) in the second section of this book.

Is there anything new to add regarding the Pole Shift?

Yes! It must be understood that this specific issue is very precise in that the shift singularly depends upon "where" the "point of rotation" is *at the exact time* of the shift. It has now been determined that the strongest probability showing up is for the *new* "Point of Rotation" to be the Sweden/Finland border which will be the new North Pole position after the shift.

This places the rest of the world in an adjusted position in relation to the newly-formed axis degree. Some warm locales will be colder while some cool regions will be warmer. Likewise, some warm ones will become tropic and some cool will become frigid. All depends upon the new longitude and latitude degree readings when all is settled.

Please refer to File VI of The Phoenix Files listed in this book. You will need to compare the longitude and latitude degree readings on this illustration to present-day ones in order to appreciate the vast climactic alterations this shift will manifest, for many icebergs will melt due to swift warming, thereby inundating all coastal regions. Conversely, many waters will begin to freeze up creating entirely new frigid areas as the separate zones re-establish themselves.

What new healing methods will there be in the future?

There will be a development of that which has been available since time began. The utilization of light, kirlian photography, and sound frequencies will evidence as the new medical technology of the Golden Age.

Was AIDS one of the new diseases No-Eyes predicted?

AIDS was but one of these foreseen.

How long will the Phoenix Days last?

The worst will be over when God wins His Battle. The Phoenix Days will be over when God decides.

When did No-Eyes foresee the polar shift happening. . .before, during or after the Phoenix Days?

There is no "after" Phoenix Days, for the Golden Age of Peace and Harmony will still be within the Phoenix Days (when the Phoenix is flying free).

The polar shift (axis adjustment) will occur moments prior to Armageddon. This is the time frame foreseen but may be altered by God Himself.

Will the Final Age of Peace and Harmony be a universal constant? In other words, will it be among all planets?

Considering that God will be walking among us during this portion of the Phoenix Days, it would naturally stand to reason that all negativity and evil will be banished from His Realms of Creation. Your answer is a definitive and absolute yes.

After all the changes are over with and everyone is living in peace with God here on earth, will the other earth intelligences reveal themselves and live among us?

This question relates to entities such as the Inner Earth dwellers (Sasquatch, Little People, Fairies, etc.). The response can only be one thing — they will join us only if they perceive it as God's will.

We know Norfolk and Virginia Beach will be safe because Edgar Cayce saw that it would be. In fact, he saw new land rising off the coast.

Know that two outcomes will always be foreseen whenever two future viewings are done "with a span of time in between." The first will be the outcome as perceived at the time. The second (more recent) will be the outcome *after* probabilities have affected the "first viewing."

When viewing a physical map of the U.S., it's clear to see how the distribution of the Continental Shelf manifests itself around the North American Continent. On the west coast, there is so little shelf that regions such as Mendocino, San Francisco and Monterey Bay have virtually no shelf at all. Yet, in the south from Texas and around Florida; and on the east coast all the way past Nova Scotia, the Continental Shelf extends for hundreds of miles into the Atlantic. Up in Alaska, the Shelf actually supports that state and the U.S.S.R. it's so massive.

So then, when a geographical region boasts of a large Continental Shelf area, it's only natural to see how "new lands" could possibly arise from this. However, what needs closer attention is the "when" factor. Do the lands arise *before* or *after* the axis shift? That is the question you must address, for the shift will place the icecap regions in a warmer temperature zone which, in turn, will create immediate melting that will inundate the oceans and bring about massive coastal flooding everywhere. Then there will also be a "backwash effect" as the planet settles — this creating a "secondary flooding" of coastal regions. The oceans and seas will virtually *swish* back and forth for a time until settling occurs. Then. . .the massive Shift Occurrence will create the additional geologic disturbances such as volcanoes, plate movement, earthquakes, geothermal activity, and sinking or rising land masses.

You see the attention that must be given to this singular issue of coastal regions? Yes, many new lands will appear. Many will sink forever. But the ocean flooding was foreseen as coming *first.*

I must know the timing for the changes so I can be ready.

Each one; you, I, and they, have inner timing mechanisms according to each one's individual purpose. Your timing may not be the same as mine. Mine may not be the same as ten thousand others. Each one is responsible to sense their own inner timing.

Many who write me express how they've managed to purchase the land they want to settle on for the future. Many are telling me of new relocations. Many express no inner need to move. And many say how they're just living day to day however their spirit leads them. And then there are folks like me who were actually given several geographical choices, but can't manage the move for various reasons. But this shouldn't be a concern if you're doing your spirit's intended work and you're following inner guidance.

If I said that the worst will manifest itself in 1992, what then? What would that mean to you? Could you be ready? What if I said the worst would begin in two months? You probably couldn't make the deadline. What then? And, what if I said not until 2007? Would you then think you had plenty of time and wait? But, most importantly, what if I said 1999 and probabilities altered that date to make the worst appear next year?

My friend, live day to day and do your best with whatever you're given to work with. Make every day count, for you may never "see" the worst of it — God may decide to call you long before anything even manifests.

We have many diverse established religions today. Will these survive the changes?

None will. . .at least not in their present form of dogma.

One universal spirituality will come out of the changes. This unified ideology will be the ultimate result of humankind's collective enlightenment about the truths.

In the future, after the cleansing period, there will be no further need for separate belief systems because the truths will then be clear to all. The truths will be self-evident as the Master walks among us. There will be but one belief system — His.

I read somewhere that western Nebraska will be the new west coast after the changes.

This just is not logical, especially when consideration is given to plate tectonics and the pattern of recrystallized eruptive and metamorphic rocks that make up the orogenic roots of North America. These latter "age" rocks span the continent in a horizontal pattern (east/west) with the exception of the west coast which runs in a vertical direction up through Canada (see File VII of The Phoenix Files).

In respect to the issue this reader raised, it could be conceivable that this vertical section of metamorphic rock could experience geologic activity that would ultimately generate an appearance of being split from the main continent. This is especially probable in view of the geothermal and seismic activity of this particular geographic region. The states that make up this metamorphic block are California, Oregon, Washington, Idaho, Western Montana, Nevada, and Western Utah. It is believed that the differing "blocks" of metamorphic rock represent historical periods in which there was a break-up of the continent by fracturing into a number of continental fragments, hence the differing "age" section of our continent. The youngest portion being the Pacific Cordilleran Orogenic Region mentioned above.

The Core Region (oldest) of the U.S. continent is also illustrated in File VII of The Phoenix Files.

Many aspects must be analyzed when considering an issue like the one this reader raised. One cannot just look at a map and draw an imaginary line down the Continental Divide and assume everything west of it will be gone. To do so is not good reason or showing logical thought. However, in view of the Orogenic Age sectioning of the U.S., it's more reasonable to envision the possibility of the Pacific Cordilleran Segment being involved with this reader's area of concern. And this, we see, does not leave Nebraska as the western coastline.

In PHANTOMS AFOOT you discovered the location of your sacred ground. We traveled up Brush Creek out of Eagle to Sylvan Lake and it was really beautiful.

Indeed, Sylvan Lake is a beautiful place. We spent many enjoyable days there while we lived in Eagle, however, this is not my sacred ground location. I never said we *ended* our journey there, instead, we kept on going up through the mountains until we reached our destination for that day's journey. When we stopped, we had actually crossed the Eagle County line so that, when I looked at my map, Eagle was actually North of me (at my head).

You were not alone in thinking that Sylvan Lake was my land location, for many assumed the same thing. Actually, that lake was more of a halfway point between Eagle and our destination.

At this time, we've not been able to afford property in that region. We've been given two other alternatives and, until we're able to purchase one of these, we'll be renting a house in the vicinity of Woodland Park. For the future, Colorado was one of the few states

No-Eyes mentioned as being prime in respect to escaping the geological and climactic alterations after the pole shift. In other words, a *least affected* state.

Will having horses be an asset for the future?

Most definitely. For some regions, this will be the only way to get anywhere other than by cycling.

Did No-Eyes list the most secure states or geographic regions for the future?

This specific question ranked high on the list of readership inquiries. And, since it's not spiritually ethical for me to tell anyone where to live, I've personally spent months of intensive research compiling The Phoenix Files. These have been opened for you in the second section of this book.

If these are studied. . .really studied, those geographic regions that will be most secure will stand out like the proverbial sore thumb. Therefore, in this manner have I responded to this very popular question.

The issue of each of us taking on one's own personal responsibility is crucial to working our individual karma. This involves the unique decision-making process of self and the corresponding aspect of the free will interplay. For me to list the suggested more secure regions would not be allowing others to utilize their free wills, exercise their intelligence through responsible reasoning, or listen to their Higher Self voice. . .all so critically important for spiritual development.

Don't hot springs represent "hot spots" for the future?

Certainly they can. Hot springs are evidence of geothermically active regions beneath the earth surface. Consequently, these are most susceptible to earth movement and will represent future areas of concern. These regions have been pointed out in File X of The Phoenix Files. See the second section of this book.

Silver Trails

The people finally did see that all Without Trails circled around and back to that which was the Beginning. . .the Within Path. And there did they find their Truth.

When I begin receiving psychic impressions, there is an associated physical shaking that evidences. What is this?

We need to go into this.

We're now entering some very critical times, both in the physical and in the spiritual realm. Considering this, there are a certain number of aware individuals who are ahead of the rest.

After the Phoenix rises completely, mankind will exist within the higher vibratory rate that the entire earth will be in (this caused from the cleansing done by higher intelligences to purify nature and our atmosphere). All surviving humans will have necessitated the raising of their own bodily vibrations to not only match that of the earth's, but also to correspond with those of the higher spiritual level vibrations. See?

Some, in the here and now, are already existing within this higher vibratory rate by which the psyches are finely attuned. A shaking type of vibration shudders through the physiological system when the high consciousness of the spirit is in recognition and in perfect alignment to the conscious mind of the individual. Simplistically, the conscious mind aligns with the superconscious at times when certain stimuli are encountered. Such stimuli can be certain herbs, spiritual masters that are inwardly encountered and recognized, healing procedures, etc. Such was the shaking I evidenced when meeting No-Eyes for the first time. Such was her response that verified the causal factor of the phenomenon.

Once the mind was bicameral (utilizing both right and left simultaneously). When this was a reality for humankind, they were exceedingly psychic because their Higher Self of the superconscious was exactly vibrationally aligned with the waking-state consciousness. Humans, through a desire for the more materialistic aspects of life, began to utilize one side of the brain rather than the synergic duality of the two. They literally unbalanced their thought process, whereby the highly sensitive psychic impressions naturally began to fade. They then only evidenced in a kind of sporadic rhythm. . .hence the "spark of psychism" that comes and goes in one's life.

You are clearly slipping back into the total duality utilization of the bicameral mind, whereby the right and left sides are working in an aligned capacity that includes the superconscious as well.

Now, what to do about it? Unless you wished to revert back to utilizing just one side of your brain (which I doubt, since everyone will be using both in the future), you need to understand the causal factor for the shaking (which I hope you do now) and then ease yourself into a gentle acceptance of it. You also mentioned that sometimes you put people to sleep when you're working on them. I can put them to sleep just by talking to them. At first I thought it was because I was boring them to death. . .then I was informed by our Advisor that it was because of the vibration I was exuding due to the raised level of same. It's very soothing to others. So you need to acquire an acceptance of this higher vibration you have and give it a welcoming reception. It's clear evidence of your spiritual advancement and inner development. There are endless ways this can be utilized for the benefit of helping others. When it evidences, mentally soothe it so that the auric emanations will be directed instead of just spiking out. Practice several visualizations for this and you'll find one specific technique that best suits your own individuality.

What is the meaning of life?

What you're really asking is what is the meaning of "your" life?

No matter who you are, you are here because your spirit wished to enter into the physical earthly plane. This was done because there were aspects in your recorded history that needed to be addressed in a positive manner.

Life itself has the purpose of providing opportunities. Think about that. Life's purpose is to provide opportunities. And we "become" physically alive again in order to utilize all opportunities life presents in our path.

Now. . .we can take the baser "physical" path or we can choose the higher "spiritual" path. This decision is a personalized one generated from each individual's free will. But know that you and I and they are here to take the spiritual one, for only through that pathway will our life be made meaningful in respect to why we initially entered. See?

So then, the meaning of life (and your's) is to take advantage of each spiritual opportunity that comes our way. These are those presented aspects that invite "action" on our part, such as helping the poor and homeless, charity, compassion, and understanding directed toward another, love that is unconditional, giving moral and spiritual support. So many opportunities does life present and, because we don't always know the specific ones we're here to take. . . we must take them all.

Is it neat to be able to "see" like you do? [from a pre-teen]

It's neat to meditate. It's neat to help others through one's spiritual abilities and, it's certainly neat to feel the touch of God through all things.

Spiritual abilities can be neat at times, like joining one's consciousness with the flying hawks, but with all things, these neat abilities also come with great responsibilities. One must never misuse them or place great importance on having them. One must never "use" their spiritual abilities for personal gain or to control others.

There are guidelines that are associated with all spiritual ability functioning. These are the "rules of right and wrong use: they must not be used to spy on another or to take unfair advantage of anyone. They must not be used to cheat, such as in gambling or picking lotto numbers or race winners.

Sometimes it's hard living with the ability to "see" and it doesn't seem such a neat thing to have. It can bring sorrow if a friend's death is seen. It brings the responsibility to not interfere in another's life when certain things are seen.

Being able to "see" is not all fun. . .there are still rules.

I seem to see a correlation between No-Eyes' philosophy and your experiences with some aspects of physics, specifically the quantum issue and the relativity factor of theories. Any comment on this?

You seem to see with exceptional clarity.

Through the visionary's own unique way of expressing ideas, she frequently stressed the beautiful interrelation of all phenomena as a naturally-occuring melding of the whole — an integral living system which harmonically interacts with all aspects in and of itself — never fragmenting into separate entities, but rather thriving as a complete interpenetrating universe of diversity of the One.

Let's make the comparisons between quantum physics and mystical realities.

• Both mystical experiences and physical science theories always have extending limitations that are unexpectedly discovered through experimentation and further development. Likewise, both are inadequately explained by the confining means of linear and conceptual language or symbols. And, both can appear mildly to severely paradoxical.

• Both prove the fallacy of previously accepted laws of nature, thereby altering the shape of the foundational database. As new and fascinating solid realities are discovered, the formerly-held validities are soon abandoned to accommodate the newfound experiential data. Therefore, both exist within a continuum status of forever reaching and extending in order to reveal wondrous perspectives of the heretofore unknown nature of nature and man. Hence, former building blocks of our conceptual belief foundations crumble away to expose yet another layer or plane of reality, laws that frequently include the fourth and finer dimensions. Therefore there are no strident fundamental foundations at all, but rather there exists a flowing continuum of interconnections.

• Both see polarity extremes as being merely aspects of the whole instead of the opposites they appear to be on the surface.

• Both view space and time from the perspective of relativity, therefore dissolving their previously-believed separateness.

One of the general principles in quantum physics contends that the result of a particle reaction can only be predicted in terms of probabilities. This is a dynamic concept which clearly parallels one of the major precepts of the spiritual universal truths of the Collective Wisdom — the Law of Probabilities which asserts that all predicted future outcomes directly hinge on the probable paths or actions (probabilities) of all affecting agents as they interpenetrate the converging space and time corridor of the specific future event as it nears manifestation.

What words does nature speak?

Nature speaks a language all its own — one of dynamically conveyed thoughts and feelings, for in truth, nature does and can communicate.

There was an experiment once conducted that verified this fact. Five plants were placed together in a room. They were hooked up with highly sensitive recording instruments.

In another room, four men participating in the experiment drew straws in order to choose the one who would violate one of the plants. Nobody knew which man was going to be the culprit. Then, one at a time, each man left the room to visit the plants. Upon his return, another man did the same while his co-experimenters waited his return. This was done until all four men had visited the plant room and returned.

The man operating the recording devices called each man back into the room with the plants. When Man Number One, Two and Three entered the plant room, the instrument gave passive recordings, but when Man Number Four entered, all five instruments literally screamed. The *plants* had accurately identified *who* the perpetrator was. They screamed that it was Number Four who crushed the living leaves of their brother.

This experiment was repeated enough times to erase all doubt in the experimenter's minds. The plants accurately screamed out each time the villain walked into the room.

Nature may not speak words, but it does convey feelings. Nature is alive and, in that life, lives a consciousness that is capable of communication and. . .memory.

What does Summer Rain think of Jesus Christ?

I believe that the man known as Jesus the Christ was the greatest psychic of all time. And that he was the son of God because he was God's child, just as we all are. Jesus was a great prophet and came to the world with a spirit purpose of bringing forth a Light that would brightly shine into the darkness of humankind. He came to bring all aspects of spirituality back into the world. He came as an example of how humankind retains within them the spark of God's spirit, and how the power of God's spirit dwells within each of us. The Jesus manifestation exemplified two aspects of God's divine trinity personality — The Son (physical aspect as one of God's children) and the Spirit (spiritual aspect as God's spiritual power within). And, of course, God the Father as Supreme but not separate, is the third Trinity aspect which nobody can represent.

I believe the entity of Jesus came to establish his spiritual concepts as a new way of living a spiritual life. This he termed his "church," meaning a "spiritual way," not a building or segregated dogma or separate religious sect.

The man known as Jesus the Christ has been greatly misread.

Did Jesus appear to the Indians?

Rather the "essence of the God Force," which has been manifested to many races throughout the term of history. God has had many emissaries.

How can I get a guide?

My friend, what makes you think you don't have one already? Please know that every spirit enters the physical plane with his/her guide immediately standing at the ready. You don't need to "get" one or to "exchange" the one you've got. You need to *listen* better, for your guide has served you well. Meditate!

What is the right way to make contact with the spirit world?

At the outset, my question to you would be: what for? I would need to know this before I could give an appropriate response.

If it's for the purpose of contacting your personal spirit guide, this is rarely done — truly. The Advisors are here to ease us along the right path that will best bring about our individual missions to a state of fruition. Meditation is a wonderful way to hear your Advisor's voice of suggestion. Please, this is *so* important.

If the purpose behind this question is to speak with discarnates, this cannot be forced but rather comes quite naturally if this is an aspect of your spiritual purpose here.

Never use automatic writing!

Never use a ouija board!

God speaks to me. He said for me to move to the mountains and await my teacher. Are you this teacher?

God would've told you if I was. We need to go into this.

There appears to be a multitude of people who are interpreting their spirit Advisor's voice as being God's. If the people aren't doing this then they're using God as a means to obtain personal goals, because God does *not* interfere in our lives — this would negate the effectiveness of the free will He gave everyone. And so He had delegated others to the task of helping to guide us.

If your guide is a true Advisor, he or she would also be able to answer your question. My source informs me that you didn't hear anyone tell you to move to the mountains and await your teacher. Please watch this tendency to "use" God or Advisors as a means to your ends. You're only fooling yourself and, in the end, ultimately delay your advancement.

How do I support myself if I don't charge for my psychic sessions?

Get a job. Part-time "free" spiritual help is far better than full-time "charged" spiritual help. Nobody has a calling to be a spiritual counselor unless they can manifest their expenses through another means. If they can't — their time has not yet come and they're trying to "force" it. This is much misunderstood.

Why were a lot of No-Eyes' concepts similar to Cayce's?

Both philosophies were made manifest from the same source — the Collective Wisdom.

What causes the tingling sensation in the brain when I pick up Summer Rain's books and begin reading?

You will find this sensation evidenced by other sources in your experience. This "tingling" is somewhat like the "shaking" I spoke of in a previous response.

You mentioned in another part of your letter, that your lower center forehead elicits the greater concentration of this sensation. This is because of the pituitary gland that hangs directly behind the bone there. And, being highly sensitive to changes in vibrational frequencies, the pituitary "picks up" on the signals sent from the superconscious. It then vibrates from the effect of higher awareness that stimulates the consciousness. The individual, on a physical level, is not aware of all this transpiring, but rather is only cognizant of the "physical" manifestation psychic awareness brings to bear on the nervous system of the body.

This tingling sensation is directly associated with the former status of humankind when the bicameral mind was the norm. The sensation is a sign that the spirit has "recognized" an aspect that is important to self. It's a throwback to our former internal "radar" sense. You're fortunate that this is in evidence, for it means that your awareness level is of a high degree.

Can you lead me to my teacher?

Only one person can do this — you.

Please understand that each individual is so incredibly unique. And, in this wonderful specialness, their spiritual development in conjunction with attained wisdom and specific psychological adjustment must be aligned proportionately for certain aspects of their advancement to manifest. This also includes the important factor of Time.

As one prepares to re-enter into the physical plane of existence, they, and their chosen spirit Advisor, take a preview of all the intended life's probabilities. Together they review what aspects must be accomplished before any additional advancement is attained. And, they see, when all is aligned, a teacher may appear.

This entire issue is not that of "finding" one's own unique physical teacher, but rather it's a matter of just "being ready" for one. It's a matter of allowing destiny to flow naturally without trying so hard to "force" same. When one is ready, the teacher does not come to the student. When one is ready, the student does not "find" the teacher. When one is ready — they meet.

This is very important, for, if one is *not* ready or properly prepared, all the teacher's words or lessons will not bring about awareness, development or enlightenment, for the teacher's words and concepts will not be understood.

How will I know my teacher when I see him or her?

When you meet a teacher and this question never comes to mind, you will know the teacher is right, for the heart and soul will immediately show recognition of same.

Do animals have souls?

The physical aspect of animals has a spirit essence that contains the consciousness and memory. The animals do not have the God Spirit Force, but rather that substance that comprises the matter of the living etheric field (a pool of energy). See?

Is it good to know one's past lives?

Not as frivolity but rather as a resolvent to present-day conflicts or dis-eases. Otherwise, past life experiences are best left within the superconscious realm. If one is seen to gain from knowing of these, they will self-manifest through the carryover memory circuitry.

I once received a letter from a former correspondent's family who, full of grief, wanted to inform me that the woman had committed suicide because of what a channeler told her she did in a past life. She just couldn't get it out of her mind and had no peace living with the knowing. This is a prime example of how some channelers know not what they do, for a true spirit entity would've never "told" this poor woman what horror she did in a previous life — the Advisor would've foreseen the result of such knowledge. Please be extremely discerning when seeking information from spirit sources. There is a vast number of lower entities who are extremely active at this time. Seeker beware. Seeker, be aware.

What type of spiritual discipline should I follow?

You cannot ask this of another. One's spiritual path MUST come from one's free will and personal inner guidance. Nobody can do your advancement and development for you, therefore, such decisions must come from within *self!* Make one attempt. Make many. A decision can only come after experiencing the many, thereby, "knowing" that which is right for you — thereby knowing that which "feels" right.

What is your opinion of today's popular New Age authors?

My opinion of these doesn't matter, for each individual must discern their own truth according to their perceptual spiritual and intellectual development.

I've precious little time to be reading all the many New Age books that are being released. My Advisors keep me informed as to their validity or lack of same. Therefore I've little interest in the matter other than being shown what is being placed before the public.

What is your opinion of Tom Brown?

I cannot give this, for I don't personally know him. I only know of his work. I believe he has developed a beautifully rewarding experiential concept for anyone wishing to understand and commune with nature. Yes, I know he charges for his courses, but his material is within the realm that allows such monetary exchange.

How does the spirit travel with consciousness?

The spirit is the house in which consciousness dwells. The consciousness can be split but spirit cannot. Therefore, the spirit can travel with consciousness while a measure of same remains with the physical. Consciousness can extend through the living "cord," while the spirit is either here or there. Conscious remote viewing is evidence of this spiritual concept.

How does one know if their teacher is on the right path?

We need to clarify the interpretation of "right" here.

Do you mean *spiritually* right? Or right for *you?*

There are myriad signs that clearly indicate if a teacher is on the right spiritual path with respect to the Collective Wisdom of the universal truths. Are all taught concepts in line with God's way? Do they teach compassion and unconditional love? Sharing? Can you comprehend everything said? Are concepts simple? These factors indicate a spiritually right belief system.

If your intent was to inquire if your teacher is right for you, then you need to go by your heart. How do you "feel" about the teacher and what is taught? Can you express disagreement freely? Can you argue with your teacher (you should be able to do this)? Do you often feel left out in the cold? Can you talk about anything? Does the teacher's actions correspond with concepts taught? All these factors help to know your heart. Rule of thumb with this issue is this: Search self. Perceive your inner guidance voice. Know the teacher by knowing self first.

In reality, it shouldn't take more than one lesson to know if the teacher is right for you.

What teachers should I be reading?

Whatever ones you're drawn to. This is an important concept to understand.

Everyone develops at differing rates of advancement. Some spend a great deal of time stuck on the "power" aspects of spirituality and never advance any higher. Some never outgrow the "sensationalism" of paranormal abilities and get hung up on the channeling aspect because of their enchantment with spirit communication. Others latch onto the great philosophers and pursue that facet. And some go far beyond all these by receiving their knowledge from within self.

So, not knowing where you are right now, I suggest you read many teachers so that you have obtained a database from which to begin the "weeding out" process as your Higher Self accepts or rejects the validity of each entry. Be careful though, if you're just beginning to walk this path there is much out there that is misleading. I suggest you begin with all of the Edgar Cayce material. Read it slowly, so that you comprehend what is said. Then think about what you've read. Contemplate on it. Meditate regularly so that your perceptions will remain clear and you maintain an open door to the voice of your Higher Self.

I've searched many spiritual paths but an emptiness remains?

Have you searched the Within Path? The Within Path must be traversed before the Without Trail is taken.

Currently there appears to be a tendency for people to delve into *all* the New Age facets, this is because there are so many new spin-offs being created. But the seeker must be discerning in his search and be careful not to fragment self. You said you searched "many" paths. This cannot be done with any kind of indepth study, for each path demands full conscious attention to all its myriad facets and, to examine a path fully, many years must be devoted to it. Therefore, the seekers go about testing this path and tasting of that one — never truly absorbing the essence of their totality. This ultimately results in a superficial skimming over the different trails. And when this occurs, the seeker is left with a void felt within for nothing experienced has filled it.

This perhaps is the crux of the matter, for the simplicity of the issue is its solution — the void cannot be force-filled by running a multitude of philosophies through it. Philosophies do not penetrate the void or fill the emptiness, for only the God Essence brings this peace. Bring God into the heart first, for his love does fill the void and emptiness of self. Then seek your path via the Without Trails. No path will be meaningful until the void within has been attended to first, for it is the Light of God dwelling within that gives depth and discernment to all future philosophies the seeker pursues.

How do I bring up my spirit for journeys?

There appears to be a great interest in being able to make spirit journeys or get out of the body. As with most paranormal functionings, the public quickly latches onto these as if they are magnetically attracted to them. They too must learn to be able to do these things. Consequently there is little or no attention given to the natural law that governs such manifestations.

What is the natural law of spirit that addresses this issue? *Spirit functioning is the extension of the advancement of same.* What does this law say? It says in very simple terms that, when one is spiritually ready the spirit will automatically extend itself to manifest new experiences. This says that such functions *must* come *naturally.* And they will as one develops.

Because the spirit is housed within the mind, there have been experimentations with "mechanically" stimulating the mind in order to elicit paranormal experiential manifestations of same. This is done with absolutely no regard to an individual's personal psychological readiness for such experiences. This is done with no consideration given to an individual's emotional stability. This is done with no regard given to one's spiritual level of personal development or degree of comprehension. The only concern given is if an individual can pay the price for the experience.

And what does this say? It says that God has been totally extricated from the New Age, for the public seeks not the beautiful essence of the spirit. . .only its powers.

My friend, meditate regularly. Contemplate upon the philosophies of the truths you've taken within your heart. Have acceptance for your own level of advancement. Love God. All will manifest according to God's will for you. Love and give your care to the spirit first and the power will naturally flow forth. To love the power first brings chaos to one's Within and Without state of being.

How does one find their guide?

Do you think your's is lost? This is not meant sarcastically. You will "find" your guide when you begin to really listen for him, for he has been with you always. Meditate regularly. Pay closer attention to those subliminal thoughts that keep spearing into your consciousness. Be more *aware* of that which is spoken to you. Open self to that which is given within self.

Where can I get true information about paranormal experiences?

It's best to thoroughly peruse the scientific aspect on this issue. In this manner you'll avoid the more sensationalized aspects of the matter that are exploited in the mass of how-to books. I recommend the book: *Psychic Discoveries Behind The Iron Curtain* by Sheila Ostrander and Lynn Schroeder. And, of course, you can't go wrong with any of the Edgar Cayce material.

Do only certain special people have the spiritual gifts to experience things like in your books?

There are no "special" people. We are all created equally. No, the spiritual gifts that created the experiential manifestations in my books are not indicative of individual specialness at all. Please understand that, because we all have beautiful spirits, we all are capable of manifesting these experiences. . .and so much more.

Each spirit is as individual as one's fingerprints. Each spirit is unique unto itself according to its specific degree of advancement and spiritual development. Therefore, there will be varying circumstances and times for each spirit to reach its point of extension that permits further learning through interdimensional pathways. And this advanced education comes quite naturally when all aspects of the individual are developmentally aligned. This is the spiritual law of it.

How does a latecomer save his soul?

The term "latecomer" is irrelevant to the question. It is in no way germane to the issue, for it's never too late to save one's soul. How is this done? By bringing God into all aspects of one's life and accepting his will as your own. This means that one lets go of the self — the ego — thereby perceiving life through a perspective of the Whole rather than the One of self. One brings God into their life and heart by living as though God was their shadow.

It bothered me that Jesus wasn't ever mentioned in your books. What did No-Eyes think of him?

It would've been impossible to pen every subject the visionary and I discussed. There were many issues we talked about that are not in any of the books.

Jesus was one. This is not to infer that he was not important. He was discussed when we spoke of the major prophets throughout history. No-Eyes shared my own perception of Jesus. Please refer to a previous response in this section for this.

You're a hypocrite if you accept royalties or advances from your spiritual books. YOU are CHARGING the POOR!

Oh boy, here we go. There are two separate concepts addressed in this reader's comment. We need to handle them separately. First I'll respond to the one that says I'm charging the poor.

My response is this: Ever heard of libraries? One great thing about books is that people can read and read, they can learn and learn without ever having to pay a cent for the books they learned from. Libraries are wonderful because one can learn (for free) just as much as the one who pays for their book learning.

Now. . .let's take a long hard look at the first aspect of this reader's comment. Because the concept of "charging for spiritual enlightenment" has been so misunderstood, I will also sequentially include other readership defensive statements on the subject. In all fairness though, I must mention that the "defensive" statements only came from those individuals who were actively "charging" for their services. On the whole, readership response to the concept of "not" charging for spiritual teaching was overwhelmingly in agreement. The arguments for charging were a small minority. Here are a few of them:

• **You're a hypocrite if you accept royalties or advances from your spiritual books.**

I was a writer long before I met No-Eyes. Writing is my profession. I make my living by the act of writing, therefore I produce a tangible product that I have incurred expenses producing. The many hours I spend at this work creating a product are worth something in the way of wages. The government views a writer's income as taxable. A product is sold.

This is the crux of the issue. If a *product* is produced such as a book, tape, or video, monetary recompense for the work of producing same is not only acceptable, it is only right. This goes for *anyone* who produces a product, spiritual or otherwise. Some of you have just *assumed* products were included in the charging concept — they weren't. It is illogical and unreasonable to think that one isn't entitled to be reimbursed or make a living from something tangible they work to produce. I'm not addressing product producers, I'm addressing the counselors.

• **People NEED to pay or else they feel they've gotten no value.**

This is extremely poor psychology. First of all, what is value? And whose definition is used? The buyer? The seller?

This is very important. A spiritual teacher views "value" in terms of *intangible* assets. In turn, the spiritual teacher conveys this to the student who clearly has false logic on the issue. The teacher needs to make the student understand what real value is. The above defense statement exemplifies how the teacher is not doing this teaching, but is instead, allowing the student to continue in error. And this is then called spiritual teaching?

Spiritually, it is not up to the teacher to weigh the value of what is taught. All spiritual teaching has value. Therefore it is up to the teacher to teach, and it is up to the student to "recognize" the value of same as information is processed within.

Spirit is intangible. Spirit only knows intangibles, and knows intangible value. It is false logic to believe spirit demands any tangible payment. Spirit does not recognize any value to money. This the teacher should teach the student.

If people "need" to pay or else they feel they've gotten no value, consider this. Where is it written that giving compassion is worth $10 and helping someone across the street has a value of $5? The speaking of kind words, what value has that? $2? $15? $250? A person can receive a wonderful uplifting feeling just from another's smile. What monetary value is due for the good feeling the smile elicited? Or is the good feeling the real value? Don't you see? All these good feelings are intangibles generated from spiritual deeds or words! Their "value" cannot be weighed in tangible gold or counted out in tangible coins! Their "value" is intangible and felt *within!* The spiritual teacher *knows* this as a natural spiritual law and therefore does not allow the student to go on believing otherwise.

SPIRITUAL VALUE IS INTANGIBLE. IT IS FELT WITHIN.

- **As a people, we tend to view things "freely given" as something suspicious. So any teacher worth his/her salt will do whatever works for them. . .including charging ridiculous sums.**

And the teacher had not the courage to show the truth, but took unto self the gold that further perpetrated the falsehood. Amen.

- **I charge because I need to eat too.**

Then get a job! As stated previously, giving part-time "free" spiritual help is far better than giving full-time "charged" help. I had to work full-time jobs because we needed to eat and I then gave "free" counseling whenever I could. Better to follow the law of it than to create your own reality with thin defense mechanisms.

- **I expend energy to channel and I deserve to earn some type of recompense for that expended energies.**

This too is a self-created defense mechanism to justify the money you want.

Listen well. One who has advanced enough to manifest the ability to channel does NOT expend energy to do so. It comes quite naturally. Point Two: a high spirit entity that is channeled will NOT deplete the individual of any energy.

So. . .what does this say then? It says that either you yourself are not developed enough to be channeling or else your "channeled" entity is not of the high caliber that should be "coming through." Either way — you lose, for your defense becomes a sieve. You clearly shouldn't be channeling, much less charging for it.

- **Whatever a person learns or gains through private consult ations from me is worth paying for.**

Clearly you're not teaching the truth of spiritual value. What other truths aren't you teaching? Your statement exemplifies the importance placed on self. Ego has no place in a spiritual teacher's heart. No one, teacher or otherwise, "owns" truth, therefore, how then can you sell that which you don't own?

• **If a person is meant to receive the information from me their reality will create the money for it.**

This one statement has got to be the most shallow of all. This "create your own reality" junk has become the catch-all for everything.

Everyone is "meant" to hear the truth. Everyone is entitled to hear it.

The singular fact that you do not know the law of spiritual value exemplifies your unworthiness to be a teacher in the first place. Or did you not know the concept of creating your own reality is a contradiction to the Collective Wisdom? Or did you not know this concept is a false one? Or *did* you know but use it as a defense mechanism? You too lose. Try another excuse, I'd love to hear how it corresponds to spiritual law.

• **Who are YOU to suddenly change the rules on this?**

I changed nothing — you did. The spiritual law of value has been a precept of the Collective Wisdom since time began. I've changed nothing. I've only shed light on the way the law reads. And because the law is not a profitable one. . .well, that clearly says it all, doesn't it.

• **I only charge on a donation or ability-to-pay basis.**

In the eyes of God, a "little" wrong is still a wrong.

• **My channeled entity is all-knowing, therefore he demands this payment as honor and respect.**

Your defense would be laughable if it wasn't such a slap in the face of God. Your "entity" first needs to quit playing games, then he needs to feel the sting of The White Brotherhood's hickory stick as he's sent back to school.

In case you've forgot — only God is all-knowing. Only God deserves the honor and respect that has been so disrespectfully claimed by you and your entity. For shame!

• I spent a great deal of money on graduate schooling to become a psychologist. I integrate the universal truths into all my counseling. Am I then wrong to charge for sessions now?

Absolutely not! Please, my friend, don't confuse a bonafide profession such as a psychologist with the New Age shops set up on every corner. You've studied long and hard for the degree you have. To incorporate aspects of the universal truths in your counseling is a beautiful manner in which to help your clients.

• Money MUST be given for spiritual counseling because it is an exchange of energy.

This is another laughable excuse that's generated as a defense mechanism from false logic.

I find it incredible that people can't understand the physical science of this issue. Spirit is spirit. Physical is physical. Spirit energy is of the spirit. Physical energy is of the physical. Apples and oranges. Night and day. Not even of the same dimension.

If you sell a product, money is an exchange. If you have spiritual aspects to give, *spiritual* energy is exchanged. How is it logical to mix the two different aspects? I fail to understand how any "spiritual" teacher doesn't know this because it's such a beginner's elementary concept.

The experienced spiritual teacher knows that the true "exchange of energy" between teacher and student comes from the *"act" of sharing knowledge* — certainly not from any form of monetary or material recompense.

I will tell you that a teacher receives a wonderful fullness of heart and spirit when they share with others — this then is the "energy" they receive in exchange for that which has been given to another. You see? The teacher's payment is spiritual in nature, it has very high spiritual value.

Any spiritual teacher who does not get this "high" from their work should perhaps become a student again.

The teacher's energy is not depleted, therefore, needing energy in exchange is not necessary. The teacher's energy is rather *revitalized!*

The teacher does not "take" energy from the student —the teacher GIVES! And, in this act of giving does the teacher also receive, for what goes out also returns tenfold.

I'm a psychology professor. One of my students sees auras around people but can't see any around dying people or those who will shortly die. Can you clarify the reason for this?

There are two main sources for auras. One is the body's energy, which emanates the wellness state of the physiological system. The second source is the spirit energy, which emanates vibrational energies that are directly associated with the level of the individual's spiritual advancement and development. There is also the mental/emotional aura field which emanates from the area surrounding the crown of the head, but this aspect is not at issue here. When an individual's spirit anticipates the separation time from the body as nearing (upcoming death), the spiritual aura field will condense closer to the body as it prepares to draw its totality onto itself for the journey out of the cord. When this occurs, the spirit aura aspect no longer spikes and flares, but rather gently wavers in a slow undulating motion quite close to the body.

Likewise, the physical aura settles into a relaxed pattern that's associated with the new state of weakened energy. The physical aura stops its spiking and conforms to more of an overall roundness about the body. It also loses its vibrant colors as it correlates to the body's illness or near-death state of existence. At the same time, this physical aura will pale considerably, frequently to such a state that it is nearly transparent.

So then, with all the auric field greatly diminished in activity and color, it is not uncommon for an individual's aura to appear nonexistent when death is imminent.

Why do you always use the masculine pronoun when referring to the Great Spirit?

This may be the time for the feminists to have their day in the sun, but if God were referred to as "she," we'd still be guilty of sexual preference or discrimination. It wouldn't be proper saying "it," meaning neither he or she, but both aspects. And to keep saying "God" or "Great Spirit" becomes very repetitious and also loses the more personal aspect. It's important to get beyond these types of things. It's important to not overdo, therefore ultimately going backward into the state of separatism which will not be a surviving state for the future.

Do I need a teacher, physical or spiritual, to start on the spiritual path?

Not at all. I found this to be a good question with respect to present-day trends because it appears that there is a strong belief that has developed. This belief says that a personal teacher is a must in order to spiritually advance and develop into a greater degree of enlightenment. This is not true, for every individual is capable of advancing just as well without a physical (or spirit) teacher. There has been a tendency to pull away from the Higher Self here. The overall tone is for the seeker to "find a teacher," "follow this channeled entity," "follow that one," "watch these videos and listen to those tapes." This New Age methodology contributes to the dangerous result of fragmenting the individual, which leads to conceptual confusion and a fractured personal spiritual database that forms a weak foundation. Consequently, this is why so many seekers find themselves in a state of continued confusion and end up feeling quite empty inside.

The idea of a teacher being a necessity is not found within the precepts of the Collective Wisdom. Why? Because the teacher is you. The teacher is your own beautiful spirit within. The teacher is your own Higher Self. The school is you. Go within and there will be found your wisdom.

What is Jesus' role in the coming times?

The intent of this question is valid, but the terminology is not.

Jesus was a child of God who experienced more than one manifestation in the physical plane. Jesus was one of God the Father's emissaries.

Now, when you speak of the "coming times," the entity of Jesus himself does not enter in, but rather the physical manifestation of God the Father himself. See? Therefore, we speak of not the Second Coming, but the First and Final Coming. This is because this will be the "first" time God the Father has manifested in the physical and it will also be the time for the "final" battle. Therefore, God the Father's role in the coming times is self-evident.

Is it wrong to be paying for papers and books from the A.R.E.?

It costs money to create a product — sometimes a great deal of money. Therefore, it's reasonable to exchange money for any product received. You choose a paperback off a drug store shelf and purchase it. This is no different.

Why can't our spirits see with more clarity?

Clarity comes with experiential development. An individual's spirit level is unique unto self and is directly associated with its overall advancement on all dimensional planes. So then, if a spirit is less advanced, does that mean the individual struggling for enlightenment on the physical plane is hampered or held back? Certainly not, for their guide is always instrumental in urging one toward the right paths that will present opportunities for the individual to attain higher learning. And this higher learning done in the physical also advances the spirit. Don't forget the beautiful learning benefits of good meditation whereby one can connect with the Collective Wisdom.

The Essenes said our original sin was ignorance. Does our spirit not remember?

You have it half-right. It's not the "spirit" that doesn't remember — it's our *physical* manifestation that doesn't recall this. The mind becomes conditioned through the religious dogma given in childhood.

In one of your books you said that we're never alone. So why is it that whenever I pray to the Earth Mother, the Four Directions or Grandfather (God), nobody ever comes?

There are two reasons for this.

One is that you're in expectation of a spiritual experience. You cannot be "open" when within expectation.

Second is that "prayer" is *active* "talking" to God. If you wish to be open in order to hear communication, you must be *passive* as in meditation.

A psychic told me that I'm to be a great teacher who's come to do the Father's work. How can I do this when there's so much I don't know? I'm so frustrated and confused.

Psychics have been known to totally confuse and frustrate people by misinformation given.

This is very important. Why is it you sought the psychic in the first place? That which you seek can be found within self! Look within for your answers. If you went to thirty different psychics you'd get thirty different "purposes" for your life. Or else they cling to the safe answers that are obscure and tell everyone they are meant to be a great healer or great teacher.

I can't tell you how many letters I've received from people who have been told by psychics and channelers that you're meant to be a great teacher, a great healer, or a great something. This just cannot be. The ratio for such is not even logical!

Because your letter distressed me so, my Advisor took compassion and informed me that you are NOT meant to be a great teacher. . .other than being the great and wonderful mother you are for your children, one of which WILL be a great teacher of children when he comes of spiritual age. Did you not think "mothering" was a great calling in and of itself?

Please, visit the psychic of self. Your craving for knowledge of the unknown can only be satisfied there — in the Within room.

Have our spirit guides left us to fend as best we can?

Is that truly what you believe? Could you really believe that our individual personal guides have such little compassion and love for us that they would do such a thing?

They are with us always. . .until we join them upon physical death.

Why do people need to rediscover religion and the reincarnation concept every time?

There is something to think about in this question.

Fundamentally, this is rediscovered because of childhood indoctrination of dogma. But the important word in your question is "need." *Do* we need to rediscover these?

An individual who experiences a long life without any religious belief system, except believing in some Supreme Power, and also lives a good and helpful life still may have balanced out all the karma he came here to clear. See? Believing in reincarnation is not a prerequisite for spiritual advancement — balancing karma is.

So your neighbor who smirks at reincarnation or spirit travel or even spirit existence may still be advancing his spirit as long as he is also balancing out his negative karma.

The advantage of *knowing* the precepts of the Collective Wisdom is that more moral and spiritual responsibility is then borne by an individual. This advantage serves as an impetus to reach for higher comprehension and spiritual accomplishments.

Why aren't the truths more straight-forward?

They are if you get them from within self. It appears that many so-called spiritual teachers and channeled entities think complexity and twenty-dollar words make them appear wise and all-knowing. In truth, these ones only serve to prolong the seeker's developmental comprehension and advancement through understanding. This, ultimately, only serves to confuse the seeker in deference to the teacher's ego for public presentation. In other words, the "show" is more important than the "substance."

Seek within self. There lies truth's beautiful simplicity.

My cat got run over by a car and suffered for two days. Did it have a bad karmic debt to pay?

My friend, animals do not incur karma — only people do.

Enclosed is $35.00 for a life reading.

Enclosed is your voided check. I do not do readings. My Advisor does not participate in this activity, for these things can be found within the sacred place of self.

I know a man who died at 96 and he never did a significant thing in his entire life. What is the purpose of a life like that?

Much more than yours unless you re-evaluate the meaning of "significant." The man you refer to balanced out all his negative karma in his life — he became completed — for he knew the meaning of significance as defined by compassion and unconditional love.

A lot of us here in our networking group believe your guide is Jesus.

I'm glad you commented on this so I can clarify this misconception. My Advisor is not Jesus. My Advisor, along with Bill's, is of the highest degree of The White Brotherhood hierarchy.

Who are you to say what is spiritual and what is not? Who appointed you God?

You give the impression that you don't know that the precepts that define spirituality are given in the Collective Wisdom of the universal truths. I have looked there and written about what I have seen. You too can look and see the same definitions and laws. They are written so that they may be read by the eyes of anyone seeking the spiritual law. However, when anger and animosity dwells within one's heart, these negatives frequently serve to blur one's perception and ability to read the written word with inner clarity.

Are you going to expand on the "little person" you saw?

There's not much to expand on. There are many realities that are multidimensional and there are also differing realities of our earth plane.

Is astrology a valid concept?

Yes, when it's calculated correctly. As detailed in *Earthway*, the concept of our physical bodies having specific vibrational frequencies is a concept that had been established in ancient times. It is no different today. Geographical regions have varying vibrational frequencies and so do all the celestial bodies. All of life vibrates. Therefore, our own systems are affected by any surrounding vibrations that are in a position to influence us at birth or throughout our life.

How can channeled information contradict each other?

This has been touched upon in previous questions that have dealt with channelers and their entities.

The spiritual function of channeling has become so popular with the public that it's become more of a fad than a developmental ability of the spirit. Therefore, in an effort for many people to be "in," they are either faking it or they're channeling the lower level entities that say whatever they think the channeler wants to hear. Clearly there is a very real danger with this practice.

It not only gives out false information, it creates a yearning for John Q. Public to want to be able to do the same and, if he can't. . .what's wrong with him? There is currently a great overkill in this one aspect of the New Age. Everything from tape cassettes to books and videos are sold by channelers. What does this say? It says that we're heading backward into darkness, not forward into enlightenment. It says that the ego of "self" is placed before the beauty of the "whole." It says that, to be somebody, you must channel a wise entity. And so, within the beautiful garden of spirituality, a multitude of weeds have sprung. The garden is no longer fragrant, fresh, and beautiful.

It's so important to know that, unless a truly wise and highminded entity is channeling, the information may contradict even the most elementary precepts of the Collective Wisdom. What is your validation for a channeler's entity? If it's "freely shared" and not "charged for."

I simply cannot stress this enough.. please listen and know that this is one of the elementary spiritual precepts — SPIRITUAL WISDOM MUST BE SHARED, NOT SOLD.

And only the highest, wise members of the spiritual plane have the integrity to hold to the law, for that integrity is what distinguishes them.

Are the appearances of the Virgin Mary valid?

More appropriately, we would advise that the one known as Jesus' mother has chosen to participate in various physical experiences for the purpose of aligning mankind to the precepts of the Law of One. . .just as her son, Jesus, has done throughout time.

Why do New Age spiritual teachers and channelers tell us there is no real evil (entities or force) in the world — only negative thoughts. I can't buy that.

Good for you. There's many erroneous concepts being bantered about as spiritual truths in the current path the New Age has taken. This is a grave one.

What did Edgar Cayce have to say on this issue? Did he not mention the Sons of Belial? The Dark Ones? Did Jesus not argue with the devil in the desert as the Evil One tried to tempt him?

My friend, I cannot say what has caused the recent shift in this belief but it does seem to go hand in hand with the concept of "creating your own reality." Both are generated from the perspective of the self. . .the wants of self. Both represent a psychology mechanism that is intended to "deny" any outside aspects that may interfere with one's own wants and desires and personal goal attainment. The misleading concepts present a great disservice to the seeking public that is trying to follow the truth.

If these so-called teachers and channelers had ever come face-to-face with one of the Sons of Belial entities, they would never again claim these ones were nonexistent. If their own life experience contained the truth of it through personal encounters, they would reverse their "truth." If their channeled "entities" were of The White Brotherhood, they would know the facts of the issue. But since the above factors clearly don't apply, I suppose they'll discover the truth of it when they witness Armageddon and these "nonexistent" entities manifest themselves in third dimensional solidity.

Are organizations such as the A.R.E. worthwhile organizations?

Please don't confuse spiritual value with those organizations or groups on a superficial level. Of course the A.R.E. is worthwhile. It has done more to preserve and share the spiritual truth than any other organization or group. Its wealth of information is based on the spiritual precepts of the law. It does not alter these for the benefit of self or changing public opinion of concepts.

How can I know my purpose?

By first knowing self. This is not a cliche or some kind of smart catch-all answer. This is the law of it.

One doesn't go to another individual such as a psychic or a channeler to be "told" what his or her purpose is. As seen, these sources will frequently respond with anything that comes into their head. They'll often reply with whatever they think the client wants to hear. But a really good psychic or channeled entity will perceive the "essence" of one's purpose and then ask the client many, many leading questions to help the client self-discover his or her own purpose. See?

This entire issue of a "purpose" is grossly misunderstood, for current belief doesn't take into consideration the many aspects of karmic debt. Rather current belief strokes the ego of self by claiming the client is to be a "great" something. And the perspective of this "greatness" is always associated with being a healer or teacher. . .everyone's supposedly here to be these. . . never a good father, never a loving and nurturing mother. Doesn't anyone have the clear sight of vision to see the wrong in this?

My friend, meditate regularly for guidance that awaits you within self. Examine your life — closely. *See* the wonderful and good spiritual aspects of your life. Recognize your *goodness* as being a beautiful *purpose* in and of itself!

Can you do some of the magic Many Heart did?

Seek the "spirit" of spirituality, not the magic of it.

I was so glad to see that your books are God-centered. So many New Age ones are not. They're centered on the ego of the "I" and the selfishness of making their own reality or gaining power.

I appreciate the give-away of your kind words. Many have expressed similar sentiments. This fact alone has served to lighten my heart and give me the encouragement to continue in the face of some adversity. The New Age sector MUST veer away from the ego aspects of centering on the self and power. It MUST set a new course that leads directly to God. . .for without him, personal power is empty and out of reach.

Aren't the "charging" teachers better than no teachers?

A real "spiritual" teacher of wisdom knows the law of it. Why bother with teachers who don't?

What was the White Light Sarah used to protect herself in the book?

This was the White Light of Protection that can be visualized as an aura of brilliance surrounding the aura of self or anyone you wish to protect.

This concept is an elementary precept and is in no way some imaginary manifestation of the mind. It is a spiritually "created" entity in and of itself. As such, it contains great power.

When properly manifested through strong visualization, the White Light is extremely effective.

Example: When I worked a full time job down in Colorado Springs, I had to commute 45 minutes from our Rainbow Valley cabin. I always visualized the White Light surrounding our truck after I got in it. One winter morning there was a terrible blizzard. The pass was extremely icy. Traffic was crawling and trying to come to a stop as a white-out obliterated visibility. I managed to come to a stop in the road as I heard vehicles crashing into each other all around me. When visibility returned, cars were surrounding the truck in a haphazard manner. . .three had stopped within four inches of my vehicle. All the others had collided. Because I had maintained dual sight (physical and spiritual visualization of the Light) while driving, the protection remained strong enough to cushion the truck from other sliding vehicles. This is just one example, for there are many others I could relay regarding this concept.

This is the same White Light that one envisions surrounding self before slipping into meditation. It is utilized at this vitally important time in order to prevent undesireable entities from being able to influence the "opened" consciousness.

Neither Cayce or No-Eyes spoke of the Rapture. Is it a valid concept?

I'm not familiar with all detailed aspects Edgar Cayce spoke on so I can only comment on what No-Eyes discussed.

The Rapture, like so many other predicted events, has been greatly misinterpreted. Some believe that *God* is going to raise up a designated number of "saved" people just before the world experiences the worst of the Phoenix Days. Some believe the Rapture will be when they are "raised" off the earth by a throng of alien spaceships. And some believe the Rapture will be when God returns to bring eternal peace on earth.

This issue needs deep thought.

If God plans on returning to earth to live among men for a thousand or two years, why would he raise up certain "good" ones and then live among the lesser? Correspondingly, why would aliens evacuate the good people when they'll be so greatly needed in such times of upheaval? Wouldn't it be more plausible for the Rapture to be the beautiful entrance of God as he brings about the Golden Age of Peace and Harmony for his children on earth? Wouldn't God's coming create a beautiful rapture in and of itself?

I'm a clairvoyant and can slip into other dimensions but I'm frightened of what I might see each time. The Dark Ones are so strong. I'm tired of this fear and want to overcome it.

(The response to this personal letter was obviously much more detailed and individualized than the following reply.)

You have a major difficulty to overcome, for my Advisors informed me that you indeed are here for a high spiritual purpose. As such, you *must* work to rid self of the fear you have of the Sons of Belial. They love frightening ones such as yourself who have returned as a completed volunteer. You must work to reinforce the strength of your protection. Practice this as often as you can. You must learn to face the Dark Ones face to face without fear.

You are strong, very strong, but your fear prevents your power from being strong. Know that these ones you fear are only "playing" with you now. They are toying with you. . .testing. This will go on whenever you journey "out." Understand that they perceive you as a warrior of light and that, as such, you may be warring with them in the future. This taunting they do is to weaken your warriorship. This may be a game to them, but for you, this is very serious. You are already marked as a future light warrior for Armageddon so you must utilize this current preparatory time to strengthen your power of protection — your shield of White Light. You MUST learn to stand up to them —especially now since this is just "playtime" for them.

The manifested dark figure you described to me is especially powerful. The fact that he actually manifested before you in the physical proves that he perceives you as a future adversary and he is attempting to shake you up — shake up your "faith" in self and God's power within self. You CANNOT allow him to do this. You CANNOT allow him to let YOU do this to self. You came to be an instrumental force. I will tell you that you'll never forgive yourself if you don't find the strength and courage to empower yourself enough to begin standing up to him now.

This has been foreseen and so has it been given.

What is truth? How do we know when to recognize it?

Truth is the wheat that remains when the chaff has been winnowed. Truth is the cream that rises to the surface.

It is known by its richness and how it nourishes the soul. It is known by how it fills the void of self.

Two different trance channelers told me to read your books. I was never so moved by anything in my life. Now they tell me we MUST meet.

And indeed, we will if it is so meant. The channeled entities didn't also say that I've discontinued all group and private meetings? However, this is irrelevant if the meeting is truly meant to be.

I've had out-of-body experiences and seen sparkling energies of light beings. I've seen auras and have taken soul flight. Why should I be allowed to have these beautiful experiences?

A better question would be this: Why not? Your questions lead me to think that you do not perceive yourself as being worthy enough to have such beautiful spiritual experiences. We are all worthy, for spiritual experiences are within the capabilities of us all — through our developed and enlightened spiritual advancement. See?

This question has been generated from the conceptual overview that "people who have spiritual/paranormal functionings are special. This just is not so! These are our spirit's beautiful right of heritage.

Does a tree have a soul of its own? Explain the energy one can feel from a tree.

Trees, as with all living things, have energy. This energy has a consciousness and even an elementary aspect of memory (as seen in a previous response in this section).

This energy is not the "soul" we associate with our own human God-Essence soul, but rather is an aspect of the great pool of conscious energy that exists in all living things. This conscious energy can convey "feelings." It is this that is felt by the perceptively aware individual.

Why would a healthy spirit choose to be born as an abnormal child?

Because to do so balances its negative karma. The physically or mentally disabled child presents the perfect resolution to the spirit's karmic need. See? This karmic need may not be for the spirit itself, but for another the child will affect in life such as its parent or sibling. Perhaps by entering as disabled, it will teach a valuable and much-needed lesson to someone the child touches in life.

Do animals follow the pattern of reincarnation?

If I answered this the way I'd like — according to the precepts, I'd have to write a novel-length explanation. To keep this as simple as I can, I will state that "energy in all life forms sustains a consciousness." And, because this consciousness also retains a modicum of memory, it is possible for it to form a relationship tie. To say more would only serve to complicate the issue, but animals do not sustain the God Essense spirit we humans do, therefore there is not "need" for the karmic balancing concept of reincarnation for them.

Can human and animal spirits interchange?

Absolutely not. . .only the consciousness aspect of the human can journey to another lifeform to attain an experiential database via the developed spirit.

I thought there was no real hell. If there is, do the souls there ever get a chance to redeem themselves?

I believe the confusion over this aspect is with terminology. "Hell," as defined as a "place of fire and brimstone" does not exist. Hell, as defined as a dimensional plane where the Sons of Belial and their evil ones congregate, does exist.

The dimension I journeyed to in the books was the latter. There, the vibrations were extremely heavy and dark as well as exuding great power. The souls there were totally evil and beyond redemption simply because they don't wish such salvation. In truth, they believe their salvation is in their own dark leader. And their vileness was an odious abomination to my spirit.

It wasn't until several years after No-Eyes left me that *I* had experiences that verified the validity of the visionary's decision to have me take that one horrifying journey, for having once experienced the viper pit, coming face to face with the occasional viper that manifests is not as shocking or fearful as it would've been. Once the snakepit is experienced, the face of the snake is known and recognized for what it is. Therefore can it be dealt with according to the known measure of power required.

Do souls there ever get a chance to redeem themselves? Those that have always been there are those souls who defied God in the beginning. They want to be there. Those souls that have joined at a later date were far beyond redemption by denying God and making their free will choice. They were free to cross the line and take whatever side they wanted.

Souls do not go to this Dark Side if there is *any hope at all* of it "wanting" God's love and redemption, for God's mercy is boundless. There is no return from the Sons of Belial camp and all who choose to join it know that.

Is it correct to assume that there are no new spirits being born now?

This is not an assumption but rather a fact. All spirits were "created" at the moment of Creation when "all" spirits were emitted from the essence of God. Only at the time of Creation were all spirits "new."

Why is the human population rising so rapidly if no new spirits are being born?

There is a transposition of concepts in this question.

First we establish that there is no such thing as a "new" spirit because *all* spirlts were *created* at the moment of Creation. So then, by "new" we're not speaking of "newly created" here. Therefore we could be speaking of "newly *entered*" spirits, which the questioner would have to be referring to.

It makes absolute sense that our world population is growing by leaps and bounds at this time. It makes perfect sense when this fact is associated with the aspect of spirit reincarnation.

Let's take a hypothetical example of why this is.

The film *A Christmas Carol* is a very good example because most everyone knows it. What kind of life did old Scrooge live? One of living for the self. One of not caring a whit for others or the good of the whole. He went about his own little narrow perspective, never giving a thought or care to the condition of his state within. And. . .when he's finally shown his upcoming death and what that death will bring in respect to results of the life he lived, he is suddenly in a state of "urgency" to make as many amends as possible.

So too is the current state of affairs on the spiritual plane. So many lower spirits spent so many thousands of years just going about their merry way without giving a care to their purpose of advancing — never wanting to put in the energy of reincarnating to balance out incurred negative karmic debts or to learn important aspects that were needed. And now. . .now they see the writing on the wall that says the Phoenix is stirring. . .that the Phoenix is anxious to prepare the world for God's final return. What would you do if you were one of these spirits? Still fool around? Dally? Or suddenly realize that "this is it!" and get your spirit behind into a body as quick as possible?

Hence is the elemental reason so many "people" are here.

Is there really a record book?

Since a "book" is physically a material object, there cannot be such in the spiritual dimensional field of existence, however the associated dimensional equivalent does exist. This is extremely difficult to properly explain in third dimensional concepts. Yet the fact of the matter is what we're dealing with in this issue, not the mechanics of it. The "recording" could be similarly compared to how a radio station records sound and that sound travels through the various air wave frequencies to come out one's radio. The "traveling" aspect of these word sounds is most associated with the record book. The "inbetween" stage best gives the most accurate concept.

Know that all an individual speaks is being recorded. Know that all deeds and thoughts are also there, just as all the past life experiential data of the spirit is.

I receive messages from God. Enclosed is a letter from Him to you. He advises that we meet as soon as possible.

You and your channeled entity should be spanked. The entity, for having the audacity to impersonate God and, you for allowing such to be transpiring, and for "using" God.

Know that my Advisors "know" when an individual is truly meant to meet with me. Know that my Advisors "know" all the others of The White Brotherhood who communicate with individuals for the purpose of carrying out the master plan. Know that God does not channel!

How can some channeled material be coming from Jesus?

The entity once known as Jesus the Christ in one of his many incarnations is not involved in such activity. Beware the impersonators.

It infuriates me when I see some New Age people call themselves teachers when they themselves were only recently made aware of the spiritual truths. How can people do that?

Because it has been foretold that ego will rule the world in the end time days. And now. . .there appears to be many participating in the big spiritual race to be "best teacher," "wisest teacher," "the channeler with the oldest entity," most famous seminar giver, one with the most native power, one with the most followers, and on and on ad nauseam. I care not for such a race of fools.

You are wise indeed to perceive the reality of this reality, for ego is truly ruling the world now.

Define "entity" please.

Generally speaking, "entity" means something separate or existing independently; a fact of existence; being.

Spiritually speaking, "entity" most frequently refers to a discarnate; a spirit.

Are all present-day urges or interests stemmed from past lives? Don't we develop interests based on the present life?

Sure we do, these depending on experiential data built in the current life. As a child, your family may have spent summer vacations by the sea. Wonderful memories of those times were incurred. And, although you live in the midwest, you may now have a great desire to return to a seaport to live. This would be one example of how current life experience affects an individual's interests or geographical magnetism.

Although it's fact that many, many present-day interests are generated by the carryover soul experiential memory, this is not to imply that they all are.

How do souls who constantly choose evil in life desire to be one with God?

Generally this paradox is generated from an individual's fear of God which one makes a subliminal aspect of their life. Although they convince themselves that they do want to choose God, they're playing a dangerous game by working both sides. Upon Judgement, God looks through one's lip-service to view one's deeds. They must justify and balance.

Karma is that which is brought over, while cause and effect may exist in one material plane only. Can you explain this?

There are two important statements made within this inquiry .

Karma is that which is brought over . Let's take this first. The aspect of this statement that could cause some confusion is "brought over." This may refer to that which is brought over "into the physical" or that which is brought over "into the spirit" plane. Karma simply refers to that which incurs unbalance. Therefore, a "balancing" must be done to reinstate equilibrium. These states of "karma unbalance and equilibrium" are recorded in the akashic record of every spirit.

So a negative act, word or deed that is done in the physical plane *must* be balanced with a positive one. Now here comes the "brought over" aspect. The "balancing" positive act, word or deed CAN be done in ANY plane, for it is not the law that the karmic balance must be done in the same plane it was created in. See ? Consequently, positive karma can be done in the spirit plane for negative deeds done in the physical plane and conversely, positive karma can be done in the physical plane for negative deeds done in the spirit plane. This is what is meant by the "brought over" aspect of the first statement.

Now. . .the second statement reads: *Cause and effect may exist in one material plane only.* The key word here is "may." Simply put, this statement says that "for every action there is a reaction." The reaction is "usually" manifested in the same dimensional plane as the action was made. A factory pollutes a river and nature downstream and downwind is affected. This exemplifies an action (cause) and reaction (effect) that occurs on the same plane. Someone speaks ill of another. The words are the cause and the hurt feelings are the effect — all occurring on the same plane of existence. See? Yet although this is the norm, the "may" aspect, it is not the law, for cause and effect may also cross dimensional boundaries.

It's important here to understand that the "cause" (if negative) will also produce the "karma" that will need balancing that can be attained on ANY plane. It's the "effect" that usually is manifested in the same plane as the cause. See?

Does one have to reach a state of total oneness with God in order not to have to return? Or are there other conditions?

It would clarify this law better if it were reworded: One must reach a state of total "completion" in order not to have to return. This then is the law of it.

Please understand that it is the "completion" state of one's spirit that must be reached first. This attained, the completed spirit utilizes the free will to either join with God's essence or to continue working *for* God. Remember that God does not *force* completed spirits into his beautiful essence, but rather gives the spirits a choice. Many return to God's essence and many choose to continue working on all dimensional levels to assist in bringing the rest (incarnated beings and discarnates) into a higher state of advancement. The White Brotherhood consists of these completed spirits. They can choose between many high missions — these being special spirit guides, to those completed spirits who have chosen to return to the physical for volunteered missions. They can choose to remain and work within the framework of The White Brother-hood on the spirit plane. They can serve as instrumental Sons of Light and join the battle against the Sons of Belial on the spirit plane. They can be teachers and advisors on the spirit plane. All the highest level positions are held by the completed spirits of The White Brotherood.

If a completed spirit of The White Brotherood decides to volunteer for a reincarnation into the physical plane in order to carry out a mission, these missions are never for self but rather for the overall upliftment of humankind. And, in the act of "returning," can open themselves to the possibly of incurring negative karma once again. Hence,to return to the physical, is one of the least attractive choices for a completed spirit because it represents dangers no other choice has. Therefore, the completed spirits who volunteer for such a physical mission, have prearranged to have their closest White Brotherhood associates as their personal spirit guide (Advisor) throughout the experiential incarnation. In this manner, the incarnated mind retains much of the spirit's knowledge and spirit functioning. . .memory of the precepts of the law. And, knowledge, not materialism, becomes the goal. *Purpose* is the operative word above all other aspects of the now physical life. And maintaining the spirit integrity of the law becomes paramount, as does the need for the completed spirit to maintain close communication with his Advisor associate because of that one's wise overview and far-sighted perspective of each situation the incarnated one encounters.

What is the difference between the physical mind and the spiritual mind?

The physical mind houses experiential and learned data obtained in the *current* incarnation. The spiritual mind houses experiential and learned data from ALL incarnations *and* that which has been ex-perienced on all planes.

The "carryover" memory of the physical mind is therefore, current data plus crossed-over memory aspects of the spiritual mind. Hence past lives are recalled as are past-life talents such as skills (woods tracking), knowledge (scientists), and talent (pianists and artists). This then is the causal factor which generates the phenomenon of child prodigies.

What other realms are there for instruction besides earth?

Many more than you can envision, for they are of every plane and dimension. And, *within* these also are the many experiential oppor-tunities for same.

Is all memory contained within our Higher Self or do we retain just enough to help in the present incarnation?

All memory is contained within the spirit mind of the Higher Self. If the current experience can benefit from selected memory fragments of the spirit mind, these will automatically carryover to the physical mind of self.

What are "spiritual forces in the earth of every nature?"

This refers to "that reality which has come from the spirit and is not interrelated to that which is associated to the materialistic manifestation of humankind." Simply said, the spiritual forces in the earth of every nature are those "forces of the spirit" that exist despite the experiential data of human knowledge. These would be all real spiritual forces that mankind currently does not understand — the myths and the realities outside his current intellectual capabilities of understanding or accepting. . .the "dynamic forces."

These include the elemental forces and beings in physical forms not accepted by current attitudes or perceptions of the general public.

How can birth in the material be death in the spiritual plane?

This does not infer that, through physical birth our spirit dies. This only means that we must live one plane of existence to the fullest extent we can. When our physical body dies, the spirit lives. When our essence leaves the spirit plane to reincarnate into the physical, our spirit mind is not usually known to the physical mind that now functions.

Must a spirit guide be at some specific level of attunement with God in order to be a guide?

Absolutely, but more accurate, the spirit guide must be at a specified completion *state* which naturally brings an understanding of the *precepts of the spiritual law.*

Therefore, when "lower" entities *play* at being an individual's spirit guide, much misinformation and confusion ensues. This is why it's so important for people to stop "opening self" to *whatever* is around. This is why so many are channeling today and, consequently this is also why so much contradictory material is given.

Are spirit guides souls that have also been in the earth plane at some other time?

Yes, and through these incarnations, they have worked out their negative karma. These guides have reached the advanced point in their development which enables them to continue their spiritual work through the dissemination of proper human guidance and the spiritual law.

Do all living things possess the spirit of life - God's creative force?

Of course. But be careful not to associate the two forces. God's *creative force* is NOT the same as God's *own* spirit essence. The concepts are not interchangeable in interpretation.

Can you explain the following statement? "When the purposes of an entity or soul are more and more in accord with that for which the entity has entered, then the soul-entity may take HOLD upon that which may bring to its remembrance that which it was, where, when and how."

This sounds an awful like Cayce material here.

This statement simply means that "when one is ready, knowledge will be known." In other words, when an individual is living their life according to the path their spirit planned for the incarnation, they are living according to their spirit's intent. The physical life and the spirit mind are in vibrational accordance and, when this frequency alignment has been established, the spirit mind sends additional information across to the physical mind in the way of past memories, spirit wisdom, or aspects that prompt and guide the individual's path toward their specific purpose. This is a very important concept to understand, for this singular Law says the following: Do not force spiritual knowledge. Do not force one's life goals. Do not force enlightenment. Do not seek the Without Trail before first walking the Within Path, for there lies the way. Gain Acceptance, for knowing self brings the knowing of the self's experiential data. . .the past lives (that which it was). . .the where (current path). . .the when (timing). . . and the how (manner of achieving one's purpose).

Can you explain the following statement? "Spiritual forces in the earth of every nature; elemental forces, fairies, those of every form — are only seen by those attended to the infinite."

This simply means that an individual who is spiritually enlightened according to the precepts of the spiritual law of God is also perceptive of the aspects of spiritual reality that coexist with the physical plane.

Does the akashic record refer to the karma we must meet as our destiny? If so, then what about free will and choosing our own destiny?

Two questions here.

Yes, the akashic record refers to the karma we must meet as our destiny. The akashic record "records" all karma incurred and balanced.

Now. . to the second associated question. What about free will and the choosing of our own destiny. My first inclination is to question the word "own" rather than the aspect of free will. The answer to this lies within the question.

What is meant by "own" destiny? Which is truly *you?* Your physical mind in the physical body? Or the spirit mind in the spirit totality of self? Which is *truly* your mind? That which controls the temporary *shell* of self? Or that which *is* the very *essence* of self? Which is the real you?

By this we see that the spirit mind is the true self. And, while in absolute consciousness of the spirit mind while still on the spirit plane, you knew your mind. You knew what your "own" mind *chose* through the use of your "own" free will. This your own spirit mind chose as the *best* destiny to bring about the karmic balance.

When incarnated, the "physical" mind now thinks *it* is the sole controler and can do whatever it pleases as its destiny in the physical plane. And, sadly, this is where the concept of creating your own reality lead so many astray, for they are using their *physical* mind to choose a pleasing destiny that is irrespective of what destiny the *spiritual* mind already chose. This is why it's so important to seek within to find self.

If I'm capable of channeling, why aren't I also aware of my OOBEs other than through vivid dreams and meditation?

Because being consciously aware of out-of-body journeys requires the splitting of consciousness and this requires a higher level of development. Be patient and stop dwelling on why this or that functioning hasn't been attained. When all lessons are learned and understood on one level, one quite naturally shifts to a higher one.

In my next incarnation, will I retain what I've learned from you or will I have to start over again from scratch?

Please remember that you're speaking of the "physical" mind here because your "spiritual" mind already knew what No-Eyes taught —it knew that and so much more.

What you recall while in the physical is uniquely up to one's own level of spiritual development. If, in your next incarnation, it is meant for you to retain the spiritual law it will be done. To worry about such now is irrelevant.

My cat actually talks to me. What metaphysical concept covers this?

None. Animals don't speak. They mentally communicate.

A wise adept master communicates to me through my cat. Can you tell me more about him?

If he wanted you to know. . .he would've told you. Please know that, although animals can teach us much, no "wise" spirit entity communicates through an animal in a *permanent* manner.

Just before I reincarnate again, can I have a choice of who my spirit guide will be?

Of course. This is the law of it. This is attained through mutual agreement.

I've heard there are places where they actually create altered states within the individual through mechanical means and by way of a regimented technique. This somehow doesn't seem right to me. Comment?

This is created through a technology that stimulates the physical mind in a manner that opens it to the spirit one. "Going within" does not refer to this spiritually unnatural method, for the safeguards of one's natural development are not in place. In essence, the child shouldn't ride the wild horse until the pony has been experienced.

Is the Corridor of Time the same as the tunnel experienced upon physical death?

No, not at all, for the Corridor of Time is rather the dimensional "current" of time and space as evidenced on a lower level. The Cross-over Corridor is on a much higher dimensional frequency.

Why doesn't my spirit guide make someone I love notice me?

This is not within their realm of "spiritual" work. Spirit guides do not play matchmaker, rather they know the wisdom of such dwells within the *physical.* . .love cannot be forced or manipulated.

You say there is no purgatory. People can't just go straight to heaven — they have to go somewhere until they're purified enough. Wouldn't purgatory be the logical place?

No, but *earth* would. Know that earth *is* the "inbetween" learning place. Earth is the school. Earth and all physical places of incarnation is the "spiritual land of opportunity." God is "home." The spirit plane is our "temporary home." Earth is our schoolroom.

I was always under the impression that group meditation was encouraged, especially to help someone. Why has that changed? God said that whenever two or more are gathered in my name, there shall I also be amidst them.

And so he shall. But remember, God did not say that, Jesus did. Don't ever confuse the two.

Jesus also wasn't referring to meditation, he refered to "gatherings in his name." Please don't mix concepts.

Meditation is the personal "listening" *for* God. Prayer is the "speaking" *to* God. They cannot and must not be perceived as the same concepts.

Meditation should be done alone, for it is a uniquely personal opening of your inner door for God to enter through. While prayer can be done alone or with the many. You mentioned gathering for the purpose of "helping" someone — this then is "prayer." This is "group *prayer.* And so this then is good.

You cannot mention "meditation" and "helping" someone all in one breath. That statement alone is an impossibility because one is "passive" while the other "active."

What does "born again" really mean in terms of when Jesus spoke about the subject? Was he referring to reincarnation?

Of course.

Man's "revised" definition has been altered to justify his own interpretation. A "born again" Christian simply means that he has found God. All people living here on earth have *already* been born again, for they are old spirits dwelling in new bodies in order to perfect their spirits through goodness toward their fellowmen and balancing out their personal negative karma.

There are many "born again" people who are not spiritually enlightened. And until they stop claiming that they are "born again," they *will* be born again and again and. . .

Is there actually an entity known as Satan?

On the spiritual plane this entity is known as Belial. Know that everything above and below has its counterpart —its polarity — even God.

I think God must be terribly disgusted with mankind. Why doesn't he just wipe us out and begin again?

Because He doesn't interfere in our lives — neither does He have to wipe us out, for mankind is doing that for Him.

In the bible, it seems to me that Judas wasn't really a betrayer, at least in the true sense of the word. What do you think?

I agree.

Judas had good intentions. He merely set up a plan for Jesus to clear himself before the Sanhedrin, which was the highest judicial and ecclesiastical council of the Jewish nation. But the plan backfired on Judas when the Sanhedrin betrayed Judas instead.

At the Last Supper, Jesus predicted to his disciples that one among them would betray him that night. He said "betray" because Jesus *knew* what the final outcome was going to be. At that time, the time of Jesus' revelation, Judas did not think the Master was referring to him because true betrayal was not in Judas' mind at all.

Judas was consumed with a deep guilt over the fact that his good intentions went awry. He killed himself because he so loved the Master, not because he wanted to harm him. If Judas had intentions of betraying Jesus, he wouldn't have been so overcome with grief over his Master's capture — he would've been glad.

Judas was betrayed by the Sanhedrin. Judas did not betray Jesus. Only the *outcome* resulted in betrayal as the true sense of the word is interpreted.

Are paranormal talents the same as the charismatic gifts of the Holy Spirit?

Yes, they are one and the same.
What is the Holy Spirit but the "spirit essence" of God within us all.

All people are judged by God when they DIE. That is the ONLY judgement upon individual souls. That intellectually negates the false reasoning behind reincarnation!

The "only" judgement? You obviously do not believe in the final judgement then. I need not comment further.

How do you find God by watching ants?

You're trying sarcasm, but what you don't realize is that it's not sarcasm. You're referring to my union with God when I'm joined with nature.
Very well. I find God by watching *all* of nature, including the "ants" because these tiny insects believe that they are the epitome of life in their world. They possess an incredible nearsightedness. They do not see the other larger lifeforms that also thrive in their world. They do not perceive the existence of "other" intelligences. They do not know of the foreign flying vehicles that travel to the distant planets and other constellations. They do not perceive their world as a planet rotating among many others. They do not have knowledge of our planet as being a miniscule speck among other universes. They do not understand the hand of power that fashioned it all in the beginning.
And, after all that, perhaps you do not see mankind itself as being very much like those tiny ants. We are so busy with our daily lives and are so consumed by our narrow preconceived notions that the very idea of expanding our awareness to encompass the paranormal, alien people, other universes and man's spiritual bond with nature is far beyond his reach, beyond his understanding, his knowledge to accept.
I "look" at the ant and I see an ordered civilization that possesses a one-minded purpose directed toward the preservation of self — I see a closed society that exists in absolute unawareness of its surrounding reality. I "observe" the ant and I perceive mankind through the saddened eye of God.

What day of the week do you keep as your sabbath?

I don't believe that people should have to make "reservations" in order to make time for God. *All* days should be a beautiful "living" expression of thinking about God. That is spirituality.

If God is all merciful, which he is, he wouldn't make us live our physical lives over and over again.

This is shallow thinking. If God is all merciful, which he is, would he condemn his children for a *first* offense? Would God give only *one* chance to prove your worth? Would you not give your own child a second chance, a third, a fourth?

God's spirit is perfectly pure. We are a part of God's spirit that needs to return back into his spirit. Our spirits therefore, require perfect purification. This cannot be accomplished in one lifetime, but rather a series of same.

How much of the bible has been lost in translation?

Sixty-seven percent!

Do you think dancing and drinking are the works of Satan?

Jesus didn't, why should you? Jesus drank wine and danced with the little children. He sang and danced with his mother.

Prove there is a God.

Prove there isn't. The burden of proof is yours, not mine.

There IS no hell. God is too merciful for such a place.

God is just. God is merciful. God is demanding — he demands justice. And for all those who have used their free wills to side with Belial, the dimension termed hell *is* justice.

I've always felt bad that all unbaptised babies are sent to limbo. Somehow that never seemed to be a fair law of a just God.

And God does agree. Therefore He never made such an inhumane law or place. All souls are old spirits. For what purpose would they have to be baptised when they *originated* from the very core essence of God

Himself? The concept of "limbo" has been a fabricated doctrine to coerce people into enlarging a religion's flock through scare tactics.

God dearly loves all His children, especially the small children.

Spiritually speaking, limbo has no place in the precepts of spiritual law of the Collective Wisdom. When consideration is given to the fact that *all* physical babies are really old spirits, the concept of limbo shatters, for it is founded on the false premise that newborns are also "new spirits" — which is certainly not the case.

Will all the atheists be condemned?

The guidelines governing the Final Judgement are within the mind of God. This is not for us to speculate upon, but I would caution you to think a little deeper on this.

An atheist in *this* life may have been a priest or rabbi in many past lives. You forget that judgement is based on the *culmination* of all experiential lives.

Isn't it obvious who will win Armageddon? Why would Satan even consider the possibility of any other outcome?

Nobody enters into a battle with the "intention" of losing — not even Belial. Obviously, the outcome is not as obvious to him and his minions as it is to you.

Where is heaven?

Do not ask the "where of it, but rather the who." Heaven is a who! Heaven is the totality of love within the essence of God.

What is spirituality?

Spirituality is the absolute belief in all God's universal truths and the immutable precepts of same. And. . .spirituality is the living of same.

When a person has premonitions, such as the death dates of friends and relatives, are those dates set in time or does the law of probabilities enter into the picture to alter these foreseen dates?

All premonitions are subject to the controlling force of affecting probabilities.

When a future event is foreseen, that event is a probability "as of the very *moment*" it is foreseen. Therefore, if the same event is then looked at on a later date, even a day or so, then the event may show an alteration because of situations that had transpired "within" that day's time to affect a *different* outcome of the event. See? This singular fact is why the predictions of specific dates of future occurrences is not a good practice.

Predicting foreseen future events can be as unstable as forecasting the stock market — changes are manifesting constantly before the event will actually take place — changes that affect the event's final outcome. Therefore, a specific death date may be foreseen, but the probabilities for altering circumstances to change it are endless.

An example of this would be when, in 1982, I had a vivid premonition dream where I saw the specter of death point a boney finger to Bill's gravestone. The dates clearly showed his birth year and his death year — 1983. I worried about him all throughout 1983 and it wasn't until the final night of that year — New Year's Eve, when I accompanied him to a service call that the foreseen event was altered. . .because I was with him. If he had gone out on the call alone, the foreseen event wouldn't have been altered. *I* was the affecting factor that changed the event.

Now, a natural question would go something like this: Then how can the future be predicted at all if so many altering probabilities are present between the event itself and the date it's foreseen? And that would be an intelligent question that shows good logic. However, many events turn out to have no probabilities affecting it. Therefore, the event will occur as foreseen. Also, many events are what are termed "concrete." You will die someday. That is a concrete event of the future. The sun will rise in the east tomorrow morning. That also is a concrete future event. But there are also future events that are just as concrete, events that can be foreseen. These events will occur no matter what alterations come *before* the event. These concrete happenings are not contingent upon their preceding circumstances. The only alterations the outcome can be affected by is that of time — but they *will* come just the same, eventually. See?

This is why precise dates can be so meaningless. This is why many good psychics have been discredited by the skeptical mind. The skeptic yells, "false prophet!" when an event doesn't occur on the exact date it was predicted. But then the skeptic will not make comment when the predicted event does occur a month or two later.

Generally, the public requires a deeper understanding of the laws that govern the enigma of future sight. And those laws are based on the *foundation* of altering probabilities.

I want to see auras. How can I do this?

Through awareness. And first seeking to know self.

Why can't psychic abilities stem from the mind? We only utilize ten percent, so why can't these talents come from the greater portion that is yet unused? Why bring the spirit into it at all?

Because the spirit *is* the mind! This is backed by the irrefutable evidence of how spirit journeys carry the "consciousness" *with* it.

If you're questioning why the spirit needs to be brought into psychic abilities, you have answered that question within your own choice of wording. If you're going to use the term "psychic," then you had better be more familiar with its meaning. Psychic stems from the word psyche, which means "of the soul or spirit." Paranormally speaking, psychic means "mind/spirit" or "spirit/mind." You simply cannot disengage the meaning of mind from the meaning of spirit when you say psychic. So then, to begin with, you need to get your nomenclature correct.

If we *were* capable of utilizing our total mental capacity, we would attain perfect enlightenment.

During the process of "soul sight," the mind's consciousness is sent out to observe and experience that which is without self. During the process of "soul flight," the mind's consciousness is at rest while the mind's superconsciousness leaves with the spirit to be free.

A brain-dead individual is without its spirit. Yes. The spirit dwells *within* the mind. But the mind *alone* is *not* the spirit. The spirit is the sum total of all personalities that it ever possessed. And where does an individual's personality stem from? The mind! The mind and the spirit are inseparable. This has not been a paradox. Remember that there is a "physical" mind and a "spirit" mind. The physical mind being that accumulation of "present-day" experiential data. While the "spirit mind" contains the experiential data since the time of Creation. They are merely different facets of each other. A thought cannot be seen within its physical casing of the brain. A spirit cannot be seen within its physical encasement of the brain either, because they both exist in tandem within the mind! Know that the mind and the spirit are indeed *one* aspect of self.

I can always tell when people are lying to me. Is this evidence of telepathy?

Not in your case.

It is rather evidence of your sharpened awareness. You cannot read the mind of others, but rather perceive falsehoods. This is as different from telepathy as black is from white.

You're fortunate that you possess such a degree of awareness. You're fortunate that others cannot lie to you. But be careful not to misuse this talent. Watch what you do with it.

What's the difference between premonition and precognition? Some people use the two terms as if they were interchangeable. Are they?

Absolutely not. The terms "premonition" and "precognition" are not interchangeable.

A "premonition" signifies the perception of a future event. A premonition represents the "event" foreseen. The term is a noun.

"Precognition" indicates the "ability" to foresee the future. Precognition represents the *ability*. The term is a verb. Since precognition denotes the "ability to see," this term therefore can indicate a *current event* happening at the "time of seeing," rather than being solely a "future" event as with a premonition. See?

Premonitions indicate warnings.

Precognition is the act of seeing.

I sometimes can physically see big ant-shaped creatures. Who are these beings? Is this a sign of my development?

This is certainly a sign of your development — a developing alcohol problem that needs immediate addressing. The ant-shaped creatures come from one source only — your martinis.

Is there really such a creature as bigfoot?

Creature? Bigfoot?

There are rarely-seen lifeforms that have inhabited this planet for centuries. The "terms" applied to these intelligences are clear evidence of humankind's absolute ignorance. Bigfoot? Abominable Snowman? Really. And we dare to call ourselves intelligent!

They are of the spirit forces of every form on earth.

Do crystal balls really work?

That depends.

Crystal balls don't come equipped with electrical cords or ON and OFF switches. They don't have video dials or frequency knobs. A crystal ball is merely a large ball of crystal — that's all you get — no product guarantee and no manufacturer warranty.

Having a crystal ball is no sure-fire method of seeing into the future, mainly because it's not the crystal that shows you visions, but rather the mind of self. The ball simply is an object on which the mind centers. A person could just as well use a bowl of water or, for that matter, the screen of his own mind. A crystal ball is merely the "focusing point" for the intense concentration of the mind. And, if the mind concentrates hard enough, the ball will work.

Many people don't have the mind force to activate a crystal, their thoughts are not nearly intense enough. Personally, I consider the utilization of crystal balls as being classed with those useless aids that are utilized by the parlor room psychics. They are not the tools of an enlightened individual — the truly adept need no tools except the mind of self.

Do tarot cards foretell the future?

You would get more out of them by trading them in for baseball cards and giving them to your son.

As with the crystal ball, tarot cards are only effective in the experienced hands of an aware individual who possesses highly-charged mental energies. These people are very rare.

Anyone can learn the card's individual meanings, but it's their absolute interpretation with respect to all corresponding cards in the layout that is most vital to the accurate forecasting.

I would caution you against the use of tarot cards as a means of foreseeing the future. You're looking in the wrong places. Search not the Without Path to enlightenment, but rather the Within Path through self.

Should I believe in the astrology forcasts in the newspapers?

I cannot tell you what to believe as your truth. I can only share that which corresponds to the precepts of the Collective Wisdom.

Aren't newspaper or magazine astrology forecasts rather general? These appear for the purpose of pure entertainment nothing more serious than that.

Astrology is a true science. It is an ancient one, for the Three Wise Men who journeyed to the nativity site in Bethlehem were renowned astrologers of their time.

Astrology demands complicated and complex research, intensive study, and absolute interpretation in order to derive at an individual's precise chart calculations for data analysis. The very "second" of one's birthtime has to be known. The "location" of one's birth must also be a known factor. There are many facets here that require consideration while working up a person's unique and individualized chart. And I could continue on with this subject for at least twenty more pages, but that would not be germane to your question.

Basically, the forecasts that are printed in popular magazines and in the daily newspapers are far too broad in scope to be helpful to anyone. You simply cannot clump all Aries folks together like one was culling sheep from cows. Each specific sign possesses massive variated factors that seriously affect each person individually according to their precise birth time and hemisphere of birth. Each sign's characteristics are *not* uniform, nor are they concrete. They are widely variable depending upon a multitude of determining factors that affect the individual chart.

I have a rather strange question. In fact, you might even think it's silly, but occasionally when I get into my car, things go wrong. Nobody else who drives the car has any problems with it, but when I get in, the wipers malfunction, it stalls out or the radio becomes static. What's the deal? I'm beginning to think I'm either crazy or that the car is an evil jinx.

Pardon my rudeness, but I laughed when I read this question. No. I don't think it's silly. Nor do I think you're crazy or that you car's an evil jinx.

I'm going to let you in on a little personal secret of my own that I think will help you feel better. If it's any comfort, I frequently experience the same thing. Occasionally I'll get into my friend's Jeep and the wipers will clear off the windshield but then they won't stop. I'll have to turn off the engine to stop them. Or the radio won't work. There've been times when I drove our truck to the store and when I got back in, the engine refused to turn over for me and I'd have to ask a stranger in the parking lot to start it for me. Now if you don't think I feel foolish after a stranger starts it right up on the first try, better guess again. If the stranger is a man, he'll usually grin at me as if to say: "women drivers!"

The fact that these are *occasional* and not constant occurrences substantiates the fact that the vehicles in question do not possess connective wayward spirits. These vehicles, yours and mine, are perfectly inanimate without forces of their own. However, they *are* capable of being adversely affected by intense outside forces of energy acted upon them — those of the operator.

You clearly are in possession of a strong auric energy field. At times, when you're rushed, upset or excited, this personal energy acts some-what like an intensive magnetic field that is in continual fluctuation — something comparable to solar flares. Consequently, this powerful field of energy strikes out and adversely affects the electrical functioning of all it comes in contact with.

I would simply advise you to remain calm whenever you know that you're going to be driving. Make firm and controlled mental efforts to tranqualize your system before getting near your vehicle. You're not crazy at all, you're merely a strong individual who just so happens to be in possession of powerful energies. You might try to consciously direct those energies into positive mental thoughts toward others. You certainly could affect beautifully helpful changes for people with that kind of energy.

Sometimes I get frightened because occasionally I'll see a dark shadow around complete strangers in a crowd. It follows them wherever they go. What is this?

Don't be frightened by this. It cannot affect you in any adverse way.

You are spiritually perceiving an individual's negative aspects of self. These may have several connotations. They may mean that the shadowed individual is unwell; mentally, spiritually, or physically. It may indicate that the individual is going to be in the transition state (death) soon. It may signify that he possesses evil intentions which would then indicate that he is a member of the opposing side of goodness.

In any case, dark shadows always represent deeply negative aspects of an individual.

But remember, never be frightened of that which is shown to you.

A lot of times I experience psychic feelings of uneasiness in certain places. Those around me will be carrying on normally. Why don't they also feel these eerie inklings?

They are not as sensitive as you.

It is possible for a sensitive individual to be a member of a group of people who enter into a highly-charged (haunted) building and nobody senses that a thing is amiss except the one individual.

You clearly can perceive the finer vibrations of a spirit's presence. And you must bear in mind that all people are different, they have varying degrees of sensitivities. Some folks can sense these types of things while others remain perfectly oblivious to them.

Do not be fearful of that which you perceive.

Sometimes I think I'm going crazy because objects frequently disappear in my house; keys, rings, watches, etc. What's going on here?

Nothing that you need to worry about.

After a quick check, I found that you are much like the lady who thought she had a jinxed car. Maybe you haven't noticed, but all your disappearing items have been composed of metal. And, if you were more observant, you also would've noticed that several of your eating utensils are slightly misshapened. Go check.

I do sympathize with your frustrating and often embarrassing situation because I too have this happen to me. When I remove my rings, they'll be very oval in shape rather than circular.

I'm going to share a very personal family joke with you —I frequently wear a metal conch belt that often decides to "hide" from me — *while I'm wearing it!* Suddenly my favorite belt will drop off of me. Embarrassed, to find it suddenly at my feet, I pick it up to find some of it *not there.* It's in *two* pieces because a couple conch links have vanished. The rest of it may not show up for several days, twice they were found out in the yard, once the decorative eagle was even found in Robin's boot. I just never know when this belt will decide to "take off" somewhere or where the missing part will be found. It has become quite a family joke. What's interesting about this particular incident is that none of the connecting links are ever found "open" —they're always tightly closed. The conch links were not "pulled," they simply disengaged from the belt.

So you see, my friend, you are not alone in this. There *are* others beside yourself who must come to grips with this frequently frustrating problem, the problem of excessive energies that are so intense that they physically affect metal objects close by. You need to exercise more so that your built-up energies have a natural means of release so that they don't become so pressurized and concentrated as to affect metal. Try to keep an even balance with your emotions and excitement. Many times this problem is merely a stage of development that causes these exasperating side effects. The problem disappears when the stage has passed. The problem disappears when the power of the excessive energy is channeled out and away from the body — preferably toward a good cause.

There's another cause of these types of manifestations — playful spirit helpers — but this aspect is not relevant to your own unique situation.

Does hypnosis regression really go back into past lives?

Hypnosis regression can go back to the creation!

It is vitally important though that this process be guided by a professional individual who has had many years of experience with the proper techniques of hypnosis and qualifies as a highly spiritually enlightened person.

There are many serious dangers that can present themselves through this process of the mind and, if it is not carefully monitored, there can be devastating results. Merely because an individual knows the methodology of hypnosis, does not also mean that they are spiritually knowledgeable and powerful enough to bring you safely through such a deeply involved experience.

Regression is not for everyone, neither should it be attempted by everyone.

What causes split personalities?

Nothing.

The closest thing to your term would be the mental aberration known as schizophrenia, and even that condition doesn't well apply.

Are there such things, or were there ever real vampires that preyed upon the innocent victims in Transylvania?

Your love of lore has been stretched beyond reality. Your fascination with the fantastic has clouded your logic. And your imagination hath runneth away with you.

My buddies and I like to work the ouija board and, lately, we've been getting messages in a strange language. Do you think we're on to something?

Most definitely. More to the point, "something" is on to *you*. Throw the board away, my friend. Do it quickly before it becomes too late!

Ouija boards are objects of great fascination for people and for spirits. They serve the function of emptying the operator's minds so that playful or harmful spirits can then do their dirty work — all to the wondrous amazement of the operators.

Listen well here. *No* enlightened spirit would ever "come through" in a *foreign* tongue! *No* enlightened spirit would *ever* confuse! What would be their purpose to communicate in code, in a foreign tongue or in a complexing language? You haven't thought this through.

My friends, you're playing with a fire that will blaze out of control — a fire that your foolish board is fueling like gasoline! Your communications are coming from a dark force —the very darkest. And if you do not immediately stop this dangerous pastime, I cannot guarantee your safety. . .or your sanity.

Is there such a thing as the "evil eye?"

Most certainly. Although it is not the "eye" that kills. We will explain.

An "evil eye" is an intensely energized "look" given to another. This look is supposed to possess so much powerful hate behind it that it actually kills. And it has been known to effect this very fatal outcome. The evil eye is real, but its mechanics has been confused, misinterpreted.

We would say here, that nobody can cause another's death with a mere intense stare *unless* the object of that stare *permits* same. And this is where the confusion arises.

I have been the object of an evil eye. It was darkly intense — into my very soul — enough to give me chills and make my hair prickle, enough to actually make me freeze for a second, but am I now speaking to you from beyond the grave? No. When I received this look, I took a few seconds to gain composure. I stood my ground and immediately shot up my protective shield, stared back into the near-black eyes of my psychic opponent and. . .smiled. I smiled and stared. The woman suddenly became visibly upset and rushed out of the restaurant. I've seen her around since then, but always she avoids my eyes. Later I discovered that she was a member of a dark group. I don't know why she was sent to me with her evil eye, nor do I care, but I'm living proof that if one *counteracts* such a psychic force, one stays alive and well to tell about it.

Only your fears can harm you. An evil eye that is given with intense power can frighten you into an awful mental state —one that becomes unaware and "accident prone."

So you must realize here that it is not the evil eye itself that kills or harms, but rather the careless frame of mind that it produces within the victim.

Can you read minds?

Is it really that important?

This is manifested only when my Advisor deems it necessary for the specific purpose of gaining valuable insights. I cannot voluntarily control such an activity. When it is needed, it's there.

Why do psychics waste their time doing movie star predictions?

I imagine it's done either for fame or fortune. . .maybe both. This is not for me to say. I suggest you write to one of them for the correct answer.

How are the spiritual abilities developed?

By putting years and years of long suffering under your spiritual belt.

No-Eyes said that your energies were very strong and that you have occasionally moved things. You must then possess the talent of psychokinesis. Do you?

Not voluntarily. . .and it continually requires efforts placed on its control.

I hear voices all the time. Does this mean I'm a medium or a channeler?

Both channeler and medium are not fully conscious while the transmissions are taking place. You are neither of these. Rather we see an aberration of the mental forces within self. We suggest you undergo psychiatric counselling at your earliest convenience.

Do Voodoo dolls actually work? If so, how?

Yes and no.

Let's just say that they *can* have the power to be effective. This effectiveness being solely dependent upon the mental strength of both the perpetrator and the intended victim.

In geographical regions such as Haiti and other areas of the West Indies where the belief in Voodooism runs high, the people are very fearful of those powerful individuals who are considered adept and powerful practitioners of this form of dark tradition.

The dolls are frequently successful there because the people "believe" in their powers, thereby *allowing* the objects to work through the individual's own foolish belief. The mind controls what the physical reacts to. If the mind believes that the body has been the image for a Voodoo doll model, then that believing mind will automatically begin to condition the body through a series of programs that will produce the unwell physical. And the victim perhaps ends up dying from the defeated mind of self.

Now, there is also another twist connected with this evil practice. If the perpetrator, the dollmaker, forms an *elemental* in conjunction with his doll, then there is little chance that the victim will escape harm even if he doesn't believe in Voodoo. This is so because an elemental is a *real* force, while the doll merely represents the perpetrator's evil desires of intent. The victim can escape unscathed only if he himself possesses powerful psychic forces of awareness and counter-protective measure techniques.

Are there places on our planet that would be considered dimensional holes or vortexes?

Yes. There are several of these portals scattered around our planet's surface, the most famous being that of the Bermuda Triangle.

This particular area also has another phenomenon affecting it at irregular intervals. Currently I can't expand too much on this for obvious reasons, for there are those who will reveal this when their time is right. However, their explanation will clearly clarify why there are times when objects disappear within the area and also why there are times when objects and humans disappear. There *is* a distinction. There *is* a difference of alternating conditions which cause varying affects upon machines, objects, and life forms. This is why there have been times when a drifting boat will be found without occupants and then there are times when both boat (or plane) *and* occupants will completely vanish without a trace. What "goes" depends upon the affecting conditions or conjunction of same that are in operation at the time that the unfortunate object enters into its field. See? And I see that perhaps I've already said too much here.

Was there actually a place called Atlantis that was inhabited by an advanced civilization?

To be sure. There was such a place and many more.

Does automatic writing actually bring messages from the other side?

Yes. But we need to go deeper into this issue.

When an individual attempts this method of communication with discarnates, he is opening himself up to an entire world of spirits (both those of light and those of darkness) who are eager to make themselves "heard" and "felt."

Be mindful that the "quality" of spirit you attract will be in direct alignment relation to the "quality" of your own spiritual advancement. This is the law. This is how it works.

If you are not an enlightened individual and you are merely playing at the parlor games or playing at being a channel, you will attract the lower level spirits who love to play games too, who are often inclined to tease in a destructive manner, or who are of evil-minded intent. This is synonymous with playing with spiritual fire — with the powerful force of darkness.

Many times these powerful unenlightened spirits will play the role of "enlightened teacher." This has become a great new game for them. They will give out messages of profound spiritual concepts, but these concepts will be given in highly complex forms that require extensive analysis and study for complete comprehension. Please, and this is most important — *any* messages that are *complex* are *not* coming from an enlightened spirit! I cannot impress this strongly enough. Listen, the truths are universal. The truths are *simple*. There is *never* the need to complicate them or to present them in terms that man must study to unravel and comprehend.

Jesus taught in terms of simple parables because that was what the people of the times understood best. The parables were simple analogies. They were never complex.

Today the Collective Wisdom remains the same — simple. There is not a complicated aspect among them. If you are deifying a spirit because of its highly intellectual manner of conveying the simple truths, then you are revering its intelligent scam. You have been cleverly duped, and justly so I might add.

Messages that give evidence of foreign tongues, complex concepts or tricks such as moving tables are proof of a deceiving spirit. God wouldn't communicate with his children in such a manner — neither would those enlightened spirits who are closest to him who come as our teachers.

God gave his Universal Truths for *all* men to comprehend — not to just the intelligent men who can decipher complexities.

Leave the automatic writing alone. Look *within* the beautiful being of self, for it is there where God speaks his simple truths to you. Why seek out the servant when you can enter the Temple?

What causes that eerie deja vu feeling?

Deja vu is simply a physical reaction to a recalled event. Deja vu is the "rememberance" of an action or situation of the past that is being reenacted in the present. The eerie feeling is a present life action that has "sparked" a subliminal memory of its identical past life counterpart. It is simply a momentary mental "flashback."

The experiential deja vu can also be caused by one other factor. . . precognitive dreaming. You dream every night. And although you don't always recall those specific dreamscapes, they occur all the same and they are imprinted upon your subconscious. Many of these dreams are precognitive, in that you've dreamed of a future event, no matter how insignificant that event might be. And, when you actually go through the physical reality of that dreamed event, the mind remembers it as being familiar — hence the deja vu feeling experienced.

What is an elemental?

An elemental is the energized product of a strong thought — a thoughtform.

Guard your thoughts, for they are living things. These things have form and energy. These things can possess powerful forces. These things have a name — elementals.

It is possible for an individual to create monsters of the mind. An evil individual can imagine a monster. He gives it all the intense mental force he can conjure up. This mental energy feeds the monster, gives it form by way of etheric energy. This individual then gives mental directions to this mindless elemental and directs it to perform harmful duties.

Be advised that this is not fantasy fiction contrived for scary entertainment, but is fact. Death wishes have become realities by the formation of an elemental from the wisher's intense energies of centered thought.

Guard your thoughts as if they were pieces of eight. For indeed, they can become powerful monsters that eventually return to turn on the sender after their work is done.

My psychic consultant says that all sickness and diseases can be cured by past-life regressions. Right?

Wrong. The consultant's premise is based on the erroneous assumption that all sickness is karmically generated.

Animals don't incur karmic debts so. . .how come they get sick too? Please apply a little logic and reason to what you hear — a small measure is all you need.

In EARTHWAY, how can you say there's six chakras when everyone knows there's seven?

Watch it when you're inclined to be all inclusive and say "everyone," for many metaphysical scholars would not want to be included in your statement.

Actually, it would be more accurate to say that there's over one hundred chakras located throughout the human body. So then, if you and they center your full attention upon seven of these, are you likewise in error? You would be if you held to the erroneous belief that these seven are the *only* ones. See?

By the above, it's clear that it could be technically acceptable to say that the human body contains one chakra (intending to infer "one of many") because it does contain one. . .and two. . .and six, seven and twenty, etc.

However, my job is not to be redundant by repeating old news in new ways. My purpose is to bring a dawning light to shine on the *basic* spiritual truths. And this light can only be illumined through the medium of simplicity. Therefore it is through this simplicity that conceptual aspects of the Collective Wisdom are brought to their basic common denominators. In this manner, the frills of the superfluous barnacles that tend to shroud basic foundational truths are relegated to their proper perspective by being scraped away.

Hence, by your initial inquiry, you yourself have scraped away over one hundred chakras in order to concentrate on only seven of them. The Brothers instructed No-Eyes to scrape one more away in order to end up with the six *main* ones — the Power Point Gates. This, of course, is not to infer that all the other chakras are unimportant, but when we want to know the bare bones facts of a concept we must dig down deeper and deeper until all that remains is the fundamental *foundation* that marks the *root* concept itself. If this isn't done, the foundational truth may be misinterpreted as being the blossom or the leaf which the root grew. See?

Although the blossom and the leaf did indeed grow from the root, they are superficial when compared to that foundational aspect which spawned them, for they could not live an existence without the life force of the root.

Cherish not the leaf, but rather look to the root and nourish same. Let not the blossom's beauty be your nectar, for the seen blossom does die while the unseen root lives on.

I cannot leave this issue without addressing an observation I made regarding popular metaphysical material on chakras. When No-Eyes gave me the Governing Gates information, it didn't take a prophet to tell me the material was completely new and that it had the potential to create a wave through the serene sea of conventional belief of the public's collective consciousness. Therefore, because I'd been away from the so-called New Age literature for so long, I decided it might be wise to take a look at current material on the subject. And I found one contradiction after another. There was no consistency. Terminology for the specific chakras was widely varied. Several accepted listings weren't even made consistent by enumerating all glands, or all organs, or all body regions. One prime example is the following chakra presentation I found:

Chakra Term	Meaning
Crown	General external head area
Third Eye	A metaphysical concept
Throat	Internal anatomy
Heart	Organ
Solar Plexus	General external region
Navel	External body point
Root	Directional term (lowest)

Another listing mixed organs with glands. Still another counted two chakra points for the adrenal glands. Yet all these lists of seven chakras have been accepted without question. Consequently, the simplicity of No-Eyes' wisdom on this subject was like a breath of fresh mountain air.

So in all searches for greater knowledge and the ensuing wisdom we hope to gain, the individual mind must at all times be keenly discerning, for you and I and they must take a personal responsibility for every belief we choose to call our truth.

You transposed the Pineal and Pituitary glands on your Governing Gate (chakra) Chart in EARTHWAY.

So glad you brought this to my attention because now I can properly address this highly confusing issue. Hopefully, through the use of a couple illustrations, this issue will be better clarified.

As with the previous question regarding chakras, I did some in-depth research in different literary works on the subject. And again I found inconsistent and contradictory information. This finding both surprised and distrubed me. For example, let's repeat the sample list of chakra points from the previous question that clearly leads to reader confusion: Crown, Third Eye, Throat, Heart, Solar Plexus, Navel, and Root.

Crown. Okay, we know that that's the top of the head, therefore, because there's nothing higher, the crown must be the uppermost chakra

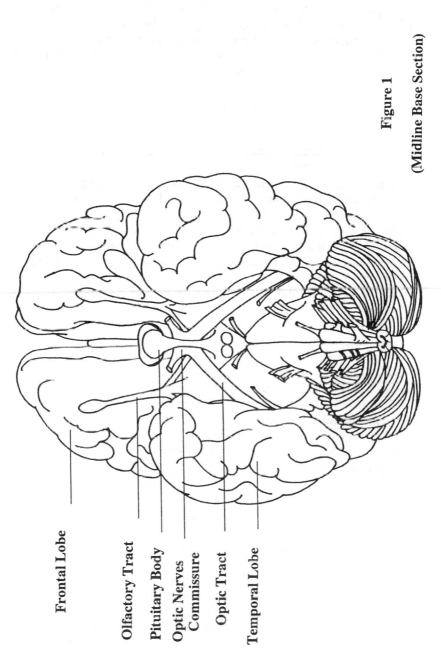

Frontal Lobe

Olfactory Tract

Pituitary Body

Optic Nerves
Commissure

Optic Tract

Temporal Lobe

Figure 1

(Midline Base Section)

on this particular listing. But what's the "gland" name for this pinnacle chakra? Some say Pineal, others say it's the Pituitary. The word "crown" is then too obscure for defining its intended purpose.

Third Eye is listed next. Ah, that one is usually called the Pineal Body or the Pineal Eye! But why is this placed in the *second* position then? If the Third Eye is listed second, then the Pituitary must be at the top "crown" location of this listing. Yes? No? And, in relation to body location, how does the term "Third Eye" tell anyone where it's at? Or which gland is intended?

Throat. Is "throat" a chakra? Or the thyroid gland located there? Are we having fun yet?

Heart is listed next. This is clearly an organ. Are organs chakras or are glands the main chakras? Which gland does "heart" infer then?

Solar Plexus. What's that? An organ? Gland? Sun spot?

Navel is an interesting chakra, especially since it's a reference point located on the body's exterior casing. Is the navel itself the chakra? Does this location represent something else in the same general region - like perhaps a gland? Which one?

Root. Somehow this calls to mind a visual of a botanical. Is there an anatomical "root" in our physiognomies? What part of our body is medically called the "root?" An organ? Gland? Is this term then a directional reference point? What is root? It says absolutely nothing.

Now, setting aside all the above chakra terms save the first two, Crown and Third Eye, we come to the basic issue of this reader's beginning statement. Based on the aforementioned "accepted" listing, it logically stands to reason that the Third Eye was meant to infer the Pineal gland which is usually illustrated to be located between the eyes. If this is so, which gland does the term "crown" then represent in this specific chakra listing?

Logic naturally points to the Pituitary. But many other lists and metaphysical illustrations claim the Pineal to be at the crown location. Clearly this evidences a great inconsistency within the belief system of this singular concept.

Because I never found one inconsistency with any of No-Eyes' wisdom (although I always looked for them), and because this chakra subject was given to her by highly intelligent beings, my Higher Self recognized her words to ring true. However, after discovering so much confusion in the metaphysical literature, I decided to study it at length in an effort to arrive at the root of the inconsistencies I was reading. It wasn't the metaphysical field I delved into, but rather, for this, different requirements were called for. I studied anatomy. . .of the brain. And I found the paradox that, I felt, led to the confusion of the Pineal and Pituitary glands in relation to the two uppermost chakra points. It

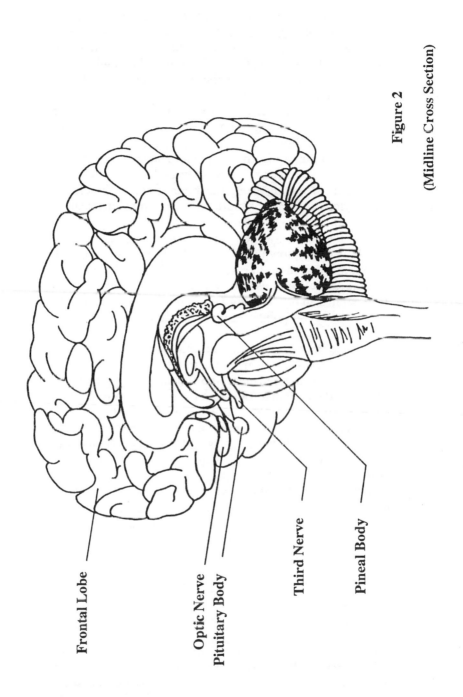

Figure 2

(Midline Cross Section)

Frontal Lobe

Optic Nerve
Pituitary Body

Third Nerve

Pineal Body

appeared that the issue was much like that of trying to determine which came first — chicken or egg.

I'm clearly not an anatomy illustrator, but the following drawings of the brain should help to clarify my findings. The confusion stems from the anatomical "placement" of the two glands in question. This then is the abovementioned paradox.

"Base of brain" does not necessarily infer "bottom" of the brain stem, but rather *center* or the midline point that's located *between* the left and right lobes (see Figure 1). The paradox comes when, anatomically speaking, the Pituitary Body is shown to stem from the "base of brain" position. Yet remember, this base of brain location simply means "center"; it means *stemming* from the brain's *root.* Therefore, this specific terminology of "base of brain" has been metaphysically confusing and consequently has been misinterpreted as being a location at the "bottom" of the brain — which is not accurate at all.

In Figure 1, it's seen how the Pituitary Body stems from the brain base root at midline and hangs like a pearl *over* the junction of the Optic Tract called the Optic Commissure. What does this singular location signify? It illustrates an orb hanging *between* the two Optic Tracts that serve each eye — a *center* point stemming directly from the brain's root base.

In Figure 2, the importance of the Pituitary Body takes on an even more revealing aspect as it's clearly seen to be located in a much more *anterior* position (*frontal* head) than the Pineal which is further back and directly *behind* the brain's root stem (or base). Figure 2 illustrates the anatomical position of the Pituitary Body as being *between* the *Optic* Nerve and the *Third* Nerve. Although this Midline Base Section view horizontally positions the Pineal slightly higher than the Pituitary Body, it is the *latter* gland which remains in the *forefront* of the brain between the two Frontal Lobes.

Although the human Pineal gland has been occasionally likened to the pineal eye of lizards (or *their* third eye), which is attached by a stalk and can be projected, this in no way correlates to the similar gland that's positioned in the human brain's *posterior* position of stemming from the Second Cerebral Vesicle.

Cayce said the Cells of Leydig are a chakra. No-Eyes said they weren't. Who's right?

Both are.

Remember that No-Eyes was *specifically* speaking of the Six Power Points of the human body. She was speaking on the *singular issue* of the Governing Gates. In the context of this specific issue then, she could not be inclusive of those chakra points that are considered the Minor

Chakras. Don't forget that there's over one hundred of these — the Cells of Leydig being only one of them.

There are over one hundred chakra points called Minor Chakras.

There are only six Major Chakras called Governing Gates.

It's important to separate out the gross concepts from their refined aspects. This prevents confusion and seeming inconsistencies.

The subject of Minor Chakras and the Major Gate Chakras can be likened to the study of biology. There are "classifications" of vertebrates — seven specific classes. These being jawless fish, sharks, the bony fish, frogs, reptiles, birds, and mammals. All of these are vertebrates, but they have separate classes because they are not the same.

Another example would be the Equine (horse) example. All the following are horses: Appaloosa, Arabian, Clydesdale, Morgan, etc. But they are also individual breeds.

So too do the more than one hundred chakras have differing characteristics and levels of status. . .some being minor and others being major.

Do you think, overall, that the current status of the New Age movement has traded in quality for quantity? Seems everyone's either a teacher, channeler, or some big time healer.

Your premise is indeed accurate. This situation was foretold. The movement is no longer serving as a guiding light. The movement is in chaos. It no longer has clear direction for the seekers. It confuses instead of clarifying. Therefore have I strived to keep No-Eyes out of it.

I saw a television show done on psychic phenomena. One woman presented has taken it upon herself to begin "certifying" psychics. How can she do this?

When one decides to call self "the judge," one can do this. A deeper question would be this: Who certifies the judge?

Clearly, this is just another sad example of how the entire subject matter has been bastardized into the present chaos state. Illegitimacy is running rampant.

What is magic?

In theatrics, magic is merely illusion. In reality, magic is a non-entity, for then it is a term applied to those physical laws physicists have yet to discover. That which *appears* to be true magic is simply the workings of lesser known laws of nature.

Please consider the "magic" a caveman would revere if he saw a helicopter overhead. To him, his first experience with fire was a form of magic. So too are the unknown natural laws of today viewed.

Magic? There is no such thing. . .unless it is the "knowledge" that unveils the unknown. Yes. The magic is *knowledge!*

Can you name some historical personalities who are now reincarnated during this critical time? And do you know them?

Only with the Advisor's permission has this answer been manifested.

Plato. Socrates. John the Baptist. Judas. Saint Germaine. Benjamin Franklin. Osceola. Rameses II. Benedict Arnold. William James. Grigori Rasputin. Anne Boleyn. Joseph and Mary. Judith, the innkeeper's daughter who helped deliver Jesus. Issac and Elizabeth, the inkeeper and his wife who were secret Essenes and had prepared the birthing place. They were the first to hold Jesus. These ones I've had present-day contact with.

How come you're so against the concept of creating your own reality?

Because it's in direct conflict and contradiction to one of the precepts of the Law of One.

Please understand that THE reality is that which you saw and chose as your lifetime while still in spirit form, before reincarnating into the physical. The reality your spirit chose was for very specific and vitally important reasons — to balance incurred karma and to advance your spirit. Then. . .when you get down here and begin facing the more difficult tribulations you were supposed to face and overcome you suddenly decide you don't like it and then go about "creating your *own* reality," that looks much greener, you try to alter your own personally chosen destiny, thereby incurring greater karmic debt to balance out in yet another lifetime. The true reality is that which lies before you. By trying to create your own better one, you're not facing the real reality you chose to live. Spiritually speaking, the concept of creating your own reality is unconscionably destructive and is counterproductive to the spirit's original purpose.

How come you criticize people who charge money for their spiritual services to others?

You haven't understood my words. I'm not in the position to criticize anyone, nor would I be involved in such. What I speak out against is "the practice" that runs in direct contradiction to the precepts of the Law of One.

In my efforts to make the public aware of No-Eyes' vision of the future, I cannot pick and choose that which I relay. She foresaw the time frame when the Golden Age of Peace and Harmony was manifested and, within this reality, there were NO charging teachers or counsellors to be found upon the land.

I cannot help that which some take exception to. I am either all inclusive in the telling, or I ignore my promise to her and never put pen to paper. It can't be both ways. What was foreseen was foreseen. I do not have the authority to be selective. It's all or nothing. I didn't write the books to be in competition with any other author. I'm not in the running for any popularity race. I'm here for a specific purpose — to just tell it like it is.

Are giants living in the hollow area of our earth?

What hollow area? Please, try a little scientific thinking about such theories as the hollow earth one. It would appear that many people have great difficulty distinguishing reality from fantasy.

This singular idea is much like the one I heard someone express when he claimed the center of our earth was a Black Hole. That specific theory is so groundless that it clearly shows no clear comprehension of what a Black Hole is.

Together, these two earth "ideas" make me skeptical about humankind's intellectual evolution.

I believe that certain spiritually completed individuals can alter or raise the vibrations of their physical being to the point of transmutating or being able to pass through solids. My friends say this is only a soul memory from ancient times. Can you settle this disagreement?

I don't know if I can "settle" this between you, because some folks will always continue to believe as they wish no matter who tries to set the record straight. So then, all I can do is stick with the facts of this metaphysical concept.

The reason (or excuse) I so frequently hear to explain away spiritual concepts that appear too complex for someone to deal with or understand is frequently this: "That's only a soul memory"; or, "You remember that from Atlantean times"; or, "Only the ancient masters could do that." But tell me, if the ancient ones could do such feats of the spirit, why isn't it still being done by someone today? See? Is it logical to believe these things are not possible today? I don't think so, for there are indeed individuals who can alter their vibrations to such an extent.

So then, take heart in your own personal belief. Respect the opposing belief of your friends — just don't bother arguing about it. They'll come into their own knowing when they've advanced to the right level of enlightenment. Arguing with them at this point will prove to be most fruitless and, for you, extremely frustrating. To some. . .the world is still flat. And so in your Knowing be not arrogant, but rather highly compassionate for the lesser enlightened.

If one has total acceptance, nothing will ever change, will it?

I'm wondering how you came to this conclusion. The state of acceptance is not synonymous with stagnation. One's destiny, in conjunction with the accompanying factor of timing, marches on with each passing day, each passing hour. Probabilities and the presentation of choices are a continuum in each one's life. Your theory doesn't take these into any kind of consideration.

Having total acceptance simply means that each day, each hour, is taken in stride as being an unfolding blossom of one's unique life. Having total acceptance means that one does not fight the unfolded events, but rather deals with them and flows harmoniously with their stream. Acceptance brings the knowing that one doesn't accomplish anything by force, but rather by *allowing* events to naturally unfold in a fruitful manner, for many times, adversities are the *only* trail to our destined goals and purposes. So then, in this light, we tread softly through the difficult times because we know we can't always see the purpose or what's on the other side, which is usually a destined direction in relation to one's specific purpose.

Total acceptance is nothing more than an understanding of the mechanics of how destiny works. It is an understanding and a deep respect for the factor of time and how it must be allowed to play its part in our lives.

I heard someone in San Francisco say that, if the Big One hit, he just wasn't going to make it part of his reality. What do you think of a statement like that?

Believe me, if the Big One hit. . .it'd certainly be part of his reality whether he wanted it or not. Can this person walk out into San Francisco Bay and not make the water a part of his reality? Can he just walk across the bottom as if he's crossing a dry prairie? Come on folks, some of this New Age thought is making fools of you. It's making God disgusted and causing the devil to laugh his ugly head off.

This crazy idea of "creating your own reality" has been generated to foster the "I." It's clearly a separatist ideology generated from a dark source for the prime purpose of creating an insulating society. The premise is more like this: "I live for the I." This then prepetrates the general perspective that aspects surrounding the I, especially the negative ones like disasters, the homeless, problems, etc., will be ignored by the individual because they want no part of them. So then, does this sound like a spiritual precept of the Law of One?

What if Moses, while standing before the burning bush said to himself, "No way, man, no *way* I'm gonna be burdened with getting all those people out of Ramses grasp. That's too big a job and I'm just not going to make it part of my reality," and he walked away from it?

Or what if Jesus, while praying in the Gethsemane garden said to himself, "I'm sorry Father, but this is just too much to ask. I can't make this part of my reality" and he snuck out the back gate while his disciples were napping?

Don't you see how important it is to live out the reality that you chose to make manifest. Don't you see how wrong it is to alter the course that you yourself chose for yourself while still in full spirit comprehension of intelligence. People get down here and at the first sign of a little trouble, right away want to turn tail and run the other way. Do you teach your children to avoid their problems. Do you teach them to be as ostriches and just stick their head in the ground so they don't *see* any adversity or problems? Is that what this concept is all about? And if it is, does having your head in the ground prevent a hurricane from blowing your behind away just because you didn't see it? Were you *really* successful in not making that hurricane part of your reality?

Please give deeper thought to these spiritual ideas that crop up out of the soil of chaos, they are not blossoms of spirituality, but rather the weeds sown by Belial's minions who throng about you.

Saint Germaine is my guide and he said I'm to be your helper.

Saint Germaine is in the *physical.* Now! He has had many names since he was known as St. Germaine. Stop fabricating! Stop fooling self! This entity does not even go by the name of St. Germaine when it is within the spiritual plane of existence!

There are many Ascended Masters who are channeling during this time. Our group believes your guides are two of these.

First there is the need to clarify the Ascended Master term.

This specific term is of the Eastern philosophy, therefore it is generated from a categorized set of ideologies with associated nomenclature that is unique to an ethnic foundational basis of thought. Therefore, the term: "Ascended Master" is confined and is not free to be aligned with the pure conceptual philosophies of the precepts of the Law of One.

The above interprets simply by stating it this way: *"All completed spirits have ascended to the highest plane of knowing and Enlightenment. . .where there is but one Master — God. "* This then is the Law of One.

In the spiritual reality, the completed ones would never, ever call themselves "Masters," for they perceive only one Master and that is God. They do not refer to themselves as *ascended* either, for they find no need to distinguish themselves in such a manner. These entities are members of the high elite known as The Great White Brotherhood, or the Brotherhood of Lights. They never refer to any term remotely resembling "ascended Masters". . .only the less knowledgeable humans do that.

And yes, I've already clarified that our Advisors are of The Great White Brotherhood.

It seems to me that, if Jesus experienced many incarnations, his earthly mother and father certainly could too. Isn't that a logical conclusion?

Yes, my friend, that is most definitely a logical conclusion. Indeed, they are both made manifest during this critical spiritual timeframe. They are both living entities of a most touchable nature in your world.

Are there any completed spirits now walking among us?

Know that there are more than a few. This singular idea should not be viewed as an improbable concept, nor should these ones be revered in any way, for they themselves do not perceive their beingness as being a greater manifestation than you or your neighbor.

Returned completed ones give no thought nor perception to anyone being viewed as "better" or "more enlightened," for they perceive *all* ones as being equal to all others — even themselves. In this manner do they set an example of perception that says: Seek the highest advancement of *self* rather than seeking out others of the highest advancement.

What does Summer Rain think of the New Age movement?

I feel the same way Jesus felt when he first saw the moneychangers conducting business on the steps of his Father's temple.

Where can I get an astrology chart done? And where can I get flower essences from?

Jyoti Wind Walsh of Boulder, Colorado does astrology charting and she also publishes a catalog on Starshine Essences called *Starshine Essences and Evolutionary Guidance* listing over 300 flower, gem, shell, and tree essences. This is in addition to her astrological services that are available.

If interested, write to: Starshine Essences, 1705 14th St., Suite 371, Boulder, CO 80302

Is the number thirteen an evil or negative number? There are thirteen in a witch coven.

And the twelve apostles plus Jesus also made thirteen.

I've tried and tried doing out of body journeys and have now come to the point that I don't believe in them as a possibility.

You never really did. That's the foundational point of fact that needs to be analyzed. And, since you lacked the initial faith, that's precisely why you've failed. Your subconscious attitude served as a solid blocking device.

Are the sightings of the Virgin Mary in the Yugoslavian town of Medjugorie valid?

Not as the public is interpreting them, for the entity once known as the Virgin Mary is presently incarnated and walks among you. The Medjugorie entity is a "representational" Being of Light. See?

I'm a Fundamentalist Christian and I see No-Eyes and you as being agents of Satan. Prophets and astrologers are of the Dark Side.

Wasn't Jesus himself a great prophet? Wasn't John the Baptist a man who roamed the biblical countryside making predictions of the King's coming?

Two of the Wise Men who followed the star to Bethlehem were astronomers and one was an *astrologer* who recognized the heaven's configurations as aligning with those that were written in ancient prophecy texts.

If you believe in the bible, then how can you logically discount the reality of prophets or those who read signs in the stars? Or is it that you believe these were only ancient time talents?

I'm a Fundamentalist Christian and you left Jesus out of all your books. Jesus is Lord!

This really needs serious addressing.

Jesus is *not* Lord! *God* is Lord! Jesus' *Father* is Lord! I see a great Christian movement to attribute God the Father's status to His son, Jesus. Jesus was the *agent* of God the Father. God is the Almighty Lord, not Jesus. When Jesus was on the cross, did he not call out to his *Father* (Lord) for mercy and forgiveness? Christians don't seem to pray to God Almighty anymore. They pray to Jesus. They say *Jesus* is in their heart. God the *Father* should be in their heart. I hear much about Jesus. . .but where are the praises to the One Greater. . .God the Father who is the *real* Lord? It won't be Jesus who comes again. . .it will be *God!*

Smoke Signals

It has been said that "Where there's smoke there's fire." Therefore am I the smoke that signals the Fire of Enlightenment that was No-Eyes' Flame of Wisdom.

What are your credentials for writing on the subject of spirituality and metaphysics?

Credentials? I wouldn't give you two cents for some of the "credentials" I've seen some metaphysical "teachers" proudly advertise.

Please, know that such certificates of knowledge can be of little evidence of one's experience or wisdom. Be discerning when these are displayed. There are no certificates for wisdom.

You have a lot of nerve saying what's what in the metaphysical and spiritual realm. I've studied for six long years to be a spiritual counsellor. Lady. . .your two years with No-Eyes ain't nothin'!

Know of which you speak.

Your premise would be viable if those two years with my beautiful No-Eyes was all there was. I've done in depth metaphysical studies since 1960; channelled our guides since 1976; been under metaphysical instruction by guides since 1976; been taught by a visionary for two years; done spirit clearings since 1984; done metaphysical counselling/teaching since 1968; and experienced paranormal functioning since childhood.

Would you consider doing some lecturing in the future? We'd sure be tickled to have you come out to Philadelphia to talk to our large group.

I'm sorry, but I don't give lectures or seminars. I'm a writer, not a speaker. Speaking engagements would only serve to take me away from my current purpose and my family. I can best accomplish what I came here to do by being available to correspond with the many who write. I do not ever want to be unavailable just because I'm traveling all over giving lectures. Family is a high priority for me.

I'm a one-on-one person. Each seeker has uniquely individualized needs based upon their own specific situations. I can only help those people by *qualifying* answers that have been tailored to their specific need or situation. I don't like answers that are given in obscure, broad-scope generalities — and that's usually what group questions elicit.

I will say that I've been informed by our Advisors that I will one day travel and speak in public. However, there are plans laid out and. . .the time for public speaking has not yet arrived. Personally, I'm not inclined toward this activity.

Since your Lodestar group isn't an actual physical living community, could you direct me to a similar one that is?

I cannot recommend any community that I haven't personally visited and spent some golden time with. There are so many of these cropping up all over now, I just couldn't manage to familiarize myself with them all.

There are advertisements for these in many New Age magazines and publications. I suggest you compose a list of important revealing questions to ask them and call around. You need to know what their goals are. How they operate in respect to their membership finances. Any community that disallows personally-held accounts needs to be avoided. Is it associated with a specific religious denomination? Do they provide separate housing? This should be expected. Can members hold outside jobs? Is there a single leader? Or is it governed democratically?

There will probably be many questions you can come up with, but above all, make sure the community you choose is not a monarchy that frowns on the expression of each member's free will.

Are you going to start a school to teach people all you've learned over the years? Or perhaps instruction books will be made available by you?

Most of what I've learned over the years cannot be taught in any book. What you're suggesting would be quite impossible. The spiritual truths can be taught because the basic concepts are concrete and universal. They are immutable. However, the "attainment of real spirituality and enlightenment does not come from reading books and attending courses, but rather from that which comes to one from deep *within* self as each level of enlightenment is opened.

A school would constitute vast amounts of money and time which I do not have. I work on an individualized basis, as *all* of No-Eyes' teachers do. A school is definitely out of the question, as are instruction books. Enlightenment comes from the spirit of God which dwells within everyone, which bestows the enlightenment of truth through the long sufferings and the deep meditations of self.

What paranormal talents do your husband and children have?

These are irrelevant. These are but physical functions of an en-lightened spirit. They are not the "prizes" to be sought after, they are simply a side-effect of spirituality. Do not concern self with such aspects, but rather the awareness of *self.*

I have some large acreage tracts that I'd like to donate to you for your work. Would you consider a branch of your Lodestar organization in Maine? If not, I'd still like to will them to you.

I cannot control what you wish to include in your personal will, but I can control what I accept from individuals. I deeply appreciate your offer, but I cannot accept such donations. We have no plans to expand into physical branches in other states because we operate on a one-on-one basis. Frequently, when a small personalized organization moves to branch out, it loses its personalization, its main purpose. It loses sight of that singular purpose. See? However, we thank you for your kind thoughts of us.

You are one CRAZY lady!

If enlightenment is synonymous with insanity, then so be it. Time will reveal the truth. Let us wait and see before the judge's gavel has sounded.

You obviously have more than a couple psychic powers. What all can you do?

Well? Let's see. . .I can "see" that you have misplaced priorities. I can "foretell" that you will not gain enlightenment by placing importance upon the physical aspects of spiritual talent functioning. I can "journey" into the future and "see" that you will need to acquire an acceptance of life before true awareness is granted to you. Please journey within self. Do not search for the "amazing" aspects *without.*

I'd like to see articles by you in women's magazines. How come you haven't done any. Seems to me you could write on health, child care, family relationships, attitudes, spirituality, nature or a score of other interesting and timely subjects. You might give it a try.

I *have* tried. It would appear that my Indian name did not lend credence to my words. That's all right, this too will change in the future. I had attempted too much before the time was right. I was, in essence, rushing too much *before* my time — but time will cross my path again.

My husband and I have read and reread your books and each time we find something new that we've missed previously. We think you're one of the most beautiful people of our time. Thank you for your inspiration and honesty.

My heartfelt thanks for your kind words. They made a beautiful give-away.

It would appear that you are not the only ones who have noticed how I "packed" the books. I didn't intentionally do so, I suppose it is natural evidence of how "well packed" my lessons were with No-Eyes.

Many correspondents have written to express how, when they reread one of the No-Eyes books, they are amazed to read things they missed the first time. Quite a few readers have written to tell me "how" they read my books. . .they read it through real fast (like eating fast food), then they start over and savor each chapter like a fine meal. This was a great compliment. No-Eyes would've been happy to hear these things.

After I finished the last page of SPIRIT SONG, I cried and cried. I just sat there and stared out the window. I wish more books contained such emotion. I gave the book to two of my best friends — they cried too. Thanks for a beautiful read.

You're quite welcome. I simply recorded a very special part of my life and the emotions that accompanied it. I'm pleased that it also touched others as it touched me.

It was a beautiful read for you because it was a beautiful experience for me. No-Eyes created all the beautiful reads.

Lady, you need your head examined!

It has been.

My head has been trampled through by several highly enlightened individuals. I have been through it many times myself. An aware individual must always be examining that which is within the head of self. This is required in order to maintain proper attitudes toward your fellows, to banish prejudice, to eradicate fears, to gain acceptance of life, and to know self.

Peace be within your loving heart.

I'd love to read a syndicated column by you. Ever consider it? You'd reach a lot of searching folks that way. Just think of all the puzzling questions you could answer for us, not to mention the helpful tips on a variety of subjects.

A syndicated column is extremely confining in respect to the writer's time. I just cannot allow myself to be tied down in such a manner. I need to be free to attend to my obligations, and I need to relate personally, not nationally.

This book is rather like what you suggest, only I get to respond to a multitude of questions rather than one or two at a time.

You don't write with your mind, but with your heart. I just LOVE reading your books. They make me cry and laugh and, most of all, they make me do some deep thinking on subjects I never before gave more than a passing thought to. You must have quite a following.

I don't have a following, for I am not a leader, I am equal among men, therefore, I walk *among,* not *before.* Follow not *man,* but *truth.*

And. . .I accept your compliments with heartfelt appreciation.

I'm a philosophy professor and I think I'm in love with you.

Now you've made me blush.

Thank you for the high compliment, but please, do not take the beauty of enlightenment and transfer that wonderful feeling to a mere person. This is natural, I know, but the tendency must be controlled, for we are all equal in the eye of God. It is natural for an enlightened individual to be attracted to another person of enlightenment. In this light, I accept your open and honest emotion of spirit.

Your husband and kids are lucky people.

As am I, for they are the lights of my life.

Could you answer questions on ANY given subject?

Could you?

Please do not make me into something that I am not. I have "access" to answers when I help people with their questions. My purpose is spiritual truths and realities — not to be a walking encyclopedia.

Please, only *God* knows all.

If you could buy anything in the world, materially speaking, what would that single thing be?

To buy a never-ending supply of food for every poor person in the entire world, and dwellings in which to house them and their food.

If you could have just one wish, what would that be?

That *all* my wishes come true.

I would have to wish that because I have too many wishes to single out. I wish for world peace, for pollution to reverse itself, for everyone to have a home, for greed to vanish, for strong family units, for fair monetary dispersion among the population, racial equality in everyone's heart and eyes, good jobs for everyone needing one, and on and on.

I think your "truths" are a bit far fetched, however, you do deserve an award for your extremely sensitive writing style. There have been few books that have "touched" me as yours have.

I gracefully accept *both* comments.

Your books have been an inspiration to myself and many of my friends. It's comforting to be getting the truths from a "living" person of enlightenment.

There are many "living" people of enlightenment — they walk silently among you. Perhaps your neighbor is one, or that quiet and shy co-worker. I used to be a secretary, a hotel maid, a dance teacher, a receptionist, and I also did composition work at a printing company.

The truths are universal. They can be found within self. I'm pleased that you were so inspired, but remember to avoid placing notoriety upon an individual, for we are all equal. See not the person, but rather the truths spoken.

Thank you for your kind words just the same.

My Spirit Advisor is of the Great White Brotherhood, as yours and Bill's are. They've validated my feelings regarding who you and Bill once were. I'm here to help if you ever need me.

You are not the first to come into this knowing and we do deeply appreciate your quiet integrity and support. Your prayers and powerful warriorship during these times has made us very grateful for your continued spiritual support.

Are your letters sorted before you see them? Do you just read the ones that are pre-selected by your staff?

What staff? Bill brings the mail home and I open and read it. Bill and I are the extent of our office operation. If I'm tied up with other aspects of my purpose, he will help lessen my workload by responding to letters. . .but I am still the one to open and initially read all the mail.

How sad that I received a form letter from you. I think it's time you rethought your direction and re-found your purpose.

At the time Lodestar received your letter, I was in the hospital having an operation. Did you wish me to answer all your questions even then?

Your six-page response to me was incredibly helpful, but the letter was typed and that made it less personal.

If I had to hand-write every response I sent to my correspondents my mail would be backed up to biblical times and I certainly wouldn't have time for any of the other aspects of my purpose, much less spend golden moments with my family.

How can you live with your empathy?

By frequently going deep into the mountain woods to release the built-up sorrows that I have absorbed. It's not an altogether negative thing because I can draw out the pain and sorrows of others, thereby helping them. But I'm most severely affected by the hungry children of the world and the homeless. Their cries are loud in my ears and their staring eyes are clear in my vision. My heart becomes swollen with a painful grief that must be frequently released into the sympathetic arms of nature.

Being an empath, I'm extremely sensitive. I'm easily "touched" by people. And I am also easily hurt. But these are also balanced out by an ecstatic love for life, the beautiful oneness that I achieve with nature and the boundless love my family gives me. There are many times that I cannot bear the pains of the suffering, and there are times that I am allowed to "share" in intense joys.

Whenever I become overburdened, I simply walk up into the mountains where the Entity of Nature awaits to unburden my heavy heart. It waits to uplift my tired spirit. . .it waits. And I raise my eyes and arms to the deep blue sky and let out my wail of grief — my soul song. Frequently I take my drum and release my pain through chanting. Afterwards I rest beside the soothing stream and I'm comforted. All around me I see evidence of the footfalls of God and I know that my song has been accepted as a simple offering at His feet.

Is your dream book out yet?

Because No-Eyes incorporated her dream material with her body, mind, and spirit healing information, I found it best to place the dream symbol interpretations in her health material that has been published as *Earthway.* This book is available to the public through any bookstore. The dream material has also been expanded in the Dream section of this book.

Is there anything I can do to get your books published any faster? Once I finish reading a new one I have a sense of being abandoned because there is no more — you're gone until next time.

That was a deeply touching compliment, and I'm truly sorry you feel abandoned when you finish each book, but there's not much we can do to get them published any faster than they are.

The former president of Donning, Bob Friedman, now president of Hampton Roads Publishing Company, once told me that Stephen King couldn't get out more than one a year. You see, publishers don't want the market "saturated" with any of their authors. . .this supposedly is not good business. I think they want the readers to get a little "thirsty" for the next installment. . .sort of like starving yourself before the big Thanksgiving dinner kind of thing. It's called. . . anticipation."

Do you sell books by mail if the bookstores don't stock them?

We're not set up to be a distributor of the No-Eyes books. The only one we handle from our Lodestar Press is the children's spiritual manual and that's strictly mail order from here. No bookstores carry it.

If a bookstore doesn't carry the No-Eyes books, all you have to do is ask your bookstore manager to order whatever title you want. The bookstores get their stock from the several large major book distributors located around the country. All of these major distributors stock the No-Eyes books and they can be sent to your bookstore within a few day's time. Don't ever let a bookstore clerk say they can't get a book. As long as it's in print — it can be ordered for the customer.

My guide told me I'm to be your next student.

Your guide is misinformed. If the entity were a true guide he/she would already be aware that taking on individual students is not within the realm of my purpose.

Please, if your guide really did say that, this is evidence of a wayward spirit or low-level entity "playing" at being a guide.

I don't take students.

There's another aspect to this reader's statement that makes me wonder if perhaps a segment of the public believes I'm gullible. Wouldn't it stand to reason that I would *know* if someone was destined to be my student? Wouldn't my Advisors or No-Eyes herself inform me of this? In reality, the latter is a fact. So I would suggest that those who believe they're to be my student (or are told this) they not proceed on the premise that I don't know the reality that exists. It must be understood that there is a plan involved with my work. Each stage will unfold at the precise time that it's destined to. And, within this block of time, there is no aspect of my purpose that involves the taking of students.

What does Summer Rain think of the government making a national holiday for Columbus?

Who?

Do you mean that Italian skipper who lost his way looking for the Far East and stumbled upon Native American land? Are you talking about the man who claimed a whole Native American continent for his own foreign Queen? Is this the Columbus who committed genocide upon the original American population? Is this the Columbus who history claims "discovered" a country that was already heavily populated with hundreds of people of various societies?

Well. I think that, logically and intellectually, you must be referring to some other Columbus because if you're talking about *Christopher* Columbus, you may as well ask me what I think of making a national holiday for General Custer.

Why haven't I ever seen you on any TV talk shows? Or did I miss them?

You haven't missed a thing. . .not a thing.

Although I've been in the position to be on several of these, I've declined. You see, I believe that whomever is presented before the public, the public then perceives the featured individual as being a notable personage. They (the public) tend to view the person as "famous" or "someone that's special." I have a hard time with this because it was *No-Eyes* who had all the wisdom I wrote about. It was *her* gentle life that people read about. *She* is the notable, not I. Therefore, it's very important to me that I try very hard to maintain this as a proper perspective to the public. It saddens me to see so many "students" who are currently basking in the light that belonged to their "teacher." No-Eyes was the light. It is *her* light that I hold up high as a bright candle to the world.

Therefore have I gone around and around with editors and my publisher on this aspect. I'm supposed to do all I can to publicize my books, yet I refuse to be featured on talk shows or be interviewed on any of the morning shows. I even shun the radio interviews. What a dud author! Yes? It appears that nobody can see the issue from my viewpoint.

Also, I feel that, because No-Eyes was such a sweet and gentle woman, and her wisdom reflected the epitome of knowledge, I simply cannot (and will not) expose her to a public who doesn't (or can't) distinguish her from the rest of the New Age people who jump at the chance to be before the public eye, TV or otherwise.

In this manner, I feel I can maintain the visionary's high integrity. She needs to be separate from the rest of today's metaphysical personages. She needs to be separate in order to prevent her from being lumped in with the general New Age pool, for she was a wise philosopher of the highest degree. And there is nobody more in control of how she is presented to the public than myself. This is solely my own responsibility. It's up to me alone to make sure her public exposure is only through organizations or medias of the highest integrity. And I am very, very selective. If she were here today, she would not appear before *any* organization or be on any talk show. She would say BLAH! Therefore, just because she is gone, am I then free to compromise her philosophy on this? I think not, for that would show a great disrespect for her.

So, whether you agree or not, this is why you haven't seen Summer Rain plastered in every New Age publication or being interviewed by anyone who's interested, or included as one of the keynote seminar speakers, or making cassettes, or. . ..

Has my lack of appearances hurt book publicity? I imagine it has, but I didn't write the books for financial gain, I wrote them to keep a very special promise. Keeping the visionary's integrity is far more important to me than any type of personal publicity. I must keep No-Eyes in the limelight while I remain in her shadow. I have no wish to share her center-stage position.

I attend all the Whole Life Expos and it seems that they always have the same speakers. My opinion is that it's getting a little stale. Why don't I ever see you there?

I continually receive appearance requests, including those from the Whole Life Expo and the Body, Mind & Spirit Expo folks. Bill spoke at length to Dr. Charles Thomas Cayce and the discussion was regarding my appearance at the A.R.E.

As I stated in a former response, my time for such public activities has not yet arrived (if they ever will). However, in my heart, I cannot understand why these requests are coming in. I find it difficult to comprehend why anyone would want to hear me. What would I talk about? I'm not a teacher or a famous person like so many other speakers are. I'm not in their league and never will be. It's beyond me why people want to hear a shy, mountain person speak. I'm no No-Eyes.

You wouldn't have to put up with that old truck of yours if you just created your own reality by charging for your correspondence and counselled meetings with people. You DO have the power to create a new vehicle for yourself.

No, I *don't* have the power to create my own new truck — to do so in this manner would be to compromise my own integrity. Or didn't the issue of integrity cross your mind?

Besides, I hadn't realized that the purpose of "charging" for one's spiritual help was to obtain material goods. Thank you for enlightening me on that. Now I know what "creating your own reality" really means. . . .

What was it in Summer Rain that was made ready so the teacher appeared?

I found this question very interesting because of the psychology behind the unspoken question that generated it. The reader is really wondering what *he* needs to ready in self so his teacher will appear. However, my circumstances cannot in any way be so easily compared with another's.

To fully respond to this question, I think it's necessary to give some detailed background regarding my own circumstances that represents the readiness in question.

Please understand that I *came* into the physical with the singular purpose of being a "voice" in matters of the spirit. I grew up with several types of paranormal functioning. Beginning in 1960 I read every metaphysical, philosophy, and spiritual book I could find. Bill and I connected in high school and shared the belief and search. We married at nineteen and, for many years, sorted out the truths that shone like lodestars in the darkness. Gathering these shining lights unto us to form our basic philosophy of the truth, I meditated and prayed daily while Bill was at work and our babies were napping.

Then, in 1976, Bill's spirit Advisor came through me while I was asleep one night. It was then when we were first informed that, although we didn't need to return to the physical again, we both volunteered to help bring some light into the world. From then on, we were involved in long nightly discussions with the Advisor. Many enigmas were resolved for us through this intense instruction period of our lives. We were then advised to move to Colorado where our work would be best fulfilled.

We sold most of our belongings and followed our guidance. Upon arriving, we found that the wage scale was minimum and we went through all our savings that was supposed to buy our land. We took turns working because we wouldn't leave our girls with babysitters.

A great urge to write a children's psychic manual came to me. I'd been ridiculed so much when I was young, I felt compelled to do something to help all those psychic children in the world who were forced into solitude because of their abilities. I didn't want them living the early life I had. So, while Bill worked nights, I stayed up and spent hours writing the material and drawing the accompanying illustra-tions. . .disappointment after disappointment was felt as each publisher's rejection letter arrived. I was told by most that the material was..."too controversial..." way before its time — if there would ever be a time. And I packed the manuscripts away.

A job opportunity up in Woodland Park opened up for Bill. He hired on as a propane company manager. After four years, we still weren't making it financially. So we sold our Blazer in trade for a pickup with a camper. We moved to Marquette, Michigan. Little did we know that Marquette's mines had closed down and much of the town was on welfare. It was when we were there when our Advisor, along with others of The White Brotherhood, shared in the dictation of a beautiful book entitled *Autumn of Man*. But when I sent out the manuscript, all the publishers said the same thing —"it's too controversial — it's way before its time." And we were devastated. Twice. Twice I'd written such spiritually enlightening books and I couldn't get anywhere with them. We wondered what our purpose was for if we couldn't get the information out? So it was then suggested we move back to Colorado where one awaited our return. We had to sell the camper off the truck for journey money. Packing the five of us in the cab, we left Marquette to return to our Rocky Mountain home.

Old friends helped with the rent on our new rental home until Bill found work. He couldn't,so he started his own gas repair business and we managed the bills on our own until he was hired at the natural gas company in Woodland Park.

At this time I was waiting to hear from the last publisher I'd sent *Autumn of Man* to. It came back with a rejection and I went into a deep depression. We weren't accomplishing our purpose. Why had we come *back* if everything was going to cause so much suffering, scraping, and tears? What was it all for? Was this all there was going to be? Was this all there is?

So I took the pickup and just drove. I drove through the blurred vision of my tears. I stopped the truck and ran into the woods...I ran right into No-Eyes...the very one who awaited me. The rest you know.

So you see, there was a master plan to everything. The aspect of "time" plays such a big part in the overall scheme of things that we seldom think about it. Things can't be forced. The Advisors were in contact with No-Eyes' spirit for a long while. They knew she would be the "vehicle" for my books — this is why she made me promise to write them. Even though I'd previously experienced such failure with my former literary attempts,she and the Advisors knew that there would be one publisher out there who would recognize the sensitivity of our experiences and the importance of the material.

I hadn't wanted to write again. I had given up on the hope of getting anything accepted. But, as always, the spirit of No-Eyes and our Advisor could see so much farther than I ever could. They had a master plan for me — and it worked. Everyone had a script but me. They know what they're doing and, although I can't always see their logic in some of their advice, I've learned over these many years to take their advice because of their future vision.

So? What was it in me that made me ready? I cannot specifically say. I only know that all unfolded as planned. And,from the time I first had a paranormal experience, the culmination of the plan took thirty-eight years.

There are over 700 members in our spiritual organization and we'd be honored to pay your way to come and give some talks.

I deeply appreciate your kind hearts and accept your offer as a beautiful give-away of the heart, however, I cannot, in all clear conscience expect anyone to "pay" to hear me speak. When the time has come for me to journey about the country, I'll be happy to include your group. I hope you can understand my position with this.

In the future, when I'm advised of the right time for such activities, I will supply my own travel expenses and not expect anyone attending my "communions" to pay anything to participate. This is the only way it can be for me, for I cannot veer away from the precepts of the Law of One and still be within the guidelines of my spiritual purpose.

Why haven't you been able to settle on your sacred ground yet? I thought you were all settled a long time ago.

So did most folks.

We haven't had the resources to purchase the various available properties that would serve our needs. Because of what is foreseen in the forthcoming economic and real estate fields, we're confined to a specific form of financing. That in itself is what creates our singular delay in the purchase of our final property.

What do you do with all your money?

All what money?

I think you've heard of too many mega-authors who make the mega-deals. That's not the norm for most writers. . .that's not the "real writing world." Or didn't you know that most writers only make an average of 35 or 40 cents per book sold. And that they only get their check every six months. That's difficult to budget for a family of seven.

Maybe you also forgot that I don't make money for doing all our spirit clearings or that I didn't charge for the five year's worth of counselled meetings I held with hundreds of readers. So what money are you even talking about?

You seem to continue having your share of troubles while trying to attain your spiritual purpose. Have you thought of trying other paths toward this goal that would be less resistant?

No path will be less resistant.

I thought this reader's suggestion came from the heart, as he was only trying to help, but there is evidence here of a spiritual aspect that was not considered. That of the tremendous ongoing battle between the Sons of Belial and the Sons of Light.

This is taking place on all levels, but the most fierce activity is on the spirit plane. Our Advisor and certain members of The White Brotherhood are heavily involved in these.

Whenever a spirit volunteers to return to the physical to accomplish a purely spiritual purpose. . .they become prime targets of the Dark Side. This must be understood, as the reality is very, very real. Therefore, each time we try to accomplish a little gained headway, every time opportunities open up for us in one way or another, the Dark Ones are right there trying to mess us up.

Our Advisor informs us of the various situations and, oftentimes, extremely complicated maneuvers are instituted in order for us to reach a satisfying conclusion. This is precisely why I need to carefully follow their advice on things. . .they've worked out a plan of action that will foil the opposition. Some of this advice will, on the surface, appear completely counterproductive to our goal, yet when all is worked through, we then see the wisdom of it all.

The agent I once had parted ways with me because she couldn't handle my decisions that "appeared" counterproductive to what we were trying to accomplish. She thought we always stopped short of goals because we didn't go straight forward into things. But she couldn't understand that, to do so, would result in failure — like running into the Dark Side's barbed wire or booby trap. It was too frustrating for her when I had to take my Advisor's suggestions and "go *around* the barbed wires." So you see, my friend, *any* path for me can be seen to be littered with enemy foxholes. . .that only our Advisor can see from his vantage point. Carefully must I quietly tiptoe through life, for this is no game. . .this is for real.

To give one more example of how this works let me try to make the concept a little more clarified.

Bill and I were journeying to a spirit clearing. Little did we know the Dark Side had planned an accident for us. They set the force in motion. Our Advisor's calm voice came into my consciousness and I told Bill to pull over for two minutes. We pulled onto the shoulder and waited exactly two minutes before he asked if it was alright to continue on now. I nodded. A mile ahead we came across a boulder that had slipped down the mountainside and landed on the road. We had to go around. I thanked our Advisor for looking out for us and I thanked God nobody else had been passing along that road.

So, on the surface, us being told to pull off the road for two minutes could've sounded ridiculous to most, but when the wisdom of such a directive is seen. . .it's far from ridiculous. Some would've had us disregard the suggestion and proceed headlong.

After seeing the spiritual matters become "prayers for a price," "long distance salvation," and "guru of the week," the No-Eyes material was indeed most refreshing to say the least.

I deeply appreciate your beautiful compliment. No-Eyes was always refreshing.

It's obvious that you're a fraud! Maybe you'd get some real inspiration from reading authors who are not, like Lynn Andrews and Carlos Castaneda. Your books are laughable and if EARTHWAY is ever printed, which I seriously doubt, I'll probably read it because I could use a good laugh.

I appreciate your right to an opinion, and I wanted to respond to you but. . .you somehow forgot to sign your letter or give a return address. Most people who write me express how my books elicit very deep emotion. I'm pleased that yours was laughter. Laughter is so good for the soul.

You think you're really hot stuff! Your humble attitude turns my stomach! Just what kind of con game are you playing anyway?

Have we sunk so low that we perceive spiritual simplicity as some kind of con game? This greatly pains my heart to see such animosity directed toward another. Statements such as this clearly verifies the great need for God's light to shine brighter among men. I wish I could've helped you with this anger but you too forgot to sign your name or supply an address for me. But that's okay, it's really not required. . .that's what Advisors are for.

I cannot express how deeply moved I was after reading all your books. The fact that you don't charge money for all the correspondence or counselling you do has solidly verified your complete genuineness.

I think it's interesting that your "proof of truth" is another's proof of a con game being perpetrated. Nevertheless, I do appreciate your kindness, for such sentiments serve as encouragement to continue on my path that contains much adversity. Your letter has provided a measure of inner strength. Thank you for your give-away of kind words.

Are you something like a hermit?

Something like? "Something like" a hermit would be a hermit crab. I've been known to be a crab at times. But a hermit, no, not at all. I just very much need my privacy and daily dose of solitude.

I was advised that this question was generated from a visit you recently made to Woodland Park. You became irritated because you inquired of me all over town. The shopkeepers either told you they never heard of me or else they didn't know my address or phone number. You also pestered the heck out of the waitresses at Grandmother's Kitchen but got nowhere.

Please understand that the Woodland Park shopkeepers are running a business and, that business is not a Summer Rain message service. The librarian will not give out my phone number, nor will those at Grandmother's Kitchen or the office supply. You even found out which real estate manages my house rental. . .they weren't any help either, although they obviously know where I live and have my number. I was also informed that you hung around my Post Office box and waited for someone to get the mail, but nobody came when you were there. Doesn't all this say something?

I understand your intentions were only the best and that you just wanted to talk to me for a bit, but it's just not polite to bother the shopkeepers or disrupt a place of business. The good folks in Woodland Park have been very patient with this, for this goes on all the time. Summer brings an inundation of people looking for me and it's reached the point where I can hardly go to town during that season because tourists pick me out in the grocery store or come up to me while Bill and I are having a quiet breakfast. They spot my truck in a parking lot and stand by it in ambush.

Please understand I too have to keep scheduled appointments and cannot be detained to discuss someone's concern or problem.

As much as I want to help everyone, I can't do it properly in a fifteen-minute parking lot consultation.

In your books you spoke of your TV being on when you came home, yet you also told of blowing out the kerosene lamp. Do you burn that out of pleasure or necessity?

Occasionally I burn the kerosene lamps around the house in winter when it gets dark, but this is just for aesthetics. Whenever I'm working on the writing of a book, I wait until everyone's in bed and turn off all the lights except for the oil lamp on the kitchen table. This seems to be the proper atmosphere most favored by my muse, as she becomes very talkative and animated then.

How could you be with No-Eyes in the fall in SPIRIT SONG, yet with Many Heart in DREAMWALKER?

This is not the inconsistency it may appear to be, for there are *two* fall seasons in two year's time.

This needs clarification.

When I wrote the manuscript of *Spirit Song,* it's important to remember that, after No-Eyes left, I sat down in the wee morning hours and wrote and wrote. I wrote as fast and furious as the memories came. There was just so *much* of it! And I thought that I was doing just the *one* book. So experiences were recorded more as an overall view in order to encompass the major issues we discussed. In essence, *Spirit Song* represented more of an outline than anything else.

When I sent the manuscript to the publisher, I also included another which had a few No-Eyes chapters at the end of it. The publisher took both books and combined them. He made the "seasons" consistent. In other words, if I had a winter experience in both books, they were combined.

Also, because I never thought to make a day-by-day "journal" of my lessons or record every time I went out to visit No-Eyes, I couldn't be exact on the moon phases or specific weather of associated dates. A full moon talked about in an experience that was recorded as the month of September could have actually been October. See? A thunderstorm written about on a specific weekend could've actually taken place "during" the week when I saw her, for I frequently visited her while the girls were at school and Bill was at work. So after two years of weekend and during-the-week visits, it was virtually impossible to pinpoint the "exact" day a storm occurred or which night the snow blizzard happened. It was by far much easier to recall what the weather was during the experiences — so the "seasons" were made the factor of consistency.

The fall season I spent with Many Heart was the "second" year. I hope this clarifies this for you.

Why do you contend that you're not a teacher when the public has learned so much from you? You're a great teacher!

No-Eyes was the great teacher the public has learned from. The only thing I might have taught anyone is that there is a right and wrong perspective for any spiritual student to have. Don't ever put your name to your teacher's wisdom, don't ever pretend your teacher's wisdom is your own, don't ever bask in the light that can only belong to your teacher. Be yourself so you can "grow" into the attained collective light of self.

I wrote to you but never heard back.

There are two reasons for this. Either I never got your initial letter or. . .you never received mine in return. And, since I don't have your name on my mailing list or have an index card for you, I never received your letter..

When each letter comes in, I look up the name in our card file and put it with the letter to be answered. If there is no card, I make one and add the name to our mailing list. We don't have computers so everything is in original hard-copy form. If there's no card — no letter was received from that individual.

So you're in the system now and I can respond to your questions.

I wrote you but didn't like getting a letter back from your secretary.

I don't have a secretary. When Robin has a free day off from her regular job, she helps me out however she can. We no longer send out any "secretary" letters as they've been replaced by the Lodestar information form letter. This is because I am frequently tied up with other aspects of my purpose and cannot also be at my typewriter answering letters.

In these two instances, I believe it rude to make the correspondent wait and wait for a response that isn't coming from me. So we send a letter stating that I'm either tied up with a manuscript or out of town on a spirit clearing. I believe that's only common courtesy of good business.

I cannot respond to letters that come in during these two situations because the mail would be too backlogged for me to attempt to answer them all like I should. I like giving golden time to each response I give and, to have hundreds of letters waiting for my attention. . .well, it just wouldn't be fair to either party. At least you heard from us and knew your letter arrived. By the way, I do read each one that comes in while I'm away. If I'm working on typing up a manuscript all day, I read them at night. If I was out of town, I read them all upon my return. No one's letter or card goes unread by me.

What organization are you associated with?

None.

Do you travel to share No-Eyes' vision?

Not at this time, for my time for such activities has not yet come. There is only a very minute probability percentage that I will one day be more public, however, the stronger probability is for my path to veer off into the woods as No-Eyes' did.

Enclosed, please find $10.00. Can you teach me to chant?

By mail? Enclosed, please find your voided check returned to you. I don't expect payment for anything I can help someone with or teach them by mail, however, chanting is an extremely personal form of personal prayer and I couldn't begin to teach this to another.

There are well qualified native teachers who do teach chanting. I suggest you take your time and check these ones out before you choose the one best suited to your own needs.

Please send me four each of your books. C.O.D.

I'm sorry, but we're not a distributor for any of the No-Eyes books. These can be ordered through any bookstore whether they stock them on their shelves or not.

The only book available through our Lodestar Press is the mail order *Mountains, Meadows and Moonbeams* manual for children.

Who do you channel and what is the entity's name?

I've channeled Bill's personal spirit Advisor, my own Advisor and several others of The White Brotherhood since 1976. Our more advanced and higher levels of spiritual instruction came from this source. These entities do not go by names, for they are eternal, however, they do give us a "reference term" to know them by. These entities are of the highest degree in the etheric hierarchy and were our closest friends on that plane of existence.

I'd like to pay for a reading from your channeled guide.

Please understand that, The White Brotherhood, being the highest level on the spiritual plane, does not subscribe to the activity of doing "readings." They assist us because of why we came here. For years they have been repelled by the lower entities who are participating in the New Age game of channeling for the fun of it. The White Brotherhood perceives this time frame as one where people are spiritually de-evolutionizing their own spiritual growth by opting for the quick and easy way to knowledge (through paid channelers) instead of utilizing their energy to spiritually evolve by going "within" and, therefore, growing and advancing.

The White Brotherhood entities will frequently give me insights when I need some special angle to a correspondent's letter. This assists me in seeing a more clear overall perspective of a reader's individual situation and/or psychological situations that are involved but not mentioned.

They will not give readings to anyone.

Will you write more of Many Heart? He was so incredibly strong, both as an individual and spiritually.

Yes, he was very strong.

I plan on writing another book on our times together, but must wait until the appointed time of his arrival manifests, for this isn't to be until after I'm settled. Events must be experienced before I can then recount them for the public.

If you're having a hard time getting the money to buy your land, why don't you move into No-Eyes place?

This is not the first time this suggestion has been made. No-Eyes' cabin (and land) was just a loan to her. The property is owned by others. It's not mine to move into.

Also, the property does not meet the criteria our Advisors gave us. It is just not the right place for us to be for the future. So even if the owners offered it to us, we'd have to decline because we're led elsewhere.

How old are your little girls now?

There is a natural tendency for the readers to think of my girls as eternally "little."

As with all ages given in books, the reader frequently forgets to add on the age of the book. If I said they were 8, 9 and 10, they'd forever be that age. Therefore, if this book is published in 1991, Jenny is 22, Aimee is 19, Sarah is 16.

You and Bill seem so close. Besides Bill's obvious feelings of love for you, what aspect of your relationship is most important *to him?*

Not a moment's thought is needed here. . .his protection of me.

Are you and Bill soulmates?

There is a great discrepancy of interpretations to this word. If you mean that we've always been together in all incarnations and on the etheric level — yes.

Will there be a PHANTOMS AFOOT II? You clarified complex concepts in your explanations and made everything so simple.

That's because it *is* simple.

No, there will not be another installment written on the issue of spirit encounters. This is because one volume, I think, is enough to get the concept across. I believe that, to do another, would only be "fishing" for ways to extend my writing. A subject is far more effective if it's not over-killed. The need to do more just isn't there.

Does Summer Rain have any type of initial perceptions when walking into a building that contains a discarnate?

You bet! But usually the "initial perceptions" come long *before* I step into one of these. Then when I enter, they become more defined as the clairaudience factor kicks in.

Your books have been so incredibly inspirational. You are truly the light of the world.

Thank you for that because No-Eyes inspired them — *she* was indeed a light in our world. She was one of the glowing embers.

Besides all your many fans in America, what other countries do you receive letters from?

I've received a great many from Germany and Canada. Readers from Israel, England, Australia, Puerto Rico, Switzerland, Finland, Belgium, Netherlands, Austria, Ireland, Spain, Denmark, Scotland, New Zealand, and China have written to me.

Does Summer Rain participate in public demonstrations such as anti-nuclear protests?

No. Although it's not that I haven't wanted to — I'm continually told to "restrain" myself on these matters that get my hackles up. I see the wisdom of the Advisors wanting to restrain me from such activities because of the possible ramifications, however, that doesn't mean I personally agree.

When the Air Force Academy near Colorado Springs permitted the "open season" for the deer on their property I wanted very much to race over there and stand between the poor tame deer and all the hunters that came for the fun.

When I see furs sold in stores my stomach turns and my heart aches for the four-legged people who were hunted down for the sole sake of their skin. For the twentieth and twenty-first century to still have skin hunters says much about our development.

I want to demonstrate for the homeless and the hungry, and dozens of other injustices such as industries that wantonly pollute, endangered species, the whales and dolphins, and I could go on forever. . .as I'm known to do.

So instead, I pray.

Many of the New Age authors/teachers/channelers have relocated to a different state than where they originally were. It seems that they've gotten what they could from the public then ran to the hills. Are you planning on doing this too?

One thing is wrong with your statement — I don't "get what I can from the public." I *give*.

Am I planning on running to the hills? I've always been *in* them. I can't say where I'll eventually end up because I don't direct my footfalls. . .spirit does.

A channeler told me that Many Heart was to be my teacher.

Your channeler's "channeled entity" needs to register with The White Brotherhood to receive his certification and guidelines to study.

Please. Please, just because someone "claims" to channel does not mean they really do! Just because someone "claims" their channeled entity is "someone wise and great" does not mean the channeler him/herself isn't being hoodwinked! This has just got to cease. So many are being misled.

Listen. Know this. Nobody can tell you who your teacher is to be!

Have you or Bill ever worked as spirit guides while in the spirit plane? If so, do you know if you will again? Could you be mine next time?

I was touched by your sincerity.

In the beginning we both worked as these after our "cycle of return" was completed. Then Bill was involved more heavily with The White Brotherhood while I became the Record Keeper and worked around books (which is why I'm currently a bookaholic now).

We will not be guides again, but I'm advised that your current one is very knowledgeable and you need to try to listen harder to her voice.

Don't you feel it's your spiritual duty to "convince" the skeptics — convert them to the truths?

Absolutely not. You see, that constitutes a "forcing" of one's will upon another. My purpose is to just "share" that wisdom that represents spiritual truths of the Collective Wisdom, not to force it down anyone's throat. Where does that leave one's free will if I did that? Nobody can "tell" you what to believe — only what they have found as truth. Once voiced, it's up to each individual to process the information according to their intellectual logic and spiritual advancement.

Enclosed, please find my manuscript. I'd appreciate your opinion and any suggestions for a publisher.

I appreciate the thought that prompted you to send me the manuscript, however, my opinion may not be that of a publishing editor you may interest.

To admit that I've not read your manuscript is not a rejection or in any way infers that I wasn't interested, but because I myself am a writer, I cannot also be in the business of reading another writer's manuscript. This is because of the very real possibility of someone claiming I plagiarized their material. This means that they believe I "copied" their work. An author must be very careful with this. And it is because of this very issue that I make it a rule to never read another person's submitted manuscript. I make every effort to send these back by return mail, but this gets very expensive for me when "return postage" is not included.

As far as suggesting a publisher for you, the best advice I could give would be for you to peruse the *Writer's Market* or the *Literary Market Place* (LMP) book that lists publishing companies and what they're looking for. Don't worry if you don't have an agent. Many times authors are better off if they deal on a one-on-one basis with their publisher or editor. Above all — have patience.

You wrote that your girls played in the mountain streams. It seems to me that your eldest daughter would be too old for such child's play.

I'm not quite sure what has generated this question, but in the summer of 1982 Jenny was 13. That may, to some, seem too old to be playing in mountain streams, but if the age of 13 is thought to be too old for that, what must folks think of a 45-year-old doing it?

Ahh, but what fun it is to be so free and playful! Sometime, when nobody's looking, you ought to try it. Loosen up, you're making yourself feel old. Be childlike sometimes — it feels wonderful. The little children can be great teachers. A child's play, like his or her perspective of life, can be very enlightening for adults to personally experience. Children have a precious innocence that many of us have lost.

Play in a stream (walk through it at first if that makes you feel less conspicuous). Hug a tree. Dance in the moonlight. Loosen up and shatter those confining strictures that (you think) spell A-D-U-L-T.

When you first started doing your metaphysical reading when a teenager, what did you read?

Because I wouldn't let the adults surrounding my younger days ridicule my strangeness, I kept the abilities hidden in order to preserve them. As a teenager, I searched out books on these abilities and I read all I could find on psychic phenomena. I'd obtained my own personal validating verification through these explanatory volumes.

This led into the issue of the world's popular enigmas such as the Bermuda Triangle, pyramids, and other supposedly unexplained matters that I recall thinking were not so mysterious at all.

Next I voraciously sought out books on the major (and lesser) religions of the world. These included books on Buddhism, the Talmud, the Kabbala, the *Tibetan Book of the Dead, Egyptian Book of the Dead, Cosmic Consciousness, The Golden Bough,* voodo, etc.

From the religions I placed my personal studies of the writers who were perceived as philosophers such as Lucretius, Francis Bacon, Gurdjieff, Confucius, Plato, Hermann Hesse, Ouspensky, Immanuel Kant, St. Thomas Aquinas, St. Augustine, David Hume, Gautama, and George Berkeley to name a few.

During high school I kept to my room with all these books and I thought long and hard on all I'd absorbed. And then. . .I read of Edgar Cayce. I then had the knowing that, to read anything more, would only be some form of repetition of the knowledge I'd already gained.

And I went within then. I meditated daily, for the Higher Self was now my teacher who taught the multi-faceted dimensional depths to all my surface reading. We built on the foundation that was to solidly support all future ventures into the spiritual realms. The next level of higher learning was orchestrated by our Advisors. And the final stage was physical interaction with No-Eyes and Many Heart.

Whenever I picture you in my mind, I always see you in flannel shirts and jeans. Is this accurate? I was wondering because I never visualize you in any kind of native clothing.

Do you do remote viewing? You're right on the mark. I wear flannel shirts and jeans in winter. In summer it's tee shirts and jeans. I'm totally mountain. Most of my native wear is in the form of footwear and outer wraps for fall weather.

What are your birth co-ordinants? I was amazed to see your birth year in the front of your books. I would've never guessed you were that old.

Boy, did I need that! Actually, the stress and agony I've been put through with my publishing legal problems (trying to get No-Eyes back from an illegal deal) sprouted many grey hairs and defined more wrinkles. Yet, through my deep caring about the books, I earned every silver thread and crevice. Going through that kind of stress for over a year would age a person at least a hundred years before their time. . .and I think it did.

Thank you for the compliment. It made my day, even though I don't feel a day over twenty. . .something.

December 12, 1945/3:05 a.m./Detroit, Michigan.

Are you Edgar Cayce reincarnated?

This is not possible, but thanks anyway.

After I finished reading SPIRIT SONG, I just sat in silence and held that book for over an hour.

You were deeply touched by No-Eyes and that's why you held onto to her for so long. You have honored her in a beautiful manner.

I hate to admit this because I'm a man, but after reading SPIRIT SONG, I cried like a baby.

Dearest friend, why did you hate to admit this? Are not men entitled to deep emotions? Cannot they be free to express them as openly as women?

Thank you for your tears of love, for I still find myself shedding them from time to time. The depth of my loss still runs deep into the heart. Although her essence is never far from me, I miss the touch of her, the sound of the rocker, her flashing ebony eyes. . .the *power* of her very being.

You act like No-Eyes was one of the wisest people on earth!

To me, she was. And I know my personal opinion may not hold a drop of water to you, but she was also considered this and more by The White Brotherhood.

Are you a Christian or a Spiritualist?

Because both terms have been so "shaded" by misinterpretations, I am neither while I am both. Don't both believe in God? A spirit life after physical death?

I'm a Christian and don't believe in your material. The things you write about are the Devil's work.

Let's examine these two statements and get a closer look at them.

First we need to define the term Christian. What is a Christian? A Methodist? Episcopalian? Baptist? Lutheran or Catholic? These all have dogma that includes the belief of a spirit life that returns to God after physical death. They believe in a "spirit" life. Are Mormons Christian? Are African natives still Christian after they've been baptized and still believe in the spirit forces? Was Jesus a Christian or Jew?

What did he call himself? Christian or Jew? If Christians believe Jesus was a Jew, why aren't all Christians Jewish or Jewish people Christians? Please don't be so concerned with "terms". . .you're only confusing yourself.

Now. . .the things I write about are the beauty of God as seen by the evidence within all of nature, the essence of God that dwells within each of us, the need for compassion and love among all humankind, the need to love God and His will for us above all else. Will these ideas come from the Devil's tongue?

Whose work would you say someone was doing if they talked to spirits? Had the power to withdraw another's sorrows or pain? Devil's work? Or God's? How about someone who could read minds? Have their spirit travel great distances or see the future and give predictions? How about a person who could see auras or know what's in another's heart? Are these abilities coming from the Devil? Are they? What about the one who did all these things and was called Jesus? What about what this Jesus said, "All these and even greater things shall you do."

My friend, it is because the spirit of the Lord (not the Devil) lives within us that these things are manifested.

Spiritually speaking, who do you personally admire?

All those fortunate individuals who maintain their strong faith in God during their times of deep tribulations. I admire all those individuals who bring justice, truth, and peace to humankind. I admire those people who suffer humiliation and ridicule for the sake of their beliefs in the truth. I admire the enlightened psychics who have chosen to remain anonymous as they go about helping their fellowmen. I admire a person for having the inner fortitude to break away from the norm in order to follow their spiritual path. I admire the seekers for having the awareness to seek the truth. And I admire all the silent teachers of the world.

I'm financially independent and could provide you with anything you need.

I deeply appreciate your statement, but I would never ask anyone for anything. Our needs have always been provided for. What are needs anyway? A roof over one's head. Food. Just enough income to make the living expenses like rent and power. All these have been provided wherever we lived. Sometimes it took a great deal of energy on our part to work enough minimum wage jobs to match the bills (and sometimes they didn't), but we've always made it through just the same. Times are usually lean, but anything over the necessities of life are not "needs" they're then "wants."

I deeply appreciate your give-away of a thoughtful offer. A give-away (no matter the form) is quite naturally manifested through one's inner prompting of their spirit.

If you don't have the funds to purchase your land, how about trying to be a "steward" on BLM or other government land. You'd certainly be the ideal person to protect a preserve or reserve.

I appreciate the compliment and, although the idea has crossed my mind, I doubt the government agencies would go for it. I imagine they receive thousands of requests to live off their land holdings or to lease same. A request from me probably wouldn't hold any more water than anyone else.

What is Summer Rain's purpose?

The overall purpose is to not judge or teach others, but just to make folks think on certain aspects of life.

I'm here
- to share
- to pass on No-Eyes' wisdom and philosophy
- to educate the public of its suppression of the native American race and to bring that culture's sensitivity and   spirituality before the eyes of the world.
- to sound a last warning for all to hear so that all may make their final decisions to heed or not.
- to prompt people into a deeper personal life purpose and urge them to recognize their moral responsibilities to their fellowmen and their living planet.
- to extend my hand to touch. . .so that others will feel freer to do the same.
- to simply be a "voice" so that some may hear the sounds.
- to blow on the embers and rekindle the fire. . .again.
- to finish all I came to do.

Who are you — really?

Really? Who would you say that I am?

You want the superfluous stripped away. And so I shall answer with the bottom-line fact. I am your sister. *We* are Children of God. That is who you, I, and they are.

Will you please place me on your mailing list.

Everyone who writes me or sends to Lodestar Press for a children's manual is placed on our mailing list.

When I hold your picture and concentrate, I get an impression that there was something unusual about your birth. Were you born with an unusual mark or something on the head area?

Your impression is acute. I didn't think anyone would've picked up on that aspect. Your psychometry abilities must be very well developed to have sensed this.

When I was born, I had an exterior tumor growth on my head. This was located on the crown just slightly right of center and a half-inch back from the forehead hairline. In 1945 it was treated by taping a radioisotope over the area. I don't know how long this treatment went on, but my baby pictures begin around the age of two and, if it wasn't for a piece of ribbon tied in a bow around a tiny piece of hair, I'd have surely passed for a little boy. Even today no hair grows from the area.

All your books were so incredibly heartwarming, but I've no adequate words to describe how deeply SPIRIT SONG touched me. Webster's Dictionary stands corrected, it should read: "Enlightenment: see SPIRIT SONG."

You have honored No-Eyes by your words. Your heart-filled sentiments were deeply appreciated.

What do you read for leisure?

Actually, I get very little leisure time unless I make it by staying up late at night. Then I read philosophy books —not popular philosophy — but ones more in line with the ancient teachers through the ages.

There are times when my work becomes so heavily saturated with the high spiritual aspects and, when I've absorbed a certain level of empathy with the readership correspondence, I need a measure of hours to totally get away from it all. These times I can't just go to bed so I stay up and read something light that will help generate the required separation. At these times I enjoy reading medical novels. I also enjoy reading historical novels set in ancient Egypt. And, when I have the time to read at least 100 pages at a sitting, I pull one of James Michener's books off my shelf.

Have you read all the New Age authors?

My Advisors have suggested that, because of my heavy schedule, it's just not necessary that I do so. They give me an overall synopsis of the current authors' material and their opinions as perceived by The White Brotherhood. I did read a couple by two authors and became depressed with what I read as their truth. Now I know why it was suggested that I not bother.

Please understand though that this is not to infer that there aren't fine New Age authors out there. As with all subjects, there are some texts that are more accurate than others and I would never step down by giving out my personal opinions (or those of The White Brotherhood) on any specific book or author. Everyone has experiences (whether they be physical, spiritual or psychological) and it's clearly up to the reading public's level of enlightenment to make their individualized discernment regarding everything that's read or heard.

Why haven't we seen any articles about you or interviews with you in any major magazines or New Age publications?

Mmmm, I think a little history is needed here.

In the time frame between the publication of *Phoenix Rising* and the release of *Dreamwalker* we were living in Leadville, where I was working on the rewrite of *Phantoms Afoot*. A writer for *Omni* came out to do an article for that magazine. The article was to cover the issues written about in *Phoenix Rising*.

The writer spent an entire day with Bill and me. We talked and talked as the reels on the recording machine were frequently replaced. The writer admitted she had more material on me than she'd gotten on Daniel Ellsburg. We resonated well with one another and she took the entire family out to dinner.

The date for the article's publication was all set and we were very excited that No-Eyes was going to be shared and so widely broadcast through a magazine with such a high readership.

Then the publication date for the article was bumped back a few months.

Then it was bumped back a couple more.

Then it was bumped into File 13. The article on No-Eyes' vision of Phoenix Rising was dead.

But Bill, sitting in the Woodland Park chiropractor's office in 1990, happened to peruse a copy of *Omni* magazine and found an article on the AIDS epidemic entitled: "Phoenix Rising."

Consequently, through my experience with journalists (who frequently misquote or negatively slant an article) I've no intention of ever giving another print interview for anyone. The same applies to media interviews. I'm just not at all interested.

In the thirty years I've been communing with my guide, I've never found him to be in error. He says you're a completed spirit and you volunteered to be in the physical during these times. Verify?

There are many completed spirits in the physical now. Please go with your feelings. Let them be your final verification.

Has your "selling of enlightenment" concept made you many enemies?

Enemies? I have no enemies. There are those involved in the selling of spirituality who have been greatly angered by my voicing of this elementary precept of the Law of One. They've written very interesting letters — unpleasant ones using strong and unkind language — but then, those only serve to underscore their own level of enlightenment, does it not?

I've received threats because of this issue, yet I cannot allow such to intimidate my stand.

Enemies are an aspect that's perceived by the individual. In this light then, I perceive no one as an enemy, but this is not to infer that no individuals exist who perceive *themselves* as enemies of Summer Rain. This then is *their* perspective, not mine. See?

I believe Summer Rain is a "chosen one."

My friend, I truly do appreciate the sentiment, but aren't we all God's chosen? I'm no different than you.

What are your future book plans so I know what to look for?

I've found that, to publicize my list of upcoming titles and associated subject matter, is not prudent for an author. I've learned this the hard way.

Five years ago, I planned out the titles and subject matter of the individual books I was going to do. They all related to my experiences with No-Eyes, spiritual philosophy or nature. When my former agent wanted to find me a larger publisher, this listing of my planned book titles and associated subject matter was sent to these publishers. Two of these future books of mine were to be what's called "pictorials" (photography books with accompanying texts). I wanted to create two beautiful Colorado scenery books with associated philosophic sayings on the opposing pages. But before my first pictorial could be published, one of the publishers who had reviewed my book plans had an Indian-related scenery pictorial released by one of their better-known authors who was famous for fiction novels. So then, when my own pictorial is released, what does that make me look like. . .a copycat writer! I was devastated when I heard this author's book was in the making. I had already had the text done three years ago because it was taken from my woodswalking notebook. I had all the photographs ready to go. The pictorial book was only waiting for it's time to come up on my planned list. I was going to be the first native writer to create such a book. But then it all fell down around me when the novelist's was released before mine was due to come out.

So a painful lesson was learned. My next five books are complete and sitting in my file cabinet for their scheduled publication year. Several major publishers know what these are going to be about. If their authors publish the same material before my own ones are released according to the schedule I laid out, then I may as well just stop writing, for, ultimately, it will have been my trusting nature that betrayed me. And if I cannot carry on an author/publisher relationship without trust, I'd just as soon forget the entire thing and go be a motel maid again. I'm not interested in participating in a business where cut-throat competition is the name of the game.

Do you have gatherings I can attend?

We no longer have the gatherings we once did. This is directly due to the many additional spiritual obligations I must attend to as other aspects of my work unfold.

How are you supported?

We're supported through our efforts directed toward hard work and the synergic sharing within the Lodestar Group as a whole.

What exactly was The Mountain Brotherhood?

The Mountain Brotherhood was the *former* organization we'd established. The intent was for it to be a spiritual information center through correspondence and to provide the public with a place to participate in informal information-sharing gatherings. The Mountain Brotherhood has been dissolved since the beginning of 1990 due to revised directions for my work. For five years the organization served its intended purpose of sharing openly with anyone who desired to do so. I met with anyone who requested a meeting, I spoke to small groups when invited to, and I personally responded to over 3,500 readership letters.

Now, since I've received many critical feminist letters lambasting me for the "Brotherhood" term, and because several new white supremacy groups are using the term "White Brotherhood," I cannot, in all good conscience retain the name of our organization. I can in no way be confused with such a destructive group.

And, since I can no longer conduct gatherings or accommodate the many requested meetings with people, the purpose of The Mountain Brotherhood has become obsolete in that context. For many readers, it gave the mistaken impression that we were a physical community set up in the mountains. Too many believed that we were highly organized with many employees and that we were technically sophisticated like the A.R.E. in Virginia Beach. It was time to clarify these misunderstandings.

So then, instead of The Mountain Brotherhood, we are *Lodestar*. We're Lodestar because I still respond to readership correspondence whenever time permits as this remains an important aspect of my spiritual purpose. We're Lodestar because, through No-Eyes' deep wisdom, I must still work to shed more light into the darkness. She was a brilliant beacon that pierced the darkness. She was my guiding Lodestar. And so it has fallen to me to keep her guiding light bright for others who have eyes to see its illumined power. Lodestar — the night's guiding light.

Know that Lodestar is not a center of any kind. Lodestar is not a physical community. It doesn't hold gatherings nor can it accommodate personal meetings. Lodestar does not hold classes nor is it a source for seminars or lectures. Lodestar is not of any physical aspect — Lodestar is of the spirit and, being such, has the singular purpose of attending to the giving of the spiritual plane's Great White Brotherhood's foundational precepts of the Law of One. Therefore, is Lodestar solely involved in the dissemination of same through the singular media of the written word.

What did No-Eyes teach you that you didn't already know?

She taught me not to be fearful of exploring that which was strange or unknown to me. She showed me how to approach the unknown with an open and discerning mind of perception.

The visionary taught me the beautiful concept of melding the consciousness with that of other living things within nature, in order to personally experience their separate existence whereby one could privately witness the unique harmonizing of the dual separateness that dwelled within the one.

She showed me the finer aspects of myself that I was unaware of and unfolded the lights of new facets of my overall purpose.

Most of all she brought me into the State of Acceptance where all of life's negativity is shed from the being of self, allowing me to perceive reality without the existence of such interfering factors of expectation, anxiety, fear, or the ego. Without these complicating and encumbering aspects, one's perception is heightened to a fine clarity.

How come photos of you aren't on the back of all your books?

I believe having photos of me on the back of four books is more than enough. I'm basically camera-shy and don't care to have my picture taken. It was originally advised that I include a few photos on some books because so many readers were requesting them. It seemed that they enjoyed referring to a photo off and on while doing their reading.

Were the group discussions of your former organization "fire and brimstone" preaching?

Why sir! Whatever gave you the impression former discussion sessions were a hell-fire kind of thing? I may get stubborn and I may tent to "rant" a wee bit, but all the group discussions we held in the past had been a wonderful open sharing of everyone's energies. You would've enjoyed them — that is, unless of course you *wanted* fire and brimstone.

I think you and your husband are walk-ins.

We are not.

We have endured too much long suffering for our purpose to have simply "walked-in" at a later date when all of the more difficult times were over.

We "volunteered" to return together (although this cycle had been over for us) for a specific purpose of the spirit. We connected in high school and have been of one mind ever since.

You're a beautiful person. It clearly shows through in all you write. Thanks for giving us the type of books that touch us — that will be read over and over again. They're classics.

I don't know about the "classics" part, but I do deeply thank you for your kind sentiments. Please remember though, it was No-Eyes who provided the experience for me to have. If any appreciation is shown, it goes to her.

Your children are so fortunate to have been raised with the truths. Would it be possible for you to photocopy your children's book for me?

This type of question came in so often that it began to prey on my mind. I went to sleep with it and awoke with it. Then a professor from Southern Colorado University began writing to me. He stressed the importance of getting *all* my writings out to the public. I commented to him that I'd been very concerned about the children's book because so many had been requesting it or at least inquiring about its availability. I told him that my publisher was interested but didn't quite know where to fit it into the schedule of other No-Eyes books. It looked as though it would sit for many more years before anything was done with it.

The professor then offered to set the type on his computer. And I was so surprised that someone would offer such a beautiful give-away that I didn't know what to say. After I found my voice we were off and running with it.

So naturally, all of us decided to self-publish and establish Lodestar Press as a division of our Lodestar. My university friend found a Pueblo printer to do up 1,000 spiral-bound manuals. A New York correspondent offered to photocopy over 5,000 of our announcement letters and the family began addressing envelopes from our mailing list. And the response was beautiful.

Mountains, Meadows and Moonbeams is now available to the public through mail order from our Lodestar Press. The 223-page manual is now in trade book format and includes over 100 black and white line drawings to illustrate the spiritual concepts. Some children are using it for a coloring book. Each manual is autographed by me and signed to the child/children of the purchaser's designation. The above was specifically designed to make this child's learning tool a very special book, therefore it cannot be available through any outlet other than Lodestar, for I personally wish to sign each one. For those interested in ordering *Mountains, Meadows* and *Moonbeams,* send a check or money order for $16.95 to: Lodestar Press, Box 6699, Woodland Park, Colorado 80866. Please include the child's name if a personalized autograph is desired. This manual is not available in Canada or foreign countries.

What can I do to help you carry on the beautiful work you're doing at Lodestar for people?

Since we don't have the room to accommodate more office help and we don't have the household room to accommodate any other type of assistance, I'd say the best help anyone could do would be to share the vision of No-Eyes wherever and whenever possible. There have been many, many people who've expressed how often they've done this and it's been a beautiful thing for me to see.

If you could be anyone in the world, who would that be?

What a strange question.

The answer is "me." The answer is me because I'm here to carry out my spirit's purpose and my spirit chose this person — this skin — to do it. To want to be anyone else would be denying my purpose. I'm quite comfortable with the blanket I've chosen to wear this time around. One does not, or cannot, walk in peace unless they have complete acceptance of that which they are "born to." While still living on the spirit plane, I *chose* to be me. To want to alter that identity in any way would be to tamper with the very purpose of my existence.

My friends think I'm seeing things and I hope you don't either, but when I visited Woodland Park, I spotted you driving your pickup. You were pulling out onto the highway and I could've sworn I saw the essence of an angel traveling just ahead of your bumper. I apologize to you if I was hallucinating.

You weren't. So now you can tell your friends to stop making fun of you.

In your opinion, what is the best and worst aspect of life?

The best is the great potential I see, both for humankind and the earth.

The worst is the vast amount of misery I see and feel, both within humankind and the earth.

Did you know that it's been rumored that Summer Rain has died?

Yes, the rumors of my death have been greatly exaggerated. One wonders how such gets started. Fortunately I was able to find out. It seems a group of native Shaman women perceived my activities during a particularly difficult spirit encounter. They thought my connecting silver cord had been severed, when in actuality, my consciousness was the aspect that had left the physical for a span of time. The Shamanesses later realized this and corrected their initial perception to correlate with the truth of it.

I heard about how another publisher illegally got control of your first four books and the great stress it caused you. How could this happen when Many Heart was the one who suggested you initially submit your story to Donning?

Your perspective is telescopic — as if you're narrowing your vision down to a pinpoint here. You need to pull way back and affix a wide-angle lens to your sights.

Brian Many Heart knew that Donning would immediately accept my submitted manuscript. He suggested them because this publisher represented the quickest manner to fulfill my purpose. And, in actuality, this proved out to be true. So then, this ends Many Heart's involvement.

Now to pull back and see the broad-scope picture. When we do this, we see many more interfering aspects.

Who I am and why I'm here is more to the point of this correspondent's issue because then the picture clearly defines those who are active light and dark warriors in the tapestry.

John Q. Public just has no perception of what these two factions are doing nor the intense battles that are being waged between them on a daily (even hourly) basis. Be it known that the beginning skirmishes of the final battle are already being waged on all levels and, the light warriors are heavily marked with battle scars. This is so serious and intense, I've no adequate words to describe what's been transpiring. This is no child's play. This is no simplistic psychic games. Shamanistic power looks like kindergarten compared to the power that is being wielded back and forth between the two eternal adversaries.

Both sides have equal power ranges. What makes the imbalance is that the dark warriors don't always stick to the rules — they too frequently cross the lines. When this happens, the light warriors (many of the Great White Brotherhood) have to request God's permission to retaliate in a like manner. When this permission is given them, it manifests in the physical as a tremendous thunderstorm with blinding lightning and heart-jarring thunder that echoes throughout our mountains.

This happened just recently when the dark warriors overstepped their battlelines. I will reveal the incident for you.

The dark warriors perceived an upcoming death-date for my daughter, Sarah. They were planning on making sure she met up with it. Meanwhile, the light warriors, who also perceived the near date were planning on making sure she bypassed it by distracting her attention.

Sarah and Mandy (Robin's nine-year-old daughter) were riding their bikes along the mountain roads surrounding our house. They went down a steep hill. The dark warriors activated two vehicles (one of which was to be Sarah's death vehicle). The light warriors saw the plan and immediately pushed Sarah off her bike so she'd be on the ground by the side of the road when the vehicles passed her. She fell, slid in the dirt and gravel, and was knocked unconscious. When she came to, she didn't know what happened nor where home was. Mandy had to lead her to the house. She was covered with deep abrasions and had a knot on her head. She kept crying and saying: "I don't know what happened. I just suddenly fell. I couldn't remember how to get home."

I debrided her injuries and kept checking her pupils. After an hour we decided to take her to the Woodland Emergency Center. Skull x-rays were negative, but her condition was deteriorating as the physician observed her. She was seeing things and getting dizzy. It was suggested we take her down to St. Francis Hospital in Colorado Springs for a CAT Scan. We did and it turned out negative. And we took her home. We can't afford medical insurance and the incident set us back $1,000 out of our land savings, but we couldn't have cared less about that. Sarah has been fine since then and her 15th birthday celebration a week later really held special significance when everyone kissed and hugged her with: "I'm so glad you're still alive today" instead of just "Happy Birthday." The incidence was a sobering experience for everyone of the family to realize how intense, the dark warriors fight against us.

I hadn't intended to reveal this incident when I was writing *Daybreak*, in fact, the few pages it took to tell this was an addendum to the manuscript page numbers. But when the correspondent's question came in, I knew it needed some very serious examples given on the reality of the powerful continuing battles that are going on daily in our lives and those of other light warriors during this so critical time frame we're in.

The incident with Sarah is only one of dozens that have happened to us while trying to accomplish our purpose. Bill and I are forever stressing to the other family members the vital need to "stay aware," to "be constantly watchful." Any situation can be an opening for the dark warriors to take advantage of. This is not playing Dungeons and Dragons — this is real! This is no game! This is war with the most powerful and conniving entities there are!

And so. . .back to the original question.

It absolutely wouldn't have made a bit of difference which publisher Many Heart recommended — there still would've been some form of antagonizing situation involved for us. The dark warriors try to hamper and frustrate us at every opportunity. Some examples of these are: us not being able to afford to purchase any property after we discovered our sacred ground area, causing accidents, making additional expenses for us, publishing problems and. . .physical manifestations by the dark warriors themselves. This latter has been only with me in an effort to present me with a visual of their incredibly powerful vibrations and to show me exactly "who" I'm up against.

Know they are *real* entities!

No-Eyes gave your Path direction. Did she ever say if your land monies would come from your books?

You began with an erroneous statement. My "direction" of spirit purpose had been given long before I ever met No-Eyes. This was back in the seventies when our spirit Advisor first manifested to us. No-Eyes was simply a "part" of that plan of destiny. See.

And no, she never brought up money nor gave any indication of what she foresaw as being the books' financial future. She did like what she saw in respect to how the public would react to them though. This then was what was most important.

The land money? Perhaps I'll always be renting a house. And, until spirit stops moving me around, it really doesn't matter if I have any money for land anyway. See?

I've heard that you're not especially receptive to those who try to seek you out. If this is true, why is this?

Receptivity isn't the correct term, for it's not the proper perspective on the issue. In truth, I'm very receptive to people. However, the real basis for this rumor doesn't pertain to my own feelings, but rather those of the public.

You first have to understand that I wrote the No-Eyes books because I made a promise to her. I didn't do them to gain notoriety or become a public figure. The books weren't written with the intent of becoming a major New Age figure (teacher, author, or leader). And this is precisely where the confusion arises. It's important to remember that I'm just an ordinary person who has always been very closely bonded with nature and the mountains. I'm basically shy and not given to being comfortable in crowds or being the center of attention. This inherent attitude alone makes me very reluctant to do anything that would give further impetus to the public's misconception of who I'm supposed to be. I did accommodate visitors for five years. I met with everyone who requested a meeting or conference, but the requests have multiplied so much that it's clear to see that people are viewing me as someone I'm not. It's the public that needs to adjust their perspective of Summer Rain, for her identity and purpose has been altered according to that which the public wishes to create of their reality instead of that which IS reality. See? Public opinion can frequently change the perspective of one's identity or purpose. . .which isn't quite fair to the individual in question who is trying to hold true to self and their purpose.

If someone says they're a gardener and the public sees them as the *creator* of the flowers, does this then make the simple gardener a creator just because of the general consensus? What is the *reality* of it? Who the someone *really* is or what the public *perceives* him/her as? Clearly then, the gardener is just a gardener *regardless* of public opinion or perspective.

So then, because I am just me, someone who wrote of her special times in order to honor a very special promise, that in no way makes me extra special in any way. And I have not changed into anyone else (famous or otherwise) because of it.

I'm a shy mountain person, nothing more. So who else would people say that I am? And, this is why some would perceive me as being unreceptive to those who seek me out, for what is so special about an ordinary mountain person? I'm only trying to maintain my true identity and discourage the public's greatly inflated perception of who I am and why I'm here.

When I wrote to you, I received your letter in response but also received an order form for your children's manual. I was disgusted to see that you too have commercialized your spiritual knowledge.

The one inquiry that is expressed more than any other in the readership letters I receive is this: "What other books are you working on? When will your next book be out? Is your children's book published yet?" And, "Do you put out a newsletter letting the public know what's going on with your work?"

So then, since I can't manage to publish a newsletter, I make an attempt to answer these questions for the reader. A high percentage ask about the books I'm working on or have recently published. And, since I can't distinguish which letter writer might or might not be interested in recently published material from me, I naturally include everyone. This, therefore, does not in any way constitute a sway toward "commercialism" by me, but rather an attempt to keep the public informed as to what I've been doing.

On your new letterhead, beneath the word "Lodestar" you have a subhead of "the Brotherhood of Light." What does that stand for?

First let me explain that the former main title of our group, The Mountain Brotherhood, disturbed me. In essence, it didn't really encompass what we were about. It was too confining to give the impression we were just a brotherhood of the *mountains*. We were about so much more than that and I wasn't restful with it.

After giving much contemplation and meditation time on it, the thought came to me that, because of our former lifetimes, we were actually here again to bring light back into spiritual concepts and to straighten out the so-called New Age aspect. In particular, I reentered this time frame to again blow on the ember and rekindle the flame of the way. So then, that, in conjunction with our close association with the highest spiritual entities of the Great White Brotherhood, led to them telling me that our group is actually a "Brotherhood of Lights" meaning the light entities — the warriors of light that encompass all highly spiritual intelligent entities. See? So although we are now generally known as Lodestar, we are also the Brotherhood of Lights. There would be no other way to word what we are. And, due to these entities of light and their beautiful explanation of this, my concern with the feminists and their shallow objections to the word "brotherhood" quickly fell by the wayside. So too did the concern over the negative groups who have coined their organizations with the word, for we are indeed their direct counterpart — we are the Brotherhood of *Lights*.

I don't know how you expect anyone to listen to you. You remind me of a clown.

Perhaps.
You see, I didn't write the books expecting anything. I merely wrote them to hold true to a very special promise made. So then, if keeping to that promise makes me a clown then, perhaps that's just what I am. . .the clown. . .the clown everyone laughed at. . . until the clown was gone.

Please don't stop writing. I know many people who are ready to buy anything you write, including me.

Your kind sentiment served as a beautiful give-away of the heart and I graciously accept it, however, I will continue writing as long as I feel I've something spiritually-meaningful to convey.

Your writings of your mountain experiences are very mystical. Do you do a few lines (cocaine) before you go into the woods? At these times, were you high on something?

You bet I was. I was high on nature! Or didn't you think there was any truth behind "a Rocky Mountain High." Who needs drugs when nature itself gives a *natural* high?

Do you know everything? You seem so knowledgeable.

A couple of major observations I've made in life are the following: those who say they know everything are the fools and, those who say they know nothing are the wise ones.

And that pretty well sums up my answer.

Do you belong to any radical organizations like Greenpeace or Save The Earth?

I'm not sure what you mean by "radical" when associating the word to the above organizations, but I don't belong to any established organization. This is because of my Advisor's caution to not be listed among the membership roster of any organizations that anyone could interpret as being somewhat radical in their methods.

However, this in no way prevents me from acting secretly and in my own manner when I see an injustice that needs to be righted. Some who know of my silent activities have more than once referred to Bill and I as "the Midnight Raiders."

Out of all the silent raids we've done, I can only speak of two because the others would be too revealing.

There was a large company that was Colorado Spring's largest employer. One of our closest friends worked there during the afternoon shift. Mostly women worked at huge machines that wrapped packages with heat-shrink plastic. In the middle of summer the building's heat climbed to over 90 and all the women were literally getting sick and fainting.

When our friend told of how unbearable it was I found that the situation had been passed to my own conscience. I laid awake that night thinking about those poor women who had complained about their hot working conditions and supervision did nothing about it. I couldn't sleep with the new burden on my mind.

So I got up and took a thick, black marker and wrote on a piece of typing paper. I wrote: PEOPLE ARE JUST DYING TO WORK AT ....!! THEY'RE DROPPING LIKE FLIES FROM THE HEAT INSIDE!! ....WHERE IS OSHA WHEN YOU NEED IT????

The next day at my own office job, I went to the copy room and quickly ran off hundreds of copies of my little sign. And that night, while our friend and her co-workers were sweating over their hot machines and all the building's doors were open to the muggy night air; we got our little girls out of bed, bundled them into our Blazer (jammies and all) and took off on a midnight run to the company. We slipped a copy of our sign beneath every windshield wiper in the car lot. We actually snuck up to the opened doors of the company and slid some flyers over the floor. Then we made sure the newspaper building got their share when Bill walked into the night copy room and just laid a dozen flyers on the counter and walked back out into the night. He then left some at the health department.

After we got back home and put the girls into bed again, we talked about what we'd done. Would it do any good? Could two people make a difference when the entire work force couldn't manage a change in their conditions? We didn't know. We did know that we felt a real uplift of spirits because we'd acted on our conscience and tried to do something to help.

The next day our friend told us about the big commotion. Everyone was talking about the mysterious Midnight Raiders. Our friend said that supervision made a big deal of it and took each employee into a room to interrogate them. Did they know who did it? Did they know anything about it? Of course, we never told our friend what we were going to do so she didn't have to lie, but I'm sure she suspected it was us. She could hardly keep a straight face in front of her supervisor.

Then we confirmed that we'd done it.

And, that afternoon when she went to work, the place was *filled* with *high-powered fans!* To this day, the Midnight Raiders have been a mystery.

That was many years ago. Since then, whenever a local injustice is brought to our attention or when big business steps on the little guy, we analyze it and, if we can help at all. . .the silent Midnight Raiders ride again.

I still have my original copy of that first flyer. And when we recount the story with our girls, they grin ear to ear to think they were a part of it. . .even though they were the Little Raiders in jammies hiding down in the truck waiting for the Mama and Papa Raiders to finish their work.

There was another incidence where a business had set up in one of the towns I was living in. An employee was a friend of mine and his story was incredible. Seems they were raking in thousands of dollars a day from one department (banks of phones). I did some investigating and found they were nothing but a "front" that operated a public scam.

I sent the owner of the company one note. It read: "I KNOW WHO YOU ARE AND WHAT YOU'RE DOING. . .SO DOES THE AT-TORNEY GENERAL."

The next day the office was closed. The employees were locked out. There was a note on the door informing the workers that they'd be closed for a week. We heard that the owners were vacating their home (moving belongings out). Then, when the employees returned, the owner was outside in his car passing out paychecks and telling the workers to cash them right away because he was closing the business account at the bank. Two days later, the office space was for rent. Businesses that take advantage of a trusting public operate all over the country but. . .not in my little town. Not while the *pen* wields such power.

So although I don't belong to any kind of activist organization, don't for a moment think I'm not plenty active. . .in my own quiet way. One (or two) *can* make a difference. What I'm silently doing can be done by anyone who sees an injustice. Everyone can be a Midnight Raider. Together, they can make a better world. So if you know of cases that bother your own conscience, don't write me about it, take the responsibility and your own initiative to take an active part in changing the world. It can be as simple as a few well chosen words to the right people.

Did you know that you were No-Eyes' mother in another life. The circle was completed when your soul returned to be her last student. The mantle was passed to you with her departure from this realm.

This thought came to you while reading the No-Eyes series, but it was just that — an idea — a possibility. It is not fact.

No-Eyes and I spent a lifetime together in 650 A.D. as members of the Spirit Clan of the Anasazi. We were not related in any way and never were. . .in any lifetimes.

Please be careful when such ideas form. Don't interpret them as solid facts. Look at thoughts as possibilities and *then* check them out before claiming them as fact.

Also, the information you provided me with gave clear indication that a portion of the public hasn't a solid grasp of who I am or what I'm about. It implies that perhaps I'm in the dark on some aspects of myself.

Please understand that with my close association with our Advisors and others of the Great White Brotherhood who comprise the Lodestar Advisory Council, I'm always well informed. I'm thoroughly cognizant of all aspects of all my past lives and, I also know the detailed plan for this life's destiny.

Our group believes that Summer Rain's main purpose for in-carnating during this time was because she's to be a bridge that unites races.

There are many working in this capacity, however, in my *own* case, my singular purpose for being here is to reveal the *entire* spectrum of the beautiful light prism of truth.

I want a teacher like Summer Rain had. I want to be taught by someone just like No-Eyes.

You will not have your teacher until you've stopped saying "I want." Until then, you will not be ready. Shed the *wants* and especially the "I." These are clear indicators that you are not living within acceptance of your destiny, for all unfolds according to a specific plan. This includes the meeting of your intended teacher *if it was deemed to be manifested.*

I heard about the major surgery you had just before Thanksgiving of 1990 and that you didn't have any medical insurance nor money to pay the medical bills. The fact that you didn't let your devoted readers know of this was like a slap in the face. Don't you think we would've been honored to be able to help you after all the help you've given us?

You made me very sad to think I've acted in a manner that compared to a slap in my reader's face. And your sentiments were indeed shared by others, yet I just could not ever burden my readers by requesting financial help. That may be impossible to comprehend, but I couldn't live with myself if I didn't follow my heart in issues such as this.

There may have been those eager to assist me in paying off the high medical bills, but there would also be those who would've been outraged at my request for help. In dealing with the public, I've learned that for everyone who would be anxious to help me out in a special time of crisis, there would also be the polarity of those made indignant by my request. So in order to avoid upsetting anyone one way or the other, I follow the lead of my heart and just keep my personal problems to myself. I regret that my silence was a slap in your face, but please try to see a portion of my own perspective on things like this. People have so much misery and sadness in their own lives. . .they don't also need to carry mine. I've come to lighten burdens, not make them heavier.

The Thanksgiving Day of that year was the best ever. My family was worried sick that God would call me Home during my operation. And God had seen fit to let me remain with them. I guess He saw that I had more work to do. That Christmas was the first one that no presents were exchanged due to my medical expenses, but God Himself gave each family member the most precious Christmas Gift possible — that of a life — a life of a family's wife and mother. It was a beautiful Christmas. It was one that brought home the precariousness of life and how incredibly happy we were that one was spared for an extended span of time. The lack of material presents beneath the tree wasn't even noticed.

So, my friend, perhaps by sharing our holiday joy will ease your mind a bit. The medical bills will be chipped away at, but they are nothing compared to the *real* gift we all received in our hearts that year.

My spirit guide is of The White Brotherhood and he inferred that your operation had a great significance. Is this true?

Every operation involving major surgery is of great significance, for it clearly provides an opening door through which the spirit may exit the physical and decide not to return through.

I experienced seven hours of intense stomach pains and later discovered that they coincided with your own gallbladder attack. What does this mean?

Because of who you are, you experienced a spiritual empathy that manifested in the physical. You were directly in tune with my own seven hours of pain.

I can't get the idea out of my mind that your operation was not caused by a physical aspect. Am I way off base with this or not?

When Bill and Sarah donned surgical gloves and dissected my gallbladder tissue in our kitchen, they found and counted out 188 stones. That is very physical. Yet those physical stones were indeed made manifest by a non-physical aspect.

I never thought someone like you could be affected by something as common as a gallbladder attack. There's something very odd about the whole thing and I can't for the life of me put my finger on it.

Your spiritual awareness is sparking, but not quite catching fire here. This is what's so troubling to you. It's like having a good thought then losing it. Perhaps if you meditate a little longer on the issue, the thought will solidify for you. Dear friends, because so many of you have had special spiritual promptings regarding my operation and have certain feelings about it, I decided to talk about it.

Many readers write me and chastise me for withholding information they know I have. They say "let *us* decide whether or not we're ready for it." And so I shall honor your request in this one instance.

First let me review the fact that I volunteered to enter the physical for this time frame. I knew there was a plan and that a specific path was laid out for my destiny here. And, in keeping with that plan, I've endeavored to tread softly through my life by following the strict directives of our guides each step of the way. There are critical junctures along my trail that must be approached and crossed. There are rigid rules and precepts that I must adhere to. Material aspects mean nothing to me. The spiritual purpose comprises my daily hours and directs my activities. I'm here for several reasons, just as I have been during most of my past lives. I cannot veer from the plan. There are designated times for each stage of my life purpose. Such is the reason I've not been a public figure. . .the time for such has not yet arrived.

So, in keeping with the above facts, I will detail the event that is causing so many of you spiritual consternation over my sudden operation.

For approximately two months before the final gallbladder attack, I'd awake several times a week with the feeling that I'd been socked in the solar plexus area. Accompanying this uncomfortable feeling was an intense ache in my upper back that corresponded with the frontal pain. I'd eat something and shortly thereafter, I'd feel better. I've never been one to run to the doctors for minor aches and pains so I dismissed the morning discomforts. During these two months though, I also was becoming more and more depressed and deeply sympathetic with the world's misery. I'd emotionally withdraw from the family. I'd become greatly irritated and very stressed out. At the drop of a hat I'd start weeping for the homeless, the abused, the poor and the hungry children of the world. My publishing problems added to the stresses I'd been piling upon myself. Our financial problems added more weight. But most of all, I couldn't stop thinking of all the incredible misery people were suffering from. I was down all the time and I was an absolute crab around those I loved. It seemed that the darkness intensified each day until I'd just sit in the living room in the evening and stare into space with all the blackness I felt with the world's negativity.

Then, on November 3rd, immediately after we'd had pizza for dinner, I began having agonizing pains in the same area in which I'd formerly felt like I'd been socked. From seven in the evening until one in the morning, I curled up in agony trying to find a comfortable position. Although Bill urged me to go to the emergency center in Woodland Park, I refused, thinking the pain would pass. Finally he and Sarah drove me down to St. Francis hospital in Colorado Springs. I was crying from the pain that wouldn't pass. Finally at 2 a.m. Sunday morning, I was given Novocaine to drink. The pain subsided enough for me to lay curled up on my side. After a sonogram was taken the doctor announced that my gallbladder had to come out. . .it looked to be full of stones.

What the medical team couldn't understand was why I didn't have months and months of acute pain before the organ got so bad. Technically, I should've been in months ago.

On Monday, November 5th, I was scheduled to be operated on. The gallbladder was going to be removed.

Bill and my three girls were there. When they wheeled me down to the operating room holding area, Bill was at my side holding my hand. The anesthesiologist came in. He was a friendly man who had bright eyes. He was all smiles and announced that his name was Dr. Gabriel. I looked over to Bill and said: "Everything's going to be just fine." The doctor's name hadn't been lost on him either.

When I was taken into the operating room, and I felt the anesthesia begin to take effect, I told the operating team goodbye. And I left. I was in recovery for an hour and a half.

When I was brought back up to my room, Bill and my girls were there. I was hooked up to a self-dispensing pain-killer machine and, every ten minutes, Sarah pressed the button that dripped morphine into my veins. I drifted in and out of consciousness.

During this time, I was making some very odd physical movements. Once I was moving my head as if I was smelling something. Bill asked me what I was doing. I said, "smelling the flowers." Then I was shaking my head. Sarah asked me what I was doing. "I'm letting the wind through my hair." I jerked my legs. "I'm running through the field of flowers." I twitched my fingers. "I'm releasing the animals from the refrigerator in the lab." I was experiencing the most beautiful visions. I was smelling flowers in front of my nose. I was running in a beautiful flower-strewn field with the wind blowing in my hair. I was freeing the helpless animals.

Finally when I awoke more, Bill informed me that the doctor said my gallbladder was the worst he'd ever seen. He estimated that it had over 100 stones in it and that I should've had months of acute pain before it got that deteriorated. Then Bill held up a plastic container. The black tissue inside was incredibly ugly. I looked at it. I looked at all the stones embedded in it. I wanted to cry, but also felt an overpowering sense of relief, for my deep and black depression had been removed with the sick organ. Although I was very sore, I felt incredibly light and happy. My family surrounded me and with tears in their eyes said, "Mom, I'm so happy you stayed with us."

Before my operation, Bill contacted several of our close friends to let them know what was going on. Two of these were Dieanna and Jim (sister and brother) who shared an ancient past life with us. Dieanna was Elizabeth and Jim was Isaac, the innkeeper and his wife who were secret Essenes. Our friend Robin was their daughter, Judith.

Dieanna was devastated that I was going to be operated on. She timed a private ceremony to coincide with the hours of my operation and recovery. By Dieanna's permission, the following reprint of her letter to me recounts what this spiritually-developed lady saw. I think her experience will explain and clarify many questions many of my readers have regarding my operation. Dieanna's letter expresses it far better than I ever could. The letter:

Hello my dear friend and sister,

After talking with Bill on the phone, he confirmed that you might want to know what transpired here while you were being operated on there. As soon as Bill told me of your operation, I knew exactly what I needed to do and fast.

I went into my special room and began a healing medicine wheel. This was to be the most special of all and the most important I ever made so far. I knew that I was very much in my power and felt confident that I would connect with Great Spirit and our many guides.

I gathered together my most sacred stones and medicine. . .I set out small medicine bundles filled with sage and tobacco in the four corners. In the center I placed your picture along with Bill's, for I knew of his great concern. To this circle I set things of the earth for grounding and Mother Love. I placed many obsidian stones and protection stones in the South. I used citrine geodes and pyrite, many healing agates and stones for purification of the body. I placed my golden beaded rosary around your pictures along with my Mother Mary medallion and picture. On top of your pictures I put a very special small, but powerful, clear quartz cluster. Many feathers, sage, cedar, etc. I took the large bundle of sage that you had given to Jim to give me that I had wrapped with red ribbon and placed over your heads. I put pointing toward your heads, a very large healing Herkimer Diamond. Over to the right of your shoulder I set a small red horse. Then I proceeded to place three large rose quartz stones then I began the outer circle of many very sacred clear crystal points On the very top in the North I set a large amethyst that I had just had energized by my friend while she was in the power spots in Sedona, Arizona. The outside of the circle I had spread tobacco.

My medicine wheel was complete except for the white candle I set in the North and the rose candle in the South.

Once everything was in place, I began burning sage to smudge my energy and the room. I calmed myself and gave thanks to Grandfather and the Keepers of the Four Directions and Gates and to Mother Earth. I gathered my energy together and called upon divine intervention of thy Father's Will to send healing energy and strength into your being-ness and body. I stated your name and situation and that I was asking with all of my love that you receive divine healing. The things I saw and felt were so profound. I had to deal with my own confusion and sadness that you had to suffer. . .I wanted to understand so that I could be clear to send more healing.

I saw the hospital. I saw and felt the drugged condition of your body in the operating room. I saw the wavering of White Light as you were leaving your body to be operated on. I saw you looking at your family and the immense love for Bill and his suffering. Yet you also knew that you had work to do. I then saw you standing outside your room naked. There was a tree nearby. In this tree was the most astounding Owl. . .so filled with wisdom and concern, so vibrant and beautiful. Then I saw on a pole, a magnificent feathered headdress blowing in the wind. I drew my attention back to your body. . .there were guides watching in a circle around you.

Then Jim called (interrupted the vision). He wanted to know what I was seeing, for he also repeated the same ceremony in his home. We had seen almost the identical scenes except for the headdress I told him that my Third Eye was in such agony and that I felt so sick to my stomach and disoriented. . .this he also was experiencing. I told him I was waiting half an hour and going back under.

I went back into my room and started some deep breathing to put me back into a deep state of acceptance. I also put my Indian flute tape on, this seemed to help me achieve a deeper level. I felt myself leaving my body. This time I was determined to find out why you had to go through this suffering. I was so concerned and knew something was happening that was of great importance.

I saw your body still on the operating table, it was open. . . there were many guides as well as yourself in a circle around your body, although energy and healing was being administered to your etheric body as well.

I saw Star Brethren as well as Archangels and someone else very special with you. He was very handsome with jet black hair and the most loving beautiful golden aura all around him. I knew it was Brian Many Heart. [It was actually Bill's Guide.]

At this time I saw them examining the gallbladder. They were shaking their heads in astonishment, the many holes and stones and dark decay. I needed understanding. . .why? Why did this need to happen?

The guides and others moved to surround the doctors and gallbladder, they were directing energy to it as if to nullify and cleanse it. I didn't know at this time that my brother would be talking to Robin in about ten minutes. I watched more intently as they moved to your body. . .[spirit] doctors and the guides and others. . .they were doing amazing things, cleansing and accelerating the bodies. They were *aware of my presence and concern. . .it was then that they implanted in my mind these words. . ."Mary sacrificed herself this day to prevent, help or stop a terrible global incident from happening." Yet this did not satisfy my mind. . .I knew there was more, gently they told me that "the decay in the body was so extreme because, for the past year, she had actually taken on the disease of the world and earth. . . that her body became a receptacle of the disease as a sacrifice. But now it was over. . .that no longer would this be necessary because all people and things must take responsibility for what they create. That you were being cleansed and prepared for new things to come.*

This made much sense to me and I had understanding. I added my energy and love to theirs as we sent healing to your body and you were ready to go into the recovery room. They would remain with you for a while and assured me that the transition into the body would not be traumatic for you.

I stayed within the energy for sometime, falling off into a deep state of meditation, then the phone rang. It was Jim asking how I was doing. I was still very out-of-it. He then proceeded to tell me that he had spoken to Robin and that she had said you came through the operation and were in recovery. . .just as I'd seen it. . .then he went on to explain how bad the gallbladder was. This I also knew. . .so I received confirmation and felt confident you would be on your way to a happier life.

When I went back into meditation, my spirit went up to your resting body after you were back in your room. I laid wild yellow and white daisies on your chest so that the aroma of nature would calm and soothe you. Then I withdrew them when I felt the guides sending you beautiful visions to enter. I didn't want to intrude on their manifestations and your interaction with them.

Mary, of course this all was only my seeing the situation as it was presented to me. . .but I have no doubt at all. . .nor do I question any longer the reasoning for this operation. Spirit was kind enough. . .knowing of my love for you to allow me to see and understand firsthand, and I believe what I saw was the truth. . .it was too real not to be. I love you Sweet Mary. . .if there is anything I can ever do to help, I am here ever ready, and you will continue to be in my heart, thoughts and prayers. [end of letter]

Dieanna's ceremonial vision has been confirmed by our guides. The antics I did after I was in my room verified the flowers Dieanna held before my nose. When I moved my nose to follow the scent, that was when she was removing them in deference to the guides' visions that were being sent. She remembered having impressions of meadows coming into view. That was when I was running and shaking my hair in the wind.

I later found out that the "global incident" that was averted was another manmade virus that was about to be loosed upon the world. It was more potent than AIDS. It would've affected millions.

I had more than a little trouble with my finite mind dealing with all of this. Yet spirit validates it for me. There are others who volunteer for such as I did, both throughout time and now. We all work to uplift conditions, both spiritual and physical. Everyone is here for a purpose, we just aren't always made consciously aware of each little step along the path that winds through the destiny our spirits chose to make manifest. All I know is that now I no longer feel depressed and filled with the intense blackness I felt right before the attack. Now I feel light and free. I still feel the world's ongoing miseries, but I don't feel "filled" with them as I did before. I'm no longer crabby at my family. I feel filled with an overflowing love for them. I'm filled with a great new desire to continue walking my path that was outlined so long ago. As far as what medically transpired, it would seem to fit the technical criteria. Yes, I should have experienced acute pain for several months. . .but I didn't. Was this because the organ needed to absorb as much as possible first? Did I experience acute pain for seven hours because it could hold no more destruction from the misery it had absorbed? Was there a reason I didn't seek medical help when the pains first hit? Was there a reason for the stones to number 188? I'm told there were reasons for all of these. But I'm really not holding my breath for the answers. It was something that was planned for me to experience. My spirit knew all about it. And so, with that, I accept. Looking back does no good. Only the current minute (and possibly the next) is what I set my sites on. I am concerning myself with making sure each step I take is aligned with the path my spirit chose to follow. For me, there is no other reality. For me, there is no other possibility.

Do you still sit in Godmother's Kitchen restaurant and write?

No. Godmother's Kitchen had a name change to Grandmother's kitchen and relocated to the other end of town. Where I used to write was the old location next to the movie theater. I haven't been in Grandmother's more than three times in the last year because every time Bill and I try to have a quiet breakfast there, someone invariably comes up to me and starts asking questions or wants a consultation.

Recently Grandmother's Kitchen was sold and the new owners know nothing of me, so please stop calling this restaurant with inquiries of my address or phone number.

Will Lodestar always be a source where people can write to with their questions?

Through The Mountain Brotherhood, then Lodestar, I've personally responded to thousands of reader's letters since 1985 when people first began writing to me. This book, *Daybreak,* was created as a reference volume that answers the public's most frequently-asked questions. Through the publication of this book and the previous No-Eyes books, most all of your questions will have been answered and most of those remaining in the public's mind should be resolved by going Within through meditation and personal guidance.

However, my path is rounding a curve in the Circle and is taking me along new courses of my purpose. Therefore, as time permits, I will continue the correspondence until my last book is released. At that time it is foreseen that I will walk into the woods and no longer be available to the public.

A channeler in California said that you think you know every-thing. That didn't sound like a very spiritual statement coming from someone who's supposed to be channeling someone who gives info from the Akashic Records.

And although you didn't reveal this to me, I also am advised that this channeler also told you to take your clothes off so he could show you how to stimulate your centers. . .and *charged* you $40.00 for the pleasure. And *that,* my friend, is definitely *not* something *any* of the Great White Brotherhood Advisors would ask someone to do. Please stop being so easily duped. Follow your inner feelings that caused you to wonder about this so-called channeler and his all-knowing entity.

People! Wake up and open your eyes! Stop letting others manipulate you. Stop *paying* to be manipulated. For God's sake, wake up before it's too late!

Out of all your books, which one took the longest time to write?

Including counting my children's book, the one destined to be my eleventh book took the longest to write, for I had to journey within one hundred times to receive the information recorded on each page.

In your dream time we spend much time together and are very close because of the work we jointly do. We need to meet in the physical.

I am rarely given the luxury of true dreams, for when one's spirit is active while the body sleeps, the consciousness is not wasted on idle dreams, but is with the totality of the spirit while it works. The issue of dream time has been greatly misrepresented. So then, during the nighttime hours, you need to know that I'm very aware of all I do, for I spend my time with the Great White Brotherhood volunteering my spirit in the participation of the warriors of light battles with the dark ones. Occasionally at night my spirit will commune with the Starborn Ones, but this is usually done through conscious physical visitations for the purpose of leaving my sleep time undisturbed in deference to my spirit's higher work with the Great White Brotherhood.

I don't deny nor discount what you see in your dreams, but please understand that they are just that. . .dreams. When I sleep at night, my spirit does not work with other earthly mortals or their spirits. And, if it ever had occasion to. . .I'd surely know who they were.

I'm collaborating with a video company to market a kit that includes most of the items from your Gateway Healing Chart. Can I have your permission to refer to the EARTHWAY book?

Permission denied. And, my friend, you merchandise that kit and you'll be hearing from my attorney for copyright infringement.

My daughter cherished your books and held No-Eyes and Summer Rain within her heart. Just before she died, she requested that some of her ashes rest upon Mary Summer Rain's sacred ground. Please, if you are not offended, sprinkle the enclosed ashes of my daughter beneath some pine trees of your land when you're finally settled.

My friend, I am far from offended and will be happy to honor your daughter's final wishes. As soon as we're able to purchase our sacred ground, I will whisper some prayers as I bring your daughter's physical essence home to rest upon my land. In the meantime, I will keep her ashes in a sacred place within my home.

I've had a hard time finding your books in bookstores, or when I do they don't have a good supply or a complete set.

Books, as long as they're in print, can always be ordered by the customer through any bookstore. You might want to request your bookstore manager to keep a complete set of the No-Eyes books in stock. Usually managers are receptive to their customer's requests. This recent situation has been directly attributable to my problems with an unauthorized publisher and his practices. You can help alleviate this aspect through personal requests made directly to your local bookstore manager.

I heard that a brand new publishing company by the name of Hampton Roads was going to publish DAYBREAK, aren't you taking a risk by going with an untried company?

Although the company itself is new, the president is not inexperienced in the publishing field. Bob Friedman, the president of Hampton Roads, was the publisher who initially accepted *Spirit Song* when I sent it to Donning. He was the man Many Heart foresaw taking my story. Since Mr. Friedman was in no way involved with the illegalities that transpired with the other publishers involved, he resigned and started a brand new company. I have a good working relationship with Bob Friedman that is based on trust and friendship.

My contractual agreement with Pocket for *Earthway* gave Pocket first option for my next work. They loved *Daybreak* and wanted it very much, but they required that I not have over 500 manuscript pages. *Daybreak* was 1,020 pages and I did not want to break up the book. I felt all the information needed to be in one large reference volume. So Pocket released their option hold on *Daybreak* because we could not resolve this aspect. Bill then immediately called Bob Friedman to see if he'd be interested in *Daybreak* and, we finalized the deal in one day.

Although Hampton Roads is indeed a new publishing company and, as such, as with all new companies, they may take a bit to get off the ground, I went with it instead of one of the several large publishers who would've snapped up *Daybreak* because Bob Friedman was the only publisher who was aware enough to recognize the light and beauty of No-Eyes back in 1984 when I sent *Spirit Song* to him, and also because he is a good man who can be trusted.

Do you and Bill ever have arguments?

We wouldn't be free-thinking individuals if we never disagreed on something once in a while. Sure, we've had some very heated "discussions," but throughout our entire marriage we've always been completely open and talked things through (sometimes for hours and hours). But the best thing about these infrequent disagreements is the "making up."

CAUTION: Never go to bed mad at your mate!

I don't mean to frighten you, but I keep having the strong feeling that Summer Rain will drown.

I already did. I drowned in a pool when I was nine and it was an amazingly gentle and painless transition.

I deeply appreciate your concern and the voicing of your warning. Your strong feeling was not a premonition, but rather was evidence of retrocognition (the knowing of a past event). You can rest easy now.

What do you like to do best?

Holding Bill and having him hold me.

What I love best is lying beside him with my head on his chest and listening to his heartbeats as I fall asleep. That gentle drumming brings the greatest comfort and serenity I've ever known. No matter what troubles life brings us, his steady heart sounds put everything in perspective. As long as I can hear them, all our problems become inconsequential; for he is my sun, my moon. He is the very breath of my life. After twenty-six years of being married, each day I find I love him more than I did the day before. Because of this, listening to his heart sounds is what I love to do best.

Walking Shadow

Above. . .Below. . .Within. . .the living Soul is made manifest throughout all dimensional vibrations. Such is the Spirit's heritage. Such is its magnificent vitality and essential beauty.

How can I talk to spirits?

My first thought would be to ask you why this is desired. If you merely want to speak with a deceased relative or other individual — this should not be done. If you wish to help the wayward spirits — this knowledge will come to you if it's meant to be an aspect of your purpose. The knowledge will naturally come into your "knowing" and will gently develop. If it's your personal guide you wish to commune with — this is accomplished by going within the self.

Teaching people to commune with spirits is not in the accepted realm of any New Age function, for such activities are directed and guided from that which is "within self."

I've read of the exchange transference of spirits. This refers to the so-called term "walk-ins." Is this possible or fantasy?

Although the term "walk-in" is not the terminology used on the spirit plane for this concept, the event itself is valid, though much more rare than the general public now believes.

Are multiple personalities evidence of spirits that hang around to influence an individual?

I'm pleased to see that you used the term "multiple" instead of "split." Yes, an individual with multiple personalities is indeed evidence of misdirected spirits.

I was amazed to find an explanation of the spirit/mind correlation in PHANTOMS AFOOT. It made the life after death concept simple to understand. You've managed another "first" in this field that's so cluttered with vague concepts.

I appreciate your kind compliment, but it also must be remembered that most all of the spiritual concepts are quite simple in theory. It's very important to keep them as such. To speak in complexities is neither wise for the teacher nor enlightening for the student.

In doing your spirit clearings, I noticed that your key ingredient was love. Your descriptions and use of logic was very confirming to me, but you didn't address the astrals. Are astrals of the same makeup as the waywards? Do astrals have the same power? Can they harm you?

You've asked four questions here. Let's take them individually.

I didn't include the astrals in Phantoms Afoot because the book was on the issue of "wayward" spirits — those discarnates who didn't go into the light after physical death. These spirit entities are not anything like astrals, therefore, the subject of astral entities had no place in the book.

Are astrals of the same makeup as the wayward spirits? No, not at all. The astral plane is comprised of the lowest types of energy forms which frequently have no individual consciousness or personality. They are rather the "mindless" types created by the wandering thoughts of physical people. When I say "mindless," this is not to infer that astrals cannot think, but rather the term is meant to suggest an "unconscionable" mind process. Therefore, the astral beings care not for the precepts of the Collective Wisdom, nor do they strive toward completion and a oneness with God.

Do astrals have the same power? All energy has power. And, when consideration is given to the former aspect of these possessing unconscionable minds, the result is even more dangerous because there is an absence of logic and reason.

Can astrals harm you? Not unless you allow same. If you are caught up in an "etheric fascination" that draws you to the more mysterious and esoteric aspects of spirituality, and you seek to open self to such, then astrals can be very dangerous because they will jump at the chance to "enter" and wreak all kinds of havoc. This havoc may come in many forms: possession in the form of giving you a multiple personality; you may begin to channel the entity; loss of reason; altered attitudes; irrational acts; and others.

You commented that our use of love while working with the waywards was very confirming to you, however, with astrals, love has no meaning.

Did it take special permission for the Indian couple in PHANTOMS AFOOT to do the earth protection they did?

All "special" projects and missions undertaken on the spirit plane requires special permission from those in the hierarchy. There is much order there and special undertakings are assigned according to a spirit's advancement and ability to perform and carry out a specific mission.

Where were your guides during your clearing process?

They remained on the spirit plane but always maintained an open line of communication. This communication is the vehicle that enlightens me on the specific background details I need to communicate with the wayward one.

You may recall the incident that took place on Thunder Mountain. Little Davey was so difficult and contrary because he held so much animosity within him. He was hurting very badly inside. I needed more information in order to help him. It was provided through my Advisor who immediately informed me that Davey's parents had searched and searched for him and that they were now in the spirit plane waiting for him.

Another example of this much-needed communication between myself and our Advisor is when we were in the Sweetwater Hotel with Josephine. You may recall that there was a very touchy moment when Bill expected me to give Josephine the information on Charles, but I was put on the spot because I hadn't received the information yet from my source. Then, a moment or two later, it began coming through for me.

I'm sure it's rather clear that, doing these clearings can be nerve-wracking work because of the precise timing of, not only the work itself, but also of coordinating the necessary communication between myself and our Advisor.

Are all psychic imprints soundless?

As with all things, there are circumstances that provide the inevitable exception to the rule. Although it's a rarity, some psychic imprints can have the additional factor of sound associated with them. This aspect directly correlates to how the sound factor relates to the event's degree of energy release.

Sound most frequently accompanies an actual spirit manifestation during a haunting.

When I was six months pregnant I had to have a C-section. When our son was three days old he died. I was devastated, but after reading SPIRIT SONG, I realized that he wasn't dead at all. I was finally able to let him go and my husband and I have had a great spiritual awakening. Thank you so much for what you've done.

I can sympathize with the physical loss you experienced, but it is greatly comforting to know that one's child is still alive and well in the spirit dimension. I appreciate your kind words, but I haven't done anything other than bringing the facts to light. The precepts of the Collective Wisdom are indeed beautiful and bestow great under-standing and clarity to life's seeming trials. The universal truths provide us with deep understanding and shed logic and reason on life.

Must one be in the physical to assist the wayward spirits?

No, not at all. As you may recall, the incident regarding little Davey in *Phantoms Afoot* exemplified the fact that higher discarnates had previously attempted to bring him home. Davey referred to these as "them other dead guys." However, there are instances, like Davey's, when the wayward spirit denies his own death and can only be open to the suggestions of a physical being.

You have to understand that, although those spirits tried to help Davey return, nobody can interfere with another's free will. The spirits cannot *force* a wayward to return. This decision, as with all choices in life, must come from the individual exercising his own free will.

We have a wayward spirit in our house. It moves things around. Can you come and send it back?

The details in your letter are not evidence of a wayward spirit but rather of psychokinetic activity generated from the over-energized mind of your daughter. You must take the time to talk more with her and attempt to find out what's bothering her. She's greatly troubled and has no release. Please provide her with one.

How come all wayward spirits can't be seen?

This depends solely on their own desire, for they themselves choose the degree of dimensional manifestation. Some appear as vaporous as a mist while others can appear as physically solid as you and I.

Along these same lines, the "manner" of presentation manifested is also their choice. They may wish to appear as they were in their last life, including style of dress, or they may desire to present themselves as a robed figure. There have been those who choose to dispense with all exterior dressings altogether. Those who either are unaware of their physical death or are within a self-generated denial of same will manifest their appearance at the time of their death.

Did you ever help the lady who manifested in your Leadville house?

We tried on several occasions, however she was not open to any type of communication from us. She knew she was dead but in no way wanted to leave her Leadville residence. She also had a sense of humor and would take great joy in quickly vanishing after suddenly manifesting before us. She didn't give us a solid foothold to build on. She enjoyed our company and, in the end, we had no choice but to be accepting of her continued presence.

Our advisor informed us that the lady had indeed "returned home" after her demise, however she chose to spend a little more time in the Leadville surrounding before her next incarnation.

This she requested and it was granted.

The theory behind such a granted request is that the spirit can gain further insights by spending an extended measure of time in the region of their last life experience. This then was why our lady was in the Leadville house. Therefore, in reality, she was not a wayward spirit at all, but rather one who wished to extend and deepen her understanding of an aspect needing same.

This exemplifies that not all spirits (manifested or otherwise) are in need of a clearing or help to home. Since we've experienced this concept, the difference between a wayward and an "intended" spirit is now distinguishable to us.

This issue possesses many, many facets.

Can the dead come back to life like a zombie?

The questioner's concept is a contradiction. Zombie's don't "come back to life" because they were never really dead in the first place. Zombies are evidence of the result of a powerful botanical's effect upon the human system which produces the state of a deathlike stupor.

Now, in this deathlike stupor, the perpetrator (or sorcerer as he is called) digs up the buried body and forces another powerful drug into the system. The buried body flutters his eyes and is helped out of the grave. He walks. He is then perceived as "the undead," But the sorcerer who has the drugs can now control the zombie because of the mental stupor his drug induces in the victim. See? There is really no "dead" person involved. . .only one who has been made to "appear" dead.

So then, an adept sorcerer who utilizes these powerful botanicals to effect a waking-state hypnosis in another can literally erase the individual's emotions, memories, values, and attitudes, thereby obtaining total control over the victim.

Know that no physically dead person can ever be brought back to life save same is accomplished through the will and the hand of God alone.

I love seances. Do you ever conduct any?

Never! And, shame on you!

I work hard to send wayward spirits back to where they peacefully *belong*. Why in God's holy name would you ask me if I ever "called" them *back?*

Listen, I've experienced some very delicate situations, situations that have placed me in grave danger while attempting to "clear" places during the process of helping these confused and frequently powerfully obstinate spirits. And people like you are trying to call them back!

Know that there is *never* a sane, intelligent reason for conducting these destructive sessions. If you desire excitement then go to an amusement park! If you're seeking a good fright then go to the movies and meet Freddy! If you like being around the dead then go sleep in a cemetery! If you like communicating with spirits then go do it in your sleep by way of your own spirit! But don't *ever* call spirits down here to your plane of existence, instead, send your own spirit out to *their* plane of existence!

I apologize if I have to be so strong here, but I simply cannot accept such an abominable practice, especially when I'm often placed in such danger to give these poor spirits some of the peace they have long deserved.

What causes an actual possession?

Now the confusion of split personalities will be clarified.

This is important, and can be a difficult concept to clearly understand. What you term a "split personality" is actually a nonexistent phenomenon simply because a *singular* personality cannot *divide*. Remember that the spirit *is* the personality and spirits cannot split and divide like cells. Spirits are separate *individuals!*

Now, at the moment of an infant's birth, a spirit enters into that baby's body. The baby will then develop its individual personality according to the quality of spirit that has entered it, and that personality will also have been affected by other outside governing factors such as planet alignments and karma. So now there is *one* baby in possession of *one* spirit (personality).

During an individual's lifetime, there are many occasions that serve to "open" that individual to the nebulous forces from without. Listen well here, please. Whenever the conscious mind is in an unconscious state such as during periods of deep sleep, inebriation, or under the effects of anesthesia, that person is "open" enough to allow the entrance of *another* spirit. Intense trauma or emotions can open an individual enough for a spirit to enter the physical being of another.

There is an unlimited number of spirits that can occupy a single body. But the individual's own personality has *not* become split, but rather his body is *shared* by many personalities (spirits) that have invaded it.

Be it known that there are thousands of spirits who would love to enter a physical body. And people offer them just as many opportunities to accommodate that entrance.

An individual in "possession" of several spirits will act and speak quite differently depending upon which spirit is in control at the time. It could be a woman, boy, man, child, foreigner, or a famous person who is deceased but wishes to speak.

There have been cases of an individual being "possessed" by the spirit of their own dead relative. Remember that an individual *cannot* possess a split personality. Remember that this misnomer merely refers to a simple fact of spirit reality — the fact of "multiple spirits inhabiting one vehicle (body)." There is no such thing as split personalities, the term would be: "multiple personalities (signifying the existence of multiple spirits)."

In your letter to me, you fully explained "multi-faceted personality, I think your readers would be interested in knowing what this is.

I agree, but am fearful they will confuse the issue with the concept of "multiple personalities." Well, here goes.

We have seen in the previous question and response that the term "multiple personality" signifies an individual's "possession" of more than one invading spirit. Please, keep that definition clear.

There is another spirit concept that elicits nearly the same psychological aberrations as the multiple personality, but this is generated from an entirely different source. An individual can "appear" to be possessed by multiple personalities when, in actuality, they are not. They may be a victim of "multi-faceted personality" instead. These are two totally separate concepts.

The conceptual term: "multiple personality" denotes "*more* than *one* personality" — *multiple* ones. . .meaning more than one spirit — possession.

The conceptual term multi-faceted personality" denotes "*one* personality" with many *facets* of the *one*. Therefore, *no* possessing spirits are manifested.

Now, since an individual's spirit is the *sum total* of *all* the spirit's experiential lives, the *one* spirit has a *memory* retention of *each* life within its database. A spirit therefore retains "facets" of each life it experienced.

An example of this would be that, at the time of Creation, spirits looked like uncut diamonds. Then, when a physical life was experienced, a "facet" was cut onto the spirit's totality. After each lifetime, another facet was cut. These facets do not alter the initial personality of the spirit, but merely give the spirit individualized facets to its initial personality. So during any one lifetime, one or more of the spirit's facets may "come forward" to share the current known personality of the individual. See? These evidenced personality facets are generated by the "carryover soul memories" of the past-life experience. Another example of "multi-faceted personality" would be myself. Through the carryover soul memory I can relate to life as Sequanu, She-Who-Sees, See-qu-aa-nu and my current personality — *all* being facets of my *one* spirit.

It's really a simple concept in theory, it's just a little difficult to explain in words.

An individual who finds it easy to learn a particular foreign language as if he/she came naturally to it is an example of how one utilizes a facet of their spirit. Clearly one of their spirit facets experienced a lifetime in that foreign country and, learning that language *now* is not a matter of actual learning, but of a "relearning" after being away from it for awhile.

Child prodigies are multi-faceted personalities. The facet of their spirit that was once a brilliant pianist comes to the forefront as if it never left. See?

I don't believe in ghosts and things that spook around and go bump-in-the-night! Save those stories for people who like to read with all their lights on and their doors bolted!

By the time we even get to send this response off to you, you will have had an encounter that will have changed your mind — forever. And peace be to you.

I'd like to be able to see wayward spirits and to help them on their way. How can I develop this helpful ability?

Rather you help the spirit of self. The blind cannot lead the blind. The ignorant cannot teach the ignorant. We are not being cruel here, but you *must* first attend to that which requires attention *within* before you can help that which is without.

What's the difference between a spirit and a guide?

All guides are spirits. All spirits are not guides.
The word "spirit" designates *form*.
The word "guide" signifies *purpose*.

How long have you been communicating with your guides?

We and our Advisors have been in communion since 1976.

Does Bill accompany you on all your clearing investigations?

You have distinguished investigations from "encounters."
Frequently I will travel alone to a site in order to obtain all the necessary background material we need. This includes interviewing the property owners, workers and anyone else who can supply additional input regarding the haunting. There are initial investigative forms that need to be filled out including permission grants that either allow or disallow me to use the people's real names if I should ever write about the location. By obtaining this information, I can also determine if the manifestation is real or not.

The actual encounter process is done by the both of us.

Isn't the mechanics of guide communication synonymous with possession of the medium?

Absolutely not. They're not the same at all. An advanced Advisor merely "shares" one's consciousness, while the medium becomes truly possessed (a condition that's frowned upon by The White Brotherhood).

What actually causes poltergeist activity? Is it from a wayward spirit or from a youngster's psychic energies?

Could be both, depending on whose interpretation you're going by. Poltergeist activity is evidenced through psychokinesis, which is the movement of physical inanimate objects by way of an intense force of psychic energy applied to them. All people possess energy. I'm not referring to their physical muscle energy, but rather to their mental/spirit force (psychic) energy.

Generally, this energy remains dormant as long as the individual maintains an underdeveloped awareness and a measure of moderate control of his emotions, especially once he's passed into adulthood.

During puberty, certain specific glands are being activated. These glands that are awakening are a vital part of the body's total glandular system that is utilized in complete meditation. An intense energy lies within these glands, and if the developing child is experiencing many severe mental frustrations or frequent bouts of anger during this fragile stage, he will also involuntarily be able to release some of the intense energy from these awakening glands. Through no fault of his own, his energies will be flung out to affect objects around him. These instances are extremely rare though. The most popular cases of poltergeist activity caused by individuals in puberty are contrived for the purpose of gaining attention through publicity.

Most all cases of poltergeist activity are caused by a wayward spirit who demands attention through its manifested tantrums. These are meaningful events because the spirit is attempting to convey a message to the living people around it. Usually this message is one of intense anger. The spirit would like the people to leave its haunt — its home. Another reason for these demonstrative and often destructive tantrums is to gain attention so that someone will help the spirit who knows of no other method of attracting the attention of the living.

Lastly, there have been situations where poltergeist activity has been caused by an evil collective force present within an area.

And, there have been cases that have been caused by the static and erratic irregularities within the earth's powerful magnetic field.

When a person in an intensive care unit is kept alive by mechanical means, doesn't that interfere with the spirit's desire to leave the physical?

This situation has no effect upon the spirit's free will to make decisions.

Nothing can prevent the spirit from leaving its physical body if it so desires. The spirit can sever the cord if it chooses to. Many people die in surgery simply because their spirits had left while under anesthesia and decided not to return. While this can happen, the cord is severed only if the spirit's time is right for such a situation. In other words, the spirit must be near one of its death dates in order for it to be accepted in the spirit dimension without being sent back.

Many times an intensive care patient that is being kept alive by machines is already dead. You can keep the body alive by maintaining a regular heart rate, but once the brain no longer shows activity — the spirit has already left.

Why on earth would a spirit enter a starving Ethiopian infant? It doesn't make sense! What could it possibly accomplish?

This question shows little understanding of the Law of Karma and the entire issue of reincarnation, for it makes perfect sense for Ethiopian infants to keep being born. The purpose? Spirit advancement!

Please remember that there is a reason for everything that happens in life. A spirit chooses an impossible life condition to enter for several spiritual reasons.

In the case of a spirit entering an Ethiopian infant that will die of starvation in a short span of time, the reasons can vary. Perhaps the spirit requires a mere few weeks of physical suffering in order to perfect itself, therefore allowing it to return quickly to God. Perhaps the spirit spent a former lifetime of cruelty to small children, thereby experiencing a child's starvation equalizes out its wrongdoing. Perhaps the spirit volunteered to enter the starving infant in order to awaken the rest of the world and incite their human compassion. And the reasons go on and on. But *nothing* happens for *no* reason.

Spiritually speaking, abortion of an unborn infant is generally considered wrong. What is it considered in truth?

An individual's free will choices constitute a solid concrete example of an unseen probability that alters a foreseen event.

When a woman becomes pregnant, a spirit may lovingly latch onto the woman with the high expectations of entering the new infant when it is born. The excited spirit hovers about and attempts to make itself felt by the mother. Suddenly, the mother gets rid of the growing fetus. The spirit is saddened over the death of what was to be its future body. The spirit sadly returns to the spirit dimension in search of another opportunity which will present it with the exact circumstances that it requires in its next lifetime in order to advance itself.

Abortion is the act of doing away with a live developing human. It makes no difference that the spirit has not yet entered the tiny body. It makes no difference that the fetus cannot live separately from its mother. It makes no difference that it's only an inch long. It is *still* a human life.

Simply put, abortion is seen as an abomination because, in the perspective taken by spirit law, a spirit has been denied a valid reentry opportunity.

My daughter insists that she sees the ghost of a tall woman in her bedroom some nights. She doesn't feel afraid, just confused. Is she experiencing a vivid imagination or an actual sighting? Who could this spirit be? I actually went as far as researching the history of the house and I couldn't find any valid reason for a haunting of this nature.

There is no evidence of a haunting indicated here.

We find that your daughter is sighting her own personal guide! Please explain this concept to her so that she will develop a close relationship with same.

There has been talk in our town about some strange feelings felt in a certain area of our state forest. I'd like to investigate it and try to get to the bottom of it. Do I need to perform any "ritual of preparation" before I go in there?

Stay away!

We find the entities there are powerful and do not wish to be returned. No preparations you would do could adequately protect you from these forces. Leave them be!

The business of "clearing" areas of wayward spirits is *serious* business. It is not fun and games. A wayward spirit possesses powerful forces. It cannot touch you, but it has *control* of forces that can. This specific wooded area has "several" angry spirits. If you mentally retain thoughts of clearing this area do NOT go near the area. They will be able to sense your intentions.

There is something evil in our house. On certain nights, someone walks up and down our cellar stairs then slams a door that isn't even there! We're ready to sell our house — GIVE it away if we have to. We're terrified! Please help us.

There is no evil in your house. You're experiencing evidence of a powerful psychic imprint with sound. There is no danger for you or for your family. If you cannot adjust to the occurrences, then I would suggest that you reside elsewhere. There is nothing that can alter the effects of a psychic imprint. It is a fact of continuing reality. I know these can be frightening when first encountered, but perhaps now that you know the cause, you will be able to ease yourself into a more acceptable perspective of it.

We live in the mountains and frequently, when friends come over, they're frightened to be outside at night. They say that they get creepy feelings like someone is watching them. We also have had the feelings at times, but it doesn't scare us — it's like having a friendly feeling of companionship. What do you think it could be?

Indeed, someone is watching them. A wayward spirit remains around your cabin. He is peaceful. He never goes within the cabin because he respects your ownership, but he remains without so as to keep a watch on his former property. He has taken a great interest in your outdoor workshop. The blacksmithing you do fascinates him, for he was once one himself. You feel his high interest as you work. There is nothing to fear from this spirit, but he really should be where he belongs. I feel that because he likes you, he is comfortable and doesn't feel threatened. You don't live far from me. Let me know what you decide to do about this "companion."

[This correspondent's property has been cleared. The entity has gone home.]

What's the difference between a troublesome wayward spirit and an evil force? What are the differentiating manifestations of the two?

A "troublesome wayward spirit" can be gently coerced through reason to return to where it belongs.

An "evil force" cannot be.

A wayward spirit will always have one singular personality being manifested through one specific concrete form such as a man, child, or woman.

An evil force will often manifest multiple personalities which present varying forms and shapes to frighten you.

The procedures for dealing with each of these separate types of manifestations greatly differ.

How do you go about clearing a location of a wayward spirit? What is the procedure?

The procedure of choice depends on the symptoms indicated. It can be simple or incredibly complex, depending on each individualized circumstance — the attitude of the spirit, it's reason for being wayward, how many spirits are involved, their extent of power, their understanding, and your degree of power.

There are few basic preparations and "points of procedure," but the circumstances greatly vary. A change in procedure can be vital toward success. A split-second alternate procedure is often unexpectedly called for. It's not a game for a weak heart or spirit. It's quite often a battle for life — the spirits *and* yours.

If you're able to communicate with guides and wayward spirits, why not help others to communicate with their beloved deceased relatives and friends? This would be a great comforting service to those bereaved who are left behind.

Your thought process is not in proper spiritual perspective, for it is greatly slanted toward the self.

Also, you're mixing concepts here — apples and oranges.

Wayward spirits are spirits who have not gone to where they should be and, consequently, need to be convinced that they should leave the earthly physical attractions that arc holding them here. The wayward spirits *need* communications that compel them forward into the Light.

Guides are there for the express purpose of helping and guiding. They're *supposed* to communicate with us in order to ease us onto our right paths — show the way.

Discarnates (spirits of deceased) are in the spirit dimension to "learn" and to "plan" and "grow" toward the advancement of their spirits. These spirits have NO reason to directly communicate with those in the living third-dimensional plane.

It is not a great comforting service to call back spirits who are busy working on their soul advancement. It would not necessarily be a great comforting service for the bereaved to talk to the spirit of their dead relative or friend. You must realize that once a spirit has left its dead casing behind, it wishes only to be about its important work of advancing itself. It does not wish further communications with those it has left behind. It does not wish its work interrupted. It does not wish to be "called back" for the purpose of parlor communication.

Is there such a thing as an incubus?

Absolutely. The term designates a wayward spirit's specific "draw" to the earth plane.

An incubus is a wayward spirit that possesses carnal desires. Such types of spirits have wasted many lifetimes and have not advanced their spirits. They have literally squandered their lifetimes, thereby prolonging their need to extend their ultimate time for soul purification. They cannot seem to adequately work out the karma they continue piling upon the spirit. Such types represent reversals for the spirit. They simply cannot shed their physical wants. A wayward spirit remains around its "physical" surroundings, while the incubus remains around a female's "body." An incubus signifies a male spirit.

The spirit counterpart of an incubus is a female spirit and is termed a succubus. The succubus remains around a physical male body. Both of these spirits can make their presence felt by physical manifestations caused by their powerful energy force.

If spirits exist in the spirit plane after physical death, how could they possibly NOT know their bodies are dead?

The key to your question is your choice of dimension. . . "spirit plane."

If the wayward were truly on the spirit plane, it wouldn't be wayward and be manifesting on the earthly plane. Therefore, waywards never make it to the spirit plane because they never went through the connecting "tunnel." So, now that we've established that the waywards exist in a dimensional frequency that is just up from earth's, it's no longer difficult to see why these unfortunate entities may not realize their bodies are not like they once were. These spirits still see and hear the living people going about the business of life. They can still stand next to their friends and relatives. . .and they wonder why nobody talks to them any more. Naturally, the spirits are drawn to the people and places it knows and they find it increasingly difficult to separate themselves from their material possessions, home and family, therefore effecting a haunting.

After a while, they don't need to be told that they're dead, but rather need to be convinced that they must get on with their spirit's advancement. They must be made to realize that they're wasting valuable time by hovering near their earthly ties.

How can you answer questions about the absolute causes of a complete stranger's spirit experiences without physically conducting an investigation? When I wrote to you a few months ago, you hit the nail right on the head. We did as you suggested and we've never been bothered again. How'd you do that?

My own perceptions and inner insights on a particular individual or situation are always double-checked and cross-referenced with our Advisor who frequently checks out the manifestation as I'm reading about it in your initial letter. By the time I'm done with the letter, I've formed my own strong impression and, because "they" have actually looked into it, I then have my theory verified through the actual facts of the case.

I usually get the basics and then I get the detailed aspects filled in. All in all, the mechanics end up being a nearly foolproof method of answering reader's letters. The answers are either from me, No-Eyes, or our Advisor. Sometimes the specific wording of my response will give clear evidence as to *who* did the actual answering. . .that is, if I've forgotten to translate back into first person singular.

How can an elemental do physical harm?

Please understand that *all* thoughts, particularly *strong* thoughts that are intensified by deep feelings, create "things." These "things" are composed of etheric matter from the mind's powerful energy — the result is an elemental.

These elementals are *not* the same as spirits, therefore, they do not possess mind/personality aspects unto itself. It is simply synonymous to a "robot of energy matter." This robot elemental will do as its creator directs. It can cause illness, accidents, and even a death. However, and this is important here, an elemental *always* "returns to its creator." What this means is that whatever you send out (thought) will always come back and return to you. So. . .watch those thoughts! They are *things!*

Our cat won't go into our old well house. I've tried to carry her in, but she'll meow and show her claws, finally leaping out of my arms. What is she sensing in there?

We see the animal senses the highly emotional residue left as an impression upon the etheric within the well house structure. A small child was frequently abused in there by her stepfather.

Research the house's older records and you will discover that, in 1891 it was owned by one known as (name withheld). This woman later married a miner known as (name withheld) who was not an ideal father for the six-year-old Jessica.

In the current time/space dimensional frequency, the animal senses the intense violence that occurred within the out-building, for the etheric retains still the emotional expressions and impressions of the child.

Why are there so many unaware and misguided people if we all have a friendly spirit that guides them?

Have you completely forgotten about humankind's greatest gift from God — the free will? Do *you* always do that which is you *know* is right?

I'm advised that your own ill-chosen paths are the direct result of the egotism within self and the desire to create your *own* reality rather than that reality your spirit came to experience.

Why do so many people die in accidents if their spirit guides are supposed to be protecting them?

You're asking why people die.

Spirit guides are continually attempting to "guide" you "safely" along your intended path. This is for the prime purpose of reaching your spirit goals in this life. Yet you do not listen. You do not heed. You, in your ignorance, wallow in your unawareness and do then *cause* the foolhardy accidental events of self.

Can you tell me what special people are returned spirits who have come with a special spiritual mission?

If *they* have not revealed self, why should we? Many spiritual mission's success depends directly upon complete anonymity! That recognition of another's enlightened spirit *must* come from within self! Attend not to the aspects of "fame" lest the seeking of same be your downfall.

Do you communicate with many highly developed spirits?

This is a matter that lies within the boundaries of my sacred ground. Seek that which lies within your *own* sacred place rather than attempting to trespass onto another's.

What is the difference between a psychic imprint and a real spirit haunting?

This was explained in *Phantoms Afoot.*

An actual "spirit inhabitation" (haunting) is when a wayward spirit frequents a particular area with its etheric presence. The *actual* spirit manifests. This spirit has an intellect to think with and to give out thoughts. It possesses an incredible reservoir of forceful power in the form of energy. It is alive, only in an altered dimensional frequency sense.

A *wayward spirit* is always emotionally disturbed. Don't forget that the spirit (soul) is comprised of the spirit essence and the mind, which includes emotions and personality and memory. This personality can be confused or enraged to the point of evidencing mental aberrations until it has been properly counseled. A wayward spirit can be an entity with a sweet personality that is merely confused, or it can be a borderline maniac. But whatever its emotional state, it is still a living and thinking force.

A *psychic imprint,* on the other hand, is only the residual energy left behind after a highly intensive emotional explosion has occurred. Just as it's true that thoughts are real things —etheric matter is formed from them, so too is etheric matter formed from intensely emotional events such as a violent crime that results in a death. When atmospheric conditions precisely meet all criteria that is associated with the "time of the event," then the "replay" of the event will be seen to occur again. The intensity of emotional energy release of the initial event creates a corresponding "image" of the event. It's like an image reflection that stays within a mirror after the real cause has moved away. The psychic image has been "caught in time" and replays itself whenever the atmospheric conditions meet the associated criteria.

A psychic imprint is like a movie segment that is played over and over again. It contains no *living* spirits who can think or have the power to direct etheric force. It never varies in its action because it is an "etheric replay" of the initial event. Physical stimuli such as living people have no effect upon it. It simply plays out its action, frame by frame, until it's done. And, when conditions again trigger the switch, it will replay the entire scene again.

A psychic imprint cannot do harm. A spirit manifestation can.

If a wayward spirit has no physical form to do harm with, what's to be afraid of?

People tend to think that a spirit is harmless because it has no physical form — no material substance. It cannot strike you, it cannot swing an axe, it cannot shoot a gun, therefore, it cannot hurt you.

But it *can* hurt you!

A spirit is "total mind." Do you realize what that means? That means it has the utilization of one hundred percent of the mind's power, while physical man has only around eleven percent at his disposal. With man's mere eleven percent we are capable of *some* paranormal talents. Think of how we would expand that functioning if we were capable of utilizing our minds to one hundred percent!

The spirit *has* that! And, consequently, the spirit can easily direct its "mental powers" to cause a multitude of harmful effects upon a physical interference — you. In essence, a wayward spirit could do anything it wants to you. The wayward spirit has nearly unlimited energy at its disposal. Fortunately, few realize this.

It's crossed my mind that, if we could use the total capacity of our brains, we would be just like God.

An illogical theory. You are "assuming" that God's mind is as small as yours. And through that false assumption, you have falsely reasoned that *your* mind's full capacity is equal in volume and mass to *God's* mind.

It would be like comparing a mustard seed to a beach ball.

In PHOENIX RISING, you talked a woman's spirit out of haunting her house. I don't understand the technicalities of this being done in the "future."

It's quite simple actually.

When the total spirit travels into the future, that future then becomes the present for the spirit. If we had traveled back into the past, that past would've been the "present" for us. See? Although it is law that a spirit cannot alter the past, the future has no such restraining rules.

The events I experienced when I accompanied No-Eyes into the future were real. They were physical happenings "at that time."

Now listen well here. The "law of altering probabilities" still holds true in respect to how they affect the future. Even though No-Eyes and I experienced "actual" future happenings, those specific happenings were the direct result of events occurring in the future, from the effects of the probabilities that were in motion *during* my *present* lifetime. Now that time has passed since that experience, I'm sure that new probabilities will affect the exact future that we experienced. Perhaps a "different" ride in a different amusement park will now be seen to break down. Perhaps a "different" woman will be murdered by a different deliveryman. But what is important to understand here is that the basic events will still occur, just the times and places may be altered by affecting probabilities. See?

We were told that there are doorways on earth that facilitate a rapid transit for wayward spirits.

Don't know who told you this, but whoever did isn't aware of the spiritual realities.

You are held responsible for your beliefs. You are held accountable for the manner by which those beliefs are gained, ascertained, and assimilated. And this responsibility brings with it a length of measured personal discretion by which the reasoning mind weighs all aspects of each conceptual idea brought forth.

There are no such doorways for wayward spirits to enter and exit through. Why would they need such a thing? Think deeper. All they require is a strong desire to advance to where they should've gone in the first place. That desire is the bottomline aspect that ultimately frees them from the heavier vibrational frequencies they've let themselves become weighted with.

We have a wayward spirit in our house. A healer came and left a spiritual ladder for him to climb whenever he was ready. I was amazed at how easy this method was.

I too was greatly amazed.

Since when are etheric "ladders" created? Since when are spirit ladders needed for a spirit to find the Corridor?

Such utter nonsense is for those who are easily fooled. Such a concept is absolutely absurd.

Our property is inhabited by a protective Indian spirit. He was a great Shaman who remains to guard it against developers. We're honored to have him with us.

Your honor is greatly misplaced.

The spirit inhabiting your property was never a Shaman, nor is he an Indian. Your imagination has been overactive through the desires of the mind.

Your spirit is a wayward. He is capable of destructive manifesta-tions. His last incarnation was of Anglo ancestry and he thinks the land is his. . .his alone.

You must not self-create your own realities in deference to *the* reality. You must stop seeing only that which you wish to see, but rather see clearly that which is.

[This wayward has since been sent Home. The property is now cleared.]

It seems that the "wayward" spirits are created when their previously deceased loved ones aren't there to greet them.

This wasn't bad logic, however, there is a misunderstanding of the general transition concept shown here.

Newly crossed-over souls meet their previously deceased family and loved ones after *exiting* the tunnel Corridor. This is the point where the communication is initiated. What makes a wayward is when the new spirit does not go directly to the light through the tunnel itself. In other words, the new spirit must first *enter* the tunnel and, this is done on one's own.

It must be understood that there are many varied layers (levels or frequencies) to the different dimensions. Upon death, the spirit first finds itself just above the physical third dimension and, those spirits awaiting the new spirit cannot usually descend down to that denser level. Therefore, it's imperative that the newly crossed-over spirit speed along to the light without looking left nor right. At the end of the tunnel Corridor, spirit friends and relatives await the newcomer. See? Many times, the new spirit will encounter a warm and welcoming spirit *within* the tunnel Corridor itself. This entity is most often the new spirits guide.

Twenty years ago my son died at the age of three. Is his spirit grown up now? Or is he still a child?

We need to go into this deeper.

A spirit is the sum total living conscious energy of all its lifetimes. This is a basic foundational fact. Therefore, when an individual crosses over, no matter the age of its former physical form, it then evidences its original spirit totality. This, of course, manifests as long as the spirit journeys all the way through the tunnel Corridor. If it doesn't do this, it remains earthbound as a wayward and, in this case, cannot experience it's spirit totality and ends up manifesting as a spirit form of it's last life (child or adult). See?

In *Phantoms Afoot*, when I relayed the encounter with the little boy, Davey, he had not journeyed through the tunnel Corridor. He was existing within an earthbound realm as a wayward shadow of his previous physical appearance. Once he finally desired to go Home where he belonged and went through the tunnel Corridor, he exited it as little Davey and rejoined his awaiting parents. *Then* he slowly transformed into his beautiful totality of spirit. . .an adult essence containing the sum total of all his conscious earthly/spirit plane experiences. He was then whole, with the *aspect* of Davey being simply one small facet of his total spirit essence.

Why aren't all spirit guides all-knowing?

My friend, please, only God is all-knowing.

And, all spirit guides aren't completely knowledgeable because people have a tendency to confuse true spirit guides with discarnates who play at being guides. There is much evidence of this in today's world.

In your last letter to me you explained how some of your lost items are manifested through materialization. Are your spirit Advisors doing this for you?

Not necessarily.

It's important to realize that our world is just chock full of spirit essences, many of these connected to our "natural" world. These can serve as "spirit helpers" and come from many different sources of nature. It is these who come to help us "find" our lost items, for the spirit helpers are very powerful.

Can the wayward spirit see your guides during an encounter?

Only if our Advisors wish the wayward to see them. Generally, neither we nor the wayward spirit visually perceive our Advisors at the encounter time because they do not manifest themselves within the specific dimensional frequency we're immediately involved in.

You have to remember that our Advisors are on the pure spirit High Plane, whereas the wayward is occupying the "in between" dimensional field that is closest to the earth's frequency. Therefore is the wayward within a much heavier and denser vibration than our Advisors.

How do you find out about the haunted areas?

Through various means such as personal feelings, our Advisor's suggestions, and through readership correspondence. Also there is the very credible source that I refer to as The Underground. These are local folks who wouldn't think of talking about such a sensitive issue with their neighbor, friends or the general public, but rather maintain high secrecy by only coming to me with their wayward situations.

Due to the tremendous backlog of wayward cases that are scheduled, I've had to decline further invitations to investigate reader's individual manifestation phenomena.

There's a wayward spirit hanging around our house. Can you come and get rid of it?

As explained in the previous question, there are many forms of spirit essences. Your's is not a *wayward*, but rather of the "nature spirit" kind. It's of a beneficent nature and may prove to be a real boon to you in the near future.

Please remember that we humans are literally surrounded by the spirit forces of nature. Just because you can't see these or understand them, doesn't mean that they don't exist. And, because you are a particularly sensitive and compassionate individual, one has attached itself to your family with the express purpose of serving as a helper.

I attend seances where the attending medium always connects with whatever spirit is being sought. Don't you think that's a wonderful success rate?

No I do not. In fact, it's a little too wonderful. A hundred-percent success rate is not even logical, for most of those she's trying to connect with (spirits) will have already reincarnated again! Or hadn't that crossed anyone's mind.

One cannot attend a seance and expect to contact any spirit they choose (whether recent or historical), for spirits are about their important work of perfecting themselves and are eager to reincarnate — not hang around to entertain seance attenders.

It occurred to me that, if a lesser spirit could manifest an appearance of anyone it wished then it could also appear as holy figures such as the Virgin Mary or specific saints.

Too bad this hasn't also occurred to others. You're absolutely right in your theory, for many manifestations of famous historical personalities (holy or otherwise) are indeed done by the lesser spirits who play-act and love duping humans in the third-dimensional plane. In truth then, the public must be much more discerning and intellectually acute than they presently are.

Also, because these current times are so critical, being the precursor hours before the Final Battle, the Sons of Belial are extremely active in many unsuspecting ways. An altered appearance manifestation is child's play for them to accomplish with amazing duplicity.

I've heard of channelers bringing through messages from Jesus, the Virgin Mary, Saint Germain and others, yet these ones have *not* remained within their historical spirit aspects, but have returned to the physical state many times since their historical personality. Other channelers claim to give messages from the Archangels Michael, Raphael, and Gabriel, but *they* do not participate in such activities.

So then, are the channelers fabricating or are the spirits themselves play-acting and fooling the mediums? Either way, the channelers lose, for they're either perpetrating a sham or they can't tell the difference between a true high spirit and a lessor mischievous one. In this case. . .everyone loses through misguidance and. . .Belial is laughing his head off.

I noticed that all your spirit clearings took place at night. Is this the time they have to be done?

The spirit encounters detailed in *Phantoms Afoot* were all cleared during nighttime hours because that's when these specific entities were most frequently seen manifesting. However, we've taken care of quite a few during daylight hours.

Night is when most wayward spirits feel most comfortable making their manifestations because they have less interference from human activity then. So too do we prefer the night hours to carry on our communications because we encounter less chances for human disruptions at that time.

There are instances where wayward spirits only manifest during the daylight hours and, in this case, we must also make our encounter during this time in order to be most effective in reaching the entity.

Nighttime is highly charged, so much more so than daylight, and the natural atmosphere of this time provides increased energy to draw from which, in turn, greatly intensifies our efforts at maintain an altered state of vibration that's required of our physical aspects.

A Golden Cord

Oh feel the metered heartbeat pulse.
See the beautiful lifeforce surge.
Hear your Mother's shared breathing.
And perceive her glowing Golden Cord.

I would like to meet you and spend a few weeks learning more about herbals, gathering, remedies, and preparations.

I understand your desire to learn of these things, however, I am not the one to teach you these. Such one-on-one instruction is not an aspect of my purpose.

There are many fine herbalists and native teachers who would be happy to accommodate you. I would suggest that you initially get some book studying under your belt before doing any type of field work. There are many good books on wild botanicals and their practical uses (both as edibles and medicinals). After you have the basics, then it will be time to seek out a teacher who can offer the type of instruction that will meet your needs.

I've stopped eating meat and expected to feel lighter, healthier and happier, but the only thing I've noticed was that family and friends are more convinced than ever that I've become a fanatic.

The key word in your statement is "expected." You stopped ingesting the meat and were in expectation as to the result. The fact that you didn't actually feel lighter, healthier, and/or happier is evidence in and of itself that vegetarianism is not the cure-all many believe it to be. Rather the key to "feeling" better through proper diet comes from eating *less* and ingesting a *balance* of required nutrients. This aspect goes hand in hand with regular moderate exercise, such as walking; getting plenty of rest and avoiding stress in your life. This combination is that which is capable of bring about the lighter, healthier, and happier state of being.

To stop eating meat and still allow stress to enter and interfere with proper assimilation is fruitless. One must give attention to all the affecting aspects of proper diet, rest, and exercise.

Another aspect of this issue is that one's degree of spirituality is in no way associated with the type of food one ingests. This has been a serious misconception for quite some time now. Consider the eating habits of Jesus, for it will be known that he has set the pattern for such. He ate of fish and fowl and even of the lamb. So, how is it that people have cleaved to the concept of "vegetarianism means a higher level of spirituality." Please, set your priorities according to those facts that are in accordance with the *precepts,* not according to false public opinion or erroneous New Age concepts.

Was AIDS generated from homosexuals? Were they the cause of it?

Cause? Rather were they one of the groups that were the targeted victims! As No-Eyes so clearly predicted, some new diseases would be engineered. And so it has been manifested. So rather than asking if a certain lifestyle caused the disease, I would put it another way. Ask who. WHO!

How can an herbalist expert be sick?

An herbalist, like a physician, is susceptible to the same viruses that everyone else is. To expect a healer to never be ill is just not reasonable. In order for an herbalist or any healer to "heal," there first must be a negative physiological condition to heal. And a negative physiological condition can strike the healer just as easily as anyone else.

If mental visualization is so healing to the body's diseases, why don't more hospitals include such therapy in their treatment programs?

There does appear to be new advancements being made in this area. Some hospitals are now incorporating the concept into their treatment programs. They are allowing the patient to attend an hour of consultation with a researcher who carefully guides them through a process of healing visualizations that have been developed specifically for the patient's individual treatment needs.

I agree with you that this type of therapy needs to be more widespread, however, that won't become an actuality until more physicians are made aware of the mind's tremendous healing capabilities in controlling the body's cells.

The mind is the body's master computer. It programs the body's systems right down to the most infinitesimal cell. The mind creates powerful energized thoughts that effect physiological reversals. One day this type of treatment will be a large percentage of a patient's total overall therapy.

I've been overweight for years. My doctor says that I don't have any physiological dysfunctions. I just like to eat all the time. What can I do about this. I hate myself.

And that's exactly why you are overweight. The more you dislike yourself the more you eat. The more you eat the more you hate yourself. You eat simply because you are unhappy with self. It's a vicious circle that only your mind can break.

Since you have no physiological causes for your problem, then it's psychological. Man possesses a self-defeating tendency to self-punish, self-destruct. This is caused by a myriad of reasons. Loneliness, depression, unhappiness, the need for attention, insecurity, frustration, and poor self-image, contributing to the psychosomatic physiological complaints, of which obesity is one.

You must first carefully analyze your life. You must be absolutely honest with yourself when you do this. What makes you happy? What makes you unhappy? What changes do you wish to make in your life besides the weight (this merely being a "side effect" to the real problem). *Facing* the problem is your first big step toward eliminating it. If you don't square off with it, face it and challenge it, you'll never come to grips with its resolution.

Will power plays a vital role in this because, once you realize how you can help yourself, if you don't have the powerful will to see it through, then you're right back to the starting line again.

Learn to accept life. Learn to love yourself and realize that you (and *only* you) have the absolute control to alter those things in your life that upset you and keep you chained to the continuing circle of unhappiness.

Is there a weight-loss diet that is safe and effective?

Many weight-loss diets fail simply because the body's total system is not free of poisons and contaminating substances. They fail because they're not maintained and regular exercise has not been adequately incorporated to act in tandem with proper eating habits.

No-Eyes outlined an effective diet program when she gave me the health material for *Earthway*. I didn't include it in the book because it's not for everyone — all people are different and therefore, require varying weight-loss programs that have been tailored to their individualized needs. There are individuals with such physiological ailments such as heart disease, diabetes, high blood pressure, cancer, etc., and those people require altered diet programs to fit their special needs.

A singular diet cannot be so broad in scope that it is healthful for everyone — each diet must be tailored to an individual's specific needs. And that is what is wrong with the popular diets that people are scrambling to try.

A quick weight-off "slim and trim," "bean pole" diet routine that has been guaranteed to make you look like Garbo will accomplish absolutely nothing if people don't realize that *total* health is involved here, and that includes the mind and its attitudes.

An entirely altered way of eating is required to "maintain" a normal weight ratio. You must understand that you cannot merely go on a special crash diet for a few weeks and then return to your usual way of eating. That's like an alcoholic who gets dried out and then goes home and hits the bottle again. *No* diet will work if your entire eating routine isn't changed.

I cannot give you a specific diet plan because I don't know your specific physical condition — ailments and such. But if you begin to eat by following the points outlined in *Earthway,* you will naturally begin to drop off excessive pounds. Avoid bulk foods, fatty meats like beef and pork, and add lots of high fiber and seeds to your daily diet. Fresh salads are mandatory. Feel good about yourself and find something to be thankful for each day of your life.

I have a mole on my face that I'd like to get rid of. What do you suggest?

I suggest that you stop viewing it as a mole, but instead, look at it as a beauty mark that accentuates your attractiveness and unique individuality.

We have become a nation of people obsessed with perfection of the body. I have two moles on my face plus a scar on my cheek from the time I was attacked by a German Shepherd when young. I used to be very self-conscious about those obvious faults that so visually marked my imperfection. But you must realize that every individual is unique, just as I did.

If you really observe the movie stars, who are idealized as the epitome of perfect beauty, you would be mildly surprised to find that there are scores of them with crooked noses, protruding chins, moles, scars, uneven teeth, and thinning hair. You probably don't notice these imperfect characteristics because you see them as stars and, being such, they are perfect in your mind. But open your eyes and look beyond the glare of their stardom and see their marvelous features that make them unique individuals.

Beauty is a qualified trait, it is not mass-produced like doll faces in a factory production line. Learn to accept those physical attributes that serve to separate you from the other faces in the crowd.

Nevertheless, if you absolutely cannot bring yourself to live with this mark of distinction, I'll give you some simple directions. Apply a mixture of equal parts castor oil and Vitamin E oil on the mole with a cotton swab. Gently massage this is a circular motion every night. Re-apply a good covering of the mixture and cover with a small bandage overnight. Keep up this treatment until the mole begins to diminish in size and lighten its pigment. Then omit the bandaged overnight treatment but continue with the nightly gentle massage with the oils.

If you think that this natural treatment will take too long, you can safely have the mole removed by a simple professional procedure that utilizes a laser beam.

Personally, I think you should accept yourself just as you are. Love self and the distinctions of same.

During the summer months my little girl frequently comes in from playing with skin rashes and scratches. What is the best medication to treat these temporary irritations with?

I can identify with your problem. When my Sarah was little, she was a wild little nature lover who was consumed with an intense headlong exuberance for life (still is for that matter). She was all over the mountainsides as she explored under bushes for puffballs and in trees for abandoned bird's nests. And she was also coming home with a mass of scrapes and skin rashes along with the newest miraculous nature find she discovered.

We use Mother Nature's own remedy — plantain. This is generally considered a troublesome weed, but it is a valuable botanical that heals most types of skin rashes, especially those caused by nature's growing things.

Plantain leaves can be collected, washed, crushed, and applied as a wash to the affected skin area. Or, to make it easier, you can purchase a jar of plantain salve at most any health food shop that sells healing botanicals.

Note: make sure your salve purchase is fresh dated.

Do you have your family on any sort of special diet?

Do bears hibernate?

Rather than to term it "diet," a better description would be "general dietary concept." We don't eat any red meats or pork. Instead we eat fish and fowl. We never fry our foods but rather either broil, bake, or steam. We limit desserts to fresh homemade fruit pies and our sweet snacks consist of cookies like molasses, nut, peanut butter, and fruit. Chocolate is a substance we greatly limit, reserving it as a rare treat.

We eat a handful of almonds daily. These gather body poisons together and carry them out of the system. Almonds are especially good for all types of tumors. We munch on sunflower seeds as these provide the body with more protein than a steak does.

Fresh salads are a large part of our weekly general dietary concept. I'm not referring solely to the lettuce and tomato type salads, but rather those salads that also include the addition of the following ingredients: sunflower seeds, fresh mushrooms, slivered almonds, freshly grated cheddar cheese, raisins, chopped raw onions, olives, garlic, fresh broccoli heads, carrot curls, tomatoes, alfalfa, and bean sprouts. *That* is our salad and it's quite a meal in itself.

All of our fresh vegetables with meals are steamed.

I don't understand how I'm supposed to plan a variety menu from just turkey.

Well you still have other fowl to choose from. And don't forget the fish. However, be careful to know where the fish came from, for many today are contaminated.

Regarding the turkey talk. . .you may have noticed that your market's meat department has been stocking a greater supply of "ground" turkey. The popularity of this product has skyrocketed because of consumer preference over ground beef. Also, this specific form of turkey opens up a whole new range of menu opportunities because the ground turkey can be used in the same way ground beef is.

Ground turkey provides the cook with options such as spaghetti, sloppy joes, turkey burgers (broiled of course), lasagna, tacos, chili, goulash, and anything else ground beef can be made into. Be creative. Ground turkey also makes a great meatloaf (even without the ground pork mixed in).

And you also may have noticed that the markets are also getting on the "turkey bandwagon" by stocking turkey hot dogs and turkey bacon and sausage. These open up even more menu options.

How often do your family members visit the doctor's office?

As infrequently as possible, and that's only for any emergencies that I can't personally handle.

In ten years, Bill has been to the doctors only twice. The first time was for a massive rupture of a spinal disc and he had to undergo an operation called Chemonucleolysis, whereby a papaya enzyme was injected into the ruptured material to dissolve it.

The second time was for a kidney stone. In the hospital emergency room the stone showed up on x-rays. He was then admitted. When another x-ray was taken in the morning to check its position — it wasn't anywhere to be found and he was released. With the help of our Advisors and much personal intense visualizations, the stone was broken up.

In ten years my girls have been to the doctors maybe twice.

These visits were for the treatment of infections such as tonsillitis.

But this is not to infer that we have not been ill or haven't had accidents. When Jenny was six she did a clever somersault off Sarah's crib and broke her thumb. I gently pulled the joint back into place and bound it for two months with a special botanical. To this day, neither of us can remember (or tell) which thumb she broke.

When Aimee was in the seventh grade she injured her tibia during gymnastics at school. She limped home and,after a "psychic" examination, I was informed that the bone was indeed cracked. The swelling was great as was her acute pain. I applied an ice pack, then a special salve under a tightly-wrapped bandage. She kept it elevated overnight and within three weeks she was as good as new. Please keep in mind that these treatments aren't being suggested for the public. Our Advisor's abilities come into play in situations like this because we frequently can't afford to carry health insurance.

Sarah went through an extended period of time when she was susceptible to infected tonsils. Every time she began to notice a slight soreness on one side of her throat, she'd say, "Mom, you have to operate again." And I'd check her tonsil and there'd be a white cluster of sacs attached. I'd remove it with a cotton swab and bathe the entire area with an antibiotic herbal. Within ten minutes, her sore throat would be gone. If the pus sacs were not removed, they would multiply and fester into a serious case of infected tonsillitis resulting in an acute sore throat and high fever. We just nipped it in the bud and she was fine until she got another bout with it. Finally, after six times of this, I marched her to an ENT (Ear, Nose, Throat) specialist and told him I wanted the tonsils OUT. She came through the operation with flying colors and never had another incident.

Bill occasionally received severe burns on his wrist from our woodstove. I immediately cut up a fresh potato and bound the slice over the burn. This was replaced hourly. This cools the pain and heals the wound.

Onions and garlic are used for infections because they are nature's antibiotic (along with a few effective others). Potatoes are used for burns. Plantain is used for skin rashes and irritations, red clover and chaparral for cleansing the system of poisons, peppermint oil for nerve pain, eucalyptus and cajeput oil for muscle pain, onion slices for severe bruises, gentian violet for athletes foot, and I could go on and on describing our highly effective country kitchen home remedies and how we care for our own illnesses. . .but then I've already adequately answered your question, haven't I?

What is cancer really caused from?

Sometimes from a virus strain, but most often from the negative activities of the mind. Contrary to popular belief, smoking does not *cause* the disease, it aggravates it when the disease is already present within the system. The most potent vectoring agent for cancer is. . .*stress* which places destructive forces upon the cellular composition of existing structures within.

If cancer is caused by stress and not smoking, why do the laboratory rats contract the disease when given smoke?

Do you see rats (or any other four-leggeds) skittering around with cigarettes in their mouths? Doesn't it seem a little "unnatural" for rats to be smoking? Or didn't you think that "forcing" smoke into an animal caused them STRESS? Animals have emotions. Animals have the same psychological range that humans do. Just because they don't have the same level of reasoning mind doesn't mean that they can't experience emotions and stress in their lives.

I'm a new mother and am concerned about several negative news reports I've seen about the baby food in jars.

Baby foods that you prepare with your own hands are best for your infant.

Are chiropractic treatments all they're cracked up to be?

This would entirely depend upon what you've heard and are referring to when you say "all they're cracked up" to be.

Generally, you have to realize that total health care means just that, a little of this method and a little of that treatment. Each type of therapy contributes to the whole. See?

The body benefits from herbal treatment, chiropractic, hydrotherapy, massage stimulation, sun therapy, mental visualization, meditation, gate alignment for vibrational balance, diet, and exercise. All of these aspects *combined* represent total treatment for the body's ailments. One *alone* will not significantly effect an absolute healing. This is important. One singular method of treatment will be ineffective unless it is combined with two or more of the others.

Chiropractic is a beautiful concept in itself, for it centers on aligning the spinal vertebrae. Nothing affects the body's Gates more than spinal misalignment. Therefore, chiropractic is a very important healing aspect.

Isn't meditation and biofeedback one and the same?

Absolutely not.

Biofeedback is a *mechanical* method of *actively* controlling the mind by *outward* means.

Meditation is a *natural* method of *passively* controlling the mind by *inner* means.

I understand your logic though. Both methods are a process of mental control. Both are utilized for the specific purpose of attaining a relaxed body. Both are placed in the cubbyhole category of an inexact science — a grey area of therapy in respect to the attitudes and application among the scientific community. However, although they share the above aspects, they are not one and the same.

If we're not supposed to eat egg whites, then how do we eat an egg?

Are you serious? You're joking, right? Where's your wonderfully creative imagination?

Boil an egg and use the yolk as crumbles in your health salad. Soft boil it and pour the yolk over toast and eat it with a fork. Make them over easy and dip your wheat toast in the yolk. Poach them and use a spoon in an egg cup. Mix boiled yolks in potato or macaroni salad. Use the yolks in your french toast batter. And omelets and scrambled eggs can be safely eaten by using three yolks to one whole egg.

Why didn't you include a beauty section in EARTHWAY?

Because exterior beauty is irrelevant.

No-Eyes did detail many types of beauty methods, several were amazing things that I would've never thought of. There were simple botanical formulas for the elimination of wrinkles, scars, stretch marks, and freckles. She gave methods and specific formulas for all types of skin types and hair conditions. And she even spoke about ways of maintaining healthful skin tone and its elasticity.

I had initially prepared these beauty secrets of hers for *Earthway's* final chapter in the health section, but after realizing how the book was shaping up, not only the long length, but also the tone of content, I decided to omit the section on external beauty — it just didn't blend well with the rest of the material.

Please remember that beauty is a qualified characteristic. It is valued and rated individually depending upon how it is seen through the eye of the beholder. Not all men prefer blondes. Not all women want to be thin. Some folks like straight noses, while others prefer turned-up ones, or think crooked ones are a mark of distinction and add individualized character to a person.

Not everyone looks good with silky sleek hair. Some are more attractive with short curls, while others are more suited to a long, straight style. Hair, makeup, nails, facial structure, and body type all contribute to an individual's total exterior uniqueness.

Do what's comfortable and satisfying for *you*. And when *you* are satisfied with self — others will be too.

What do your kids eat for breakfast?

Now you've really gone and done it! This is going to get me into a hot pot of water with some mothers out there.

Since my girls are grown now and can take care of themselves, I'll need to backtrack to their younger school days since this is the age you're inquiring about.

Every evening, I'd give my girls a choice for next morning's breakfast. These were apple spice pancakes, blueberry waffles, cinnamon French toast, cheese omelets, or "dippin' eggs" (sunnyside up eggs that they dip their wheat toast in).

A good nourishing breakfast that fills them up is most important so that their "hunger pangs" will be put off until they get to their lunches at school. I don't consider cold cereal or just toast to be an adequate breakfast for anyone, much less for the growing young bodies of kids. I do buy the boxed cereals but they're reserved for those nightly snack attacks kids get.

Now I hear some of you moaning and groaning that you don't have the time to prepare this sort of breakfast for your kids. You say "well fine, that's wonderful for *her,* but *I* have a job to get to." So did I. You can also make the time because I fixed one of the above breakfasts for four kids each morning (sometimes *more* than one choice) and I was still able to be sitting in my restaurant doing my writing by eight a.m. And I've even showered beforehand.

If you need to roll your little sleepyheads out of their warm sacks a wee bit earlier — then do it, but they deserve to have the best possible start for their long day.

What do you think about artificial heart implants?

Not much at all. But rather than asking what my opinion is, inquire as to the "spiritual" opinion.

Artificial hearts are not life extenders, they never will be. They are not the miracle machines that we could've had by now. A machine that man must forever be dependent upon in order to sustain and extend his life is not a sign of medical advancement. Understand that I'm not speaking about pacemakers or kidney machine equipment here. There is a vast differentiation between those helpful types of aids and an artificial mechanical heart.

People must decide at what point they are going to draw the line. We must determine how far we are willing to go, what methods we will utilize for this extension of life. There is going to be a point that will prove to be too far. Perhaps we have already reached it.

I don't believe that an individual's life should be extended by mechanical means. If a person cannot live naturally, then it is time for him or her to die naturally and let their spirit free of its terminally ill encasement. This is the opinion of my Advisors who are well versed in spiritual law.

What do you think about organ transplants?

I think they are wonderful techniques, as long as the organs were donated by "humans." There is a world of difference between "human" organ transplants and "animal" organs or "artificial" organ transplants. Human organs belong in human bodies and as long as the recipient body accepts the donor organ, then the life of the recipient was "meant" to be extended in this natural manner.

It is important to remember that one of the most beautiful things we can do for our fellow human beings is to donate our bodies to medical science. I cannot express this with enough emphasis. At the moment of physical death, the spirit quickly leaves. Now nothing is left but a useless body — unless that body has been donated to a medical school or a hospital organ bank.

It is a most foolish thing to waste good organs that could be utilized by the saving of another's life. Yet we continue our ignorant traditions of choosing to let bodies decay in the earth rather than donating them as life savers for the living.

This then is also the perspective of our Advisors.

I have very dry skin. What commercial body cream do you recommend?

None.

I have not found a commercial body cream product that performs satisfactorily for the excessively dry skin that the Colorado high country brings. Instead, I make up my own formula from ingredients that are readily available in any marketplace.

I mix peanut oil, sunflower oil, olive oil, and castor oil with a few drops of liquid myrrh. This needs to be shaken well before each application because the ingredients create a suspension. If this formula is gently massaged into the skin, it not only eases the dryness, but it will also eventually eliminate scars, stretch marks and pigmentations such as freckles and moles.

The secret to this effective use is continual *regular* use and utilizing the *massage* action upon application.

What do you do for burns?

This response needs to be qualified. Serious burns require immediate evaluation and treatment by a medical professional. I do not recommend that you personally treat serious burns yourself. It takes much experience with burns to be able to personally evaluate their seriousness.

Minor burns can be quickly relieved by immediately placing a slice of fresh raw potato on the skin surface and wrapping it with a rag or Ace Bandage. This remedy may also prevent skin blistering and later scarring, depending on how quickly you've responded.

What do you give your family for desserts?

Now I'm in hotter water with the mothers of the world!

For desserts we bake. This baking is in the form of *homemade* fruit pies, banana nut breads, blueberry muffins, and spice cakes. Occasionally, if I'm particularly busy, the girls will do the baking. Aimee is particularly fond of baking breads, although they don't last long around here.

What is your opinion of the Christian Scientist's view toward the use of doctors?

I will not denigrate a specific religion's belief system, but I can comment upon the general premise of the question.

What do I think about the practice of people believing that God alone is their physician? That an accident or illness wouldn't have happened unless it was the will of God and, therefore, meant to be?

We have to bear in mind that God does *not* interfere in our lives. Therefore, God neither wishes, wills, nor causes, humanity's ills. And, if God *did* call an individual back to him, that person would die no matter *what* the medical profession did to save his life. When *God* calls a spirit — it goes!

Basically, everything within "reason"should be done to save a life. The medical profession does not interfere with God's will — nothing can. To say that it can, or does, infers that it (the treatment) is more powerful than God. See? God does not will harm to his children.

Would you ever consider endorsing a health or beauty product on a television commercial?

Only if I fully approved of it and actually used the product myself. The issue of your question is not a likelihood.

Commercial endorsements are effective only if they are made by nationally-famous personalities like movie stars and sports notables who grace the television screen with their sparkling smiles. Since I'm basically a very shy person, I wouldn't be a good choice, nor would I look great in a commercial.

Do you or Bill ever have an alcoholic drink?

Rarely. Then it's only a glass of wine with a special dinner.

Do you ever cheat with your eating regiment? Do you ever sometimes have a "Big Mac attack" or sneak a no-no?

I couldn't hold onto my integrity if I said I didn't. Although the concept of "right" eating was detailed in *Earthway,* it comprised No-Eyes' wisdom on the subject. This is not to infer that I or my family members always go "by the book." We generally follow the given guidelines, but don't feel as though we've committed a sin if we veer from it now and then.

Nobody's perfect. That's not an excuse either — that's just plain reality. As with everything, moderation is the key.

My little girls love bubble baths. Do you think they get them clean enough?

Cleanliness is not the point of issue here.

Baths, in themselves, do not get the body clean enough unless a long rinse period from the shower follows it up. Baths leave a dirty film on the hair and body. So, first of all, if you give baths to your children, be sure to have them rinse clean under a warm shower.

Now, as to the subject of bubble baths. Bubble baths are a fun thing to experience. They can fascinate and amuse a child in the bath water for hours. They give a small child the incentive to wash off his or her comfortable dirt. And they can give vaginal infections.

Forget the bubbles and buy bath toys instead. Play it safe.

Would you let your daughters smoke when they get old enough?

The key words here are not "smoke," but rather "let" and "old enough."

It is important for a parent to realize *when* to cut those damaging "apron strings." Many a family has been ruined and torn apart forever because of those strings.

Listen well here, please. When children reach adulthood they're no longer children, they're adults. Parents oftentimes don't see this. They continue to perceive these new adults as their eternal children, their babies who need their continued wise guidance.

A wise and mature parent recognizes the time to let go. They may not always agree with what their grown children do in life, but they gracefully accept it without interference. This is not to infer that mature parental input should not be given, indeed, it should be. Open lines of mature communication should *never* be severed, yet if the grown child holds his ground, the parent must accept and make the best of it without further recriminations that will strain and possibly ruin the relationship forever.

So, your question has been qualified. When my daughters are old enough to be perceived as adults, there will be no "letting" involved anymore. Whether they wish to smoke or not is their own personal adult decision — not mine.

Are diet soft drinks all right for the system?

Not if they contain *any* type of artificial sweetener in them. You would be farther ahead by drinking *less* of the "regular" type of soft drink than you would be by ingesting *more* of the "diet" ones that contain the artificial sweeteners.

If you care enough for your health that you drink "diet" drinks, you would naturally care enough to not want to be ingesting harmful sweeteners. This doesn't make any sense. It's a clear contradiction.

Nitrates are dangerous carcinogens for the body. So how do we eat lunch meats without eating the nitrates? Our family goes through a lot of sandwiches in a week.

Purchase "fresh" meat, cook it up, refrigerate it, and then slice it.

You must reprogram your thinking. Reprogram it back to the natural way of cooking and eating. Erase the mental program entitled: "Processed Foods."

I have a scar on my face. It's not real noticeable, but I feel that it detracts from my looks. How can I get rid of it?

Change your attitude toward it and you won't even notice it. Remember that it is the efforts applied *within* that affect that which is *without.*

I'm a heavy smoker. I'm also pregnant. Does smoking really have any negative effects upon the fetus?

What you're really looking for is a reason to continue smoking. With this question, you've just opened up a can of worms.

This real issue of the question is not the smoking aspect at all, but rather the pregnancy itself.

During my own three pregnancies I never took one puff on a cigarette. I abstained from smoking for each nine-month period. I didn't touch a glass of wine and I ate all the right foods. But most importantly, I kept a light heart and right attitudes.

Not *only* is the fetus really adversely affected by the mother's ingestion of substances, it is *also* adversely affected by the mother's negative emotions and attitudes!

What if I were to make a statement that went something like this: "A child will be afraid of lightning if the mother was fearful of same while pregnant with the child." Sounds rather like a preposterously foolish old wive's tale, doesn't it? And you'd probably laugh at it — but don't. Most folk tales and old wive's tales have been based on some remnant of a singular fact — just as the above statement is.

Recently, researchers have conducted tests that have conclusively proven beyond a shadow of a doubt that "memory imprints" are transferred through the umbilical cord. I do not have room here to detail the precise experimentation, but know that this is reality.

So, in conclusion, while pregnant, don't smoke, drink alcohol, get stressed out or, above all, don't do drugs.

What can I do for the ugly stretch marks left from childbirth?

What? Aren't you proud of your mark of accomplishment?

If you're not, deep massage the abdominal area with a mixture of peanut oil, castor oil, olive oil, Vitamin E oil, and liquid myrrh. Massage this on nightly and after your showers. Be consistent. In time, the marks will blend in so that they are less noticeable.

Can a forceps delivery contribute to the possible mental retardation of a baby?

Infrequently, for the scull bones of an infant are not fused together but are separate soft plates that overlap to accommodate the journey through the pelvic region.

What is better for the mother and child, natural childbirth or regular childbirth?

You want me to say regular, don't you? You want to hear that because you've been intimidated by women friends who've been through a natural childbirth and you're frightened. You're frightened of their recriminations if you don't go through with it too. You're afraid of the pain and your inability to bear it.

Well, you have every right to those natural feelings. Natural childbirth is not always the brave experience that it's touted to be.

The experience of "natural" childbirth can be a beautiful one or it can result in an ugly memory. This all depends on each individual experience. But certainly, going into childbirth with fear, just because a woman thinks it's *the* thing to do, is *not* the decision of choice. Recent professional medical findings have inferred that woman who chose natural childbirth are evidencing a higher percentage of heart problems than those woman who didn't deliver by the natural method.

I would advise expectant mothers to think deeper on this issue. I would advise them to disregard the "grandiose" connotations that are implicated with the natural method and, therefore, place themselves in the capable hands of a professional obstetrician who can best advise the individual woman.

Know that the endurance of natural childbirth pain does *not* a better mother make.

Are all diseases caused by karma?

If this question was asked shortly after the time of Creation, the correct response would be a definitive "yes." However, this would not be a logical or reasonable answer today. The pollution factor and man-made chemical aspect of our times, in conjunction with the issues of stress and emotional ills account for most diseases that invade our systems. Radiation alone generates a high percentage of disease. This being borne out by Three Mile Island and other geographical regions where nuclear accidents or radioactive discharges have contaminated the atmosphere with airborne elements. To say that these were karmically-vectored is more than ridiculous — it's downright ludicrous and absurd. The theory shows little comprehension of the spiritual laws and their mechanics in respect to the totality of their ramifications. Many diseases are the direct result of individual free will choices in the current lifetime — not destiny.

In your book EARTHWAY, does one have to do all twenty-five alignments in order to bring about a healing?

Not at all. These were listed in order to provide the reader with an all-inclusive and comprehensive aspect scope. The individual may choose which ones are more convenient to use, or then again, all may be utilized. The important thing to remember is that whatever treatment aspects are used, they will be directly vibrationally-aligned with the illness and the Power Point Gate that it affects. If someone just wanted to use stones and scents, those will still provide a vibrationally-aligned treatment. See? Gateway Healing therefore provides a multitude of choices for the individual who utilizes the treatment.

On page 220 of EARTHWAY, line 5, was a word left out? It reads "the patient visualizes a brilliant white being pulled down through the head with each breath inhaled." I think the word "light" was omitted.

Yes, the word "light" was indeed omitted. We certainly don't want to be pulling "beings" down through us. The correct wording is: "the patient visualizes a brilliant white *light* being pulled down through the head with each breath inhaled."

I want to learn how to identify and gather the wild plants. Will you teach me this?

This type of learning takes a great deal of time, for it involves many weeks of field work in various regions of the country where the various botanicals grow.

You have to remember that, because this aspect of No-Eyes' wisdom was of lesser importance than the spiritual aspect, the visionary didn't spend a lot of time on the issue of the wild plants. It was more of a crash course for me as I made notes on her instructional lectures. We had precious little time to actually go out roaming the mountainsides and valleys to do real field work. She just didn't feel we could afford the time on this subject.

I suggest that you inquire at your local university to see if they have an extension division for this type of interest. Many universities and colleges have agricultural and horticultural departments that are more than happy to provide the public with bulletins, pamphlets, and books regarding the botanicals that are indigenous to your specific geographic region.

If you have access to a Nature Center in your area, many of these routinely conduct nature walks for the specific purpose of learning to identify local flora.

If these fail to be fruitful for you, check your local bookstore or library for regional botanicals and herbs. There are many fine publications on this subject. The following are good examples:

Earth Medicine Earth Food by Michael A. Weiner
Indian Herbalogy of North America by Alma R. Hutchins
American Indian Medicine by Virgil J. Vogel
Medicines From The Earth by Richard Evans Schultes
Native Harvests by Barbie Kavasch
Field Guide to Medicinal Wild Plants by Bradford Angier

If you're interested in some real hands-on field experiences and you have the time to be away from home for a few weeks, Tom Brown, Jr. conducts nature survival courses in New Jersey. This will cost you, but I hear the experience is well worth one's time.

What causes psychosomatic illnesses?

"Psycho" means of the "mind." The mind!

These ailments are generated from an individual's psychological need for emotional fulfillment or a diversion from an intolerable life situation.

Psychosomatic illness is the result of negative thought patterns due to affecting factors such as stress, unhappiness, hate, jealousy, insecurity, aloneness, and other emotional negatives. The phenomenon is a splintered form of a psychological escape mechanism which saves the individual from fearful situations.

All the above generating forces can evidence a psychosomatic illness or dis-eased physiological state of being. And frequently, an individual may self-generate a psychosomatic illness because they have a great need for attention from those around them.

How can Reiki cost $225 just to learn First Degree?

My friend, as with all new ideas (contrived or otherwise), they are seen as a "marketing medium." The more outrageous ways and means to expand an issue, such as healing, offers the creators untold avenues of new wealth. As was foretold, the End Times would see an influx of many, many ways and means being perpetrated. Why so much money? Well because you're being shown a very "unique" technique and are being "trained" to be one of those who're "certified" for it. And, if you believe that, I've got a great bridge for you to buy too.

The idea of selling New Age training (healing or otherwise) is a scam. How about I charge to teach the intricate Earthway Healing Way of No-Eyes? After all, most of her information came from her "brothers" (other intelligences). That should be worth, ohhh, say at least $2,500. Especially since it encompasses all the Aligned Vibratory healing aspects of exactness, for I'd have to charge you for a First Degree level that included Proper Lifestyle and General Dietary Guidelines. The Second Degree could then include the "secrets" of proper "Element Utilization" which would instruct you on the correct use of stones, totems, metals, etc. The Third Degree would be quite expensive because then you'd be into the deeper aspects of learning the "Vibrational Rate Alignments" of all elements as they're associated with the corresponding Power Point Gates of the spinal vertebrae. And, Fourth Degree would make you a *Master Earthway Healer* because then. . .then you would have the total "Secret Knowledge" and could then be "certified" to go out and charge the same amount to teach others.

This would be nothing different from the "pyramid" type of selling so common with many commercial retail companies that depend on the teacher/student/teacher scenario. It's a method of generating income.

So then, if the issue of money is removed, what is left?

What's left is a give-away. And so the *Earthway* book does serve as my health teachings to everyone. . .it is my give-away so that "everyone" can know, learn and utilize the method of Gate Alignment Healing taught by No-Eyes through her information from her Starborn Brothers. What makes this Healing Way so beautiful is that you need no teacher or "healer" other than yourself. It is a "self-healing" way. And, if you get the book through a library or borrow it from a friend — it didn't cost you a single red penny.

How can color play a role in healing?

All color variations vibrate to differing frequencies. These various frequency vibrations can be directly aligned to the psychic Power Points of the body and specific spinal vertebrae. By correlating the same vibrational frequencies of all elemental healing aspects, great power is applied to the precise point of the illnesses source .

If color wasn't a major aspect, the Power Point Gates would have no specific corresponding color. However, they're very sensitive and responsive to this important vibratory aspect that serves to play a major role in affecting Gates, Spinal Points and, ultimately, healing.

What do you suggest using as a soothing agent for hemorrhoids?

Almond oil will shrink these. NOTE OF CAUTION: this may slightly burn upon initial application, but the sensation will quickly dissipate.

Pure petroleum jelly will act as a soothing agent when applied after each bowel movement. Be sure to also thoroughly clean area with a mild soap and warm water after each movement and before applying the jelly.

Warm sitz baths several times a day can also be soothing. Warm water is a wonderful healer.

What do you personally use as a hair shampoo? Do you make your own?

I don't make my own shampoo. I lather up a bar of Packer's Pine Tar Soap. It's also an excellent facial cleanser and body soap that leaves the skin moisturized and soft. The black bar may not look so appealing, but it cleanses well and doesn't leave a film.

What do you suggest for a chronic pain that's high in the stomach?

A trip to your doctor. You may have an ulcer or other serious internal problems. Don't guess at these. Don't procrastinate either. A pain that's chronic is already a clear sign that it's not going away any time soon.

No-Eyes suggested we not eat of the pork meats, yet Cayce said bacon was okay as long as it was done crisp.

All kinds of pork variations come from a "hoofed" animal, and so No-Eyes abhorred the ingestion of same.

However, it would appear that there are times when my own Advisors see a need for me to ingest bacon (crisp). This is for various personal health reasons they perceive I require and so advise me of same. But on the whole, the regular or routine ingestion of bacon (crisp or otherwise) is not a good practice.

You must remember that there are extenuating circumstances to many dietary guidelines. Many of these depending upon the individual's unique requirements at any given time.

Eating meats is not spiritual nor does the habit contribute to a spiritual body.

Really? What a conflicting and contradictory concept that is.

Please know that spirituality is of the spirit and, being such, is of an intangible nature.

The physical body is of the physical and is, therefore, a definitive tangible.

Intangibles and tangibles do not and cannot mix nor affect each other. Please keep these two separate as are their inherent natures.

Please recall that Jesus ingested meat. Did that make him less spiritual?

What botanicals or foodstuffs are good antitoxins?

Kelp (for radiation), red clover and chaparral (tumors), onions, garlic and lettuce (blood purifiers).

It's been said that the ingestion of honey is no better than cane sugar. I'm confused.

This has been said in relation to "surface" comparisons by nutritionists and such who haven't delved into the more far-reaching benefits of honey.

When ingesting honey processed in your own region or state, it acts not only as a sweetener replacement for cane sugar, but also as an immune-builder against local pollen allergens. And, most importantly, sugar is acid-producing while honey is *alkaline.*

Wherever possible, purchase and consume locally-processed *un*filtered honey.

Edgar Cayce suggested that, along with fish and fowl, lamb was a good source of meat. Yet No-Eyes suggested differently. Can you clarify why?

I can only comment on the visionary's reasoning here. She knew that the higher animals (hoofed ones) had a greater capacity for emotional expression and sensitivity. Therefore they were perceived as a slightly lesser level of mankind's "brothers." The killing and eating of hoofed brothers was highly repulsive to her and her view of our animal kingdom relationship.

Why would the application of honey be a healing agent for cysts and skin infections?

This is because honey is one of nature's own antibiotic substances.

Can you explain why mullein is recommended for colds, cancer, boils, acne, and lymph ailments?

All of the above represent an acid condition within the body. They all also indicate an infection or invasion of harmful or toxic cells and/or conditions. And since mullein is an agent that balances the acid-alkaline ratio, this is a highly effective substance for these ailments. Also, mullein acts to bind up the toxins so they can then be eliminated from the system.

Why are my sinuses giving me so much trouble all year around? Is this karmic?

Absolutely not. It's beer-ic! Avoid those hops!

What over-the-counter medication is good for a child's vomiting and diarrhea?

Emetrol can control the vomiting. Imodium A-D for the diarrhea. You need to get these under control first. Then give the child plenty of liquids to replenish the body fluids. The least upsetting and most beneficial of these would be liquids such as chicken broth, plenty of water, have him suck on popsicles for these also replace lost sugar for energy, mullein tea, Vernor's Ginger Ale (this has a particular stomach-calming effect).

Is there something in my diet that's causing my daily headaches?

The daily chocolates.
The nightly beers.

Why do I feel so sluggish most of the time?

The rare beef steaks, the daily beef hamburgers, the weekly pork roasts, the morning rubbery bacon, and the weekly ham dinners are the culprits generating your sluggishness. With this type of diet you're setting up a prime pre-cancerous condition, especially when you're not controlling your stress levels!

What kind of margarine is best to use?

Most margarines are made from vegetable oils. These are not advised. It would be far better for your system to use small amounts of real butter.

My daughter has a bad case of acne. Is it something she's eating?

The *corn* foods. She snacks too much on corn chips. Remove all corn from her diet and have her wash her face with Packer's Pine Tar soap twice a day. Her makeup is also clogging her pores — leave off the foundation cream base she's wearing. She also needs to refrain from much of the fried foods she eats.

What type of vegetable oil should I be using. There's so many kinds available. Sunflower oil? Corn Oil? Peanut Oil?

Canola, olive or peanut oil are the three best choices for cooking with. The olive oil has the added benefit of also lowering the bad cholesterol levels in the system.

There's so many hair conditioners on the market. Can you suggest a "natural" one?

A weekly oil treatment is best to condition dry or damaged hair. Pour oil in your palm and generously coat all the strands from scalp to ends. If the hair is short, wrap the head in a cotton scarf and leave it overnight (or an entire day). If the hair is long, braid it. The oil does not have to be "hot," but is better if it's room temperature.
Peanut oil for light colored hair.
Walnut oil for darker colored hair.

How many eggs are in the ovaries and when do they develop?

A woman's reproductive system contains two ovaries. Each one houses approximately 250,000 eggs. That's around 500,000 total. And, perhaps about 450 will be released in the woman's lifetime.
The second part of your question is not clear. If you meant to ask when these egg cells manifest within the ovaries, then the answer is that they're already there at birth. A woman is born with them there. If you're asking when the egg cells develop into new life, then that would be when fertilization occurs. . .conception.

Where is the mind located within the brain?

Medically speaking, thought is generated by neuron stimulation and interaction. The location of the mind is still listed as. . .unknown.
Spiritually speaking, the mind is wherever the spirit is.

What's causing the migraine headaches I get in the evenings?

This is seen as not being classed as a migraine, but rather what is termed "cluster" headaches. . .these being located on one side of the head behind the eye.
In your effort to weather-proof your home, you've closed off any and all available "make-up" air for your furnace.
Carbon monoxide is forming within the home. Please provide adequate make-up air. . .you're poisoning your family! Literally!

My daughter's had headaches, dizziness, and blurred vision for several weeks now. I've treated them with herbs but nothing seems to work. What do you suggest?

Listen carefully here. Herbs are wonderful healers, but there are times when more professional help is required for a specific condition. Your daughter needs to see a neurologist *immediately*. Please see to it.

Will modern medicine find a better way to deal with bad burn victims?

Oh, absolutely! In fact, this new healing method for serious burn victims will come from seed oils, and honey is being utilized today in China. Later, after the Phoenix is flying free, there will be even more miraculous ways of healing severe burns.

I live in Colorado Springs. Can you suggest a natural health shop that has knowledgeable employees?

The owners of R & A Natural Foods are extremely knowledgeable. They're located in Old Colorado City. The address is:2631 W. Colorado Avenue, Colorado Springs, CO 80904. (719) 632-2516. Ray Wells, Owner

I wrote you with a health problem but you said you could no longer answer specific health questions. Why is that?

This is because everything is already in *Earthway*. You have to understand that I'm not a healer like No-Eyes was and don't treat people with health problems. I passed on the healer's methods and information through the health book so that the public could learn and gain from it. For me to pretend I'm No-Eyes or have her capabilities would just never due. Therefore, I've made it a policy to refrain from dispensing medical advice to those who write with such questions or problems. Anything that's not covered in *Earthway* should be directed to a qualified physician or some type of bona fide medical practitioner. Even when I did assist people with health questions (such as in some of the former questions and responses), I always finalized the information with a statement that advised the individual to check with their doctor. Alternative methods of healing or treating medical symptoms can be wonderful, but only after the causal problem is properly diagnosed by a qualified physician. I've seen too many people who misdiagnose their symptoms, thereby further complicating the condition by mistreating it. So see your physician. Or see several to get a solid diagnosis. Listen to the doctor's advice and then go from there by following your own inner guidance regarding the best course of treatment.

One word of caution though: be extremely careful of many of the so-called New Age healing techniques. . .most you can successfully accomplish all by yourself without having to learn "secret techniques," or pay hundreds of dollars for them.

What's best to use for taking eye makeup off with?

You have to be extremely careful with anything used around the eyes. For years, I used to take my makeup off with a wonderful natural preparation called Golden-Myrrh that contained pure herbal ingredients. But suddenly, my eyes started becoming very red and my first thought was that the makeup had become contaminated so I tossed it all out and bought fresh. The redness continued. Then I thought I might have developed an allergy to the makeup and stopped wearing it. The eyes cleared up. When I tried it one more time, the eyes reddened again. So I stopped to think about *everything* I used whenever I did my eyes. And I came up with the Golden-Myrrh I used to take it off. A few weeks prior, I had noticed that they'd changed the product label. And, when I read the *ingredient* of the "new packaging," I found that they'd added one. . .Benzoin! And this singular ingredient is definitely NOT for the eyes! I was just sick that the manufacturers of such a wonderful natural product had completely adulterated it by adding such an ingredient. So. . .lesson learned here is to always double-check ingredients of a product that had its label changed. As has been proven. . .oftentimes more than the packaging has been altered.

So then, what to use to take your eye makeup off? *Pure* petroleum jelly. Nothing works better or is safer.

Your book EARTHWAY was like an encyclopedia. It was everything I thought it would be.

I appreciate the compliment. The book took more than a year to organize, due to the reams of notes I'd made from No-Eyes' health lessons, and it was quite a project to collate into a single book. I wanted to make it be all-inclusive of the many health aspects that, heretofore, has been only available by forcing the public to search through many separate volumes. This is why I combined all her material to make just a single resource book that would make natural healing referencing so much easier for the public. The only material that didn't come directly from No-Eyes was the section called: "The Earth Mother's Pharmacy." I thought most people would be impressed by today's modern medicinal use of botanicals in their doctor's prescriptions and pharmacology preparations. It proves that the utilization of natural botanicals and other substances (such as spider's webs and frog glands) are not the "voodoo medicine" some professionals would have the public believe. I had to do a little arguing with my editor to keep this section in the book. They kept wanting to pull it out because it didn't come from No-Eyes. I'm glad they kept it in because it will enlighten a lot of people who thought the use of botanicals for healing was just for witch doctors and native medicine men.

In the Gateway Healing section of EARTHWAY, does one use "all" the botanicals listed for each ailment?

Using all the suggested botanicals at once would be unhealthy for the system. These natural herbals are listed as those that are most beneficial for a specific ailment. The individual chooses from these and finds which botanical is most effective in their own system.

Just as there is individual preference for headache pain relievers for each person (Aspirin, Tylenol, Advil, etc.), so too do people find certain botanicals more efficient for their specific system. One wouldn't take Aspirin, Tylenol, Advil together for a headache, likewise, one doesn't take all the botanicals listed for a specific ailment in the Gateway Healing Section. One self-discovers which botanicals work best for them.

Can you tell me if there are any Gateway healers in North Carolina that I can go to?

Gateway Healing is nothing at all like Reiki or any of the other New Age types of natural healing, because Gateway healing is inherently designed for "self-healing." That's the most beautiful aspect of it. You don't *need* anyone else to work it for you. See? It's totally self-contained and meant to be simple enough for each individual to utilize themselves.

There will not be Gateway practitioners taking your money. This method of natural self-healing was given by No-Eyes and no other individual has the authority to capitalize on it in any way, shape or form. One does Gateway healing on themselves only.

I'd be very interested in hearing of anyone claiming to be a Gateway healing practitioner (utilizing the format outlined in *Earthway*). Yes, I would be very interested. . . so would my attorney.

In the "Gateway Healing" section of EARTHWAY, the use of solarized water was listed as an aspect. Where can these colored jars or bottles be purchased?

I'm not familiar with a specific outlet for these, however, you can use any colored bottle, such as washed-out wine bottles.

My Advisor has a more simple suggestion. Take any "clear" glass bottle and wrap a solid colored piece of 100% cotton around it. As these cloths become faded with the sunlight they'll need replenishing to keep their brilliance and energy. It will be important to use cloth with the pure colors, such as forest green as opposed to a lime green.

Are condoms a valid safeguard against AIDS?

No. Likewise, many types of surgical gloves present the same risks.

You mentioned using Packer's Pine Tar Soap . Where can I get it?

Some Wal-Mart stores carry it. You can also order it through the Heritage Store, P.O. Box 444-MR, Virginia Beach, VA 23458 (1-804-428-0100)

I heard that cocoa butter was good for diminishing fresh scars. If this is true, does any cocoa butter cream work?

Cocoa butter is an excellent aid for diminishing fresh scars, however, two points need to be known. The cocoa butter has to be 100% *pure* and it must be applied on a *daily* basis (several times per day if possible.)

I've looked at all the cocoa butter lotions and creams that are currently available and none of them are pure, in fact, they have a very disagreeable smell. These will not help to heal scars.

When I was very young and was bitten by a dog, I was left with a large facial scar. The physician had me apply cocoa butter to my face throughout each day (every few hours). This pure product is still available today under the same trade name and it has a very agreeable scent. It comes in a push-up tube style for ease of application. This pure cocoa butter is made by the Woltra Company and should be available through your local pharmacist or by ordering it from the Heritage Store (address above).

Doesn't lobelia have the potential to be dangerous? Yet in EARTHWAY you suggest it for memory and for children's learning disabilities.

You're absolutely right in your statements. Whenever lobelia is suggested, its use needs to be monitored by an accredited herbalist. This statement was inadvertently omitted from the book, therefore I recommend lobelia not be ingested by anyone not fully acquainted with it.

Laughing Eyes

The ones with smiling hearts are the Hope of the world. The ones with open minds are the New Teachers. The ones with laughing eyes and spirits free are the Innocents. Smiling hearts. Open minds. Laughing eyes. Spirits free.
The Children.

Are talented child prodigies the result of a carryover soul memory?

Yes. Child prodigies are best recognized through the evidence of their musical abilities, however, there are also those young ones who excel in many other intellectual areas of science, mathematics, and spiritual law.

These recalled aspects of knowledge stem from an *active* facet of the spirit's multi-faceted personality that comprises the totality of same.

My little boy has been begging me for a gerbil. Animals can transmit diseases to children. What do you advise? Have your kids ever had any pets besides your dog?

Loosen up, mom. Pets are one of the best things you can buy your son.

• Currently we have two dogs, a parakeet, and a cat. Throughout the years we've had gerbils, guinea pigs, stray cats who've walked into our home and stayed, lizards, fish, and baby wild birds that have fallen from their nests that Sarah brought home to save. We've taken wild birds with broken wings to our veterinarian, and once, when a hawk flew into our window, we wrapped it to keep it warm and had to travel quite a distance to take it to the Department of Wildlife's "hawk lady" who is licensed to care for these protected wild ones. We had the chance to care for a wolf pup (which I would've loved to have), but I had somehow lost the name of the woman who wanted to give it to me. I'd love to have a couple of llamas too.

Animals provide a great deal of love — the unconditional kind — and companionship. Our dogs, Rainbow and Magic (both part coyote) have such tender sensitivities that are so human-like. They perceive our moods and respond accordingly. Both take turns curling up beneath my desk to be near me whenever I'm typing. They'll nudge my elbow with their nose or place a paw on my lap or arm when I'm writing, just to say they love me.

My obvious advice to you would be to go ahead and buy your son that gerbil. It will give him a sense of responsibility as he cares for it. It'll give him a little companion and something to talk to and play with.

Pets have been found to be an invaluable method of mental therapy for people of all ages, but particularly for children and the elderly because both of these segments of society frequently find themselves alone with nobody to talk to.

The only caution I would give to you about a gerbil would be to make certain that it can't get out of its cage or, only let it out in a small enclosed room. You'll save yourself and your son a lot of anxiety in case it should ever escape into the house like Sarah's once did.

So loosen up, mom. Buy the little furry critter — you won't be sorry.

I love nature and have decided to leave the merry-go-round workaday life to give my attention to that aspect of life, however, my daughter wants to be a veterinarian. Should I foresake my new trail into nature or go back to work to finance her education?

I found your question interesting because the aspects of it parallel my own situation. Since I cannot tell you what to do about this, the best thing would be for me to let you in on our own tentative plans.

My Sarah is the same age as your daughter. Sarah, since she's always loved animals, also wants to be a veterinarian (or a nature artist since she's artistically talented). I can't afford to put money away for Veterinary School, so we've decided it would be best if she could get a job as a veterinary assistant. This would be part-time, of course while she's still in school. This part-time job would allow her to save up her money while gaining invaluable hands-on learning experiences in the field she's chosen. Our local vet has offered to take her under her wing and begin teaching Sarah the fundamentals by letting her attend routine examinations and observe the various operations. In this manner, your daughter, like Sarah, can get a real feel for the field long before she's old enough to apply for schooling. And, she will have saved up her tuition for it in the meantime. There's no reason why your daughter can't attend school and, at the same time, work a part-time job to save for her specialized schooling after graduation. Most of our friend's children have worked their own way through college. And, don't forget the aspect of personal value that affects this issue: when an individual personally works to obtain a goal, that goal is so much more valued.

So, ultimately, what you choose to do here is up to you, but I hope I've given you a viable alternative by sharing our own situation.

I had a miscarriage three years ago and didn't release the child's spirit. I had a hysterectomy six months ago and feel grief that I can't bring the spirit into the world now. My teacher (name withheld) released the spirit into the cosmos, but two days ago I heard "Mommy" whispered in my ear. Can you help me?

I sympathize with the grief you experienced with your miscarriage, for I've had four and know the emotional pain they cause. However, we must go into the factual spiritual mechanics of this because both you and your teacher do not have a complete understanding of them.

A developing fetus does not yet have a spirit contained within it. A developing fetus *may* have an *associated* spirit who awaits entry at the time of birth. *A spirit awaiting entry into a newborn can perceive the probabilities that may negatively affect the development of the fetus.* That statement is so important for us to realize. This underscores the fact that, if a miscarriage is foreseen as being a strong probability, no spirit will associate itself to the pregnant woman until the probable threat has *passed.* Therefore, a miscarriaged fetus *has* no spirit associated with it. Consequently, there is *no* spirit to release! This is so important to grasp because this is truly the "way of it."

The "spirit" you *think* has remained attached to you has long ago reincarnated again. You are now and *have always been* "free" of that spirit.

I cannot account for what "teachers" are telling the public, but I do see much grief experienced by an overly-trusting public. This grief runs deep into the mind's psychological aspects, so much so that one may even begin "hearing" the mind's self-generated voices that serve to deepen the grief and make it real.

Please, my friend, know the reality of the precepts of spiritual law. Know how these things work. If your teacher isn't in full cognizance, then it's up to you to be responsible for the knowing.

My four-year-old sometimes appears to have an invisible playmate. I don't want to do the wrong thing with this so can you help me out?

The young children can be extremely sensitive to the spiritual forces of reality. They may frequently perceive a "presence" that you cannot. Generally it's best to let this situation alone and it works itself out quite naturally.

Two children in our own household experienced a "presence" as a playmate. The situation was temporary. Because I could also perceive these playmates, and knew their source, the family members acknowledged their existence and left it at that.

There are two main sources for a "playmate presence" who manifests to a physical child. One is a wayward child spirit who is lonely. Frequently the spirit's interaction with a living child will be the very impetus that makes it realize the truth. The spirit likes the interaction but isn't fulfilled. Soon it's situation becomes less and less enjoyable and this creates the condition that makes the spirit "open to better options," thereby creating a willingness to listen to its spirit helpers.

The second source for a child's invisible playmate is the child's own spirit guide as in my own case in childhood. These very caring and loving entities manifest in one's childhood for a wide variety of reasons. Sometimes they come to instill the child with early knowledge. They may come to preserve psychological stability if the child is being abused in any way. They may come to establish a spiritual foundation for the child, for a child who has had "experiential spiritual data," will not veer from the truths he or she has experienced when young.

The only time a "spiritually knowledgeable" psychologist should be consulted is if the child's established behavior is altered in a negative manner or if the child gives any indication that his/her playmate says or does bad things. This would indicate a wayward child spirit who is extremely angry or negatively influenced. But, on the whole, you should be advised that this is a rarity.

What causes stillbirths?

Stillbirths are caused either by a fetus that didn't physiologically develop right or by the associated spirit who either missed the entry moment or changed his/her mind at the last minute. It's possible, but not very probable, that there was no associated spirit awaiting entry.

We want to relocate to Arizona, but are afraid of upsetting our kids. Did your's give you a hard time about moving whenever you relocated?

A family's geographic relocation can be traumatic on children, but only if they don't already have a solid emotional foundation. This is important here.

Since moving to Colorado in 1977 we've moved eleven times. Some of these moves were to other homes in the same area and some were across entire mountain ranges. All moves were advised by our guides. All were necessary and never frivolous. And although many of them represented the girls attending new schools and making new friends, they never complained. Why? Because they knew that, as long as they were still going to be a part of their loving family unit, there'd be nothing to fear.

Our girls have learned one important thing during all these moves — to have faith in yourself and those you love. Although many moves were made without knowing what jobs we were going to work for income, the girls saw that we'd work whatever we had to in order for the monthly household expenses could be met. Most often the income was just enough, other times it didn't quite make it and we strived to work as much overtime as we could. But through all of this, the bottom line was always that the children knew they were greatly loved and that, although circumstances frequently changed, nothing else would. At a young age they learned that, no matter where one lived or how many times they moved about, you needed to keep your eyes open for every opportunity to take advantage of, thereby having faith in yourself and those you love. In this manner there is no fear involved in relocating to a completely strange town or area. You learn self-reliance and you learn the responsibility of making your way in any situation.

As far as new schools and friends, sure it's difficult for children to be doing this. Isn't it a little nerve-wracking to start a new job? You don't know the routine or the people. You're the new one in the office. Will your co-workers like you? Kids are no different in dealing with this type of personal situation, but by going through it several times, they also learn that friends are found everywhere. Their self-image and inner fortitude is strengthened. They then realize that they too can make their way among strangers in new surroundings. They become self-reliant "within." And, they have learned, that they are not the only ones who move, for their own friends relocate to other areas or states. This then shows children that life is ever changing and, to be resilient, one must personally accommodate all those changes by meeting them with acceptance.

The important aspect to remember here is that as long as there is a strong and loving family unit *core,* all peripheral changes are superfluous to the members. And, my friend, that "strong family core" is *your* responsibility.

How do I tell my children about the changes without scaring them?

If your child needed an operation how would you explain it? Psychologically, what attitude would you convey. What terminology? Would you say: "They're going to knock you out, take a sharp knife and cut out your tonsils?" Hardly. You would approach the subject in a compassionate manner and use terminology that instills the proper attitude that doesn't generate any fear. You would stress the many benefits of the "outcome" rather than dwelling on the mechanics of the operation itself. See? You emphasize the "goodness" of the issue and center on the wonderful "result."

Children are not stupid little people running around our houses. They see the television newscasts. They hear the radio broadcasts . They hear adults talking . They're not the dreamers many adults perceive them to be. They worry about war. They are concerned about pollution and nuclear plants and radioactive waste . They're not dumb. They know their world isn't paradise, so why *not* tell them things will get much better in the future? Telling children about the Golden Age of the future when the Phoenix flies free would be a wonderful ray of hope to most children. My own can't wait for it all to come about .

So in response to your question I say that the "how" of telling your children about the changes dwells in the proper attitude and perspective. You have that choice. You can stress blood and guts destruction or you can emphasize the beauty of living in a world with no pollution, no threat of nuclear war or accidents, and no unjustice or hate. The ugly or the beautiful. It's your call.

My son told me that he "flys" around during his sleep. Is he just dreaming or is he actually having out-of-body experiences? I'm not sure I know the proper way to explain this ability to him. He's six. I feel it's important that these children receive the right terminology in terms they can easily grasp.

I've been advised that your son is doing both.

And yes, I absolutely agree with you regarding the use of proper terminology that clearly conveys these concepts in terms a small child can readily grasp. Young children are the segment of our society who most frequently experience evidence of the paranormal such as spirit flight during the sleep state. And, if these experiences are not fully and accurately explained, they'll grow up to become the mature skeptics who have all but forgotten their own childhood encounters with spirit reality.

God said that we need to become as little children. And little children possess free spirits and marvelously open minds — until the adults close them with a loud slam.

Explain to your son that, while he sleeps, his physical body is like a big spaceship. His beautiful spirit is like an astronaut that can float through space. Tell him that his spirit can never get lost because it's safely connected to his spaceship by his glowing safety line (the silver cord). Explain that his silver cord is like a big rubber band that can stretch forever and ever without breaking. And, it allows his spirit to go wherever it wants until he is ready to wake up and the cord pulls him back to his spaceship.

I gave you the analogy that I've used when my own girls were very young. You can use it in your own words and drawings.

My child frequently verbalizes what I'm thinking. He says that he can read my mind. Is he telepathic? It was scary at first, now it's just a normal part of our daily lives.

And that is how it should be, for this is a very "normal" aspect of the spirit. Yes. Your son is indeed telepathic. Please be aware of this at all times. My advice to you would not be to guard your tongue, but rather your "thoughts."

My child says she sees colored lights around people. Is she seeing auras? How do I teach her about these abilities? How do I explain the reality of auras to a seven-year-old child?

We see that the youngster easily perceives auras. She has a highly-developed spirit and came from an advanced former lifetime. She has retained this function, but is also saddled with a child's untrained mind.

I'm saddened when I hear of cases like yours, and I hear of so many. This saddens me because so many of these advanced spirits are here now for a specific spiritual purpose, and unless they're nurtured by aware parents who will encourage them and understand them, they will be greatly hampered. They will have to begin again when they reach adulthood when their nebulous inner promptings tell them that they have an important service to accomplish and, not knowing that they'll have to break away in order to find the searching path that the spirit within guides them to.

Your daughter is one of the fortunate ones who have parents who are aware enough to recognize the symptoms of awareness and desire to protect that awareness. The issue of auras is addressed in my children's manual. For now, explain to your daughter that all things in life, both living and non-living, have energy that comes from it. Living things have a greater energy than non-living things. This energy can be seen by certain people. It is normal to be able to see this energy. It is a real part of life. Tell her that just as some people are born blind and some are born with eyesight, there are also people who can see some things that others can't. She is simply one who can see them.

It is also vital that you impress upon her the importance of secrecy regarding her sight ability. This is the most sad aspect, for, if she speaks about it, her peers will jeer and make fun of her and the adults (teachers and such) will advise you to take her to a psychologist. Give her your love and support. Within the safe confines of your home, discuss this with her freely and begin to expand her awareness of the other beneficial paranormal functions that are "normal" for *normal* people to possess.

If the world wasn't so ignorant, our aware children could be free to develop their spiritual skills naturally — the way they were intended.

Where does a stillborn baby's spirit go to after it dies?

A stillborn baby *has* no spirit. The spirit enters a newborn at the precise second the baby breathes its first breath on its own.

Besides, where *would* a spirit go to other than back to the spirit dimension it came from?

I took great care while pregnant. Why was my baby born with so many physical defects?

Before your baby was born, its spirit *knew* of the defects it would be experiencing. And it still chose to enter. This is because these physical difficulties were accepted by the spirit as being the best possible manner of balancing out its previously incurred negative karma. This physical condition was indeed a chosen one.

How can siblings who are being raised as equals in the exact same environment have such opposing personalities? Or, for that matter, how can identical twins be so different in personality?

One answer can serve both situations.

"We" are not the product of physical genes. We, meaning each individual (whether or not they be twins), are the product of each's "composite personality" as formed through all past experiential incarnations.

Each newborn brings to its new life an old spirit that has been imprinted with facets of every life it previously lived. This then is responsible for the uniquely individualized personalities that have been separately influenced long before birth.

My three-year-old has a powerfully strong will. He's constantly testing me to see how much he can get away with. I'm about worn out and ready to just let him have his way.

Yes, let him have his way. Let him do as he wishes and you'll have raised a self-centered monster.

Listen carefully here. Little children can possess incredibly strong wills. That's just part of their growth pattern to test and test those of authority. But you were the one who became pregnant with this child and, hopefully, that pregnancy was wanted. With this desire for a child also comes the desire for a "good" child who will grow to be a responsible adult. You want your child to be an asset to humanity.

Good solid values are not taught to a youngster by letting *him* be the parent. *Your* will must ever remain the strongest, must ever prevail. If he is always winning out, then you're definitely doing something wrong in your disciplinary technique. You're doing a grave disservice to your young child. You must always be firm. You must also always be consistent. You must always be strong. . .yet loving at the same time.

I see more and more disturbing evidence in our society of parents who are either too busy to properly discipline their wayward children or they simply don't care. The kids are strong. They're persistent. They'll beg and beg until I hear the parent's usual reply after they let out an exasperated sigh. They'll simply reply, "Oh go ahead, I don't care." But the parent really does care, they're just tired of the constant hassle and the begging, therefore they give into the child's wants by defeatedly saying that they don't care — and the child smiles and happily skips off to wherever he wanted to go.

Don't *ever* answer your child's requests with the reply of "I don't care." Rather say "alright," or "yes, that's okay with me," or "I guess you can do that," but *never* respond with that horrible "I don't care" attitude.

The next time you're too worn down to maintain the upper hand, think about what kind of adult your child will grow to be if you let him have his way all the time. He'll grow into a man who is so self-centered and egotistical that he'll treat others (even you) like servants and will, in the end, be a very unhappy individual who has no respect for the feelings of his fellowmen.

A responsible parent cares.

My grown children are all moving out of state. They're deserting their mother. I'll be all alone. How can children be so thoughtless and cruel?

I couldn't accurately respond to your situation unless I knew more of what the other side of the coin looked like, and I was apprised of the total picture.

I believe that it is thoughtless and cruel to expect your children to remain with you all of your life. It is thoughtless because it's selfish. It's cruel because you are keeping them from growing and seeking their own guided way in this life.

I never mean to intentionally pry into one's personal life, but I needed a rounded perspective of your situation and I was advised that all your children offered to take you with them and even buy you a house in their new neighborhood. But, you said, you refused to move to another state.

Dear lady, your children are grown adults and they're separate entities from you. Once they've left the home nest, they're responsible for themselves and their families. They're not intentionally trying to hurt you. You must stop trying to manipulate them with your negative self-centered emotions. You must stop playing upon their sensitivities. Perhaps this sounds stone-hearted to you. It would, simply because of how you're thinking. Your children do love you very much — love them back and set them free. Or, better yet, take their offer and go with them.

If you let your children move away from you, please see that the decision was not theirs, but rather yours, for you were given a choice to be with them.

How did you raise your children in respect to discipline?

I was a strict parent. I demanded obedience and got it. I also got the respect that goes with it.

I cannot simply set rules down for you here because correct discipline is a qualified concept depending on the personal relationship the individual family shares between its members. The best way to explain my technique would be to tell you about our own family relationship.

From the time my girls were very young I gave them responsibilities such as putting all their toys away before bed and making their beds in the morning. (A mother is not a maid.) They made their beds. A three-year-old can make her bed. It may not *look* like it's been made but that's not what's relevant. These daily responsibilities gives a small child a real sense of helpfulness and of being a total part of the household.

If they were doing something wrong I'd tell them nicely to stop and, after the second request, if they continued, they'd have to stand in a corner. Usually this hurt their feelings enough to make them never do the thing again.

Both parents must agree on discipline. Both must be always consistent.

We constantly reinforce our love for all the girls. We're a family that hugs and kisses a lot. Love *must* outweigh the discipline.

Since they were small children, they've been openly exposed to the facts and realities of life. Nothing was ever hidden from them. Consequently, today they are well adjusted young ladies who understand the technicalities of sexuality and also possess healthy attitudes about the subject . It's important that all questions be answered for a child . Don't ever answer more than the child asks. As she grows, she'll ask more and then you can answer more.

Our unique closeness has come from open and frequent expressions of love in conjunction with playful bantering. We frequently use sarcasm. This may sound highly unusual, but it's made us a family that deeply understands each other It's been a way of maintaining equal ground. Too frequently, parents and their children are miles apart — vertically. The parents are up in the sky somewhere while the children are down in the pits. If common ground can be continually maintained, a natural understanding of each other's feelings and situations comes naturally .

Always be fair and treat each child equally. We've passed the "standing in corners" and the "grounding" stages now because they' re young ladies who appreciate our "input" in respect to their personal problems. And we spend long hours talking them out .

Very young children are always testing . This isn't because they want to be ornery, but rather because they have a mind of their own and are always exercising their individuality and their right to think. A parent must "allow" a measure of freedom for the child here. But the parent must also draw a firm line. I see far too many parents who let the *child* dictate the rules simply because the parent doesn't want a "scene." Children can really take control in a public place and they know it. Don't let your child intimidate you in public.

Generally, we found that our form of discipline advanced to the stage where control was maintained just by our tone of voice or a certain look.

Always be consistent in your discipline. Never allow a child to get away with something one time and then send him/her in a corner the next time. This leads to confusion in the child's mind. It leads to unstable discipline.

Most of all, give unbounded love. . .lots and lots of hugs.

Our young people are going crazy with their wild music and their outrageous fads of dress. Don't you think this is the type of thing that is contributing to the eventual downfall of our nation?

Are not the young — our youth — entitled to free expression?

Think back to your own youth. Each generation of young people is different than the one preceding it. They have different likes and dislikes that are evidenced through their dress and choice of music style.

The dress and music of your own youth were an abomination to the adults of that particular time. The dress and music of my own youth (miniskirts and Elvis) was a disgrace to the adults of that time. They were often viewed as "the devil's work." You see, it's simply a situation that becomes relative to the altered viewpoints of the observer. The viewpoint is altered to fit the mind of the viewer — the participant sees it one way and the onlooker sees it another.

You must realize that the youth of any nation are merely the products of those who have preceded them. The youth *is* the result — not the cause. The "times" are a continuum evolution in lifestyle and, this includes music and modes of dress. So too do the youth evolve and eventually mature into their own adulthood, but rarely are they permanently damaged or "made evil" by a measure of youth spent listening to music adults disapprove of. Many of the baby boomers that loved the music of Elvis are now surgeons, rabbis, and company presidents.

Why do you think there is such an increase in youth suicides?

The youth of today are intelligent and restless with a deep desire for stability (inner and outer) and world peace. They want to be assured that there will be a world worth striving for when they finally reach adulthood. Even the very young children are afraid of war. They have nightmares and frightening daydreams of their world ending with bombs or radioactive pollution that brings a final end to their world.

The young are basically afraid of the reality of a non-existent future world. They see much negativity around them — declining economic stability, warring nations, seemingly irreversible pollution, drugs, famine, etc. They temporarily escape their haunting fears with the euphoric drugs. They've become unconcerned with the damaging negative effects of such drugs because they reason that it really doesn't matter anymore — they'll all be dead from radiation anyway. Acid rain, nuclear reactors, civil unrest, chemical and germ warfare, environmental disasters, increasing unemployment, etc., all continue to invade the minds of the young. Is it any wonder they feel so defeated before they've even had the opportunity to be in a position to fight? Their parents are busy with jobs — the young are alone, defiant, and contrary. They see no future, no viable reason to discipline themselves for a productive bright future.

It isn't the young people who have gone awry — the adults simply haven't left anything that's worth inheriting. Therefore, we must not blame this depression on the youth, but on the adults who have allowed the world's negatives to persist and worsen. The adults *must* work hard to correct the negatives and turn them around into positives that give a loud and clear message: "The world will be beautiful once again! Life's worth living! We're *doing* something and. . .WE WANT YOU TO HELP!"

A lot of television isn't good for children. What sort of programs do you let your kids watch?

This is a good question, but first we need to reestablish the fact that my "kids" are adults now.

When they were young, they could watch anything except explicit sex and extreme violence. These two were banned because neither belong in the home as entertainment. Basically, because we've always been a family that continually enjoyed open communication on "any subject," my girls were always welcomed to discuss *whatever* they had questions on, or were in any way curious about. And long discussions would then ensue until they were in complete understanding. I've always believed that the developing minds of children should never be confined, but rather exposed to the world and the ways of life. In this manner they've grown into sharply perceiving adults who've learned, since childhood, to accept and deal well with realities (both in their own lives and in their world). They've become extremely responsible people because of this early exposure to long discussions and analytical thought. Nothing is taken at face value because they know there are always many facets to every situation, event, and individual. Needless to say, I'm very proud of my girls. Their early exposure to life and the long conversations have made them responsible and mature individuals.

I'm a single parent and my young son is starting to ask about sex. I can't bring myself to talk about it with him. I'm so embarrassed. How do I handle this?

By getting *un*embarrassed. Sex is a natural part of life. Your son wouldn't be here if you hadn't participated in that part. A child who is beginning to become curious about sex and the physical differences of the sexes will develop a healthy attitude if the issue is taught right along with other aspects of the body's functions, such as digestion, respiration, etc. This means that the subject of sex should not *wait* until the child asks about it, but should be included in the earliest instructions or discussions about the body. Early on, when a parent is teaching a young one the names of his or her body parts such as eyes, ears, and mouth, all other parts should likewise be named and pointed to. In this manner, the youngster learns to perceive the genital region as nothing more mysterious or secretive than his ears. Where babies come from and how they begin is a very natural aspect of life. To ignore the issue until the child is older then makes the subject a taboo one that has been set apart from previous lessons. If a child isn't brought up with the facts of life early on, then he or she may develop unhealthy perceptions of it as its learned from unknowledgeable peers who may be slanting it toward being something dirty rather than it being a natural aspect of life.

There are several good children's books on this subject and these should be read to the youngsters right along with their other favorite picturebooks. A child who grows up with the facts of life that are treated in a straightforward manner will have a healthy attitude toward them as a young adult.

Now that your son is asking questions, you would best serve his curiosity by responding in a forthright manner. Your attitude will be perceived by him so you may as well admit your embarrassment by telling him that although sex is very natural, it's a little difficult for you to discuss it with him. Tell him that you also understand that he too may be a little embarrassed but by talking about it, you'll both feel more comfortable. Let him know that you don't want him having any misconceptions on the subject and that he can come to you whenever he has future questions.

Sometimes, very young children are exposed to the conversations of older youth, such as school bus rides. One day when we were all sitting at our dinner table, Mandy (Robin's seven-year-old daughter), asked something out of the blue. "What's a lesbian?" she said. Although we all had a tendency to grin at the suddenness of the question, we maintained nonchalance while Robin replied in a very matter-of-fact manner, "a lesbian is a woman who is attracted to another woman instead of a man." Mandy thought on that then all she said was, "oh, okay." That evening, mother and daughter went into the issue more fully so Mandy wouldn't think that someone was a lesbian just because they had women friends.

So the point is that making your answers as speedy and as honestly as possible is very important. As with all things, parents and children must be open and straightforward at all times, no matter what the subject of the question or discussion is on.

My youngest child is five years old and I caught her pinching our dog's ear. I was shocked to see her do something so cruel. I saw a real mean streak and it really frightened me.

Settle down, mom. Your other children probably did the same thing when they were that age — you just didn't catch them at it.

Many children, especially those with older siblings frequently go through a span of time when the "pecking order" becomes too great for them and they, in turn, need to dominate or "boss over" someone or something beneath them. And, oftentimes, there is nothing beneath them but the family pet.

It is upsetting for a parent to see their child pinch or squeeze a family pet, but it certainly doesn't mean that the child in question has a cruel or mean streak in them. Most often it's just a manifestation of the child's frustration (sometimes a way of gaining attention if done in front of an adult). So you need to talk to your child to find out the real reason behind the unexpected act you caught her in. If she's frustrated, find out why. If she's feeling low man on the totem pole, she needs to be made to feel more a part of things or more important in your life. Above all, don't give negative input. Don't center or dwell on the "badness" of her act, but rather try to dig down and find the cause that generated the act. Talk things through with your daughter. Show her you care about her feelings. Make her feel important in your life. After you're done discussing her feelings and talking about them, stress the loving character of your family pet and how these animals are around just to be our companions and give us love in return for the love we also give to them. Don't tell her she did a shameful or cruel thing, just stress the innocence of the pet — she'll take care of the shame part all by herself.

Heart Sounds

Nothing makes a greater sound than whispers from the heart.

I've found my soulmate but he doesn't want anything to do with me. How can I convince him otherwise?

It's not your place to "convince" him of anything. Know that soulmates are not *always* meant to have experiential lifetimes *together*. Frequently they must live incarnations as separate individuals due to a requirement of their spiritual advancement and development.

During the time frame I was known as She-Who-Sees, Bill was not my life mate, however he was still close by and was instrumental in that lifetime. This was the only life experience we spent apart because of the different roles required to play as associated aspects of one purpose. See?

So although you strongly feel that your friend is truly your soulmate, this doesn't necessarily mean that you must spend this time as mates, but rather as co-workers striving toward the fruition of a singlular purpose. To attempt an interference of this "set plan" creates a strong probability that the spirit purposes of *both* incarnations may be greatly hampered or even nullified.

Can you shed any light on the current male/female imbalance? Women are giving and doing so much, while the men appear so nonsupportive and unresponsive.

Sounds much like *women* before the 70's. Your perspective comes from experiencing the "shoe being on the other foot." Know that this period of time is *not* experiencing a male/female "imbalance," but rather the time frame where the balancing is being manifested. See? For centuries, it was the male that took all the responsibilities and risks while the female role was to attend to the domestic (family) facet. Now there is the balancing period when the female catches up and takes responsibility and risks in the totality of life's aspects. This is not an imbalance at all, but rather an "equalizing" evolutionary factor of society. This must not be seen as a "women's age," but rather as an "equalizing age," where both male *and* female begin to exercise their rights of responsibility in the world. This must be done in order for the future world to manifest into that which has been foreseen. However, great devolution will occur if women, during this "emergence time" perceive only the "female" aspect of life and power instead of understanding that their emergence is actually for the purpose of bringing about the beautiful "synergic" essence of *both* male and female facets, thereby creating the *melding* of both aspects manifesting within each individual. See? This is so important to comprehend. This is so important to understand now because, in society, I see a dangerous trend for women to center on *only* this new "female power." By doing this they over-compensate and therefore do create their own inner imbalance.

A prime example of this "over-compensated imbalance" is clearly evidenced when feminists write me and chastise me for using the pronoun "he" when referring to God. Or when they took exception to the name of our former organization, The Mountain "Brotherhood." This then is clearly the self-same attitude that will "hold" them in an *unbalanced* state — until they can effectively meld their male facet with their female, and perceive themselves as a beautiful manifestation of a balanced whole. The feminists are, in essence, working hard to maintain an imbalanced state, both within and without. "I am woman" means "I am of man." The very word "woman" is male inclusive, therefore should be the perspective that manifests the balance.

The emergence of "female" aspects into the world is not a *gender* issue at all. Spiritually speaking, the entire issue is meant to equalize the feminine sensitivity in males and the male responsibility in females. It is a balancing for *both* sexes to fully experience. To misinterpret the basic concept is to warp the beautiful intent.

When the "new women" perceive the spiritual intent as being a "physical" or purely social manifestation, they raise up their new image of power and perceive it as a *weapon* to fight with rather than perceiving it as a *balancing factor*. They disfigure the concept and, by doing so, help perpetuate the "separateness" the concept is trying to eradicate.

It's time for women to view themselves as equal to men, not better or more powerful. Feminism is fine, but when it over-compensates, it becomes a threat to the beautiful *equality* "women power" was meant to bring about. Men have feminine aspects and feminine powers to balance their totality. Women have male aspects and masculine powers to balance their totality. For either sex to center on *one* of these disrupts the very balance that is required for *true totality* of being.

Once a person has gained a full comprehension and a firm grasp of the truths, it is very hard to live the everyday life. The truths appear to shed a pallor over everything else, making it seem mundane. How can I keep an even balance between my everyday lifestyle and the brilliance of the truth?

This has been noticed by many.

It is simply due to the fact that the spiritual truth, when fully realized, is so brilliant in its light that the everyday work-a-day world around you is dulled by comparison. It is because you feel the inner importance and exhilaration of the truth,and those aspects which caused happiness for you before, just cannot begin to compete.

What you have to remember is that you returned to the physical for a specific purpose. That purpose being different for each and every individual. You still have jobs to perform, families to raise, incomes to earn, etc. Your business on earth is very important to the business of the spirit. You simply cannot ignore your physical surroundings because you have become in touch with the spiritual truths. No matter how menial your job is, it is important, and you must do your best at it. You must seek out a happy medium between your physical existence and your spiritual knowledge in order to put that knowledge to good use. What good does it do a man to obtain the knowledge of the truth and then squander it away in physical unhappiness and discontent?

Jesus was but a human when he came. He retained all truths and abilities, yet he had to maintain the existence of a mere carpenter's son. A fine balance *must* be kept between the brilliant truths and the physical life that those truths bridge. You must *utilize* the truths to "connect" with your fellowmen. It's the "bringing" of the spiritual knowledge and light *into* the physical surroundings that generates the manifestation of a meaningful existence whereby one individual can make a marked difference in the world.

Therefore, perceive not the "difference," but rather the beautiful "blend" of both spiritual and physical aspects.

Does suicide cause negative problems for the spirit?

God said that he would not overburden his children. However, with the free use of your free wills, you find yourselves frequently overburdening *self!* Don't forget that if only you would place your lives in God's capable hands, you would forego the worries and the problems that plague your physical lives. This is very important here. *We* try to *force* our personal desires into becoming a manifested reality. We, through our inacceptance of the natural unfolding process, stress our *own* lives. It's our own desires and lack of acceptance that most frequently pushes us past endurance. God is always available to help in times of greatest need. Yet he is completely forgotten about. People need to learn to seek God within self. Seek him not through pleading prayers, but through quiet and open meditations. He is forever there..look! He is standing ever on the other side of your door just waiting for you to open it up to him. Open it!

The taking of a precious human life is an abomination to spiritual law. When the act of suicide is committed, is not that the taking of a precious life? Even if it is your very own life, you do not have the authority to do with it as you would wish. You have the responsibility to care for and to nurture the precious God Essence within your physical casing. You have the responsibility to care for that casing which is the Holy Temple of God's Spirit. Only *God* can decide when a physical life can be terminated.

When the spirit of a suicide reaches the spirit dimension, it is terribly disoriented and hopelessly confused. It is guided to an area of peace where it rests for a prolonged period of time. Many times this spirit will be shown the torment and the grief that it had caused for those loved ones left behind in the physical. Or it might be shown the future that was waiting its physical if it had stayed in the physical and had weathered through its troubles. Many times this future vision is one of happiness and contentedness. The spirit is then filled with remorse that it hadn't had the fortitude to play out its life and to seek the solutions it needed within the comfort of God.

Suicide is merely self-murder. Also, don't forget that anyone committing such a shortening of its physical life is only creating additional karma for self. This karma results in the cutting off of that spirit's reason and accomplishments for his specific initial entering into the physical. The spirit did not carry out his specified purpose in that life, therefore, it creates the need to return again to carry it out to fruition.

If the spirit is so advanced, why then is it so hard for the physical mind to deal with things here? It almost seems that the spirit, with its infinite knowledge and wisdom, is a separate entity from the physical intelligence of the individual. It would appear that there is the physical me AND a separate SPIRIT of me. Maybe this is too confusing to sort out.

Not really. There's really no confusion here. It's a very good question and it's also very clear what you're saying. I understand your feelings.

At times it would appear to be the case, however, know that the spirit and all of its knowledge is *not* a separate entity from your mind. Understand this, please. Yes, it is extremely difficult for the physical mind to deal with certain aspects of physical life. You know that your spirit knows what is right and directs your actions in the physical. But, you say, sometimes what my spirit wants to do — I do not! If you would only look at the situation from a distance. Pull away from it for a better perspective. On the one hand there is the Higher Self, the spirit. And on the other, there is the physical mind with all of its physical problems of life contained within its boundaries.

Now, the spirit, with all of its incredible faculties to see into the future and to view all possible probabilities, directs the actions of the physical. And, the physical mind, with its shortsightedness and limited view of what is ahead, *prefers* to follow the most visible path and the most logical current choices. This then is in direct conflict, of course. But when you realize that the spirit is *you,* that the spirit is only a higher fragment of self, you will understand the wiseness of following the spirit's wise guidance. It is similar to viewing a beautiful scene from the ground. You only see a limited area. But when viewed from an airplane, such as your spirit sees it, you would appreciate the complete beauty of it all and realize the absolute scope of it also.

Know that your spirit *is* you. Know that it will guide you on the straight and most proven path. Do not let your physical short-sightedness overrule your judgement. Get in touch with the spirit of self through regular meditations and you'll indeed become more intune with your Higher Self's good judgements. You'll become more comfortable with the feelings that you and the "spirit of you" are one!

I'm an aware individual and I find it difficult to accept the ignorance and narrow-mindedness of those I'm in daily contact with. People are so unbelievably unaware. Any suggestions as to how I can best ease this situation?

I appreciate your situation. It is difficult moving about among the unaware masses. But hopefully, things will change.

You'll have to draw upon your deep well of understanding and accept these unaware people. You cannot change them, but your patience and spirituality *can* affect them. You might never realize that you're affecting the people you come into daily contact with, but if you *utilize* your awareness by giving off an attitude of absolute acceptance, you'll be inadvertently helping those around you, thereby, helping self.

Never buck what you cannot alter. Ride the tide peacefully. It will take you into calmer waters.

What are the spiritual implications connected with birth control?

Implications? There are none. Better the child not ever exist than to exist unloved and unwanted! We speak *only* of those methods of "preventing" the initial conception of same.

Since a spirit does not enter a newborn's physical vehicle until it takes its first voluntary breath, a fetus is spiritless.

The prevention of initial conception by birth control measures has no negative spiritual implications.

In the spirit dimension, a spirit doesn't usually begin searching for its vehicle (infant body) until the fetus has at least entered into its final trimester developmental stage. Although there are some spirits who are so anxious to return to the physical that they hover near the chosen mother when she is only a few weeks pregnant, they do not do this unless it is foreseen that the mother will indeed "keep" the developing fetus to fruition.

Choosing the pregnant mother that will give the spirit the precise life circumstances it requires for advancement is an exacting process. Therefore, when a spirit discovers a pregnant woman whose child will meet its needs, it is anxious to get to know her. But a spirit has nothing to do with a barren womb. A "prevented" conception, therefore means that no implications are involved.

It has occurred to me that homosexuality might have negative ramifications for the spirit. Does it?

This reader evidences some very deep thinking.

Yes, you have the right idea here. In order for a spirit to reach completion, it must have experienced an "equal ratio" of male and female lifetimes.

When the spirit is in the spirit dimension, it reviews its record and decides what type of future incarnation will best serve its needs to advance. Frequently a spirit will choose too many lifetimes in succession as the same gender. It then becomes overly-comfortable with that sex and is reluctant to make the needed change in order to balance out its experiences. Then the higher spirits intervene to guide the spirit into realizing that it requires a lifetime as the sex opposite of the former incarnations.

Let's say that a spirit has been choosing to be a female for many, many lifetimes. Now it has been prompted to enter its next incarnation as a male. The spirit dutifully complies because it knows that it requires this experiential aspect.

Now, when in the physical, the male individual is having a difficult time adjusting to its new sex. The spirit within the male's mind has too many carryover memories of being a female for so long, and the physical mind (with remembered tendencies) cannot make the new adjustment. There were too many lifetimes of relating to men (as a female) and now this male cannot relate well to females. Consequently, he is naturally drawn to a male because that is the sex he has been drawn to in all the former incarnations.

The negative ramifications are that, because he "requires" a male experience for the advancement of his spirit and since he cannot adjust, he will have to return again and again as a male until he works out a satisfactory male/female relationship.

Homosexuality is evidence of a spirit's excessive lifetimes as the opposite sex resulting in a current inability to reverse roles. Homosexuality *extends* the spirit's "return cycle." It represents a wasted lifetime in respect to the spirit's ultimate purpose and advancement. Homosexuality incurs karma. The male/female *balance* must be equalizing. It must be balanced both within the "physical" entity *and* the "spirit."

Simply stated, a *male* homosexual has spent too many lifetimes as a female interacting with males. A *female* homosexual has spent too many lifetimes as a male interacting with females. Both of these are experiencing an inability to accommodate their new gender, thereby holding onto the comfortable relationships that *feel* more natural due to former incarnation experiential tendencies. This clearly explains why male homosexuals frequently display female characteristics and female homosexuals elicit male characteristics. . .they find it extremely difficult to break former life tendencies.

I'm going to be traveling to Colorado this summer. Should I fly or drive? Bring the children or not?

This really isn't up to me, but generally it's always better to be the one in control of any vehicle. You didn't say why you *wouldn't* consider bringing your children, but "family" units stay closer if journeys or vacations are experienced together. I've seen too many women leave their children behind as they journey about the country "seeking their own reality." A *mother's* reality IS her children!

How does one deal with people's ignorance?

By first accepting it and then by being a light through example.

People tell me that I work too hard, that I'm not happy unless I'm busy. What's so wrong with being active all the time as long as I'm content?

Since you're single, nothing is so wrong except that perhaps you're making others feel guilty — they don't like that.

Listen, there's absolutely nothing wrong with keeping busy all the time as long as it doesn't adversely affect your mental or physical health.

There is a vast difference between a continually active individual and one who is a workaholic. As long as you get enough rest and mental relaxation, you can remain as busy as you wish. As long as your busy activities don't prevent you from performing your responsibilities to self and others — carry on.

People personally feel guilty when someone around them is always active. They feel that they're lazy or perhaps being unproductive. They're comparing themselves to you. Therefore, they'll tell you to slow down and attempt to place some type of negativity to your lifestyle in order to justify their own slower pace.

I thoroughly understand your situation. I too must be ever busy with something. If I'm not physically active, then my *mind* is racing like a film on FAST FORWARD. I'm far from being the nervous type, I'm merely continually thinking — unless, of course, I'm writing or typing or. . ..

I struggle with the concept of having no expectations. Working on total acceptance is hard, but I do "expect" people to respect nature and animals. Must we give up all our expectations for the best?

You're mixing conceptual terminology here. Expectations is not the same as goals.

Expectation infers the "best" outcome. Goals suggest something to strive for. We can have a "goal" for ourselves and others, but to retain "expectations" for those goals is not reasonable, for the outcome may still be fruitful — but not manifesting according to your *own relative* vision of it. See?

Let's look at this "best" word. You said that you do expect the best. But, my friend, what is your personal interpretation of this "best?" Is your idea of best associated with *your* best? Is it correlated with someone else's best? My best might not live up to your best. See? So when there are expectations for the best, we must not qualify that "best" by grading it by our own value, but rather we must "accept" the best outcome as being the highest effort attainable by *another*. Therefore, we are free to "accept" *best* when we don't "expect" it to correlate to our own value of same.

Should I have a child out of wedlock?

Spirits enter newborns irregardless of marriage certificates. That is the way of it. You ask me not a question of spiritual law, but rather one of moral societal ethics. This then is not within my realm, for it is a personal free will choice of self.

You seem a little slanted against the wealthy who have successfully obtained material possessions in life. Would you perhaps be a smidgen jealous?

I chuckled when I read this question, for I've not a jealous bone in my body. You see, jealousy comes only when one is covetous of another's possessions or status. There is nothing I want in life and all my "needs" are provided for. Therefore of what could I be envious of? As far as being jealous of another's status, which would be fame or notoriety, well. . .I certainly don't care for that either. The limelight has no attraction for me.

Know that jealousy is one of the dragons of the mind that is terribly destructive. Its effects are far-reaching because its green tentacles stretch out into all areas of life to encompass many other emotions. Jealousy destroys relationships and eats away at the mind of self. No, I wouldn't ever be jealous or envious of anyone. I view material possessions as those things that pass away — they're inconsequential and superficial in respect to the "valuables" that the spirit needs to amass for its advancement.

Now, there is some misunderstanding here in regard to my attitude toward those successful individuals who do have material possessions or financial wealth. Please understand that I don't dislike the wealthy. Let's get that straight right from the beginning. When I've ever spoken about people's material things, it's been in deference to the future changes and the great need for one to place importance on obtaining survival goods rather than placing priorities on video equipment, new vehicles, and adult toys. It's evident that the wealthy are more skeptical about the future, perhaps because they don't wish to face the probable fact that they'd lose all their material possessions — they don't want to deal with that possibility.

I certainly am not against the wealthy, especially those who've attained their success through their own ingenuity and personal efforts and are not opposed to contributing to the underprivileged in society. These deserve a lot of credit.

All people are equal in my eyes. The trash man possesses the same beautiful spirit as the bank president. It's the "spirit" I see in all people — not the thickness of their wallets.

All my life I've worked hard just to maintain a liveable life for my family. I hate those people on welfare, yet I suppose you'll tell me I'm wrong for thinking that way.

You must be psychic. Of course that's what I'd tell you.

First of all, you cannot "hate" anyone until you've walked a while in their shoes. My friend, if you did, you wouldn't hate the "person" then, you'd hate the *circumstance* you found self in. You just cannot be so biased against those who are less fortunate than yourself. Your statement insinuates that those individuals on welfare don't work hard, that they don't put out any effort to improve their state in life. That is wrong too.

Most folks on welfare are not free-loaders. They're conscientious people who hate being in the depressing situation of having to accept handouts. They're on welfare, but not because they choose to be. Welfare can be degrading, and those people are humiliated and feel up against the wall of life.

Your attitude needs to be reversed. I would agree that there are many people who like being on welfare and feel comfortable with it. But for every one of those, there are a hundred others who would like nothing better than to be proud of themselves once again, to have a good steady job (not minimum wage) that gets them firmly on their feet — forever.

Try to have a little more compassion for those good people who have been beaten down by life's hard knocks.

You're dead wrong! Everyone is NOT equal! It's people like YOU who would ROB everyone of their unique individuality. This nation is NOT homogenized! NEVER will be!

It doesn't take a psychic to see your anger here. Anger wouldn't have filled your being if you had correctly perceived my viewpoint.

I *agree* with you — totally.

We will never become a "homogenized" nation because we're a colorful patchwork quilt. Our people are all colors and hail from myriad cultures. You can't homogenize such a diverse mixture to make it into a pure singular race of one.

Somewhere along the line you've misinterpreted my intent. I never meant to "rob" anyone of their unique and beautiful individuality. That very individuality is the one characteristic that makes folks unique and their own person. I personally have never followed the crowd in respect to fashions, hairstyles, etc. I would not have our nation going around in Mao suits. I would not have a "grey" world.

Everyone is different and therefore should exercise that beautiful difference by their mode of dress and choices of possessions What needs to be unified are not the superflous "outerness," but rather the *attitudes* that reflect a higher level of awareness of the *spirit*. See?

We are all equal in the sense of Creation. We were total spirit and, in being so, *all* spirits had the same degree of brightness and goodness. You must shift perspective and perceive people as "spirits" for the "without casing" is only temporary. How you personally "view" those casings greatly affect your own measure of spiritual evolution (or deevolution). The without casings are merely the fluctuating state of one's metamorphosis continuum.

I'm thirty-three years old and my mother still tries to run my life. What should I do?

This appears to be a situation that's sweeping the nation. It has reached epidemic proportions, and is a common problem.

You need to politely confront your mother and calmly attempt to make her see that she is no longer responsible for your life. Many parents feel a personal reflection upon themselves by what their grown children do. Many parents don't realize that their adult children can have opinion, attitudes, and belief systems that greatly differ from their own. They tend to think that their children are an extension of themsel-ves. . .indeed they are, but an extension with its own unique in-dividuality.

Try to help your mother realize these important things. That you have to be free to live your life according to *your* attitudes and beliefs — not hers. Whatever you do — stay calm and be understanding. Many parents feel the only way to stay close and "in touch" with their adult children is to give continual input through opinions. Keep your mother involved in your life through other means, such as doing things together. Express your love for her and do little things to show you care. Frequently an overbearing or domineering parent is evidence of loneli-ness or a painful feeling of being left out. This must first be addressed and resolved before your mother will loosen her apron strings.

What do you think about the subject of divorce?

What I personally think about this issue is not important. More to the point would be the facts of the matter.

Divorce appears to be a necessity of life that allows peace of mind and the continuance of an individual's productive life and spirit advan-cement.

Divorce wouldn't be a fact of life at all if the mates had truly known one another *before* they married. Divorce occurs because of a lack of deep love and committment. Many problems can be overcome in a marriage, but people are too stubborn, too self-centered, too uncom-municative to endure the hardship of working things out.

Granted, if one mate simply packs up and leaves, then nothing is left to work out. What must be analyzed here is the "reason" that the mate left in the first place.

I'm sorry that divorce is so common, but then, people do change throughout life. Their likes and dislikes change. They may take up drugs or drinking. They may become abusive. They may change life goals. All these personality and lifestyle alterations contribute to the growing number of divorces.

On the whole, a good and strong marriage must have mates who know how to give and take, how to suppress one's depressive feelings in deference to helping the other pull through bad times, how to communicate openly, how to be completely honest, and how to show how much you care — always how much you care.

Sometimes people are so beset by their physical and mental troubles that suicide is the only way out for them. Surely these people have had too much to bear and have become so out of touch with everything that they find it comforting to resort to this end. Please comment on this.

Suicide may appear to be an out that's "physically" comforting, but it surely won't be "spiritually" comforting when the individual's spirit reaches its destination. And, I would comment further by saying that God does *not* overburden us. We do that all by ourselves.

Don't forget that the physical life was voluntarily chosen by the spirit before it was even born into the physical. The spirit could see certain adverse conditions and situations that would present themselves, and the spirit came anyway because those very adverse aspects were precisely what it required to experience for its advancement. It "needed" those negatives in order to balance the incurred karma.

Granted, once the spirit is actually "living" through those negative conditions, the physical mind feels overburdened and oftentimes defeated. But the life was chosen and the mind must generate an adjustment in order to see it through. Suicide is not the way out. Suicide merely serves to deepen the pit because then the spirit not only has to "finish" out what it left unfinished on earth, it also has to now make up for the "murder" it committed upon self!

Suicide only complicates and extends the work of the spirit.

Many times life would seem to be so black that it will never again be lightened by better times. But every day brings a new daybreak light that shines on opportunities. Adversities cross our paths to strengthen us, not to wear us down. These negatives present themselves to not only test one's faith in self, but also one's faith and trust in God.

I'm an adult with a life of my own, but my relatives are always complaining and talking about everything I do. Why do you think this is?

You also said that you blazed your own path in life — a path far different from theirs. This is an important factor here.

Your relatives are always talking about you because they're basically too judgemental.

People complain because they lack the acceptance needed to let things be. They judge the actions of others by how they themselves would have responded in the same situation. As long as people continue to be judgemental of others, there will always be the complaining. . .the "talking" behind your back.

This constant tendency for people to complain about others has been a fact of life for a very long time. Perhaps you've just recently become aware enough to notice it. It can be very tiring to hear. Those who strike out on their own and cleave to their own separate beliefs and lifestyle are those who feel free to express their beautiful individuality. Frequently relatives resent this beautiful freedom and, the only way to deal with it is to criticize it. You must have acceptance for this sorry attitude of your relatives, for in their hearts, they may actually be very jealous of your freedom.

My mother is continually getting sick enough to be hospitalized and it's usually right around the Christmas holidays. How can a sickness chronically occur with such routine regularity?

By being programmed by the mind! Remember that the mind is the body's controlling computer.

Examine your family relationships. Are get-togethers a strain of any kind? Do all members get along or are they just cordial? Perhaps if there is evidence of serious friction between family members, your mother would just as soon have a valid reason to *not* attend a family gathering. She simply *creates* an alternate reason to not attend. She simply creates her own valid reason.

There are many reasons why an illness presents itself each holiday season — all psychosomatic.

I've worked hard to get where I am today. I deserve all the material possessions I have. I have more than any of my neighbors and I have a RIGHT to be proud of my success!

I think you do too, just maintain the proper perspective of success. Success can be a gentle thing or it can be flaunted.

Why is it that whenever I'm down and out I have lots of sympathy, but whenever I'm successful, nobody is there to share it with me?

Two words, "gloat" and "envy" respective. Misery loves her company, but success can be a lonely lady.

How should I respond to a family that has disowned me?

By not disowning *them!* Two wrongs don't ever make a right. Show them you're bigger.

My family wants me to get into a "respected" profession. I want to pursue my painting interests. How do I handle them?

By *not* handling them. Handle your *own* affairs.

You must realize that you're your own person. And each person must recognize his own destiny. Every individual is uniquely suited to that occupation he was "meant" to participate in. There are many professionals who are unhappy because they didn't follow their feelings — their inner instincts — but rather were good little children and followed the path that their parents layed out for their life.

As an adult, you must make decisions that will affect your future — a future you alone have to live out and justify. Each generation improves life — not stagnates it.

This subject of "respected" occupations is merely another negative concept of an unaware society. *All* occupations deserve respect. There is not a demeaning one around because all occupations are necessary for the gears of a civilized society to run smoothly.

And what constitutes a "professional" individual? A fine blacksmith is a talented professional. An experienced and honest repairman is a professional. The very word "professional" indicates one who does high quality workmanship and has integrity.

Our attitudes and perspectives are grossly out of line.

My boss is always putting me down and making me feel inferior or ignorant. I need this job but I don't know how much longer I can take this verbal abuse.

You can do one of two things. You can quit the job or you can change your attitude toward your boss.

I had this same problem once. Every time my boss stood face-to-face with me and made an unkind comment I looked him in the eye and smiled. Whenever I did this, he would blush and become so flustered he'd forget what he was saying. He'd just walk away trying to figure me out. But I did eventually quit. That may sound like a coward's way out, but I personally can't tolerate being around an ignorant egotistical person for eight hours a day. His superior attitude and demeaning comments were something I didn't have to witness.

Tactfully confronting an individual such as this does no good, because you're then letting him know how much he's getting to you and also because he'll never change anyway.

If you choose to quit, don't do so until you have another employment position lined up. If you choose to remain, you must alter your attitude toward yourself and your employer. View him as a poor ignorant individual who doesn't know any better. These highly egotistical people truly are evidencing their ignorance, for they haven't the commonest courtesy toward others. See yourself as someone more aware, more humane than him. See yourself as an enlightened person who can ignore the puffed up egotism of others around you. Nobody should have to endure such uncivilized treatment, especially from a boss who should have better leadership abilities.

I tend to look people directly in the eye whenever I'm talking to them, yet many times this will make them extremely uncomfortable. Why is that?

Many people avoid direct eye contact because it makes them nervous and gives them the uncomfortable feeling of somehow being exposed.

People of today are generally very private individuals. They don't like being in uncomfortable situations. Direct eye contact is a form of "touching" another, and most folks simply don't care to be touched anymore.

There is nothing esoteric about the situation you've noticed. It's not a psychic feeling or evidence of "forces," it's simply psychological. I wouldn't suggest that you change your ways. You "reach" people when you look them in the eye. Continue reaching out to them.

I'm a fairly pretty woman. I'm shy and good-natured, however, I often experience dislike from other women who don't even know me. Can you explain this?

Beauty has its price.

Other women who see you for the first time are envious of your attractiveness. They also equate physical beauty with self-assuredness and egotism. You could be the sweetest, most timid individual in the world, but if you're also pretty enough to turn heads, then you've automatically gained the additional characteristic of being vain (as assumed by other women).

I know this is a terrible unfairness, but regardless, it's true. I have a friend with your problem. She's extremely shy and good-hearted. Men turn their heads for a better look, while women sneer.

I'm sorry that you experience this sort of ignorant snobbery. You just have to ignore it. You haven't done anything wrong to warrant such bad manners directed toward you. You can't help the fact that you were born pretty. Just remember that these people are unaware and you should feel sorry for their bad manners and prejudgements.

There's nothing wrong with true beauty, especially when someone like yourself also has the "inner beauty" to go with it.

I was very well-liked when I functioned within the mainstream, yet when I struck away from the establishment to follow the inner promptings of my own path, people criticized me and laughed behind my back. What makes people suddenly become turncoats like that? I'm basically the same person I was before.

Sure you are and, if they were half the friend they professed to be, they'd see that too.

I could make this a very lengthy answer, but what it basically comes down to is the fact that when an individual breaks away from the norm in order to follow his/her own inner promptings, people don't generally like that. They don't like it because *they* would've liked to be able to do that too, but for various self-imposed superficial reasons, they couldn't bring themselves to actually activate their own desires. This negativity you're experiencing from friends and family is simply evidence of their "sour grapes" attitude toward your adventuresome determination and strong individuality. You had the *courage* to "step in time with your own drummer, while they forced themselves to listen to the old tune called tradition.

When I'm happy, I'm bubbly and ecstatic about life, yet when I'm down, I feel suicidal and nothing matters to me. These mood swings can shift in an instant. What's wrong with me?

You're a manic depressive, but you're not alone. There are literally thousands of people who experience these sort of emotional extremes. Try to remain more on an even keel. Take each day as it comes and when you have your "down" days, go out for a walk and watch the little children at play. Learn how to properly meditate. This will serve to calm the system and fill it with an all-encompassing feeling of inner well-being. When you're feeling bad — go into yourself and bathe in the peace you find there.

If the above suggestions don't help to alleviate the mood swings or lighten their intensity, seeing a psychologist counselor may be a good alternative.

Some people think I'm nuts because I love to watch bad thunderstorms. I'm a real storm freak. Is this a psychological aberration?

If it is, my husband is in real trouble. There is absolutely no psychological aberration connected with the activity of watching thunderstorms.

There are some people who love to watch thunderstorms because of the intense energy that is released and violently displayed. They feel this powerful force within their being and they relate the storm's explosive power to that of God.

Some folks like to watch these storms because they feel physically and mentally energized and renewed from the intensive ionization of the air. They feel refreshed and envigorated.

And then there are those who simply like to stand out in a bad storm to tempt their fate. They enjoy the challenge between man and nature.

My mother is always telling me how sick she feels or how many big bills she has to pay. I hate it whenever she calls because it's so depressing talking with her. Should I confront her about her incessant complaining or what?

You need to take the "or what" path here and use reverse psychology with her.

People who have the tendency to continually accentuate the negative aspects of their life are seeking sympathy. They moan about their high utility and/or medical bills. They groan about household or automobile repairs that they've had to have done. Their aches and pains are on the top of their list of things to tell you about. All their own expenses and pains will *always* be more and worse than yours. And all because they want your sympathy.

Next time you talk to your mother, listen sympathetically to her lengthy list of woes and then ask her to tell you about all the "good" things that've happened in her life since you last talked together.

People don't accentuate the negative just to irritate you. They don't do this unless they have a deep psychological void in their life. They're unfulfilled in some way. The negative needs to be reversed into positive attitudes. Try to get *behind* her surface negativity. Try to get to the *source* of her sympathy-seeking ploy. Find out *why* she's using this type of "mechanism" to cloak her need for sympathy.

My sister is always bragging about her latest household acquisition, especially the more expensive ones. I'm not rich and it seems like she's just rubbing in the fact that her husband is doing better than mine. I'm sick of the situation! What should I do?

What you need to do depends on what is *actually* transpiring here.

First, before you do any confronting, you have to make some absolute observations regarding the situation. Are you positively certain that you're not just jealous, thereby making your sister's actions "appear" vindictive? Perhaps she is simply innocently excited about her new acquisitions and wishes to share that excitement with you. Perhaps she is not the one who is guilty of doing the comparison here. If, after closer analyzation of the problem, you find this to be true, please readjust your own perspective toward your sister. You have done her a grave injustice. She obviously doesn't realize the hurt she's causing you. This hurt wouldn't exist if you were rid of your envious feelings. Don't ever blame others for causing negative attitudes of self. Don't ever blame another person for their success. And. . .don't ever compare others with self.

Now, if you conclude that you're *not* jealous but are purposely being made to feel inferior and unsuccessful by your sister's actions, you still need to readjust your own perspective rather than confronting her.

Most people who feel the need to flaunt their possessions have a severe psychological problem. And, on top of that, they are simply very unaware individuals. There is no way to verbally change these people. All you can do is to consider the source and accept their ignorance. Perhaps one day they will wake up and realize how self-centered their bragging was. Until then, try to ignore her strutting and proud crowing.

Everyone is a unique individual. There are different goals for different folks. One person's definition of value will greatly vary from another's. Clearly, your sister's perception of value is in material "things." Where is your perception of value? In things? Your hardworking husband? The love shared between you? Your shared happiness together? Know that personal value is the determining factor in this issue.

I'm a college student. I'm popular, however, I'm beginning to tire of the juvenile ways of my friends. I like being popular but would also like to break away from this group. I'm afraid I'll lose my popularity if I do.

Watch your priorities so you can be true to self.

When you've graduated from college and all your close friends have scattered, what will be most important then? Your college pranks or your personal growth?

This popularity business is clearly a means of retarding individual growth. See it for what it is.

Everyone desires to be well liked, but don't betray self for popularity. Don't trade in your unique individuality for temporary popularity. First and foremost — be true to self!

How would you handle a hypochondriac parent?

Sympathetically.

She is crying inside for attention. She needs to extend her own attention outward toward others instead of turning into self, thereby causing adverse physiological conditions that will eventually do her great physical harm. She requires an externalization. Perhaps she could do volunteer work or something in that line whereby she would then transfer the attention from self to others.

Also, many times the reason behind a hypochondriac parent is the parent's wish for you to feel guilty for not being around to help out. Don't ever fall for this psychological mechanism. This constitutes a mental manipulation by the parent. See it for what it really is!

My best friend's husband is a real basket case! Consequently they're having constant marital problems. I've told her that she should leave him but she remains anyway. What else can I do to convince her?

Nothing. . .you've done too much already.

There is more to the situation than the one side that you see and hear. You must remember that the bond of marriage is consummated between *two* people — husband and wife — *not* between husband and wife and wife's friend!

The united couple have vowed to remain together for better *and* for worse. You have no right to interfere. Your friend must work her marital problems out according to how *she* sees the situation, not by what you see.

The best thing you can do for your friend is to offer her your friendly comfort, your loyal companionship, and your silence. You stated that your friend's husband was a "real basket case. Many a basket case has been helped by an understanding mate who sticks it out to "heal" with their unconditional love. Leaving someone who needs help is not in keeping with why we're all here.

I'm terribly attracted to a married man who works with me. He also has begun to show his amorous feelings toward me. I know what you'll say about this, but I guess I need to hear your reasoning. Doesn't this attraction mean that we were "meant" for each other? Besides, he says he's unhappy at home now.

I'm sure he does say that. Fits right in, doesn't it? You are attracted to him. He is not attracted to you — he is "dis-tracted" by you. There's a deep difference.

He says he's unhappy at home only because you've seduced him. Quit your job before you do something that will cause a great deal of pain for many people.

When a man is wearing a wedding band, that means that he is already spoken for — he is unavailable. What makes you think you've the option of choosing a "married" man for your conquest? Does the marriage bond mean nothing to you? Once a person marries, their "roving eye" days are over.

Grow up. Be mature. You're acting like a child who insists on touching all the "no-nos" in life. You're being grossly immature, unspiritual, and a destructive force. If you already knew what I would say about this situation then you already knew that you are wrong. How could you ever be at peace with a relationship knowing that you've torn a family apart? Where's the logic? Where's the awareness? Where's the justice?

Your rationale of this relationship of being "meant" is flimsy at best. If the man is already married, it certainly was *not* meant. Stop making excuses for inexcusable actions. Wake up and open your eyes. Face reality and stop trying to create your own here.

Physical attraction happens all the time — even with married people — it's a fact of life. However, most mature people keep it in perspective.

I have been happily married for eight years. Lately I enjoy getting out alone in the evening for a few hours. I'll go to the library or a local restaurant for a cup of coffee and take a book with me. My husband doesn't understand this. He thinks I'm trying to get away from him. How do I handle this problem?

Why do you act as if he's wrong? You are trying to get away from him. Be honest. Getting away from others *is* wanting solitude.

I could say that your husband has a jealous possessiveness of you, but with respect to the content of the details of your total letter, this conclusion would not be accurate.

Your husband loves you a great deal. He looks forward to coming home each night because *you* are there. He enjoys your company, your conversation, and your companionship. When you're gone in the evening he feels as though he is without a vital part of himself.

You should feel fortunate that this bond of love is so strong in your mate. You should feel proud that your husband cherishes your evening hours together. Don't turn his beautiful deep love into something negative. He is not trying to confine or restrict your outside activities, he just wants to be with you.

Your son is in school all day long. Let the laundry go. Let the dishes set. Get out during the day. But set aside the evening hours for your loving husband. Treasure your times together, especially when they mean so much.

Do you think an engaged couple should have a lot of interests in common in order for a marriage to survive?

That depends. It depends upon the depth of love shared.

I could say that true love surpasses all, but that conceptual cliche has lost most of it's real meaning for most.

A marriage will survive if both partners show an interest in their mate's individual hobbies and views. I didn't say "become involved," I simply said "shows an interest."

Couples need to share the things that make them excited. They need to communicate their viewpoints and attitudes to a mate who will listen to them and offer intelligent responses. This type of open sharing of each other's interests is required, not specifically the action of physical participation. See?

Major interests such as spiritual beliefs, attitudes toward child discipline, and future goals should definitely coincide. Minor interests such as sports activities, hobbies, etc., need not. But, the communication aspect of these minor interests are most important. Each partner should take a cordial interest in the unique individualized activities of the other.

What causes hypochondria?

A deep void in one's life and/or unhappiness caused from lack of purpose.

What makes me despise one race and have sympathies toward another without ever having experienced any outstanding negative or positive encounters with either one?

The terminology of the question is in error.

Something cannot be held despicable nor sympathized with unless there has first been an experiential event which generated the emotional response. It's a former life experience in this case, and the carryover memory imprints from past lives. The hate and sympathy aspects are karmic. The "hate" facet must be karmically balanced in this lifetime. Please, overcome this.

Why can't people accept others as they are?

Because of personally-held perceptions. If another individual holds differing viewpoints or belief systems or breaks from tradition, they are not accepted by those whose perspective is based upon the "established mean" of tradition. In this manner it is evidenced that people are consumed with personal and "qualified" prejudgements. They believe that they are forever in the right while their fellowmen are in the wrong.

What is the real underlying cause of hate?

Ignorance. Unawareness. And to be sure. . .darkness of mind!

What one singular attitude do people need more of?

One? Unconditional love. Then awareness is spawned. Then enlightenment blossoms within.

How did you gain acceptance of life?

Through the final realization that I'm here only for the purpose my spirit chose. This dawning light came after much long-suffering and spiritual growth.

I love life! People are always telling me to take off my rose-colored glasses. Maybe THEY should borrow mine!

Oh yes, I do agree. Indeed, your friends surely do need to borrow *yours* so that you will be *without* them to finally perceive reality with clarity.

There is nothing wrong with a bubbly and happy disposition, but when it covers up the seriousness of life, then it does become a blindness, an unawareness. See?

What makes people so obsessive with their material possessions?

Misplaced priorities that stem from an ignorance or denial of the spiritual truths. Unawareness. Egotism.

This probably sounds like I'm a real idiot, but what IS awareness?

I don't think that's an idiotic question at all. If the terms aren't adequately clarified within self, how will you then understand them enough to "live" them? An idiot wouldn't admit ignorance nor the need for clarification.

Awareness is simply a total sensitivity to one's surroundings. This is inclusive to sensitivities toward your fellows, being sensitive and watchful in your actions and speech. It is the continual attention given to basic spiritual ethics. It's the lack of negative attitudes and prejudices.

Awareness is the "living" of spiritual truths every day. It's being watchful of world and social situations that are unfolding.

Having compassion and empathy is living within awareness. Attending to the needs of others is living in awareness. See?

I credit you with the intelligence of requesting this clarification.

I'm a psychic and I see that you are NOT one. You just want to make a lot of money.

You said you were a psychic?

If it were true that I just wanted to make a "lot of money," I certainly wouldn't have spent years of hard suffering for my purpose. And I certainly wouldn't be responding to your letter without first receiving a consultation fee.

Your opinion of me has merely served to discredit your own claim of enlightenment. Any enlightened individual who possesses spiritual paranormal functioning would not be of like opinion, for they know who I am and from whence I've come.

Please examine the vindictive motives of self, for they're generating great destructive forces within you.

I've believed the truths for years now, but because of my family's firm beliefs in an "established" religion, I've had to go along with theirs and keep mine in the closet. I'm very disgusted.

You *should* be disgusted with closeting your beautiful beliefs! Your "uncomfortable" feelings have been trying to tell you something. Listen! *Never* sacrifice the beliefs of self for those of another's!

Your secretive actions are self-demeaning, not to speak of also demeaning your own beautiful belief system. By closeting your true beliefs, you're saying that you are not "allowed" to think for yourself or cleave to a different belief. You're smothering your wonderful individuality. . .your beliefs. . .self. . .and your beautiful free spirit!

Please, for your own sake, let the butterfly *free!*

Sometimes when my eyes connect with those of a complete stranger, I'll get an awful sinking feeling. What is this caused from?

This is a sensation that accompanies a spirit recognition, or is a psychic signal of your awareness of the other person's negative force. Both causes have negative connotations and come from "within" as a warning caution.

A "sinking" feeling is a physiological response to the psychic perception of a negative force within close range. Learn to deal with these by sharpening your awareness and keeping your power of protection reinforced.

What makes instantaneous likes and dislikes felt toward people I meet in this life for the first time?

This immediate internalized emotion is generated from two causal factors.

Many people are very sensitive to another's level of spiritual development. And, when an aware spiritual person meets up with another individual who is also spiritually aware, but is in possession of primarily negative aspects to his awareness, the first individual will experience an immediate dislike. The opposite holds true too. An instantaneous positive attraction will result from a recognition of like-minded and near-equal spirits.

Now, for the second cause. Frequently we cross paths with certain individuals we have known in previous incarnations. These individuals will be those who we've had intense relationships with. And, the sole determining factor that qualifies the "manner" of recognition in *this* life when your paths again cross, is dependent upon whether these highly energetic relationships were positive or negative.

If you had a good relationship with an individual in a former incarnation, you'll automatically be drawn to them when you meet again in this life. Have you ever met someone and felt like you've known them all your life? Conversely, if you had a negative relationship in a former life, you will naturally be repelled by them when you meet them again.

Watch for these important inner feelings, especially the negative ones, for it's these that could be important factors in the advancement of your spirit. The negative feelings of immediate dislike and the accompanying unexplained repulsion could very well signal the fact that you need to rectify these feelings in *this* life. It could signify a particular spiritual purpose you need to accomplish or it could also signify the importance of "avoiding" the individual. Your inner promptings will distinguish between the two.

My husband and I want to relocate to another state, but my mother is in a nursing home. What should we do?

Leaving an elderly parent who is still vitally energized with their own lifestyle is one thing, but leaving one who is so dependent as to be in need of the professional care in a nursing home is not conscionable.

To leave her there alone while you move to another state would not be spiritually or morally ethical. In the end, it would indeed create additional karmic debts for both yourself and your husband.

I think beauty pageants should be banned. What do you think of these? I think they're offensively chauvinistic.

In light of your expressed reasoning, I would certainly tend to agree. Beauty is a beautiful thing in and of itself, however, for society to continue to judge beauty on physical appearance and body shape serves to exacerbate the issue of women being pleasurable "things" to look upon. As long as physical characteristic are emphasized in respect to women, this issue will not evolve into true equality. As long as the ladies continue to "participate," they themselves are perpetuating the continuum of the sexist attitude beauty pageants generate.

Why do people want the Creator's powers?

Because, somewhere along the way, there came into being a satanic concept that people are gods.

In our never-ending search for who we are, the Sons of Belial interjected negative pathways for some to tread upon. These being freely littered with highy-damaging spiritual concepts that tend to equate humanism with divinity. And, of course, many accepted and then "fell" into the belief of same.

Although it's true that Jesus himself once said we would do great things, this in no way infers that we are little gods walking around. We have the inherent spiritual ability to reach great levels of enlightenment and, correspondingly, to be able to spiritually perform accordingly, but this is our beautiful heritage of spirit and does not at all mean we are *as* God or that we *are* gods. The very idea is a terrible affront to God. . .just as the Sons of Belial planned it to be.

Does thinking negative thoughts actually create negative?

Like attracts like. That is the precept of the law. Above (mind), so also below (reality). You are what you think. Thoughts are things. Thoughts are energy and, energy is a force. Know the precepts of the law, for they will not deceive.

How do we forgive? How do we have compassion?

Through living within acceptance. Through living without expectation. Through unconditional love. In this manner of living is forgiveness and compassion manifested.

I finally located your house, but Bill wouldn't let me see you. I thought that was terribly rude.

I had been up for two days and an entire night tending to a sick daughter. Her fever had finally broke and I'd just gone to bed while the rest of the family sat down to dinner. From what I heard of the incident, Bill was exceptionally polite to you and, although he didn't feel the need to explain our family situation, he reminded that I'd written you telling you that I was no longer meeting with people. You came just the same.

How come you treat your dogs like people?

Because they're people of the "four-legged" variety. Tell me this, how would you treat someone who loved you very much? Someone who could communicate with you? Who sensed your every mood and played with you when you were happy. . .and gave you comfort when you were sad? How would you treat someone who lived to protect you from strangers? Someone who never mistreated you but only lived to be by your side? How would *you* treat someone who did all the above? Because I have *two* someones like this and, because they are like this in spite of not having the human capability of reasoning intelligence, is all the more reason to treat them with respect and love. Just because they are furry does not mean they do not have the capacity to breach the language barrier and communicate their own emotions and love to another. And, in so doing, do the four-legged variey of people frequently surpass the two-legged kind.

I was at a New Age lecture and was shocked to hear (name withheld) speak against Mary Summer Rain. It seems your concept against the "selling of enlightenment" has ruffled many famous feathers.

And rightly so, for the light has been shed onto the precept of the Law of One on this issue. The public is seeing that light. And it would seem, there are those (famous or otherwise) who would prefer the light of this subject not shine forth and be seen.

I'm tired of giving and giving without receiving anything in return.

And what would you consider "return value?"

My friend, the act of living with expectation is a spiritually and emotionally draining act. But the act of living unconditionally is truly a spiritually and emotionally fulfilling act indeed.

Unconditional living fills one's vessel, while living with expectation dries the vessel until it cracks and crumbles.

I'm a high school senior. I'm troubled by the gross lack of responsibility I see in those around me. Why is this?

Are you asking why you're concerned or why nobody around you seems to have any measure of responsibility?

You're concerned because you *have* a deep sense of responsibility and are wondering why others your age don't.

You're wondering why those others don't have this sense of responsibility because you're worried they won't be able to make their way in life without it.

You are not alone in this recognition. The world is full of people going about their lives by following the crowd. They don't bother to think for themselves or make their own personal decisions. They want to confer with their peers or a teacher or a psychic before making any personal moves. They either don't trust their own mind or they don't care to take the responsibility to excercise their beautiful free wills to make choices. This is seen in all aspects of society. More and more people are wanting others to make their life decisions for them — to tell them what to do. Personal responsibility is not a priority, for it is too much work and, ultimately, it's much easier to place the blame on someone else for bad advice that was followed.

Indeed, it would almost seem as though there is a new generation of robots out there who choose to let others do their thinking —to let others program their every move. How sad it is that so many place their entire lives and futures in the hands of others. How sad it is that so many wish to be ruled by the whims of others. It would almost seem that we've become a society that can no longer think for itself, but rather must be "told" what to do and where to go.

I too see so much of this. Something is gravely wrong when I get a letter inquiring what kind of container to store water in. Or where an individual should relocate to. Or should they marry who they're dating. Where has personal responsibility gone?

Yes, I too am concerned. The concern is real, for the reality of nonthinkers has been manifested. And a society of nonthinkers is a dangerous ground of fertile soil for the Sons of Belial to cultivate with ease.

A Blanket Shared

You do not live over there. . .
I do not live over here. . .
What you do affects me. . .
What I do affects you. . .
Yours is mine. And mine is yours.
Ours is Earth. . .a Blanket shared.

Our prisons wouldn't be so crowded if capital punishment was enforced for murderers and drug dealers. What do you think?

I think you're right. Overcrowding certainly wouldn't be nearly as bad if capital punishment was meted out to these criminals. However, I'm only addressing the issue of "crowding" here.

I wonder at your theory of "murder being a solution." The very premise of capital punishment suggests an accepted social practice that justifies the act of murder according to the type of crime. If the taking of another's life is a serious crime in the framework of societal behavior, how then do you justify the *law's* right to do same? Does *being* the law create the accepted "exception." Does being the law make one *above* the law? Does being the law make murder an acceptable action of retaliated justice? Doesn't that thinking constitute a double standard? Murder is murder. And it can't get any more concrete than that. How can murder by an individual be a crime while murder by the law be justice?

Was there ever a true oil crisis several years ago?

While I was under No-Eyes' wise tutelage I often asked her such questions regarding the past. This happened to be one of those subjects that I inquired about.

She responded with a grin and a simple shrug. She merely said, "There be a play on words with this. There been big crises in minds of scheming men — not in reality."

You're outspoken about how man is destroying the planet but you haven't given any solutions on how to fix anything.

I'm not sure I have the solutions to fix the mess, but I have made some observations over the years. Some of my ideas are already manifesting, for the ecosystem of our planet has become a greater concern of the public's mass consciousness.

The wasting of precious energy appears to be a major cause of pollution. The more society uses, the more coal is needed to fuel the power plants, and coal is a major cause of acid rain. Therefore, I view our "drain of power" as an important aspect to be addressed by everyone. This drain corresponds to our desire for conveniences. Our laziness has generated a demand for technology to develop myriad ways to accommodate this modern day attitude by developing, manufacturing, and providing the public with a wide variety of labor-saving devices. I see the need to stop buying frivolous appliances that waste our precious energy sources. Blenders, dishwashers, shavers, curling irons, facial saunas, pencil sharpeners, plant lights, electric toothbrushes, deep fryers, juicers, massagers, nail dryers, electric knives, etc., are all non-necessities. They're all using up our valuable energy and placing a high demand on our power plants. Getting rid of these unnecessary appliances would greatly reduce our energy usage.

Use fluorescent light bulbs in homes and offices.

Manufacturers of products need to stop packaging their goods in non-biodegradable or non-recyclable containers. The use of styrofoam and like materials should be banned. There's been a great increase in the manufacturer's use of plastic to package everything from tools to toys. What was wrong with the "boxes" they used to package these in?

Mass consciousness needs to shift their attitude on the "color" of paper products. Bleached paper products contain dioxin.

Every household, business and office needs to separate their rubbish according to recyclable material. Paper, plastic, aluminum, glass, metals, etc. need to be taken to a recycling center instead of bagged together for the dump.

Retail stores, including grocery markets, need to do away with their plastic bags and return to the paper ones that can be recycled by the consumer. The retailers then need to purchase the "recycled" bags to use instead of new ones.

Skylights should be built into the roofs of buildings to take advantage of the sun's thermal energy.

Coal-generated power plants need to be converted into ones utilizing alternative natural energy sources. Wind energy should be used instead. Or solar energy. These two sources have been tried experimentally and have been found to be powerful enough to successfully provide large cities with all their electrical needs. We have not yet gone far enough in the right direction, but the earth's own magnetic field can also be utilized to more than satisfy the world's energy demand.

Accept, develop, and manufacture the suppressed schematics that've been submitted for a non-gasoline vehicle engine. These utilize the simplistic application of magnetic fields and small crystals. A non-polluting, absolutely clean energy source for powering our vehicles is a must. This source does not refer to the electric cars that are now available. We must get away from the idea that "oil" and "gas" is the only source of energy. Those who control these sources must not be allowed to continue holding the axe over those who develop the natural alternatives. Greed has got to give way to moral responsibility for the good of the whole. It just isn't reasonable, nor is it logical that, if we have developed the technology to walk on the moon, we can't also develop the technology for magnetic power. It just doesn't wash.

The government needs to prioritize their values in respect to the "whole" earth and its precarious ecosystem. This means much more attention given to the forests, barrier reefs, and other finely-balanced systems. Entire forests are being infested with destructive insects. Once the forests are dead, an entire scope of forces are set in motion then. The probability for forest fires greatly increases, soil erosion becomes a threat, animal life is endangered. The government must do far more to clean up the mining districts that are leaching a vast array of poisons into the land and water courses. The government must take a firm hand to shut down manufacturing plants and all other industries that are found polluting the air, ground, or water.

Forget we ever learned the word "nuclear" and dismantle all the nuclear plants. There *is* a far better way. Our scientists have not been given free rein here.

Don't burn coal in woodstoves.

Stop manufacturing so many synthetic fabrics. What ever happened to good old cotton? Wool? Silk? There could be a wealth of new fabrics if textile mills thought harder on it — all natural.

Take all "artificial" additives such as coloring and flavoring out of products. These, more than you know, cause a wide variety of physical and psychological ills.

Getting back to the "plastic mentality" — everyone needs to be more aware of how much plastic they're buying and using. Didn't children's blocks used to be made of wood. . .pop bottles be glass. . .groceries bagged in paper? The fruit and vegetables you bag in plastic at the market will go bad in a day if not removed. . .that's very bottom line. And where are all the old paper cups? Walk into any convenience store and you find more and more plastic and styrofoam. Fast food eateries are styrofoam city. Straws are plastic, not paper. Bread bags aren't waxed paper anymore. Little boy's toys. . .from fire engines to big riding things. . .are plastic. Little girl's toys. . .from dolls to jewelry. . .are plastic. Infant baubles are even worse. The "consumer" needs to be aware of what they purchase, for if the *demand* is not there, neither will be the "plastic" supply. The *consumer,* more than anyone else, has the power to change this "plastic consciousness" in all phases of society.

Now you might say that I've not addressed the "food" aspect. This means the real rotting, stinking *garbage.* Well, my first question would be why is food being thrown away in the first place when so many people are starving in the world? Sound a little like your mother when you were young and didn't clean your plate? You bet! What's creating the "throwaway food?" Do we prepare more than we can eat? Why? If there's enough dinner left over for one person's next lunch, then shame on you for not saving it. Food scraps can go to your pets or, if you live in a country or mountain atmosphere, leave them out for the animals. How much bread scraps do you discard? How about leaving them out for the birds? The "normal" food waste such as fish bones can be buried in your garden or shrubbery. Make a compost pile. Those who have no ground for such should have a garbage disposal. The garbage disposal is not a frivolous energy user, for they're capable of drastically cutting down on our nation's garbage.

After mowing the grass, add the clippings to a compost pile instead of putting it out front in plastic bags for the garbage collector. In autumn, add your raked leaves to the pile.

In a nutshell, get rid of all unnatural materials and you've gotten rid of chemical plant pollutants and 87 percent of the rubbish. You've also eliminated 88 percent of toxic dumping.

Now that we've got the Earth Mother happy. . .we need to make verbal war on physical war and finally make our peace with Peace.

I'd like you to comment on the scientific use of animals by researchers in lab experiments.

There has been increased utilization of various animals in the research laboratories by medical, technical, and cosmetic researchers. This sad situation has developed because of a general unawareness toward the "worth of life."

Humankind views itself as the pinnacle of the evolutionary pyramid. Therefore, all lesser life forms are inconsequential when it comes to improving the quality of man's life. All types of animals are used within the laboratories. All types of animals are experimented on behind locked doors. These are subjected to operations in which electrical probes are permanently inserted into all parts of their small bodies. They're blinded by the researchers in the laboratories of the cosmetic companies. . .this being done for the sake of beauty products. Thousands of animals are maimed, tortured, and killed in the name of scientific or technological advancement. And these atrocities are all carried out so that we, the superior species, can advance our technology. How then can we do this type of inhumane research and still perceive ourselves as "superior."

Man forgets that the lower life forms feel acute pain, that they're capable of thought, that they communicate, that they're a living facet of our beautiful world.

The Indian people respected the animals so much that they called them "brothers."

Question: Since man considers the lower life forms of animals so insignificant that he uses them for painful laboratory experimentation, what would we then think of a *higher* alien race who also thought *they* had the same rights toward us? I suppose that would be all right since humanity would then be the *lower* life form! Think on that.

There has been a raising of consciousness in the past few years that has evidenced the protest of such experimental laboratory research, as well as the use of furs and leathers. As it should be, we are slowly, but surely, learning to respect the life of all life.

I've read several technical books regarding other countries utilization of paranormal gifts to gain secret military information about the U.S. On the surface, this would appear to make America look backward in their own secret military techniques. How can a person justify using their abilities for this end?

You've done some good reading here, however, you haven't carried your reasoning far enough.

It's true that a certain country has been working with people who possess acute paranormal functioning. They've been researching this for many years. Their advancements in the field of parapsychology are far beyond those of America's. Americans remain ignorantly skeptical while their world counterparts are making milestone advancements with the paranormal facets of man.

One secret aspect of our government is now in its infant stage of this research. They've finally begun to realize the massive far-reaching advantages of utilizing such abilities, but sadly enough, they're too far behind, they woke up too late to effectively accomplish anything of value with it.

In response to the final segment of your question, there *is* no justification for an individual using his/her paranormal functioning for the purpose of government spying or war. Perhaps these people are being coerced in some way. Most individuals with this type of functioning find it difficult to just turn it on and off at a command, but that's certainly not to infer that there are those who could.

World history bears out the fact that it has experienced many religious wars. Is there any justification for these?

Historically, there were even Popes who sanctioned "holy" wars, But think! Since when does an evil or destructive *means* ever justify an end? Any killing is murder, and murder is a direct act of commission against God's law!

You may then think of a clever rebuttal to this that goes something like this: If a religious war is against God's law, then what about the Final Battle between good and evil? All historical battles were also between good and evil.

Well my friends, that Final Battle is God's and God's alone to wage. It is his judgement upon mankind and all the dark forces in existence. Remember, since *all* life originally came from God, he *alone* possesses the right to take it as he deems justifiable. God createth — God taketh.

Also, don't fool yourself into thinking that all the historical religious wars were fought between good and evil. What about the continuing troubles in Ireland? Are the Catholics evil? Are the Protestants evil? There is *never* justifiable cause for warring between religious factions.

Is the Pope really infallible?

As seen through the singular example in the previous question, the Pope, as historically recorded, has sanctioned wars. To one who is well versed in religious history as a scholar, it is clear that throughout history, politics has played an intertwined role in the early Church years. Kings have been extremely influential with certain reigning Pope's decision-making. And, at the Council of Constantinople, several major precepts had been stricken from the belief system. . .one being reincarnation.

Over the years, Popes have altered or negated Church aspects that were once considered to be solid facets of its belief system. An example of this is the long-held belief that St. Christopher was the patron saint of protection and, to wear his medal would provide protection. Then suddenly, the belief was disavowed.

There are other reversals that were done over the years and, if the Pope were indeed infallible, how is it that one Pope can uphold all the teachings of the Church as "truth" and another one strike some of these same truths from the belief system?

My friend, only *God* is infallible. God does not alter or negate any of his truths.

I think the theory of evolution is an unintelligent one. It's just plain stupid.

In depth research into our planet's historical development absolutely supports this theory. Have I gone against my own belief system? Absolutely not.

The continually debated theory of evolution is always discussed and argued in an all-encompassing sense of the term. There are massive amounts of proven instances of the evolution of animals, plants, and even human life. Yes. . .human life.

Dentists are now seeing more and more children who have no wisdom teeth appearing on their x-ray scans. This is evidence of how our physiological systems are weeding out those physical aspects that are no longer required for the human body. This is indisputable proof of our evolving species. All species of all living organisms, from the most simple single-celled organisms all the way up to man, have made verifiable evolutionary adjustments according to their environment.

However, just because all living organisms have been shown to evolve, does not mean that man was once an ape. There is a median ground between the evolutionists and the creationists. Both are correct but they continue to draw a definite demarcation line. There is none. God created the original man. God created lesser life forms. Both had evolutionary changes according to their environmental time alterations.

What do you think of the bestseller list?

Not much. If all my books made this list, I wouldn't be thrilled. If all my books never made this list, I wouldn't be disappointed.

The bestseller list is merely a barometer that measures the *quantity* of books sold — not the *quality* of those books. I keep an eye on what's selling. This is a good measurement for gauging the mentality of our society. Something is gravely amiss when people are reading thousands and thousands of horror stories that are dipped in blood. Something is seriously wrong when thousands and thousands are groveling between the pages of the explicit romance novels. Murder, crime, espionage, and sex. This is escapism at its lowest level. When these types of books remain on the bestseller list I think it's time to take a long hard look at ourselves as a whole. And then you wonder why our youngsters are fed up with life. Why do they do drugs? What beauty have they been exposed to? They've become desensitized to the respect for life.

No, I'm sorry, but the bestseller list means nothing to me as a writer. As a human being, the list is frequently a source of great disappointment.

If Summer Rain could change one thing about the world's people, what would that one thing be?

Not a second of deep thought is required here.

I would uplift the world's awareness level. It's because the world lacks this singular mental characteristic that we're now experiencing the problems that we are. Awareness would prevent bigotry, hatred, jealousy, egotism, materialism, prejudice, crime, hunger, welfare, unemployment, and all other negative aspects of humankind's life.

Awareness brings one into a higher understanding and compassion toward life as a unified whole. Technology would advance in great strides when total awareness is present within the mind. Our environment would reverse its failing health with the addition of awareness, peace would reign worldwide and the family of humankind would be united in a common goal of deeply felt humanitarian attitudes

I feel that it's our young mens' patriotic duty to defend our country. You sound as if you support the resistors and the draft dodgers.

You're assuming here.

When a nation is threatened by an invasion, I would naturally expect all able-bodied men to rally their patriotism toward its strong defense.

However, I do sympathize with those young men and their loved ones when they're forced to defend foreign countries in an "undeclared" war. Mind you, I said an undeclared war. There's a chasm of difference here.

No one nation is supreme over other world nations. No one nation can expect to be the world peace keeper. No one nation should think that they're so right, so powerful, that they expect their young men to give their vital lives in order to settle the warring differences between the quarrels of all other nations. This is like a father expecting his only son to physically fight to settle all his friend's disagreements. It's all right to fight for yourself, but to expect a son to fight *all* the fights of others is a bit unfair and would ultimately constitute an interference in the affairs of others.

Giving military aid in the way of wizened and experienced mediators and negotiators is one thing, but when it comes to using a peaceful nation's men to fight the wars of other nations — that's quite another.

Negotiate for other nations — don't kill our youth for them. Send peaceful mediators — not killing machines.

Isn't land development synonymous with progress?

It could be.

Most developers are too eager to build as many high density housing tracts as they possibly can and then get out with a pocketful of money. They've no respect for the aesthetic value of the beautiful land they choose to level.

In most areas, there is no rhyme or sane reason given to the control of architectural design in regard to a pleasing continuity. And most of the more expensive new house designs end up looking more like a wooden mine shaft than a comfortable home.

Land development *can* be synonymous with progress if the city planners drafted building guidelines that controlled the developers like the developers in turn strive to control their buyers.

I'm not against land development, but from how I see it being done, just don't ever do it near me.

Covenants are drafted for the "protection" of the buyers.

You're clearly defending yourself here. You're either a home owner with a list of restrictions to obey or you're a developer.

Well that's fine. I've no argument with you. You see, I believe that covenants are indeed a form of protection for the home buyer. A suburban homeowner certainly doesn't want a flock of chickens squawking in his neighbor's yard.

Yet, you must realize that everyone is different. Everyone doesn't wish to be crowded into controlled, safe, protective tract housing like a stack of dominos. Different folks have different ideas for their ideal home. Personally, the only reason I don't like covenants is because I happen to be one of those different folks. When I'm ready to purchase my home, it will be situated on forested mountain land. We want to feel "free" on our own property — not confined within another person's idea of what we can and cannot have or do there. If we want a couple llamas, we also want the freedom to have them. A person's property isn't really their own if another individual dictates what can or cannot be allowed on that property.

So you see, I don't actually disagree with your defensive statement, it's simply not for me. You would do well to gracefully accept the opinions of others rather than wasting your energies trying to counter them without getting all the facts. Recognizing and accepting differences of opinions is a sign of mental maturity and an awareness of the rights of others to disagree.

Are botanicals really sensitive to human emotions?

Of course! Check your local library for any of the large number of factual research books that verify this reality.

What is your opinion of an arms buildup?

The action is synonymous with the contest between two very young children who are carefully attempting to make their stack of blocks higher than the other's. In the end, they both topple — nobody wins. . .they both lose.

I know your opinion of hunting for sport, but can you clarify your reasoning?

I can make this very explicit for you

When the white man came to America and desired the Indian's land, the white men percieved the natives as less than human, for they weren't so-called "civilized." The natives were pagans, were "primitive" and were perceived "simple" in intelligence. They had no rights. Therefore, being viewed as undesireables, the white military thought nothing of herding the natives off of valuable land. This was done through any means that proved effective including massacres of entire villages. The "seemingly" *higher* intelligent race *hunted* down the primitive one. And it was not called murder or a criminal offense — it was called *progress.* It was called the "taming of the wild west."

So too do the sport hunters perceive the lower intelligent life forms upon the land, for they have not the eyes to perceive them as brothers.

And so, these self-same hunters will be the first to scream "barbarism!" to the first "higher intelligent *alien*" who comes to earth to harvest *their* lower life form for sport. This will not be called murder or a criminal offense by the aliens — it will be called progress. It will be called the "taming of the wild earth."

Fortunately, the "higher intelligent aliens" *are* higher in intelligence, for they perceive us as brothers.

It appears that our weather is becoming more violently forceful, but what actually causes the intensity to increase like that?

You're observant. I'm speaking about being observant with your awareness, not simply with your eyes. Many people comment about the weather's increased force without equating it with the Phoenix Days changes.

All the increased weather intensities were explained in *Phoenix Rising.* You have to remember that all aspects of man's life are being allowed to follow their own natural courses. Many of the world's disasters directly correspond with a specific area's civil unrest or negative forces applied by the people of that region. Be acutely aware of this fact of reality and watch for your own verification of this.

Also, as the time approaches for the changes to become a reality in full-swing, the forces of nature are gathering energy through released natural causes such as solar flares, sun spots, ionization bombardment of our atmosphere, alterations in the magnetic fields of earth and otherplanets, and also the increased plate movements and internal earth activity, they release energy with greater force. See?

Nature is no longer the docile lady she once was. She's come into her own. Her time is rapidly approaching.

I live in a small coastal town that's been quiet and quaint for as long as I can recall. But lately, the developers have been building and building. Why do they have to destroy the beautiful quaint surroundings with high-rise condos?

So that they may gild their golden calf named "profit."

I've always been a peaceful person, but I think it'd be good if we had a revival of the demonstrations of the sixties. Individually people can't fight against corporate and governmental powers, but collectively they can peacefully voice their dissatisfactions and perhaps bring about beneficial changes for the betterment of humankind

I would normally agree with that strategy, however, I see many forms of demonstrations as being harmful to the participants.

Although the sixties have reached Europe and great changes are being brought about by the foreseen civil unrest, America is experiencing the quiet hour before the stormy turbulent future. In time, the sixties will indeed be revived here with a ferocity that even you had not wished for nor imagined.

Do you think a woman would be good in the White House? Also, who do you think would make a good president?

Are you trying to get me in trouble with the Women's Liberation Front? Anyway, what I think doesn't matter.

I'm going to answer this question by saying that I disregard the gender of an individual when it comes to justice, peace, awareness, intelligence, and humanitarianism. An individual with the above qualities would be a wonderful leader for our country. The first part of your question is one that enforces the concept of separatism (man/woman). This ideology within the mass consciousness must be purged so that gender is never a consideration, but rather one's overall leadership qualities that correlate to spiritual law.

In regard to your second question, No-Eyes foresaw a black person who possessed all of the above attributes. However, she was saddened that she also foresaw this gentle and aware man being defeated because of our nation's unenlightened voters.

I worry about the widespread use of computers.

And well you should.

The utilization of computers are a reflection of how we've come to allow the good minds of men to atrophy. Labor saving devices were bad enough, but when it comes to saving "mind energies," we've indeed signed our own death certificates.

Computers can have their place. We've become infatuated with the thinking machines that would appear to possess qualities and abilities that far surpass those of our own minds. In time, these wonderful products of man's highly advanced technology will become silent monsters that no longer have life. For a span of time, the computers will prove to be a useless invention and billions of bytes will have been taken out of man's development.

I don't think it's right to transplant monkey hearts into humans. Am I wrong or what?

Or what.

Medical research has played follow the leader with the technical and scientific community of researchers. Advancements in energy, weapons, and science have all taken a wrong turn years back. They've continued to develop their sciences along the wrong lines — they never got back on track. And. . .medical research is the caboose of the runaway train.

By now you'll have realized where I stand on the utilization of animal organs in human bodies. Species were not meant to be physically intermixed. It's not a medical breakthough to have successfully transplanted a monkey's heart into the chest of a human infant, but rather it's a definitive medical giant step back to the time of Ra-Ta who was so instrumental in "separating" animal from human form.

People must be aware that the use of just *any* method applied to the successful preservation of a human life is not necessary morally right and good. People are dangerously toying with the idea of playing God. A human life is human. It possesses a living spirit that has a specific purpose for being here on earth. And many times that spirit has intentions of surviving in an infant for a mere few hours, days, or weeks.

Medical doctors cannot judge a spirit's purpose for entering into the physical form of an unwell infant. By attempting such major operations on the child, the physicians are interferring with it's purpose.

Animal and human organs are *not* interchangeable. That is not the medical perspective — that is the spiritual perspective.

I think movie star salaries are exorbitant! They're outrageous and unfair.

Think deeper. You sound as though you're envious.

You have to realize the facts here. Each individual occupation, from the file clerk and the waitress to the market analyst and the movie star have their separate wage scale. That is fact. And, simply because one occupation happens to have a higher range wage scale, doesn't mean that it's automatically unethical or unjust.

I agree that movie stars do rake in incredible salaries that would indeed appear way out of line, but who are we to judge what one is worth in any specified occupation or what the price of that worth is?

Judge not another. What's important here is not how much money one *earns,* but rather what one *does* with that money. See?

The wealthy, more than any other segment of society, have a great karmic responsibility. Wealth provides untold opportunities for an individual's advancement. . .or untold paths into karmic debt.

Be not envious of the wealthy, rather be prayerful for their burden.

I don't understand why so much hunger exists in our modern age. What causes this deplorable situation?

We find this causal factor summarized within a singular word: "Politics." Governmental politics. Spiritual politics.

It would appear that much of politics is self-serving instead of serving the people the politicians were elected to represent. Why is this?

This is because of the "way of it," the "manner" by which the political machine has evolved.

In order for the people to be heard, their local representative needs to be heard on the floor of the House or Senate. And, in order for this designated individual to be effectively (influentially) heard, he needs to have a certain amount of internal clout. He or she gains this internal influential clout by first serving self through an internal process of achieving recognition by his/her superiors who have long-term experience. Granted, it's a wasteful machine, but that's the way it is.

Once your representative has proven himself among his/her influential and experienced government constituents, then and only then does the voice of the people he/she represents become loud and clear. It works, but only after too much personal clout-gathering has been done.

The IRS stormed into my friend's home and raided it for records. How can they take people's homes away because of innocent oversights on tax returns? This really frightens me because it's rings of being a police state.

Yes, this would appear to be true. I've known a few of these unfortunate people myself. Many God-fearing good people within our nation have the same fears.

People shouldn't have to fear their government. Something is gravely amiss if this is so. No segment of a government should have the right to simulate storm troopers, to suppress freedoms that were granted, to strip away anyone's rights or property. People are indeed fearful to exercise their opinions, their constitutional right to speak out against transgressions and/or unconstitutional actions by the government.

No, it's not right that we have become a nation of fearful people because the IRS or the CIA or the FBI will put you on a "subversive" list just because you exercise your constitutional right to utter a word of disagreement. The Hoover administration clearly exemplified this reality when he had so many innocent people put under surveillance and maintained files on them simply because he harbored paranoid unfounded suspicions of them.

Since when does personal opinion constitute a subversive person? We've become a nation of people who are afraid to disagree with the government for fear of having our possessions taken away or put in prison for subversion. Does that remind you of any other type of government? To me, it rings a bell, a bell that tolls a reverberating death knell.

Listen well here, because my above words would seem to be prime material for placement on the FBI's list of subversives. However, the words are not malice against the government, they're merely the truth that I and many others see and read about in the newspapers. I see these words to be true — but I also see a nation of good, good people. I see a nation with many influential men and women who are working hard within our government to change things. I see a nation of proud people who're working in awareness to uplift the quality of life for all. No where in the world is there a government that grants so many freedoms to its people. Yes, it has its weaknesses, it has become paranoid, but that too will change —that too will pass from this world.

It seems that our black people still have a way to go in gaining equality in terms of white mass consciousness.

Sadly, this appears to be so, yet their advancements and achievements are still decades ahead of the native American people. Have you noticed that, whenever the term "minorities" is used, only blacks, Hispanics, and Asians are listed or meant? The Native American race most often isn't even included. That alone signifies how far back into the mass consciousness Native Americans are relegated. By comparison, blacks should be proud of their accomplishments in view of Native Americans being perceived as non-entities. . .still.

Soon there will be no more middle-class people. As the rich become richer and the poor get poorer, there will be no inbetween — nothing will be left but affluent neighborhoods and slums. Am I right?

No, you are not.

It would appear that we are indeed headed in that direction —but that's merely a superficial perspective. There's not time left for this clear division of the classes to manifest into physical reality.

At about the time for this separation to begin, other aspects will also be beginning — things that will accompany the birth of the Phoenix.

What makes a college degree take priority over years and years of applied experience? I've had twenty years' experience in my occupation, yet young men just out of college will be hired over me. I don't understand the logic.

You don't understand the logic because there is none.

You're right, there has never been a better source for knowledge than good hands-on experience.

This injustice will change though. Book learning cannot begin to fill the shoes of experience. One day those who've had the college education will be praying for someone with experience to help them — to teach them.

What form of government is best for all-around peace?

A government that is aware enough to place true humanitarianism above all else, a government that is truly for and by the people.

I think the beauty pageants are a disgrace. All the entries have such perfect forms and are so beautiful. It's demeaning to be parading around the way they do.

Your statements address several different areas. But initially I would ask you what's wrong with beauty? A beautiful individual, like the wealthy, has a great responsibility to use that asset in a positive manner.

In respect to the beauty pageants and the "perfect forms," you need to understand that the idea of a "perfect body" is a highly relative factor that's dependent upon individual perception and preference. In this light, there is no perfect shape. Now, it sounds like you'd be interested in knowing that, during a recent beauty pageant when the participants were interviewed, they freely admitted going through "body shops." Many of the entrants had surgical procedures done such as nose jobs, face lifts, liposuction, etc. Their perfect forms had been "surgically sculptured" — what I call going through a body shop. I was surprised to learn this was allowed in the competition arena, but evidently the practice has no bearing on an individual's entry qualifications or restrictions. So next time you happen to see a beauty pageant, know that many of those perfect forms are the result of slight-to-extensive "body work."

The most important aspect of this issue is not the beautiful forms you see, but the *comparing* of same with that of self. We're all different shapes and sizes. Beauty is relative. And true beauty is not even seen — it's felt.

I believe our present society has become too soft. We look for the quickest and easiest way to do everything. We've become a people obsessed with creature comforts.

Creature comforts are not *all* bad. Washing machines, irons, vacuums, and such allow a busy mother to spend more time with her children. These types of machines are time savers. However, when technology says that we require machines to perform faster, then we're getting into the issue of needless creature comforts.

A microwave will prepare a supper with the greatest of ease and with the rapidness of a speeding bullet. . .but a broken seal exposes ourselves to radiation. A bread maker will blend ingredients, mix the dough and bake the loaf. . .and we call it "homemade." Machines chop, slice, curl, swirl and even make our ice. They all save our valuable time and sap our precious energy resources.

Creature comforts can be good, but not to the extent of draining our energy resources and atrophying our bodies. One day humankind will have to rely upon his own manual skills — then where will he be?

What's to be done about the juvenile drug problem? Why does it even exist?

I noticed how you qualified the question. Drugs are not only a "juvenile" problem, but an adult one as well. There wouldn't *be* a juvenile drug problem if the kids weren't supplied by the adults in the first place.

As long as there's money to be made by the commerce of any product, that product will continue to be bought and sold. It makes no difference if it's legal or not — underground supply lines, the black market, contraband materials, etc., all remain active and profitable outlets. Did prohibition stop the hidden stills? As long as there remains a demand, the supply will continue to be endless.

The demand for drugs stems from a dissatisfaction within oneself and an inability to face the harsher realities of life by taking personal responsibility in deference to an escape route. It stems from a need to search for worthwhile meaning and satisfaction in one's personal life. Think on this. If people were content and satisfied with their lives, if they had acceptance, they wouldn't give a thought to using drugs. And, if people were more aware of their spirit's powerful abilities to function on a higher level, a level that often is representative of their drug-induced effects, they'd never again have urges for their expensive and damaging substances.

But the entire scenario is one big malevolent merry-go-round. The rotating machine has to be dismantled in order for the riders to be freed from its evil operators.

The suppliers will be put out of business only when those who demand the product wake up and shed their primitive ignorance.

Do you think prostitution should be legalized?

If I could be insulted, that question would certainly do it. Fortunately, I'm above that. What do *you* think I think?

Prostitution is a cancer of society. Those who fuel it (the johns) are the reason the sickness thrives. As with the drug issue — the "demand" regulates the supply.

Sex is a function that has a two-fold purpose. It serves to protect our civilization from extinction and it serves as a beautiful expression of the deep love between married people.

Why are so many horror movies popular? I can't imagine why people would want to sit and view such films, much less enjoy them.

What's even doubly shocking is that many of the horror films were originally born from books. The horror films have reached their lowest level by being coined the "splatter" films. That term in itself says it all.

The widespread popularity of films and books such as these represent our society's general downgraded respect for life. We beat our breasts and wail with a great lament over our history's eras of atrocities, praying that we'll never again experience the evil and horror that emanated from the sick minds of madmen such as the Chivingtons, Hitlers, and the Colonel Patrick Connors. Yet what does society enjoy for "entertainment?"

Oh, but that's not reality! some claim of the films. But what's the difference? I can't see the distinction? Blood is blood. Murder is murder. These books and their subsequent films are concrete evidence of why the future changes are approaching so soon. There is something afoot among a race of people who watch other people getting hacked and then call it entertainment. Indeed, watch out, there is some *thing* that is silently afoot among us.

Whatever became of fine craftsmen? Everything today is cheaply mass produced.

Your statement needs qualifying.

There are many products made today that've been produced by mass means and have shoddy quality. However, there are also many good products that have retained their high standards of quality. Not "everything" is cheaply made.

In respect to your inquiry regarding the whereabouts of good fine craftsmen, I'm pleased to say that they're still around. Their numbers are increasing daily, for more and more individuals are being drawn to the old arts of quality handiwork. The master craftsmen of old have not left. They've not died away with the past, but are here among us, ready to take up the slack when their time is ripe. They'll teach those who will survive the changes and will be ready to carry on when all the mass production machinery has been silenced.

Are ancient relics really powerful?

No object possesses a power of itself, rather the foundation substance of same.

No matter what sort of relic you hold in your hand, it won't contain powers to bless, protect, or save. Objects are mere objects, nothing more. A sliver from the crucifixion timbers would have no more powers than your picnic table wood.

You must remember that it's the *spirit* that possesses the power! And simply because a certain spirit is "associated" with a specific object does not mean that the object also possesses the same power that the *spirit* did. Objects are powerless things until an enlightened spirit affects them. When the spirit leaves, the object does not retain any of the spirit's former powerful effects — it's simply an object once again.

Relics may have once been in the personal possession of a saintly individual, but they're still merely objects. Relics grant no miracles but through the will of God Himself.

Base metals and crystals and natural materials carry their own vibrational and magnetic frequency fields of power, but they do not generate miracles as in the misconception of relics.

Do secluded monks and such types of people do any good with their fasting, vows of silence, and prayers for the world?

They serve to help uplift the heavy vibrations that man has burdened the world with. These vibrations play a major role in the degree of our self-induced woes. A geographical region that is continually beset by the destructive forces of nature, such as devastating earthquakes, will be found to also be areas that possess an excessive amount of negative vibrations sent up by the actions of its people — many times this action being civil unrest or war. Just as the action of the earth's plate movement affects the geologic surface unrest, so too does the affecting vibrations the people generate there.

Monks and such could better serve mankind by "touching" them, by going out into the world and walking among those who most need spiritual guidance and uplifting. To remain sequestered behind their walls of stone is not nearly effective enough, especially as times for man become negatively intensified.

Please understand that this is not to infer that prayers don't work. But what the world needs are prayers "holding hands" with enlightened people — the physical manifested among us. See?

I've recently seen a television special about the Holy Grail. Would you comment on its existence and whereabouts?

Rather we would comment on its non-existence.

The man known as Jesus was a simple man during his incarnation. He was the son of a hard-working carpenter. And being this simple man, he avoided luxuries and any of the accouterments of the wealthy sect. Jesus was a man of the people, therefore, he utilized simple utensils.

The cup of the Last Supper was a crude wooden bowl type object. It was a well used cup. And, it has since returned to its source — the earth.

We would caution you to avoid the tendency to glamorize such objects. We would warn you to refrain from the desire to make a simple wooden cup into a goblet of gold. Cherish not the material remnants of this man, but rather his holy *words*. Tarry *not* over objects — but rather that which eternally endures —his spoken truths!

If the original story of Adam and Eve didn't exist, then how do you account for all the "begats" in the bible?

God created five earth races. He created five mates. The bible's begats merely cover the descendants of a singular race. There are four *more* lists of begats. And that's just of this earthly civilization. What of all the other civilizations on all the *other* planets in other galaxies that were created concurrently with humankind on earth?

It's not that the story of Adam and Eve never existed, but rather that it has been recorded with a gross neglect to the concept's totality.

If the idea of five different races being created at the moment of Creation is difficult to accept, consider this. If a Swedish couple were placed on a new planet by God and told they were to be its first man and woman, their descendants would all be fair-haired and round-eyed. This original couple couldn't biologically carry any genes for a black race or an oriental one, therefore, the new planet would only have a singular race. See?

When the moon is new, and we look out onto the horizon of the mountains, we can see faint flashes of light. Please explain these.

Nature must be perceived as a living entity.

Our planet is a living and breathing entity. It's in continual motion. This motion is not generally perceived by most folks, however, to those who are aware, the planet constantly moves and breathes — it lives — it's always giving proof of its life.

The faint flashes of light that you occasionally observe during a darkened night are energy releases of the planet. An enlightened individual who has become attuned to his environment can see this light all the time. It gently hovers ever so faintly above the surface of the earth. This light shoots up in frequent split-second flares of release that are visible to the naked eye.

Remember that many forces affect the earth. It's affected by sun spots, solar flares, planet alignments, magnetic fields of other planets, the phases of the moon, etc. Our earth breathes in and out (the tides) and the plates are always in continual motion beneath our feet. An energy pressure is continually being built up by these outside forces upon the earth and, consequently, the earth compensates by regular intervals of pressure release. This regularity is also evidenced by the visual rhythm in which Old Faithful erupts.

If this energy had no regular release pattern, our earth would retain it until it exploded with a big bang out into the universe — a "big bang" that had come full circle.

What's your opinion of the Big Bang theory (solar system beginnings)?

It would seem that the moment of Creation *would* be a big bang. God never does things in little ways. So too would His Creation hour be the biggest Fourth of July event ever imagined. However. . .we're not doing God justice by giving out impressionistic visuals of a Big Bang. Creation of the universe was a meticulously ordered event that was accompanied with the harmony of a Moonlight Sonata. Indeed, it was a beautiful symphonic orchestration of the spheres whereby the stanzas and meters of the music can be numerically measured.

What established religion of today most resembles what God originally intended for His people?

The only way to answer this is by chronicalling the spiritual way of living as God originally intended. You decide which "established" religion best conforms.

The following major points are God's truths — God's facts.

1. The Ten Commandments.
2. One Supreme Power (God the Master)
3. The Spirit of God dwells within the Spirit of each individual
4. All people are created equal.
5. Life after death.
6. Concept of soul rebirth (reincarnation).
7. Unified bond between humanity and all living things.
8. The force of evil.
9. The Final Battle (Armageddon).
10. Spiritual talents (paranormal functioning).
11. Existence of other intelligent lifeforms.
12. Spirit heritage of knowledge (one's right to truth).
13. Multiple dimensional planes.
14. Hierarchy of spirits.

There are more of course, but the above are the basics. Now, show me an "established" religion that teaches all these tenets of God's truths.

What type of house structures harmonize best with the earth?

Those made of materials *of* the earth and are round in shape.

Only Americans should live in America. Our country is being over-run by foreigners who are taking all our jobs and buying all our land.

Hmmm. I believe the Indians once said that too.

Who *is* American though? Seems it's a fact that nearly all the whites in American once came from somewhere else. England, Ireland, France, Germany, Spain, and more are the homelands of most American ancestors. So then, what conclusion can we draw from this fact?

The bottomline is this: The only "Americans" who *didn't* come to this continent from a foreign country were the Indians.

So using your own premise, you too are a foreigner here.

A spade is still a spade. It cannot alter its shape for the sake of convenience. America has become a melting pot of foreigners who've blended to make a unified country. That *is* what America is. . .a beautiful harmony of diverse people. No other nation can match its diversity. America the beautiful. So if you're unsettled with what this country is, perhaps your own ancestral nation would suit you better. . .but don't try to wish a spade into something else. And, since you are not a native

American, you too are one of the foreigners whose ancestors came here from somewhere else.

What is the origin of music? The first song?

Music originated during the first seconds of Creation when the Music of the Spheres was composed as the first sound.

Likewise, the first song was that of the first spirits' Spirit Song of joy and adoration of their Creator.

Today many songs and sounds of music pass through this world unheard by humankind. Such being the music of the forests and the seas and deserts. Wind song. Celestial music of the singing spheres of stars and planets as they rotate. Singing waters of rivers, streams, and creeks. Dimensional music that can be heard crossing over to the Third. The lyrical hum of magnetic fields. The chantlike rhythm of the Standing Stones. The Singing Stones. The music of nature. Of God.

In your letter to me, you mentioned how plastics are such an environmental threat. I'm happy to tell you that the plastic bags I now get in my grocery store are biodegradable.

And so they are.

They are "photodegradable." This means that long-term exposure to sunlight will eventually degrade the material. However, if you've ever visited a real trash dump site, you'll see that most refuse is piled then bulldozed under the earth and "buried." So then, how is it that the sunlight as a chance to degrade your plastic grocery bag?

The issue of plastics cannot be placated so easily. Many manufacturers are now claiming that they "recycle" the plastics. In this manner they're being an "environmentally-conscious" company. And, on the surface, this would appear to be so. But for those who look beneath the surface, they see the toxic pollutants manufacturer's spew into the air as the "recycling" of their plastics are manifested.

I recently noticed a restaurant's posted notice that claimed how environmentally conscious they were because they recycled their containers into playground equipment. Sounds utopian, but how many people realize the toxic pollutants the plants emit as the containers are reformed into playground equipment? Chemicals are chemicals. And materials such as plastics and styrofoam have to go. They will have no place in our world once the Phoenix is flying free.

That's not speculation or dreaming — that's just plain fact.

I've never heard of you appearing at any Earth Day gatherings (April 22nd). Don't you celebrate this beautiful occasion?

This question can be equated to the idea of reserving one day a week to worship God (Sunday). I find ways to worship and pray to God everyday and, therefore, don't require a special "mandatory" day to set aside for God.

So too is the Earth Day issue, for *every* day is my Earth Day. I need no special one day of the year to be designated as such. Hopefully, neither will everyone else. The earth needs to be a living part of everyone's heart and soul — *every* day. I was celebrating Earth Day long before it became a "popular" thing for the public to do.

The government's using our Social Security taxes to bring down the deficit and make it look smaller to the people. Don't you think people should stop paying this tax when the reserve funds are being spent instead of saved for our old age?

Is this an entrapment question? Methinks you want me to condone civil disobedience here. Do you work for the FBI?

I could respond to this question with an affirmative or a negative reply. Instead I take the Fifth.

How much are we manipulated and deceived by the government?

You must understand that I cannot and do not use spiritual gifts to undermine another person or organization. I won't expose anyone's faults — even the government's.

It's important to realize that although you may believe that our government conceals its plans from the general public and manipulates the people by way of secretive maneuvers, our system of government is still the best there is and you should be grateful that you live in this beautifully free country.

All governments have their basic problems, mainly because a government is comprised of so many different people — all human — with the capacity for human error and frailty. Perhaps the initial quality of "Big Brother's" protectiveness occasionally shows his over-eager face as a bully with strong-arm tactics, but on the whole, a big brother is not a bad person to have on one's side.

No one individual is without faults, just as no one government is. You would do well to accentuate the positive rather than to seek out and zero in on the negative.

How does one geographically relocate without contacts in the new state?

If the relocation is going to be in a larger city or town, there will always be some type of living quarters to move into such as apartments or house rentals. And there will always be some type of employment that you can get right into until something more attractive or suitable opens up.

If the relocation is going to be in a smaller town, it would be best if you first wrote the Chamber of Commerce and request they send you the local newspapers and also get in touch with several real estate agents.

Did No-Eyes ever mention anything unusual about our sun?

You're referring to certain theories that claim our sun is hollow or that an intelligent civilization lives on/or in its sphere. I've heard all these postulations.

The visionary didn't speak of the sun's composition nor of anything remotely relating to the above theories. However, very early on in my lessons, while we were sitting out in the autumn sunshine, she announced that we were going to take a special journey. This was a spirit journey. And we traveled up toward the sun, through the licking and spearing flames. . . into an incredibly peaceful chamber. . .where other beings of all civilizations were being energized while meditating. The inner feeling was quite beyond description, for it felt just like resting in the Hand of God.

More I cannot tell you, for, more is unknown to me.

Why is there such an influx of mystical paintings done at this time? It seems that everyone is getting on the bandwagon.

I hope you're ready to climb aboard, for the bandwagon has a name. . .The Golden Age of Peace and Harmony.

My friend, what you've perceived is the emergence of a new and wonderful awareness of how humans are so clearly connected —interconnected — with all of life, including the *spirit* of same. And, correspondingly, the arts should indeed reflect that new and bright awareness. Art and literature will blossom with the New Reality that is manifesting so that the world can then be eased up into its destined lighter vibration.

What's your opinion of the practice of holding dolphins in swim pens for the public to see?

This can't be answered without qualifying the response because there are more than one marine facility that hold these mammals, likewise, there are various reasons for doing so.

Dolphins are far more intelligent than anyone realizes and it's a travesty upon their species to use them as a circus sideshow by having them perform tricks. This is far beneath them. And it is not humane.

There are a few marine facilities that utilize the dolphins for the benefit of mentally deficient individuals. In this instance, both the dolphins and the humans benefit through a synergistic relationship. The dolphins do recognize the human's deficiency and are more than willing to be of assistance in bringing out a noticeable developmental improvement. This would be the *only* acceptable use of dolphins in light of how they're currently being utilized.

Lastly, the most unconscionable use of the dolphins is being perpetrated by the U.S. Navy. Dolphins are kept in small pens and trained to be marine weapons. The military mentality, in this case, proves to be far less advanced than the dolphins themselves.

When a popular national news documentary team investigated the Navy's use of these mammals they were met with armed guards who confiscated their tapes and were told to leave the premises.

What's your solution to household insects? I hate using chemicals on them.

I should hope so! Why would you use any kind of chemicals on these little crawling or winged people anyway?

Forget the chemical sprays and forget swatting them. Get yourself a paper cup (a bug cup) and "catch" them. . .then gently let them loose outside. We've been doing this for years.

If you have some type of infestation such as ants, sprinkle a line of Capsicum (Cayenne Pepper) around their trails and also around your house foundation, entryway door thresholds and window sills.

Moth balls or peppermint oil soaked rags will discourage the wild rodents such as field mice, chipmunks, and gophers.

Is our weather ever directly affected by God?

Although He can and sometimes does affect the weather, the earth's weather is due to the planet's aura of magnetic field and how it is affected during various points in its orbital rotation around the sun. The sun's specific activity also strongly affects the earth's magnetic field as does the proximity of other celestial bodies.

Strong vibrations can also interfere with the earth's magnetic field, therefore we see the human condition affecting the weather more often than is realized.

I think it's wonderful that some U.S. nuclear plants are being converted to natural gas. We'd have a much safer world if they all were. I know you'd agree.

Not necessarily, not necessarily at all.

Natural gas is a resource we do not require and, in itself, has the great potential to be a dangerous energy source.

In the future, no fossil fuels will be utilized to power *anything*. In the future we will have no requirements for power plants of *any* kind, for furnaces and all appliances and *vehicles* will be powered by a simple device that utilizes the earth's natural magnetic field.

This energy device will make all of the following obsolete: power plants, electric companies, natural gas (and propane), oil, etc. We will have no more electric lines strung across the nation nor will we have gas companies and their underground pipelines. We will have no more gas stations, and we will have no more *pollution!*

This revolutionary energy device has already been manifested in the world. I know the inventor and have talked to him. His twenty-year battle to get a patent has worn him down, for the U.S. Office of Patents and Trademarks wanted to destroy his device and all prototypes. Wall Street was warned to have nothing to do with his invention and, technological companies were likewise warned away. Yet scientists from all over the world visited the inventor and were amazed to discover that the device put out more energy than it took in. This in itself shattered the currently-accepted rules of physics and made the scientists begin to reevaluate their accepted physical laws. Several U.S. Presidents have been made aware of the energy device but have done nothing to bring about its development. The inventor has been battling the power people for over twenty years. The Supreme Court refused to listen to his appeal to the highest court of the land. At the time of this writing, the inventor is still battling to bring about a new pollution-free world by fighting for his well-deserved U.S. patent! Sadly, because of its ramifications for the present-day energy businesses it has been suppressed and smothered by the people in control who wish to keep this beautiful earth in a pollution-spewing state, which produces continuing profit for the few. But take heart, my friends, this too will change. Although this energy device has been successfully suppressed so far, I do see the day ahead when its time has come. Oh yes. . .come it *will*, for the world of earthly mortals is indeed destined for a beautiful time when no form of chaos or negative distrubances will be allowed to exist upon the land.

Note: Please don't write to me inquiring of this inventor or the energy device for I cannot say more on the subject. For the obvious reasons I must tread lightly with certain dangerous issues and, perhaps I've already said too much. . .but then I am here to bring the truth to light — in so doing, there are times I place myself in great risk. Please respect my precarious position for some of the things I know but cannot yet *fully* speak of.

DREAM SYMBOLOGY

The symbology in dreamscapes is frequently quite a play on words and phrases. These specialty interpretations most often combine more than one symbol to complete the intended meaning. Examples of these "play on word" interpretations are as follows:

- a pigeon on a stool = a stool pigeon
- someone pinching a penny = a penny pincher
- laced in a straight line = someone who is strait-laced
- a human with a pig's head = someone who is pigheaded
- someone who is turning his coat around = a turncoat
- pins in someone's hair = a pinhead
- someone with a yellow stomach = yellow-bellied
- path lined with flowers = a primrose path (life of ease)
- loving a puppy = puppy love
- someone being pushed over = a pushover
- racing rats = a rat race situation

- a red penny = red cent (meaning poor)
- cashing coupons in = redeeming self
- a red hand = caught red-handed
- neck of rubber = rubberneck (to gawk)
- two fiddles = second fiddle
- two guesses = second guess
- two hands = second hand
- two mortgage papers = second mortgage
- placing something on a shelf = shelving something
- shoe lace = shoestring (lack of funds)
- blue stockings = bluestocking (a scholarly woman)
- a blue shirt collar = bluecollar worker
- throwing a stone = a stone's throw away

The following interpretations represent those dreamscape symbols that were inquired about in readership letters. These serve to greatly expand the symbology listing in *Earthway* and increase the public's correct interpretive database.

AARDVARK represents a tendency to hide from problems. This infers a "burrowing" down away from reality.

ABACUS denotes a need to "refigure" an old situation or condition.

ABALONE symbolizes the inherent beauty of spiritual gifts, talents or knowledge.

ABANDON connotes an individual or situation that has been left unattended or voluntarily shed from one's life or thoughts.

ABBEY represents an immediate need to regain one's spiritual sacredness toward beliefs.

ABDOMEN most frequently refers to the solar plexus region that spiritual (psychic) sensations are felt. This is an indication to take heed of one's inner promptings.

ABDUCTION denotes the spiritual "unlawfulness" of "taking on" a belief system that has not yet come to one naturally. This would be a prime dreamscape symbol for an individual who has recently delved deeply into native ceremonies without the prerequisite deeper understanding of same.

ABHOR symbolizes a deep negative feeling that is not expressed in one's waking hours.

ABOLISH denotes a warning to "get rid of" something in one's life that is (or will be) damaging to self or others.

ABORIGINE represents simplicity. This can refer to a situation, condition or belief system in one's life. This means that one needs to go back to basics.

ABORTION symbolizes the "willful killing" of a relationship, situation, or belief system. This is, of course, meant to warn the dreamer that this killing is wrong.

ABRASIONS (skin) refer to those individuals, situations, or beliefs that are causing "friction" in the dreamer's life.

ABSCESSES connotate aspects of the dreamer's waking life that will lead to infectious conditions. This may refer to any of the three aspects of man (mental, physical, or spiritual).

ABSENT refers to an obvious void in one's life.

ABSINTHE symbolizes a self-imposed "bitterness" in the dreamer's life. This is most often a warning to forgive the past transgressions of others and to accept life in order to progress.

ABSOLUTION connotates the need to shed one's self-imposed sense of guilt that is serving to hold one back.

ABSORBENT represents that which is "taken in." This is usually an indication that the dreamer needs to absorb a concepts deeper meaning or to gain a fuller understanding of something.

ABSTINENCE refers to one's necessity to "abstain" from something. This is a warning that clearly tells the dreamer to "stop" doing something that will prove to have negative effects for him or her.

ABSTRACT (painting) symbolizes the dreamer's mental confusion and the need to clarify conceptual ideas or beliefs. This may also refer to relationships or situations.

ACCENTS indicate the dreamer's need to "accent" or place more importance on something. The dreamer will know what this symbol refers to in his/her life.

ACCESS is a symbol that literally points the "access route" to whatever the dreamer is seeking.

ACCESSORY represents that which the dreamer doesn't need. This may denote something in a belief system, a situation or another individual.

ACCOLADES always represent personal praise for something the dreamer has accomplished in life.

ACCOMPLICE denotes a "partner," usually inferring something negative done in life. This may also symbolize someone in the dreamer's life who has led him/her spiritually astray.

ACCORDION refers to those life relationships, situations, or beliefs that are in "accordance" with the precepts of the Law of One.

ACCOUNTS connotate the balance of payments (karma). What condition were the accounts in? Were they in the red? Balanced?

ACCREDITATIONS symbolize "readiness." This usually refers to spiritual aspects of the dreamer's life. Were you accredited for that which you claim to know? Or were you turned down, indicating further study needed?

ACHIEVEMENT TESTS represent that which the dreamer has achieved in life. High scores are required on these in order for the dreamer to expect to advance.

ACQUAINTANCES denote those individuals the dreamer meets in his/her waking life who will affect changes.

ACQUIESCE connotes a "giving in." This is usually a warning for the dreamer to either do so or refrain from giving in. This applies to another individual, situation, or belief system.

ACRES symbolize extent of spiritual attainment. **Acres** may also refer to the dreamer's future geographic attainment.

ACROBAT means the "contortions" one goes through to gain a goal. This is not necessarily a negative aspect, but may indicate the needed twists and turns one's path must take.

ACTIVIST symbolizes "active involvement."

ACTOR/ACTRESS is a dreamscape symbol that comes as a warning to stop "acting" in one's waking life. This is a strong caution to start being yourself. This symbol infers dishonesty.

ADDER (snake) represents a "venomous" nature.

ADJUSTING refers to that which needs adjustment in one's life. Check to recall what was being adjusted in the dreamscape. Was it a situation? Hair (thoughts)? A relationship?

ADMONISHMENT is a symbol that clearly represents a warning. **Who** was doing the admonishing? You? Then that means you need to set someone straight. Was someone admonishing you?

ADOBE represents a down-to-earth condition or attitude.

ADOPTING connotes a "taking in" of something or someone. This may refer to spiritual belief systems as well.

ADRIFT denotes a "drifting" or "lost" sensation or condition. Since drifting can only be done on water, and water symbolizes spiritual aspects, this refers directly to one's spiritual belief system or spiritual life path.

ADULTERY comes as a symbol to warn against the taking of that which cannot be yours. This is a clear warning to abide by the precepts of the Law of One.

ADVISING represents the need for the dreamer to either be advised or for him/her to advise another. Either way, it infers that the dreamer is not doing as he/she should.

ADVOCATE symbolizes to need for the dreamer to "support" an individual or situation or belief system. This dreamscape symbol comes only when there is a need for the dreamer to be actively involved in something.

AFFLUENT signifies "riches." These may be material or spiritual, but the important point is what is done with these. Some dreamers don't know they're spiritually rich until a dreamscape clearly points out the fact.

AFTERGLOW denotes inner light and the warm feelings of same.

AFTERNOON represents a time of day that will be important for the dreamer to accomplish something.

AGENDA represents the need to take serious responsibility for that which the dreamer must give attention to.

AGENT refers to a "middleman" that is not necessary in the dreamer's life. This particular dreamscape element indicates that the dreamer must begin taking responsibility for his/her own life decisions.

AGITATION (as a washing machine) represents an aspect in the dreamer's life that is causing great mental/emotional disturbances. Frequently these are not admitted to, but when a dreamscape clearly indicates this disturbance, it's important to take action to alleviate the condition before it gets worse.

AGONY will signify something the dreamer is agonizing over. This may also refer to someone else in the dreamer's life.

AGREEMENTS represent that which must be resolved in the dreamer's life. This may also refer to an agreement already sealed, but needs undoing.

AIR CONDITIONER can represent the need to cool off or it can refer to a "cold" situation, relationship, or individual. Surrounding aspects will clarify this intention for the dreamer.

AIR LOCK signifies that which the dreamer shuts off from self. This dreamscape symbol comes as a serious warning to stop separating self from that which will benefit him or her.

AISLE connotates a "pathway" through to one's goal or purpose.

ALABASTER refers to a "hard coldness." This is certainly a negative connotation that warns the dreamer of another individual's inner feelings or personality. This may also infer the dreamer him/herself.

ALADDIN symbolizes one's wishes and represents the deep desire for easy access to goals or possessions. This is definitely a warning to stop striving for the easy way.

ALAMO symbolizes a final confrontation. This may be for the dreamer or for someone he/she knows.

ALBINO connotates lack of individuality.

ALCOVE represents places of respite in which one rests.

ALIBI refers to guiltlessness. This may be generated from the dreamer or someone they're acquainted with. What's important here is if the alibi is valid or not. The surrounding aspects will verify this fact for the dreamer.

ALIEN connotates that which is foreign. This may refer to an individual, situation, or belief system in the dreamer's life. Though something foreign may have entered the dreamer's life, this symbol represents the need to familarize self with it.

ALIMONY refers to reparations required.

ALLEGATIONS signify "unproven claims" made. The emphasis is on "unproven," for this dreamscape symbol can be one that clearly points out a very destructive situation for the dreamer.

ALLEGIANCE connotates "support" needed.

ALLERGY symbolizes negative aspects that the dreamer will experience with association with an individual, situation, or belief system.

ALLOWANCE (money) represents the need to make allowances. This dreamscape facet is evidenced when more understanding is needed on an individual's part. This signifies a strict or judgemental personality that needs to loosen up.

ALLURING connotates temptations.

ALLIES refer to friendships that are true.

ALOE is represented in dreamscapes to indicate the need to "soothe" a burning situation or desire.

ALPENGLOW denotes the gentleness of one's nature.

ALPHABETICAL signifies the need to bring proper order into one's life or to get priorities in place.

ALTAR symbolizes adoration. What is on the dreamscape altar? Is the adoration misplaced? What condition is the altar in? Does it have cobwebs covering it? Is it black? White?

ALTERATIONS represent changes needed.

ALTITUDE SICKNESS signifies a "high attitude or position" that is not yet deserved. This important dreamscape fragment warns that the dreamer (or associated individual) must face reality instead of trying to be better or know more than is truly manifested.

ALUMINUM indicates the need to "reflect" or contemplate upon one's spiritual beliefs.

AMATEUR NIGHT symbolize the allowance of "hearing out peers." This dreamscape aspect usually refers directly to the dreamer's life relationships.

AMAZEMENT connotates a revelation of some type that literally amazes the dreamer.

AMAZON denotes confusion of one's life. This represents the tangled jungle the dreamer (or associated individual) walks through in daily life. This must be corrected.

AMBASSADORS represent goodwill and personal helpfulness. This dreamscape facet will clearly indicate those people in the dreamer's life who are willing and capable of helping by way of being an intermediary or go-between.

AMBIDEXTROUS denotes duality. This symbol most frequently indicates an individual who is capable of seeing the polarity (pros and cons) of any situation or condition.

AMBLING connotates nonchalance or loss of clear direction or purpose. This is a warning symbol that manifests to spur the dreamer into a more enthusiastic sense of purpose.

AMISH signify simplicity and cooperation in relationships.

AMMUNITION denotes validations. Do you have ammunition to back up your claims? In the dreamscape, are you out of ammunition?

AMNESIA indicates forgetfulness (including self-induced). This dreamscape facet is a clear warning that the dreamer has forgotten something important or else he/she has chosen to forget same.

AMNESTY signifies total and absolute forgiveness.

AMPLIFIERS represent a need to "hear better." This would indicate a great need to **listen** with a heightened degree of attention and awareness. The dreamer is, in essence, hearing — but **not** hearing.

ANABIOTIC (coma state) denotes complete unawareness. This symbol comes as a severe warning from the Higher Self for the dreamer to "wake up."

ANAGRAM represents solutions available within the problem itself. This dreamscape fragment advises of the capacity to solve one's problems with what they already have to work with. The major solution components are already provided.

ANALGESICS represent painless resolutions. These are important to recall, for they will provide the dreamer with resolutions that were before one's eyes, yet overlooked.

ANALYSIS means to analyze something. Clearly, this dreamscape facet wouldn't present itself if the dreamer were already thinking deeply upon a problem or situation.

ANCIENT connotates old and wise.

ANDROID symbols come as warnings for the dreamer to stop acting like a mindless robot and to start "thinking for self." This may also refer to someone in the dreamer's life.

ANECDOTE represents lessons needed. An acecdote is like a moral to a story and, in this light, carries a much-needed message.

ANEMIA signifies poor nutrients. This, of course, can refer to any of mankind's aspects. Is the dreamer eating correctly? Is the dreamer spiritually starved for conceptual basics? Is the dreamer emotionally distant and uncommunicative?

ANGLING (fishing) represents spiritual inactivity. In other words, one is nonchalant about his/her belief system and is whiling away time waiting for some spiritually-important aspect to enter one's life.

ANIMATION in dreamscapes denote immaturity. This infers a real serious perception that life is nothing more than a cartoon. . .a joke.

ANKHS symbolize peace and spiritual knowledge.

ANNALS (historic) signify lessons to be learned from the past.

ANNEX denote the need to become active; to join.

ANNIHILATE represents the need to "get rid" of something in the dreamer's life.

ANNIVERSARY symbolizes important dates in the dreamer's life. These will be those dates that mark a special occasion or event.

ANTHEM denotes loyalties.

ANTIBIOTICS signify a poisonous relationship, situation, or belief system. The dreamer will understand which is inferred by recalling the surrounding aspects of this dream.

ANTICHRIST connotes all that is negative and evil. This may also enter one's dreamscape to verify a misconception of spiritual truths such as the nonexistence of evil in the world.

ANTICIPATION comes as a dreamscape symbol to underscore the dreamer's emotional response of same. This does not represent "expectation" however.

ANTISEPTICS reveal the need to guard against a "germ infested" condition, relationship, or belief system. This comes as a clear caution that whatever the dreamer is doing or believing in his/her waking hours has the potential to poison.

ANUBIS symbolizes "judgement upon death." For Anubis to be manifested in a dreamscape means that the dreamer is not paying attention to personal ramifications of actions done or beliefs held in his/her waking hours.

ANVILS represent the need to "reshape" something in the dreamer's life. This most frequently refers to basic foundational aspects.

APERITIFS refer to the lack of good nutrition. Again, this may not infer the physical system, but may indicate one's mental, emotional, or spiritual aspects. One (or more) of these need to be better stimulated with fortifying nutrients or knowledge.

APERTURES (lens openings) signify "sight" or "awareness." This directly refers to one's perceptions of life or belief systems.

APEX denotes the "pinnacle." This dreamscape fragment signifies the very top of one's path or knowledge.

APHIDS signify a mentally and emotionally draining personality.

APHRODISIACS represent misplaced methods and motives.

APHRODITE symbolizes love and the manner of attainment. Usually a manifestation of Aphrodite infers that someone is using love to gain ends. Ill-gotten love or ends is a severe warning from the Higher Self.

APIARY refers to one's industrious nature (or lack of same). Recall the physical condition of the apiary and of the attending bees.

APOCALYPSE represents some type of personal "revelation." The surrounding dreamscape aspects and fragments will clearly identify the intent here. Oftentimes this dream aspect will present itself as a clear warning for the dreamer to "shape up" and pay attention to the truth of his future.

APOLLO comes as a dreamscape fragment as a symbol of male beauty. This, of course, will infer the "inner" type of beauty so many men deny themselves.

APOLOGIES represent the admission of guilt. This can refer to the dreamer him/herself or it can be associated with someone the dreamer knows.

APOSTLE comes as a dreamscape fragment to identify those individuals who are following the right path as outlined in the precepts of the Law of One.

APPARITIONS manifest in dreamscapes as helping entities who come with important messages for the dreamer. Recall these, for they're very critical.

APPETIZERS represent aspects that prompt further actions such as gaining deeper knowledge.

APPLAUSE always comes as a commendation, but may also caution the dreamer that he/she should give appreciation where and when due.

APPLICATIONS signify one's need to "apply" self.

APPRAISALS denote the need to understand true value in life.

APPRENTICE means a "helper." This may refer to the dreamer being this new learner or it may infer someone in the dreamer's life.

APTITUDE TESTS manifest as dreamscape fragments to clarify the dreamer's learning capacity or ability. Surrounding dreamscape fragments may indicate this refers to spiritual concepts, personal relationships or work positions.

ARBITRATORS denote mediation and the necessity of same. Clearly, this dreamscape facet does not manifest unless there's something important going on in the dreamer's life.

ARBORS signify spiritual inner beauty of one's gifts. Recall what condition and color this arbor was in.

ARCHANGELS denote critical spiritual messages from the highest level of the spiritual hierarchy. Pay close attention to these messages, for they wouldn't come if they weren't needed.

ARENAS connotate aspects of life that one deals in. What was going on in the arena? Who was present? Was it a battle? A demonstration?

ARMADILLOS signify defense mechanisms. This dreamscape facet refers to those "hard shells" we put up to separate us from others or threatening situations. Usually we're cautioned to "face" these rather than to curl up into ourselves as we can present a hardened exterior to others.

ARMBANDS represent the showing of emotions. What color was the dreamscape armband? Did it have an insignia or symbol on it?

ARMOIRES symbolize hidden aspects of self.

ARMOR is manifested as dreamscape fragments to illustrate the dreamer's level of "protection." This may refer to emotional, physical, or spiritual shielding.

ARMIES signify force capability.

ARRESTS connotate "being caught" or justice served. For arrests to occur in dreamscapes, the dreamer usually thinks a deed will have been the perfect crime or that he/she will not be caught doing something illegal, unethical or unspiritual.

ARROWS represent a straight course.

ARROYOS denote dangerous probabilities that are present.

ARSENALS refer to the storage of ammunition supplies and the condition of same. This, of course, directly refers to one's level of credibility and validating proof the dreamer has stored.

ARTIFACTS denote validating aspects in one's life.

ARTIFICIAL signifies the lack of genuineness or credibility. This dreamscape facet clearly represents imitations.

ASBESTOS represents the duality of one's spiritual gifts. They can protect and be used for good or they can turn against one if they're used in a negative manner.

ASCENDING indicates one's advancement.

ASPHALT denotes a serious separation from the "grounding" qualities of one's life.

ASPIRIN signifies the need for respite.

ASSEMBLY LINES caution against continual conformity. This dreamscape fragment warns the dreamer to begin thinking for self.

ASSIGNMENTS are a symbol from the Higher Self that cautions the dreamer to "be about his/her spiritual purpose." This fragment comes when the dreamer has severely veered from the intended goal.

ASTERISKS signify a critical warning for the dreamer to pay close attention to something. An *asterisk* is always very important for the dreamer to give attention to.

ASTRINGENTS signify a harsh and severe personality.

ASYLUMS refer to a "possible ending place" for the dreamer if he/she doesn't get back on course.

ATHEISTS connotate those in the dreamer's life who would tear down his/her spiritual beliefs.

ATLAS (maps) represent the need for geographic awareness.

ATOLLS signify spiritual serenity through protection.

AUDIENCES symbolize "watchers" that are ever-present in one's life. What is the audience doing? Applauding? Booing? Leaving? Asking for an encore?

AUDITS denote "suspected transgressions committed." Who is being audited? Is it the dreamer? Is the dreamer doing the auditing on someone else? What is being audited?

AUTISM indicates the hiding of one's inner light and knowledge.

AUTOGRAPHS denote misplaced priorities. Is the dreamer signing autographs? Then the dreamer has an egotistical perception of self. Is the dreamer seeking someone's autograph? Then the dreamer is not viewing everyone as his/her equal in life. If the dreamer has an autograph of a historical figure, this will have an important message. Lincoln refers to honesty. Satin denotes the dreamer admires evil. Whoever has signed the autograph will clearly hear a message for the dreamer.

AUTOPSY signifies the need to analyze a past action, relationship, or belief system.

AVALANCHES denote spiritual smothering being done.

AVALON symbolizes fantasy goals and utopian dreams.

AWLS symbolize the presence of lies. There are "openings" or "holes" in a situation, relationship, or belief system.

B

BABBLING (talk) signifies mental confusion or ignorance.

BACHELORS signify a selfish tendency. This is not to infer egotism or homosexuality, but rather a self-centerdness based on an inability to sustain a successful interrelationship with a mate. Frequently, **bachelors** suggest a individual incapable of committment.

BACKBONES denote strength of character. Check to recall the condition of the backbone. Was it the dreamer's? Someone the dreamer knows? Was the spine shriveled? Crooked? Strong and straight?

BACKDROP signifies a false past. Backdrops are different painted scenes used in the theater. These then represent those make-believe backgrounds that people contrive for themselves.

BACKFIELD symbolizes a secondary position of support. Is the dreamer in the backfield? Is someone else? This dreamscape fragment manifests when someone is taking a major role when, in reality, they should be a minor player.

BACKFIRE (vehicle) connotes repercussions. This will indicate that a plan, relationship, situation, or path will not manifest according to one's desire or goal.

BACKHOE denotes the need to "dig back" for more information. This directly relates to something in one's past; a relationship, situation, or belief system that one is currently involved with.

BACKLASH indicates a negative reaction.

BACKLOG signifies something unfinished. This dreamscape fragment usually infers that something important isn't being attended to.

BACK SEAT represents one's rightly designated position. Do you need to take a back seat instead of being the driver? Does someone else need to get out of the driver's seat and let you do the leading? This directly refers to one's authority or right to lead their own lives.

BACKSLIDING connotates regression. Who is backsliding? This dreamscape aspect comes as a warning from one's Higher Self.

BACKSTAGE indicates one's proper position. This is a warning when someone takes center stage when, in reality, they should be in the wings or backstage.

BACKSTITCH signifies the need to make amends.

BACKSTROKE represents a need to review spiritual concepts. This dreamscape facet would clearly indicate a "forgetting" or "falling away" from one's spiritual belief system.

BACKTRACKING refers to a wrong path taken. One must backtrack to get back on the right pathway. This comes to reveal how one has gone too far too fast and has clearly missed something.

BACKWASH symbolizes an aftermath in turmoil. This indicates that a path taken will have serious repercussions.

BACTERIA denotes germs or a dangerous situation, relationship, or belief system that will **infect** the dreamer. This is a definitive warning symbol for the dreamer.

BADLANDS symbolize a "bad situation."

BAFFLES represent lack of success. This particular dreamscape aspect forewarns of a relationship or situation in the dreamer's life that will be thwarted. . .it will fail to succeed.

BAGGAGE signifies excesses in life.

BAIT represents enticements. Watch yourself when this dreamscape fragment is presented, for it means that the dreamer is either **being baited** or that he/she is the one baiting another. Either way, it's a serious warning for the dreamer from the Higher Self.

BALANCE SHEETS directly refer to karma and one's personal Akashic Record state of affairs. How does the balance sheet look? Is there a debit? Credits? Is it grossly unbalanced? This specific dreamscape fragment comes as a beautiful insight into one's own spiritual condition.

BALCONIES designate perceptual clarity.

BALLAST signifies excess weight in relation to emotions, mental, or spiritual aspects. This does not usually refer to physical overweight. This dreamscape aspect will indicate that one is carrying around excessive beliefs that are unproductive and unnecessary.

BALLOONS refer to exaggerations; something blown up.

BALLOTS designate one's right to have a say.

BANKBOOKS represent wealth. If the bankbook is silver, this refers to spiritual wealth. If the bankbook is gold, it infers material wealth. If it's black, it signifies a lack of wealth which indicates one who doesn't share that which he/she has.

BANKROLLS (moneyroll) represents sharing wealth. To bankroll someone or a project means to give money (or other types of wealth) to it.

BANKRUPT signifies a spiritually devoid type of wealth. In other words, this means that one is indeed wealthy, but does not share. This dreamscape fragment may also be a literal symbol which would mean that the dreamer may indeed go bankrupt.

BARGES indicate a lethargic spiritual progression.

BAROMETERS denote amount of pressure one is under. If this is a high number, the dreamer is cautioned to ease up on life's activities, or to stop letting everything pressure him or her.

BARRACKS refer to lack of individuality; repression.

BARRELS symbolize a large amount of something. Recall what the barrels contained. What condition were the dreamscape barrels in? Were they in a dry warehouse or floating in water?

BARRETTES represent contained thoughts. It's important to recall what *type* of barrette was presented in the dreamscape. Was it in a specific shape of something?

BASSINET signifies spiritual respite. This dreamscape fragment indicates the need to rest along one's spiritual path because a rebirth is occuring.

BATHYSPHERE designates a journey into the deeper aspects of spiritual concepts.

BATONS indicate an egotistical personality.

BATTLEMENTS represent heightened spiritual protection. Who is on the battlement? What condition was it in?

BAYONETS indicate one's personal protective preparedness.

BAYOU indicates a sluggish spiritual perception or belief system.

BAY WINDOWS refer to clear perceptions and acute awareness.

BEDLAM symbolizes complete confusion. Surrounding dreamscape aspects will clarify if this symbol refers to the dreamer's emotional, physical, or spiritual life.

BEDOUINS denote spiritual separatism. This is not the negative connotation it may appear to be, for many individuals must separate their learned truths from those of the mainstream religionists.

BEDROCK represents strong foundations. This dreamscape facet may refer to any of mankind's aspects.

BEESWAX refers to an industrious nature.

BEGGING indicates desperation. Who is doing the begging. What is begged for?

BEHEMOTHS symbolize a "mammoth" size of something. This may relate to nearly anything in the dreamer's life. Recall the surrounding aspects of the dream for specifics on this symbol.

BELFRY denotes "alarming" situations or persons. This will specifically be associated with **mental/emotional** aspects of an individual, whether it be the dreamer or an acquaintance.

BELLBOYS represent servitude.

BELL JARS signify narrow-mindedness; a closed mind.

BERMUDA TRIANGLE symbolize spiritual mysteries or conceptual vacillation. This is a serious warning, for it means that spiritual beliefs are not solid.

BEST MAN (wedding) refers to male support in life.

BETEL NUTS indicate a hypnotic or mesmerised state of mind.

BEWITCHED means a lack of independence or absence of individual thought. This is a clear warning from the Higher Self that is cautioning the dreamer against associating with persons who capture one's free will.

BILE signifies bitterness. This may reveal a secretive bitterness felt by the dreamer or someone associated with him or her. It may indicate a situation or relationship or belief system that will leave the dreamer extremely bitter in the end.

BILL OF HEALTH indicates condition of one's health. This dreamscape fragment may refer to any of man's aspects.

BILL OF SALE represents the selling of something. What was sold? Was it a belief? A person?

BIOPSY symbolizes something that's questionable. This infers that something in the dreamer's life requires examination to determine if it's a healthy or destructive force.

BIRD DOG denotes a "hounding" being done. Who has the bird dog? Is it the dreamer? If it is, then this is a caution to stop hounding someone or something.

BITTERSWEET (bush) refers to that which has the capability of causing both happiness and pain. This dreamscape fragment will directly refer to those aspects in one's life that have a duality of nature.

BLACK BALLS represent negative decisions.

BLACKBOARDS denote messages. What was written there? Was it blank?

BLACK EYES indicate misdeeds. Who had the injury? If it was the dreamer, then this symbol is a warning to stop interfering in another's business or life.

BLACKJACKS (weapon) denote lawlessness. This dreamscape facet will indicate an unscrupulous personality.

BLACK LISTS indicate prejudices.

BLACKOUTS (electrical) refer to sporadic perception. This means that an individual **chooses** what he/she wishes to see or understand. This indicates a selective personality.

BLACK WIDOWS (spiders) infer a poisonous individual or situation.

BLIND ALLEY symbolizes a dead end path that has been entered without awareness.

BLIND SPOTS represent karmic reality. This dreamscape fragment indicates those aspects in one's life that are **meant** to be manifested upon one's path. These being those aspects that are vital to experience.

BLOATED indicates excesses. This symbol may connote any of man's aspects.

BLOODLETTING signifies misconceptions.

BLOOD SUCKERS denote a draining personality. This may indicate one who drains another's energy, emotions, wealth, or spirituality.

BLOOD THIRSTY symbolizes an unethical and unscrupulous personality. This may also indicate one who is vengeful.

BLOODY MONEY connotes a traitor or ill-gotten wealth.

BLUE BOOKS represent market value. This does not necessarily indicate true value, but rather that which the general public perceives as value.

BLUE CHIPS indicate good probabilities.

BLUE NOSES represent puritanical perceptions. These will indicate a strait-laced personality.

BLUSHING signifies embarrassments.

BOARDWALKS connote a voluntary separation from spirituality.

BOMB SHELTERS indicate one's fear of the future. This dreamscape facet specifically reveals one's lack of self confidence and faith in God. It clearly reveals one's lack of priority as one places more importance on the physical rather than the spiritual aspects in life.

BOOKCASES signify knowledge. Recall what titles were on the bookcases. Were the bookcases full? Empty? Old? New?

BOOK REVIEWS designate literary quality and personal relevance. This particular dreamscape fragment is extremely important, for it comes from one's Higher Self to reveal specific book titles and if they're important to the dreamer or not.

BOONDOCKS denote a spiritual remoteness.

BOTTLENECKS symbolize complications.

BOUNTY HUNTERS represent misplaced priorities and/or ulterior motives.

BRAIDING signify the voluntary complication of matters, relationships, situations, or thoughts. Whoever is doing the braiding in the dream is the one who is "twisting" things.

BRAIN CORAL denotes spiritual intelligence and/or higher knowledge.

BRAINSTORMING indicates deep thinking and/or analyzation. This may also suggest complex planning being done.

BRAMBLES represent painful problems.

BRASS symbolizes a harsh personality.

BREAKWATER signifies a spiritual barrier. This dreamscape fragment may be a positive symbol if it refers to a "controlled intake" of spiritual concepts and belief systems.

BREASTPLATES signify emotional protection. This symbol refers to that which protects one's heart.

BRIDGES always refer to connections. It's important to recall what the bridges connected and what condition they were in.

BRUISES indicate a relationship, individual, situation, belief system, or mental/emotional condition that will cause a minor setback.

BUDDHA signifies spiritual concepts.

BULBS (flower) denote a spiritual budding that's occuring.

BULBS (light) represent new awareness or forthcoming problematic resolutions. This dreamscape fragment directly refers to the "idea." Is the bulb tiny? If it is, then more thought must be applied.

BULLDOGS represent a bullish friend.

BULLDOZERS denote an overbearing personality or an individual who is manipulative.

BULLET-PROOF VESTS indicate an emotionally devoid personality.

BULLHORNS signify the need to stress one's attitudes, thoughts or beliefs.

BUS BOYS refer to correcting wrongs done. Who is the represented bus boy in the dream? Is it you? If so, then this is a warning for you to take responsibility to clean up your own messes instead of making someone else do it.

BUZZARDS indicate a gloating personality.

BY-PASSES represent a "going around." This may be advised in the dream or it may be presented as something for the dreamer to **avoid.**

BYSTANDERS signify remoteness. Is the dreamer being advised to be "just a bystander" or is he/she advised to NOT be one?

C

CABAL denotes schemers. This dreamscape fragment can be very revealing for the dreamer. If he/she is part of a cabal then the Higher Self is warning the dreamer to **get out.**

CABLE CARS indicate dangerous thoughts.

CABOOSE represents the **end** of something. Surrounding dreamscape aspects will clarify this intended meaning for the dreamer's personal life.

CACHE means high value; a motherlode.

CACTUS indicates protected spiritual concepts.

CALLIGRAPHY denote important messages. Recall what was intricately written out.

CALLING CARDS signify one's true intentions. Recall what the calling card said. What was the occupation? Business? Line of work?

CAMOUFLAGE (clothing) symbolizes an untrusting personality or one with hidden/ulterior intentions.

CANALS inticate spiritual connections.

CANNIBALS denote overbearing personalities or manipulative ones.

CARAVANS refer to an individual's protected path in life. This may mean protection being done by self or others around the dreamer such as friends or spirit advisors.

CARD CATALOGS represent further book studying needed. This dreamscape fragment infers that the dreamer needs expanded knowledge on a certain subject. Check which subject was presented.

CARGO signifies that which we perceive as personally valuable.

CARNIVALS denote unrealistic perceptions of life.

CAROUSELS refer to a fruitless path chosen.

CARPETBAGS symbolize self-interests and self-gain.

CARTOUCHES represent important messages that reveal those in the dreamer's life who are meaningful.

CASHIER'S CHECKS indicate true value that is guaranteed.

CATACOMBS connotate repressed spiritual belief systems.

CATAPULTS represent those aspects in the dreamer's life that will serve as an impetus toward advancement. This advancement may or may not be a positive aspect. Check surrounding dreamscape fragments for clarity of this intent.

CATNIP symbolizes a type of sedation in the dreamer's life. This is definitely a warning symbol, for acute awareness should be a constant perceptive quality in everyone's life.

CAULKING connotates the need to seal something in one's life.

CAUTERIZE denotes the need to heal a wound. This, of course, may refer to an emotional, physical, or spiritual wound.

CAVERNS represent nature's hidden aspects in relation to the extended realities.

CAVIAR signifies spiritual arrogance.

CEDAR refers to spiritual cleansing and/or protective measures.

CEMENT denotes solidification. This refers to an aspect in the dreamer's life that needs to be absolutely resolved.

CENSORS symbolize those who are overly critical.

CENTURIONS represent one who is always on guard.

CESSPOOLS signify the basest aspects.

CHAIR LIFTS symbolize unearned spiritual paths. This means that the easiest and quickest "way" is being sought after. This is a definite warning from one's Higher Self.

CHAISE LOUNGES signify nonchalance.

CHARLATANS denote those individuals in the dreamer's life who are not what they outwardly present. Is the dreamer him/herself the charlatan?

CHAUFFEURS indicate dependency and lack of initiative in respect to one's individual life or spiritual path. If the dreamer is presented as being the chauffeur then this is a warning for the dreamer to stop leading others around and start letting them think for themselves.

CHIMES almost always represent a "calling." This may be a calling of the dreamer's attention to something important. Recall surrounding dreamscape fragments for clarity of intention with this symbol.

CHIPMUNKS denote a spiritual hoarding being done.

CHURN (butter) symbolizes hard work and personal energy applied to one's path.

CISTERNS indicate personal spiritual knowledge. What condition was the cistern in? Was it full of water or empty? What was the water's quality? Clear and pure? Contaminated? Muddy?

CLINGING VINES signify a smothering personality.

CLOUD SEEDING denotes a forcing of spiritual attainment or knowledge. This is always a warning symbol in dreamscapes.

CLOVER indicates spiritual abundance available to the dreamer.

CLUBHOUSES refer to one's tendency toward wanting to belong.

COATTAILS represent associations and one's readiness to join up with others. This is most often a warning symbol.

COBRAS connotate a threatened personality and/or an individual who is frequently dismayed by others.

COCOONS denote spiritual respite before higher enlightenment is achieved.

COFFINS symbolize a comatose state of being, or it may, in fact, be a symbol manifested to forewarn of an impending death.

COMIC BOOKS indicate unrealistic perceptions and outlooks on life.

CONFESSIONALS signify the need for honesty; to get something off one's chest and come clean so that advancement can continue.

CONNOISSEURS represent those who have a higher level of knowledge on a given subject. The surrounding dreamscape facets will clarify this important intent.

CONTESTS denote a competitive personality. This is a definite warning symbol.

CONTRACTS represent agreements. Recall what type of contracts were manifested in the dream. Recall what condition these were in. What color paper were they on?

COSMOS always signifies the higher spiritual forces at work.

COUNTDOWNS mean that time is running out.

CREMATORIUMS connotate the end of a relationship or situation.

CROWBARS signify a "forcing" being done. Remember that, if something is truly meant to be, one never needs to force it. . .it will manifest when the time is right.

CRUISE SHIPS symbolize a perspective that spiritual seeking is a journey of leisure and not taken seriously. This usually is presented in a dream when the dreamer perceives spiritual seeking as a game or a part of the "in thing" to participate in. The dreamer views the seeking as a fun fad.

CRUSADES represent misplaced spiritual concepts. In other words, the use of spirituality for unspiritual ends.

CRYPTOGRAMS connote confusing messages. This dreamscape fragment refers to the dreamer's desire for spiritual knowledge and the attainment of same before he/she is ready.

CRYSTAL BALLS denote an obsession with the future. This is a definitive warning dream symbol that cautions the dreamer to attend to the "moment" and not have their sights set on what their future holds.

CUBBYHOLES indicate a judgemental personality; one who prejudges others.

CUCKOO CLOCKS signify those individuals who are a slave to time rather than letting events unfold naturally. This indicates a personality who is extremely regimented in daily life.

CULVERTS refer to spiritual channelling. This "channeling" is not associated with mediumship, but rather the "directions" and personal "guidance" one manipulates their abilities toward.

CURFEWS represent personal guidelines set.

CUSPS symbolize turning points in one's life.

CUSTODIANS signify the designated or qualified keepers. Surrounding dreamscape fragments will clarify the precise intent of this symbol.

D

DABBLING connotates a lack of seriousness. What was the dreamscape person dabbling in? Occult aspects? Ancient truths?

DAGGERS signify harmful aspects in the dreamer's life. These may be any one of the aspects of man: physical, emotional, mental, or spiritual.

DAGUERREOTYPES symbolize old relationships. These will most frequently have a present-day association for the dreamer's current life.

DANDELIONS represent hidden benefits.

DANDRUFF signify the need to shed misconceptions.

DAYDREAMS denote desires. These are not necessarily negative aspects if they're applied in a positive manner.

DEAD LETTERS refer to unproductive communications or relationships.

DEADLINES indicate time is running out.

DEAD WEIGHTS symbolize extraneous aspects to one's life. This is a very revealing dreamscape fragment from the Higher Self that clearly shows the dreamer what is not important in his or her life.

DEATH MASKS represent danger. This may refer to an individual in the dreamer's life or a situation or belief system that will ultimately prove to be completely unsuccessful or reach a deadend. Occasionally a death mask will also forewarn of a physical death.

DEATH WARRANTS come as a warning from the Higher Self to caution against something in the dreamer's life that will be the "death of him or her." Recall **who was signing** this warrant. If the dreamer was, then it means that the dreamer is doing something that will end his or her physical or spiritual life.

DEBATES signify the need to listen to another's perspective.

DEBRIS connote the unnecessary aspects of one's life.

DECAY symbolizes a decomposing relationship, situation or belief system.

DEFECTIVE (items) mean that there's something not working right in the dreamer's life. This could be his or her thinking, beliefs, actions or relationships.

DEFROST connotates the need to soften and be less rigid.

DELICATESSENS signify karmic connections. These being the "ready-made" situations or relationships that were destined to manifest upon one's path.

DELIVERY ROOMS (birthing) symbolize the right timing for something to manifest in the dreamer's life.

DEMITASSE (cups) signify a very small amount. Surrounding dreamscape facets will clarify this intent.

DEMOLITION represents the absolute destruction of something in the dreamer's life. Who is doing the demolition? What is being demolished?

DEODORANT denotes lies; a cover-up.

DESTROYERS (ships) signify a relationship, situation, or belief system that will destroy the dreamer.

DETERGENT refers to the need to clean up something in the dreamer's life.

DIAGNOSTICIANS connote the need to analyze something. This may refer to the dreamer's relationships, situations, personal motives, or belief systems.

DIAL TONES (phone) denote unfruitful communications.

DICTATORS signify manipulative personalities. This is a clear warning from the Higher Self to reveal those individuals in the dreamer's life who are "dictating" to him or her.

DIETS indicate the urgent need to "shed" something in the dreamer's life. Although this may refer to one's physical weight, it may also intend a relationship, situation, or belief system.

DIKES (dams) signify the misuse of spiritual beliefs as shields to hide behind.

DIME NOVELS connote unproductive thoughts and a wasting of one's intelligence.

DIMMER SWITCHES symbolize the need to "tone down" one's over-rambunctiousness. This is usually associated with a braggart, a manipulator, or a religious fanatic.

DINOSAURS indicate outdated attitudes or beliefs.

DIRECTORIES represent the need to do research. This symbol is a clear indication that the dreamer is letting others provide the information instead of doing it him or herself.

DISC JOCKEYS signify selectiveness. This dreamscape fragment infers that the dreamer is either being too selective in what he or she wishes to hear or that he/she is letting others tell them what to believe.

DISCONNECTED (phone) symbolizes "cut off" communications.

DISCOUNTS indicate alternate paths leading to the same end.

DISCOVERIES connote revelations. Surrounding dreamscape fragments will clarify these for the dreamer.

DISGUISES denote hypocrisy.

DISINFECTANTS represent unhealthy aspects in the dreamer's life. This may refer to relationships, situations, or belief systems.

DISPATCHERS connote the Higher Self. This directly refers to that which one is supposed to accomplish.

DISTORTIONS symbolize poor perspective being given by the dreamer. What was distorted?

DIVORCE represents a failed relationship, but not necessarily that of a marriage. This may be associated with a business, other relationship, or even a belief system.

DOG DAYS denote time periods of inactivity or lack of advancement.

DOLLS signify misplaced relationships.

DOLPHINS connote spiritual friendships and loyalties.

DOODLES indicate subconscious thoughts. Recall what was being drawn. This dreamscape fragment can be extremely revealing.

DOSSIERS symbolize background knowledge of an individual, situation, or belief system.

DOUBLE BOILERS signify increased activity needed. This infers the necessity toward speed, but without burning oneself out.

DOUBLE CROSSES refer to a treacherous personality or a betrayer in the dreamer's midst.

DOUBLE FACED (two-faced) indicates a betrayer.

DRAFTING BOARDS signify the need to plan out something better.

DRAGNETS refer to spiritual gullibility.

DRAIN PIPES symbolize spiritual waste. This dreamscape fragment infers that the dreamer is harboring unnecessary or erroneous spiritual beliefs that need to be disgarded.

DRESS REHEARSALS indicate a misconception of reality. There are no dress rehearsals in life. Life is the real thing.

DRIFTWOOD represents a spiritual drifting being done.

DROUGHTS symbolize spiritual starvation that is self-imposed by the dreamer.

DUMBBELLS denote that which is utilized to strengthen self. This may not be a positive dreamscape facet if the presented strengthener is ultimately a negative or destructive one.

DUMBWAITERS connote self-reliance.

DUNES (sand) indicate one's "shifting" thoughts, beliefs, or ideals. This a definitive warning from the Higher Self.

DUST DEVILS signify mental vacillations.

E

EARMUFFS represent a closed mind; choosing what one wants to hear.

EASTER EGGS signify a "slanted" spiritual belief; a "colored" perception that has been "decorated" and embellished.

ECLIPSES (sun) denote a partial acceptance of spiritual truths.

EGGBEATERS symbolize confusion; "scrambled" perceptions.

EIGHT BALLS indicate a problematic situation or relationship.

ELASTIC connotes a "giving" or workable relationship or situation in the dreamer's life.

ELECTIONS refer to the need for a firm decision on something.

ELECTONIC EYES signify being watched by another. This does not refer to one's spiritual aspects, but rather is directly associated with one's physical life.

ELEVENTH HOUR connotes last minute chance to accomplish something in the dreamer's life. This is a "fair warning" symbol.

ELOPING represents individuality and one's sense of freedom to follow their own path in life.

EMBROIDERY signifies embellishments and elaborations. This is a warning to be forthright and not exaggerate.

ENCORES denote the need to repeat something. Surrounding dreamscape factors will clarify this intent for the dreamer, for this symbol may mean to "keep on the current path" or to "go back and relearn or restudy" something. It may mean that something in the dreamer's life was missed.

ENGRAVE signifies an unalterable truth. It refers to something that cannot be changed.

ESCALATORS denote laziness of mind.

ESTIMATES symbolize that which cannot be pinpointed or predicted in an absolute. This particular dreamscape fragment will mean a "probability" foreseen in the dreamer's future.

EXCAVATIONS signify the need to "dig deeper." This will refer to a current problem, situation, or belief system in the dreamer's life.

EXHAUST (vehicle) means a lack of energy or a run-down condition. This dreamscape facet may also indicate a "finality," in other words, the "last" of something — all avenues exhausted.

EXHIBITIONS symbolize overall perceptions.

EXORCISMS connote "getting completely rid" of something in the dreamer's life.

EXPLOSIONS indicate emotional upheavals.

F

FABLES represent moral or spiritual parables; truths clothed in a storyline.

FACE-LIFTS signify hypocrisy.

FAIRGROUNDS symbolize a "fair ground" to work within.

FALLING STARS denote disappointments.

FALLOUT connotates repercussions forthcoming.

FALSE BOTTOMS refer to misconceptions. This indicates that the dreamer has perceived he or she has gotten to the bottom of something when, in fact, there is much more to be seen or understood.

FAMILIES represent unity.

FANATICS indicate lack of logic and reason.

FANFARE serves to "stress" something in the dreamer's life. Surrounding dreamscape aspects will clarify what this is.

FASHION SHOWS signify public opinion or popular beliefs. This symbol defines what is "in," not necessarily what is right or true.

FAWNS indicate an emotionally sensitive nature.

FEATHER BEDS connote a down-to-earth personality.

FEMME FATALE represents a devious personality; one who gains through insincerity and ruse. This indicates one who misuses their charms.

FEVERS refer to obsessions or fanaticism.

FIDDLES denote insincerity. It infers a sense of just fooling around (fiddling) with something instead of taking it seriously.

FIELD DAYS denote times of great enjoyment.

FIELD TRIPS connote the need for "hands-on" learning experiences.

FILIGREE signifies complexities or entanglements.

FINGER BOWLS represent "washing one's hands" of something. This indicates a clear wish to be separated from an individual or situation.

FISHBOWLS indicate transparencies. This dreamscape fragment reveals to the dreamer that his or her character or deeds are not as hidden as they believe them to be.

FIVE WHEELS denote extra or unnecessary aspects; a "fifth wheel" type of situation or relationship.

FLEECE (lamb's wool) refers to fraudulent activities. This represents a cheater and a swindler.

FLUTES connote personal power. How this power is utilized will be clarified by the dreamscape's surrounding aspects.

FOLKLORE refers to those aspects of truth that have been preserved through the unwritten word.

FOOL'S CAPS signify foolishness. Who is wearing the cap? This is a revealing symbol from the Higher Self, especially if the dreamer is the one wearing it.

FOOTBRIDGES denote connective aspects to one's path in life.

FOOTLOCKERS represent the more important material aspects of one's life. This is a representation of priorities.

FORECLOSURES indicate situations in the dreamer's life that will not be fulfilled. This may also relate to a specific path or desired goal.

FORK LIFTS signify those aspects in the dreamer's life that can be utilized to ease one's burdens.

FORTUNE HUNTERS symbolize materialism and those who seek same.

FOUL LINES indicate misdeeds or intentions.

FOUNTAINS represent spiritual abundance; gifts and talents. Recall what type of flow the fountain had. Did it have a color to it?

FRANKINCENSE refers to a prominent past-life in biblical times.

FREIGHT TRAINS infer that one is carrying excessive aspects along tried and true paths. This is a serious warning to shed that which is not necessary and to strike out on one's own path.

FRUITCAKES symbolize unawareness and illogical thought.

FRUIT FLIES represent destructive spiritual aspects.

FUDGE indicates falsehoods and/or exaggerations.

FUNGUS denotes inactivity. This is a dreamscape fragment that will advise the dreamer that he or she needs to wake up and be more actively pursuing their purpose or life path.

G

GALLERYS (art) signify aspects that are admired or appreciated. It's important to recall what type of art was presented. This will clearly indicate the dreamer's preferences and whether they are correct or not.

GALLOWS indicates a situation that may be "left hanging" by the dreamer. This clearly advises the dreamer to take care of business.

GATECRASHERS symbolize a lack of respect. Generally this dreamscape fragment will infer that an individual does not live within acceptance, but rather tries to force his or her own desired reality.

GAUGES represent levels or amounts. Recall what type of gauges were presented. What were their readings?

GAUNTLETS signify karmic debts and what must be endured or "gone through" in one's life in order for the balance to be attained.

GAUZE denotes a "flimsy coverup" being done.

GAVELS represent a final decision or judgement on something in the dreamer's life.

GEISHAS connote servitude for personal gain. This would clearly indicate an individual who is a hanger-on or a groupie in order to gain acceptance or personal advancement of self.

GELATIN denotes cohesiveness or binding aspects.

GHOSTWRITERS represent the use of another's ideas. This dreamscape fragment infers that an individual is not thinking for oneself.

GIANT SEQUOIAS indicate ancient truths as associated with spiritual talents.

GLADIATORS connote poor reasoning for actions taken.

GLITTER represents those aspects that fascinate one. This may be a severe warning for an individual to stop placing his or her attention on the "fascination" but rather to place it on the **cause.**

GLOBES (earth) refer to earthly matters that need attention.

GLOSSARY denotes a need for correct terminology to be used. This dreamscape facet infers that the individual does not have a good comprehension of certain word or conceptual meanings.

GNATS signify mental irritations. What or who were the gnats flying around?

GODFATHER connotates "using" others for personal gain.

GOLDSMITHS denote misplaced priorities; those who place material possessions above their spirituality or spiritual purpose in life.

GOLEMS signify misuse of spiritual abilities.

GOSSIPMONGERS represent a warning to "hold one's tongue" and stop spreading rumors. It's important to recall who was doing the gossiping. Was it the dreamer?

GOVERNESS signifies care of children and the manner of same.

GRAMOPHONES denote "old tunes." This dreamscape fragment will advise against making old excuses for actions taken. This infers that one is placing blame or using reasons that are not relevant to one's life.

GRANARY symbolizes amount of personal talent or skill. Is the granary full? Empty? Contaminated? What is stored there?

GRAND PIANOS signify great potential of one's personal talent. What was the condition of the grand piano? What was its quality of sound?

GRANITE represents a solid foundation.

GRAPEFRUIT denotes the need to shed excesses. This may refer to body weight or anything in one's life that is foreseen as being unnecessary.

GRAVE ROBBERS refer to those who take advantage of those less intelligent than themselves. This dreamscape fragment comes as a serious warning that clearly advises one to stop preying on the less fortunate for personal gain.

GRAVEYARD SHIFTS denote a warning to bring the "light" into one's life.

GRAVY represents easy access. Whether this is a positive or negative symbol will be clarified by the **color** of the gravy. Is it light or dark?

GREASE PAINT clearly symbolizes hypocrisy; the desire to "put on a false face" before others.

GREEN DRAGONS connote jealousy; an envious nature.

GRIDLOCK symbolizes a "deadlocked" situation, relationship, or life/spiritual path.

GROUPER (fish) indicates one who is a follower. This is definitely a warning to be one's own person and to think for self.

GUARDS signify the need to "guard" and protect. What was presented as being guarded? Who was the guard?

H

HACKLES symbolize personal irritations or defensiveness.

HACKSAWS represent difficult solutions. This dreamscape fragment will advise that there are solutions to a problem, but they may be difficult or complex to carry out.

HAGS denote old grudges.

HAIRBALLS indicate misconceptions (those thoughts, ideas, or conceptions that must be gotten rid of — regurgitated).

HAIR SHIRTS connote self-**reproach**; guilt.

HAIR TRIGGER (gun) signifies an explosive personality, situation or relationship.

HALLOWEEN connotates personal revelations. This dreamscape facet is associated with allowing the dreamer to have clear insights into another's true character. What are the dreamer's friends wearing for costumes? What is the dreamer wearing?

HAMMOCKS indicate laziness.

HAMPERS represent that which is unclean. What was in the hamper? What condition was the dreamscape hamper in? This will indicate whether or not the individual cares to clean up his or her act.

HANGOVERS symbolize repercusions to unawareness and irresponsibility.

HARBORS denote spiritual respite. This refers to those aspects that offer a type of spiritual retreat or resting place for the seeker.

HARD-ROCK MINERS indicate great energy expended to advance along one's life path.

HARVESTS symbolize the fruits of one's goodness.

HAWK-EYED denotes acute awareness.

HAYWIRE represents a state of complete confusion. This is not only in reference to one's mental state, but may also indicate one's relationships or spiritual life.

HEADBANDS indicate confined thoughts. These need to be unbound and allowed to be free to expand and develop.

HEAD-HUNTING denotes vengeance.

HEADLINES represent important messages from one's Higher Self. Recall what the exact headlines were.

HEADRESTS denote intellectual respite. This may be advising to rest the mind or it may be a caution that the rest time is over and the individual now needs to get "thinking" again. The surrounding dreamscape aspects will clarify which is intended.

HEARTHSTONES signify family foundations and condition of same. Recall what the hearthstone's condition were. What color?

HELICOPTERS indicate a mental state that frequently vacillates.

HERCULES denotes mighty strength. The important aspect associated with this dreamscape symbol is "how" this strength is utilized and what level it's at.

HOARDING signifies selfishness.

HONEYMOON connotates a harmonious relationship.

HOT SPRINGS symbolize underlying anger.

HOUSEFLIES represent negativity associated with one's homelife.

HURDLES indicate obstacles that need to be overcome. These may refer to any of man's aspects.

HYDROELECTRIC PLANTS connotate spiritual energy. Is the plant operating to its fullest capacity? Is it shut down? Is there even water?

HYENAS refer to one's lack of seriousness.

HYPNOTIST symbolizes a manipulative personality.

I

IDENTICAL TWIN symbolizes one's alter ego.

ILLUSTRATIONS are visual messages for the dreamer. What was clearly illustrated for the dreamer?

IMMORTAL (state of being) signifies one's misconceptions of the physical self. This dreamscape fragment infers that an individual is egotistical and perceives self to be indestructible.

IMPLANTS (medical) signify the need to "replace" a negative in one's life. This may indicate a physical, mental, or spiritual aspect.

IMPRINTS refer to that which has gone before. Whether these imprints should be followed or not will be clarified by the dreamscapes surrounding aspects.

INCH WORMS represent a slow, but steady progression. The specific "condition" of the inch worm will clarify whether this is a warning to **speed up** or if it's a verification that the slow pace is recommended.

INCOME TAXES connote required payments or dues. This relates directly to karmic debts.

INFECTIONS denote negative aspects in the dreamer's life.

INFESTATIONS (insect) signify destructive forces that have invaded an aspect of one's life. **Insects in the house** refer to homelife. **Insects in a garden** refer to one's skills. **Insects in water** indicate one's spiritual life or belief system. **Insects in the air** refer to one's mental state or the emotions.

INFINITY (symbol or design) represents a never-ending state; immortality of the spirit.

INHERITANCE signifies that which is handed down.

INOCULATIONS represent one's protection against negatives, either physical or spiritual.

INQUESTS denote the need to fully investigate something in the dreamer's life.

INSPECTORS denote those in high authority; frequently one's own Higher Self.

INSTALLMENTS (payments) signify the step-by-step balancing of one's karmic debts.

INTERPRETERS indicate clarifications required. The manifestation of this specific dreamscape fragment indicates that an individual is not understanding something important.

INTERROGATIONS symbolize dispelling misconceptions; getting to the truth of a matter.

INTERSECTIONS (roadways) refer to life choices.

INTERVIEWS connote the need to know the background on something important in the dreamer's life. This dreamscape fragment is manifested to advise the dreamer that more information is required.

INTRODUCTIONS represent the need for new aspects in the dreamer's life. This will relate to those new people or situations or beliefs systems that will advance one's enlightenment or quicken one's spiritual purpose or path.

INVASIONS signify negative intrusions.

INVENTORIES is a warning to "take stock" of one's life or direction.

INVESTIGATORS relate to the need for deeper studies. The dreamer needs to investigate something important in life.

INVISIBLE INK means hypocrisy.

INVITATIONS denote requests. Recall what the invitation was for and what the color and condition of it was. If it was verbal, who offered it and what was the tone.

IODINE symbolizes that which will soothe and heal. This may refer to an individual, a relationship or a situation in the dreamer's life that caused some type of personal wound.

IRON (metal) denotes high energy and strength. Was it rusted? What shape was it in? Was it being shaped?

ITALICS signify something important; an emphasis. What word or phrase was italicized? Was it a specific color?

ITCHING refers directly to a restlessness. This is a clear indication that an individual is not within acceptance in life.

J

JAIL represents a confinement. Frequently this is a symbol that indicates an individual's "self-confinement."

JAWBREAKERS refer to difficulties, particularly conceptual complexities. These, of course, can always be broken down and, this dreamscape fragment would advise the "breaking down" of anything difficult to understand so it's in clear pieces. This symbol comes as a warning from one's Higher Self to "stop trying to ingest too much at once."

JAYWALKING symbolizes the taking of "short-cuts" on one's path.

JAZZ signifies mental confusion.

JEEPS denote one's perseverance.

JEKYLL AND HYDE signify hypocrisy and falsehoods.

JESTERS connote nonchalance and a lackadaisical attitude toward life or one's spiritual purpose or path.

JESUS signifies the precepts of the Law of One.

JUICE denotes aspects that ease something. This may refer to a relationship, situation, or emotional aspect.

JUKE BOXES represent that which one chooses to listen to. This comes as a warning to stop being so closed-minded.

JUMPING JACKS indicate an individual who doesn't think for oneself. This is a clear warning from the Higher Self to begin taking responsibility for one's own life and path.

JUMP-STARTS (vehicle) represent the need to connect with one who will prompt and serve as a renewed impetus. This would not be manifested in a dreamscape if the dreamer were not in a slump or point of inactivity.

JUNCTION BOXES denote mental analysis and reasoning ability. What were the junction boxes condition? Were they live with electrical power? Were they being built? Installed? Dismantled?

K

KELP represents spiritual health. What condition was the kelp in? What color was it?

KEROSENE denotes one's ability to energize others. This refers to an individual who can "start a fire" beneath others. And it may refer to encouragement or excitement.

KETCHUP signifies elaborations; the need to spice things up.

KETTLES connote something brewing. What was in the kettle? What color was it? Who was tending it?

KINDLING symbolizes exacerbations; aspects that make something worse.

KINGDOMS refer to egotism and associated material desires.

KINGPINS represent major players in a relationship or situation. These will signify those in control.

KIOSKS connote the need for more information.

KITTENS signify gentleness and innocence of character. This may also infer an individual who is helpless or at another's mercy. Surrounding dreamscape fragments will clarify this intended meaning.

KLEPTOMANIACS symbolize lack of individuality or resourcefulness. This infers an individual who must always "take from another."

KOSHER represent the proper manner or process.

L

LABORATORY represents work needed to be done, particularly in reference to self-discovery.

LABOR UNIONS symbolize justice in the workplace.

LACE denotes an individual who is extremely particular or fussy. This dreamscape fragment reveals those who are reluctant to get their feet wet in life or "get involved"; an aloof personality.

LAGOONS signify spiritual tranquility.

LANDMARKS come as personal messages for the dreamer. Recall what the landmark was. What state? Did it represent a specific historical site or individual?

LANTERNS connote more light needed. This may refer to an individual's relationships, belief systems, or path.

LARDERS signify personal prepardness. What condition was the dreamscape larder in? Was it full or empty? Were the contents outdated? New?

LASSO refers to those methods of attainment that are unethical.

LAUNCH PADS indicate the need to get something off the ground. Surrounding dreamscape aspects will clarify this intent for the dreamer.

LAXATIVES represent negative aspects that need to be gotten rid of in the dreamer's life.

LEAKS indicate a lack of one's protection.

LEAPING is a warning from one's Higher Self to slow down and stop going so fast — there are important aspects that are being missed.

LEAPFROG (game) means an individual is "getting ahead of oneself" and that they're using others for self-attainment. This is a clear warning from one's Higher Self.

LEFTOVERS indicate the need to utilize one's complete potential.

LEGENDS represent truths.

LEMONS connote bitterness and/or misdeeds.

LETTERHEADS represent messages that point out importance. What does the dreamscape letterhead read? What color was lettering? What style of type?

LEVEL (tool) indicates stability.

LIFE INSURANCE refers to an unhealthy or dangerous situation or condition is present in the dreamer's life.

LIMBO symbolizes a state of inactivity or ineffectiveness; nonaction.

LINT signifies that which is in a stagnant state and "collects dust." This is most frequently a warning type of dreamscape symbol that cautions the dreamer to get actively involved.

LIQUIDATIONS represent a "selling out." This may indicate an individual or a situation.

LITTERBUGS symbolize a disregard for others. This, of course, may also include a disregard for nature (which represents spiritual aspects of one's soul talents).

LIVERS signify fortitude. **Animal livers** represent an unhealthy state of affairs which may refer to any of man's aspects.

LIVE WIRES denote unchanneled energies.

LIZARDS connote a unscrupulous personality.

LLAMAS exemplify those who ease burdens.

LOAN SHARKS signify self-gain through negative means.

LOCKETS symbolize treasured relationships. Recall whose photograph was in the dreamscape locket.

LOCUSTS connote that which will totally destroy spiritual belief systems.

LOFTS refer to high-minded attitudes.

LOGJAMS signify mental/emotional confusion in association with spiritual concepts.

LULLABYS represent those aspects which tend to "lull" one into a sense of false security.

M

MACHETE represents a forcing of one's advancement or enlightenment. This dreamscape fragment is clearly indicating an individual who has no respect or appreciation for the spiritual concepts that are presented along the path.

MACHINE SHOPS denote the creation of examples, models, or molds. What condition are the templates in? What color? Shape? Are they defective in any way?

MACHINISTS signify those who are followed or looked up to.

MACKINAWS exemplify those close to nature and natural laws.

MACRAME (braided rope) symbolizes twisted truths or concepts.

MAELSTROMS represent mental and spiritual confusion.

MAESTRO denotes an individual who is capable of leading groups. Be careful with this one. If the maestro is conducting, what sounds are being created? Harmonious? Chaos? And, do you know this maestro?

MAFIA exemplifies manipulation for self-gain.

MAGGOTS symbolize a self-serving personality who gains from others.

MAGI denote individuals who have attained spiritual knowledge.

MANNEQUINS represent those who are easily manipulated and aren't interested in thinking for themselves. Who was presented as a mannequin? Was it the dreamer?

MARIONETTES, like mannequins, represent a lack of personal responsibility or thought.

MAROONED signifies a personal state of remoteness. Frequently this state if self-created.

MARQUEE denotes an important message for the dreamer. What words were spelled out on the dreamscape marquee? Was it lighted? Were the lights also blinking for attention?

MASSACRES connotate a massive misdeed done or foreseen.

MATHEMATICIANS signify the need to "figure" something out. Clearly, the numbers aren't adding up in the dreamer's life.

MATTRESS indicates manner of rest. The "type" of mattress is most important here. What was its condition? Composition? Color?

MAZES exemplify mental confusion or illness.

MEDIATORS signify the urgent need for help with a personal relationship.

MEDUSA comes as a severe warning to straighten up one's thoughts before they become dangerous.

MELODRAMAS represent gross exaggerations.

MEMENTOS signify those aspects in one's life that should remain important.

MEMOIRS come as a prompting to record one's life events and remember same. This will be presented as a dreamscape fragment if this recording and recalling will bring revelations to the dreamer.

MEMORIALS denote the need to remember something or someone. What was the memorial for? A historical event? A person?

MERGERS signify a blending; a bringing together. This may be a positive aspect (suggestion) or a negative one (warning). The surrounding dreamscape aspects will clarify this for the dreamer.

MERLIN symbolizes the manifestation of one's spiritual talents and the utilization of same for the benefit of others.

MERRY-GO-ROUND represents unproductiveness or fruitless. This may refer to an individual's relationship, situation, path, or spiritual belief system.

MESH signifies the need to interact or merge; to join harmoniously.

MIGRATION (birds) connotes the need to physically relocate.

MINE SWEEPER denotes the presence of a danger in one's life and the need to discover and disarm it.

MISCARRIAGE signifies the shedding of an erroneous spiritual belief.

MISERS represent selfishness; one who hoards.

MITER BOX exemplifies the need to be precise; exactness.

MONOGRAMS represent important initials that will have specific meaning for the dreamer.

MUSIC BOXES signify melancholia.

MYSTIC (person) connotes an over-emphasis on the paranormal aspects of spirituality.

N

NARCOTICS signify an escape from reality associated with a lack of acceptance and responsibility.

NARCS denote those individuals who reveal the faults or misdeeds of others.

NARROW GAUGE (railway) represents a "straight and narrow" path. This is not necessarily a positive dreamscape fragment to manifest, for few true paths follow such a set course as a railway. Each must make his or her own way according to the spirit's promptings.

NATIONAL GUARD (soldiers) denotes massive upheaval present or forthcoming in the dreamer's life.

NAVAL BASES signify spiritual protection is needed.

NECTAR connotes that which is sweetest; attained goals; fruitful conclusions.

NETTLES exemplify "stinging" aspects in life.

NIGHT BLINDNESS symbolizes an individual's ignorance or self-denial of life's negative aspects. This would also indicate a vulnerable personality.

NIGHTHAWKS represent extreme awareness.

NIGHTMARES almost always represent one's inner fears.

NIGHT OWLS signify watchfulness and heightened spiritual protection.

NIGHT SCHOOL denotes the need for immediate learning. What is being taught? Who is doing the teaching?

NIRVANA signifies euphoria. This is not a positive dreamscape fragment, for it infers that the dreamer is living in a fantasy world and not within acceptance of reality. This indicates one who lives in their own world.

NITROGLYCERIN denotes a highly explosive personality, situation, relationship, or belief system.

NOMADS represent an individual who is free to follow their personal path of purpose.

NOSEBLEEDS exemplify an individual who interferes in another's life or business.

NOSEDIVES connotate a "headlong" dive into something. This may be positive or negative depending upon surrounding dreamscape aspects that clarify the intended meaning.

NUCLEUS is a symbol that manifests to caution the dreamer to "get to the core or center" of something. This means that it's being advised that the dreamer understand the "cause."

NUTCRACKERS signify the need for resolutions and/or solutions.

NUTSHELLS denote personality shells that are self-constructed for one's protection. This may infer the use of psychological defense mechanisms. These need to be cracked in order to see with clarity and understand a situation or another individual.

O

OAKS (tree) represent an unyielding personality.

OATHS denote promises that must be kept.

OBELISKS signify an important aspect for the dreamer. Dreamscape shapes such as obelisks refer to spiritual concept truths.

OBESE connotes overindulgence. The dreamer will know what this refers to in his or her life.

OBSIDIAN represents the beauty of the more esoteric spiritual concepts.

OINTMENTS refer to those aspects in the dreamer's life that will serve to soothe over negative or uneasy aspects.

OLIVE BRANCHES signify peace offerings.

OLIVE OIL symbolizes quelling aspects in the dreamer's life.

ONE-WAY (sign) denotes a warning that there's no "turning back."

ONIONS exemplify healing aspects. Onions heal bruises and serve as natural antibiotics for wounds, hence the "healing" aspect of same.

OOZE signifies that which cannot (or will not) be contained. This dreamscape fragment comes as a warning that the dreamer is trying to hide something that will not be hidden.

OPIUM denotes that which dulls one's senses, intelligence, reasoning, or awareness.

ORACLES connotate prophecies.

ORCHARDS represent an individual's skills or talents. What condition was the orchard in. Was it bearing fruit? Was the fruit healthy?

ORCHESTRA denotes harmony within a group.

OSIRIS connotates renewal and rebirth.

OUTPOSTS represent resting points along one's right path. This dreamscape fragment assures the dreamer that, although his or her path may be far from others, there have been others who've gone before and they're not alone.

OVERALLS denote the need for protection.

OVERHAULS exemplify the need for re-evaluations of self.

OVERLOOKS indicate that a wider view is required for proper perception.

OVERSHADOWING refers to a suffocation being done. Who is overshadowing another? Is it the dreamer?

OVERSPENDING signifies the over-extensions of self. This may also indicate an individual who exaggerates or inflates their self-worth.

OVERSTEPPING symbolizes an individual who interferes in another's affairs.

OVERTIME represents the need to work harder at something. Surrounding dreamscape fragments will clarify what this is.

P

PACKAGES denote those material goods one perceives as being important in their life. What are in the packages? What type of packages are they? Boxes? Bags? Gift-wrapped?

PACK TRAINS indicate those aspects that are unnecessary for one's path.

PADDLES (canoe) signify one's ability to pass "gently" through their spiritual destiny. Are paddles being used? How? What condition are they in?

PADDLE WHEELS symbolize aspects which serve as spiritual promptings or an impetus.

PAGODAS connotate spiritual misconceptions associated with the truths as related to the precepts of the Law of One. This dreamscape fragment would clearly represent an individual's tendency to build altars or harbor misdirected or misplaced priorities.

PAILS exemplify the amount of spirituality one utilizes in life. What is the pail made of? Is it full? Empty? What quality is the content?

PAINT signifies a cover-up of some type.

PAMPHLETS indicate information. This dreamscape fragment may be positive or negative depending upon what the dream pamphlet was about. The surrounding aspects such as condition and color will help to clarify the intended meaning for the dreamer.

PANIC BUTTONS clearly represent high anxiety or an extreme state of confusion. Recall surrounding dreamscape aspects.

PANSYS denote an extremely fearful personality. This dreamscape facet refers to those who are holding back their personal development or advancement because of reprisals from others.

PANTHERS symbolize caution. This may be required of the dreamer or it may come as a warning that the dreamer is being overly cautious without reason.

PAPERWEIGHTS exemplify the need to retain important ideals or belief systems.

PAPYRUS indicate a delicate or fragile aspect. Recall who or what was associated with the dreamscape papyrus.

PARABLES denote important lessons needed to learn or relearn.

PARADISE connotates unrealistic ideals, thoughts, or belief systems.

PARAFFIN represents the need to preserve or seal something. The surrounding dreamscape aspects will clarify this intended meaning for the dreamer.

PARAPETS symbolize awareness; a broad perspective.

PARASITES come in dreamscapes to warn of aspects that are draining the dreamer. These may be situations, relationships, business dealings, individuals, or belief systems.

PARASOLS indicate a frivolous spiritual attitude or belief system.

PARKING METERS represent a specified span of time. The surrounding dreamscape fragments will help to clarify this intent. How much time was left on the meter? Was it "expired"?

PARTITIONS denote separations. These may be indicated as needed or warned against. The dreamer will know the intent.

PARTNERS signify close associations or associates.

PARTY LINES (telephone) represent a warning that reveals a lack or loss of privacy unbeknownst to the dreamer.

PASSWORDS denote aspects in one's life that serve as "keys" or "gateways."

PASTE represents a temporary cohesiveness required. This dreamscape fragment would infer the need to quickly make attempts to resolve a current problem or negative situation.

PASTRIES indicate that which is perceived as being "sweet." This would be associated with an individual's personal perspectives and not necessarily be a true indication. Recall what the pastry was and what condition it was in. Was it dripping with honey? Was it loaded with sugar or nuts? Was it stale? Underbaked?

PASTURES signify one's voluntary usefulness in life. Is the dreamer out to pasture? Who is in this dream pasture? What are they doing? What condition is the pasture in? Is it full of flowers or weeds? Is it completely barren?

PATCHWORK (designs) come in dreamscapes to emphasize the importance of variety in one's life. This symbol frequently infers that the dreamer is not expanding his or her scope of perceptions.

PAYCHECKS indicate true value of one's deeds, beliefs, or relationships. What amount was the paycheck for? Was it minimum wage? Was it for overtime put in?

PAYMASTERS signify spiritual law; those who know and understand the value of deeds done.

PAYOLA denotes misdeeds and misplaced priorities. This dreamscape fragment refers to an individual who would do anything for money.

PEA SOUP connotates cloudiness. This may refer to the dreamer's perception of a relationship, individual, situation, or belief system.

PEAT symbolizes aspects that are capable of enriching.

PEAT BOGS denote a "bogged-down" situation.

PEBBLES exemplify diversity.

PECTIN signifies aspects that can solidify. This may refer to a relationship, situation, problem resolution, or personal belief system.

PEDIGREE (certificate) represents a "certification" of some type. Recall the surrounding dreamscape aspects for clarity here. Usually this symbol will not be lost on the dreamer.

PEELER (kitchen utensil) comes as dreamscape fragments as a warning to "peel away" something that is blocking perceptual clarity. Surrounding dreamscape aspects will define this intent.

PENNANTS connotate loyalties. This may be a positive or negative aspect. Check the condition of the dream pennant.

PEPPER MILLS indicate the need for "finer" perceptions or awareness to be utilized.

PERCOLATORS represent a state of "brewing." What is brewing? Who is doing the brewing? Does the aroma have a positive or negative scent?

PERMAFROST indicates a "frigid" personality; one with a cold shell.

PEROXIDE refers to the need to cleanse or heal. This may also refer to a "whitewash" or "bleaching" being done. Surrounding dreamscape aspects will clarify this intended meaning for the dreamer.

PERPETUAL MOTION (device) connotates high energy or something that has been put into motion.

PERSPIRING exemplifies great energy applied.

PERVERSIONS symbolize misdirection or misplaced priorities.

PEYOTE represents sacred aspects.

PHANTOMS signify one's fears; or personal spiritual messages. Surrounding dreamscape aspects will clarify this symbol's intention.

PHARAOHS refer to spiritual domination. Who was the pharaoh?

PHEASANTS indicate spiritual seeking.

PHILOSOPHERS come in dreamscapes to represent higher learning and deeper thought.

PHOSPHORESENCE represents illuminating aspects in the dreamer's life. These dreamscape symbol lights come to point out those aspects that will serve to enlighten the dreamer.

PHOTOCOPIERS connotate repetitiveness. The condition and color or the dream photocopier will clarify whether or not the dreamer actually needs to repeat something or if this is a warning for him or her to "stop" repeating or copying something or someone. This symbol may also infer that the dreamer is "repeating" past mistakes.

PICKPOCKETS indicate lack of resourcefulness; cheating.

PICNICS signify respites needed in life.

PIGGYBACK represents personal irresponsibility. Recall **who** was **riding** piggyback and who was **carrying** another. This can be an extremely revealing dreamscape fragment.

PIGGY BANKS indicate lesser amounts of value. Was the piggy bank full? Was it filled with silver or gold? Dollars?

PIGPENS symbolize disorder.

PILGRIMS represent searching or discoveries required.

PILLOWS indicate an individual's true temperament, state of mind, or level of reasoning. What were the pillows made of? What color were they? Their condition?

PIMPS refer to a "user" personality.

PINCERS represent a "tight" aspect in one's life. This may refer to another individual, relationship, business deal, personal situation, or belief. Who is using the pincers? What is being pinched?

PIRATES connotate unethical personalities who gain by stealing.

PLACEBOS exemplify those aspects which serve as replacements in one's life. These will be those facets that are phoney or false. Frequently these refer to one's mental or psychological excuses for not following their Higher Self guidance.

PLAGUES denotes negative aspects in the dreamer's life that could be emotionally or spiritually fatal.

PLANETARIUMS indicate a need to expand one's perceptions.

PLANKTON refer to foundational facts or "the basics."

PLANTATIONS signify the quality and quantity of talents. Recall who was working on the plantation? What was planted? What was the condition of the growing vegetation?

PLASTIC connotates lack of quality. This dreamscape fragment may refer to an individual or one's own attitudes.

PLAYER PIANOS denote lack of individuality or reason. This symbol infers that an individual depends upon others to be original. This represents an individual who "plays another's tune" instead of following their own.

PLAYGROUNDS connotate a lack of seriousness.

PLEDGES indicate promises. Recall what was promised. This may be a dreamscape warning that cautions the dreamer that a promise has been made and the necessity to hold to them.

PLUGS represent voluntary "holds" or stoppages.

PLUMB LINES denote rightness or straightness. This dreamscape fragment may be revealing the dreamer's path in life, his or her belief system, or relationships.

PLUMS signify something of high quality as perceived by the dreamer. This may not necessarily be in truth though.

PLUNGERS signify the need to "unclog" something. The dreamer will understand this personal intent.

POLAR BEARS exemplify spiritual aloofness.

PORTALS indicate spiritual perceptions. Was the dreamscape portal clouded? All wet? Dry and clear? What was seen through the portal?

PORTRAITS signify true revelations of people. What type of portrait was it? What was represented in the portrait? Was it a beautiful painting? Grotesque? A caricature? A cartoon? A clownish representation?

POSSE refers to assumptions and prejudgements.

POSTAGE STAMPS connotate the value of communications. What was the postage stamps on? A letter to whom?

POSTMARKS indicate a specific date for communication. Recall what date the postmark was stamped. This will have personal meaning for the dreamer.

POSTSCRIPTS symbolize afterthoughts and the need to express same.

POTLATCHES represent unconditional sharing of one's talents and gifts.

POWDER KEGS exemplify "explosive" aspects. This dreamscape fragment may refer to one's own emotions, attitudes, or mental state. This may also indicate a relationship, situation, or belief system.

POWDER PUFFS indicate a fragile nature or sensitive personality.

POW WOWS represent a need to communicate; a get-together required.

PRETZELS connotate a "twisted" perception. Who had the pretzels? Was someone selling them? Who? Was the dreamer eating them?

PRIMA DONNAS indicate egotism.

PRINT-OUTS symbolize the need for "hard copies." This represents "proof" of something.

PRIVATE DETECTIVES refer to the need for each individual to do his or her own thinking and searching.

PRIVATE SCHOOLS symbolize the need for "individualized" thought.
PRIZES signify goals or attainments as personally perceived. These, of course, may not be aligned with right or true goals.
PROBATION OFFICERS indicate those individuals in one's life who serve to guide and advise. Be careful with this one, for someone presented as a probation officer may not be correct for the dreamer. Recall what they wore? How they acted? Colors that were associated with the dream person?
PROFIT SHARING signifies synergistic relationships. This dreamscape fragment refers to those aspects in the dreamer's life that are harmonious and assist in bringing about the balance of one's karma.
PROOFREADING comes as a clear warning to be careful what one accepts as their truth in regard to literature or what one reads.
PROPOSITIONS signify probabilities presented. Not all of these will be a benefit to the dreamer and this is why this dreamscape fragment is so important. What type of proposition was it? Who did it come from? What colors surrounded the proposition? What was the mood of the players?
PROSECUTORS (legal) exemplify higher judgements of the spiritual plane. These will come to give clear revelations for the dreamer regarding his or her actions or path.
PROSPECTORS denote a search. Surrounding dreamscape fragments will clarify whether or not this search is worthwhile. If it's for gold, it's not. If it's for silver, it is. What condition was the prospector in? Was he or she being successful? Was the dream prospector digging in the earth or panning in water?
PROVISOS connotate ulterior motives or special provisions.
PROWLERS signify stealth. Who was the dreamscape prowler? Was it the dreamer?
PROXY represents loss of input. This means the dreamer has lost (or is losing) his or her freedom of individuality.
PUMICE STONES are the need to smoothe something out.
PUNTING (football) refers to the need to take an alternate route.
PURITANS signify narrow-mindedness.

Q

QUARRELING clearly represents disagreements. Recall who was doing the quarreling and what it was about.
QUARTERBACKS indicate those individuals who "call the signals." This may be a positive or negative dreamscape fragment depending upon the individual dreamer's situation. Does the dreamer need to STOP calling another's shots? Does the dreamer need to call his or her own?

QUARTZ signifies spiritual purity. Usually this refers to the truths as they relate to the precepts of the Law of One.

QUESTS symbolize that which is needed to accomplish; a specific personal goal that is required.

QUESTIONNAIRES denote self-examination. This dreamscape fragment will manifest specific questions the dreamer must ultimately face with the honest responses. What questions were asked?

QUETZALCOATL refers to spiritual rebirth.

QUICK BREAD exemplifies one's "quick fixes" or the short cuts to "rising up." This may refer to one's physical life path or to his or her spiritual searching for enlightenment.

QUININE signifies that which heals. This dreamscape fragment may refer to any of man's aspects.

R

RABBIT FOOT represents the belief in luck rather than oneself. This includes those individuals who would like to think that they can create their own reality instead of dealing with their intended chosen one.

RABIES signifies a fatally negative aspect in the dreamer's life.

RACCOONS symbolize an industrious personality.

RACEHORSES represent the competitiveness. This dreamscape fragment most frequently refers to the desire to be better and faster than others; to get ahead of the rest; to win in everything.

RACETRACKS denote the "fast track."

RACKETS (sports) connote where responsibility lies. Is the dreamer whacking the ball back into another's area? Is someone else giving the ball to the dreamer? What is the racket's color and condition?

RADIAL SYMMETRY signifies outward radiation from a single source, usually an individual. This dreamscape fragment refers to the importance of giving; sharing one's abilities.

RAFFLE TICKETS exemplify chances taken when opportunities manifest.

RAFTS symbolize spiritual ingenuity as associated with one's path of developed enlightenment.

RAILINGS (hand) signify those aspects one "leans" on in life. Recall the condition, composition, and color of these.

RAIN CHECKS denote postponements; promises to fulfill at a later date.

RAMBLING indicates a shiftless personality; no clear direction.

RANGE FINDERS signify one's personal priority to follow their path.

RANSOMS symbolize the "price of attainment." This is a clear warning symbol, for there should be no price involved with enlightment.

RASHES (skin) represent emotional irritations or psychological difficulties.

RATCHET (tool) indicates the need for backtracking to attain one's ultimate advancement, success, or purpose.

REAR GUARD exemplifies protection one needs for their past or a warning not to leave self unprotected.

REBATES signify the rewards for deeds done; benefits.

RECESSES denote periods of rest that are being advised for the dreamer. This dreamscape fragment infers that the dreamer is going too far too fast.

RECIPES connote proper steps needed or required aspects for one's path.

RECITALS represent the need for personal life reviews or a reveiw of one's acquired knowledge.

RECLUSE symbolizes a remote and distant personality.

RECRUITERS signify an individual who has a tendency to coerce others into their way of thinking.

RED HERRINGS connote aspects that divert one's centered attention. This dreamscape fragment infers that an individual is being misled or is losing sight of their path or purpose.

RELAY RACES indicate an individual's dependence on others for his or her advancement.

RELICS symbolize misplaced spiritual priorities.

RELIEF MAPS denote the need for an individual to gain a clearer perspective of their geographic location. This may refer to future relocations.

REMNANTS connote unnecessary aspects to one's purpose or path.

REPAIRMEN symbolize the need to remedy or "fix" something in one's life.

REPELLENTS (chemical) represent an individual's use of negativity. This dreamscape fragment would indicate a personality who has a tendency to be "stand-offish".

RESERVOIRS denote the quantity of one's spiritual aspects. Check to recall how much water was in the reservoir. What was its quality. What color?

RESIDUE exemplifies that which is "left behind." This dreamscape facet usually refers to "aftermaths."

RESPIRATORS connote those aspects in that serve as life-saving factors in one's life.

RESUMES represent the need for an honest review of one's accomplishmen and goals.

RETIREMENT indicates finalizations; completion of a life stage.

RETRIEVERS (dog breed) refers to the need to "go back"; something important has been left out of the dreamer's life.

RETROGRADE symbolizes a backward movement. This dreamscape fragment may be advising the dreamer to "review" something or to attend to something in their past. It may also mean for the dreamer to STOP living in the past. Surrounding dreamscape aspects will clarify the intention of this symbol.

REUNIONS signify the importance of past relationships and the need to "keep in touch."

REVISIONS represent a need to reassess one's life, goals or path direction.

REVIVALS denote a warning to revitalize something in one's life.

REVOKING comes as a caution for the dreamer to "take back" or rescind something in their life. This may refer to a deed done, a loyalty, or a personal belief system.

RHYMES connotate an individual's juvenile attitude or personal perspective. This dreamscape fragment usually refers to one who rarely shows developed reasoning or logic.

RIDGEPOLES denote that which serves as one's personal shield or means of protection. This may refer to an individual's physical, emotional, or spiritual protection.

RIGOR MORTIS indicates a dead state; an individual who maintains "stiff" thinking or reasoning.

RINDS exemplify that which harbors fruitful aspects. This dreamscape fragment refers to the "tough" path or exterior that serve as the outlying regions of one's direction or fulfillment.

RINGSIDE (seats) represent an "onlooker"; one who prefers not to participate or become involved.

RINSING symbolizes an individual's need for clarity on something. This infers that misconceptions or confusion is involved.

RIOTS indicate discontent; demonstrative voicing of opinions.

RIPCORDS represent life-saving aspects in an individual's life. This may refer to any of man's aspects.

ROLL CALLS signify names on a list. What purpose was the roll called? Whose names were included. What does the dreamscape list represent to the dreamer? Does the dreamer's name belong on the list? Should it be deleted?

ROLLER COASTERS indicate an individual's unstable path or personality.

ROUND TRIPS symbolize one's nonadvancement; a circling state of affairs.

RUMBLE SEATS denote dissatisfaction with self for not taking control of one's life. This is a severe warning.

RUNWAYS connotate pathways leading to one's purpose.

RUSTIC (atmosphere or decor) exemplifies one's down-to-earth perspective and general reasoning.

S

SABBATICALS indicate periods of additional learning needed. This usually refers to one who considers self to be a teacher or leader.

SABOTEURS represent a two-faced personality.

SACCHARIN/NUTRASWEET symbolizes one's tendency to be content with imitations. This is usually a warning that cautions an individual to be true to oneself and strive for the "real" aspects of reality.

SACHETS denote a coverup being done; a replacement scent or aspect being utilized.

SACKCLOTH connotates self-imposed guilt; unnecessary punishments.

SACRED COWS signify misplaced priorities in life. This may be social or spiritual.

SAFE-DEPOSIT BOXES indicate that which one places priorities in or highly values.

SAFETY BELTS (vehicle) represent those aspects in life an individual chooses to utilize as their protective shields.

SAGUAROS (cactus) indicate protected spiritual aspects of an individual.

SAINTS represent unrealistic spiritual goals.

SALADS indicate diversity. What was the condition of the salad? What type of foods comprised its variety?

SALOONS signify states of unawareness or reason.

SANCTUARY symbolizes respite. This dreamscape fragment may refer to one's emotional, mental, or spiritual aspects.

SANDBAGS represent spiritual withdrawal.

SANDBOX denotes immaturity of thought and reason.

SAND FLEAS connotate an individual's irritations in life. These most often refer to one's juvenile relationships.

SAND TRAPS designate one's problems in life. This dreamscape fragment represents karmic aspects that are intended to test the individual.

SATIN (fabric) signifies one's desire for a smoothe life and path.

SAWDUST represents that which is "left over" or "left behind."

SCABS (wound) denotes healing aspects in one's life.

SCANDALS connotate reprisals of deeds done.

SCAVENGERS exemplify resourcefulness.

SCHEMATICS indicate the necessity of detailed plans.

SCIENCE FICTION symbolizes unrealistic attitudes or belief systems.

SCOOPS (utensils) represent aspects leading to positive opportunities.

SCOUTS indicate the need to do "advance" research or investigations in one's life before proceeding.

SCREWDRIVERS denote pressures in one's life. These may be referring to self-induced pressures or problems. Who is holding the dream screwdriver? Is it being used to *un*screw something? This would mean a **lessening** of pressure.

SCRIPTS (actor's) denote the need to "play by the rules." This dreamscape fragment infers that an individual is not holding to his or her pre-chosen life path or purpose.

SCYTHES connote the need to "cut through" excesses or unnecessary aspects in one's life.

SEAFOOD represents spiritual knowledge. Recall what condition and color this dreamscape seafood was for additional clarification.

SEALING WAX exemplifies "privacy." Who was using the sealing wax? What color was it? Was it impressed with a symbol or initial? Who needs this new privacy?

SEANCE symbolizes misplaced spiritual priorities.

SEASICKNESS connotates an individual's state of spiritual confusion; spiritual "dizziness" or nausea from taking in too much too fast.

SEEDLINGS indicate the birthing of new understandings in the dreamer's life. What were the seedlings? What color? Were they healthy? Were they being watered and cared for or left dry and fallow?

SEISMOGRAPHS connote watchfulness. This dreamscape fragment refers to the need to be aware of "undercurrents" in one's relationships, business or personal situations in life.

SEQUELS denote continuation; not the end of something.

SEXTANTS indicate the need for precise spiritual path planning and watchfulness so one doesn't veer off course.

SHARECROPPERS symbolize sharing for the good of the whole.

SHARKSKIN (fabric) denotes a spiritually unethical personality.

SHARPSHOOTERS signify the need for discernment and accurate judgements.

SHELL GAMES exemplify a swindle or an unethical personality.

SHOCK WAVES come in dreamscapes to warn of future repercussions expected from a deed done.

SHOEHORNS represent the need for an individual to take "larger" steps toward advancement or one's goal instead of always trying to "stuff" self into a confined path.

SHOOTING STARS indicate the loss of an important spiritual belief. This dreamscape fragment means that someone has ignored, forgotten, or allowed to "die out" major spiritual truths.

SHORT CIRCUITS exemplify mental confusion or severe misconceptions.

SHOVELS connote an individual's tendency to overindulge. This dreamscape facet may refer to the **intake** or **output** aspects.

SHOWCASES signify what one values; one's priorities. What was in the dreamscape showcases? Was the showcase glass clear or clouded? Was it colored? Cracked? What color and condition were the items within the showcase?

SHRAPNEL represents those aspects in one's life that leave permanent damage behind.

SHREWS denote personalities who are never satisfied. These refer to those who are always complaining.

SHUTTERS (window) symbolize openness of mind. Are the dreamscape shutters closed tight? Opened wide? Part-way? What color are they? What are they made of? Their condition?

SHUTTLE (vehicle) indicates intermediate paths or directions in one's life.

SIDE SHOWS denote those aspects in one's life that are ridiculous or outrageous in respect to one's serious path or purpose.

SIDEWINDERS (snake) connotate a "shifty" personality. This denotes an individual who is not forthcoming or up-front.

SIGHTSEEING represents cursory knowledge. This dreamscape fragment usually comes as a warning to start doing more indepth research or study.

SILT signifies spiritual aspects that are unnecessary to one's personal advancement or development.

SINKHOLES indicate spiritual pitfalls upon one's path.

SIRENS always symbolize warnings. Surrounding dreamscape aspects will clarify the intended meaning for the individual dreamer.

SKETCHING represents a "mapping out" being done or needed.

SKEWERS symbolize a very dangerous or negative aspect about to appear in one's life. What is on the skewers? Who is holding them?

SKIMMING comes in dreams to represent a warning for the dreamer to stop doing cursory work. This may refer to one's efforts applied to purpose, business, or spiritual seeking.

SKYDIVES indicate psychological negatives. This would refer to an emotionally unstable personality.

SKYLIGHTS represent open-mindedness; a willingness to "let the light in." Recall if the skylight was a specific color. What was its condition?

SKYWRITING is always a message from one's Higher Self. Be sure to recall what was written — exactly. Was the skywriting done in a specific color?

SLEEPING PILLS exemplify one's desire to escape life.

SLOT MACHINES symbolize the chances taken in life. These referring to those not intended as personal probabilities, but rather those that appear to be shortcuts.

SNAKE CHARMERS indicate a manipulative personality. Recall who the snake charmer was. Was it you? Was it a friend? A business associate?

SNAKESKIN (leather) signifies a shiftless personality; a swindler.

SNOWPLOWS denote paths through spiritual difficulties. This refers to complex spiritual concepts that an individual has "plowed" through and managed to understand.

SNOWSHOES denote spiritual respect.

SOUNDING BOARDS signify the need for an individual to share their thoughts or emotions with another.

SOUND STAGES connotate the need to be aware of one's actions and words. What type of set was the sound stage? Who else was interacting on the set? Was it lit up or dark?

SPARK PLUGS indicate those aspects in the dreamer's life that serve as an impetus toward action or advancement.

SPEED TRAPS come in dreamscapes to warn of the pitfalls of going too fast along one's path.

SPILLWAYS (water) represent spiritual excesses or that which is spiritually unnecessary for the individual dreamer.

SPIRAL (shape) connotates aspects in the dreamer's life that are interrelated.

SPOTLIGHTS come as dreamscape fragments to point out and reveal important aspects for the dreamer to give attention to in his or her life.

STAMPEDES represent loss of one's personal control; one who is easily led by others or gives in to emotionalism rather than keeping one's wits and reason about self.

STEAMROLLERS denote negative control. Who is operating the dreamscape steamroller?

STEEL WOOL signifies a harsh or coarse personality; insensitivity.

STENCILS indicate a template which to follow; an example. Whether this template is right for the dreamer or not will be clarified by the dreamscape's surrounding fragments. What color was the stencil? What shape was it in? What was the stencil's precise condition?

STOCKPILES symbolize a tendency for an individual to "hoard." This may be **advised** in the dream or it may be a warning to **stop** keeping things to self and begin to share with others. This will be clarified when attention is given to the stockpile itself. What was stockpiled? What condition was it in? Color?

STORM CELLARS connotate one's personal preparedness. This may be a physical or spiritual aspect. It may even refer to one's emotional/mental state of mind.

STRAINERS exemplify the need to "sift" through something. This usually refers to an individual's knowledge or research. It cautions to stop "taking everying in" indiscriminately.

STRAIT JACKETS indicate a clear need to "straighten out" one's life, thoughts, emotions, or belief systems.

SUNSTROKES denote an inability of self-control.

SWITCHBACKS represent the need to retain past knowledge. This dreamscape fragment infers that the dreamer is not retaining that which has been learned. He or she is not applying the knowledge gained throughout life.

T

TABERNACLES represent sacredness or; that which the dreamer perceives as being sacred. What was In the tabernacle? What color was it? What condition was the dream tabernacle in?

TACHOMETERS indicate speed. This dream interpretation will be clear to the dreamer as surrounding aspects are recalled. Is the dreamer being cautioned to "slow down?" Speed up? Recall the tachometer reading and ALSO the condition and color of the instrument.

TACKLE (fishing) connotes spiritual accessories that are unnecessary for enlightenment or development.

TAFFY symbolizes difficulties in life. This refers to an individual having to "pull" oneself up and persevere.

TAILGATING represents lack of individuality. This is a warning to stop "following another so closely."

TAILSPINS connotate the need to straighten out one's emotions, mental state, or belief system. It means total confusion.

TAIL WINDS denote those aspects in one's life that serve as an impetus or prompting aid toward advancement and development.

TARGETS indicate goals. These may or may not be a positive aspect for the dreamer. Recall surrounding dreamscape fragments for clarity of intent.

TARPAPER signifies one's spiritual protection. What condition was the tarpaper in?

TEDDY BEARS connote the soothing and comforting aspects in one's life.

TERM PAPERS exemplify one's complete knowledge on a given issue or subject. What was the term paper on? Could the dreamer write a good one? Could the dreamer recall all the information needed to write this dream term paper? These responses will clarify if the dreamer needs to learn more on the presented subject or will advise him or her if enough knowledge has been attained.

TEST PILOTS connotate self-confidence.

TEST TUBES indicate personal experiments. Does the dreamer need to experiment more with something? Has enough experimentation already been done? Surrounding dreamscape fragments will clarify this intention for the dreamer.

TEXTBOOKS reveal type of study needed for the dreamer.

THANKSGIVING DAY symbolizes one's thankfulness or gratitude.

THEOLOGIANS represent the need for deeper spiritual study. This infers that the dreamer does not know as much as he or she thinks they do.

THIMBLES indicate a very small amount of something. What was in the thimble? Who was using it? What was it used for?

THISTLES refer to the "thorny" aspects in one's life. Surrounding dreamscape fragments will clarify these for the dreamer.

THREADBARE indicates a "worn out" aspect. This may refer to one's relationship with another, a mental or emotional state, a personal situation or one's belief system.

THUNDER denotes a spiritually "attention-getting" warning. This doesn't come as a dreamscape fragment unless the dreamer needs to give important awareness to a spiritual aspect in life.

TIC-TAC-TOE (game) connotates the need for deeper thought and calculations.

TIME BOMBS designate an explosive aspect presented. This may refer to any of man's aspects.

TIMECLOCKS the need to stop racing the clock in life. Everything as a prescribed time to manifest. Wasting energies on watching the clock is not productive.

TOASTERS indicate a situation, relationship, or belief that will ultimately end up in disagreement with the dreamer.

TOMBSTONES represent a death which may be literal or symbolic. Most often the dreamer will be able to clarify this intent by recalling the surrounding dreamscape fragments associated with the tombstone.

TOOTH FAIRIES symbolize a lack of reality in one's life.

TORPEDOS indicate spiritual warfare. This will be associated with one's personal life relationships.

TRADEMARKS denote revelations. This dreamscape fragment will reveal true attitudes, beliefs, and intentions of others. Recall what symbols and colors the trademark was.

TRADING POSTS exemplify the need for "give and take"; bartering; sharing.

TRAFFIC LIGHTS symbolize the rightness of one's path. Does the light show green...yellow (slow down)? Does it indicate that it's time to take a turn?

TRANSVESTITES signify an individual's identity confusion.

TRAVOIS indicate a journey is required for the individual's path advancement.

TRAWLERS represent spiritual "dragging." This comes as a caution for the dreamer to stop dragging his or her feet and get spiritually active on their purpose or path.

TREATIES denote agreements. Whether this dreamscape fragment is advising the **sealing** or **breaking** of an agreement will be clarified by the surrounding aspects associated with the treaty.

TRENCHES connotate perseverance and personal faith in self.

TRIVETS symbolize the need to separate self from a "burning" or "hot" relationship, situation, or belief system.

TROJAN HORSE exemplifies stealth.

TRUANT OFFICER denotes one's Higher Self.

TUITION represents one's personal sacrifices for the attainment of knowledge.

TUNING FORKS indicate that adjustments are required in order to be back within a harmonious state.

U

UGLY DUCKLING represents misconceptions associated with first impressions.

ULCERS (stomach) indicate stress and the need to alleviate same.

ULTIMATUMS connotate last resort choices in life.

UMBILICAL CORD signify vital connections.

UNABRIDGED (literary work) denotes the need for "complete" information or knowledge.

UNANIMOUS (communication) exemplifies a spiritual message, usually from one's Higher Self or spirit advisor.

UNBRIDLED (horse) indicates an "uncontrolled" state. This dreamscape aspect may refer to one's emotions, mental reasoning, or energies.

UNCHARTED (course) signifies lack of meaningful direction.

UNCLES come as a warning to admit mistakes or errors made.

UNCONVENTIONAL (means) refers to a veering away from the norm or accepted way. This usually comes as advice for the dreamer to "step out of convention" and follow his or her own path or destiny.

UNCOVERED refers to somthing exposed. Does something in the dreamer's life need to be exposed?

UNDERCLASSMEN indicate those who are less knowledgeable in the dreamer's life.

UNDERCOVER denotes secrecy. Surrounding dreamscape aspects will clarify whether or not the dreamer **needs** this secrecy.

UNDEREXPOSED (film) means that an aspect in the dreamer's life needs "more developing."

UNDERGROUND represents the need for an individual to keep certain aspects of his or her life to self. This may also advise the dreamer to "get out in the open." Surrounding dreamscape fragments will clarify the intent.

UNDERHAND signifies unethical practices.

UNDERLINED expresses important emphasis. Recall **what** was underlined for emphasis. This will be what the dreamer needs to give awareness or importance to in his or her life.

UNDERSTUDY connotates being tutored by a mentor. Who was the dream understudy? Who the teacher? What was being studied?

UNDERTAKER symbolizes those who have a tendency to profit or gain from another's grief. Please recall who this dream undertaker was.

UNDER-THE-COUNTER signifies misdealings or unethical practices.

UNDERTONES denote "implications." This may also refer to the dreamer's tendency to make erroneous assumptions. Watch this.

UNDERWORLD exemplifies "hidden" aspects in one's life. This may refer to the dreamer's or those associated with him or her.

UNEMPLOYED connotates an "unproductive" state.

UNFINISHED represents the need to complete something important in the dreamer's life.

UNICYCLES denote resourcefulness and individuality.

UNIFORMS signify specific attention required. What did the uniform represent? A policeman? A judge? Maids or waiters?

UNLOADING symbolizes the need for honesty in one's life.

UNLOCKING cautions the dreamer against "locking self away" from others.

UNMASKING exemplifies one's need to perceive others with clarity.

UNPACKING symbolizes a permanent situation.

UNPLUGGING represents a "disconnection" being done. What was unplugged? Who did the unplugging? Surrounding dreamscape fragments will clarify the intent for the dreamer.

UNRAVELING denotes new understandings and clarifications being done by the dreamer.

UNSCREWING signifies the lessening of pressures in one's life.

UNVEILING connotates discoveries.

UPDATES refers to current information and the ability to keep up with new knowledge.

UPROOTING symbolizes a disconnection of some type. This may refer to an individual's personal relationships, a plan or it may indicate an actual geographical relocation in the offing.

URANIUM denotes a "contaminating" aspect in the dreamer's life.

V

VACANCY SIGN signifies availability. This may refer to the dreamer's personal state of openness.

VACATIONS connotate the need to get away and relax.

VAGABONDS denote one's freedom to follow their own path.

VALENTINES symbolize amorous attitudes and emotions. Recall who the valentines were associated with. What color were they? What were their condition? All valentines are not positive aspects.

VALETS connote servitude. Who was the dream valet? Was it the dreamer? An associate or relative of the dreamer?

VANDALS represent destructive personalities. Were these dreamscape vandals anyone the dreamer knew? Was the dreamer participating in the destructive group force?

VAPORIZERS indicate one's need for spiritual refresher studies.

VELVET signifies a soft and soothing situation, relationship, or state of mind.

VENDETTAS connote family discord associated with revenge.

VERMICULITE symbolizes those aspects in one's life that serve to uplift and nurture.

VERMIN indicate severe negatives in one's life.

VESTIBULES refer to entryways to one's destined path or purpose.

VETERANS exemplify experienced persons. This may or may not be a positive aspect. Just because one has experience doesn't necessarily mean they're an asset.

VETOES usually come as important messages that advise one which choice to make.

VIEW FINDERS signify the necessity of clear perception and insight.

VIGILS denote perseverance.

VIRGA designates spiritual unfulfillment.

VIRUSES represent contaminating negatives in one's life.

VOLUNTEERS signify selfless giving of oneself. This may or may not be a positive aspect. What did one volunteer for? What did the volunteers represent to the dreamer?

VORTEX represents an opening; an unconventional way to something.

VOWS signify promises.

VOYEURS symbolize personal inadequacy and self-image. This dreamscape fragment may have nothing at all to do with sexual aspects, but come to reveal personalities who are incompetent and dependent upon others.

W

WAGERS represent one's degree of self-confidence. How much was the wager for? What was it for?

WAGON TRAINS denote a lack of personal direction or inability to gain confidence in one's sense of purpose.

WAIFS connote the less fortunate one's in life; those who are the innocent victims of circumstances.

WAITING ROOMS symbolize expectations. Recall what type of waiting room was presented? Was it a delivery room? Then the dreamer is waiting for a new birth, a "rebirth." If the surrounding dreamscape fragments give a negative feeling then the intent of the waiting room is a caution for the dreamer to *stop* waiting around and get to work.

WAIVERS signify an individual's voluntary refusal of something. This will represent something the dreamer has decided to decline.

WALLOWING denotes self-pity.

WALL STREET exemplifies economic aspects that are not solid.

WARTS symbolize a negative aspect that is irritating the dreamer.

WASTEBASKETS signify that which is discarded. What was in the dream wastebasket? Did it really belong there?

WATER BOYS indicate a helpful personality; one who has the capacity to refresh others.

WATERLOGGED denotes spiritual drowning. This comes to warn the dreamer that he or she has tried to progress too far too fast and has not absorbed (comprehended) that which was studied.

WATERPROOF represents a personality who is devoid of spirituality; one who voluntarily chooses to separate self from same.

WATER WHEELS signify spirituality as being the driving force.

WEANING connotes a growing away from something.

WEATHERPROOF represents the effectiveness of one's protection. This may refer to emotional, physical, or spiritual.

WEBS exemplify complexities that an individual weaves in life. This may indicate emotional, mental, or spiritual complications.

WELFARE indicates situations that require the assistance of others.

WHEELCHAIRS denote the inability to stand on one's own feet. This may not be a negative aspect if it's a literal message of forewarning.

WHISPERING symbolizes secrets. This may be a dreamscape fragment that **advises** secrecy or one that cautions against it. Surrounding dreamscape aspects will clarify the intended meaning for the dreamer.

WHITTLING signifies a calculated path advancement; one that is taken a little at a time.

WICKS denote that which generates illumination.

WIDOW'S WALK (small high balcony) indicates watchfulness in life; awareness.

WILDWOODS exemplify individuality of self and one's path.

WINDBAGS connote lack of meaningful communications; lack of useful knowledge. This represents an individual who continually talks but never really says anything meaningful.

WIND TUNNELS symbolize mental confusion; aberrations.

WOLVES signify self-interest and the wanton seeking of gratifications.

WRECKAGES represent destructive ends. Recall what was wrecked. Was it associated with a vehicle? A relationship?

WRENCHES indicate a forcing of something. This is a clear cautionary dreamscape fragment that warns against forcing one's way, ideals, or paths.

Y

YARN represents falsehoods or that which may lead to complications.

YEARBOOKS symbolize the need to review one's recent past activities or relationships.

YODELING indicates a braggart personality. Who was doing the yodeling?

YOGIS signify a misplaced spiritual attitude; one placing priority on showmanship or self-interest.

YOLKS (egg) denote an aspect that serves as the main factor or importance of something in the dreamer's life.

YO-YOS connote an unstable emotional life or one's lack of decision-making capabilities. This dreamscape fragment will infer that an individual has a frequent tendency to vacillate.

YUCCA represents those aspects surrounding an individual that have the natural capacity to "cleanse." This may refer to one's emotions, mental attitudes, or belief systems that are in a negative state.

Z

ZEPHYRS (soft breezes) represent new thoughts or ideas that serve to renew one's stale perspectives.

ZOOM LENS (camera) symbolize the need for a closer look at something in the dreamer's life. Was the zoom lens focused on something in particular? What was the camera being used for? Was it facing the person using it? This would clearly indicate the person's need for self-examination.

THE PHOENIX FILES

The information provided in the following Phoenix Files has been provided for your personal information This information serves as reference material which you make your own responsibility in personal decision-making. I cannot tell anyone where to live nor where to relocate to, this is a personal free will choice each of us must make individually. The following information will assist in that choice. Study it. Meditate upon it. Listen to the guiding voice of your own spirit. Take up the personal responsibility to follow your own path. Nobody can tell you where to live, therefore The Phoenix Files have been opened to provide you with a valuable decision-making aid.

Phoenix File I
US Nuclear Plants

Note: This listing of nuclear plants represent those that are in various stages of being On Order, Under Contract, Under Construction, or fully On-Line.

ALABAMA (7)

Utility: Alabama Power Company
Plant Name: JOSEPH M. FARLEY #1
Type: Pressurized Water Reactor
Manufacturer: Westinghouse
County: Houston
City: Dothan

Utility: Alabama Power Company
Plant Name: JOSEPH M. FARLEY #2
Type: Pressurized Water Reactor
Manufacturer: Westinghouse
County: Houston
City: Dothan

Utility: Tennessee Valley Authority
Plant Name: BROWNS FERRY #1
Type: Boiling Water Reactor
Manufacturer: General Electric
County: Morgan
City: Decatur City

Utility: Tennessee Valley Authority
Plant Name: BROWNS FERRY #2
Type: Boiling Water Reactor
Manufacturer: General Electric
County: Morgan
City: Decatur City

Utility: Tennessee Valley Authority
Plant Name: BROWNS FERRY #3
Type: Boiling Water Reactor
Manufacturer: General Electric
County: Morgan
City: Decatur City

Utility: Tennessee Valley Authority
Plant Name: BELLEFONTE #1
Type: Pressurized Water Reactor
Manufacturer: Babcock & Wilcox
County: Jackson
City: Scottsboro City

Utility: Tennessee Valley Authority
Plant Name: BELLEFONTE #2
Type: Pressurized Water Reactor
Manufacturer: Babcock & Wilcox
County: Jackson
City: Scottsboro City

ALASKA (0)

ARIZONA (3)

Utility: Arizona Public Service Company
Plant Name: PALO VERDE #1
Type: Pressurized Water Reactor
Manufacturer: Combustion Engineering
County: Maricopa
City: Wintersburg

Utility: Arizona Public Service Company
Plant Name: PALO VERDE #2
Type: Pressurized Water Reactor
Manufacturer: Combustion Engineering
County: Maricopa
City: Wintersburg

Utility: Arizona Public Service Company
Plant Name: PALO VERDE #3
Type: Pressurized Water Reactor
Manufacturer: Combustion Engineering
County: Maricopa
City: Wintersburg

ARKANSAS (2)

Utility: Arkansas Power & Light

Company
Plant Name:
ARKANSAS NUCLEAR ONE #1
Type: Pressurized Water Reactor
Manufacturer: Babcock & Wilcox
County: Pope
City: Russellville

Utility: Arkansas Power & Light
Company
Plant Name:
ARKANSAS NUCLEAR ONE #2
Type: Pressurized Water Reactor
Manufacturer: Combustion Engineering
County: Pope
City: Russellville

CALIFORNIA (7)

Utility: Pacific Gas and Electric Co.
Plant Name: HUMBOLDT BAY
Type: Boiling Water Reactor
Manufacturer: General Electric
County: Humboldt
Locale: Humboldt Bay

Utility: Pacific Gas and Electric Co.
Plant Name: DIABLO CANYON #1
Type: Pressurized Water Reactor
Manufacturer: Westinghouse
County: San Luis Obispo
City: Avila Beach

Utility: Pacific Gas and Electric Co.
Plant Name: DIABLO CANYON #2
Type: Pressurized Water Reactor
Manufacturer: Westinghouse
County: San Luis Obispo
City: Avila Beach

Utility: Sacramento Municipal Utility
District
Plant Name: RANCHO SECO #1
Type: Pressurized Water Reactor
Manufacturer: Babcock & Wilcox
County: Sacramento
Locale: Clay Station

Utility: Southern California Edison
Company
Plant Name: SAN ONOFRE #1
Type: Pressurized Water Reactor
Manufacturer: Westinghouse
County: Orange

City: San Clemente

Utility: Southern California Edison
Company
Plant Name: SAN ONOFRE #2
Type: Pressurized Water Reactor
Manufacturer: Combustion Engineering
County: Orange
City: San Clemente

Utility: Southern California Edison
Company
Plant Name: SAN ONOFRE #3
Type: Pressurized Water Reactor
Manufacturer: Combustion Engineering
County: Orange
City: San Clemente

COLORADO (1) (Permanently closed)

Utility: Public Service Company
of Colorado
Plant Name: FORT ST. VRAIN
Type: High Temperature Gas-Cooled
Graphite Reactor
Manufacturer: General Atomic
County: Weld
City: Platteville

CONNECTICUT (4)

Utility: Connecticut Yankee Atomic
Power Company
Plant Name: HADDAM NECK
Type: Pressurized Water Reactor
Manufacturer: Westinghouse
County: Middlesex
City: Haddam Neck

Utility: Northeast Utilities
Plant Name: MILLSTONE #1
Type: Boiling Water Reactor
Manufacturer: General Electric
County: New London
City: Waterford

Utility: Northeast Utilities
Plant Name: MILLSTONE #2
Type: Pressurized Water Reactor
Manufacturer: Combustion Engineering
County: New London
City: Waterford

Utility: Northwest Utilities
Plant Name: MILLSTONE #3
Type: Pressurized Water Reactor
Manufacturer: Westinghouse
County: New London
City: Waterford

DELAWARE (0)

DISTRICT OF COLUMBIA (0)

FLORIDA (5)

Utility: Florida Power Corporation
Plant Name: CRYSTAL RIVER #3
Type: Pressurized Water Reactor
Manufacturer: Babcock & Wilcox
County: Citrus
City: Red Level

Utility: Florida Power & Light Company
Plant Name: TURKEY POINT #3
Type: Pressurized Water Reactor
Manufacturer: Westinghouse
County: Dade
Locale: Turkey Point

Utility: Florida Power & Light Company
Plant Name: TURKEY POINT #4
Type: Pressurized Water Reactor
Manufacturer: Westinghouse
County: Dade
Locale: Turkey Point

Utility: Florida Power & Light Company
Plant Name: ST. LUCIE #1
Type: Pressurized Water Reactor
Manufacturer: Combustion Engineering
County: St. Lucie
Locale: St. Lucie

Utility: Florida Power & Light Company
Plant Name: ST. LUCIE #2
Type: Pressurized Water Reactor
Manufacturer: Combustion Engineering
County: St. Lucie
Locale: St. Lucie

GEORGIA (4)

Utility: Georgia Power Company
Plant Name: EDWIN I. HATCH #1
Type: Boiling Water Reactor
Manufacturer: General Electric
County: Appling
City: Baxley

Utility: Georgia Power Company
Plant name: EDWIN I. HATCH #2
Type: Boiling Water Reactor
Manufacturer: General Electric
County: Appling
City: Baxley

Utility: Georgia Power Company
Plant Name: ALVIN W. VOGTLE #1
Type: Pressurized Water Reactor
Manufacturer: Westinghouse
County: Burke
City: Waynesboro

Utility: Georgia Power Company
Plant Name: ALVIN W. VOGTLE #2
Type: Pressurized Water Reactor
Manufacturer: Westinghouse
County: Burke
City: Waynesboro

HAWAII (0)

IDAHO (0)

ILLINOIS (16)

Utility: Commonwealth Edison Company
Plant Name: DRESDEN #1
Type: Boiling Water Reactor
Manufacturer: General Electric
County: Grundy
City: Morris

Utility: Commonwealth Edison Company
Plant Name: DRESDEN #2
Type: Boiling Water Reactor
Manufacturer: General Electric
County: Grundy
City: Morris

Utility: Commonwealth Edison Company
Plant Name: DRESDEN #3
Type: Boiling Water Reactor
Manufacturer: General Electric
County: Grundy
City: Morris

Utility: Commonwealth Edison
Company
Plant Name: ZION #1
Type: Pressurized Water Reactor
Manufacturer: Westinghouse
County: Lake
City: Zion

Utility: Commonwealth Edison
Company
Plant Name: ZION #2
Type: Pressurized Water Reactor
Manufacturer: Westinghouse
County: Lake
City: Zion

Utility: Commonwealth Edison
Company
Plant Name: QUAD CITIES #1
Type: Boiling Water Reactor
Manufacturer: General Electric
County: Whiteside
City: Cordova

Utility: Commonwealth Edison
Company
Plant Name: QUAD CITIES #2
Type: Boiling Water Reactor
Manufacturer: General Electric
County: Whiteside
City: Cordova

Utility: Commonwealth Edison
Company
Plant Name: LA SALLE #1
Type: Boiling Water Reactor
Manufacturer: General Electric
County: LaSalle
City: Seneca

Utility: Commonwealth Edison
Company
Plant Name: LA SALLE #2
Type: Boiling Water Reactor
Manufacturer: General Electric
County: LaSalle
City: Seneca

Utility: Commonwealth Edison
Company
Plant Name: BRAIDWOOD #1
Type: Pressurized Water Reactor
Manufacturer: Westinghouse
County: Will

City: Braidwood

Utility: Commonwealth Edison
Company
Plant Name: BRAIDWOOD #2
Type: Pressurized Water Reactor
Manufacturer: Westinghouse
County: Will
City: Braidwood

Utility: Commonwealth Edison
Company
Plant Name: BYRON #1
Type: Pressurized Water Reactor
Manufacturer: Westinghouse
County: Ogle
City: Byron

Utility: Commonwealth Edison
Company
Plant Name: BYRON #2
Type: Pressurized Water Reactor
Manufacturer: Westinghouse
County: Ogle
City: Byron

Utility: Commonwealth Edison Company
Plant Name: CARROLL COUNTY #1
Type: Pressurized Water Reactor
Manufacturer: Westinghouse
County: Carroll
City: Savanna

Utility: Commonwealth Edison
Company
Plant Name: CARROLL COUNTY #2
Type: Pressurized Water Reactor
Manufacturer: Westinghouse
County: Carroll
City: Savanna

Utility: Illinois Power Company
Plant Name: CLINTON #1
Type: Boiling Water Reactor
Manufacturer: General Electric
County: De Witt
City: Clinton

INDIANA (I)

Utility: Public Service Company of
Indiana
Plant Name: MARBLE HILL

Type: Pressurized Water Reactor
Manufacturer: Westinghouse
County: Wabash
City: Wabash

IOWA (2)

Utility: Iowa Electric Light and Power Co.
Plant Name: DUANE ARNOLD
Type: Boiling Water Reactor
Manufacturer: General Electric
County: Linn
City: Palo

Utility: Iowa Power & Light Company
Plant Name: VANDALIA
Type: Pressurized Water Reactor
Manufacturer: Babcock & Wilcox
County: Jasper
City: Vandalia

KANSAS (1)

Utility: Kansas Gas and Electric Co.
Plant Name: WOLF CREEK
Type: Pressurized Water Reactor
Manufacturer: Westinghouse
County: Coffey
City: Burlington

KENTUCKY (0)

LOUISIANA (3)

Utility: Gulf States Utilities Co.
Plant Name: RIVER BEND #1
Type: Boiling Water Reactor
Manufacturer: General Electric
County: Pointe Coupee
City: St. Francisville

Utility: Gulf States Utilities Co.
Plant Name: RIVER BEND #2
Type: Boiling Water Reactor
manufacturer:
General Electric County:
Pointe Coupee City: St. Francisville

Utility: Louisiana Power & Light Company
Plant Name: WATERFORD #3
Type: Pressurized Water Reactor
Manufacturer: Combustion Engineering

County: St. John the Baptist
City: Taft

MAINE (1)

Utility: Maine Yankee Atomic Power Company
Plant Name: MAINE YANKEE
Type: Pressurized Water Reactor
Manufacturer: Combustion Engineering
County: Lincoln
City: Wiscasset

MARYLAND (2)

Utility: Baltimore Gas and Electric Co.
Plant Name: CALVERT CLIFFS #1
Type: Pressurized Water Reactor
Manufacturer: Combustion Engineering
County: Calvert
City: Lusby

Utility: Baltimore Gas and Electric Co.
Plant Name: CALVERT CLIFFS #2
Type: Pressurized Water Reactor
Manufacturer: Combustion Engineering
County: Calvert
City: Lusby

MASSACHUSETTS (2)

Utility: Boston Edison Company
Plant Name: PILGRIM #1
Type: Boiling Water Reactor
Manufacturer: General Electric
County: Plymouth
City: Plymouth

Utility: Yankee Atomic Electric Company
Plant Name: YANKEE ROWE
Type: Pressurized Water Reactor
Manufacturer: Westinghouse
County: Franklin
City: Rowe

MICHIGAN (7)

Utility: Consumers Power Company
Plant Name: BIG ROCK POINT
Type: Boiling Water Reactor
Manufacturer: General Electric
County: Charlevoix
City: Charlevoix

Utility: Consumers Power Company
Plant Name: PALISADES
Type: Pressurized Water Reactor
Manufacturer: Combustion Engineering
County: Van Buren
City: South Haven

Utility: Detroit Edison Company
Plant Name: ENRICO FERMI #2
Type: Boiling Water Reactor
Manufacturer: General Electric
County: Monroe
City: Lagoona Beach

Utility: Indiana & Michigan Electric Co.
Plant Name: DONALD C. COOK #1
Type: Pressurized Water Reactor
Manufacturer: Westinghouse
County: Berrien
City: Bridgman

Utility: Indiana & Michigan Electric Co.
Plant Name: DONALD C. COOK #2
Type: Pressurized Water Reactor
Manufacturer: Westinghouse
County: Berrien
City: Bridgman

And 2 in Midland with Reactor
Construction Permits

MINNESOTA (3)

Utility: Northern States Power Company
Plant Name: MONTICELLO
Type: Boiling Water Reactor
Manufacturer: General Electric
County: Wright
City: Monticello

Utility: Northern States Power Company
Plant Name: PRAIRIE ISLAND #1
Type: Pressurized Water Reactor
Manufacturer: Westinghouse
County: Goodhue
City: Red Wing

Utility: Northern States Power Company
Plant Name: PRAIRIE ISLAND #2
Type: Pressurized Water Reactor
Manufacturer: Westinghouse
County: Goodhue
City: Red Wing

MISSISSIPPI (2)

Utility: Mississippi Power & Light Co.
Plant Name: GRAND GULF #1
Type: Boiling Water Reactor
Manufacturer: General Electric
County: Claiborne
City: Port Gibson

Utility: Mississippi Power & Light Co.
Plant Name: GRAND GULF #2
Type: Boiling Water Reactor
Manufacturer: General Electric
County: Claiborne
City: Port Gibson

MISSOURI (1)

Utility: Union Electric Company
Plant Name: CALLAWAY #1
Type: Pressurized Water Reactor
Manufacturer: Westinghouse
County: Callaway
Locale: Within Callaway County

MONTANA (0)

NEBRASKA (2)

Utility: Nebraska Public Power District
Plant Name: COOPER
Type: Boiling Water Reactor
Manufacturer: General Electric
County: Nemaha
City: Brownville

Utility: Omaha Public Power District
Plant Name: FORT CALHOUN #1
Type: Pressurized Water Reactor
Manufacturer: Combustion Engineering
County: Washington
City: Fort Calhoun

NEVADA (0)

NEW HAMPSHIRE (2)
Utility: Public Service Company of New
Hampshire
Plant Name: SEABROOK #1
Type: Pressurized Water Reactor
Manufacturer: Westinghouse
County: Rockingham
City: Seabrook

Utility: Public Service Company of New Hampshire
Plant Name: SEABROOK #2
Type: Pressurized Water Reactor
Manufacturer: Westinghouse
County: Rockingham
City: Seabrook

NEW JERSEY (4)

Utility: Jersey Central Power & Light Co.
Plant Name: OYSTER CREEK
Type: Boiling Water Reactor
Manufacturer: General Electric
County: Lacey
City: Oyster Creek

Utility: Public Service Electric and Gas Co.
Plant Name: SALEM #1
Type: Pressurized Water Reactor
Manufacturer: Westinghouse
County: Lower Alloways Township
City: Salem

Utility: Public Service Electric and Gas Co.
Plant Name: SALEM #2
Type: Pressurized Water Reactor
Manufacturer: Westinghouse
County: Lower Alloways Township
City: Salem

Utility: Public Service Electric and Gas Co.
Plant Name: HOPE CREEK #1
Type: Boiling Water Reactor
Manufacturer: General Electric
County: Lower Alloways Township
City: Alloway

NEW MEXICO (0)

NEW YORK (7)

Utility: Consolidated Edison Co. of New York, Inc.
Plant Name: INDIAN POINT #2
Type: Pressurized Water Reactor
Manufacturer: Westinghouse
County: Rockland
City: Buchanan

Utility: Power Authority of the State of New York
Plant Name: INDIAN POINT #3
Type: Pressurized Water Reactor
Manufacturer: Westinghouse
County: Rockland
City: Buchanan

Utility: Power Authority of the State of New York
Plant Name: JAMES A. FITZPATRICK
Type: Boiling Water Reactor
Manufacturer: General Electric
County: Oswego
City: Scriba

Utility: Long Island Lighting Company
Plant Name: SHOREHAM
Type: Boiling Water Reactor
Manufacturer: General Electric
County: Suffolk
City: Brookhaven

Utility: Niagara Mohawk Power Corporation
Plant Name: NINE MILE POINT #1
Type: Boiling Water Reactor
Manufacturer: General Electric
County: Oswego
City: Oswego

Utility: Niagara Mohawk Power Corporation
Plant Name: NINE MILE POINT #2
Type: Boiling Water Reactor
Manufacturer: General Electric
County: Oswego
City: Oswego

Utility: Rochester Gas and Electric Corporation
Plant Name: ROBERT E. GINNA
Type: Pressurized Water Reactor
Manufacturer: Westinghouse
County: Monroe
City: Rochester

NORTH CAROLINA (8)

Utility: Carolina Power & Light Company
Plant Name: BRUNSWICK #1
Type: Boiling Water Reactor

Manufacturer: General Electric
County: Brunswick
City: Southport

Utility: Carolina Power & Light
Company
Plant Name: BRUNSWICK #2
Type: Boiling Water Reactor
Manufacturer: General Electric
County: Brunswick
City: Southport

Utility: Carolina Power & Light
Company
Plant Name: SHEARON HARRIS #1
Type: Pressurized Water Reactor
Manufacturer: Westinghouse
County: Wake
City: New Hill

Utility: Duke Power Company
Plant Name: WILLIAM MC GUIRE #1
Type: Pressurized Water Reactor
Manufacturer: Westinghouse
County: Lincoln
Locale: Cowans Ford Dam

Utility: Duke Power Company
Plant Name: WILLIAM MC GUIRE #2
Type: Pressurized Water Reactor
Manufacturer: Westinghouse
County: Lincoln
Locale: Cowans Ford Dam

Utility: Duke Power Company
Plant Name: THOMAS L. PERKINS #1
Type: Pressurized Water Reactor
Manufacturer: Combustion Engineering
County: Davie
Locale: Davie County

Utility: Duke Power Company
Plant Name: THOMAS L. PERKINS #2
Type: Pressurized Water Reactor
Manufacturer: Combustion Engineering
County: Davie
Locale: Davie County

Utility: Duke Power Company
Plant Name: THOMAS L. PERKINS #3
Type: Pressurized Water Reactor
Manufacturer: Combustion Engineering
County: Davie
Locale: Davie County

NORTH DAKOTA (0)

OHIO (3)

Utility: Central Area Power
Coordination Group
Plant Name: PERRY #1
Type: Boiling Water Reactor
Manufacturer: General Electric
County: Lake
City: North Perry

Utility: Central Area Power
Coordination Group
Plant Name: PERRY #2
Type: Boiling Water Reactor
Manufacturer: General Electric
County: Lake
City: North Perry

Utility: Central Area Power
Coordination Group
Plant Name: DAVIS-BEESE #1
Type: Pressurized Water Reactor
Manufacturer: Babcock & Wilcox
County: Ottawa
City: Oak Harbor

OKLAHOMA (0)

OREGON (1)

Utility: Portland General Electric
Company
Plant Name: TROJAN
Type: Pressurized Water Reactor
Manufacturer: Westinghouse
County: Columbia
City: Rainier

PENNSYLVANIA (10)

Utility: Central Area Power
Coordination Group
Plant Name: BEAVER VALLEY #1
Type: Pressurized Water Reactor
Manufacturer: Westinghouse
County: Beaver
City: Shippingport

Utility: Central Area Power
Coordination Group
Plant Name: BEAVER VALLEY #2

Type: Pressurized Water Reactor
Manufacturer: Westinghouse
County: Beaver
City: Shippingport

Utility: Metropolitan Edison Company
Plant Name: THREE MILE ISLAND #1
Type: Pressurized Water Reactor
Manufacturer: Babcock & Wilcox
County: Londonderry Township
Locale: Three Mile Island

Utility: Metropolitan Edison Company
Plant Name: THREE MILE ISLAND #2
Type: Pressurized Water Reactor
Manufacturer: Babcock & Wilcox
County: Londonderry Township
Locale: Three Mile Island

Utility: Pennsylvania Power & Light Co.
Plant Name: SUSQUEHANNA #1
Type: Boiling Water Reactor
Manufacturer: General Electric
County: Columbia
City: Berwick

Utility: Pennsylvania Power & Light Co.
Plant Name: SUSQUEHANNA #2
Type: Boiling Water Reactor
Manufacturer: General Electric
County: Columbia
City: Berwick

Utility: Philadelphia Electric Company
Plant Name: PEACH BOTTOM #2
Type: Boiling Water Reactor
Manufacturer: General Electric
County: Lancaster
Locale: Peach Bottom Township

Utility: Philadelphia Electric Company
Plant Name: PEACH BOTTOM #3
Type: Boiling Water Reactor
Manufacturer: General Electric
County: Lancaster
Locale: Peach Bottom Township

Utility: Philadelphia Electric Company
Plant Name: LIMERICK #1
Type: Boiling Water Reactor
Manufacturer: General Electric
County: Montgomery
Locale: Limerick Township

Utility: Philadelphia Electric Company
Plant Name: LIMERICK #2
Type: Boiling Water Reactor
Manufacturer: General Electric
County: Montgomery
Locale: Limerick Township

RHODE ISLAND (0)

SOUTH CAROLINA (7)

Utility: Carolina Power & Light Co.
Plant Name: H. B. ROBINSON #2
Type: Pressurized Water Reactor
Manufacturer: Westinghouse
County: Darlington
City: Hartsville

Utility: Duke Power Company
Plant Name: OCONEE #1
Type: Pressurized Water Reactor
Manufacturer: Babcock & Wilcox
County: Oconee
Locale: Lake Keowee

Utility: Duke Power Company
Plant Name: OCONEE #2
Type: Pressurized Water Reactor
Manufacturer: Babcock & Wilcox
County: Oconee
Locale: Lake Keowee

Utility: Duke Power Company
Plant Name: OCONEE #3
Type: Pressurized Water Reactor
Manufacturer: Babcock & Wilcox
County: Oconee
Locale: Lake Keowee

Utility: Duke Power Company
Plant Name: CATAWBA #1
Type: Pressurized Water Reactor
Manufacturer: Westinghouse
County: York
Locale: Catawba Dam

Utility: Duke Power Company
Plant Name: CATAWBA #2
Type: Pressurized Water Reactor
Manufacturer: Westinghouse
County: York
Locale: Catawba Dam

Utility: South Carolina Electric & Gas Co.
Plant Name: VIRGIL C. SUMMER #1
Type: Pressurized Water Reactor
Manufacturer: Westinghouse
County: Union
Locale: Parr Reservoir

SOUTH DAKOTA (0)

TENNESSEE (4)

Utility: Tennessee Valley Authority
Plant Name: SEQUOYAH #1
Type: Pressurized Water Reactor
Manufacturer: Westinghouse
County: Hamilton
City: Daisy

Utility: Tennessee Valley Authority
Plant Name: SEQUOYAH #2
Type: Pressurized Water Reactor
Manufacturer: Westinghouse
County: Hamilton
City: Daisy

Utility: Tennessee Valley Authority
Plant Name: WATTS BAR #1
Type: Pressurized Water Reactor
Manufacturer: Westinghouse
County: Rhea
City: Spring City

Utility: Tennessee Valley Authority
Plant Name: WATTS BAR #2
Type: Pressurized Water Reactor
Manufacturer: Westinghouse
County: Rhea
City: Spring City

TEXAS (4)

Utility: Houston Lighting & Power Co.
Plant Name:
SOUTH TEXAS PROJECT #1
Type: Pressurized Water Reactor
Manufacturer: Westinghouse
County: Matagorda
Locale: Matagorda County

Utility: Houston Lighting & Power Co.
Plant Name:
SOUTH TEXAS PROJECT #2
Type: Pressurized Water Reactor

Manufacturer: Westinghouse
County: Matagorda
Locale: Matagorda County

Utility: Texas Utilities Generating Co.
Plant Name: COMANCHE PEAK #1
Type: Pressurized Water Reactor
Manufacturer: Westinghouse
County: Somervell
Locale: Somervell County

Utility: Texas Utilities Generating Co.
Plant Name: COMANCHE PEAK #2
Type: Pressurized Water Reactor
Manufacturer: Westinghouse
County: Somervell
Locale: Somervell County

UTAH (0)

VERMONT (1)

Utility: Vermont Yankee Nuclear Power Corp.
Plant Name: VERMONT YANKEE
Type: Boiling Water Reactor
Manufacturer: General Electric
County: Windham
City: Vernon

VIRGINIA (4)
Utility: Virginia Electric and Power Co.
Plant Name: SURRY #1
Type: Pressurized Water Reactor
Manufacturer: Westinghouse
County: Surry
City: Gravel Neck

Utility: Virginia Electric and Power Co.
Plant Name: SURRY #2
Type: Pressurized Water Reactor
Manufacturer: Westinghouse
County: Surry
City: Gravel Neck

Utility: Virginia Electric and Power Co.
Plant Name: NORTH ANNA #1
Type: Pressurized Water Reactor
Manufacturer: Westinghouse
County: Louisa
City: Mineral

Utility: Virginia Electric and Power Co.
Plant Name: NORTH ANNA #2

Type: Pressurized Water Reactor
Manufacturer: Westinghouse
County: Louisa
City: Mineral

WASHINGTON (4)

Utility: Department of Energy
Plant Name: HANFORD
Type: Graphite Reactor
Manufacturer: Department of Energy
County: Franklin
City: Richland

Utility: Washington Public Power
Supply System
Plant Name: WPPSS #1
Type: Pressurized Water Reactor
Manufacturer: Babcock & Wilcox
County: Franklin
City: Richland

Utility: Washington Public Power
Supply System
Plant Name: WPPSS #2
Type: Boiling Water Reactor
Manufacturer: General Electric
County: Franklin
City: Richland

Utility: Washington Public Power
Supply System
Plant Name: WPPSS #3
Type: Pressurized Water Reactor
Manufacturer: Combustion Engineering
County: Grays Harbor
City: Satsop

WEST VIRGINIA (0)

WISCONSIN (4)

Utility: Dairyland Power Co-op
Plant Name: LA CROSSE
Type: Boiling Water Reactor
Manufacturer: Allis Chalmers
County: Vernon
City: Genoa

Utility: Wisconsin Electric Power
Company
Plant Name: POINT BEACH #1
Type: Pressurized Water Reactor
Manufacturer: Westinghouse

County: Manitowoc
City: Two Creeks

Utility: Wisconsin Electric Power
Company
Plant Name: POINT BEACH #2
Type: Pressurized Water Reactor
Manufacturer: Westinghouse
County: Manitowoc
City: Two Creeks

Utility: Wisconsin Public Service Corp.
Plant Name: KEWAUNEE
Type: Pressurized Water Reactor
Manufacturer: Westinghouse
County: Kewaunee
Locale: Carlton Township

WYOMING (0)

Source: Public Utility Guide

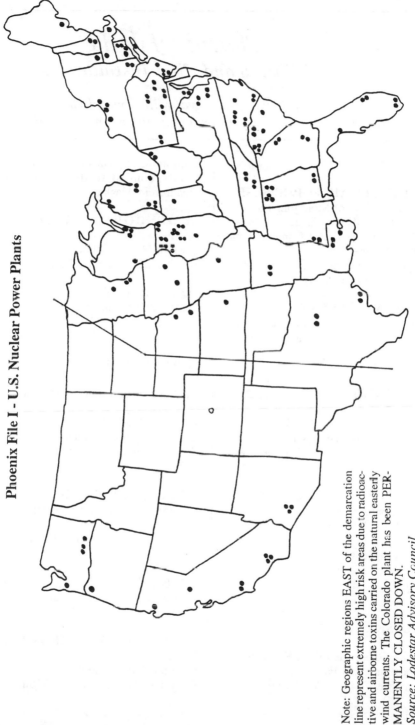

Phoenix File I - U.S. Nuclear Power Plants

Note: Geographic regions EAST of the demarcation line represent extremely high risk areas due to radioactive and airborne toxins carried on the natural easterly wind currents. The Colorado plant has been PERMANENTLY CLOSED DOWN.
Source: Lodestar Advisory Council

Phoenix File II
Military and Civil Installations

Note: The following listing of Military and Civil Installations represent the major facilities and is not meant to be all-inclusive.

ALABAMA

MAXWELL AIR FORCE BASE
Location: NW of Montgomery
Facilities: (Military Education)
Air War College, Air Command and Staff College,
Squadron Officer School, Air Force Senior NCO Academy

FORT McCLELLAN
Location: 3 miles N of Anniston
Facilities: Military Police School

FORT RUCKER
Location: 8 miles W of Ozark
Facilities: US Army Aviation School

REDSTONE ARSENAL
Location: Near Huntsville
Facilities: US Army Missile Command

ANNISTON ARMY DEPOT
Location: Anniston
Facilities: Weapons Depot

HAYES INTERNATIONAL
Location: Birmingham
Facilities: MX C3 System development

ALASKA

EIELSON AIR FORCE BASE
Location: Near Fairbanks
Facilities: 343rd Composite Wing -
trains and equips tactical air support
* only combat-ready air control squadron in Alaska

ELMENDORF AIR FORCE BASE
Location: N of Anchorage
Facilities: 21st Tactical Fighter Wing

FORT GREELY
Location: 105 miles SE of Fairbanks
Facilities: Northern Warfare Training Center & Cold Regions Test Center

FORT RICHARDSON
Location: Near Anchorage
Facilities: 172nd Infantry Brigade

FORT WAINWRIGHT
Location: E of Fairbanks
Facilities: Fourth Battalion, Ninth Infantry

ADAK NAVAL STATION
Location: Adak Island in center of the Aleutian chain
Facilities: Naval Security Group Activity

ARIZONA
(ICBMs Scattered Underground Across State)

DAVIS-MONTHAN AIR FORCE BASE
Location: SE of Tucson
Facilities: Headquarters for 836th Air

Division and the 355th Tactical Training Wing, 5th Fighter Interceptor Squadron, F-106 on alert with nuclear missiles

LUKE AIR FORCE BASE
Location: 20 miles W of Phoenix
Facilities: Headquarters for 405th Tactical Training Wing - trains special pilots in sophisticated fighter planes

WILLIAMS AIR FORCE BASE
Location: SE of Phoenix
Facilities: Largest underground pilot training base

FORT HUACHUCA
Location: Outside of Sierra Vista
Facilities: US Army Intelligence Center, US Army Communications Command, US Army Intelligence School

YUMA PROVING GROUND
Location: 23 miles N of San Luis
Facilities: Tests weapons and aircraft armament systems and military equipment for desert warfare

YUMA MARINE CORPS AIR STATION
Location: Yuma
Facilities: Air Combat maneuvering Range/Instrumentation System 1.5 million acres of bombing ranges: air-to-air combat fighter training in the most sophisticated planes

FLAGSTAFF WEAPONS ARSENAL
Location: Between Flagstaff and Williams
Facilities: Weapons Depot

UNIDYNAMICS PHOENIX, INC
Location: Phoenix

Facilities: Arm/disarm devices

GOODYEAR AEROSPACE COMPANY
Location: Litchfield Park
Facilities: MX Transportation and Handling Equipment

ARKANSAS
(ICBMs Scattered Underground Across State)

BLYTHEVILLE AIR FORCE BASE
Location: NW of Blytheville
Facilities: Stragic Air Command's 42nd Air Division and 97th Bombardment Wing, 150 nuclear bombs, 60 attack missiles

FORT CHAFFEE
Location: Fort Smith
Facilities: Infantry Training

LITTLE ROCK AIR FORCE BASE
Location: Near Jacksonville
Facilities: Headquarters for the 314th Tactical Airlift Wing, the 308th Strategic Missile Wing of SAC, Nuclear Airlift Support, base for weapons transmission

PINE BLUFF ARSENAL
Location: Pine Bluff
Facilities: Nuclear Weapons Depot

CALIFORNIA
(ICBMs Scattered Underground Across State)

BEALE AIR FORCE BASE
Location: W of Lake Tahoe and Reno
Facilities: Headquarters for 14th Air Division and other units

CASTLE AIR FORCE BASE
Location: N of Fresno
Facilities: 43rd Bombardment Wing and 84th Fighter Interceptor Squadron
*Los Alamos nuclear weapons sister plant

EDWARDS AIR FORCE BASE
Location: E of Rosamond, 100 miles NE of L A
Facilities: Test Wing, USAF Test Pilot School, USAF Rocket Propulsion Lab, US Army Aviation Engineering Flight Activity
*Test center is responsible for the management of the 1.7 million acres of the Utah Test and Training Range

GEORGE AIR FORCE BASE
Location: 37 miles N of San Bernadino
Facilities: 35th and 37th Fighter Wings which utilize Phantom Fighters

LOS ANGELES AIR FORCE STATION
Location: El Segundo S of L A
Facilities: US Key Installation in the Space Program
*   Restricted Areas

MARCH AIR FORCE BASE
Location: E of Riverside
Facilities: 22nd Bombardment Wing (Heavy) SAC

MATHER AIR FORCE BASE
Location: SE of Sacramento
Facilities: Department of Defense Navigational Training, 323rd Air Base Group

McCLELLAN AIR FORCE BASE
Location: NE section of Sacramento
Facilities: Air Logistics Center

NORTON AIR FORCE BASE
Location: San Bernadino
Facilities: 63rd Military Airlift Wing and 3 Squadrons of C-141 Starlifters

TRAVIS AIR FORCE BASE
Location: 50 miles NE of San Francisco
Facilities: Pacific Airfield

VANDENBERG AIR FORCE BASE
Location: Vandenberg Village, Mission Hills and Lompoc
Facilities: First Strategic Aerospace Division
Rocketry where ICBMs are tested out over the Pacific

FORT ORD
Location: Monterey Penninsula
Facilities: 7th Infantry Division (Bayonet Division)

PRESIDIO OF MONTEREY
Location: Subpost of Fort Ord
Facilities: Defense Language Institute

BARSTOW MARINE CORPS LOGISTICS BASE
Location: E of Barstow in the Mojave Desert
Facilities: Marine Equipment Center for West of Mississippi

CAMP PENDLETON
Location: SE of San Clemente
Facilities: First Marine Amphibious Force, First Marine Division, Marine Aircraft Group (MAG) - 39

EL TORO MARINE CORPS AIR STATION

Location: N of Camp Pendelton, S of Santa Ana

Facilities: Third Marine Aircraft Wing

SAN DIEGO MARINE CORPS RECRUIT DEPOT

Location: San Diego

Facilities: Basic Training Post

TWENTY-NINE PALMS MARINE CORPS AIR GROUND COMBAT CENTER

Location: Twentynine Palms

Facilities: 7th Marine Amphibious Brigade, Marine Corps Communication-Electronics School

*Depot for combined arms designed to fight a Soviet-type threat

ALAMEDA NAVAL AIR STATION

Location: San Francisco Bay Penninsula Facilities: Naval Rework Facilities, Port of *USS Enterprise* and *Coral Sea*

US NAVAL WEAPONS STATION

Location: Los Angeles

Facilities: Weapons Depot

CHINA LAKE NAVAL WEAPONS CENTER

Location: N of Barstow

Facilities: Naval Ordinance Test Station for Missiles

* Restricted land and airspace

CONCORD NAVAL WEAPONS STATION

Location: Diablo Valley in San Francisco Bay Area

Facilities: Transshipment point for ammunition and other hazardous cargo, Home Port and Logistic Support Facility for Pacific Fleet auxiliary ammunition ships

CORONADO NAVAL AMPHIBIOUS BASE

Location: San Diego Bay

Facilities: Headquarters for: Commander Naval Surface Force, US Pacific Fleet, Naval Beach Group One, Naval Special Warfare Group One (including SEAL Team One and Underwater Demolition Teams Eleven and Twelve, Tactical Air Group One and others)

EL CENTRO NAVAL AIR FACILITY

Location: W of El Centro, N of Mexicali, Mexico

Facilities: Support Group for the Operational Fleet units of bombing and gunnery practice Has a simulated carrier deck and landing area

* Permanent Unit of Attack Squadron 174

LEMOORE NAVAL AIR STATION

Location: SW of Fresno

Facilities: Heart of training readiness for carrier-based aircraft Very important role in National Defense Headquarters for Commander, Light Attack Wing, US Pacific Fleet, 15 Attack Squadrons, 3 Carrier Wings

MARE ISLAND NAVAL SUPPORT ACTIVITY

Location: N extension of San Francisco Bay

Facilities: Headquarters for Mare Island Naval Shipyard, Naval Support Activity, Combat Systems Technical

Schools
Command, Engineering Duty Officer
School and others

MIRAMAR NAVAL AIR STATION
Location: N of San Diego
Facilities: Master Jet Station and
Home for all Pacific Fleet Fighters
Early Warning and Reconnaissance
Squadrons

MOFFETT FIELD NAVAL AIR STATION
Location: S of San Francisco
Facilities: Headquarters for Antisubmarine Warfare, 2 Patrol Wings and 8 Patrol Squadrons

NAVAL CONSTRUCTION BATTALION CENTER
Location: Port Hueneme area of Ventura County
Facilities: Headquarters to 7 US Naval Mobile Construction Battalions

NAVAL POSTGRADUATE SCHOOL
Location: Monterey
Facilities: Preflight School

NORTH ISLAND NAVAL AIR STATION
Location: San Diego Bay
Facilities: One of the most important Naval Air and Sea Bases Headquarters for 57 Commands and Activities

PACIFIC MISSILE TEST CENTER
Location: Point Mugu
Facilities: Tests missile systems and related devices
*Restricted Areas

POINT SUR NAVAL FACILITY
Location: N of Big Sur
Facilities: Oceanographic Research Station

SAN DIEGO NAVAL STATION
Location: San Diego
Facilities: Home of Navy's major West Coast Logistics Base for Surface Operations, Fleet Training Center

SKAGGS ISLAND NAVAL SECURITY GROUP ACTIVITY
Location: Shore of San Pablo Bay (N half of San Francisco Bay)
Facilities: Naval Radio Transmissions Unit

TREASURE ISLAND NAVAL STATION
Location: San Francisco Bay
Facilities: Headquarters for 47 Commands

YUBA CITY ARSENAL
Location: Yuba City
Facilities: Weapons Depot

SACRAMENTO ARMY DEPOT
Location: Sacramento
Facilities: Weapons Arsenal

FORT BRAGG
Location: N of Mendocino
Facilities: Military Reservation

CAMP ROBERTS MILITARY RESERVATION
Location: N of Paso Robles
Facilities: General Military Camp

HUNTER LIGGETT MILITARY RESERVATION
Location: NW of Paso Robles

Facilities: General Military Camp

LOS ALAMITOS NAVAL AIR STATION
Location: Los Alamitos
Facilities: Naval Air Station

FORT IRWIN
Location: N of Barstow
Facilities: Nuclear Weapons Depot

ROCKWELL PLANT
Location: Garden Grove
Facilities: Production of B-1 Bomber Parts

LAWRENCE-LIVERMORE PLANT
Location: Livermore
Facilities: Nuclear Weapons Design

ROCKWELL INTERNATIONAL
Location: Anaheim
Facilities: Flight computer and integration of components into guidance and control systems

ROCKWELL INTERNATIONAL
Location: Canoga Park
Facilities: Stabe IV propulsion systems development

SCIENCE APPLICATIONS, INC
Location: La Jolin
Facilities: MX Software

TRW
Location: Redondo Beach
Facilities: Missile Engineering, Targeting and Analysis Studies, Development of the Advanced ICBM Weapon System

WESTINGHOUSE
Location: Sunnyvale
Facilities: MX Canister production

ENDEVCO
Location: San Juan Capistrano
Facilities: Dynamic data measurement system of 750 channels for MX testing

LOCKHEED MISSILE SYSTEMS COMPANY
Location: Sunnyvale
Facilities: MX Ordnance Initiation sets/flight termination ordnance sets.

COLORADO

LOWRY AIR FORCE BASE
Location: Aurora
Facilities: Technical Training Center, Air Training Command

PETERSON AIR FORCE BASE
Location: Colorado Springs
Facilities: Headquarters for 46th Aerospace Defense Wing (SAC)

FORT CARSON
Location: Colorado Springs
Facilities: 4th Infantry Division

NORAD
Location: Cheyenne Mountain near Colorado Springs
Facilities: Early Warning Command Center for North America

ROCKY MOUNTAIN ARSENAL (PERMANENTLY CLOSED)
Location: 10 miles E of Denver
Facilities: During 40's manufactured deadly GB nerve gas, incendiary bombs, mustard gas, napalm, white phosphorous bombs, and Lewisite. Shell Oil then used facility to manufacture lethal insecticides (aldrin and dieldrin) Presently both Shell and the Army are working on the

massive clean-up of soil and water table pollutants

ROCKY FLATS
Location: Commerce City
Facilities: Rockwell International manufacturs plutonium bomb triggers

MARTIN MARIETTA
Location: Denver
Facilities: MX Weapon System assembly

YARDNEY ELECTRONIC COMPANY
Location: Denver
Facilities: Missile Guidance Components

CONNECTICUT

NEW LONDON NAVAL SUBMARINE BASE
Location: New London/Groton
Facilities: Largest base of its kind in the free world. Home for vessels and crews of Submarine Group Two (one of the most powerful Naval Flotillas in the world) 20 nuclear attack submarines

BLOOMFIELD WEAPONS PLANT
Location: Bloomfield
Facilities: Rockwell International manufactures B-1 Bomber Parts

ENERGY RESEARCH CORPORATION
Location: Danbury
Facilities: MX Ground Power Advanced Development Program

OLIN
Location: Stamford

Facilities: Produces propellants for Titan Missiles and MX

NORDEN SYSTEMS
Location: Norwalk
Facilities: MX C3 System Development

DELAWARE

DOVER AIR FORCE BASE
Location: 3 miles S of Dover
Facilities: Headquarters for 436th Military Airlift Wing and the largest cargo aircraft in the world (36 C-5 Galaxys)

DISTRICT OF COLUMBIA

BOLLING AIR FORCE BASE
Location: S of Washington
Facilities: 1100th Air Base Wing

WASHINGTON NAVY YARD
Location: Washington
Facilities: Headquarters for Naval District Washington

FORT MCNAIR
Location: N of Bolling Air Force Base
Facilities: General Activity

NAVAL RESEARCH LABORATORY
Location: S of Bolling Air Force Base
Facilities: Sea Warfare Research

THE WHITE HOUSE

FLORIDA

EGLIN AIR FORCE BASE
Location: Choctawatchee Bay
Facilities: Home of Armament Division of the Air Force Systems Command

HOMESTEAD AIR FORCE BASE
Location: S Florida between Miami and Everglades
Facilities: 31st Tactical Training Wing which trains F-4 combat aircrews

HURLBURT FIELD
Location: Hurlburt
Facilties: First Special Operations Wing, 442nd Tactical Control Group, Air Ground Operations School, 823rd Civil Engineering Squadron, Special Operations Control Team and Air Commandos

MACDILL AIR FORCE BASE
Location: Tip of Tampa Bay
Facilities: Home for 56th Tactical Fighter Wing and Headquarters for US Central Command (Readiness Group) Also responsible for Avon Park Air Range (largest bombing range of its kind in the Tactical Air Command)

PATRICK AIR FORCE BASE
Location: Cape Canaveral
Facilities: Headquarters of the USAF Eastern Space and Missile Center

TYNDALL AIR FORCE BASE
Location: Panama City
Facilities: Fighter Weapons Training, Weapons Center

CECIL FIELD NAVAL AIR STATION
Location: Jacksonville
Facilities: Headquarters for Light Attack Wing One, Air Antisubmarine Wing One, Carrier Wings Three and Seventeen and others

JACKSONVILLE NAVAL AIR STATION
Location: Jacksonville
Facilities: Home for Commander, Sea Based Antisubmarine Warfare Wings Atlantic, Patrol Wing Eleven, Helicopter Antisubmarine Wing and others

KEY WEST NAVAL AIR STATION
Location: Key West
Facilities: Home for Tactical Electronic Warfare and Attack Fighter Squadrons

MAYPORT NAVAL STATION
Location: Mayport, N of St Augustine
Facilities: Home for Cruiser-Destroyer Group Command, Naval Surface Force Atlantic Readiness Support Group and Fleet Training Center

ORLANDO NAVAL TRAINING CENTER
Location: Orlando
Facilities: Recruit Training, Service School, Administration and Personnel Support Activity

PENSACOLA NAVAL AIR STATION
Location: Pensacola
Facilities: Home of Chief Naval Education and Training Commands and Blue Angels

WHITING FIELD NAVAL AIR STATION
Location: Milton
Facilities: Home to Training Air Wing Five and Helicopter Squadrons

ROCKWELL INTERNATIONAL PLANT
Location: Melbourne
Facilities: Constructs B-1 Bomber parts

GENERAL ELECTRIC PLANT
Location: Pinellas Park
Facilities: Manufactures neutron generators for weapons

HONEYWELL, INC
Location: St Petersburg
Facilities: Specific force integrating receiver production

SYSTEMS ENGINEERING LABORATORIES
Location: Ft Lauderdale
Facilities: Computers for MX Program

AMERICAN BERYLLIUM
Location: Sarasota
Facilities: Main memory sub-system for MX electronics and computer assembly

GEORGIA

WARNER ROBINS AIR FORCE BASE
Location: S of Macon
Facilities: Air Logistics Center for Air Force missiles

FORT BENNING
Location: S of Columbus
Facilities: Training and Maneuvers for Infantrymen & Ranger Courses

FORT GORDON
Location: SW of Augusta
Facilities: Signal Corps Training Center

FORT MC PHERSON
Location: SW of Atlanta
Facilities: Headquarters for US Army Forces Command, controls Fort Gillem which is home for the US Army Readiness and Mobilization Region IV and Army Special Operations Forces

FORT STEWART
Location: SE of Savannah
Facilities: Largest installation E of Mississippi River
24th Infantry Division and Nuclear Units

ALBANY MARINE CORPS LOGISTICS BASE
Location: SW Georgia
Facilities: Supply Depot and Formal Schooling

ATLANTA NAVAL AIR STATION
Location: Marietta
Facilities: Active Duty and Reserve Personnel

LAWSON ARMY AIR FIELD
Location: SW of Columbus
Facilities: General Facility

ROBINS AIR FORCE BASE
Location: S of Macon
Facilities: General Facility

DOBBINS AIR FORCE BASE
Location: S of Marietta
Facilities: General Facility, 116th Tactical Fighter Wing (Nuclear Capability)

NAVAL SUBMARINE SUPPORT BASE
Location: King's Bay
Facilities: Home for Poseidon nuclear submarines and Nuclear weapons

depot for over 408 warheads

HAWAII

HICKMAN AIR FORCE BASE
Location: W of Honolulu
Facilities: 15th Air Base Wing

WHEELER AIR FORCE BASE
Location: 20 miles N of Honolulu
Facilities: Helicopter Training

SCHOFIELD BARRACKS
Location: Island of Oahu
Facilities: 25th Infantry Division
Headquarters

KANEOHE BAY MARINE CORPS AIR STATION
Location: N side of Oahu
Facilities: Home of Marine Aircraft
Group 24 and First Marine Brigade

BARBERS POINT NAVAL AIR STATION
Location: W of Pearl Harbor
Facilities: Headquarters for Commander, Patrol Wing Two, Fleet
Composite Squadron One, 5 patrol
squadrons, helicopter antisubmarine
squadron and Army's 147th Aviation
Company

PEARL HARBOR
Location: Oahu
Facilities: Navy's most important
Pacific base — 50 Commands here
Naval Station, Submarine Base,
Shipyard, Supply Center, Fleet Training Group

DILLINGHAM AIR FORCE BASE
Location: NW side of Oahu
Facilities: Readiness Base

FORT RUGER MILITARY RESERVATION
Location: S Honolulu
Facilities: General Facility

IDAHO

MOUNTAIN HOME AIR FORCE BASE
Location: SE of Boise
Facilities: Home for the 366th Tactical Fighter Wing

IDAHO NATIONAL ENGINEERING LABORATORY
Location: W of Idaho Falls
Facilities: US Atomic Energy Commission Reservation (571,000 acres
where spent fuel from Naval reactors
are processed and also serves as a
military nuclear waste storage site)

ILLINOIS

CHANUTE AIR FORCE BASE
Location: Chanute
Facilities: 3330th Technical Training
Wing, trains in weapons systems support, electronics, weather and aircraft
maintenance

SCOTT AIR FORCE BASE
Location: NE of Belleville
Facilities: Home for Military Airlift
Command, 375th Aeromedical Airlift
Wing and over 40 other Commands
FORT SHERIDAN
Location: Shore of Lake Michigan N
of Chicago
Facilities: Headquarters of the US
Army Recruiting Command and US
Army Readiness and Mobilization
Region V

ROCK ISLAND ARSENAL
Location: Vicinity of Davenport

Facilities: Home of the US Army Armament Material Readiness Command responsible for production of carriages, recoil mechanisms, for towed and self-propelled artillery and for tank armament
* Major Germ Warfare Installation

GREAT LAKES NAVAL TRAINING CENTER
Location: On Lake Michigan near Zion
Facilities: Service School Command

US ARMY ARSENAL
Location: S of Joliet
Facilities: Nuclear Weapons Depot

ROCKWELL INTERNATIONAL
Location: Des Plaines
Facilities: Manufacturing of B-1 Bomber parts

INDIANA

GRISSOM AIR FORCE BASE
Location: N Central Indiana
Facilities: Home to 305th Air Refueling Wing which flies KC-135 Stratotankers in support of the Strategic Air Command's B-52 Bomber Force

ARGONNE NATIONAL LABORATORY
Location: Argonne
Facilities: Department of Energy Nuclear Waste Management

CRANE NAVAL WEAPONS CENTER ARSENAL
Location: W of Bedford
Facilities: Major Arsenal

JEFFERSON PROVING GROUND
Location: N of Madison
Facilities: Artillery

BUNKER HILL ARSENAL
Location: S of Peru
Facilities: Major Air Force Arsenal (Air to Ground Warheads stored)
* Nuclear Weapons Depot

FORT BENJAMIN HARRIS
Location: NE of Indianapolis
Facilities: General Reservation

IOWA

DES MOINES MUNICIPAL AIRPORT
Location: Des Moines
Facilities: 132nd Tactical Fighter Wing (Nuclear Capability)

SIOUX CITY MUNICIPAL AIRPORT
Location: Sioux City
Facilities: 185th Tactical Fighter Group (Nuclear Capability)

AMES LABORATORY
Location: Ames
Facilities: Iowa State University with Department of Energy (DOE) for nuclear research and material testing

KANSAS

McCONNELL AIR FORCE BASE
Location: Wichita
Facilities: Home to 381st Strategic Missile Wing, Bombardment Wing, 184th Tactical Fighter Group (Nuclear Capability)

FORT RILEY
Location: Manhattan
Facilities: General Military Reservation: 1st Infantry Division, nuclear-

capable artillery battalions

FORT LEAVENWORTH
Location: Leavenworth
Facilities: Army's Command and General Staff College Disciplinary Barracks

KENTUCKY

FORT CAMPBELL
Location: S of Hopkinsville
Facilities: 101st Airborne Division (Screaming Eagles Air Assault) Nuclear Battalion Units

FORT KNOX
Location: S of Louisville
Facilities: Armory Center and Weapons Development for Tactical Use Gold Treasury

BLUE GRASS ARMY DEPOT
Location: SE of Richmond
Facilities: Nuclear Weapons Depot

NATIONAL GUARD ARMORY
Location: W side of Lexington
Facilities: Arsenal

LOUISIANA

BARKSDALE AIR FORCE BASE
Location: E of Shreveport
Facilities: Headquarters for 8th Air Force and Second Bombardment Wing — also 917th Tactical Fighter Group (flies A-10s and Thunderbolt II)
* Nuclear Weapons Storage Depot

ENGLAND AIR FORCE BASE
Location: NW of Alexandria
Facilities: Headquarters for 23rd Tactical Fighter Wing that flies the sophisticated rapid-fire, high velocity

Thunderbolts and carry air-to-surface Maverick missiles

FORT POLK
Location: NE of Alexandria
Facilities: 5th Infantry Training Division, Nuclear Artillery Battalion

NEW ORLEANS NAVAL AIR STATION
Location: S of New Orleans
Facilities: 2 Naval Reserve Squadrons and 5 Tenant Commands, US Coast Guard Air Station, US Customs Service, Air Support Branch

MAINE

LORING AIR FORCE BASE
Location: Near Limestone and Fort Fairfield
Facilities: 42nd Bombardment Wing (heavy) of Strategic Air Command (SAC).

BRUNSWICK NAVAL AIR STATION
Location: Brunswick
Facilities: Support System for Antisubmarine Operations of 6 Squadrons of Patrol Wing Five Storage of over 100 nuclear depth bombs

CUTLER NAVAL COMMUNICATIONS UNIT
Location: Cutler (on Atlantic peninsula)
Facilities: Operates and maintains powerful radio transmitters

CASWELL AIR FORCE STATION
Location: N of Caribou
Facilities: Nuclear Missiles Depot

BUCKS HARBOR AIR FORCE STATION
Location: E of Jonesport
Facilities: Nuclear Air-to-Ground Missiles

MARYLAND
(Radon Level High In State's Soil)

ANDREWS AIR FORCE BASE
Location: SW of Washington, D C
Facilities: Aerial Port of Entry for visiting foreign Heads of State and Presidential Plane Major Units are: 76th Airlift Division, 89th Military Airlift Wing, 1776th Air Base Wing and others
* National Emergency Command Post

FORT MEADE
Location: S of Baltimore
Facilities: First US Army and National Security Agency

FORT RITCHIE
Location: 8 miles from Waynesboro
Facilities: US Army Communications Command's Seventh Signal Command
* Alternate National Military Command Center (ANMCC) (Secret Underground Military Command Bunker)

PATUXENT RIVER NAVAL AIR STATION
Location: Southern tip of Maryland
Facilities: Naval Air Test Center which tests and evaluates Aircraft Weapons Systems and components
* Principle test site for the most advanced weapons systems known

BLOSSOM POINT PROVING GROUNDS
Location: N of Riverside
Facilities: Nuclear testing (missiles)

EDGEWOOD ARSENAL
Location: Edgewood
Facilities: Nuclear Weapons Depot

NAVAL SHIP RESEARCH AND DEVELOPMENT CENTER
Location: E of Annapolis
Facilities: Development of advanced sea weaponry

NAVAL SURFACE WEAPONS CENTER
Location: White Oak
Facilities: Nuclear Weapons Arsenal

ROCKWELL INTERNATIONAL
Location: Baltimore
Facilities: Manufacture of B-1 Bomber Parts

GODDARD SPACE FLIGHT CENTER
Location: N of New Carrollton
Facilities: Advanced Research

OAO CORPORATION
Location: Beltsville
Facilities: MX software studies and analysis

MASSACHUSETTS

HANSCOM AIR FORCE BASE
Location: NW of Boston
Facilities: Headquarters for Electronic System Division, Develops equipment and techniques for sophisticated communications

NORTH TRURO AIR FORCE STATION
Location: E of Provincetown, Cape Cod

Facilities: Home of 762nd Radar Squadron (part of NORAD) and one of several Long Range Antiballistic Radar Sites

FORT DEVENS
Location: S of New Hampshire border
Facilities: Headquarters for Army Readiness and Mobilization Region I, Army Intelligence School, Tenth Special Forces Group (Air)

SOUTH WEYMOUTH NAVAL AIR STATION
Location: South Weymouth
Facilities: Weapons Depot

WESTOVER AIR FORCE BASE
Location: Holyoke
Facilities: Readiness Air Wing

CAMP EDWARDS MILITARY RESERVATION & OTIS AIR FORCE BASE
Location: W of Hyannis
Facilities: Arsenal

ROCKWELL INTERNATIONAL
Location: Lynn
Facilities: Manufactures B-1 Bomber Parts

HARVARD
Location: Cambridge
Facilities: Chemical and Germ Experiments

NATICK LABORATORIES
Location: Boston
Facilities: Development of Germ Warfare

GTE-SYLVANIA, INC
Location: Needham Heights
Facilities: Command, Control and Communications Systems

SOFTECH, INC
Location: Waltham
Facilities: MX JOVIAL Compiler Systems

MICHIGAN
(ICBMs Scattered Underground Across State)

K I SAWYER AIR FORCE BASE
Location: Marquette (Upper Michigan)
Facilities: Home of 410th Bombardment Wing's B-52H Stratofortresses and KC-135 Stratotankers, 87th Fighter Interceptor Squadron which flies the F-106 Delta Dart Fighter, stores nuclear bombs and missiles

WURTSMITH AIR FORCE BASE
Location: 100 miles NE of Saginaw
Facilities: Strategic Air Command's 379th Bombardment Wing, Nuclear bombs and missiles stored

US ARMY MOBILITY COMMAND ARSENAL
Location: Madison Heights
Facilities: Nuclear Weapons Depot

FEDERAL REGIONAL CENTER
Location: Battle Creek
Facilities: Underground civil Defense Command Center

ROCKWELL INTERNATIONAL
Location: Kalamazoo
Facilities: Manufactures B-1 Bomber Parts

ENVIRONMENTAL RESEARCH INSTITUTE OF MICHIGAN
Location: Detroit
Facilities: Defense development of lasers, detectors and guidance sys-

tems for cruise missiles

MINNESOTA

WHITE BEAR ARSENAL
Location: White Bear
Facilities: Nuclear Weapons Depot

ROCKWELL INTERNATIONAL
Location: Minneapolis
Facilities: Manufactures B-1 Bomber Parts

MISSISSIPPI

COLUMBUS AIR FORCE BASE
Location: N of Columbus
Facilities: Pilot Training

KEESLER AIR FORCE BASE
Location: Biloxi
Facilities: Home of 3300th Technical Training Wing, 3380th Air Base, Seventh Airborne Command and Control Squadron, 53rd Weather Recon Squadron and others

GULFPORT NAVAL CONSTRUCTION BATTALION CENTER
Location: 30 miles W of Biloxi
Facilities: Center for 10th Naval Construction Regiment, Marine and Naval Reserve Centers and Training Center
* Weapons Depot

MISSOURI
(ICBMs Scattered Underground Across State)

WHITEMAN AIR FORCE BASE
Location: E of Kansas City
Facilities: Home to the 351st Strategic Missile Wing, 150 Minuetman II missiles around base, the OSCAR Launch

Control Facility for SAC

FORT LEONARD WOOD
Location: NE of Camdenton
Facilities: US Military Training Center

ROCKWELL INTERNATIONAL
Location: Kansas City
Facilities: Manufactures B-1 Bomber Parts

BENDIX CORPORATION
Location: Kansas City
Facilities: Manufactures Electronic Bomb Components

MONTANA
(ICBMs Scattered Underground Across State)

MALMSTROM AIR FORCE BASE
Location: E of Grand Falls
Facilities: Home to 341st Strategic Missile Wing
*200 Minuteman missiles around base

NEBRASKA

OFFUTT AIR FORCE BASE
Location: S of Omaha
Facilities: Headquarters for Strategic Air Command SAC has more than 350 B-52 Bombers and 1,000 Minuteman missiles

NEVADA

NELLIS AIR FORCE BASE
Location: 8 miles NE of Las Vegas
Facilities: Nuclear Testing Site (Nellis Range), Primary Weapons Testing Sites (Frenchman Flat & Yucca Flat Atomic Weapons Testing (Yucca and

Pahute Mesa), Home of USAF Tactical Fighter Weapons Center. Central Nuclear Storage Site (over 260 nuclear bombs and missiles)

FALLON NAVAL AIR STATION
Location: Fallon
Facilities: Weapons Delivery Training
(1.5 million acres for 4 impact areas in nearby desert)

HAWTHORNE ARMY AMMUNITIONS PLANT
Location: Hawthorne
Facilities: Nuclear Arsenal

INDIAN SPRINGS AIR FORCE BASE
Location: Indian Springs
Facilities: Air-to-Ground Warheads

STEAD AIR FORCE BASE
Location: N of Reno
Facilities: General Facility

NEW HAMPSHIRE

PEASE AIR FORCE BASE
Location: W of Portsmouth
Facilities: 509th Bomb Wing and 3 other Tactical Units, 715th Bombardment Squadron, 509th Refueling Squadron and
45th Air Division — stores nuclear bombs and missiles

PORTSMOUTH   NAVAL SHIPYARD
Location: Portsmouth
Facilities: Major Naval Port (Nuclear Missile Submarines)
*Restricted Area
NEW JERSEY

GIBBSBORO AIR FORCE STA-TION
Location: 44 miles NE of Atlantic City
Facilities: 772nd Radar Squadron which provides air surveillance and radar data for Philadelphia and S Jersey areas

MC GUIRE AIR FORCE BASE
Location: 18 miles S of Trenton
Facilities: 22 organizations including Airlift Wings, National Guard — (Nuclear capable)

FORT DIX
Location: N of Browns Mills
Facilities: Largest Military Installation in NE US Basic Infantry Training

EARLE NAVAL WEAPONS STATION
Location: Near Freehold and Long Branch
Facilities: Main supplier for ammunition ships (Nuclear Weapons Port)

LAKEHURST NAVAL AIR ENGINEERING CENTER
Location: Lakehurst
Facilities: Command ensures effectiveness of Navy's Air arm by researching, developing, and testing to support the world's most sophisticated aircraft — (Nuclear storage site)

MILITARY TRAFFIC MANAGEMENT COMMAND, BAYONNE
Location: New York Harbor
Facilities: Commands Terminals and Regional Storage Management Office for all branches of the Armed Forces

PICATINNY ARSENAL

Location: Dover
Facilities: Army Armament Research and Development Center
Army Materiel Command, Army Large Caliber Weapon Systems Laboratory, Nuclear Munitions Project Office

NEW MEXICO
(ICBMs Scattered Underground Across State)

CANNON AIR FORCE BASE
Location: 8 miles W of Clovis
Facilities: 27th Tactical Fighter Wing (nuclear weapons)

HOLLOMAN AIR FORCE BASE
Location: SW of Alamogordo
Facilities: Base for 833rd Air Division's 49th Tactical Fighter Wing and 479th Tactical Training Wing

KIRTLAND AIR FORCE BASE
Location: SE side of Albuquerque
Facilities: Department of Energy's Sandia National Laboratories, 1550th Aircrew Training and Test Wing, Systems Command's Contract Management Division, Air Force Test and Evaluation Center, Air Force nuclear weapons storage site

WHITE SANDS MISSILE RANGE
Location: E of Las Cruces
Facilities: Test guided missiles and rockets for Navy Fleet

LOS ALAMOS
Location: Los Alamos, W of Santa Fe
Facilities: Advanced research and development of chemical and nuclear weaponry

CARLSBAD NUCLEAR DIS-

POSAL SITE
Location: Carlsbad
Facilities: Underground radioactive waste dump site

NEW YORK

(ICBMs Scattered Underground Across State — Second largest site for nuclear warhead storage — 1,900)

PLATTSBURGH AIR FORCE BASE
Location: Plattsburgh on shore of Lake Champlain
Facilities: Base for 380th Bomber Wing
* Nuclear Weaponry Depot

GRIFFISS AIR FORCE BASE
Location: Rome
Facilities: 416th Bombardment Wing whose mission is to keep the cruise missile-equipped B-52G Bombers flying
* Nuclear Warheads

FORT DRUM
Location: Watertown
Facilities: Training facility for National Guard and Reserve Units

FORT HAMILTON
Location: Long Island
Facilities: Long Island District Recruiting Command and Entrance Station for New York City

SENECA ARMY DEPOT
Location: S of Geneva (near Five Finger Lakes)
Facilities: Storage and handling of conventional weapons and munitions

* Restricted Area - largest U S Army nuclear weapons depot in the world

BROOKHAVEN NATIONAL LABORATORY
Location: Long Island
Facilities: Experimental Research for War

NORTH CAROLINA

POPE AIR FORCE BASE
Location: Fayetteville
Facilities: Trains Paratroopers

SEYMOUR JOHNSON AIR FORCE BASE
Location: Goldsboro
Facilities: Fourth Tactical Fighter Wing SAC's 68th Bombardment Wing (Heavy) — mission is to maintain strategic deterrent force capable of immediate nuclear response
* 24 megaton bombs stored

FORT BRAGG
Location: Fayetteville
Facilities: Airborne Units

BEAUFORT MARINE CORPS AIR STATION
Location: Beaufort (N side of Port Royal Sound)
Facilities: Home for Marine Air Group 31 with 6 Fighter Attack Squadrons of F-4 Phantom Jets

CAMP LEJEUNE
Location 5 miles W of Jacksonville
Facilities: Several different Commands - all Support and Air Groups

CHERRY POINT MARINE CORPS AIR STATION
Location: Havelock
Facilities: Second Marine Aircraft Wing and Naval Air Rework Facility

NORTH DAKOTA

(ICBMs Scattered Underground Across State — Third largest U S site for nuclear warhead storage - 1,510)

ANTIBALLISTIC RADAR CENTER
Location: Grand Forks
Facilities: Center for Antiballistic Radar Detection 319th Bombardment Wing, 321st Strategic Missile Wing — 150 missile silos around base

* Nuclear weapon storage

MINOT AIR FORCE BASE
Location: N of Minot
Facilities: Major SAC Command Base, Headquarters for 57th Air Division 91st Strategic Missile Wing, 5th Bombardment Wing, Fifth Fighter Interceptor Squadron, 91st Combat Support Group and 91st Security Police Group
* Nuclear Warheads on B-52 Bombers ready throughout state

GRAND FORKS AIR FORCE BASE
Location: Grand Forks
Facilities: 321st Strategic Missile Wing, 319th Bombardment Wing, 321st Combat Support Group
* B-52 Bombers poised to soar with nuclear warheads

OHIO

WRIGHT-PATTERSON AIR FORCE BASE
Location: NE of Dayton
Facilities: Headquarters for Worldwide Logistics System and Research and Development Center

Tactical Fighter
Group (nuclear capable)

DEFENSE CONSTRUCTION SUPPLY CENTER
Location: Whitehall
Facilities: General Construction Depot

RICKENBACKER AIR FORCE BASE
Location: S of Columbus
Facilities: 121st Tactical Fighter Wing (nuclear capable)

ROCKWELL INTERNATIONAL MISSILE SYSTEMS DIVISION
Location: Columbus
Facilities: Stage III Rocketry Development for Weapons

ROCKWELL INTERNATIONAL
Location: Springfield
Facilities: Manufactures B-1 Bomber Parts

ROCKWELL INTERNATIONAL
Location: Akron
Facilities: Manufactures B-1 Bomber Parts

MONSANTO LABORATORIES
Location: Miamisburg (Mound Lab)
Facilities: Manufactures detonators for missiles and bombs

OKLAHOMA

ALTUS AIR FORCE BASE
Location: 2 miles from Altus
Facilities: Base for the largest and most powerful aircraft in the world: 5 C-5 Galaxies and 17 C-141 Starlifters, 443rd Military Airlift Wing, and 340th Air Refueling Group

TINKER AIR FORCE BASE
Location: Oklahoma City
Facilities: Air Force Logistics Command, 2854th Air Base Group, 552nd Airborne Warning Control Wing and others

VANCE AIR FORCE BASE
Location: S of Enid
Facilities: 71st Flying Training Wing of Air Training Command

FORT SILL
Location: NW of Lawton
Facilities: General Army Post

MCALESTER ARMY AMMUNITION PLANT
Location: McAlester
Facilities: Manufacture of artillery

ROCKWELL INTERNATIONAL
Location: Tulsa
Facilities: Manufactures B-1 Bomber Parts

OREGON

NAVAL WEAPONS SYSTEMS TRAINING
Location: Boardman
Facilities: SAC B-52 bomber range

COOS HEAD NAVAL FACILITY
Location: Charleston
Facility: Sound Surveillance System processing station

KINGSLEY FIELD
Location: Klamath Falls
Facilities: 318th Fighter Interceptor Squadron

MT HEBO AIR FORCE STATION
Location: Hebo

Facilities: 14th Missile Warning Squadron
689th Radar Squadron

NORTH BEND AIR FORCE STATION
Location: North Bend
Facilities: 761st Radar Squadron, Coast Guard LORAN-C Monitor Station

PORTLAND INTERNATIONAL AIRPORT
Location: Portland
Facilities: 142nd Fighter Interceptor Squadron

PENNSYLVANIA

CARLISLE BARRACKS
Location: 18 miles W of Harrisburg (Cumberland Valley)
Facilities: US Army War College and US Army Military History Institute

PHILADELPHIA NAVAL BASE
Location: On Delaware River
Facilities: Naval Shipyard, Ship Systems Engineering Station, Naval Damage Control Training Center, Destroyer Squadron

WILLOW GROVE NAVAL AIR STATION
Location: Willow Grove
Facilities: Naval Reservist Training Center for Antisubmarine Warfare

NAVAL SUPPLY DEPOT
Location: W of Camp Hill
Facilities: General Military Supply Depot
* Nuclear Depository

DEFENSE SUPPLY DEPOT
Location: Philadelphia
Facilities: Weaponry Arsenal

NEW CUMBERLAND ARMY DEPOT
Location: S of New Cumberland
Facilities: Weaponry Arsenal

GENERAL ELECTRIC
Location: Philadelphia
Facilities: Adaptation of MARK 12 re-entry vehicle for MX

HONEYWELL, INC
Location: Horsham
Facilities: MX ground power advanced development program

RHODE ISLAND

NAVAL EDUCATION AND TRAINING CENTER
Location: Narragansett Bay
Facilities: 31 separate Commands, mostly for Training and Support

SOUTH CAROLINA
(ICBMs Scattered Underground Across State, Ranks first in US sites with largest number of nuclear warheads stored — 1,962)

CHARLESTON AIR FORCE BASE
Location: Charleston
Facilities: Military Airlift Command

MYRTLE BEACH AIR FORCE BASE
Location: Myrtle Beach
Facilities: 354th Tactical Air Fighter Wing which can deploy worldwide

SHAW AIR FORCE BASE
Location: W of Columbia near Sumpter
Facilities: Tactical Fighter Squadrons and Recon Squadrons — major use of

the Phantom Fighters

FORT JACKSON
Location: Charlotte
Facilities: Infantry Training Center

PARRIS ISLAND
Location: S of Charleston
Facilities: Marine Training Center

CHARLESTON NAVAL BASE
Location: Charleston
Facilities: Naval Ship Port
Naval Weapons Station (stores approximately 1,482 warheads)

DU PONT INDUSTRIES (Savannah River Plant)
Location: S of Augusta
Facilities: Produces enriched Plutonium, Tritium and Deuterium
* Dump site for the radioactive waste
** Government ordered restricted area

AIKEN MANUFACTURING PLANT
Location: Aiken
Facilities: Produces Bomb Detonators and Plutonium and Tritium

SOUTH DAKOTA
(150 nuclear warheads underground)

ELLSWORTH AIR FORCE BASE
Location: E of Rapid City
Facilities: 44th Strategic Missile Wing and 28th Bombardment Wing's B-52 and KC-135 Stratotanker Aircraft, 365 nuclear warheads around base — stores nuclear bombs and missiles

SOUTH DAKOTA NATIONAL GUARD CAMP
Location: Rapid City
Facilities: General Military Barracks

TENNESSEE

ARNOLD AIR FORCE STATION
Location: S of Nashville
Facilities: Aerospace Testing for Department of Defense, NASA, and other Federal agencies

MEMPHIS NAVAL AIR STATION
Location: Millington
Facilities: Naval Air Technical Training Center

MEMPHIS DEFENSE DEPOT
Location: Memphis
Facilities: Weapons Arsenal

MILAN ARSENAL
Location: Milan
Facilities: Nuclear Weapons Depot

FORT CAMPBELL
Location: Clarksville
Facilities: Military Reservation (Army)

OAK RIDGE NATIONAL LABORATORY
Location: Oak Ridge
Facilities: Oak Ridge National Laboratory - production of warheads and uranium assemblies, nuclear materials testing

ARNOLD ENGINEERING DEVELOPMENT CENTER
Location: Manchester
Facilities: Weapons Research

TEXAS
(ICBMs Scattered Underground Across State)

BERGSTROM AIR FORCE BASE
Location: Austin
Facilities: Headquarters for 12th Air Force and 67th Tactical Reconnaissance Wing, Military Intelligence Battalion (nuclear capable)

BROOKS AIR FORCE BASE
Location: San Antonio
Facilities: Air Force Human Resources Lab
USAF Occupational and Environmental Health Lab
* Sophisticated aerospace Medical Research
** Restricted Area — Germ Warfare Experimentation

CARSWELL AIR FORCE BASE
Location: NW of Fort Worth
Facilities: Air Division, Bombardment Wings and Fighter Groups, Nuclear weapon bombs and missiles stored, 301st Tactical Fighter Wing, stores nuclear bombs and missiles

DYESS AIR FORCE BASE
Location: Abilene
Facilities: Air Divisions, Bombardment Wings, Nuclear weapon bombs and missiles stored

GOODFELLOW AIR FORCE BASE
Location: SE of San Angelo
Facilities: Cryptological Training

KELLY AIR FORCE BASE
Location: San Antonio
Facilities: San Antonio Air Logistics Center, Management and Inventory of aircraft and 350 Patrol German Shepherds — Controls Air Force nuclear weapons

LACKLAND AIR FORCE BASE
Location: SW of San Antonio
Facilities: Technical Training for Basic and Advanced Security Police and Law Enforcement Personnel including Patrol dog-handler

LAUGHLIN AIR FORCE BASE
Location: E of Del Rio
Facilities: Undergraduate Pilot Training Command

RANDOLPH AIR FORCE BASE
Location: Campbell Lake
Facilities: Air Force Training Command, Manpower and Personnel Center, Recruiting Services, Flying Training Wing

REESE AIR FORCE BASE
Location: W of Lubbock
Facilities: Air Training Command's Training Wing

FORT BLISS
Location: El Paso
Facilities: Army's Air Defense School, Nuclear Artillery Battalions

FORT HOOD
Location: S of Waco
Facilities: Largest Armored Post training of men and machines of the Cavalry and Armor Group Nuclear Support Group

FORT SAM HOUSTON
Location: San Antonio
Facilities: Academy of Health Sciences, Health Services Command, Brooke Army Medical Center

CHASE FIELD NAVAL AIR STATION
Location: Beeville
Facilities: Training Air Wing

CORPUS CHRISTI NAVAL AIR STATION
Location: Corpus Christi Bay
Facilities: Chief of Naval Air Training

KINGSVILLE NAVAL AIR STATION
Location: S of Corpus Christi
Facilities: Training Navy Pilots

ROCKWELL INTERNATIONAL
Location: Amarillo
Facilities: Manufactures Weapon Components
* Bomb Assembly Plant

CASTNER RANGE
Location: El Paso
Facilities: Missile Range

PANTEX PLANT
Location: Amarillo
Facilities: Assembles Bombs

E-SYSTEMS
Location: Greenville
Facilities: Researches and conceals MX Missile locations

UTAH

HILL AIR FORCE BASE
Location: W side of Great Salt Lake
Facilities: Air Logistics Center, Backup Support to 56 Air Activities

DUGWAY PROVING GROUND
Location: W of Vernon
Facilities: Conducts, evaluates, and reports results of developmental testing on munitions and other materials, including Chemical weapons, Chemical and Biological systems, flame systems, incendiary devices, and smoke-obscurant systems

OGDEN DEFENSE DEPOT
Location: Ogden
Facilities: Nuclear Weapons Arsenal

DESERT RANGE EXPERIMENTAL STATION
Location: SW of the Confusion Range of Mountains
Facilities: Germ Warfare Experimentation
* Restricted Access

HERCULES
Location: Magna
Facilities: Stage III Propulsion Systems and Nuclear Hardness and Survivability Research

MORTON THIOKOL
Location: Brigham City
Facilities: Stage I Propulsion Systems Development

HERCULES
Location: Bacchus
Facilities: Graphite Composite Launch Tubes for MX Canisters

VERMONT

VERMONT AIR NATIONAL GUARD
Location: Burlington
Facilities: 158th Tactical Fighter Group (nuclear capacity)

VIRGINIA

LANGLEY AIR FORCE BASE
Location: N of Hampton
Facilities: Tactical Air Command's Headquarters, Air Defense, Tactical Air Command Communications Division, Fifth

Weather Wing and others, Nuclear capability

ARLINGTON HALL STATION
Location: Arlington
Facilities: US Army Intelligence and Security Command

FORT BELVOIR
Location: S of Alexandria
Facilities: Defense Mapping School, Computer Systems Command and Defense Systems Management College

FORT EUSTIS
Location: NW of Hampton
Facilities: Principle Training Post for Army Transportation Corps

FORT LEE
Location: E of Petersburg
Facilities: Army Quartermaster Corps (one of the most important military installations) — Quartermaster is responsible for maintaining a central point for logistical information, training, and techniques

FORT MONROE
Location: S side of Hampton
Facilities: Home of Army's Training and Doctrine Command Battlefield Training

FORT MYER
Location: W of Washington, D C
Facilities: US Army Fife and Drum Corps, Third Infantry

VINT HILL FARMS
Location: 9 miles from Warrenton
Facilities: Home of Army Garrison, Army Electronics Material Readiness Activity and Intelligence and Security Command

QUANTICO MARINE BASE
Location: W of Quantico
Facilities: Headquarters for Marine Development and Education Command, Officer Basic School, Amphibious Warfare School, Command and Staff College

NORFOLK NAVAL BASE
Location: Norfolk
Facilities: Navy Fleets in Port
Navy Nuclear Weapons Suppy Depot
Ocean Fleet Surveillance Center

OCEANA NAVAL AIR STATION
Location: Virginia Beach
Facilities: Attack and Fighter Squadrons on alert (Nuclear Capable)

YORKTOWN NAVAL WEAPONS STATION
Location: Yorktown
Facilities: Testing and evaluation of weapons

NATIONAL CHIEFS COMMAND CENTER
Location: Berryville
Facilities: Underground bunker for Second in Command in event of war

READINESS, INTELLIGENCE AND SECURITY COMMAND
Location: Warrenton and Falls Church
Facilities: Highest Security Command Post in event of war

ARMY DISPOSAL AREA
Location: Norfolk
Facilities: Nuclear waste dump site

YORKTOWN ARSENAL
Location: Yorktown

Facilities: Nuclear Weaponry Depot

HAMPTON ARSENAL
Location: Hampton
Facilities: Nuclear Weaponry Depot

CAMP PEARY
Location: NE of Williamsburg
Facilities: General Military Facility

LITTLE CREEK NAVAL AMPHIBIOUS BASE
Location: Virginia Beach
Facilities: Navy Amphibious Training and Readiness

SYSTEMS TECHNOLOGY LABORATORY, INC
Location: Arlington
Facilities: MX Basing Studies

COMPUTER SCIENCES CORP
Location: Falls Church
Facilities: MX C3 System Development

WASHINGTON

FAIRCHILD AIR FORCE BASE
Location: W of Spokane
Facilities: Air Division, Bombardment Wing (Heavy), Combat Crew Training and others — stores nuclear bombs and missiles

McCHORD AIR FORCE BASE
Location: Between Tacoma and Fort Lewis
Facilities: Military Airlift Wing, 25th NORAD Region

FORT LEWIS
Location: Near Tacoma
Facilities: Yakima Firing Range, Infantry Division

BANGOR NAVAL SUBMARINE BASE
Location: Across Puget Sound from Seattle
Facilities: Squadron of Trident Submarines — nuclear weapons stored at Silverdale

NAVAL UNDERSEA WARFARE ENGINEERING STATION
Location: Keyport (along Puget Sound)
Facilities: Proves, tests, maintains, and repairs undersea weapons

PUGET SOUND NAVAL SHIPYARD
Location: Puget Sound
Facilities: Maintaining Sea Vessels

WHIDBEY ISLAND NAVAL AIR STATION
Location: N of Oak Harbor
Facilities: Home for all Navy Electronic Warfare Squadrons flying the EA 6B Tactical jamming Aircraft and Intruder Attack Bombers, Nuclear capability

YAKIMA FIRING RANGE
Location: Yakima
Facilities: Missile Proving Ground

SAND POINT NAVAL AIR STATION
Location: Seattle
Facilities: Readiness Command

HANDFORD SITE
Location: Richland
Facilities: Cruise Missile Depot and Nuclear Weaponry Arsenal

SEATTLE ARSENAL
Location: Seattle
Facilities: Nuclear Weaponry Depot

BOEING AEROSPACE
Location: Seattle
Facilities: Blast and Shock testing for
nuclear missiles

ROCKWELL INTERNATIONAL
Location: Seattle
Facilities: Manufactures B-1 Bomber
Parts

WEST VIRGINIA
(1 Research Facility)

WISCONSIN

**FORT McCORD MILITARY
RESERVATION**
Location: Tomah
Facilities: General Military Facility

WYOMING
(ICBMs Scattered Underground
Across State)

F.E. WARREN AIR FORCE BASE
Location: Cheyenne
Facilities: Home of Air Division and
Strategic Missile Wing,
200 Minuteman III missiles in silos
around base

US EXPERIMENTAL STATION
Location: Cheyenne
Facilities: Warfare Experimentation

Source: U.S. Department of Defense

Phoenix File II
State by State Military Facilities

STATE	MILITARY FACILITIES	NUCLEAR FACILITIES
Alabama	70	6
Alaska	210	42
Arizona	52	14
Arkansas	44	7
California	299	79
Colorado	78	11
Connecticut	33	2
Delaware	12	1
District of Columbia	15	0
Florida	135	33
Georgia	55	15
Hawaii	76	30
Idaho	27	12
Illinois	73	8
Indiana	35	6
Iowa	29	7
Kansas	48	9
Kentucky	18	7
Louisiana	45	10
Maine	43	16
Maryland	85	35
Massachusetts	71	17
Michigan	53	18
Minnesota	36	7
Mississippi	38	6
Missouri	218	12
Montana	254	19
Nebraska	118	10
Nevada	32	15
New Hampshire	12	2
New Jersey	53	12
New Mexico	25	18
New York	132	29
North Carolina	70	14
North Dakota	361	21
Ohio	74	11
Oklahoma	46	6
Oregon	34	12
		10

State by State Military Facilities

STATE	MILITARY FACILITIES	NUCLEAR FACILITIES
Pennsylvania	124	10
Rhode Island	35	6
South Carolina	45	13
South Dakota	180	9
Tennessee	34	5
Texas	140	24
Utah	72	11
Vermont	9	3
Virginia	109	32
Washington	106	27
West Virginia	1	0
Wisconsin	41	5
Wyoming	85	8

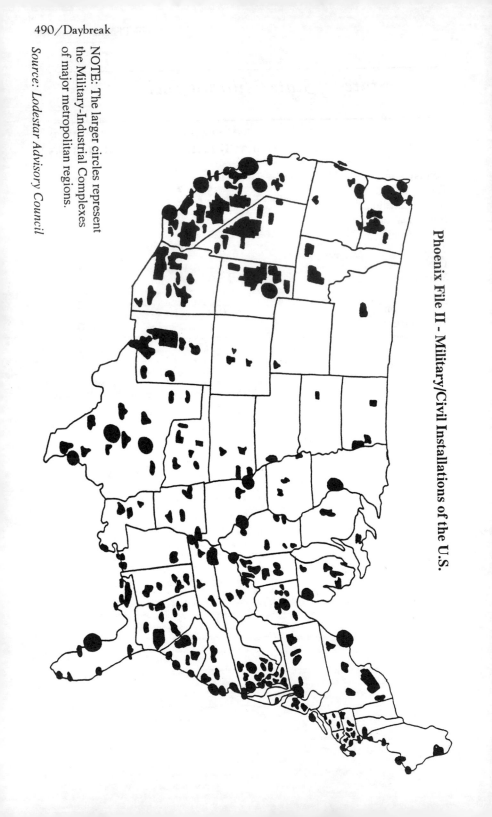

Phoenix File II - Military/Civil Installations of the U.S.

NOTE: The larger circles represent the Military-Industrial Complexes of major metropolitan regions.

Source: Lodestar Advisory Council

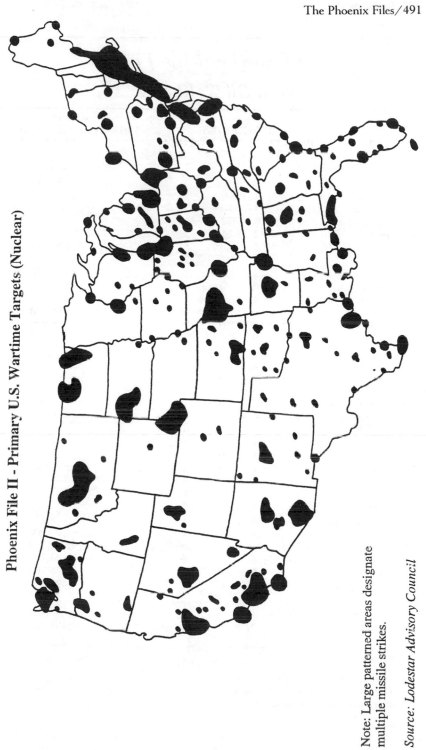

Phoenix File II - Primary U.S. Wartime Targets (Nuclear)

Note: Large patterned areas designate
multiple missile strikes.

Source: Lodestar Advisory Council

Phoenix File III
U.S. Oil Refineries

STATE	REFINERIES OPERATING	IDLE	TOTAL	CRUDE OIL DISTILLATION CAPACITY BARRELS PER DAY
Alabama	3	1	4	149,600
Alaska	6	0	6	229,850
Arizona	1	0	1	9,600
Arkansas	3	0	3	58,400
California	0	32	32	2,206,150
Colorado	2	1	3	91,200
Delaware	1	0	1	140,000
Georgia	1	1	2	33,079
Hawaii	2	0	2	131,500
Illinois	6	0	6	882,600
Indiana	4	1	5	431,150
Kansas	8	0	8	351,700
Kentucky	2	0	2	218,900
Louisiana	19	3	22	2,590,847
Michigan	3	0	3	117,100
Minnesota	2	0	2	252,100
Mississippi	6	0	6	368,400
Montana	4	0	4	139,650
Nevada	1	0	1	4,500
New Jersey	6	0	6	458,900
New Mexico	4	0	4	77,800
New York	1	0	1	41,850
North Carolina	1	0	1	3,000
North Dakota	1	0	1	58,000
Ohio	4	0	4	484,600
Oklahoma	6	0	6	387,500
Oregon	1	0	1	0
Pennsylvania	8	0	8	739,315
Tennessee	1	0	1	60,000
Texas	34	2	36	3,918,350
Utah	6	0	6	154,500
Virginia	2	0	2	56,700
Washington	7	0	7	490 700
West Virginia	2	0	2	31,700
Wisconsin	1	0	1	33,000
Wyoming	5	0	5	169,725

Source: Department of Energy,
Energy Information Administration
Petroleum Supply Annual 1989, Vol 1

The Phoenix Files/493

Phoenix File III
U.S. Oil Refineries
Major Producers

(Companies with a capacity of producing over 100,000 barrels per day)

Chevron U.S.A. Inc.	1,621,000
Port Arthur, Texas	329,000
Pascagoula, Mississippi	295,000
El Segundo, California	286,000
Richmond, California	270,000
Philadelphia, Pennsylvania	175,000
Perth Amboy, New Jersey	80,000
El Paso, Texas	66,000
Honolulu, Hawaii	53,000
Salt Lake City, Utah	45,000
Kenai, Alaska	22,000
Exxon Co. U.S.A.	1,147,000
Baytown, Texas	426,000
Baton Rouge, Louisiana	421,000
Linden, New Jersey	130,000
Benicia, California	128,000
Billings, Montana	42,000
Shell Oil Co.	1,078,600
Wood River, Illinois	274,000
Deer Park, Texas	215,900
Norco, Louisiana	215,000
Martinez, California	140,100
Carson, California	120,000
Anacortes, Washington	85,000
Odessa, Texas	28,600
Amoco Oil Co.	984,000
Texas City, Texas	415,000
Whiting, Indiana	350,000
Mandan, North Dakota	58,000
Yorktown, Virginia	53,000
Salt Lake City, Utah	40,000
Casper, Wyoming	40,000
Savannah, Georgia	28,000
Mobil Oil Corp.	838,000
Beaumont, Texas	275,000
Joliet, Illinois	180,000
Chalmette, Louisiana	160,000
Torrance, California	123,000
Paulsboro, New Jersey	100,000
	172,000
	167,500

BP America Inc./BP Oil Corp.	756,640
Belle Chasse, Louisiana	213,640
Marcus Hook, Pennsylvania	172,000
Lima, Ohio	167,500
Toledo, Ohio	126,100
Ferndale, Washington	77,400
Star Enterprise	615,000
Port Arthur/Neches, Texas	250,000
Convent, Louisiana	225,000
Delaware City, Delaware	140,000
U.S. Steel Corp	603,000
Marathon Petroleum Co.	
Garyville, Louisiana	255,000
Robinson, Illinois	160,000
Texas City, Texas	69,500
Detroit, Michigan	68,500
Rock Island Refining Corp.	
Indianapolis, Indiana	50,000
Sun Co Inc.	510,000
Marcus Hook, Pennsylvania	175,000
Toledo, Ohio	125,000
Tulsa, Oklahoma	85,000
Sun Refining & Marketing	
Philadelphia, Pennsylvania	125,000
Atlantic Richfield Co.	414,000
Arco Products Co.	
Los Angeles, California	222,000
Ferndale, Washington	167,000
Arco Alaska Inc.	
Prudhoe Bay, Alaska	13,000
Anchorage, Alaska	12,000
E I Du Pont De Nemours & Co.	406,500
Conoco Inc.	
Westlake, Louisiana	159,500
Ponca City, Oklahoma	140,000
Billings, Montana	49,500
Commerce City, Colorado	48,000
Santa Maria, California	9,500
Ashland Oil Inc.	346,500
Catlettsburg, Kentucky	213,400
St. Paul, Minnesota	67,100
Canton, Ohio	66,000
Koch Industries Inc.	310,000
Koch Refining Co.	
St. Paul, Minnesota	185,000
Corpus Christi, Texas	125,000

Phillips 66 Co.	305,000
Sweeny, Texas	175,000
Borger, Texas	105,000
Woods Cross, Utah	25,000
Texaco Refining & Marketing Inc.	300,000
Anacortes, Washington	117,000
El Dorado, Kansas	78,000
Wilmington, California	57,000
Bakersfield, California	48,000
Trans-America Natural Gas Corp.	300,000
Trans-America Refining Co.	
Norco, Louisiana	300,000
Lyondell Petrochemical Co.	290,000
Houston, Texas	290,000
Citgo Petroleum Corp/	282,000
Petroleos De Venezuela	
Citgo Petroleum Corp.	
Lake Charles, Louisiana	282,000
Solomon Inc.	277,100
Hill Petroleum Co.	
Texas City, Texas	119,600
Houston, Texas	66,000
Krotz Springs, Louisiana	57,500
St. Rose, Louisiana	34,000
Coastal Corp., The	275,300
Coastal Eagle Point Oil Co.	
Westville, New Jersey	104,500
Coastal Refining & Marketing Inc.	
Corpus Christi, Texas	85,000
Coastal Derby Refining Co.	
El Dorado, Kansas	30,400
Wichita, Kansas	28,800
Coastal Mobile Refining Co.	
Chickasaw, Alabama	26,600
Unocal Corp.	222,100
Wilmington, California	108,000
Rodeo, California	73,100
Arroyo Grande, California	41,000
Total Petroleum Inc.	190,100
Ardmore, Oklahoma	60,500
Arkansas City, Kansas	56,000
Alma, Michigan	45,600
Colorado Refining Co.	
Commerce City, Colorado	28,000
Fina Oil & Chemical Co.	165,000

Port Arthur, Texas	110,000
Big Spring, Texas	55,000
Mapco Petroleum Inc.	163,850
North Pole, Alaska	103,850
Memphis, Tennessee	60,000
Diamond Shamrock Refining & Marketing Co.	161,000
Sunray, Texas	110,000
Three Rivers, Texas	51,000
Kerr-McGee Corp.	156,800
Southwestern Refining Co. Inc.	
Corpus Christi, Texas	104,000
Ker-McGee Refining Corp.	
Wynnewood, Oklahoma	45,000
Cotton Valley, Louisiana	7,800
Uno-Ven Co.	147,000
Lemont, Illinois	147,000
Crown Central Petroleum Corp.	146,000
Pasadena, Texas	100,000
LaGloria Oil & Gas Co.	
Tyler, Texas	46,000
Tosco Corp.	131,900
Martinez, California	131,900
Petroleos De Venezuela	130,000
Champlin Refining & Chemical Inc.	
Corpus Christi, Texas	130,000
Sinclair Oil Corp.	125,500
Sinclair, Wyoming	54,000
Tulsa, Oklahoma	47,000
Little America Refining Co.	
Evansville, Wyoming	24,500
Horsham Corp.	121,600
Clark Oil & Refining Corp	
Blue Island, Illinois	64,600
Hartford, Illinois	57,000
Murphy Oil U.S.A. Inc.	121,000
Meraux, Louisiana	88,000
Superior, Wisconsin	33,000

*Source: Department of Energy, Energy Information
Administration, Petroleum Supply Annual 1989, Vol. 1.*

Phoenix File III
U.S. Oil Refineries
(Complete Refinery Listing)

Refinery	Location	Barrels per Day Operating	Idle
Alabama			
Coastal Mobile Refining	Chickasaw	26,600	0
Hunt Refining Co	Tuscaloosa	33,500	0
LL&E Petroleum Marketing	Saraland	80,000	0
Vulcan Refining Co	Cordova	0	9,500
Alaska			
Arco Alaska Inc	Anchorage	12,000	0
	Prudhoe Bay	13,000	0
Chevron U.S.A. Inc	Kenai	22,000	0
Mapco Petroleum Inc	North Pole	103,850	0
Petro Star	North Pole	7,000	0
Tesoro Petroleum Corp	Kenai	72,000	0
Arizona			
Sunbelt Refining Co	Coolidge	9,600	0
Arkansas			
Berry Petroleum Co	Stephens	3,700	0
Cross Oil & Refining Co	Smackover	6,700	0
Lion Oil Co	El Dorado	41,000	7,000
California			
Arco Products Co	Los Angeles	222,000	0
Chemoil Refining Corp	Long Beach	14,200	0
Chevron U.S.A. Inc	El Segundo	286,000	0
	Richmond	270,000	0
Conoco Inc	Santa Maria	9,500	0
Eco Asphalt Inc	Long Beach	0	10,550
Edgington Oil Co	Long Beach	41,600	0
Exxon Co U.S.A.	Benicia	128,000	0
Fletcher Oil & Refining	Carson	29,500	0
Gibson Oil & Refining	Bakersfield	0	9,600
Golden West Refining,	Santa Fe Springs	44,700	0
Huntway Refining	Benicia	8,600	0
	Wilmington	5,500	0
Kern Oil & Refining	Bakersfield	21,400	0
Lunday Thagard	South Gate	8,100	0
Mobil Oil Corp	Torrance	123,000	0
Pacific Refining	Hercules	55,000	0
Paramount Petroleum	Paramount	46,500	0
Powerine Oil	Santa Fe Springs	37,000	7,000

Refinery	Location	Barrels per Day Operating	Idle
San Joaquin Refining	Bakersfield	14,300	10,000
Shell Oil	Carson	120,000	0
	Martinez	140,100	0
Sunland Refining	Bakersfield	12,000	0
Tenby Inc	Oxnard	4,000	0
Texaco Refining & Marketing			
	Bakersfield	48,000	0
	Wilmington	57,000	0
Tosco Corp	Martinez	131,900	0
Ultramar Refining	Wilmington	69,000	0
Unocal Corp	Arroyo Grande	41,000	0
	Rodeo	73,100	0
	Wilmington	108,000	0
Witco Corp	Oildale	0	0
Colorado			
Colorado Refining Co	Commerce City	28,000	0
Conoco Inc	Commerce City	48,000	0
Western Slope Refining	Fruita	0	15,200
Delaware			
Star Enterprise	Delaware City	140,000	0
Georgia			
Amoco Oil Co	Savannah	0	28,000
Young Refining Co	Douglasville	5,079	0
Hawaii			
Chevron U.S.A. Inc	Honolulu	53,000	0
Hawaiian Independent Refinery Inc.	Ewa Beach	78,500	0
Illinois			
Clark Oil & Refining	Blue Island	64,600	0
	Hartford	57,000	0
Marathon Petroleum	Robinson	160,000	0
Mobil Oil Corp	Joliet	180,000	0
Shell Oil Co	Wood River	274,000	0
Uno-Ven Co	Lemont	147,000	0
Indiana			
Amoco Oil Co	Whiting	350,000	0
Indiana Farm Bureau Cooperative Assoc.	Mount Vernon	21,200	0
Inter-Coastal Energy Services Corp	Troy	0	1,250
Laketon Refining Corp	Laketon	8,700	0
Rock Island Refining	Indianapolis	50,000	0

Kansas

Refinery	Location	Barrels per Day Operating	Idle
Coastal Derby Refining	Augusta	0	0
	El Dorado	30,400	0
	Wichita	28,800	0
Farmland Industries	Coffeyville	56,500	0
	Phillipsburg	26,400	0
National Cooperative Refinery Assoc.	McPherson	75,600	0
Texaco Refining & Marketing	El Dorado	78,000	0
Total Petroleum	Arkansas City	56,000	0

Kentucky

Refinery	Location	Operating	Idle
Ashland Oil	Catlettsburg	213,400	0
Somerset Refinery	Somerset	5,500	0

Louisiana

Refinery	Location	Operating	Idle
American International Refinery Inc	Lake Charles	0	27,000
BP Oil Corp	Belle Chasse	213,640	0
Calcasieu Refining	Lake Charles	13,500	0
Calumet Refining	Princeton	4,207	0
Canal Refining	Church Point	8,000	0
Citgo Petroleum Corp	Lake Charles	282,000	0
Claiborne Gasoline Co	Lisbon	7,500	0
Conoco Inc	Westlake	159,500	0
Dubach Gas Co	Dubach	10,000	0
Exxon Co. U.S.A.	Baton Rouge	421,000	0
Hill Petroleum Co	Krotz Springs	57,500	0
	St. Rose	34,000	0
Kerr-McGee Refining Corp	Cotton Valley	7,800	0
Marathon Petroleum Co	Garyville	255,000	0
Mobil Oil Corp	Chalmette	160,000	0
Murphy Oil U.S.A. Inc	Meraux	76,000	12,000
Pennzoil Products Co	Shreveport	46,200	0
Placid Refining Co	Port Allen	46,000	0
Sabine Resources Group	Stonewall	0	10,000
Shell Oil Co	Norco	215,000	0
Star Enterprise	Convent	225,000	0
Trans-America Refining	Norco	0	300,000

Michigan

Refinery	Location	Operating	Idle
Crystal Refining	Carson City	3,000	0
Marathon Petroleum	Detroit	68,500	0
Total Petroleum Inc	Alma	45,600	0

Minnesota

Refinery	Location	Operating	Idle
Ashland Oil Inc	St. Paul	67,100	0
Koch Refining Co	St. Paul	185,000	0

Mississippi

Refinery	Location	Barrels per Day Operating	Idle
Amerada Hess Corp	Purvis	30,000	0
Chevron U.S.A. Inc	Pascagoula	295,000	0
Ergon Inc	Vicksburg	20,600	0
Petro Source Resources	Vicksburg	6,000	0
Southland Oil Co	Lumberton	5,800	0
	Sandersville	11,000	0
Montana			
Cenex	Laurel	41,450	0
Conoco Inc	Billings	49,500	0
Exxon Co. U.S.A.	Billings	42,000	0
Montana Refining Co	Great Falls	6,700	0
Nevada			
Petro Source Refining Partners	Tonopah	4,500	0
New Jersey			
Amerada Hess Corp	Port Reading	0	0
Chevron U.S.A. Inc	Perth Amboy	80,000	0
Coastal Eagle Point Oil	Westville	104,500	0
Exxon Co. U.S.A.	Linden	130,000	0
Mobil Oil Corp	Paulsboro	100,000	0
Seaview Petroleum Inc	Paulsboro	44,400	0
New Mexico			
Bloomfield Refining Co	Bloomfield	16,800	0
Giant Refining Co	Gallup	19,000	0
Navajo Refining Co	Artesia	38,000	0
Thriftway Co	Bloomfield	4,000	0
New York			
Cibro Petroleum Products	Albany	41,850	0
North Carolina			
GNC Energy Corp	Greensboro	3,000	0
North Dakota			
Amoco Oil Co	Mandan	58,000	0
Ohio			
Ashland Oil Inc	Canton	66,000	0
BP Oil Corp	Lima	167,500	0
	Toledo	126,100	0
Sun Co Inc	Toledo	125,000	0
Oklahoma			
Barrett Refining Corp	Thomas	10,000	0
Conoco Inc	Ponca City	140,000	0
Kerr-McGee Refining Corp	Wynnewood	45,000	0

Refinery	Location	Barrels per Day Operating	Idle
Sinclair Oil Corp	Tulsa	47,000	0
Sun Co Inc	Tulsa	85,000	0
Total Petroleum Inc	Ardmore	60,500	0
Oregon			
Chevron U.S.A. Inc	Willbridge	0	0
Pennsylvania			
BP Oil Corp	Marcus Hook	172,000	0
Chevron U.S.A. Inc	Philadelphia	175,000	0
Pennzoil Products Co	Rouseville	15,700	0
Quaker State Oil Refining	Smethport	6,700	0
Sun Co Inc	Marcus Hook	175,000	0
Sun Refining & Marketing	Philadelphia	125,000	0
United Refining Co	Warren	60,000	0
Witco Corp	Bradford	9,915	0
Tennessee			
Mapco Petroleum Inc	Memphis	60,000	0
Texas			
Amoco Oil Co	Texas City	415,000	0
Champlin Refining & Chemical Inc	Corpus Christi	130,000	0
	El Paso	66,000	0
Chevron U.S.A. Inc	Port Arthur	329,000	0
	Corpus Christi		
Coastal Refining & Marketing,		85,000	0
	Pasedena		
Crown Central Petroleum		100,000	0
Diamond Shamrock Refining	Sunray	110,000	0
& Marketing Co.	Three Rivers	51,000	0
	Jacksboro	1,800	0
Eagle Refining Corp	El Paso	25,500	0
El Paso Refining Co Ltd	Baytown	426,000	0
Exxon Co U.S.A.	Big Spring	55,000	0
Fina Oil & Chemical Co	Port Arthur	110,000	0
Hill Petroleum Co.	Houston	66,000	0
	Texas City	119,600	0
Howell Hydrocarbons	San Antonio	1,500	3,000
Koch Refining Co.	Corpus Christi	125,000	0
LaGloria Oil & Gas Co.	Tyler	46,000	0
Leal Petroleum Corp.	Nixon	15,900	5,000
Longview Refining Assoc.	Longview	13,300	0
Lyondell Petrochemical	Houston	290,000	0
Marathon Petroleum Co.	Texas City	69,500	0
Mobil Oil Corp.	Beaumont	275,000	0
Petrolite Corp.	Kilgore	1,000	0
Phillips 66 Co.	Borger	105,000	0
	Sweeny	175,000	0

Refinery	Location	Barrels per Day	
		Operating	Idle
Polo Chemical Inc.	San Leon	0	7,000
Pride Refining Inc.	Abilene	28,500	14,250
Rattlesnake Refining Corp.	Wickett	0	8,000
Shell Oil Corp.	Deer Park	215,900	0
	Odessa	28,600	0
South Hampton Refining	Silsbee	0	0
Southwestern Refining	Corpus Christi	104,000	0
Star Enterprise	Port Arthur/Neches	225,000	25,000
Trifinery	Corpus Christi	27,000	0
Valero Refining Co.	Corpus Christi	20,000	0
Utah			
Amoco Oil Co	Salt Lake City	40,000	0
Big West Oil Co	North Salt Lake	24,000	0
Chevron U.S.A. Inc	Salt Lake City	45,000	0
Crysen Refining Inc	Woods Cross	12,500	0
Pennzoil Products Co	Roosevelt	8,000	0
Phillips 66 Co	Woods Cross	25,000	0
Virginia			
Amoco Oil Co	Yorktown	53,000	0
Primary Oil & Energy	Chester	3,700	0
Washington			
Arco Products Co	Ferndale	167,000	0
BP Oil Corp	Ferndale	77,400	0
Chevron U.S.A. Inc	Richmond Beach	0	0
Shell Oil Co	Anacortes	85,000	0
Sound Refining Inc	Tacoma	11,900	0
Texaco Refining & Marketing	Anacortes	117,000	0
U.S. Oil & Refining Co	Tacoma	32,400	0
West Virginia			
Phoenix Refining Co	St. Mary's	19,200	0
Quaker State Oil Refining	Newell	12,500	0
Wisconsin			
Murphy Oil U.S.A. Inc	Superior	33,000	0
Wyoming			
Amoco Oil Co	Casper	40,000	0
Frontier Refining Co	Cheyenne	38,670	0
Little America Refining	Evansville	24,500	0
Sinclair Oil Corp	Sinclair	54,000	0
Wyoming Refining Co	Newcastle	12,555	0

Source: Department of Energy, Energy Information Administration, Petroleum Supply Annual 1989, Vol. 1

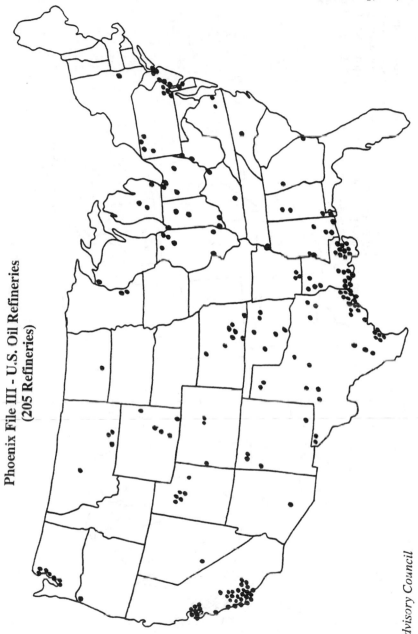

Phoenix File III - U.S. Oil Refineries
(205 Refineries)

Source: Lodestar Advisory Council

Phoenix File IV — U.S. Active Mountains

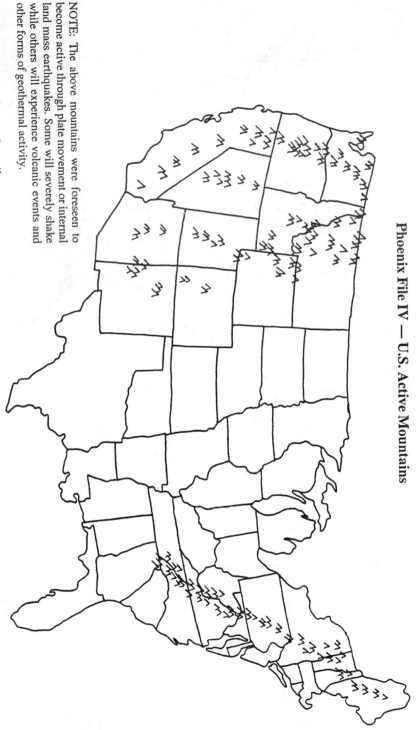

NOTE: The above mountains were foreseen to become active through plate movement or internal land mass earthquakes. Some will severely shake while others will experience volcanic events and other forms of geothermal activity.

Source: Lodestar Advisory Council

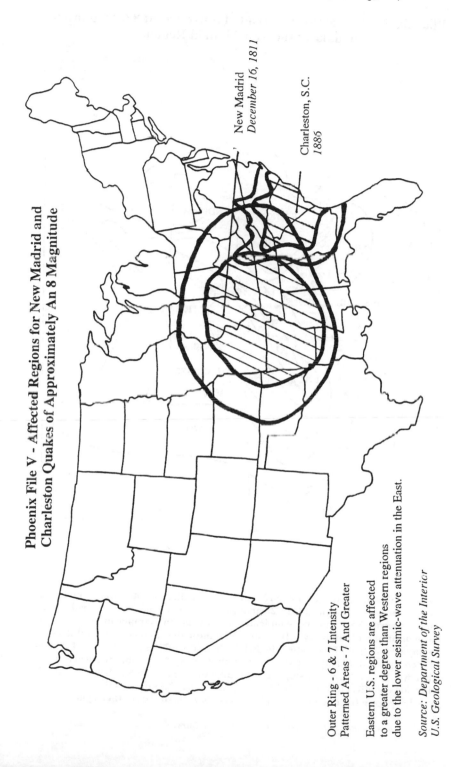

Phoenix File V - Affected Regions for New Madrid and Charleston Quakes of Approximately An 8 Magnitude

New Madrid
December 16, 1811

Charleston, S.C.
1885

Outer Ring - 6 & 7 Intensity
Patterned Areas - 7 And Greater

Eastern U.S. regions are affected
to a greater degree than Western regions
due to the lower seismic-wave attenuation in the East.

*Source: Department of the Interior
U.S. Geological Survey*

Phoenix File V - Intensity Spread of a Recurrent 8.6 Magnitude Quake of the New Madrid Region

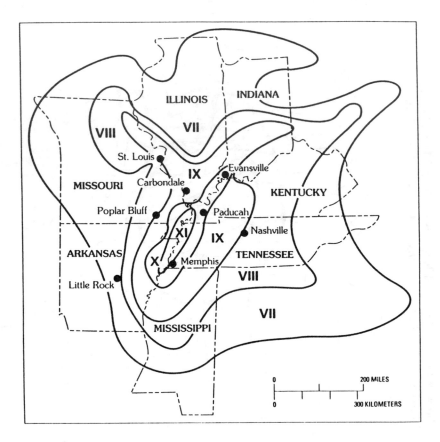

Regional distribution of estimated Modified Mercalli intensities that would result from a recurrence of the 1811-12 earthquake series in the New Madrid seismic zone. Intensity VIII and above indicates that structural damage might occur in a large number of buildings. Intensity VII indicates principally architectural damage. Intensity VI indicates widely felt shaking and items knocked off shelves. This composite intensity map shows a distribution of effects more widespread than what would result from a single earthquake of magnitude 8.6, because the distributions of effects were plotted for magnitude 8.6 earthquakes that could occur anywhere from the northern end of the seismic zone to the southern end.

Source: Department of the Interior U.S. Geologic Survey

Phoenix File VI
Pole Shift Realignment Configurations

Because it's difficult to imagine the new global axis position after the shift, it would be easier to reach specifics by rearranging an old globe. If you have one, disengage the two pole points and reposition the North Pole on the border of Finland and Sweden. The South Pole will be affixed on the Anarctic Circle just to the left of 150°. Once this is done, hold a black marker pen at the zero placement on the globe arm (this will be the Equator) and turn the globe to mark the new equatorial position. Do this with each consecutive 15° increments both North and South. This will give you the new degree positions of geographical locations around the globe.

For those who don't have an old globe to make adjustments on. The following is a partial listing of the new degree positions and their corresponding geographic locations. Keep in mind that this entire scenario is *only* if the axis shift occurs at the *exact* "point of rotation" the event was foreseen occuring.

Geographic locations bisecting new degrees

75°N
N. Germany
Central Poland
S. of Moscow
N. Ural Mountains
E. Coast of Iceland
Wick, Scotland

60°N
N.E. Spain
Sicily
S. Greece
S. Turkey
N. tip of Iran
Atasu, Russia
Kemerovo, Russia
Cape Farewell, Greenland

45°N
Brooks Range, Alaska
S. Central Hudson Bay
Central Quebec
S.W. Newfoundland
Santa Cruz (Canary Islands)
S. Algeria
S. Libya
Central Saudi Arabia

S. Iran
N. Central Pakistan
N.W. China
Central Mongolia
Korkodon, Russia

30°N
Unalaska (Aleutian Islands)
Queen Charlotte Island
Shelby, Montana
Mott, N. Dakota
Rochester, Minnesota
Dayton, Ohio
Richmond, Virginia
Sargasso Sea
Sao Tiago (Cape Verde Islands)
Central Ghana
S. Nigeria
S. Central Ethiopia
Hyderabad, India
S. Bangladesh
N. Burma
Chungking, China
Border of N and S Korea
N. Hokkaido Is., Japan

15°N

Pasadena, California
Phoenix, Arizona
El Paso, Texas
Bay City, Texas
Havana, Cuba
Santo Domingo
Martinique
N. Angola
S. Zaire
S. Central Tanzania
Nicobar Islands
Central Cambodia
Bonin Island (Volcano Islands)

Equator

Kauai Island (Hawaiian Islands)
Bogota, Colombia
Manaus, Brazil
Carolina, Brazil
Central South West Africa
Central Kalahari Desert
Manakara, Madagascar
Mauritius Island
S. Sumatra
Central Borneo
Guam

15°S

Lima, Peru
Miranda, Brazil
Sao Paulo, Brazil
Central New Guinea
Ebon Island (Gilbert Islands)

30°S

La Serena, Chile
Buenos Aires, Argentina
Perth, Australia
Townesville, Queensland, Australia
Vanikoro Island, (Santa Cruz Islands)
Eiao Island (Marquesas Islands)

45°S

Deseado, Argentina
Stanley (Falkland Islands)
Mt. Gambier, South Australia, Australia
Newcastle, New South Wales, Australia
Ata Island (West Samoa)
Mauke Island (Cook Islands)
Easter Island

60°S

Adelaide, Antarctic Peninsula
Greymouth, New Zealand
Wellington, New Zealand

75°S

Little America, Ross Ice Shelf, Antarctica
Emerald Basin
Byrd Land, Antarctica

If the calculated *Point of Rotation* is indeed accurate at the time of Axis Shift, the evidence of great climactic changes, in conjunction with altered ocean and wind currents will be the forces that bring about major alterations. As seen by the new degree alignments, icecaps will instantly begin melting and will cause ocean levels to rise dozens of feet. New ice regions will form. Formerly cold regions will experience a new temperate climate while some warm ones will be tropical due to their new equatorial position. Likewise, many warm regions will be colder. It's also extremely important to remember that, even if the Point of Rotation is altogether different at the exact time of axis shift, although the new degree alignments will be different from what I've outlined, THE CLIMACTIC ALTERATIONS WILL STILL BE JUST AS SEVERE.

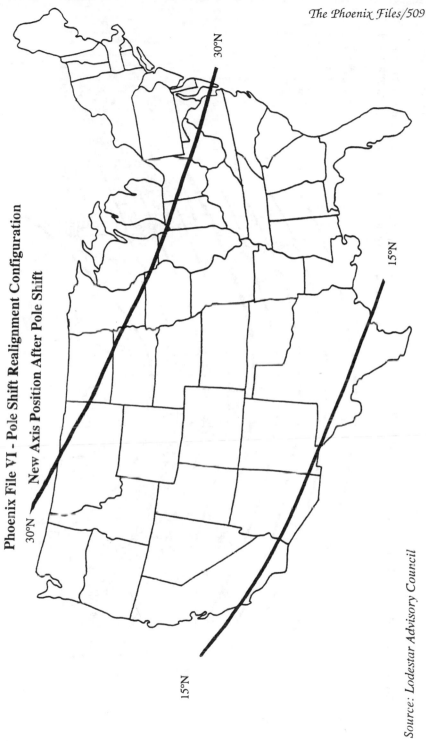

Phoenix File VI - Pole Shift Realignment Configuration
New Axis Position After Pole Shift

30°N

15°N

30°N

15°N

Source: Lodestar Advisory Council

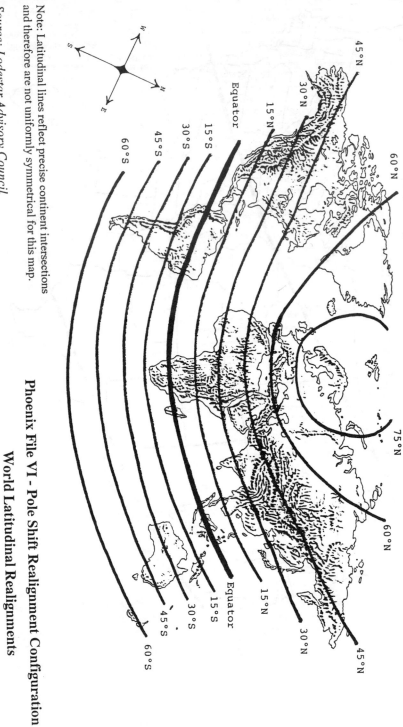

Phoenix File VI - Pole Shift Realignment Configuration

World Latitudinal Realignments

Note: Latitudinal lines reflect precise continent intersections and therefore are not uniformly symmetrical for this map.

Source: Lodestar Advisory Council

Phoenix File VII - Orogenic Roots of the United States

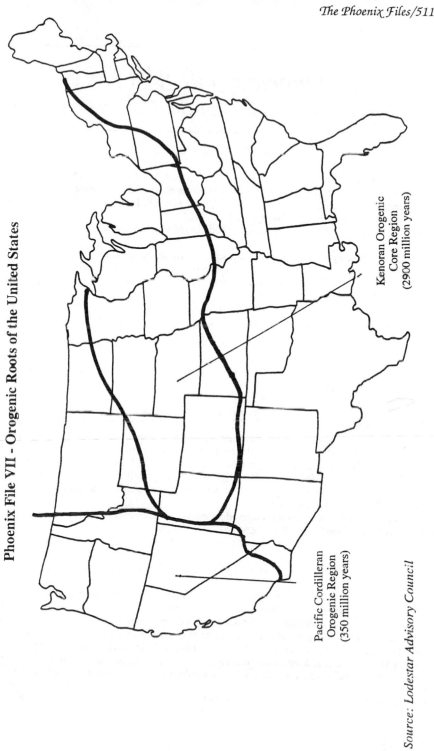

Kenoran Orogenic
Core Region
(2900 million years)

Pacific Cordilleran
Orogenic Region
(350 million years)

Source: Lodestar Advisory Council

Phoenix File VIII
Earthquake Regions of the United States

THE MERCALLI SCALE

The scale used in The Phoenix Files is the Modified Mercalli Intensity Scale which evaluates the *degree of damage* from earthquakes. As opposed to the Richter Scale, which measures an earthquakes *magnitude,* the Modified Mercalli Intensity Scale clearly indicates the extent of an event's damage.

The following is a list of the 12 levels of Modified Mercalli intensities.

I. Not felt except by a very few under especially favorable conditions.

II. Felt only by a few persons at rest, especially on upper floors of buildings.

III. Felt quite noticeably by persons indoors, especially on upper floors of buildings. Standing vehicles may rock slightly.

IV. Felt indoors by many, outdoors by few during the day. At night, some awakened. Dishes, windows, doors disturbed; walls make cracking sound. Sensation like heavy truck striking building. Standing vehicles rock noticeably.

V. Felt by nearly everyone; many awakened. Some dishes, windows broken. Unstable objects overturn. Pendulum clocks may stop.

VI. Felt by all, many frightened. Some heavy furniture moved; a few instances of fallen plaster. Damage slight.

VII. Damage negligible in buildings of good design and construction; slight to moderate in well-built ordinary structures; considerable damage in poorly-built or badly-designed structures; some chimneys broken.

VIII. Damage slight in specially-designed structures; considerable damage in ordinary substantial buildings with partial collapse. Damage great in poorly-built structures. Fall of chimneys, factory stacks, columns, monuments, and walls. Heavy furniture overturned.

IX. Damage considerable in specially-designed structures; well-designed frame structures thrown out of plumb. Damage great in substantial buildings, with partial collapse. Buildings shifted off foundations.

X. Some well-built wooden structures destroyed; most masonry and frame structures destroyed with foundations. Rails bent.

XI. Few, if any (masonry) structures remain standing. Bridges destroyed. Rails bent greatly.

XII. Damage total. Line of sight and level are distorted. Objects thrown into the air.

Another measure of the relative strength of an earthquake is the *size of the area over which the shaking is noticed.* The extent of the associated felt areas indicates that some comparatively large earthquakes have occurred in the past in places not considered by the general public to be regions of major earthquake activity. For example, the three shocks in 1811 and 1812 near New Madrid, Missouri, were each felt over the entire eastern U.S. The 1886 Charleston, South Carolina earthquake was also felt over a region of approximately 2 million square miles, which includes most of the eastern United States.

Source: U.S. Geological Survey, Denver, CO.

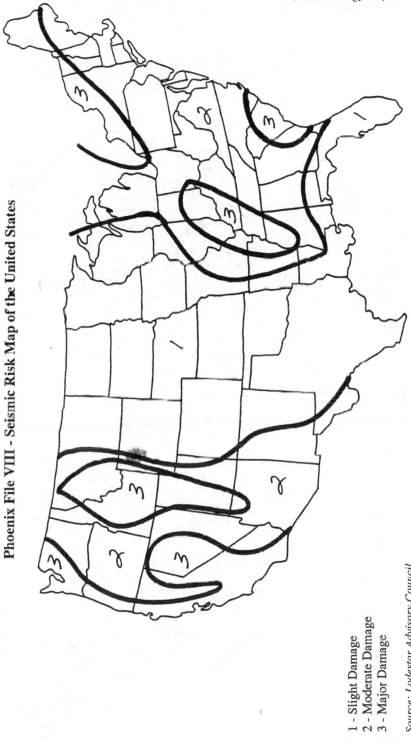

Phoenix File VIII - Seismic Risk Map of the United States

1 - Slight Damage
2 - Moderate Damage
3 - Major Damage

Source: Lodestar Advisory Council

Source: National Oceanic and Atmospheric Administration

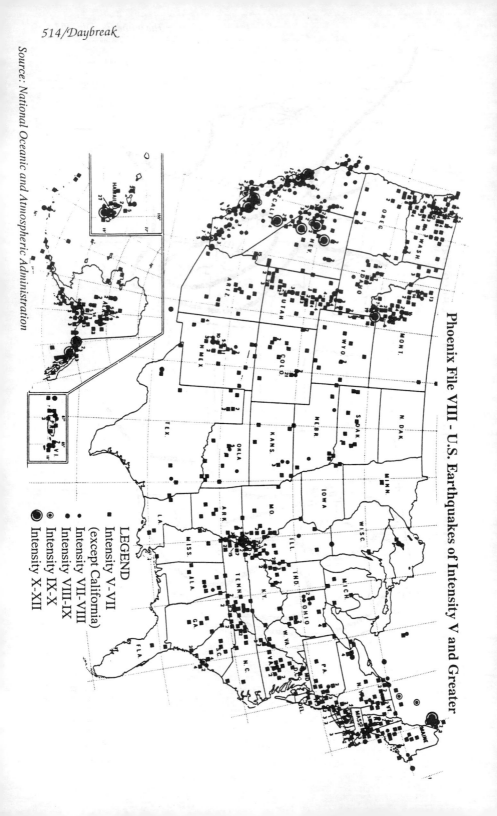

Phoenix File VIII - U.S. Earthquakes of Intensity V and Greater

LEGEND
■ Intensity V-VII
  (except California)
• Intensity VII-VIII
⦿ Intensity VIII-IX
◉ Intensity IX-X
● Intensity X-XII

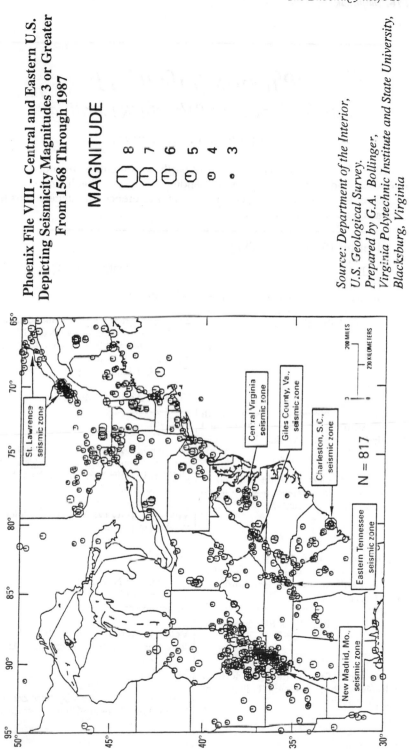

Phoenix File VIII - Central and Eastern U.S. Depicting Seismicity Magnitudes 3 or Greater From 1568 Through 1987

MAGNITUDE

8
7
6
5
4
3

Source: Department of the Interior,
U.S. Geological Survey.
Prepared by G.A. Bollinger,
Virginia Polytechnic Institute and State University,
Blacksburg, Virginia

St. Lawrence seismic zone
Central Virginia seismic zone
Giles County, Va., seismic zone
Charleston, S.C., seismic zone
Eastern Tennessee seismic zone
New Madrid, Mo., seismic zone

N = 817

200 MILES
200 KILOMETERS

Phoenix File VIII
Earth Movement Weekly Recordings

(For 1990, and part of 1991)

The following listing is comprised of earth movements as recorded during one week, and is specified by the date ending the week. This listing is not all inclusive, therefore, it is provided as a general reference that underscores the increasing activity of our earth.

During 1990 week ending:

Jan. 5th

Earthquakes: central Greece, northern Papua, New Guinea, Guam, Tonga Islands, and Nevada/California border.

Volcanic Activity: Redoubt volcano in Alaska

Jan. 12th

Earthquakes: Newcastle (New South Wales, Australia), northeastern India, and Bangladesh, central Alaska, Yugoslavia, and Lima, Peru.

Volcanic Activity: Redoubt volcano in Alaska, Mount St. Helens in Washington State, Mount Etna in Sicily.

Jan. 19th

Earthquakes: Bangladesh, Mexico, northwest China, western Australia, Taiwan, northern, and southern California, and Maryland.

Volcanic Activity: Mount Etna in Sicily.

Jan. 26th

Earthquakes: Tehran, Iran (2), northern Philippines, Peru, southern Indiana, and New England.

Volcanic Activity: Mount Etna in Sicily.

Feb. 2nd

Earthquakes: southern Indiana, northwestern Kentucky, New Mexico, Nepal, Athens, Aleutian Islands, Algiers, Puerto Rico, Dominican Republic, and Hokkaido Island off Japan.

Volcanic Activity: Mount Etna in Sicily.

Feb. 9th

Earthquakes: Iran, Philippine city of Cebu, northern Venezuela, eastern Caribbean, California, northern India, and Soviet Uzbek Republic.

Volcanic Activity: Mount St. Helens in Washington State

Feb 16th

Earthquakes: New Zealand, central Japan, northern Italy, southern Mexico, and western Nepal.

Volcanic Activity: Mt. Kelud volcano in Java, Redoubt volcano in southern Alaska.

Feb. 23rd

Earthquakes: South Pacific, New Zealand's North Island, central Japan, southwest

Mexico, Vanuatu, western Nepal, northern Algeria, South Carolina, northern and southern California, Puerto Rico, and the Virgin Islands.

Volcanic Activity: Kilauea Volcano in Hawaii, Mt. Kelud Volcano in Java, Redoubt Volcano in Alaska.

March 2nd

Earthquakes: San Francisco Bay, and Los Angeles, California, southern Yugoslavia, southwestern Pakistan, and western Nepal.

Volcanic Activity: Redoubt Volcano in Alaska, Mount Lewotobi LakiLaki Volcano in Indonesia, Mount Etna.

March 9th

Earthquakes: western Pakistan, South Pacific (2), Aegean sea, Illinois, Idaho, and southern California.

Volcanic Activity: Quiet

March 16th

Earthquakes: Mombasa, Kenya; Kuril Islands off Japan, Aleutian Islands, and Montana.

Volcanic Activity: Redoubt Volcano in Alaska, Bezymyanny Volcano on Soviet Kamchatka Peninsula.

March 23rd

Earthquakes: northern New Zealand (2), Reykjavik, Iceland; southern California.

Volcanic Activity: Quiet

March 30th

Earthquakes: Costa Rica, Mindanao Island in Philippines, central Japan, western Nepal, eastern Iran, and Republic of Tadzhikistan.

Volcanic Activity: Quiet

April 6th

Earthquakes: English Midlands in Britain (5.6), southern Yugoslavia, Nicaragua, Costa Rica, San Diego (5.3), central Chile, and border of Washington State and British Columbia.

Volcanic Activity: Kilauea Volcano in Hawaii.

April 13th

Earthquakes: San Francisco Bay Area/Concord, and Walnut Creek, California; central and northern Japan, New Zealand, and southern Kazakhstan.

Volcanic Activity: Quiet

April 20th

Earthquakes: San Francisco Bay Area and southern California, northwestern China/Soviet Union border, Pacific Northwest from southern British Columbia to Seattle, Washington; eastern Indonesia, central Taiwan, Manila, and southern Indiana and Ohio.

Volcanic Activity: Kilauea Volcano in Hawaii, Redoubt Volcano in Alaska.

April 27th

Earthquakes: northwestern China, southern Italy, southern islands of Japan, Chile's central coast, eastern Turkey, Yugoslavia, and central Alaska.

Volcanic Activity: Quiet

May 4th

Earthquakes: Qinghai Province in China (killed over 100 and left thousands homeless), eastern San Francisco Bay Area, southern Alaska, central Japan, Costa Rica, and Panama.

Volcanic Activity: Kilauea Volcano in Hawaii.

May 11th

Earthquakes: south of Naples, Italy; Western Australia Panama, New Mexico, Iran, and southern California.

Volcanic Activity: Kilauea Volcano in Hawaii.

May 18th

Earthquakes: New Zealand, central and southern Chile, Soviet Sakhalin Island, central Japan, southern Mexico, and Greece.

Volcanic Activity: Nevado del Ruiz Volcano in Colombia.

June 1st

Earthquakes: Acapulco, Mexico; western Iran, Portugal, West Germany, southern Sudan, Soviet Armenia, Kodiak Island. Powerful quake rocked huge area from the Baltic to the Black Sea for 45 seconds killing people in Romania, and carving destruction from Bucharest to Moscow. Damage was also in Istanbul and Greece. More than 100 people killed from a quake in Peru.

Volcanic Activity: Quiet

June 8th

Earthquakes: Mere Lava Island off Vanuatu, northeastern Peru, and buildings in Tokyo swayed for 20 seconds.

Volcanic Activity: Sabancaya Volcano in Peru, Kilauea Volcano in Hawaii.

June 15th

Earthquakes: Northeastern Peru, swarm of hundreds of quakes in Costa Rica, Istanbul, Laguna Beach, California; southern Philippines, eastern Romania, Soviet/China border, and in the Pyrenees.

Volcanic Activity: Sabancaya Volcano in Peru, Kilauea Volcano in Hawaii.

June 22nd

Earthquakes: Northwestern Iran (more than 1,900 killed), northwestern Greece, Pakistan.

Volcanic Activity: off Chile coast a newly discovered underwater volcano was responsible for earthquakes and tidal waves in region, and also was the cause of water boiling within a radius of one quarter mile.

June 29th

Earthquakes: Northern Iran, deserts of Southern California, northern Colombia, and central Italy. Underwater seismic activity off Mexico's southern coast produced a tidal wave that swept away 300 homes in the fishing village of Cuajinicuilapa.

Volcanic Activity: Quiet

July 6th

Earthquakes: Costa Rica, and San Francisco Bay Area.

Volcanic Activity: Quiet

Flooding: 4,340 homes destroyed in flooding of China's Hunan Province. 1,000 homes destroyed, and more than 70 killed in Vietnam flooding.

July 13th

Earthquakes: 150 buildings damaged with western Java quake, northern Iran, northwestern British Columbia, the Yukon, Alaska, and Sudan.

Volcanic activity: Quiet

Flooding: 33 killed, and 10,000 homeless from China floods.

July 20th

Earthquakes: Hundreds killed in worst quake in 14 years in Luzon Province in the

Philippines. Chile, Argentina, Peru, Taiwan, central Japan, southern Turkey, Pakistan, Romania, and Nebraska

Volcanic Activity: Quiet

July 27th

Earthquakes: Intense seismic activity in Philippines have triggered new geothermal activity in Abra Province where loud underground explosions have been heard. Seismologists say they were caused by steam exploding huge boulders. A moderate quake jolted Iran.

Volcanic Activity: Santiaguito Volcano in Guatemala.

August 10th

Earthquakes: 500 homes destroyed in quake striking Sino/Soviet border in Kazakhstan. Manila, northern Luzon Island, Aleutians, Greece, western Java, central Japan, northern, and southern California.

Volcanic Activity: Quiet

Flooding: 3 million people affected by flooding in northern India, and northwestern Bangladesh.

August 17th

Earthquakes: Central Ecuador, Kenai Peninsula of Alaska, San Francisco Bay Area, northeastern Taiwan, Iran, and Mexico's Michoacan coast.

Volcanic Activity: Quiet

August 24th

Earthquakes: 40,000 killed in initial tremor of Iran quake, central Japan (3 quakes at least 5.0), Kenai Peninsula of Alaska, south of San Francisco, and Sakhalin Island of Soviet Far East.

Volcanic Activity: Quiet

August 31st

Earthquakes: Jamaica, Cuba, northern coastal Chile, Italy's northern Adriatic coast, and San Francisco Bay Area.

Volcanic Activity: Quiet

Sept. 7th

Earthquakes: Iran, southeastern Cuba, southern Philippines, central Ecuador, western Yugoslavia, southern California, and Tennessee.

Volcanic Activity: Quiet

Flooding: 108 killed in Taiwan, and China's mainland. 350,000 left homeless in western Ethiopia.

Sept. 14th

Earthquakes: Acapulco, Mexico; San Francisco Bay Area, and northeastern Kentucky.

Volcanic Activity: Quiet

Flooding: 84 killed, and 52 missing in Korean flood. 80 villages disappeared under water.

Sept. 21st

Earthquakes: Northeast Caribbean, Aleutian Islands, Iceland, and eastern Oklahoma.

Volcanic Activity: Quiet

Sept. 29th

Earthquakes: New Madrid Fault (2 quakes) affecting 6 states, South African city of Welkom (4.7), northwestern Iran, central Japan, Beijing, and central California.

Volcanic Activity: Quiet

Flooding: 45 killed in Chihuahua, Mexico flood.

Oct. 5th

Earthquakes: Puerto Rico (4.5), western Japan, east-central Idaho, and East China Sea.

Volcanic Activity: Volcano near New Zealand's White Island in the Bay of Plenty sent an ash cloud 10,000 feet into the air.

Oct. 12th

Earthquakes: Lima, Peru (6.5), California aftershocks

Volcanic Activity: Quiet

Flooding: 5,000 fishermen missing off Bangladesh coast, and tens of thousands homeless.

Oct. 19th

Earthquakes: Charletonville, South Africa; Indian Ocean, northern Thailand, western Nepal, central Philippines, southeastern Iran, and central California

Volcanic Activity: Kilauea Volcano in Hawaii.

Flooding: several thousand were left homeless in southern Brazilian city of Blumenau. Northeastern India floods affected 1.5 million people, and 2,670 villages in Assam were inundated.

Geothermal Explosion: Western El Salvador geyser exploded leveling homes, and killing 13 people.

Oct. 26th

Earthquakes: Western China (6.2), northern Afghanistan in the Hindu Kush range, northern Pakistan city of Peshawar, Sierra Nevada region tremor caused rockslide that closed three roads near Yosemite National Park, Iran, Costa Rica, eastern Canada, the Chesapeake Bay region, Southern California, and southern Illinois.

Volcanic Activity: Quiet

Flooding: northern Thailand's 100 villages were submerged, 34 people, and 3,000 farm animals drowned in flooding that inundated 1.3 million acres of farmland, and 2,480 villages.

Nov. 2nd

Earthquakes: Northern Colombia, northern Chile, Guerrero coast of Mexico, and southeastern Missouri.

Volcanic Activity: Redoubt Volcano in Alaska.

Nov. 9th

Earthquakes: Southern Iran (6.6) killed more than 20 people, and left 21,000 homeless. Indonesian Province of Irian Jaya, Mariana Islands, the Aleutian Islands,, and the California/Nevada border.

Volcanic Activity: Mount St. Helens violently shook and sent an ash cloud 30,000 feet above Washington State.

Nov. 18th

Earthquakes: Sumatra Island in Indonesia that shook buildings in Thailand, and Malaysia (strongest quake in area since 1936), northern Peru, northwestern Yugoslavia, Soviet Republic of Kazakhstan, the Soviet Far East, Taiwan, Panama, South Carolina, and Oklahoma

Volcanic Activity: Quiet

Flooding: Orissa, India flooding left 150 dead, and sparked a cholera outbreak. 20,00 left homeless in Honduras flood.

Nov. 30th

Earthquakes: Yugoslavia's Adriatic coast experienced a strong tremor; Australia's Northern Territory, Cyprus, western Colombia, and central Alaska.

Volcanic Activity: Mount Kelud Volcano in east Java killed 4 people.

Dec. 7th

Earthquakes: Soviet Republic of Kirgiziya (destroyed 1,000 homes, and left 3,000 homeless); Peruvian Andes, coastal Tunisia, and eastern Yugoslavia.

Volcanic Activity: Quiet

Flooding: 50,000 homeless in Honduras floods. Avalanches and mud slides killed 16 people. 500 homes were washed away west of Dhaka, Bangladesh.

Dec. 14th

Earthquakes: Violent tremor rocked Sicily; Azores, Kirgiziya, Taiwan, northern Tokyo and southern Alaska.

Volcanic Activity: Quiet

Dec. 21st

Earthquakes: Powerful tremor jolted coastal Iranian Province of Bushehr killing at least 20 people, and causing landslides. Taiwan experienced over 1,600 aftershocks of two strong quakes that struck the island Dec. 13-14. Southern, and central Panama, coastal Peru, northern Armenia, northwestern Indiana, and two in central California.

Volcanic Activity: Quiet

Dec. 28th

Earthquakes: Greece, Bulgaria, Yugoslavia, Romania, Taiwan, Costa Rica (destroyed 100 homes), Philippine Island of Luzon, Iran, Soviet Republic of Georgia, Washington State, and near Yellowstone National Park.

Volcanic Activity: Quiet

Flooding: Guam declared a disaster area to help rebuild 2,000 homes destroyed.

During 1991 week ending:

Jan. 4th

Earthquakes: Papua New Guinea's New Britain Island, swarm of at least two dozen quakes rattled western Nevada, Soviet Republic of Azerbaijan, Japan's central Pacific coast, southern Quebec, Mexico's Jalisco coast, southern Alaska, and Washington State.

Volcanic Activity: Quiet

Flooding: 500 families homeless, and 6 killed in Peru's central highlands flood, tens of thousands left homeless in northeastern Mexico flood, flooding caused hundreds to flee in Indiana, Ohio, and West Virginia flooding. Flooding caused 100 people to flee their homes in Montreal.

Jan. 11th

Earthquakes: Mandalay city in Burma (quake so powerful it overloaded seismic instruments in neighboring Thailand, and rocked skyscrapers 800 miles away in Bangkok. Strong tremor jolted Lima, Peru.

Volcanic Activity: Quiet

Flooding: Northeastern Australia (worst flooding since 1954).

Jan. 25th

Earthquakes: Managua, Nicaragua; southern Alaska, Rat Island of the Aleutian Islands, Iran, northern Burma, and Taiwan.

Volcanic Activity: Mt. Hekla Volcano in Iceland erupted for first time since 1981.

Feb. 1st

Earthquakes: New Zealand's South Island (2 quakes), Deception Island along the Antarctic Peninsula (7.0) that generated a tsunami. Mexico's Guerrero State, eastern Indonesia, Japan's Honshu coast, Tadzhikistan, and near Cleveland, Ohio.

Volcanic Activity: Keireki Volcano near the Azerbaija capital of Baku.

Feb. 8th

Earthquakes: More than 1,000 killed in Himalayan quake in Pakistan, and Afghanistan. Large-scale destruction of homes in Soviet Republics of Tadzhikistan, and Uzbekistan to northern Pakistan where 40 lives were lost to avalanches. Other quakes this week were felt in coastal Chile, the Mexican state of Chihuahua, northern Alaska, and on California's Big Sur coast.

Volcanic Activity: Quiet

Flooding: southeastern Iran (worst flooding of the century destroyed 168 villages, and left at least 50,000 homeless). Floods in seven Ecuadoran provinces killed 14 people, and destroyed thousands of crop acres.

Feb. 15th

Earthquakes: Solomon Islands, Istanbul, Guam, Argentina's Santiago del Estero province, southwestern Iran, and the Arkansas/Tennessee border.

Volcanic Activity: Unzen Volcano of Japan spewed smoke 1,500 feet into the air near Nagasaki. The Peteroa Volcano in Chile erupted.

Feb. 22nd

Earthquakes: Sichuan Province in China, Greece, southern British Columbia, southern Alaska, the Bering Sea, New Zealand's South Island, and southern Philippines.

Volcanic Activity: Quiet

March 1st

Earthquakes: 120 homes destroyed in China's Zinjiang Region near the Soviet border. Pakistan, northern Italy, Albania, Vancouver Island, and along the

Peru/Brazil border.

Volcanic Activity: Quiet

March 8th

Earthquakes: Strong quake hit the city of Bengkulu in southern Sumatra; northern Chile, Costa Rica, Tokyo vicinity, and between San Diego and Tijuana.

Volcanic Activity: Quiet

March 15th

Earthquakes: Strong quake in Kalgoorlie, Australia; eastern Siberia, southern Iran, eastern Columbia, Taiwan, northern Chile, central Alaska and the San Francisco Bay area.

Flooding: 750 villages in southern Iran, 472 people dead, and thousands homeless from flash flooding in East African nation of Malawi, floods struck fertile valleys and closed roads in Morocco between Rabat and Tangier.

March 22nd

Earthquakes: Crete (along the Greece-Albania border) measuring 4.8 and 5.1, Alaska measuring 5.1), and 3.8 in Virginia

Flooding: 20 people died in flooding in San Paulo, Brazil where flood waters surged 6 feet high in the worst flooding in the city's history. Heavy tropical rainstorms paralyzed Hawaii's Oahu where shores were cut off from Honolulu by mud, boulders, and rain-swollen streams. Torrential rains flooded parts of Pretoria, Johannesburg, western Transvaal, and western Orange Free State in Southern Africa.

Hail: 60 people and 4,500 farm animals killed in freak hailstorms in Hunan province in China.

Drought: China's capital Beijing is suffering from its worst crop drought in 30 years causing 60% of the wheat crop to be seriously threatened.

April 5th

Earthquakes: S Burma, S Thailand, central Alaska, Panama, central and southern Mexico and the Peru-Ecuador border.

Volcanic Activity: Taal Volcano S of Manila.

April 12th

Earthquakes: Peru and northeastern India

Volcanic Activity: 3,000 people fled their homes near two Philippine volcanoes. 1,318 people fled their homes after Mt Pinatubo in Zambales began spewing steam after 520 years of inactivity.

April 19th

Earthquakes: Okinawa, N Afghanistan, Washington State, S Indiana, metropolitan New York and California.

Volcanic Activity: Mt Colima spewed lava, rock and plumes of ash in its most violent eruption since 1913.

April 26th

Earthquakes: Worldwide seismic activity rose sharply this week. Costa Rica and Panama (7.4) where 77 people died and thousands were left homeless. Anatolia, Turkey (5.0), Philippines (5.6), S central Alaska (5.0), Lima, Peru (4.5), Quito, Ecuador (4.2), Hokkaido Island in Japan (5.6), Soviet Frontier (5.0), Dominican Republic (4.2), Utah (4.0), West Virginia (3.5) and California (4.1) and (3.6).

Volcanic Activity: Fernandina Island in the Galapagos, Mt Pinatubo NW of Manila showing signs of increased activity.

Nuclear: Nuclear Regulatory Commission and Department of Energy's data show that in 1990, the 111 licensed nuclear plants in the U.S. suffered 177 automatic shutdowns, 1,921 breakdowns of systems, 894 violations of safety regulations, 125 activations of emergency core-cooling or emergency power systems, 38 NRC-designated "significant events" that potentially threatened public safety and 404 failures of reactor safety systems involving multiple component breakdowns.

May 3rd

Earthquakes: Soviet Georgia (7.1) killed more than 360 people and 80% of buildings damaged in Dzhava, Oni, Ambrolauri and Sachkhere. Lima, Peru (5.3), Yugoslavia (5.7), central Afghanistan (4.9), southern Philippines (5.3), S central Alaska (5.2) and Arizona-Utah order (4.0).

Floods: 20 inches of rainfall caused widespread flooding that affected thousands of homes in Louisiana and S Mississippi.

Tropical Storms: 145 mile/hr winds and 20 foot waves inundated Bangladesh leaving over 150,000 people dead.

Source: EARTHWEEK

Phoenix File IX
Toxic Waste Sites of the United States

The information in this section relates directly to the Environmental Protection Agency's (EPA) most critically contaminated U.S. sites. These sites have been prioritized according to the highest hazard risk and are designated sites for the government's National Priorities List (NPL). These are specifically targeted for the Superfund Cleanup Project. Sources for this section have been taken from the EPA National Priorities List on Hazardous Waste Sites.

Types of Toxic and Hazardous Contamination

TOXIN	SITES CONTAINING RAW MATERIAL	SITES CONTAINING DERIVATIVES	TOTAL SITES
Petrochemicals			
Acetylene	0	56	56
Benzene	19	113	132
Butane	0	8	8
Butylene	0	8	8
Butadiene	0	0	0
Ethylene	0	97	97
Methane	1	44	45
Napthalene	2	0	2
Propylene	0	14	14
Toluene	23	30	53
Xylene	12	6	18
Waste Oil	35	0	35
Inorganics			
Ammonia	6	22	28
Antimony & compounds	1	0	1
Arsenic & compounds	10	0	10
Barium sulfide	0	0	0
Berylium & compounds	0	0	0
Bromine	0	2	2
Cadmium	5	0	5
Chlorine & compounds	5	197	202
Chromium & compounds	18	1	19
Cobalt	1	0	1
Copper	6	1	7
Hydrogen flouride	2	1	3
Lead & compounds	11	0	11
Mercury	16	0	16
Nickel	4	0	4
Nitric acid	1	0	1
Phosphorous & compounds	6	8	14
Potassium hydroxid	1	0	1
Selenium	1	0	1

TOXIN	SITES CONTAINING RAW MATERIAL	SITES CONTAINING DERIVATIVES	TOTAL SITES
Sodium hydroxide	0	39	39
Sulfuric acid	3	35	38
Stannic(oud) chlorides	0	0	0
Zinc	9	2	11

Hazardous Materials and their Precursors

MATERIALS FOUND ON SITE	PETROCHEMICAL AND INORGANIC CHEMICAL PRECURSORS
Acetic Acid	Butane, Ethylene, Methane, Propane
Acetone	Benzene, Propylene
Aldrin	Acetylene, Chlorine, Pentane
Alkyl Benzene Sulfonate	Benzene, Propylene, Sulfuric acid
Allyl Ether	Chlorine, Copper, Sodium hydroxide Sulfuric acid, Propylene
Asbestos	Natural mineral
Benzene Hexachloride	Benzene, Chlorine
Carbofuran	Acetic acid, Ethylene, Chlorine, Methane
Carbon Tetrachloride	Chlorine, Methane, Propane
Chloranilic Acid	Benzene, Chlorine
Chloroform	Chlorine, Methane
Chromic Acid	Chromium, Sulfuric acid
Cumene	Benzene, Phosphoric acid, Propylene
Cyanide	Ammonia, Methane
Cyclohexamine	Ammonia, Benzene, Sulfuric acid
Dibromochloropropane	Bromine, Chlorine, Propylene
DDT	Benzene, Chlorine, Sulfuric acid
DEF	Butylene, Chlorine, Phosphorus, Sodium, Hydrogen sulfide
Dichlorobenzene	Chlorine, Benzene
Dieldrin	Acetylene, Chlorine, Pentane
Dichloroethane	Chlorine, Crude oil, Natural gas
Dichloroethylene	Chlorine, Ethylene
Dimethyl Sulfide	Hydrogen sulfide, Methane
Dioxane	Ethylene, Sodium hydroxide
Dioxin	Acetic acid, Chlorine, Phenol, Sodium hydroxide
Endosulfan	Butylene, Chlorine, Pentane, Toluene, Sulfuric acid
Endrin	Acetylene, Ethylene, Chlorine, Pentane, Hydrochloric acid, Sodium hydroxide
Ethanol	Ethylene
Ethylbenzene	Benzene, Coal, Ethylene, Xylene
Ethyl Acetate	Butane, Ethylene
Ethylene Dibromide	Bromine, Ethylene
Ethylene Glycol	Ethylene, Sodium hydroxide
Freon	Chlorine, Ethylene, Methane, Hydrogen flouride
Heptane	Crude Oil
Heptachlor	Acetylene, Chlorine, Pentane
Hexachlorobenzene	Benzene, Chlorine
Hexachlorobutadiene	Butylene, Hydrochloric acid
Hexachlorocyclopentadiene	Chlorine, Pentane
Hexane	Crude oil
Hydrogen Sulfide	Hydrogen, Sulfur

MATERIALS FOUND ON SITE	PETROCHEMICAL AND INORGANIC CHEMICAL PRECURSORS
Kepone	Aluminum, Chlorine, Pentane
Lindane	Benzene, Chlorine
Lithium	Natural metal
Methacrylic Acid	Ammonia, Benzene, Propylene
Methane Gas	Natural gas
Methyl Ethyl Ketone	n Butane, Butylene
Methylene Chloride	Chlorine, Methane
Mirex	Aluminum, Chlorine, Pentane
O-Nitoaniline	Ammonia, Benzene, Sulfuric acid
Parathion	Ethanol, Chlorine, Methane, Phosphorus, Ammonia, Sodium
Polybrominated Biphenyls	Benzene, Bromine
Polychlorinated Biphenyls	Benzene, Chlorine
Pentachlorophenol	Benzene, Chlorine, Phenol, Toluene
Phenol	Benzene, Sodium hydroxide, Sulfuric acid, Toluene
Sodium	Natural metal
Sodium Aluminum Hydroxide	Aluminum ore, Sodium hydroxide
Styrene	Benzene, Ethylene, Xylene
Tetrachlorobenzene	Benzene, Chlorine
Tetrachloroethylene	Ethylene, Chlorine
Trichloroethane	Ethylene, Chlorine
Trichloroethylene	Acetylene, Chlorine, Ethylene
Trimethylsilanol	Ammonia, Chlorine, Bromine, Methane
Tris (Tromethamine)	Ammonia, Methane
Vinyl Chloride	Acetylene, Ethylene, Hydrochloric acid, Sodium hydroxide
Zinc Chloride	Chlorine, Hydrochloric acid, Zinc

OTHER MATERIALS

Acids	Nitric acid, Chromic acid, Sulfuric acid
Alkaline Wastes	Sodium hydroxide, Potassium hydroxide
Aromatic Hydrocarbons	Benzene, Butylene, Butadiene, Napthalene, etc.
Chlorinated Organics	Benzene, Chlorine
Coal Tars	Napthalene, Toluene, Benzene
Explosives	Methane, Ammonia, Nitric acid
Fly Ash	Mineral salts, Heavy metals
Herbicides	Arsenic, Benzene, Chlorine
Nitrates	Nitric acid, Ammonia
Pesticides	Arsenic, Benzene, Chlorine
Petrochemicals	
Polynuclear Organics	Benzene, Napthalene, Toluene
Solvents	Butylene, Butadiene, Napthalene, Benzene
Toxic Metals	Cadmium, Chromium, Lead, Mercury
Uranium Radiation	Uranium
Volatile Organics	Methane, Acetylene, Benzene, Butane
Waste Oil	Napthalene, Toluene, Xylene

NATIONAL PRIORITIES LIST SITES PER STATE/TERRITORY

State/Territory	Current NPL	Proposed Non-Fed	Fed	Total
New Jersey	85	8	2	95
California	19	34	7	60
Michigan	47	12	0	59
New York	29	28	1	58
Pennsylvania	39	9	1	49
Florida	29	6	0	35
Minnesota	23	11	0	34
Ohio	22	6	0	28
Texas	10	13	2	25
Washington	13	7	3	23
Wisconsin	20	3	0	23
Illinois	11	8	3	22
Indiana	17	4	0	21
Massachusetts	16	5	0	21
Missouri	6	7	2	15
Colorado	9	3	2	14
New Hampshire	10	1	0	11
South Carolina	10	0	0	10
Virginia	4	5	1	10
Alabama	7	0	2	9
Delaware	8	0	1	9
Kentucky	7	2	0	9
Utah	1	5	3	9
Montana	5	3	0	8
Puerto Rico	8	0	0	8
Tennessee	6	1	1	8
Arkansas	6	1	0	7
Kansas	4	3	0	7
North Carolina	3	4	0	7
Rhode Island	6	1	0	7
Arizona	5	1	0	6
Connecticut	6	0	0	6
Hawaii	0	6	0	6
Iowa	3	3	3	6
Louisiana	5	0	1	6
Maine	5	0	1	6
Maryland	85	8	2	95
West Virginia	19	34	7	60
Georgia	47	12	0	59
Oregon	29	28	1	58
Idaho	39	9	1	49
Nebraska	29	6	0	35
New Mexico	23	11	0	34
Oklahoma	22	6	0	28
Mississippi	10	13	2	25
Vermont	13	7	3	23
American Samoa	20	3	0	23

State/Territory	Current NPL	Proposed Non-Fed	Fed	Total
Commonwealth of Marianas	3	3	0	6
	4	2	0	6
Guam	3	1	1	5
North Dakota	3	1	1	5
South Dakota	4	0	0	4
Trust Territories	0	3	1	4
Wyoming	4	0	0	4
Alaska	3	1	0	4
District of Columbia	1	1	0	3
Nevada	2	0	0	2
Virgin Islands	1	0	0	1
Totals	538	212	36	786

EPA National Priorities List
of Toxic Sites by State

Proposed Sites are classified in Group Numbers

(* signifies state's highest priority site)

SITE / POSITION ON NPL

ALABAMA

Ciba-Geigy Corp. (McIntosh Plant) / 124
McIntosh

Mowbray Engineering Co. / 118
Greenville

Olin Corp. (McIntosh Plant) / 320
McIntosh

Perdido Ground Water
Contamination / 511
Perdido

Stauffer Chemical Co. (Cold Creek Plant)
/ 204
Bucks

Stauffer Chemical Co. (Lemoyne Plant) /
467
Axis

Triana/Tennessee River (Redstone Arsenal) / 31
Limestone/Morgan Counties

Proposed
Alabama Army Ammunition Plant /
Group 8
Childersburg

Anniston Army Depot / Group 3
Anniston

ALASKA (O)

AMERICAN SAMOA

Taputimu Farm * / 92
Island of Tutuila

ARIZONA

Indian Bend Wash Area / 280
Scottsdale/Tempe/Phoenix

Litchfield Airport Area / 217
Goodyear/Avondale

Mountain View Mobile Home Estates* /
91
Globe

19th Avenue Landfill / 115
Phoenix

Tucson International Airport Area / 68
Tucson

Proposed
Motorola, Inc. (52nd St Plant) / Group 6
Phoenix

ARKANSAS

Cecil Lindsey / 395
Newport

Frit Industries / 325
Walnut Ridge

Gurley Pit / 310
Edmondson

Industrial Waste Control / 509
Fort Smith

Mid-South Wood Products / 219
Mena

Vertac, Inc. / 18
Jacksonville

Proposed
Midland Products
Ola/Birta

CALIFORNIA

Aerojet General Corp / 110
Rancho Cordova

Atlas Asbestos Mine / 220
Fresno County

Celtor Chemical Works / 510
Hoopa

Coalinga Asbestos Mine / 221
Coalinga

Coast Wood Preserving / 233
Ukiah

Del Norte County Pesticide Storage Area
/ 389
Crescent City

Iron Mountain Mine / 70
Redding

Jibboom Junkyard / 525
Sacramento

Koppers Co., Inc. (Oroville Plant) / 450
Oroville

Liquid Gold Oil Corp / 246
Richmond

McColl / 287
Fullerton

MGM Brakes / 421
Cloverdale

Purity Oil Sales, Inc. / 247
Malaga

San Gabriel Valley (Area 1) / 281
El Monte

San Gabriel Valley (Area 2) / 282
Baldwin Park Area

San Gabriel Valley (Area 3) / 530
Alhambra

San Gabriel Valley (Area 4) / 531
La Puente

Selma Treating Co / 176
Selma

Stringfellow * / 32
Glen Avon Heights

Proposed
Advanced Micro Devices, Inc. / Group 8
Sunnyvale

Aliviso Dumping Areas / Group 5
Aliviso

Applied Materials / Group 10
Santa Clara

Beckman Instruments (Porterville Plant) /
Group 9
Porterville

Castle Air Force Base / Group 8
Merced

Fairchild Camera & Instrument Corp /
Group 10
Mountain View

Fairchild Camera & Instrument Corp /
Group 8
South San Jose

Firestone Tire & Rubber Co. / Group 11
Salinas

FMC Corp / Group 7
Fresno

Hewlett-Packard / Group 11
Palo Alto

Intel Corp / Group 10
Mountain View

Intel Corp / Group 10
Santa Clara

Intel Magnetics / Group 10
Santa Clara

IBM Corp / Group 11
San Jose

J. H. Baxter Co / Group 9
Weed

Lawrence Livermore National Laboratory
(USDOE) / Group 6
Livermore

Lorentz Barrel & Drum Co / Group 9
San Jose

Louisiana-Pacific Corp / Group 9
Oroville

Marley Cooling Tower Co / Group 10
Stockton

Mather Air Force Base (AC&W Disposal
Site) / Group 11
Sacramento

McClellan Air Force Base (Ground Water
Contamination) / Group 2
Sacramento

Monolithic Memories, Inc / Group 6
Sunnyvale

Montrose Chemical Corp / Group 9
Torrance

National Semiconductor Corp / Group 8
Santa Clara

Norton Air Force Base / Group 7
San Bernardino

Operating Industries, Inc., Landfill /
Group 4
Monterey Park

Precision Monolithic, Inc / Group 10
Santa Clara

Raytheon Corp / Group 8
Mountain View

Sacramento Army Depot / Group 5
Sacramento

San Fernando Valley (Area l) / Group 6
Los Angeles

San Fernando Valley (Area 2) / Group 6
Los Angeles/Glendale

San Fernando Valley (Area 3) / Group 6
Glendale

San Fernando Valley (Area 4) / Group 8
Los Angeles

Sharpe Army Depot / Group 6
Lathrop

Signetics, Inc / Group 10
Sunnyvale

Southern Pacific Transportation Co /
Group 7
Roseville

Teledyne Semiconductor / Group 6
Mountain View

Thompson-Hayward Chemical Co /
Group 6
Fresno

Van Waters & Rogers, Inc / Group 3
San Jose

Westinghouse Electrical Corp / Group 7
Sunnyvale

Coecon Corp/Rhone-Poulenc, Inc /
Group 10
East Palo Alto

COLORADO

Broderick Wood Products / 410
Denver

California Gulch / 72
Leadville

Central City-Clear Creek / 147
Idaho Springs

Denver Radium Site / 239
Denver

Lincoln Park / 487
Canon City

Lowry Landfill / 180
Arapahoe County

Marshall Landfill* / 81
Boulder County

Sand Creek Industrial / 36
Commerce City

Woodbury Chemical Co / 229
Commerce City

Proposed
Eagle Mine / Group 4
Minturn/Redcliff

Rocky Flats Plant (USDOE) / Group 1
Golden

Rocky Mountain Arsenal / Group 2
Adams County

Smuggler Mountain / Group 5
Aspen

Uravan Uranium Project (Union Carbide Corp) Group 5
Uravan

COMMONWEALTH OF THE MARIANAS

PCB Warehouse / 100
Saipan

CONNECTICUT

Beacon Heights Landfill / 203
Beacon Falls

Kellogg-Deering Well Field / 316
Norwalk

Laurel Park, Inc.* / 80
Naugatuck Borough

Old Southington Landfill / 113
Southington

Solvents Recovery Service of New England / 228
Southington

Yaworski Waste Lagoon / 374
Canterbury

DELAWARE

Army Creek Landfill / 9
New Castle County

Delaware City PVC Plant / 504
Delaware City

Delaware Sand & Gravel Landfill / 208
New Castle County

Harvey & Knott Drum, Inc / 498
Kirkwood

New Castle Spill / 339
New Castle County

New Castle Steel / 507
New Castle County

Tybouts Corner Landfill* / 2
New Castle County

Wildcat Landfill / 501
Dover

Proposed
Dover Air Force Base / Group 8
Dover

DISTRICT OF COLUMBIA (0)

FLORIDA

Alpha Chemical Corp / 249
Galloway

American Creosote Works / 50
Pensacola

Brown Wood Preserving / 222
Live Oak

Cabot/Koppers / 376
Gainesville

Coleman-Evans Wood Preserving Co / 213
Whitehouse

Davie Landfill / 64
Davie

Florida Steel Corp / 216
Indiantown

Gold Coast Oil Corp / 66
Miami

Hipps Road Landfill / 479
Duval County

Hollingsworth Solderless Terminal Co / 235
Fort Lauderdale

Kassauf-Kimerling Battery / 125
Tampa

Miami Drum Services / 120
Miami

Munisport Landfill / 466
North Miami

Northwest 58th St Landfill / 167
Hialeah

Parramore Surplus / 361
Mount Pleasant

Pepper Steel & Alloys, Inc / 480

Medley

Pickettville Road Landfill / 252
Jacksonville

Pioneer Sand Co / 138
Warrington

Reeves Southeastern Galvanizing Corp / 46
Tampa

Sapp Battery Salvage / 187
Cottondale

Schuylkill Metals Corp / 42
Plant City

Sherwood Medical Industries / 319
Deland

62nd Street Dump / 170
Tampa

Taylor Road Landfill / 149
Seffner

Tower Chemical Co / 240
Clermont

Tri-City Oil Conservationist, Inc / 327
Tampa

Varsol Spill / 237
Miami

Whitehouse Oil Pits / 132
Whitehouse

Zellwood Ground Water Contamination / 142
Zellwood

Proposed
City Industries, Inc. / Group 10
Orlando

Davidson Lumber Co / Group 9
South Miami

Dubose Oil Products Co / Group 9
Cantonment

Montco Research Products, Inc /
Group 11
Hollister

Peak Oil Co/Bay Drum Co / Group 2
Tampa

Pratt & Whitney Aircraft/United
Technologies Corp / Group 4
West Palm Beach

GEORGIA

Hercules 009 Landfill / 133
Brunswick

Monsanto Corp / 392
Augusta

Olin Corp (Areas 1,2,&4) / Group 5
Augusta

Powersville Site / 398
Peach County

Proposed
Robins Air Force Base / Group 3
Houston County

GUAM

Ordot Landfill* / 96
Ordot

HAWAII

Proposed
Kunia Wells I / Group 7
Oahu

Kunia Wells II/ Group 7
Oahu

Mililani Wells/ Group 6
Oahu

Waiawa Shaft / Group 6
Oahu

Waipahu Wells / Group 7
Oahu

Waipio Heights Wells II / Group 9
Oahu

IDAHO

Arroom (Drexler Enterprises) / 523
Rathdrum

Bunker Hill Mining & Metallurgical/ 107
Smelterville

Pacific Hide & Fur Recycling Co / 273
Pocatello

Union Pacific Railroad Co / 122
Pocatello

ILLINOIS

A & F Materials Reclaiming, Inc / 102
Greenup

Acme Solvent Reclaiming, Inc / 478
Morristown

Belvidere Municipal Landfill / 538
Belvidere

Byron Salvage Yard / 442
Byron

Cross Brothers Pail Recycling / 285
Pembroke Township

Galesburg/Koppers Co / 418
Galesburg

Johns-Manville Corp / 342
Waukegan

LaSalle Electric Utilities / 284
LaSalle

Outboard Marine Corp* / 82
Waukegan

Velsicol Chemical Corp (Illinois) / 178
Marshall

Wauconda Sand & Gravel / 126
Wauconda

Wauconda

Proposed
Joliet Army Ammunition Plant /
Group 10
Joliet

Kerr-McGee (Kress Creek/West Branch
of Dupage River) / Group 7
DuPage County

Kerr-McGee (Reed-Keppler Park) /
Group 7
West Chicago

Kerr-McGee (Residential Areas) / Group
7
West Chicago/Dupage County

Kerr-McGee (Sewage Treatment Plant) /
Group 9
West Chicago

NL Industries/Taracorp Lead Smelter /
Group 7
Granite City

Pagel's Pit / Group 6
Rockford

Petersen Sand & Gravel / Group 7
Libertyville

Sangamo Electric Dump/Crab Orchard
National Wildlife Refuge (USDOI) /
Group 1
Carterville

Savanna Army Depot Activity / Group 6
Savanna

Sheffield (U.S. Ecology, Inc) / Group 9
Sheffield

INDIANA

American Chemical Service, Inc / 414
Griffith

Bennett Stone Quarry / 465
Bloomington

Envirochem Corp / 210
Zionsville

Fisher-Calo / 137
LaPorte

Lake Sandy Jo (M&M Landfill) / 341
Gary

Lemon Lane Landfill / 522
Bloomington

Main Street Well Field / 265
Eklhart

Marion (Bragg) Dump / 407
Marion

Midco I / 211
Gary

Neal's Landfill / 255
Bloomington

Ninth Avenue Dump / 309
Gary

Northside Sanitary Landfill, Inc / 215
Zionsville

Poer Farm / 363
Hancock County

Reilly Tar & Chemical Corp / 437
Indianapolis

Seymour Recycling Corp* / 53
Seymour

Wayne Waste Oil / 272
Columbia City

Wedzeb Enterprises, Inc / 488
Lebanon

Proposed
Fort Wayne Reduction Dump / Group 6
Fort Wayne

International Minerals & Chemical Corp
(Terre Haute East Plant) Group 4

Terre Haute

MIDCO II / (Group 4)
Gary

Neal's Dump / Group 8
Spencer

IOWA

Aidex Corp* / 90
Council Bluffs

Des Moines TCE / 274
Des Moines

Labounty Site / 8
Charles City

Proposed
Chemplex Co / Group 3
Clinton/Camanche

U.S. Nameplate Co / Group 10
Mount Vernon

Vogel Paint & Wax Co / Group 10
Sioux City

KANSAS

Arkansas City Dump* / 99
Arkansas City

Cherokee County / 56
Cherokee County

Doepke Disposal / 191
Johnson County

Johns' Sludge Pond / 388
Wichita

Proposed
Big River Sand Co / Group 10
Wichita

National Industrial Environmental Services/ Group 7
Furley

Strother Field Industrial Park / Group 10
Cowley County

KENTUCKY

A.L. Taylor (Valley of the Drums)* / 94
Brooks

Airco / 459
Calvert City

B.F. Goodrich / 461
Calvert City

Distler Brickyard / 231
Jefferson County

Lee's Lane Landfill / 324
Louisville

Newport Dump / 359
Newport

Proposed
Maxey Flats Nuclear Disposal / Group 10
Hillsboro

Smith's Farm / Group 10
Brooks

LOUISIANA

Bayou Bonfouca / 517
Slidell

Bayou Sorrell / 422
Bayou Sorrell

Cleve Reber / 177
Sorrento

Old Inger Oil Refinery* / 77
Darrow

Petro-Processors of LA, Inc. / 290
Scotlandville

Proposed
Louisiana Army Ammunition Plant / Group 11

Doyline

MAINE
McKin Co / 33
Gray

O'Connor Co / 481
Augusta

Pinette's Salvage Yard / 438
Washburn

Saco Tannery Waste Pits / 251
Saco

Winthrop Landfill / 394
Winthrop

Proposed
Brunswick Naval Air Station / Group 5
Brunswick

MARYLAND

Limestone Road /505
Cumberland

Middletown Road Dump /520
Annapolis

Sand, Gravel & Stone /293
Elkton

Proposed
Kane & Lombard Street Drums /Group 11
Baltimore

Mid-Atlantic Wood Preservers, Inc /Group 6
Harmans

Southern Maryland Wood Treating /Group 9
Hollywood

MASSACHUSETTS

Baird & McGuire / 14
Holbrook

Cannon Engineering Corp (CEC) /317
Bridgewater

Charles-George Reclamation Trust Landfill / 194
Tyngsborough

Groveland Wells / 300
Groveland

Hocomonco Pond / 230
Westborough

Industri-Plex / 5
Woburn

Iron Horse Park / 253
Billerica

New Bedford Site* / 76
New Bedford

Nyanza Chemical Waste Dump / 11
Ashland

Plymouth Harbor/Canon Engineering Corp / 106
Plymouth

PSC Resources / 332
Palmer

Re-Solve, Inc / 183
Dartmouth

Silresim Chemical Corp / 257
Lowell

Sullivan's Ledge / 463
New Bedford

W.R. Grace & Co., Inc / 38
Acton

Wells G&H / 258
Woburn

Proposed
Haverhill Municipal Landfill / Group 11
Haverhill

Norwood PCBS / Group 11

Norwood

Rose Disposal Pit / Group 10
Lanesboro

Salem Acres / Group 9
Salem

Shpack Landfill / Group 11
Norton/Attleboro

MICHIGAN

Anderson Development Co / 495
Adrian

Auto Ion Chemicals, Inc / 474
Kalamazoo

Berlin & Farro / 13
Swartz Creek

Burrows Sanitation / 502
Hartford

Butterworth #2 Landfill / 106
Grand Rapids

Cemetery Dump / 434
Rose Center

Charlevoix Municipal Well / 349
Charlevoix

Chem Central / 343
Wyoming Township

Clare Water Supply / 337
Clare

Cliff/Dow Dump / 429
Marquette

Duell & Gardner Landfill / 423
Dalton Township

Electrovoice / 405
Buchanan

Forest Waste Products / 333

Otisville

G&H Landfill / 171
Utica

Grand Traverse Overall Supply Co / 399
Greilickville

Gratiot County Landfill* / 74
St. Louis

Hedblum Industries / 364
Oscoda

Ionia City Landfill / 486
Ionia

K&L Avenue Landfill / 346
Oshtemo Township

Kentwood Landfill / 404
Kentwood

Liquid Disposal, Inc / 24
Utica

Mason County Landfill / 433
Pere Marquette Township

McGraw Edison Corp / 458
Albion

Metamora Landfill / 400
Metamora

Northernaire Plating / 58
Cadillac

Novaco Industries / 344
Temperance

Organic Chemicals, Inc / 462
Grandville

Ossineke Ground Water Contamination /
448
Ossineke

Ott/Story/Cordova / 128
Dalton Township

Packaging Corp of America / 143
Filer City
Petoskey Municipal Well Field / 261
Petoskey

Rasmussen's Dump / 483
Green Oak Township

Rose Township Dump / 155
Rose Township

Shiawassee River / 496
Howell

Southwest Ottawa County Landfill / 321
Park Township

Sparta Landfill / 477
Sparta Township

Spartan Chemical Co / 294
Wyoming

Spiegelberg Landfill / 119
Green Oak Township

Springfield Township Dump / 139
Davisburg

Sturgis Municipal Wells / 278
Sturgis

SCA Independent Landfill / 420
Muskegon Heights

Tar Lake / 179
Mancelona Township

U.S. Aviex / 451
Howard Township

Velsicol Chemical Corp / 134
St. Louis

Verona Well Field / 202
Battle Creek

Wash King Laundry / 313
Pleasant Plains Township

Whitehall Municipal Wells / 401

Whitehall

Proposed
Avenue "E" Ground Water Contamination / Group 10
Traverse City

E.I. DuPont De Nemours & Co., Inc / Group 7
Montague

Lacks Industries, Inc / Group 9
Grand Rapids

Lenawee Disposal Service, Inc., Landfill / Group 8
Adrian

Michigan Disposal Service (Cork St Landfill) / Group 8
Kalamazoo

Motor Wheel, Inc. / Group 4
Lansing

North Bronson Industrial Area / Group 9
Bronson

Roto-Finish Co., Inc / Group 7
Kalamazoo

South Macomb Disposal Authority (Landfills #9 and (A) / Group 9
Macomb Township

Thermo-Chem, Inc / Group 3
Muskegon

Torch Lake / Group 5
Houghton County

Waste Management of Michigan / Group 8
Holland

MINNESOTA

Arrowhead Refinery Co / 243
Hermantown

Boise Cascade/Onan/Medtronics / 165

Fridley

Burlington Northern / 205
Brainerd/Baxter

FMC Corp / 17
Fridley

General Mills/Henkel Corp / 385
Minneapolis

Joslyn Manufacturing & Supply Co / 238
Brooklyn Center

Koppers Coke / 105
St. Paul

Lehillier/Mankato Site / 266
Lehillier/Mankato

MacGillis & Gibbs Co/Bell Lumber &
Pole Co / 181
New Brighton

Morris Arsenic Dump / 340
Morris

New Brighton/Arden Hills / 43
New Brighton

Nutting Truck & Caster Co / 354
Faribault

NL Industries/Taracorp/
Golden Auto/ 315
St. Louis Park

Oakdale Dump / 101
Oakdale

Perham Arsenic Site / 348
Perham

Reilly Tar & Chemical Corp / 39
St. Louis Park

South Andover Site / 402
Andover

St. Louis River Site / 473
St. Louis County

St. Regis Paper Co / 130
Cass Lake

Union Scrap Iron & Metal Co / 262
Minneapolis

Washington County Landfill / 279
Lake Elmo

Waste Disposal Engineering / 156
Andover

Whittaker Corp / 314
Minneapolis

Proposed
Adrian Municipal Well Field /Group 10
Adrian

Agate Lake Scrapyard /Group 10
Fairview Township

Koch Refining Co/N-Ren Corp /Group 10
Pine Bend

Kummer Sanitary Landfill /Group 6
Bemidji

Kurt Manufacturing Co /Group 10
Fridley

Long Prairie Ground Water Contamination /Group 10
Long Prairie

Oak Grove Sanitary Landfill /Group 5
Oak Grove Township

Olmsted County Sanitary Landfill /Group 10
Oronoco

Pine Bend Sanitary Landfill/Crosby
American Demolition Landfill / Group 3
Dakota County

University of Minnesota (Rosemount
Research Center) / Group 5
Rosemount

Windom Dump / Group 7
Windom

MISSISSIPPI

Flowood Site* / 97
Flowood

Proposed
Newsom Brothers/Old Reichhold
Chemicals, Inc / Group 5
Columbia

MISSOURI

Ellisville Site* / 86
Ellisville

Fulbright Landfill / 303
Springfield

Minker/Stout/Romaine Creek / 373
Imperial

Quail Run Mobile Manor / Group 11
Gray Summit

Shenandoah Stables / 516
Moscow Mills

Syntex Facility / 241
Verona

Times Beach Site / 312
Times Beach

Proposed
Bee Cee Manufacturing Co / Group 11
Malden

Findett Corp / Group 7
St. Charles

Lake City Army Ammunition Plant /
Group 10
Independence

Lee Chemical / Group 5
Liberty

North-U Drive Well Contamination /
Group 11
Springfield

Quality Plating / Group 7
Sikeston

Solid State Circuits, Inc / Group 8
Repulbic

Weldon Spring Quarry (USDOE/Army) /
Group 3
St. Charles County

MONTANA

Anaconda Co. Smelter / 47
Anaconda

East Helena Site / 29
East Helena

Libby Ground Water Contamination /
358
Libby

Milltown Reservoir Sediments / 242
Milltown

Silver Bow Creek / 21
Silver Bow/Deer Lodge Counties

Proposed
Burlington Northern Railroad
(Somers Tie-Treating Plant) / Group 8
Somers

Idaho Pole Co / Group 7
Bozeman

Mouat Industries / Group 10
Columbus

NEBRASKA

Proposed
Cornhusker Army Ammunition Plant /
Group 4
Hall County

Hastings Ground Water Contamination / Group 6
Hastings

Lindsay Manufacturing Co / Group 4
Lindsay

Waverly Ground Water Contamination / Group 8
Waverly

NEVADA (O)

NEW HAMPSHIRE

Auburn Road Landfill / 383
Londonderry

Dover Municipal Landfill / 368
Dover

Kearsarge Metallurgical Corp / 335
Conway

Keefe Environmental Services / 19
Epping

Ottati & Goss/Kingston Steel Drum / 127
Kingston

Savage Municipal Water Supply / 362
Milford

Somersworth Sanitary Landfill / 16
Somersworth

South Municipal Water Supply Well / 393
Peterborough

Sylvester* / 23
Nashua

Tinkham Garage / 248
Londonderry

Proposed
Coakley Landfill / Group 11
N. Hampton

NEW JERSEY

A.O. Polymer / 526
Sparta Township

American Cyanamid Co / 161
Bound Brook

Asbestos Dump / 323
Millington

Beachwood/Berkley Wells / 275
Berkley Township

Bog Creek Farm / 250
Howell Township

Brick Township Landfill / 57
Brick Township

Bridgeport Rental & Oil Services / 35
Bridgeport

Burnt Fly Bog / 40
Marlboro Township

Caldwell Trucking Co / 51
Fairfield

Chemical Control / 199
Elizabeth

Chemical Leaman Tank Lines, Inc / 189
Bridgeport

Chemsol, Inc / 259
Piscataway

Ciba Geigy Corp / 159
Toms River

Combe Fill North Landfill / 182
Chester Township

Cooper Road / 372
Voorhees Township

CPS/Madison Industries / 10
Old Bridge Township

D'Imperio Property / 73
Hamilton Township

DeRewal Chemical Co / 390
Kingwood Township

Delilah Road / 168
Egg Harbor Township

Denzer & Schafer X-Ray Co / 307
Bayville

Diamond Alkali Co / 403
Newark

Dover Municipal Well 4 / 527
Dover Township

Ellis Property / 424
Evesham Township

Evor Phillips Leasing / 377
Old Bridge Township

Ewan Property / 163
Shamong Township

Fair Lawn Well Field / 264
Fair Lawn

Florence Land Recontouring, Inc.,
Landfill / 192
Florence Township

Friedman Property / 444
Upper Freehold Township

Gems Landfill / 12
Gloucester Township

Goose Farm / 184
Plumstead Township

Helen Kramer Landfill / 4
Mantua Township

Hercules, Inc / 308
Gibbstown

Hopkins Farm / 435
Plumstead Township

Imperial Oil Co., Inc/Champion Chemicals / 445

Morganville

Jackson Township Landfill / 345
Jackson Township

Jis Landfill / 225
Jamesburg/South Brunswick Township

Kin-Buc Landfill / 157
Edison Township

King of Prussia / 195
Winslow Township

Krysowaty Farm / 104
Hillsborough

Landfill & Development Co / 453
Mount Holly

Lang Property / 174
Pemberton Township

Lipari Landfill / 1
Pitman

Lone Pine Landfill / 15
Freehold Township

M&T Delisa Landfill / 468
Asbury Park

Mannheim Avenue Dump / 381
Galloway Township

Maywood Chemical Co / 152
Maywood/Rochelle Park

Mataltec/Aerosystems / 172
Franklin Borough

Monroe Township Landfill / 270
Monroe Township

Montgomery Township Housing Development / 350
Montgomery Township

Myers Property /446
Franklin Township

Nascolite Corp /153
Millville

NL Industries / 129
Pedricktown

Pepe Field / 447
Boonton

Pijak Farm / 244
Plumstead Township

Price Landfill* / 6
Pleasantville

PJP Landfill / 535
Jersey City

Radiation Technology, Inc / 263
Rockaway Township

Reich Farms / 121
Pleasant Plains

Renora, Inc / 306
Edison Township

Ringwood Mines/Landfill / 131
Ringwood Borough

Rockaway Borough Well Field / 271
Rockaway Township

Rockaway Township Wells / 528
Rockaway Township

Rocky Hill Municipal Well / 351
Rocky Hill Borough

Roebling Steel Co / 295
Florence

Sayreville Landfill / 367
Sayreville

Scientific Chemical Processing, Inc / 71
Carlstadt

Sharkey Landfill / 175
Parsippany/Troy Hills

Shieldalloy Corp / 45
Newfield Borough

South Brunswick Landfill / 123
South Brunswick

Spence Farm / 218
Plumstead Township

Swope Oil & Chemical Co / 391
Pennsauken

Syncon Resins / 245
South Kearny

Tabernacle Drum Dump / 371
Tabernacle Township

U.S. Radium Corp / 335
Orange

Universal Oil Products (Chemical Division)/ 109
East Rutherford

Upper Deerfield Township Sanitary Landfill/ 454
Upper Deerfield Township

Ventron/Velsicol / 148
Wood-Ridge Borough

Vineland Chemical Co., Inc / 41
Vineland

Vineland State School / 298
Vineland

W.R. Grace & Co, Inc / 198
Wayne Township

Williams Property / 305
Swainton

Wilson Farm / 440
Plumstead Township

Woodland Route 532 Dump / 413
Woodland Township

Woodland Route 72 Dump / 491

Woodland Township
Proposed
Cinnaminson Township (Block 702)
Ground Water Contamination /Group 8
Cinnaminson Township

Fort Dix (Landfill Site) /Group 8
Burlington County

Fried'Industries /Group 10
East Brunswick Township

Glen Ridge Radium Site /Group 4
Glen Ridge

Lodi Municipal Well /Group 10
Lodi

Jame Fine Chemical /Group 10
Bound Brook

Montclair/West Orange Radium Site
/Group 4
Montclair/West Orange

Naval Weapons Station Earle (Site A)
/Group 8
Colts Neck

Pomona Oaks Residential Wells /Group
10
Galloway Township

Waldick Aerospace Devices, Inc /Group
5
Wall Township

NEW MEXICO

AT&SF / 455
Clovis

Homestake Mining Co / 432
Milan

South Valley* / 83
Albuquerque

United Nuclear Corp / 508
Church Rock

NEW YORK

American Thermostat Co / 456
South Cairo

Batavia Landfill / 164
Batavia

Brewster Well Field / 352
Putnam County

Facet Enterprises, Inc / 207
Elmira

Fulton Terminals / 382
Fulton

General Motors (Central Foundry
Division) / 301
Massena

GE Moreau / 52
South Glen Falls

Hooker (Hyde Park) / 419
Niagara Falls

Hooker (S Area) / 145
Niagara Falls

Hudson River PCBs / 108
Hudson River

Kentucky Avenue Well Field / 322
Horseheads

Love Canal / 136
Niagara Falls

Ludlow Sand & Gravel / 369
Clayville

Marathon Battery Corp / 512
Cold Springs

Mercury Refining, Inc / 234
Colonie

Niagara County Refuse / 318
Wheatfield

Old Bethpage Landfill / 44
Oyster Bay

Olean Well Field / 236
Olean

Pollution Abatement Services (PAS)* / 7
Oswego

Port Washington Landfill / 223
Port Washington

Ramapo Landfill / 232
Ramapo

Sinclair Refinery / 117
Wellsville

Solvent Savers / 416
Lincklaen

Syosset Landfill / 114
Oyster Bay

Vestal Water Supply Well 1-1 / 353
Vestal

Vestal Water Supply Well 4-2 / 276
Vestal

Wide Beach Development / 69
Brant

York Oil Co / 186
Moira

Proposed
Anchor Chemicals / Group 8
Hicksville

Applied Environmental Services /
Group 6
Glenwood Landing

Byron Barrel & Drum / Group 8
Byron

BEC Trucking / Group 10
Town of Vestal

Claremont Polychemical / Group 10

Old Bethpage

Clothier Disposal / Group 9
Town of Granby

Colesville Municipal Landfill / Group 11
Town of Colesville

Cortese Landfill / Group 10
Village of Narrowsburg

Endicott Village Well Field / Group 8
Village of Endicott

FMC Corp (Dublin Road Landfill) /
Group 10
Town of Shelby

Goldisc Recordings, Inc / Group 10
Holbrook

Griffiss Air Force Base / Group 9
Rome

Haviland Complex / Group 10
Town of Hyde Park

Hertel Landfill / Group 10
Plattekill

Hooker Chemical/Ruco Polymer Corp /
Group 4
Hicksville

Johnstown City Landfill / Group 4
Town of Johnstown

Katonah Municipal Well / Group 9
Town of Bedford

Kenmark Textile Corp / Group 10
Farmingdale

Liberty Industrial Finishing / Group 4
Farmingdale

Nepera Chemical Co., Inc / Group 7
Maybrook

North Sea Municipal Landfill / Group 9
North Sea

Pasley Solvents & Chemicals, Inc /
Group 7
Hempstead

Preferred Plating Corp / Group 9
Farmingdale

Robintech, inc/National Pipe Co / Group
10
Town of Vestal

Sarney Farm / Group 10
Amenia

Suffern Village Well Field / Group 8
Village of Suffern

SMS Instruments, Inc / Group 8
Deer Park

Tronic Plating Co., Inc / Group 5
Farmingdale

Volney Municipal Landfill / Group 10
Town of Volney

NORTH CAROLINA

Chemtronics, Inc / 515
Swannanoa

Martin Marietta, Sodyeco, Inc / 141
Charlotte

PCB Spills* / 95
210 Miles of Roads

Proposed
Bypass 601 Ground Water Contamination
/ Group 8
Concord

Celanese Corp (Shelby Fiber Operations)
/ Group 4
Shelby

Jadco-Hughes Facility / Group 6
Belmont

North Carolina State University
(Lot 86, Farm Unit #1) / Group 3

Raleigh

NORTH DAKOTA

Arsenic Trioxide Site* / 87
Southeastern North Dakota

OHIO

Allied Chemical & Ironton Coke / 201
Ironton

Arcanum Iron & Metal / 28
Darke County

Big D Campground / 500
Kingsville

Bowers Landfill / 158
Circleville

Buckeye Reclamation / 411
St. Clairsville

Chem-Dyne* / 78
Hamilton

Coshocton Landfill / 328
Franklin Township

E.H. Schilling Landfill / 428
Hamilton Township

Fields Brook / 227
Ashtabula

Fultz Landfill / 326
Jackson Township

Laskin/Poplar Oil Co / 386
Jefferson Township

Miami County Incinerator / 65
Troy

Nease Chemical / 197
Salem

New Lyme Landfill / 490
New Lyme

Old Mill / 387
Rock Creek

Powell Road Landfill / 485
Dayton

Pristine, Inc / 408
Reading

Skinner Landfill / 514
West Chester

South Point Plant / 212
South Point

Summit National / 135
Deerfield Township

United Scrap Lead Co, Inc / 54
Troy

Zanesville Well Field / 396
Zanesville

Proposed
Alsco Anaconda / Group 4
Gnadenhutten

General Electric Co / Group 4
Coshocton

Industrial Excess Landfill / Group 2
Uniontown

Republic Steel Corp Quarry / Group 11
Elyria

Sanitary Landfill Co (Industrial Waste
Disposal Co., Inc) / Group 10
Dayton

Van Dale Junkyard / Group 10
Marietta

OKLAHOMA

Compass Industries (Avery Drive) / 380
Tulsa

Hardage/Criner / 154
Criner

Sand Springs Petrochemical Complex /
Group 11
Sand Springs

Tar Creek / 55
Ottawa County

OREGON

Gould, Inc / 472
Portland

Teledyne Wah Chang / 116
Albany

United Chrome Products, Inc / 494
Corvallis

Proposed
Martin-Marietta Aluminum Co /
Group 5
The Dalles

Umatilla Army Depot (Lagoons) / Group
10
Hermiston

PENNSYLVANIA

Berks Sand Pit / 476
Longswamp Township

Blosenski Landfill / 503
West Caln Township

Brodhead Creek / 493
Stroudsburg

Bruin Lagoon / 3
Bruin Borough

Centre County Kepone / 226
State College Borough

Craig Farm Drum / 536
Parker

Dorney Road Landfill / 214
Upper Macungie Township

Douglassville Disposal / 103

Douglassville
Drake Chemical / 334
Lock Haven

East Mount Zion / 296
Springettsbury Township

Enterprise Avenue / 299
Philadelphia

Fischer & Porter Co / 524
Warminster

Havertown PCP / 338
Haverford

Heleva Landfill / 162
North Whitehall Township

Henderson Road / 288
Upper Merion Township

Hranica Landfill / 140
Buffalo Township

Industrial Lane / 268
Williams Township

Kimberton Site / 519
Kimberton Borough

Lackawanna Refuse / 379
Old Forge Borough

Lehigh Electric & Engineering Co / 513
Old Forge Borough

Lindane Dump / 146
Harrison Township

Lord-Shope Landfill / 329
Girard Township

Malvern TCE / 206
Malvern

McAdoo Associates* / 26
McAdoo Borough/Kline Township

Metal Banks / 460
Philadelphia

Mill Creek Dump / 169
Erie

Moyers Landfill / 360
Eagleville

Old City of York Landfill / 441
Seven Valleys

Osborne Landfill / 112
Grove City

Palmerton Zinc Pile / 254
Palmerton

Presque Isle / 304
Erie

Resin Disposal / 357
Jefferson Borough

Stanley Kessler / 443
King of Prussia

Taylor Borough Dump / 497
Taylor Borough

Tysons Dump / 25
Upper Merion Township

Voortman Farm / 537
Upper Saucon Township

Wade / 378
Chester

Walsh Landfill / 452
Honeybrook Township

Westline Site / 484
Westline

Proposed
Ambler Asbestos Piles / Group 9
Ambler

Brown's Battery Breaking / Group 8
Shoemakersville

Domino Salvage Yard / Group 5
Valley Township

Hunterstown Road / Group 4
Straban Township

Letterkenny Army Depot (SE Area) /
Group 9
Chambersburg

Middletown Air Field / Group 8
Middletown

Modern Sanitation Landfill / Group 9
Lower Windsor Township

Shriver's Corner / Group 5
Straban Township

Westinghouse Elevator Co Plant / Group
8
Gettysburg

Whitmoyer Laboratories / Group 5
Jackson Township

PUERTO RICO

Barceloneta Landfill / 292
Florida Afuera

Fibers Public Supply Wells / 406
Jobos

Frontera Creek / 291
Rio Abajo

GE Wiring Devices /489
Juana Diaz

Juncos Landfill / 464
Juncos

RCA Del Caribe / 492
Barceloneta

Upjohn Facility / 286
Barceloneta

Vega Alta Public Supply Wells / 277
Vega Alta

RHODE ISLAND

Davis Liquid Waste / 193
Smithfield

Landfill & Resource Recovery, Inc / 166
North Smithfield

Peterson/Puritan, Inc / 311
Lincoln/Cumberland

Picillo Farm* / 75
Coventry

Stamina Mills, Inc / 436
North Smithfield

Western Sand & Gravel / 150
Burrillville

Proposed
Central Landfill / Group 5
Johnston

SOUTH CAROLINA

Carolawn, Inc / 475
Fort Lawn

Geiger (C&M Oil) / 469
Rantoules

Independent Nail Co / 61
Beaufort

Kalama Specialty Chemicals / 62
Beaufort

Koppers Co., Inc / 151
Florence

Leonard Chemical Co., Inc / 200
Rock Hill

Palmetto Wood Preserving / 336
Dixianna

SCRDI Bluff Road* / 79
Columbia

SCRDI Dixiana / 302
Cayce

Wamchem, Inc / 188
Burton

SOUTH DAKOTA

Whitewood Creek* / 20
Whitewood

TENNESSEE

Amnicola Dump / 297
Chattanooga

Gallaway Pits / 499
Gallaway

Lewisburg Dump / 457
Lewisburg

Murray-Ohio Dump / 209
Lawrenceburg

North Hollywood Dump* / 93
Memphis

Velsicol Chemical Corp / 185
Toone

Proposed
American Creosote Works, Inc / Group 9
Jackson

Milan Army Ammunition Plant / Group 2
Milan

TEXAS

Bio-Ecology Systems, Inc / 412
Grand Prairie

Crystal Chemical Co / 34
Houston

French, Ltd / 22
Crosby

Geneva Industries/Fuhrmann Energy Corp / 37
Houston

Harris (Farley St) / 439
Houston

Highlands Acid Pit / 356
Highlands

Motco, Inc* / 27
La Marque

Pig Road / Group 6
New Waverly

Sikes Disposal Pits / 30
Crosby

Triangle Chemical Co / 534
Bridge City

United Creosoting Co / 365
Conroe

Proposed
Air Force Plant #4 (General Dynamics) /
Group 7
Fort Worth

Bailey Waste Disposal / Group 3
Bridge City

Brio Refining, Inc / Group 4
Friendswood

Crystal City Airport / Group 10
Crystal City

Koppers Co., Inc / Group 10
Texarkana

Lone Star Army Ammunition Plant /
Group 10
Texarkana

North Cavalcade Street / Group 8
Houston

Odessa Chromium #1 / Group 6
Odessa

Odessa Chromium #2 (Andrews Hwy) /
Group 6
Odessa

Pesses Chemical Co / Group 11
Fort Worth

Petro-Chemical Systems, Inc. (Turtle Bayou) / Group 11
Liberty County

Sol Lynn/Industrial Transformers / Group 7
Houston

South Cavalcade Street / Group 7
Houston

Stewco, Inc / Group 4
Waskom

TRUST TERRITORIES

PCB Wastes* / 88
Trust Territory of the Pacific Islands

UTAH

Rose Park Sludge Pit* / 98
Salt Lake City

Proposed
Hill Air Force Base / Group 4
Ogden

Mayflower Mountain Tailings Ponds / Group 5
Wasatch

Monticello Radioactively Contaminated Properties / Group 9
Monticello

Ogden Defense Depot / Group 5
Ogden

Olson/Neihart Reservoir / Group 9
Wasatch County

Portland Cement Co (Kiln Dust Sites 2&3) / Group 1
Salt Lake City

Sharon Steel Corp (Midvale Smelter) / Group 1

Midvale

Tooele Army Depot (North Area) / Group 7
Tooele

VERMONT

Old Springfield Landfill / 415
Springfield

Pine Street Canal* / 84
Burlington

VIRGIN ISLANDS (O)

VIRGINIA

Chisman Creek / 196
York County

Matthews Electoplating* / 89
Roanoke County

Saltville Waste Disposal Ponds / 518
Saltville

U.S. Titanium / 417
Piney River

Proposed
Avtex Fibers, Inc / Group 9
Front Royal

Culpeper Wood Preservers, Inc / Group 5
Culpeper

Defense General Supply Center / Group 9
Richmond

IBM Corp (Manassas Plant Spill) / Group 7
Manassas

L.A. Clarke & Son / Group 9
Spotsylvania County

Rhinehart Tire Fire Dump / Group 11
Frederick County

WASHINGTON

American Lake Gardens / 532
Tacoma

Colbert Landfill / 289
Colbert

Commencement Bay, Near
Shore.Tideflats / 283
Pierce County

Commencement Bay, South Tacoma
Channel / 111
Tacoma

Frontier Hard Chrome, Inc / 60
Vancouver

FMC Corp (Yakima Pit) / 330
Yakima

Greenacres Landfill / 533
Spokane County

Harbor Island (Lead) / 426
Seattle

Kaiser Aluminum (Mead Works) / 347
Mead

Lakewood Site / 267
Lakewood

Pesticide Lab / 521
Yakima

Queen City Farms / 430
Maple Valley

Western Processing Co., Inc / 48
Kent

Proposed
Bangor Ordnance Disposal / Group 11
Bremerton

Fort Lewis (Landfill #5) / Group 6
Tacoma

McChord Air Force Base (Wash Rack/

Treatment Area) / Group 5
Tacoma

Mica Landfill / Group 9
Mica

Midway Landfill / Group 3
Kent

Northside Landfill / Group 11
Spokane

Northwest Transformer / Group 9
Everson

Quendall Terminal / Group 6
Renton

Silver Mountain Mine / Group 11
Loomis

Toftdahl Drums / Group 7
Brush Prairie

WEST VIRGINIA

Fike Chemical, Inc / 384
Nitro

Follansbee Site / 449
Follansbee

Leetown Pesticide / 375
Leetown

West Virginia Ordnance* / 85
Point Pleasant

Proposed
Moray Chemical Corp / Group 5
New Martinsville

Ordnance Works Disposal Areas / Group 8
Morgantown

WISCONSIN

City Disposal Corp Landfill / 370
Dunn
Delavan Municipal Well #4 / 529

Delavan

Eau Claire Municipal Well Field / 397
Eau Claire

Janesville Ash Beds / 63
Janesville

Janesville Old Landfill / 59
Janesville

Kohler Co Landfill / 256
Kohler

Lauer I Sanitary Landfill / 260
Menomonee Falls

Lemberger Transport & Recycling, Inc /
427
Franklin Township

Master Disposal Service, Inc., Landfill /
190
Brookfield

Mid-State Disposal, Inc., Landfill / 409
Cleveland Township

Moss-American (Kerr-McGee Oil Co) /
470
Milwaukee

Muskego Sanitary Landfill / 144
Muskego

Northern Engraving Co / 331
Sparta

Oconomowoc Electroplating Co., Inc /
482
Ashippin

Omega Hills North Landfill / 49
Germantown

Onalaska Municipal Landfill / 269
Onalaska

Schmalz Dump / 173
Harrison
Scrap Processing Co., Inc / 431

Medford

Waste Research & Reclamation Co / 471
Eau Claire

Wheeler Pit / 67
La Prairie Township

Proposed
Fadrowski Drum Disposal / Group 10
Franklin

National Presto Industries, Inc / Group 7
Eau Claire

Stoughton City Landfill / Group 10
Stoughton

WYOMING

Baxter/Union Pacific Tie Treating / 366
Laramie

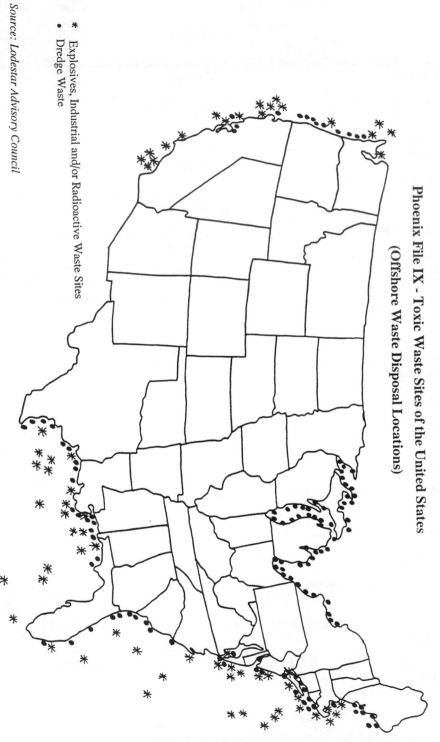

Phoenix File IX - Toxic Waste Sites of the United States
(Offshore Waste Disposal Locations)

* Explosives, Industrial and/or Radioactive Waste Sites
• Dredge Waste

Source: Lodestar Advisory Council

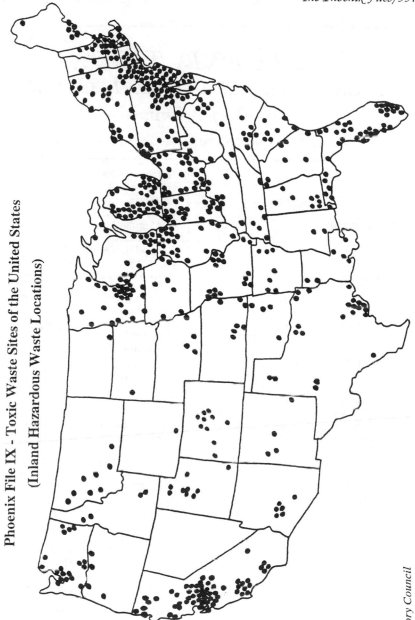

Phoenix File IX - Toxic Waste Sites of the United States
(Inland Hazardous Waste Locations)

Source: Lodestar Advisory Council

PHOENIX FILE X
Geothermal Regions of the United States
(Major Springs)

Note: The words *BOILING, HOT, WARM* replace unknown temperatures.

Spring Name
(Region) ....Temperature °F

ALASKA (108)

Hot Springs On Adak Island
(ADAK)..........154
Fumaroles On Kanaga Island
(ADAK)..........219
Hot Spring On Tanaga Island
(ADAK)..........HOT
Fumaroles On Gareloi Island
(GARELOI ISLAND)..........HOT
Fumaroles On Gareloi Island
(GARELOI ISLAND)..........144
Fumaroles On Little Sitkin Island
(RAT ISLANDS)..........HOT
Fumaroles On Little Sitkin Island
(RAT ISLANDS)..........HOT
Fumaroles On Little Sitkin Island
(RAT ISLANDS)..........HOT
Hot Spring On Little Sitkin Island
(RAT ISLANDS)..........HOT
Hot Spring On Kagamil Island
(SAMALGA ISLAND)..........HOT
Chuginadak Hot Springs
(SAMALGA ISLAND)..........HOT
Hot Spring On Seguam Island
(SEGUAM)..........HOT
Hot Springs On Atka Island
(ATKA)..........HOT
Hot Springs On Atka Island
(ATKA)..........HOT
Hot Springs On Atka Island
(ATKA)..........167
Hot Springs On Great Sitkin Island
(ADAK)..........210
Hot Spring On Attu Island
(ATTU)..........WARM
Makushin Volcano Fumaroles
(UNALASKA)..........310

Hot Springs Near Summer Bay
(UNALASKA)..........HOT
Hot Springs Near Makushin Volcano
(UNALASKA)..........HOT
Hot Springs Near Makushin Volcano
(UNALASKA..........94
Hot Springs On Bogoslof Island
(UMNAK)..........HOT
Thermal Springs In Okmok Caldera
(UMNAK)..........212
Hot Springs Near Hot Springs Cove
(UMNAK)..........158
Hot Springs Near Hot Springs Cove
(UMNAK)..........192
Hot Spring On Umnak Island
(UMNAK)..........149
Hot Springs Near Beyser Bight
(UMNAK)..........214
Hot Springs Near Geyser Bight
(UMNAK)..........216
Hot Springs Near Geyser Bight
(UMNAK)..........HOT
Hot Spring On Amagat Island
(FALSE PASS)..........HOT
Hot Springs Near Morzhovoi
(FALSE PASS)..........145
Hot Spring On Unimak Island
(UNIMAK)..........HOT
Hot Springs On Akun Island
(UNIMAK)..........HOT
Hot Springs On Akun Island
(UNIMAK)..........HOT
Hot Springs Near Hot Springs Bay
(UNIMAK)..........181
Bailey Hot Spring
(KETCHIKAN)..........198
Bell Island Hot Springs
(KETCHIKAN)..........165
Dalton
(Craig) Hot Springs
(CRAIG)..........109
Hot Spring Near Port Moller

ARKANSAS (6)

CALIFORNIA (304)

(OURAY).........156
Lemon Hot Spring
(PLACERVILLE)..........91
Eldorado Springs
(ELDORADO SPRINGS)..........79
Idaho Springs
(IDAHO SPRINGS)..........115
Hartsel Hot Springs
(HARTSEL)..........126
Rhodes Warm Spring
(FAIRPLAY WEST)..........75
Conundrum Hot Springs
(MAROON BELLS)..........100
Dotsero Warm Springs
(DOTSERO)..........90
South Canyon Hot Springs
(STORM KING MOUNTAIN)..........118
Glenwood Springs
(GLENWOOD SPRINGS)..........124
Penny Hot Springs
(REDSTONE)..........133
Routt Hot Springs
(CRAIG-ROCKY PEAK)..........147
Steamboat Springs
(STEAMBOAT SPRINGS)..........102
Hot Sulphur Springs
(HOT SULPHUR SPRINGS)..........111
Juniper Hot Springs
(JUNIPER HOT SPRINGS)..........100

FLORIDA (2)

Little Salt Spring
(MURDOCK)..........81
Warm Mineral Springs
(MYAKKA RIVER)..........86

GEORGIA (7)

Thundering Spring
(SUNSET VILLAGE)..........75
Barker Spring
(SUNSET VILLAGE)..........73
Warm Springs
(WARM SPRINGS)..........88
Tom Brown Spring
(MANCHESTER)..........68
Parkman Spring
(SHILOH)..........77
Lifsey Spring
(ZEBULON)..........79
Taylor Spring
(ZEBULON)..........75

HAWAII (11)

Akins Spring
(PAHOA NORTH)..........84
Warm Vapor
(PAHOA SOUTH)..........WARM
Steam Vents
(PAHOA SOUTH)..........HOT
Isaac Hale Park Spring
(KAPOHO)..........97
Steam Vents
(MAUNA LOA)..........HOT
Steam Vents
(KILAUEA CRATER)..........HOT
Steam Vents
(MAUNA LOA)..........HOT
Steam Vents
(KILAUEA CRATER)..........HOT
Steam Vents
(KILAUEA CRATER)..........HOT
Steam Vents
(MAKAOPUHI CRATER)..........HOT
Waiwelawela Point Spring
(PAHALA)..........90

IDAHO (232)

Blackfoot River Warm Spring
(HENRY)..........79
Blackfoot Reservoir Warm Spring
(HENRY)..........72
Henry Warm Spring
(HENRY)..........86
Portneuf River Warm Spring
(PORTNEUF)..........93
Soda Springs
(SODA SPRINGS)..........82
Steamboat Hot Spring
(SODA SPRINGS)..........88
Pescadero Warm Spring
(NOUNAN)..........79
Mound Valley Warm Spring
(ONEIDA NARROWS RESERVOIR)..........WARM
Treasureton Hot Springs
(ONEIDA NARROWS RESERVOIR)..........95
Cleveland Hot Springs
(ONEIDA NARROWS RESERVOIR)..........151
Maple Grove Hot Springs

(SUNNYSIDE)..........90
Abel Spring
(THE WALL)..........115
Moon River Spring
(HOT CREEK BUTTE)..........92
Unnamed
(MOSQUITE CREEK)..........HOT
South Mosquito Creek Ranch Springs
(MOSQUITO CREEK)..........95
Fish Springs
(FISH SPRINGS)..........WARM
Upper Warm Spring
(UPPER FISH LAKE)..........106
Upper Warm Spring
(LITTLE FISH LAKE)..........95
Old Dugan Ranch Hot Springs
(LITTLE FISH LAKE)..........102
Hot Creek Ranch Hot Spring
(HOBBLE CANYON)..........180
Hot Creek Valley Spring
(BLUE JAY SPRING)..........142
Saulsbury Warm Spring
(SAULSBURY BASIN)..........86
Warm Springs
(WARM SPRINGS)..........145
Spring
(TONOPAH)..........86
Charnock Springs
(CARVERS)..........80
Big Blue Spring
(CARVERS)..........90
Darroughs Hot Springs
(CARVERS)..........203
Indian Springs
(SAN ANTONIO
RANCH)..........WARM
Double Spring
(GILLIS CANYON)..........WARM
Wedell Hot Springs
(WALKER LAKE)..........144
Unnamed
(AURORA)..........110
Soda Springs
(SODAVILLE)..........100
Walleys Hot Springs
(MINDEN)..........160
Spring
(WELLINGTON)..........WARM
Nevada Hot Springs
(WELLINGTON)..........144
Hot Spring
(YERINGTON)..........HOT
Doud Springs

(MT. SIEGEL)..........70
Wilson Hot Spring
(YERINGTON)..........83
Spring
(ELY)..........83
Cherry Creek Hot Springs
(ELY)..........144
Upper Shellbourne Spring
(ELY)..........74
Lower Shellbourne Spring
(ELY)..........77
Monte Neva Hot Springs
(ELY)..........176
Campbell Ranch Springs
(ELY)..........76
Schoolhouse Spring
(MCGILL)..........84
McGill Spring
(MCGILL)..........84
Lackawanna Hot Springs
(EAST ELY)..........95
Thompson Ranch Spring
(DIAMOND SPRINGS)..........68
Giocoecha Warm Springs
(COLD CREEK RANCH)..........76
Big Blue Spring
(GREEN SPRINGS)..........WARM
Siri Ranch Spring
(GARDEN VALLEY)..........95
Shipley Hot Spring
(GARDEN VALLEY)..........106
Hot Springs
(WALTI HOT SPRINGS)..........180
Walti Hot Springs
(WALTI HOT SPRINGS)..........162
Little Hot Springs
(WALTI HOT SPRINGS)..........HOT
Sulphur Spring
(GARDEN VALLEY)..........74
Bartine Hot Springs
(BARTINE RANCH)..........108
Warm Spring
(BARTINE RANCH)..........WARM
Klobe Hot Spring
(ANTELOPE PEAK)..........156
Spencer Hot Springs
(SPENCER HOT SPRINGS)..........162
Unnamed
(WILDCAT PEAK)..........HOT
Potts Ranch Hot Springs
(DIANAS PUNCH BOWL)..........113
Hot Spring
(DIANAS PUNCH BOWL)..........124

Belknap Springs
(MCKENZIE BRIDGE)..........160
Foley Springs
(MCKENZIE BRIDGE)..........178
Cougar Reservoir Hot Springs
(MCKENZIE BRIDGE)..........111
Cook Creek Hot Spring
(WAPSHILLA CREEK)..........97
Unnamed
(ELGIN)..........WARM
Warm Spring
(COVE)..........85
Hot Lake Springs
(CRAIG MOUNTAIN)..........176
Union Station Hot Springs
(CRAIG MOUNTAIN)..........HOT
Medical Hot Springs
(FLAGSTAFF BUTTE)..........140
Kropp Hot Spring
(NORTH POWDER)..........109
Bingham Springs
(BINGHAM SPRINGS)..........93
Lehman Springs
(LEHMAN SPRINGS)..........142
Hidaway Springs
(LEHMAN SPRINGS)..........100
Warm Mineral Spring
(FLY VALLEY)..........83
Well Spring
(WELL SPRING)..........80
Mount Hood Fumaroles
(MOUNT HOOD)..........194
Swim Warm Springs
(MOUNT HOOD)..........79
Austin Hot Springs
(FISH CREEK MOUNTAIN)..........186

SOUTH DAKOTA (2)

Hot Brook Springs
(MINNEKHATA)..........75
Hot Springs
(HOT SPRINGS)..........87

TEXAS (9)

Unnamed
(INDIAN WELLS)..........90
Hot Springs
(BOQUILLAS)..........106
Rio Grande Village Spring
(BOQUILLAS)..........97
Springs/Las Cienegas

(CERRO ORONA)..........86
Capote Springs
(CAPOTE FALLS)..........99
Nixon Spring
(CAPOTE FALLS)..........90
Ruidosa Hot Springs
(RUIDOSA HOT SPRINGS)..........113
Red Bull Spring
(INDIAN HOT SPRINGS)..........99
Indian Hot Springs
(INDIAN HOT SPRINGS)..........117

UTAH (116)

Warm Spring
(MANCOS MESA)..........79
Lefevre
(PANGUITCH)..........90
Tebbs
(PANGUITCH)..........68
Red Canyon
(KANAB)..........72
Irvine Spring
(CENTRAL)..........70
Veyo Hot Spring
(VEYO)..........90
Dixie Hot Springs
(HURRICANE)..........108
Snow Spring
(ST. GEORGE)..........70
Berry Springs
(HURRICANE)..........75
Virgin River Spring
(HURRICANE)..........70
Green Spring
(ST. GEORGE)..........75
Warm Spring
(ST. GEORGE)..........75
Warner Valley Spring
(HURRICANE)..........70
Salt Spring
(SALINA)..........72
Unnamed
(FILLMORE)..........72
Meadow Hot Springs
(TABERNACLE HILL)..........106
Hatton Hot Spring
(FILLMORE)..........100
Richfield Warm Springs
(RICHFIELD)..........73
Coyote Spring
(CRUZ)..........68
Springs

(RAYS VALLEY)..........68
Castilla Springs
(SPANISH FORK PEAK)..........104
Hobo Warm Spring
(SALTAIR)..........84
Big Warm Springs
(TIMPIE)..........72
Utah Fish and Game Dept.
(TIMPIE)..........75
Unnamed
(TIMPIE)..........68
Redlum Spring
(TOOELE)..........70
Grantsville Warm Springs
(TIMPIE)..........77
Unnamed
(TIMPIE)..........72
Horseshoe Springs
(TIMPIE)..........73
Desert Livestock South Springs
(TIMPIE)..........73
Desert Livestock South Spring
(TIMPIE)..........72
Desert Livestock
(TIMPIE)..........75
Morgans Warm Spring
(STOCKTON)..........80
Russells Warm Springs
(STOCKTON)..........72
Davis
(FAUST)..........68
Blue Lake Spring
(WENDOVER)..........84
Gancheff Spring
(TRENTON)..........88
Patio Springs
(HUNTSVILLE)..........68
Ogden Hot Spring
(OGDEN)..........135
Como Springs
(MORGAN)..........81
Coyote Spring
(MONUMENT PEAK)..........109
Udy Hot Springs
(RIVERSIDE)..........124
Cutler Warm Spring
(CUTLER DAM)..........73
Blue Creek Spring (HOWELL)..........82
Bothwell Warm Springs
(THATCHER MOUNTAIN)..........75
Crystal Hot Springs
(HONEYVILLE)..........129
Springs

(THATCHER MOUNTAIN)..........72
Little Mountain Hot Spring
(PUBLIC SHOOTING
GROUNDS)..........108
Stinking Hot Springs
(BEAR RIVER CITY)..........118
Poulsen Spring/Salt
(EAST PROMONTORY)..........72
Utah Hot Springs
(PLAIN CITY)..........138
Unnamed
(POKES POINT)..........77
Compton Spring
(PROMONTORY POINT)..........72
Hooper Hot Springs
(OGDEN BAY)..........140
Pugsley
(PARK VALLEY)..........73
Head Spring
(YOST)..........70
L G Carter Springs
(PARK VALLEY)..........77
Larson Springs
(PARK VALLEY)..........70
W R Carter Springs
(PARK VALLEY)..........70
Warm Spring
(YOST)..........81
Spring/Hot
(GROUSE CREEK)..........108
Warm Spring
(PROHIBITION SPRING)..........68
Kimber Spring
(TOMS CABIN SPRING)..........68

VIRGINIA (11)

Hot Springs
(HEALING SPRINGS)..........106
Healing Springs
(HEALING SPRINGS)..........86
Rockbridge Baths
(GOSHEN)..........72
Falling Spring
(COVINGTON)..........77
Layton Spring
(COVINGTON)..........72
Sweet Chalybeate Spring
(ALLEGHANY)..........75
New River White Sulphur Springs
(EGGLESTON)..........85
Alum Springs
(WHITE GATE)..........72

Bragg Spring
(BURNSVILLE)..........75
Bolar Spring
(BURNSVILLE)..........73
Warm Springs
(WARM SPRINGS)..........95

WASHINGTON (30)

Klickitat Mineral Springs
(KLICKITAT)..........81
St. Martins Hot Springs
(BONNEVILLE DAM)..........120
Rock Creek Hot Springs
(BOONEVILLE DAM)..........HOT
Collins Hot Springs
(HOOD RIVER)..........122
Moffetts Hot Springs
(BOONEVILLE DAM)..........97
Warm Springs Canyon Warm Spring
(ZANGAR JUNCTION)..........72
Simcoe Soda Springs
(YESMOWIT CANYON)..........90
Mt. Rainier Fumaroles
(MT. RANIER)..........162
Longmire Mineral Springs
(MT. RAINIER)..........77
Ohanapecosh Hot Springs
(PACKWOOD)..........122
Packwood Hot Spring
(PACKWOOD)..........100
Orr Creek Warm Springs
(GREEN MOUNTAIN)..........72
Mount Adams Fumaroles
(MOUNT ADAMS)..........150
Fish Hatchery Warm Spring
(OUTLET FALLS)..........75
Green River Soda Spring
(ELK ROCK)..........86
Mt. St. Helens Fumaroles
(MOUNT ST. HELENS)..........190
Garland Mineral Springs
(BLANCA LAKE)..........84
Scenic Hot Springs
(SCENIC)..........122
Goldmeyer Hot Springs
(SNOQUALMIE PASS)..........127
Lester Hot Springs
(GREENWATER)..........120
Olympic Hot Springs
(MOUNT CARRIE)..........118
Sol Duc Hot Springs
(BOGACHIEL PEAK)..........122

Hot Lake
(OROVILLE)..........122
Poison Lake
(OROVILLE)..........122
Dorr Fumarole Field
(MOUNT BAKER)..........194
Sherman Crater Fumaroles
(MOUNT MAKER)..........266
Baker Hot Spring
(MT. SHUKSAN)..........108
Sulphur Creek Hot Springs
(DOWNEY MOUNTAIN)..........99
Gamma Hot Springs
(GLACIER PEAK)..........140
Kennedy Hot Spring
(GLACIER PEAK)..........100

WEST VIRGINIA (5)

Old Sweet Spring
(ALLEGHANY)..........73
Thorn Spring
(SUGAR GROVE)..........72
Minnehaha Springs
(MINNEHAHA SPRINGS)..........70
Swan Pond Spring
(MARTINSBURG)..........72
Berkeley Springs
(HANCOCK)..........72

WYOMING (173)

Saratoga Hot Springs
(SARATOGA)..........129
Warm Springs/Immigrants Washtub
(WHEATLAND)..........70
Douglas Hot Springs
(CHALK BUTTES)..........86
Alcova Hot Springs
(ALCOVA)..........129
Horse Creek Springs
(HORSE CREEK SPRINGS)..........75
Sweetwater Station Warm Springs
(HAPPY SPRING)..........90
Steele Hot Springs
(FREMONT BUTTE)..........102
Auburn Hot Springs
(PRESTON)..........144
Johnson Springs
(PRESTON)..........115
Thermopolis Hot Springs
(THERMOPOLIS)..........133
Wind River Canyon Spring

Hot Springs on Lewis Lake (WEST THUMB)..........199
Hot Springs, Heart Lake Geyser Basin (WEST THUMB)..........201
Heart Lake Geyser Basin, Middle Group (WEST THUMB)..........174
Hot Springs, Heart Lake Beyser Basin (WEST THUMB)..........201
Bechler River Hot Springs (OLD FAITHFUL)..........194
Rustic Geyser (WEST THUMB)..........199
Hot Springs on Lewis Lake (WEST THUMB)..........154
Hot Springs on Upper Snake River (MOUNT HANCOCK)..........167
Hot Springs (HUCKLEBERRY MOUNTAIN)..........142
Snake Hot Springs (HUCKLEBERRY MOUNTAIN)..........136

Crawfish Creek Hot Springs (HUCKLEBERRY MOUNTAIN)..........138
Crawfish Creek Hot Springs (HUCKLEBERRY MOUNTAIN)..........136
South Entrance Hot Springs (HUCKLEBERRY MOUNTAIN)..........156
Huckleberry Hot Springs (HUCKLEBERRY MOUNTAIN)..........BOILING
Boundary Creek Hot Springs (WARM RIVER BUTTE)..........181

Source: U.S. Department of Commerce, National Oceanic and Atmospheric Administration Environmental Data and Information Service, National Geophysical and Solar-Terrestrial Data Center, Boulder, Colorado.

Special acknowledgement to Joy Ikelman for her invaluable assistance in providing information for this section in the form of a reference book she co-authored with Paul J. Grim and George W. Berry entitled *Thermal Springs List For The United States*.

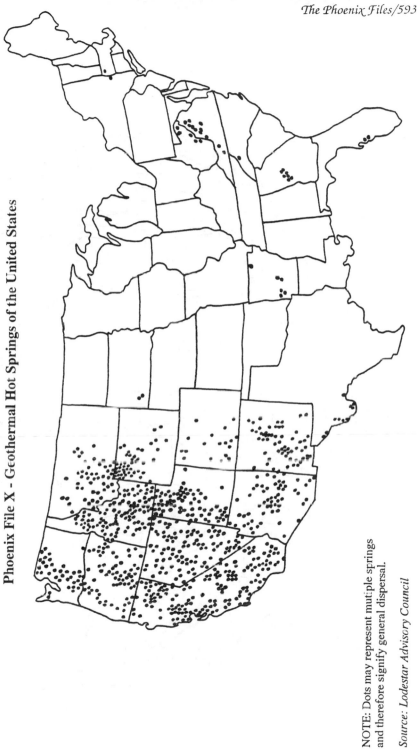

Phoenix File X - Geothermal Hot Springs of the United States

NOTE: Dots may represent multiple springs and therefore signify general dispersal.

Source: Lodestar Advisory Council

Source: U.S. Department of Energy

Phoenix File X - Geothermal Regions of the United States
(Patterned Areas)

Phoenix File XI
Hurricane Hazard Regions of the United States

Saffir/Simpson Hurricane Scale

Scale Number	Winds (Mph)	Damage
1	74-95	Minimal
2	96-110	Moderate
3	111-130	Extensive
4	131-155	Extreme
5	over 155	Catastrophic

The above scale ranges are used in the following reference sections.

Phoenix File XI - Hurricanes

(Deadliest Hurricanes in U.S., 1900 - 1989)

Hurricane	Year	Category	Deaths
1. Galveston, TX	1900	4	6000
2. Louisiana	1893	-	2000
3. Lk. Okeechobee, FL	1928	4	1836
4. SC & GA	1893	-	1/2000
5. GA & SC	1881	-	700
6. FL (Keys)	1919	4	600
7. New England	1938	3	600
8. FL (Keys)	1935	5	408
9. AUDREY (LA & TX)	1957	4	390
10. NE U.S.	1944	3	390
11. Grand Isle, LA	1909	4	350
12. New Orleans, LA	1915	4	275
13. Galveston, TX	1915	4	275
14. CAMILLE (MS & LA)	1969	5	256
15. Miami, FL	1926	4	243
16. DIANE (NE U.S.)	1955	1	184
17. SE Florida	1906	2	164
18. Pensacola, MS & AL	1906	3	134
19. AGNES (NE U.S.)	1972	1	122
20. HAZEL (SC & NC)	1954	4	95
21. BETSY (FL & LA)	1965	3	75
22. CAROL (NE U.S.)	1954	3	60
23. FL, LA, MS	1947	4	51
24. DONNA (FL & E U.S.)	1960	4	50
25. GA, SC, NC	1940	2	50
26. CARLA (TX)	1961	4	46
27. S. California	1939	-	45
28. Velasco, TX	1909	3	41
29. Freeport, TX	1932	4	40
30. South Texas	1933	3	40
31. HILDA (LA)	1964	3	38
32. SW Louisiana	1918	3	34
33. SW Florida	1910	3	30
34. CONNIE (NC)	1955	3	25
35. Louisiana	1926	3	25

Source: U.S. Department of Commerce
National Oceanic And Atmospheric Administration
National Hurricane Center

Phoenix File XI - Hurricanes

(Costliest Hurricanes in U.S., 1900 - 1989)

Hurricane	Year	Category	Damage $
1. HUGO (SC)	1989	4	7,000,000,000
2. BETSY (FL & LA)	1965	3	6,321,225,000
3. AGNES (NE U.S.)	1972	1	6,279,000,000
4. CAMILLE (MS & AL)	1969	5	5,128,727,000
5. DIANE (NE U.S.)	1955	1	4,108,598,000
6. New England	1938	3	3,515,940,000
7. FREDERIC (AL & MS)	1979	3	3,427,000,000
8. ALICIA (N TX)	1983	3	2,340,000,000
9. CAROL (NE U.S.)	1954	3	2,318,830,000
10. CARLA (TX)	1961	4	1,884,960,000
11. DONNA (FL & E. U.S.)	1960	4	1,784,070,000
12. JUAN (LA)	1985	1	1,635,000,000
13. CELIA (S. TX)	1970	3	1,526,610,000
14. HAZEL (SC & NC)	1954	4	1,413,430,000
15. ELENA (MS, AL, NW FL)	1985	3	1,362,500,000
16. Miami, FL	1926	4	1,286,880,000
17. Galveston, TX	1915	4	1,152,400,000
18. DORA (NE FL)	19644	22	1,132,500,000
19. ELOISE (NW FL)	1975	3	1,058,400,000
20. GLORIA (E. U.S.)	1985	3	981,000,000
21. NE U.S.	1944	3	905,000,000
22. BEULAH (S. TX)	1967	3	826,000,000
23. Galveston, TX	1900	4	691,440,000
24. FL, LA, MS	1947	4	688,600,000
25. AUDREY (LA & TX)	1957	4	681,000,000
26. CLAUDETTE (TX)	1979	TS	596,000,000
27. CLEO (SE FL)	1964	2	582,105,000
28. SW FL, NE FL	1944	3	570,150,000
29. HILDA (LA)	1964	3	566,250,000
30. SE FL	1945	3	527,400,000
31. ALLISON (N. TX)	1949	TS	500,000,000
32. DAVID (FL & E. U.S.)	1979	2	476,800,000
33. IONE (NC)	1955	3	434,720,000
34. ALLEN (S. TX)	1980	3	402,000,000

Note: TS signifies a Tropical Storm

Source: U.S. Department of Commerce
National Oceanic And Atmospheric Administration
National Hurricane Center

Source: Lodestar Advisory Council

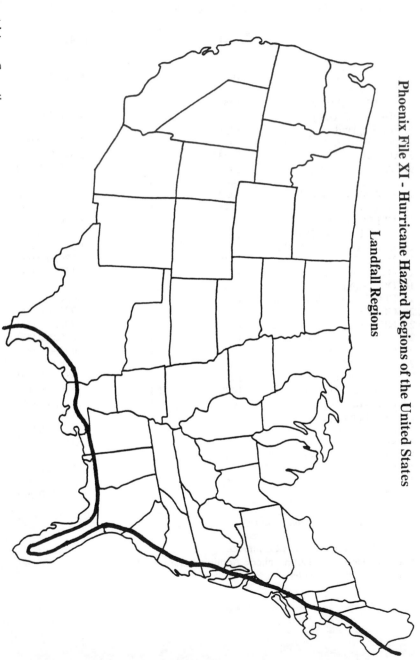

Phoenix File XI - Hurricane Hazard Regions of the United States

Landfall Regions

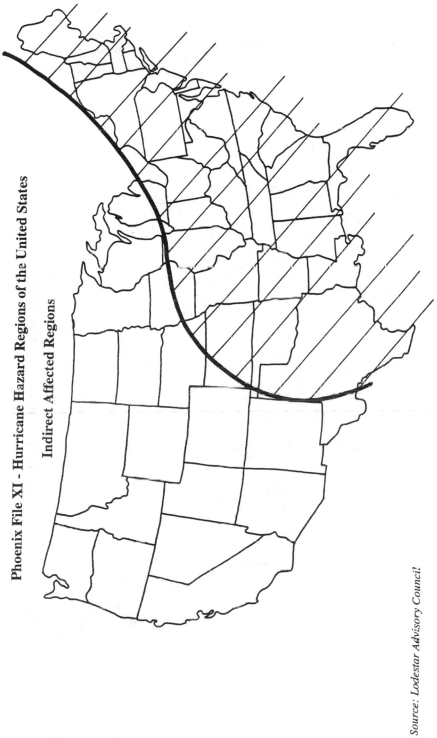

Phoenix File XI - Hurricane Hazard Regions of the United States

Indirect Affected Regions

Source: Lodestar Advisory Council!

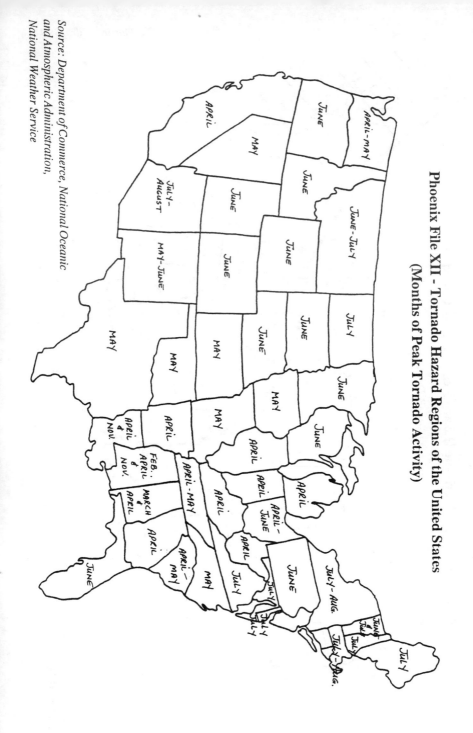

Phoenix File XII - Tornado Hazard Regions of the United States
(Months of Peak Tornado Activity)

Source: Department of Commerce, National Oceanic and Atmospheric Administration, National Weather Service

Phoenix File XII - Tornado Hazard Regions of the United States
(Average Number of Tornadoes and Deaths)

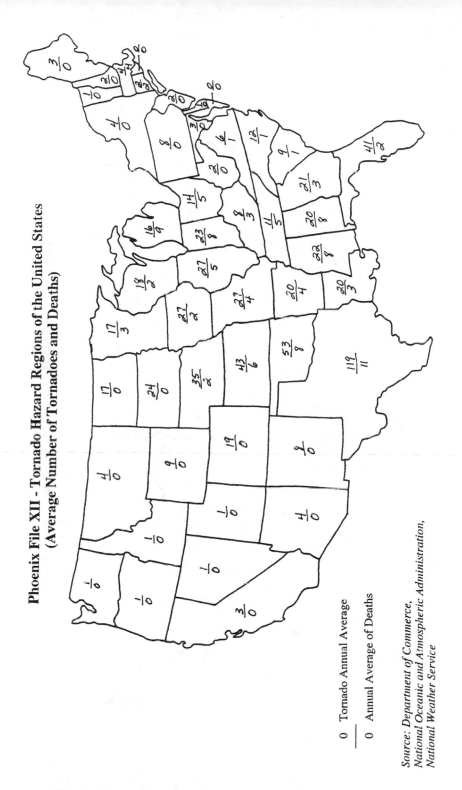

0 Tornado Annual Average

—
0 Annual Average of Deaths

*Source: Department of Commerce,
National Oceanic and Atmospheric Administration,
National Weather Service*

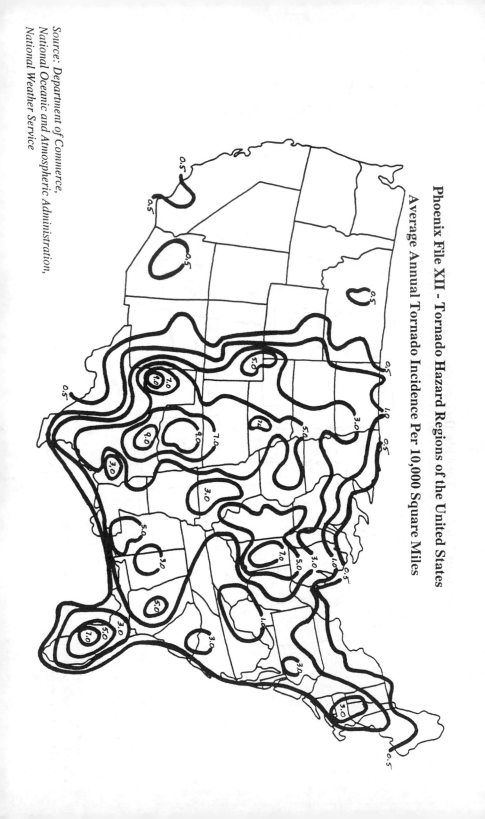

Phoenix File XII - Tornado Hazard Regions of the United States
Average Annual Tornado Incidence Per 10,000 Square Miles

Source: Department of Commerce,
National Oceanic and Atmospheric Administration,
National Weather Service

Phoenix File XII - Tornado Hazard Regions of the U.S.

The following six maps depict six of the nation's worst tornado outbreaks. They are called the "deadly half dozen."

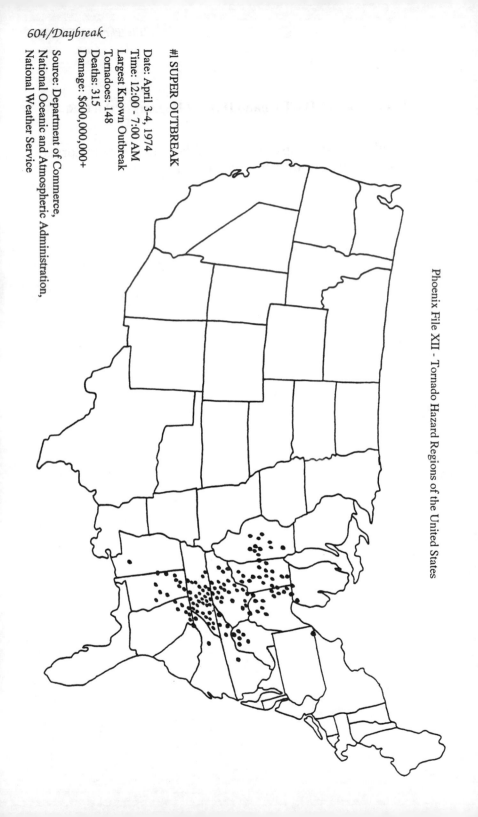

#1 SUPER OUTBREAK

Date: April 3-4, 1974
Time: 12:00 - 7:00 AM
Largest Known Outbreak
Tornadoes: 148
Deaths: 315
Damage: $600,000,000+

Source: Department of Commerce,
National Oceanic and Atmospheric Administration,
National Weather Service

Phoenix File XII - Tornado Hazard Regions of the United States

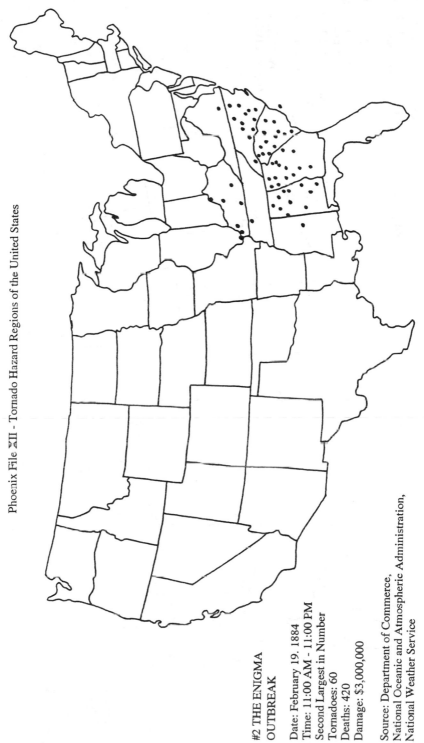

Phoenix File XII - Tornado Hazard Regions of the United States

#2 THE ENIGMA
OUTBREAK

Date: February 19, 1884
Time: 11:00 AM - 11:00 PM
Second Largest in Number
Tornadoes: 60
Deaths: 420
Damage: $3,000,000

Source: Department of Commerce,
National Oceanic and Atmospheric Administration,
National Weather Service

#3 PALM SUNDAY
OUTBREAK

Date: April 11 - 12, 1965
Time: 1:00 PM - 1:00 AM
Third Largest in Number
Tornadoes: 51
Deaths: 256
Damage: $200,000,000+

Source: Department of Commerce,
National Oceanic and Atmospheric Administration,
National Weather Service

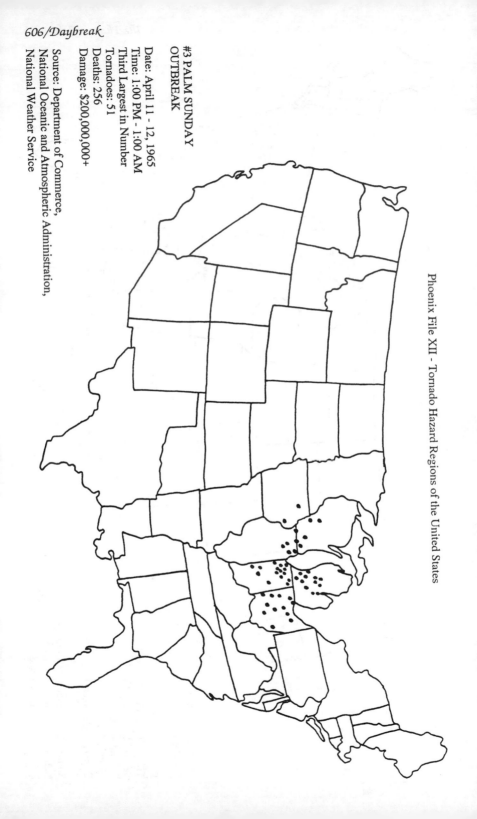

Phoenix File XII - Tornado Hazard Regions of the United States

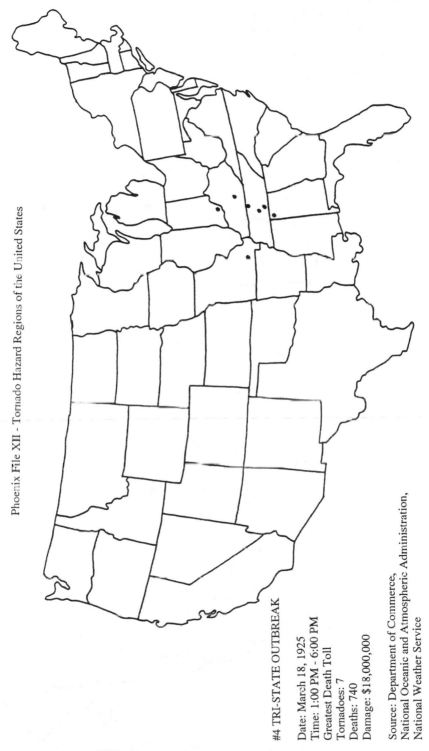

Phoenix File XII - Tornado Hazard Regions of the United States

#4 TRI-STATE OUTBREAK

Date: March 18, 1925
Time: 1:00 PM - 6:00 PM
Greatest Death Toll
Tornadoes: 7
Deaths: 740
Damage: $18,000,000

Source: Department of Commerce,
National Oceanic and Atmospheric Administration,
National Weather Service

#5 TUPELO -
GAINESVILLE OUTBREAK

Date: April 5 - 6, 1936
Time: 8:00 PM - 9:00 AM
Second Greatest Death Toll
Tornadoes: 17
Deaths: 446
Damage: $18,000,000

Source: Department of Commerce,
National Oceanic and Atmospheric Administration,
National Weather Service

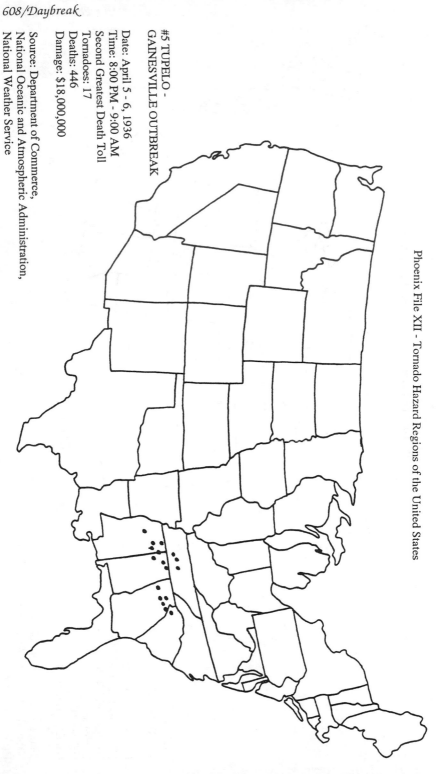

Phoenix File XII - Tornado Hazard Regions of the United States

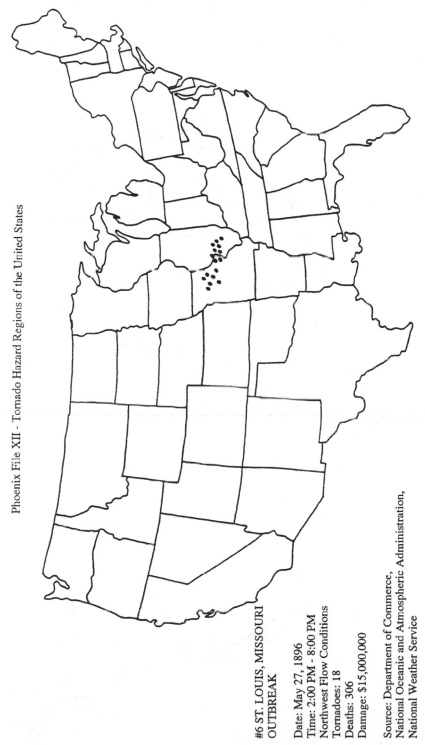

Phoenix File XII - Tornado Hazard Regions of the United States

#6 ST. LOUIS, MISSOURI
OUTBREAK

Date: May 27, 1896
Time: 2:00 PM - 8:00 PM
Northwest Flow Conditions
Tornadoes: 18
Deaths: 306
Damage: $15,000,000

Source: Department of Commerce,
National Oceanic and Atmospheric Administration,
National Weather Service

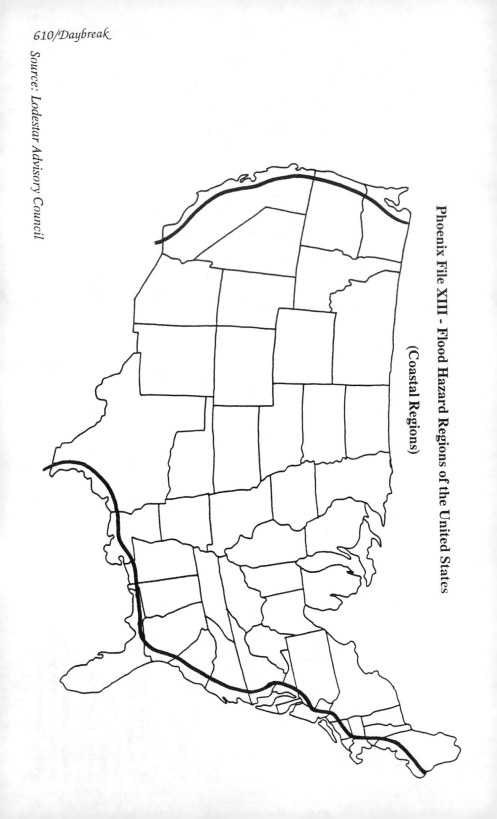

Phoenix File XIII - Flood Hazard Regions of the United States

(Coastal Regions)

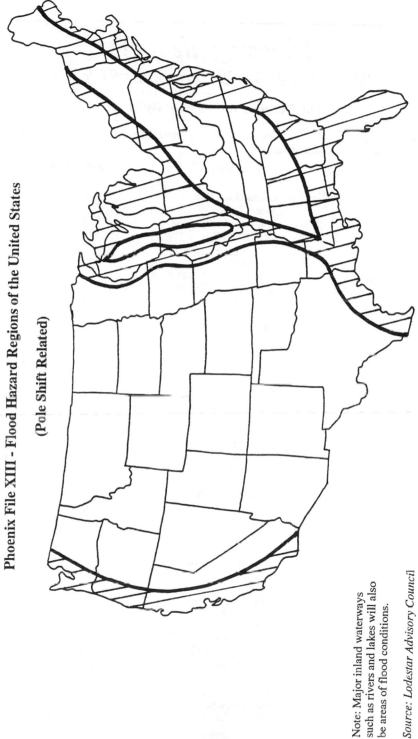

Phoenix File XIII - Flood Hazard Regions of the United States

(Pole Shift Related)

Note: Major inland waterways
such as rivers and lakes will also
be areas of flood conditions.

Source: Lodestar Advisory Council

Phoenix File XIV
Deep Mines of Conterminous U.S.A.

The Deeper Mines Listed By State

Note: The following is provided as an informative reference and, therefore, is not meant to serve as an all-inclusive listing.

State	County	Mine Name	Depth (FT)
Arizona	Cochise	Contention Mine	800
		Moore Mine	800
		Tombstone Extension	550
	Gila	Columbia Mine	550
		Dripping Springs Mine	550
		Melrose Mines	60
		Regal Group (Mine)	700
	Graham	Black Beauty Group	Unknown
		Safford Deposit	804
	Greenlee	Dover Copper Group	600
	La Paz	La Cholla Placers	84
		La Paz Placers	60
		Red Cloud Mine	535
	Mohave	Aztec Mine	700
		Big Jim Mine	750
		Gold Road Mine	900
		Katherine Mine	900
		Payroll Mine	600
		Telluride Mine	700
	Pima	Black Princess Mine	80
		Copper Queen Mine	700
		Mineral Hill Mine	700
		Mission Mine	990
		New Cornelia Mine	5,000
		Paymaster Mine Group	-100
		Prosperity Mine Group	600
		Senator Morgan Mine	900
		Twin Buttes Mine	800
		Yellow Star Mine	60
	Pinal	Bluebird Mine	535
		Glory Hole Mine	650
		Silver King Mine	987
	Santa Cruz	Bonanza Mine	635
		Montana Mine	750
	Yavapai	Alaska Mine	730
		Cherry King Mine	60
		Climax Mine	600
		Dove Mine	70
		Ethiopia Mine	75
		Hackberry Mine	900
		Hidden Treasure-Gold	80

State	County	Mine Name	Depth (FT)
Arizona	Yavapai	Howard Copper Mine	558
		Little Jessie Mine	600
		Loma Prieta Prospect	600
		Monarch Mine	600
		Monica Mine	700
		Senator Mine	835
		Southern Cross Mine	70
		Tip Top Mine	800
		U.S. Navy Mine	550
		Union Mine	660
		Zonia McMahon Mine	874
	Yuma	King of Arizona Mine	750
		Little Dome Mine	60
California	Mono	Black Rock Mine	600
	San Bernardino	Beck	65
	Shasta	American	800
	Tulare	Herbert and Crab	74
Colorado	Chaffee	Rock King Prospect	-100
		Sedalia Mine	725
	Custer	Cloverdale Mine	700
		Terrible Mine	700
	Freemont	Devil's Hole Quarry	75
		Leeks Lode	60
		School Section Mine	75
	Park	J & S Group	66
	Saguache	Eagle Mine	650
Connecticut	New Haven	Jinny Hill Barite Mine	600
Idaho	Blaine	Homestake Mine	700
		Triumph Mine	850
	Boise	Banner District	600
	Butte	Wilbert Mine	800
	Custer	Montana Mine	565
		Redbird Mine	700
		Yankee Fork District	600
	Elmore	Buffalo Mine	670
		Monarch Mine	600
	Lemhi	Kentuck Mine	800
		Pittsburg-Idaho Mine	650
		Pope-Shenon Mine	900
	Owyhee	DeLamar Mine	900
		Poorman Mine	950
	Shoshone	California Mine	600
		Marsh Mine	900
		Silver Summit	5,500

State	County	Mine Name	Depth (FT)
Idaho	Shoshone	Star-Morning Mine	9,100
	Washington	Climax Prospect	600
Missouri	St. Francois	Bonne Terre	61(M)
Montana	Beaverhead	Comet Group	600
		Lone Pine Mine	850
	Cascade	Dacotah Mine	700
	Granite	Black Pine Mine	700 (M)
		Granite-Bimetallic	800 (M)
	Jefferson	Ruby Mine	600
	Lewis & Clark	Piegan-Gloster Mine	750
		Spring Hill Mine	600
	Madison	Golden Rod Mine	800
		Mayflower Mine	980
		Regal Mine	60
	Mineral	Amador Mine	601
		Nancy Lee Mine	640
New Mexico	Eddy	IMCC Mine	992
	Grant	Georgetown District	600
		Steeple Rock District	600
	Guadalupe	Stauber Mine	60
	McKinley	Ann Lee Mine	735
		Dysart No. 2 Mine	550
		Mary No. 1 Mine	630
	Rio Arriba	Joseph Mine	60
	Sandoval	Lone Star Mine	800
	Santa Fe	Cash Entry Mine	600
Nevada	Churchill	Bernice Mine	400
	Clark	Searchlight District	900
	Esmeralda	16 To 1 Mine	550
	Humboldt	Baldwin Mine	76
		Cordero Mine	600
		Niebuhr Mine	60
	Lander	Ruby Hill Mine	750 (M)
	Lincoln	Hanos Property	60
		Mendha Mine	900
	Lyon	Buckeye Mine	400
	Nye	Rainbow, Sunrise	72
	Pershing	Esther Mine	60
New York	Putnam	Croton-McCollum	60
		Tilly Foster Magneti	630
	Saratoga	Unnamed	80
Oregon	Baker	Iron Dike	950

State	County	Mine Name	Depth (FT)
Oregon	Jackson	Ashland Mine	900
	Jefferson	Axehandle Mine	80
		Oregon King Mine	700
S. Dakota	Lawrence	Homestake	7,216
	Pennington	Addie Lode	800
		Golden Slipper-Gold	650
Utah	Beaver	Beaver Carbonate	700
		Black Rock Mine	300
		Cactus Mine	600
		Garnet #1 Claim	96
		Harrington-Hickory	604
		Mowitza Mine	90(M)
		Strategic Metals Mine	60
		Sundown Mine	90
	Emery	A. Y. Clark Mine	75
		Baker Incline Mine	75
		Black Dragon Mine	600
		Black Jack	75
		Brown Dog Claims	70
		Camp Bird 12 Group	70
		Cancer Cure #1 Mine	65
		Commonwealth Mine	75
		Consolidated	55
		Delta Mine	700
		Desert Moon	75
		Dexter 7	75
		Dirty Devil 3 & 4	750
		Flewelling Incline	75
		Incline #10 Mine	60
		Incline #16 Mine	60
		Incline #7 (West) Mine	75
		Lone Tree Group	60
		North Mesa	700
		Payday Mine	60
		Plymouth Rock Mine	75
		Red Butte	600
		School Section #36 Mine	60
		Snow Mine	640
		Standard Ore	600
		United Prospectors	600
		Vanadium King 6	75
		Virginia Low Mine	75
	Garfield	Oak Creek Prospect	70
	Grand	A-Group Mine	600
		Big Chief	55
		Cottonwood Mine	700
		Matchless Mine	60
		Mineral Mine 60	60

State	County	Mine Name	Depth (FT)
Utah	Grand	Sage	700
		Unknown	600
		Unknown	55
		Utah School Section	600
	Juab	Bell Hill Mine	51 (M)
		Dyke #1 Claim	500+
		Harrisite Mine	64
		Oversite Mine	80
		Unknown Shaft	70
	Kane	Kanab Creek Road	70
	Millard	Tremolite #1	60
	Piute	Annie Laurie Mine	800
		Bully Boy Mine	700
		Deer Trail Mine	760
		Mineral Products	600
	San Juan	Al Rogers	60
		Big Hole Mine	75
		Blue Jay	60
		Blue Lizard Mine	80
		Bluebird-Suspender	80
		Bonanza Group	60+
		Bradford 5	80
		C Group	65
		Calliham	600
		Camel Mine	80
		Camel No. 1 Prospect	60
		Chess Ridge #3	65
		Chess Ridge 1	60
		Coal Bed Canyon Unknown	75
		Copperhead Mine	60
		Cottonwood #1	70
		Cottonwood #2	70
		Dead Buck Mine	60
		Delaware Chief	75
		Divide Incline	650
		East Woodenshoe	60
		Fiddle #2	75
		Freeda #2	60
		Fry No. 4 Mine	80
		Giveway	80
		Glade Mine	90
		Happy Jack Mine	600
		Hatchet #3	85
		Indian Creek No. 2 Mine	70
		Jean #1 Mine	60
		Jomac Mine	60
		Last Chance	60
		Lifter	60
		Little Peter Mine	60
		Lone Butte No. 1	80
		Lone Butte No. 4	60

State	County	Mine Name	Depth (FT)
Utah	San Juan	Lookout Mine	95
		Lucky Strike	60
		Margaret	60
		Monument 3	75
		Notch #1 & 4	80
		Old Rattler	80
		Payday	60
		Peavine Queen Mine	60
		Point	80
		Rim Shaft	780
		Royal Flush	80
		Rusty Little Mae	60
		Saddle Mine	607
		Sandy No. 2 Mine	60
		School Section 32 Mine	600
		Tree Mine	60
		Unnamed	60
		Unnamed	90
		Unnamed	60
		Unnamed	80
		Unnamed	70
		Unnamed	80
		Unnamed	75
		Unnamed	60
		Unnamed	70
		Unnamed	60
		Unnamed	75
		Unnamed	60
		Unnamed	60
		Unnamed	70
		Unnamed	60
		Unnamed	60
		Unnamed # 34	80
		Ute Mine	60
		Vanadium Queen Mine	60
		View	70
		W.N. Mine	80
		Wee-Hope Mine	80
		West Incline	670
		Wilson Shaft	650
		Yankee Girl	60
		Yellow Jack #10	600
	Summit	Ontario Mine	760
	Tooele	Cannon Mine	55
		Confidence Property	70
		Gold Hill Mine	900
		Prosperity Property	80
Virginia	Botetourt	Bonsack Prospect	90
	Campbell	Grasty MN Mine	93

State	County	Mine Name	Depth (FT)
Vermont	Orange	Elizabeth Mine	800
Washington	Clallam	Peggy	85
	Okanogan	Eureka Silver Prospect	65
	Stevens	Deep Creek Mine	750
		Germania Mine	540
		Pioneer Mine	75
Wyoming	Sweetwater	Big Island Mine	850

*Source: U.S. Department of the Interior,
Geological Survey/Bureau of Mines,
Minerals Information Office*

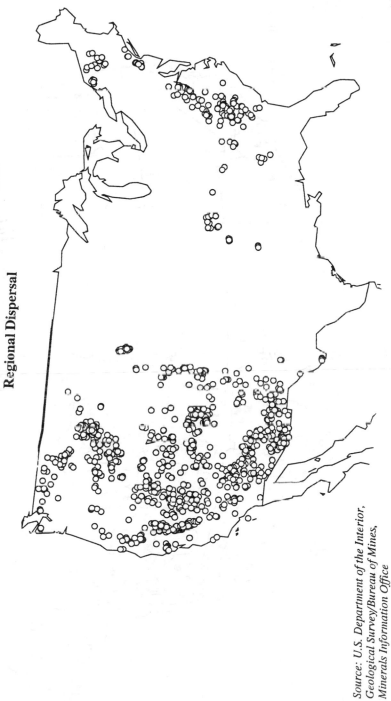

Phoenix File XIV - Deep Mines of Conterminous USA

Regional Dispersal

*Source: U.S. Department of the Interior,
Geological Survey/Bureau of Mines,
Minerals Information Office*

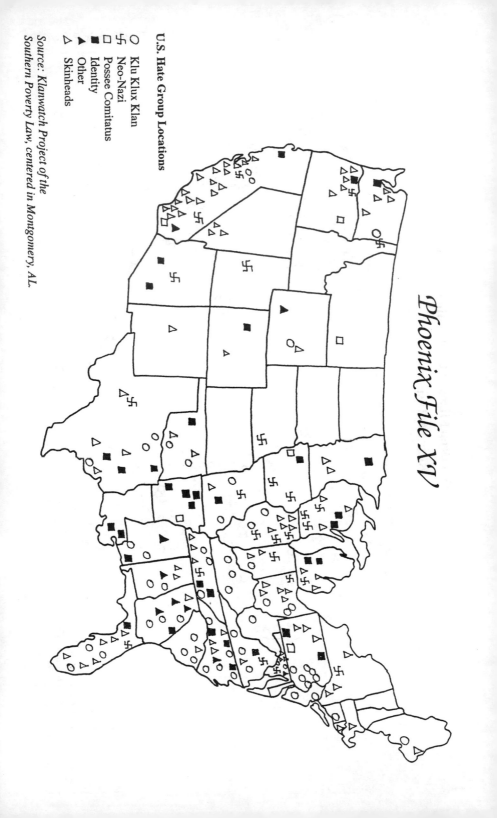

Phoenix File XV

U.S. Hate Group Locations

○ Klu Klux Klan
卐 Neo-Nazi
□ Possee Comitatus
■ Identity
▲ Other
△ Skinheads

Source: Klanwatch Project of the
Southern Poverty Law, centered in Montgomery, AL.

*May all your gathering Clouds of Darkness
be pierced by the dawning Ember
of a golden Daybreak.*

**For a color catalog of
Carole Bourdo's beautiful and sensitive artwork,
please send $2.00 to:**

Carole Bourdo
P.O. Box 62522
Colorado Springs, CO 80921

To order Mary Summer Rain's children's book,
Mountains, Meadows and Moonbeams,
please send $16.95 to:

Lodestar Press
Box 6699
Woodland Park, Colorado 80866

To obtain a personal autograph by the author,
please provide the name of the child (or adult!).
This book is no longer available outside the United States.

If you are unable to find *Daybreak* at your local bookstore, please
feel free to contact the publisher:

Hampton Roads Publishing Co., Inc.
891 Norfolk Square
Norfolk, Virginia 23502
804-459-2453